Brothers of Myghal

Brothers of Myghal

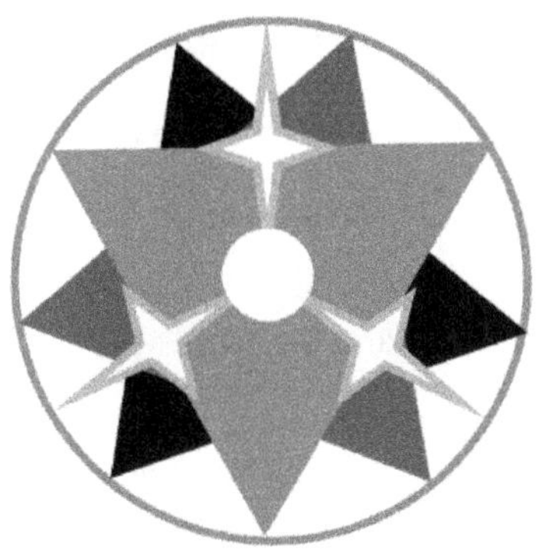

Book 3 of

Heirs to the Taxiarch

Terry Lee Martin

Primary BISAC:
FIC009020 Fiction / Fantasy / Epic

Additional BISAC:
FIC009090 Fiction / Fantasy / Romantic
FIC009120 Fiction / Fantasy / Dragons & Mythical Creatures
FIC071000 Fiction / Friendship

ISBN: 978-1-7320138-8-9 (Hardcover)
ISBN: 978-1-7320138-9-6 (Paperback)
ISBN: 979-8-9994630-0-5 (E-book)

First Edition

Library of Congress Control Number 2025914430

Brothers of Myghal is Book Three of the Epic Fantasy Series:

Heirs to the Taxiarch

Contact the author:
tmartin@silvergobletpress.com

1251 Briarcliff Ct.
Gallatin, Tennessee, 37066
USA
www.silvergobletpress.com

For Laura

Brothers of Myghal

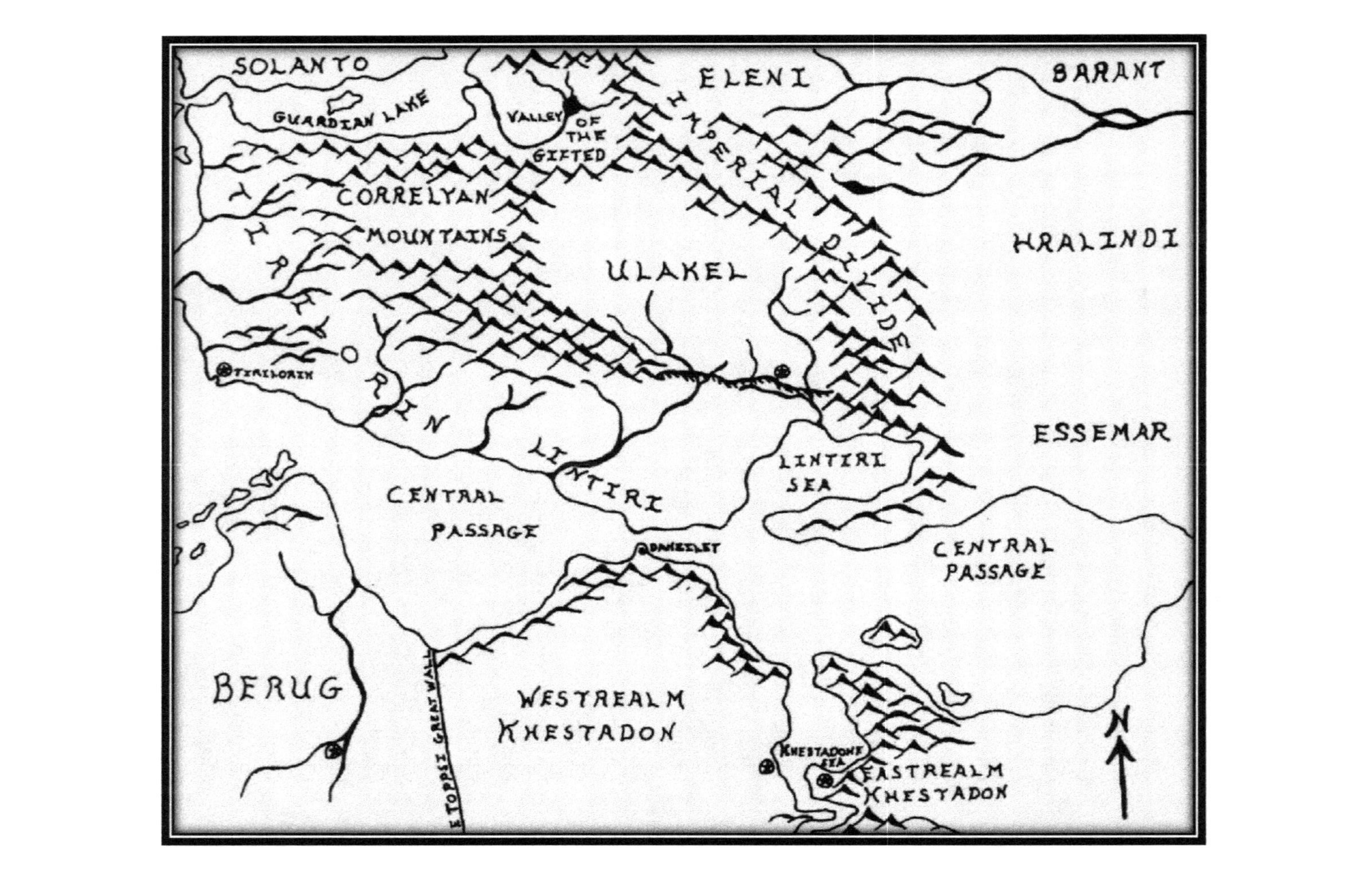
SOLANTO
GUARDIAN LAKE
VALLEY OF THE GIFTED
ELENI
BARANT
IMPERIAL DIVIDE
CORRELYAN MOUNTAINS
ULAKEL
HRALINDI
ESSEMAR
LINTIRI
LINTIRI SEA
CENTRAL PASSAGE
CENTRAL PASSAGE
BERUG
WESTREALM KHESTADON
EASTREALM KHESTADON
N

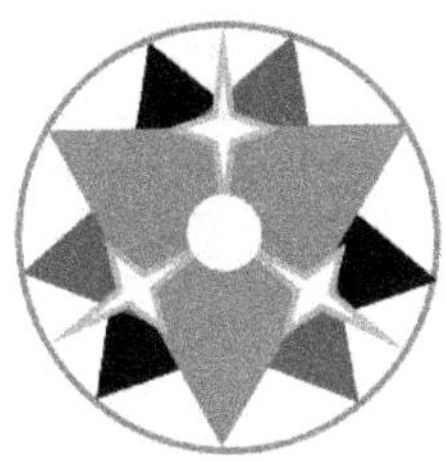

Chapter 1—The Abduction

The sun burst through dispersing rain clouds, and the escort of Solantine Kingsmen removed their cloaks, cheering the break in the weather. Even so, the sudden sun could not break through the clouds in the princess's mind. Traveling on the Northern Road not too far from Davos, Isatura sat dry in her coach reflecting on the recent King's Council in Ferostro. She had sat beside her father throughout, and despite her advice and that of Grand Duke Mannago and Father Marco, his indecision was upsetting. Indeed, her father was growing old, she thought. Unlike past decades when he deftly handled the barons during the Reforms, that former energy and forceful personality had given way to a sweet old man who wanted nothing more than peace and contentment for all. The warning that Curdoz had brought to the king prior to leaving the country could not overcome Carlomen's desire to try to avoid conflict at all cost...at *any* cost, even the honor of the kingdom, it seemed.

Well, it wasn't quite that bad, she knew. At least not yet. Though that nasty Prince Filiddor threatened, the king had bought them all a little time by refusing a final decision for three months. Which left two more months remaining.

It was not what she would have done. Isatura would have made it plain that despite the old document the prince presented, four hundred years of history had intervened. Nor was anyone mollified by the fact that though the document also placed Tulesk under Hescian jurisdiction, the prince pretended he did not want it out of regard for his "brother, the Duke Amerro." As if demanding the whole of the Tolosian Peninsula had not already been enough to infuriate the duke and turn him into his life-long enemy. They already hated each other and so had their fathers before them.

If Duke Snoffit of Ascanti and some of his barons had not spoken in Filiddor's favor, the demand likely would have ended with a firm rejection the moment it was made. She was disgusted to think that at this moment she was on Ostin's turf as she traveled on the road towards Tulesk. The young baron was one of the more outspoken during the arguments. It angered her, for she knew that Ostin's father, the former count, had been one of the great supporters of the Reforms. The son's support for Filiddor was inconsistent with his family's former views. She suspected gold was involved. She would *not* seek lodgings at his estate and was glad Chernis was not on the main road. It might have been seen as an insult if she had passed by without at least calling politely at his manor. She'd always had a good rapport with his wife.

Instead, she expected to make it to Thorune sometime after nightfall. She trusted old Count Ilmore. It would be delightful to stay a night or two at the old castle; he and the countess converted it into a grand palace after the last war, for with the acquisition of Stavenland from the Ice Tribes, Thorune was no longer on the frontier. Ilmore had spoken bravely against his own duke in the Council in favor of Amerro's position. Like the majority, he was opposed to Filiddor's demands and favored the status quo.

It was unfortunate that the minority was as vocal as it was, for that is what led to her father's indecision. Duke Snoffit's defense of Prince Filiddor's rights by way of the old Terianh document came as a surprise, and for whatever reason, this made the king feel the need for a period of review and reflection.

The document certainly came as a surprise. It was a great shock when it was presented and translated in Council. It was unfortunate Curdoz had not discovered it on his little spying expedition, for its existence, let alone its contents, muddied everything. And there was still the question of Ice Tribesmen spotted in Hesk. Mannago and Marco had told her the details. She knew it was sinister to begin with, but unfortunately her father did not. Carlomen had it settled in his mind that the presence of Tribesmen was nothing more than what that wily Filiddor had pretended it was: a *trade* delegation. The grand duke had called the prince out on it in the middle of the Council, and it came as a jolt to most, but her father was willing to give the prince the benefit of the doubt. She told her father it was wrong to take Filiddor's word over the warnings of Curdoz and the rest, but he dismissed her concerns.

It made her angry at the time, for she believed the king's position had been swayed by the arguments, yet she couldn't bring herself to fault openly her kind-hearted, peace-loving old father. Yet she herself was not deceived. She was absolutely on the side of Mannago and Marco: Filiddor was at the least attempting a diplomatic rapport with the dangerous northerners. She and the others worried there was more to it. Indeed, they were preparing for more.

She felt for Duke Amerro of Tulesk. She was on her way now to Felto in the guise of visiting the twins' mother, Elisa, and to offer her friendship and cheer in the absence of her husband and the twins. And besides, Isatura was much intrigued by the whole Fothemry family now that she had met the twins and understood they were part of some great plan on the Guardian's part. She had a desire to know this family better. But she had arranged a secret meeting to take place with Duke Amerro while there. Felto was out of the way, and it would offer the privacy they all wanted to debate strategy.

She looked out the coach window. There was Matteo. Her face softened. A ray of sunlight shone in her mind. Or, perhaps more correctly, her heart. Mannago's oldest son was with her to represent his father at the upcoming meeting. She approved of her official 'escort', Matteo and his younger brother Olaron, who had come with him. She thought the brothers handsome and dashing as they rode their steeds beside her coach, cloaks swung back in the sun, revealing them as the able young lords that they were. Matteo clearly enjoyed the company of his younger brother despite the two being several years apart; they spoke and laughed much together as they rode along.

The smile came to her face as she eyed Matteo. She was not unaware of Mannago's hopes on that front, as he had insinuated much over the years both to her father the king and to her directly. She so much liked Matteo. Very much indeed. This journey had allowed them their first opportunity to spend useful time together, apart from all the eyes and ears of the court, though they had been dance and dinner partners at palace parties since they were quite young. They had come to enjoy one another's company on this trip, engaging in much conversation, both political and not. He was intelligent and engaging like his sociable father, with a hot energy and a warmly enveloping but non-domineering masculinity that drew her.

Until quite recently, she had never allowed herself to feel this way about a man before. But, lately, when he would look at her—the confident smile he offered, the casual wink now and again, his deep voice that she liked so well (there was a delightfully teasing ring to it when he would utter the words *Your Highness*)—she could no longer help the way her heart danced. She'd had suitors over the years, including some promising young lords and princes from Eleni, but she had recently come to admit that Matteo was the best of the lot. When she became queen, he was just the sort of consort, and man, she wanted at her side.

Hmm, she thought. Did that mean she had made a decision? She looked deep into her heart. She knew he was waiting for her to indicate something. He had, unlike most of the men in his father's clan, put off Bonding. It seemed to her most of the grand duke's family and even their distant cousins Bonded quite young. As crown princess, of course, it was her call to make. He was much too gentlemanly to overstep his position with her and force the issue. Yet he had, she concluded, waited long enough. He had retained his honor and held in reserve his passion. He was the subject of no little—or big—scandals, no liaisons or illegitimate progeny, according to the ears and eyes with which she communicated. It said something about him and his self-discipline. She knew he had done this...for her.

Yes, she said to herself in order to settle her mind, and the sunlight seemed to grow even brighter. The time was right. She believed she was ready for such a commitment. Matteo understood what he was getting into; if he didn't, he would have aimed elsewhere years ago. He would be a powerful and influential consort considering his connections and personality, not to mention the father of a royal dynasty, though the way the kingdom's law worked the Grand Duchy of Escarant would instead pass from Mannago to Olaron in such an event. Matteo had surely weighed such pros and cons, had even insinuated that some things were more important to him than others. Again, he was referring to her.

Her father would be pleased she had made up her mind. Just maybe, she thought, a new sense of joy in their family after the loss of the queen so many years ago would give the king a new lease on life and snap him out of his near malaise and even to face Filiddor's threats with more resolve. Bringing Matteo, and by extension, Mannago, into the family orbit might solidify a union of minds in confronting Filiddor and the other dangers in the world.

Those threats seemed to diminish as she smiled to herself and allowed her thoughts to wander in bliss over the next few hours. She looked often out the window of her coach. At one point, Matteo happened to be looking at her from his position astride his horse, just as she was looking at him.

He winked.

Her heart leapt.

They came to Davos, which she knew was the town where Lord Curdoz was from. Townsfolk came out, excited to see the princess's procession, and she waved as they passed through. Before long they passed the more southerly of two side roads that led westward to Chernis, the seat of County Ostin. A little further on, an inviting green hill loomed out of the forest on the east side of the road. Having basked in a hot sun since noon, she anticipated it would be dry enough. It was teatime. She called a halt.

"We shall picnic here," she said as she stepped from the coach. Matteo was instantly there and held out his hand to her. She held to it a little tighter than she ever had before.

"Shall I escort you to the hilltop, *Your Highness*?" he asked. There was that playful ring again. "It should have an enjoyable view!"

"Surely!" she replied with a nod and a little wink of her own. "Indeed, my dear, there is something I wish to speak to you about!"

Some were surprised when she ordered that a little private affair be set up for herself and Matteo upon the hilltop, yet the servants did as they were told. Olaron seemed to think the situation interesting, grinned at his older brother and disappeared through the trees on his horse. Olaron loved to race off on his own and explore whenever he had a chance.

This country between Davos and Thorune was lovely, with low green hills interspersed with stretches of forests. A little further north, the Ascantian plains opened out again. At the tip top of the green hill upon which they had their picnic, the princess and Matteo could see far in the east the line demarcating the Escarpment. Despite the fact that the unsavory Principality of Hesk was so near, the scene was beautiful with a dramatic sky. Birds flew overhead and cool breezes blew.

After the servants had set out everything and disappeared down the hill to wait by the road with the Kingsmen, Matteo himself poured Isatura's tea. They sat on a layer of blankets and engaged in small talk for a while, eating little sandwiches and treats out of a basket.

The small talk gave way to a bit of flirtation, and Isatura invited Mateo to sit a little closer. Shifting nearer, he seemed quite pleased by this.

"I have come to the conclusion, Matteo, dear," she began with a pretense at aloofness, "to honor your request."

His eyebrow shot up. "Ah, Your Highness, but I have requested nothing of you, as you know quite well! I am your devoted servant, of course."

"Perhaps then 'tis time for you to do so. Yet, I would prefer it should you address me in such settings as *Isatura*. Do you not know?" She beamed and blushed, and then looked away for a moment. Then she looked back into his face with a sweet smile and waited. He had a handsome look: black scruff on a face unshaved for a few days, on a chiseled, dark olive face. The Nantian descent was strong in his family. He paused for a little. The whole time his eyes seemed to dance.

From his point of view, Matteo, though delighted at the portents of these last several minutes, was, in a way, taken aback. The protocol required a crown prince or crown princess to, as it were, 'do the asking'. And of course, he would never have presumed to press her. Did the princess harbor a little wish of the 'old fashioned' when it finally came down to the actual deed?

All hesitation melted as he realized she was offering him a little gift. He had daydreamed about this moment for a long time, always playing in his mind phrases he considered both daringly rakish and chivalrously gallant. Tones and words he would never have really used in the actual presence of the woman who would one day be ruling Queen of Solanto, but rather for the woman of intelligence, of beauty, of charm, of...his many desires.

It seemed she knew this and was allowing him an opportunity to...be himself. To be the daring and courageous man he hoped he was. And if *that* didn't, in a moment's time, double his devotion and love for her...

He stood. He breathed in a magnificent breath and looked all around. Whether or not the servants and Kingsmen at the bottom of the hill were paying attention was irrelevant. The world around him had never seemed so extraordinary, and so exquisitely detailed, as it did at this moment. The sun lit up a crystalline sky, the breezes were especially refreshing, the colors of the grass and trees bore shades of green he had not noticed before. He knelt before her and looked into her stunning green eyes. They were the verdant shade he knew best, for how often had he looked into them and noted their depth? He reached out and took her hand from her lap, in itself a daring move. The formality between them fell away.

"Darling Isatura! Oh, the subject of all my dreams. I love you with all that I have, and with all that I am. Would you, dear one, consent to Bond me? And, throughout our joint lives, face the joys and challenges of this world...together?"

There was nothing particularly rakish in that, yet it was certainly from the heart. He then kissed her non-resistant hand and looked purposefully into her eyes.

"Yes, dear Matteo! I will!"

He could hardly believe his ears, nor could he contain his joy as they then kissed ardently on that sunlit hill. Perhaps he did employ a dash of the rake in that kiss.

Young Olaron was on his horse trotting through a stretch of forest. The road was just off to his left, and every once in a while, he could catch a glimpse of it if he strained his eyes in that direction. He loved exploring the woods and countryside alone, in harmony with his surroundings. He had a great love of nature.

Yet as he rode, something seemed a little odd. He couldn't put his finger on it. He pulled up and stopped, listening.

There were no birds singing nor any other sound. He also realized there had been no traffic on the road for some time. For whatever reason this did not please him. He decided teatime would soon be over anyway, and he had just turned his horse in the direction of the road in order to return quickly to his brother when he heard a voice. It was north and a bit east of his position.

In fact, there were several voices, all men.

Curiosity getting the better of him, he dismounted, tied the reins around a stump and made off in the direction of the voices. Before him was a low fold in the land. He descended, then climbed. The voices were just the other side of the hill. Not wanting to be seen, he lay flat at the top of the rise and looked down into a cleared hollow. Below were at least two hundred soldiers on horseback.

But they were not Kingsmen.

Suddenly, just off to his right a horseman galloped over the rise and down to the others. Thankfully, Olaron was in such a position he was invisible to the rider.

When the rider reached the others, he began to talk animatedly and point, southward. Olaron could not make out what was said, but he knew this wasn't right. Not right at all. He crawled backward a little way, and in a few more minutes he was racing on his horse to the road and back to the others.

Kingsmen and palace servants were staring up the hill. Some were surprised and some were smiling. The maids seemed particularly pleased.

"Oh, I always hoped!" said one. "Lord Matteo is such a good one, too!"

"And so handsome!" said another.

Suddenly, Olaron galloped in, looking around. He quickly found the captain of the guard. "Hescian horsemen, Captain Cludder! At least two hundred of them!"

The captain was in shock for a long moment, then suddenly began issuing orders. Everyone scrambled.

Olaron raced his horse straight up the hill.

"Olaron!" Matteo did not appreciate the interruption. "Whatever are you doing?"

Unfazed, Olaron leapt from his horse and bowed to the princess. "I...I am sorry! But there are Hescians ahead, Your Highness! Well-armed soldiers and knights on horseback!"

Matteo stood. "What! Where, Olaron? How many?"

"At least two hundred of them east of the road in the woods about three miles north!" Quickly he explained precisely what he saw, including the runner who had come up from the south.

"You mean they might be both south and north of us?"

Isatura spoke swiftly. "It is an ambush, Matteo! Don't you see? Consider the Council! Think what would happen if Filiddor had me as a hostage!"

Matteo's mind worked quickly. "Yet there are others traveling. It's a busy road! How could they get away with it?"

"But...but there is no one on the road!" offered Olaron. "I noticed it just before I discovered the Hescians!"

"They've blocked the road?"

"That would be Count Ostin's doing." said Isatura. "You heard for yourself how he took Filiddor's part on that old boundary document!"

Matteo raised an eyebrow. "Of course! And between here and the Ramp are Nees and Mere. They are great supporters of Filiddor. But what a vicious turn of events for them to act in this way! It is treasonous, I tell you! We must get you out of here, Isatura!"

Leaving the tea things, they raced back down to the others. The captain had all the servants back in the coaches, and one of the maids had donned one of Isatura's cloaks and sat regally in the princess's coach.

A disguise was exactly what Matteo had in mind as well, and Isatura adopted a plain traveling cloak.

Then occurred the newly betrothed's first disagreement.

Matteo had mounted his horse and reached down for Isatura. His brother was ready to assist the princess. "Step up, dear! Quickly! We'll travel northwest and around! I must get you to Thorune. I know Captain Santher at the barracks, and you'll be safe in Ilmore's territory.

"No! I shall ride myself. Get me a horse, Captain Cludder!"

The captain went about choosing.

"But I can carry you more swiftly, my dear!" pleaded Matteo.

"Foolish. Of course, you cannot! But you shall certainly defend me as we ride!"

Matteo nodded. This was not an argument he would win. Captain Cludder produced a swift gelding from among the Kingsmen's own.

She mounted. She was a good rider and had been since she was a little girl. "And hand me a long knife! The first Hescian that touches me I'll slash his throat!"

Matteo smiled. He appreciated her fierceness. He was then giving Olaron instructions to ride back to Davos and see if he could get word south about what was happening.

"I will do no such thing! Send another! I am riding with you, *Prince Consort!*" Obviously, Olaron discerned quickly what had actually taken place on the hill while he was temporarily away and winked at his older brother. He mounted his own horse again and reached down to make sure his sword was in its place. "Oh. And congratulations, Brother!" And then he nodded to the princess. "And to you, Your Highness!"

It was determined that only a small number would accompany the princess, they to ride secretly through the woods and hills westward and northward with the hope of entirely skirting the Hescian force. It did seem better to try to get to Thorune which was much closer than any point south besides Davos which was a part of County Ostin and could provide little protection. There was no stronghold or barracks there, whereas Thorune was a large town and offered several. The rest were to proceed on the road with the caravan as if everything were normal. Hopefully, should the Hescians surround the caravan, it would take them a little time before they realized the princess was gone.

Cludder dispatched four of his best to go with the Escarantine brothers and the princess. The seven set off immediately. It would, unfortunately, take them a little closer to Chernis and Count Ostin's seat, and there was the second Chernis Road they would have to cross. Yet going east seemed even more dangerous considering the Hescians apparently had that region under watch. They had definitely come from that direction; the Ramp lay that way.

They rode swiftly, though they tried to stay close together. Matteo was not pleased. "You are the *only* woman with us!" he called out to her. "If they catch up with us, they will see through the disguise quickly. Would that it were night and we could manage this more secretively."

"Would that I had time to dress up like a Kingsmen!" She pondered for a moment and spoke again. "I'm not happy about any of it, Matteo. Do you know what this means?"

"Yes. It means Filiddor is perfectly prepared for a war with the rest of the country if he doesn't get what he wants. Yet he can't, by himself. He must have help!"

Olaron put in. "You mean the Ice Tribes?"

Isatura nodded at whom she hoped would someday be her brother-in-law. "Yes. Exactly that, Olaron. Your father suspected this."

"Yet he expected no such aggressive move until long after the king made his decision about Tolos," added Matteo. "None of us did."

"Filiddor has become impatient," said Isatura. In fact, she thought to herself, it was as if he were pressing the issue. "He actually *wants* to fight a war? But why? What if he could gain Tolos without a fight? Why does he not wait for my father to issue his decision on the matter?"

"Because Amerro would go to war against him in any regard. I don't think we should pretend differently, Isatura. I know Amerro. He's my cousin and a bit hot-headed. I like him, certainly, but as you and I have discussed before, it was an error for your father to grant him the Peninsula. At the least he should have given it to another. Despite Hess Fothemry's exploration, Amerro doesn't deserve Tolos anymore than does Filiddor. Your father should have granted it to Fothemry in the first place, if you ask me."

"Kodi and I got to know each other well when he came through with his sister and the Lord Curdoz," said Olaron as they rode. "He told me his father really didn't want jurisdiction over such a large land. He was content with County Fothemry and the ambernut trade."

"Yet men should respond to duty when called upon," said Isatura. "He is clearly talented, and men follow him."

"But that's just it, begging your pardon, Your Highness," said Olaron. "Kodi said his father would prefer to be his own man without always being subject to another, but he felt obligated to Amerro. He said that's why he thinks Hess made Kodi stay at home so long, afraid that just like his father, he would subject himself and feel trapped into the bidding of others. Amerro especially. Of course, Kodi's not like that. Kodi's one to want to go out and conquer the world. In a good way, if you understand me."

"Of course, I do, Olaron, dear," said Isatura. "I discerned that when I met him."

"Sometimes I wish I could have gone off with him. He's a cousin, too, you know. We kept calling each other 'Cousin Ko' and 'Cousin O' out of fun. We got to be good friends."

Isatura smiled in his direction. He did have a certain amount of wisdom. Even so, Matteo was right. If her father had designated Tolos a new duchy and given it to Hess, or to another if Hess refused it, then the current political situation might not be as volatile.

"If Filiddor has you as hostage, it would prevent your father from siding with Amerro. Surely that is what he is after," said Matteo.

She considered this as they rode through the woods. It was distressing to realize, but Matteo's observations regarding Amerro and Filiddor were right. There would be war. It was mostly a matter of which of the two would begin it. Filiddor, it seemed, was desperate for an advantage. If he could indeed capture her, it would complicate her father's position and decision-making. She wished it would not. She didn't like thinking of herself as a pawn in a hostage negotiation.

She called a momentary halt, and the other six gathered in a circle about her. "Who's the fastest rider?" she asked, commandingly.

They all shifted. Most of them looked at Olaron—the youngest one there, though tough, muscly, and within a few months of traditional manhood. He grinned. "I am the best, Your Highness!"

The unabashed confidence of a fifteen-year-old boy, she thought, and yet presumed, particularly considering that Matteo did not argue, he was probably right. He did have a way with horses.

In fact, Matteo looked at his brother and admitted, "He wins all the races."

She issued Olaron a direct order. This time he didn't argue. He nodded his understanding, reached out and undertook the soldier's grip with his brother, and disappeared northwards through the woods.

Matteo looked at Isatura. "It is to be hoped still that we will outmaneuver the Hescians."

She nodded. "Yet if we do not, he will raise the alarm, and your friend Captain Santher may be our best hope. And if there is to be a fight, your young brother is out of the way."

"Thank you, Your Highness," he said. "It is a good thing you did not make that part plain, otherwise he would have resisted. But give him another year or two, and he will be a powerful knight-in-arms."

"Like you, my dear?"

He grinned boyishly.

"They will not harm me, you understand?" she added.

"What is your point, Your Highness?"

She trotted forward, and they continued on their way. She allowed Matteo to catch up. She spoke loudly enough that the other Kingsmen could also hear. "The point is that, if we are outnumbered, I want you to save yourselves, allow them to capture me, and then..." she paused and glared with a determined face when Matteo was about to protest, "I expect you to come after me. Whatever it takes, you will not allow Filiddor to *keep* me! He cannot be allowed to have his way. *You* must rescue me, Matteo, from that vile man!"

That last went without saying, yet what it did was give Matteo permission to ignore any orders to the contrary that might come from her father. "I am yours, Isatura."

"Yes, you are, Matteo," she said, with a bit of humorous condescension. She decided a moment of fun was called for, both to ease the tension, but also to make it clear to him exactly how she felt; their time on the hilltop was cut short. "You must preserve yourself, for the future of my House is in your hands, Matteo. Actually, it is in your trousers."

The Kingsmen guffawed. This was what she hoped, a joke to endear them to her and make her seem more human and not some distant, unseen royal in a palace. Matteo would need willing volunteers if events went badly.

Matteo grinned hugely. "I can happily manage that, Your Highness!"

"Now enough of this, and let us be a little quieter, shall we? We are attempting to elude capture, are we not?"

"*You* are the one creating a clamor, Your Highness!" said Matteo.

"You should not accuse a princess," she responded teasingly.

"Of course not, *Your Highness*! I am glad to know your mind on..." he cleared his throat, "all these matters!"

She laughed. To have someone with whom to drop her guard and play with in such a way was a new joy to her. She so hoped events would not turn out as grimly as they might. Then, for the very first time she said the words, "I love you, Matteo."

He reached across for her hand and held it for a moment as they rode, "and I love you, Isatura."

Though they were ready to depart, Captain Cludder held the caravan in place for another quarter hour. Delay should aid the princess and the grand duke's sons. He could not send out any scouts, for if the Hescians knew he was scouting, they would realize he knew of their position and cause them to react too quickly. He only hoped they were not currently being watched, though he didn't think so based on Olaron's details. Smart boy, that one. Cludder was angry with himself for not having noticed all traffic on the road had ceased. It was a clear clue that something wasn't right.

Eventually, he called the group to move. Additional delay would arouse too much suspicion. This was what Matteo and he had agreed upon beforehand. He had the caravan move at a snail's pace. There was no point in rushing this.

He looked around at his men. These were some of the best from King's Valley, he thought. He knew they would acquit themselves well if it came down to defending the princess's servants. Yet Isatura was convinced that this situation was all about her. She doubted the Hescians would fight except to get to her, and only if the Kingsmen insisted upon mounting a defense.

The question in his mind was whether they should initiate such a defense in order that it might gain the princess that much more time. Matteo had left that up to him to determine based on the situation as it presented itself. If the boy Olaron's information was correct, they were hopelessly outnumbered. He wished he had more men. There were only thirty of them. Twenty-six, now, he realized. He had sent off four with the princess. Thirty had seemed plenty as an escort for a princess's caravan through a kingdom at peace.

This would change everything. There was nothing about this situation that remotely implied peace could prevail. War was coming, and that was assured whether the princess was taken or not. Obviously, Prince Filiddor was expecting it and even preparing for it. The princess as his hostage would give him leverage. To save the princess from Filiddor, the king would hesitate to side with Duke Amerro in the coming conflict.

Perhaps it was wrong of the princess to undertake this journey to Tulesk in the first place, considering recent events. However, it was the belief of the court that for the time being—at least until King Carlomen issued his decision on the Tolosian matter—all would continue as before.

Yet, with the exception of Thorune and County Ilmore, they were now in a part of Ascanti that was both geographically and historically tied closely to the Principality. And now there was a sizeable force of Hescians on horseback close by. Duke Snoffit was too easily bought, it seemed, as were some of his barons. He hoped Count Ilmore was still a friend. Matteo and the princess were insistent that he was. Santher, he thought, was the better hope. Cludder had known Santher for years and knew him to be an able officer. He had five-hundred horsemen and two-hundred foot soldiers and archers under his command in Thorune. If they could make it to the barracks in the middle of the town, the princess would be safe.

They had traveled only a half hour when suddenly before them was a contingent of perhaps twenty Hescian soldiers, most in the red and white colors of the Principality.

"Halt! Halt I say!" said the leader, a knight in chain mail.

The caravan halted and the captain rode forward. "Who are you to demand us halt on the king's roads? You are Hescians! What are you doing here in Ascanti? The roads are under the jurisdiction of the King of Solanto!"

"We will return them to *your king*," the man scoffed, "the moment you turn over to us Her Royal Highness, the Princess Isatura!"

"How dare you threaten the princess! She may travel wherever in her father's kingdom she pleases!" He drew his sword and the Kingsmen behind him immediately surrounded the coaches and took up a defensive posture. "I command you to turn about your mounts and return to the Principality!"

He spoke imperiously, pretending there were only the twenty Hescians before him. He didn't wonder but a moment where the rest were. Suddenly on all sides, coming out of hidden folds and forest growth and surrounding them in a thick ring, was the rest of the force. The boy was right. There were two hundred at least.

The Kingsmen all drew their swords and waited for a command. Despite the odds, they would willingly fight if the captain ordered it.

The Hescian knight in mail spoke again. "You are outnumbered, Captain. A fight between our forces is not required. Hand over the princess, and we will return to the Ramp forthwith. The rest of you may go free. His Highness Prince Filiddor promises to keep Her Highness Isatura safe from all harm."

"So, you intend to take her as a hostage?"

"Exactly that, Captain. I'm sure you are not stupid to the current political crisis."

The captain fumed. "I am not! And you must understand that it was not a *crisis* until you yourself appeared upon the road armed for war and with this outrageous demand! You are declaring open enmity with the king! Go back to Hesk, I tell you! Or better yet, turn yourselves over to me and I will guarantee your safety! Follow not a Prince of Hesk who dares to terrorize a royal lady on the roads!"

"That I cannot do, Captain. Now submit to my demand, or we shall be required to take her by force!"

There was little more Cludder could do at this point. He had tried to gain as much time as he could. Fighting was not a good choice; they would be overcome, and they would die without cause. If the princess were still with them, perhaps...yet there was still hope for her.

"Allow me to speak to Her Highness and see if she agrees to your demand."

"I am glad you finally see it my way, Captain."

He did not, of course, but he retained his silence on that subject as he trotted back to the princess's coach. He dismounted and stepped inside. After delaying several more minutes he stepped out of the coach and ordered his men to stand down. They all sheathed their swords and withdrew to the rear of the caravan.

The captain waited by the coach as the Hescian knight stepped forward.

"I would have your name, m'lord," said the captain.

"Indeed! Tell His Majesty when you see him that it is Valgene, Son of High Lord Ultrech, Earl of Varn, who will escort his daughter in perfect safety to His Highness Filiddor." Then he turned to the coach and called out loudly. "Come out, Your Highness! I'm sure the good captain here has informed you what is afoot! Come out!"

With that, the chambermaid stepped out in Isatura's rich satin cloak. The man stared for a moment.

"You are not the princess!" Valgene was livid. He came forward and slapped the woman so hard she fell sprawling to the ground, blood dripping from her mouth. If he'd been wearing gauntlets, he'd have done much damage. As it was, he had removed them when Cludder ordered the stand down. He turned to the captain. "I have a mind to gut you!"

The captain ignored him and bent down to assist the poor maid. "Whatever did you do this for, brute? You are no lord and gentleman!"

"She is just a lowly servant and a woman; why do you care? Search the caravan!" he called to his men.

It took all of ten minutes, but finally the man named Valgene had to admit he had been duped.

"Where is she?" he yelled in the captain's face. "I've a mind to slaughter the lot of you!"

The captain laughed in his face. "You won't, though. Though war may come, I think you've been ordered not to begin the fighting. Suffice it to say Her Highness is not here. Now begone back to your Ramp! And once inside, I recommend you lock the gates, and should you ever come out of them again we'll see who guts who!"

Valgene ignored the provocation. The captain was right; he had been ordered at all costs not to fight unless absolutely necessary in order to take the princess into custody. He issued orders and within two minutes the Hescian force had disappeared.

It was over, yet the captain was unhappy. He said to the servants as they went about aiding the brave chambermaid and to the soldiers in earshot, "He realized the only place Her Highness would have gone is to Thorune. It's the only safe haven for her. He has sent them all in that direction. I'm afraid they will cut them off at the second Chernis Road."

Olaron came abruptly upon the second Chernis Road. There was no traffic here either. To his right he saw two horsemen, Hescians certainly, in red and white. They were looking in the other direction, but the moment he began to cross they turned, yelled, and charged at him full gallop. Olaron urged his mount forward and plunged into the woods ahead. He had a good head start. *They'll never catch me,* he said to himself. Indeed, they did not follow him far, and he was soon free of pursuit. It was to be hoped they would view him simply as a local boy on a horse. Nevertheless, he was much distressed. Their presence and their attempt to catch him meant the road to Chernis was being watched as well, though they expected it might be. He had no idea if his brother and the princess could cross it without being pursued and caught. They could not move as fast as he could by himself. He was tempted to go back and warn them to perhaps try a different route, but he knew it would likely lead the Hescians to follow.

He had to get to Santher in Thorune, yet he must return to the Northern Road at some point, or he'd never manage it in time for a warning to do any good. He didn't know this part of the country well enough to navigate without getting lost. Asking local folk and farmers to direct him on routes cross country would take too much time. In a few hours it would be dark. He wondered how far northwards the Hescians were monitoring the Northern Road. All he could do was make a guess, and after another half hour in the woods, he struck off in that direction.

Unlike Olaron, the princess's party approached the second Chernis Road from a different angle and at a slightly more open location, therefore their approach was not as abrupt. They could see no one, and this cheered them. If they could cross without being seen, their chances of making it to Thorune safely were much improved. One of the Kingsmen, Kalob by name, was more familiar with this country and said there were many farms on the plains beyond the woods, and they could take refuge in a barn until nightfall. Once it was dark, they could navigate more secretively. Beyond the woods they would be in County Ilmore. It seemed their best hope, for they presumed Count Ostin and his folk in Chernis were now in the pay of the Hescians. They did not dare go that way.

The six crept to the roadside. From behind trees, Matteo dismounted and walked to the road. All was quiet as he looked this way and that. He returned to the princess and mounted again.

However, just as they began to ride across, they could hear suddenly a troupe of horsemen galloping from the east in their direction. They crossed quickly, but too late. A cry went up. They had been spotted.

Another cry came close from the west.

"Ride!" called Matteo.

They plowed through the trees, the Hescians pursuing. There were at least eight in red and white garb coming from the east and two from the west, angling towards them in the woods, and they were gaining.

"They're determined!" cried the princess. "They must realize who I am! Oh, Matteo!"

Her cry was desperate. She had not expressed real fear until now, and the panic on his betrothed's face set Matteo on fire.

"Halt!" he called. The four Kingsmen turned with him. Two had their bows quickly in hand and shot in the direction of the rapidly approaching Hescians. One of the pursuers fell. He would prove the first casualty in this northern war. Then another.

Suddenly the rest were upon them, and the resulting swordfight was fierce. Two went after the princess—her cloak was a poor disguise. In the heat of the moment, the princess's courage returned. True to her word, when the first reached out to grab her, in a flash she whipped out the long knife she had been hiding under the cloak and, swinging outward in a huge arc, slashed the rider's throat. Blood spurted everywhere and the man fell from his horse dead. There was a moment of shock for Isatura, and the other horseman was suddenly there and knocked the knife out of her hand.

Matteo plunged forward and unbalanced the man, stabbing him in the back as he fell. It was going well for the defenders, but suddenly there were more Hescian horsemen, at least thirty, bearing down on them.

They were quickly surrounded. At least twenty arrows were aimed at the men.

"Drop your arms!" called out a knight in mail.

"Do as he says!" Isatura screamed. "Remember what I told you, Matteo!"

Infuriated, Matteo tossed his sword to the ground, and the other Kingsmen followed suit. Remarkably, they were all uninjured. "Who by the Guardian are you? Why are Hescian cavalry pursuing us in the woods of Solanto!"

The knight smiled. "Matteo, is it? I've heard of you. You are the son of that interfering Mannago, are you not? Father said you both spoke hotly against him and His Highness at the Council!"

"You are Ultrech's son? I see the resemblance."

The knight nodded. "Very good. Valgene is my name! I have come, as you already realized, for the princess. Now back off! Or I'll slaughter the lot of you like pigs! You gave us the slip back there on the main road, but you won't do it again."

"You are starting a war, you realize, Valgene!" said the princess courageously. "My father will give in to no one's demands!"

Valgene looked at her scathingly. "What would *you* know! Keep silent, woman!"

He then pulled her forcefully from her horse onto his. It was all Matteo could do to not interfere.

Valgene sneered triumphantly at him. "Your captain already knows this, but you tell your old king that the princess will be kept safe. Her life is in no danger if you leave us alone, but tell him, if he ever wants to see his daughter again, he had better make the right decision regarding His Highness Prince Filiddor's claim on the Tolosian Peninsula. There may be other demands, as well. We expect our messengers to be treated with respect and their safety assured, and His Highness promises likewise." Then to his followers present he said, "Retrieve their arms and those of the dead and gather up our own horses."

It seemed he had said all he was going to say to the Solantines and turned to leave.

"Your days are numbered, Valgene!" exclaimed Matteo hotly.

"Really? That pathetic captain of the guard said much the same thing. This is what I say to that!" He came up to Matteo and backhanded him across the face. Matteo fell from his horse, face bloodied. However, he stood again. He looked first at the distraught princess to assure her he was alright, then he looked coldly at Valgene.

"You will regret that," he said, this time with deadly cold eyes.

"No. I don't think so," said Valgene unconcernedly. "Now ride for the Ramp, men! Let us leave this place!"

With that the Hescians took off eastwards.

They were without weapons, but at least Matteo and the four Kingsmen were sound and still had their horses. Valgene obviously didn't want even more riderless mounts to manage than those of the three dead Hescians, yet it was a wonder he didn't have the beasts shot. Maybe it was his contempt for Matteo, thinking he was no longer a threat. He probably thought a cowed Matteo would hustle back to the king in Ferostro with his message. Perhaps if he had known of the betrothal and Matteo's determination, he would have done otherwise.

Overlooked by Valgene's men, Matteo found the bloodied long knife used by Isatura. He looked at the man the princess had slain and felt an upwelling of pride in her willingness to fight. He presumed, now the Hescians had what they came for, the entire force would vacate the area and head east towards the Ramp with all speed. Matteo hoped they themselves would not run into any of Ostin's people. He was in a murderous mood. He took a minute to drink from his water bottle, cleaned up his bloody face, and then the five men raced to find the Northern Road through the woods, just as Olaron had done an hour earlier. They eventually found it and before long had caught up with the caravan.

There was much disappointment when the servants and the Kingsmen realized Isatura had been abducted. Some of her maids wept.

"This isn't over," said Matteo grimly.

They knew the servants were in no more danger, and so the captain decided to leave only ten guards with the caravan. After discussing the situation with Matteo, it was determined that the procession should turn around and make their way back to Ferostro with all speed and spread the news as they went. The captain had already sent out two riders to Thorune earlier, as soon as he knew the Hescians had departed, but now he dispatched two more with the firm news that Isatura had indeed been taken by the Hescian force.

Matteo and the four with him were quickly armed again, and even as the sun began its descent in the west, the remainder of the Kingsmen, some sixteen, along with Captain Cludder and Matteo, rode cross country in pursuit of the Hescians. They did not plan to overtake them with so few to force a fight, yet they had high hopes that Olaron would get through to Santher, and if all went well they would meet and engage the Hescian force before they reached the Ramp.

This course of action seemed their best hope in trying to retrieve the princess, for once behind the great gates at the bottom of the Ramp, it would be difficult to get her back other than through negotiations. Negotiations that would put King Carlomen and Solanto at a huge disadvantage. The old king would be heartsick. Despite Isatura's brave words to Valgene, Matteo foresaw the king giving in to any demand in order to get his daughter returned safely.

Even as they rode, Matteo kept plotting how he could keep his promise to Isatura. She had virtually ordered him to do whatever it took to rescue her. They did have some new spies in Aster, agents of his father Mannago. And he was privy to Lord Curdoz' little organization centering on that ancient librarian, Theneri. He could try disguising himself. The problem with that was his obvious Escarantine looks. He was decidedly darker than most northerners; he might attract one too many second glances. A Monastic, maybe? There were Monastics and Healers in Aster that hailed from Escarant. Yes, that might work quite well. The biggest problem was how to get onto the Highland and into the Principality in the first place. After this abduction and the almost certain closure of the Ramp gates, what was he going to do? Climb the sheer Escarpment? And even if he could do that, how was he supposed to, if all went perfectly, get the princess out of Hesk? He could hardly drop her off the bluff. The only other good way in was the pass from Eleni on the other side of the Imperial Range, but it would take two or three months to get around to that point, and yet Filiddor would likely close that as well. It would be no easier than the Ramp.

Well, he thought, he'd figure that part out later. Maybe there were those in Ferostro who knew of some way north out of King's Valley over the hills and through the Durn marshlands. Yet even if there were such a path, it would be slow and perilous to try to return with Isatura that way.

He hoped for a miracle. Maybe, if threatened with battle, Valgene would let the princess go. Apparently, he was under orders to avoid a fight if possible; Filiddor did not want a war to begin too soon.

Yet, in retrospect, it seemed hopeless. If Santher came and confronted the Hescians before the Ramp, what if Valgene threatened the princess's life in order to assure safe passage? The man was a brute. And as far as Matteo knew, there could be another force at the Ramp ready to assist Valgene. Not to mention Counts Nees and Mere.

"I'm stabbing that proud pecker Valgene," shouted Captain Cludder as they galloped along. It had been several hours, and it was dark now. However, the land though still hilly was more open here with fewer woods, and the moons and stars gave them light.

"Not before I take off his head," replied Matteo. The fury in his mind at what had happened threatened to overcome him. He tried to settle it with a memory. Just a few hours ago he was newly betrothed to the woman he had carefully wooed for so long. It was a memorable moment frozen in time, and he would never forget how wonderful it was. He still felt their first kiss on his lips. How awfully it had ended when his brother raced up that hill with the news. If he went back there right now, he would find all the tea things and baskets still on blankets at the top. Some locals or travelers would find them. Would they even wonder what they represented: a moment when true love shone for a bright few minutes in the sunshine?

I will come after you, my love, he said both to himself and the mystical cosmos. *My princess.* For him the sun would not shine again until he held her close once more.

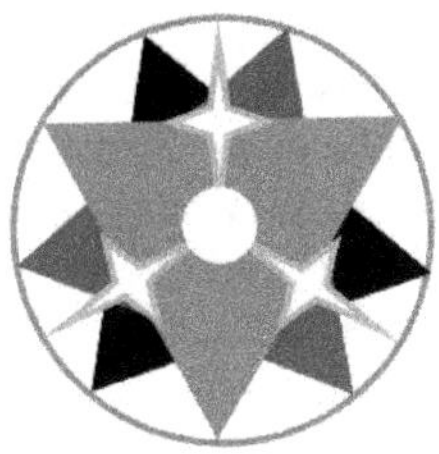

Chapter 2—Rescue Attempt

Sometime after dark, an exhausted Olaron stumbled into the Barracks in Thorune and begged the concerned guards to take him immediately to Captain Santher.

When they brought the boy before him, Santher exclaimed, "Master Olaron! Master Olaron! Whatever are ye doing here in Thorune? Bring the boy food and drink! My, my, have ye grown so tall! Ye be a man, now!"

Olaron was grateful to hear that familiar voice. He had known Santher since he was a little boy, for the soldier had trained under his father and was close to the household. Not long ago he Bonded a woman from Thorune, and Mannago had arranged for him to be placed here to be near the woman's family.

He plunged into his tale, and as it unfolded, Santher's face went from one level of astonishment to another. If it had been some local boy, Santher would have dismissed the tale as foolishness. Yet he had complete trust in Olaron. "That bastard! That bastard Filiddor! Vicious cur! How dare he!"

He was on his feet issuing orders like a general. Messages were sent off to the castle and Count Ilmore, and within an hour well over three hundred Kingsmen horsemen had gathered in the barracks courtyard.

Old Count Ilmore himself arrived with an escort of thirty heavily armed knights of the realm, just as Santher's men were about to set off. Such a level of efficiency in the old count was astonishing, a remnant of the days when his land was on the border with the Ice Tribes of old Stavenland.

"What is this all about, young Olaron? Her Highness Isatura is in trouble?" The old man talked loudly as if everyone around him were deaf. It was he himself who was losing his hearing.

Olaron explained it all over again. Ilmore then directed that some riders be sent to scour the county southwards to try to find the princess, just in case she was able to elude the Hescians.

Olaron listened as Santher spoke to Ilmore. "Ye Duke Snoffit must be in league, Your Grace! I am not so sure ye are safe here anymore. He may try to sway ye to take a new side on these matters. Perhaps ye and the lady should go south!"

"I am old, and I don't care. You hear me, Captain?" He shouted. "We must look to the safety of Isatura! My son and grandsons are in Ross; therefore, I'll have to do it myself. I'll wield a sword one more time if need be!" He reached down and patted the scabbard at his side. It was touching to see the old man, a hero from the last war, act with such courage. "More of my knights will meet us on the eastward road. If the Hescians have the princess, we must race to the Great Ramp! If we are fast, we may get there first. I will do battle for her, for she will be our queen someday. She is most worthy. If I fall, I fall, and you bury me by my folks in the back garden, you hear me, Santher?"

Olaron, after a good meal and a short rest, was ready again. His brother had told him to stay put in Thorune, but Olaron had no intention of missing out on anything. However, he'd have to borrow another horse, for he had run his own hard. Santher resisted, but old Ilmore said, "Let the boy ride! His father'd be proud, he would! He has his own sword, does he not? That means his father thinks him good enough. He's of Bagarro's breed! Brave heroes all! Heroic times are coming. Now ride beside me, son!"

What the old man might have foreseen in Olaron's future could not be determined, though it made the boy feel bigger and braver than ever. A fresh horse was provided for him, and they set out. Just as they arrived at the intersection of the Northern and Hescian Roads, two Kingsmen rode up from the south having been dispatched by Captain Cludder. They confirmed Olaron's story and the number of Hescians.

"Valgene, son of Ultrech? Bastards both!" exclaimed Ilmore loudly. He could probably be heard throughout the whole town. "How I despise those over-proud asses!"

Nothing had been seen nor heard of Isatura and Matteo, and it seemed unlikely they would receive more news, for Santher's contingent and Ilmore's knights traveled fast. There was nothing they could do now except presume that the Hescians likely captured the princess, and their only hope was to get to the Great Ramp before they did. Yet even if they did not have Isatura, Santher was prepared to teach them a lesson. He was a King's man through and through, and Ilmore's knights were just as ready to do glorious battle. The Hescians had come down off their Highland with wicked intent, and they would pay.

One uncertainty was what Counts Mere and Nees might do. Their lands stood between County Ilmore and the Escarpment. Ilmore was irate at their presumed complicity. He knew the only reason a large Hescian force was riding through these lands was because those two barons allowed it, young Ostin, too, apparently, which irked him enormously having known his father for years. And he agreed with Santher on the likelihood they had approval from Duke Snoffit, or at the least he was turning a blind eye.

As they traveled, they were able to pick up other Kingsmen patrollers, and by daybreak, when they had come to the borders between counties Ilmore and Nees, Santher's little army had grown, and with Ilmore's knights, altogether there were just over four-hundred-fifty armed men.

And one determined fifteen-year-old boy.

Along the way the Kingsmen rested for short bouts at streams for the horses' benefit. Yet time was of the essence, so they never stopped for long. They gathered little useful news. None of Count Nees' officials were on the roads and the villagers in the towns they passed were not privy to what had transpired. They were, as a matter of fact, surprised to hear that the Hescians had come down off their perch on the Highland, and doubly so to hear that the king's daughter might have been abducted by them. On the other hand, though they themselves were loyal to king and country, local gossip held to the belief that the count was close to the lords of Hesk and to the political positions of Prince Filiddor.

It seemed a bit foolhardy for Santher or Ilmore to send runners to Count Nees' estate and demand explanation. Who knew whether such runners would be received well and allowed to return, particularly if Count Nees had, as suspected, allied himself with Prince Filiddor? They could not afford to deplete their numbers.

The same held true when they at last entered County Mere, the last Ascantian county that bordered the Principality in the region of the Ramp. It made some sense to Captain Santher. That the locals had not seen nor heard of any Hescian soldiers meant Valgene's force had traveled away from the main road southwest across Mere's and Nees' personal lands from the moment they entered the plain at the base of the Ramp—probably at night, four- or five-days past—in order to be in place in Ostin's territory in time for the princess's caravan to pass.

"Mere and Nees both have strong castles, and each have about forty vassal knights connected to their households," said Ilmore. "But they will have few local folk or common archers to heed a call. As you see, most of the commoners who live in these parts don't care for them."

Having been schooled in politics by his father, Olaron understood why. Mere and Nees had resisted instituting Curdoz' Reforms, and it was the Reforms which gave all these folks or their parents land and independence and what freed the villages from interference by the local lords. They did not think well of rich lords who had maneuvered against their interests, even if it was thirty years ago. They had long memories. Most of the locals wished the Kingsmen well, expressing hopes that the princess would be found safe. They even went so far as to tell them to 'beat the bastard Hescians into oblivion.'

"Then it would really make it hard, wouldn't it, sir, for Duke Snoffit to take Filiddor's side in a war?"

"Oh, it would certainly, Master Olaron!" exclaimed Count Ilmore. "These eastern parts of Ascanti could witness civil war between the commoners and the barons. Snoffit is sly, though. Known him for years. Knew his hot-headed father, too. All-in-all, it doesn't benefit Snoffit to take Filiddor's part, unless...unless Filiddor is offering him some sort of bribe or promises. Could be he's just going to try to play a neutral position. Fool. His own duchy might prove to be a theater of war. I don't look forward to the next several months, I can tell you. Filiddor might be trying to avoid a war, and it could be he's pinning all his hopes on hostage negotiation with the princess in his control. Yet at the same time he acts as though he is prepared for war. I believe war will come if I know Duke Amerro of Tulesk. He won't give up Tolos, at least not to someone he despises as much as Prince Filiddor. Amerro is your cousin, isn't he?"

"Yes, sir. My brother Matteo says the same as you, that Amerro will fight a war to keep Tolos. It might not matter to him one way or the other whether the other lords help him against Filiddor."

"Amerro will not be alone," said Ilmore.

Just then a horseman galloped swiftly in from the rear. He was one of Santher's own from the barracks and had ridden like the wind without rest in order to catch up. He brought the terrible news confirming now that the princess had indeed been captured by the Hescians, and that Valgene was racing to the Ramp. It was definitely a blow to all to hear this.

"It gives him the advantage, it does, then," said Captain Santher.

"We'll see about that," said Ilmore.

"What about my brother, Matteo, son of Mannago?" asked a concerned Olaron.

"Lord Matteo has been re-armed, and he and Captain Cludder and some sixteen from the princess's guard were preparing to follow them cross country," said the messenger.

Olaron was relieved to hear his brother was safe but was disappointed, as they all were, to hear the princess had not escaped in the attempt to skirt the Hescian force. Yet that meant Santher and Ilmore had acted appropriately and had moved with speed. If they could rescue the princess before Valgene locked her behind the gates, they would be considered heroes, and his own part would be viewed as very important indeed.

He hoped. Yet he felt Santher was right that Valgene held the advantage as long as he had the princess. He hadn't himself met this Valgene, yet he was already plotting revenge.

Halfway into the second night and with prospects of reaching the Ramp by noon the next day, Santher and Ilmore rested on the roads. In the end man and horse needed to have strength to fight. It was a risk to take the time, but it was believed that the Hescian force would be slowed by terrain and forests; there was a reason there was no good road in those parts. Therefore, they too would have some need of rest. Olaron took advantage and slept hard on the grass under the stars.

Just before dawn he was awakened by Santher. "Horsemen approach, Master Olaron! Mount up!"

The force from Thorune was soon ready.

"Who do you think it is?" asked Olaron as he found his own horse and jumped on its back. He double-checked that he could reach his sword easily.

In the distance could be seen the Escarpment and even the cutting with the rising sun behind. This land was more open with fewer woods, though there were folds in the land southward, and little could be seen in that direction. There was no way to determine whether or not Valgene and his force were near.

"'Tis likely knights in the service of Count Lis of Mere," said Ilmore. He strode to the front with Santher.

In the foreground on the road a troop of perhaps thirty riders could be seen galloping towards them. In a minute they had arrived.

"Lord Ilmore!" called out the foremost rider. "Whatever are you doing here? You look as if you are prepared for battle!"

It was Count Lis of Mere himself. He seemed shocked by the presence of Kingsmen.

"Explain *yourself!*" said the undaunted old Count Ilmore. "Hescians ride across your lands and have abducted Her Highness the Princess Isatura! Are you a man of the King of Solanto or do you follow the Prince of Hesk? Yet I think we all know the answer."

Mere seemed taken aback for a moment. He then put on a sly face. Refusing to admit anything he said, "You understand you are now within my jurisdiction? I recommend you turn around and go back to your own land, Lord Ilmore."

An impatient Santher spoke up. "Your jurisdiction? The roads be the king's! And we be one kingdom and ye be a part of it! Or ye *were*. How much gold is Filiddor paying ye? Promised ye land and riches in Tolos, has he?"

The count's face flushed. "I will not answer to a commoner captain! How dare you speak to me in such fashion!"

"In the name of the king," Santher began as he drew his sword for emphasis. All the men behind followed suit, as did Ilmore and his knights. "I will run ye down if ye do not vacate the king's road immediately! Reevaluate where your loyalties lie, Lord Mere! We be going to the Ramp, and we will stop that foul Valgene before he makes off with the princess! And after that, I will deal directly with ye! So be off! Fortify your little castle if ye wish, with all the folk ye can muster, if ye think ye can hold out. Or better yet I can arrest ye now and have ye taken straight to the king, and he can judge ye for your treason!"

"And Nees and Ostin, too!" said Ilmore. "We know you are in league with the Hescians! You helped plot the princess's abduction!"

Count Mere drew his own sword as did his knights behind him. "I will do as I please in my own land! The king is weak! As you will soon see. I will no longer answer to Carlomen! 'Tis unfortunate you came, old man."

Ilmore laughed in his face. "You were not expecting us, were you, Lis? You thought Valgene would have the princess secure behind the Ramp gates long before the king's forces could muster a response! Isatura would be hostage, and all would be worked out in your favor in negotiations? You did not expect a fight, did you? Obviously, the king is stronger than you think he is!"

"Aye, that he is!" agreed Santher. "I am the king's man, as be all here behind me! Now get off the road! Or do ye intend to fight? Ye have ten heartbeats to decide!"

Santher waited exactly two heartbeats before ordering his men into position. Four hundred were prepared to run down thirty, and Lis of Mere seemed to realize how dangerous his position was. Without another word to Ilmore or Santher he ordered his men to ride south. They were soon gone.

"They will try to find Valgene," said Santher. "They will swell his force. We have not seen the last of them this day."

"Why did you not go ahead and fight them?" asked Olaron curiously. "He admitted his treachery at the end of that."

"One thing at a time, Master Olaron," said Santher patiently. "We must be fit for our confrontation with Valgene. We do not know what to expect. Hopefully our numbers will remain favorable, but if we fight too many little wars before we get there, we won't have a chance. We still may not, especially if more Hescians emerge from the Ramp. That is me fear. Hopefully, we can engage long before we get there."

Olaron had an idea to try to find his brother who would surely be close on the tail of the Hescians, and after expressing his wish to Santher and Count Ilmore, Ilmore not only approved, but decided to take half his knights and go with Olaron. "If we found Lord Matteo and joined up with him, we could strike a strong blow from behind once Captain Santher engages them and if the Hescians choose to fight rather than give back the princess."

Santher agreed there was potential in such a plan. Therefore, some twenty-five were pulled from Ilmore's force and, with the old man and Olaron, made off south and a bit east. Santher was to continue with his own men and half of Ilmore's knights along the Hescian Road with the intention of turning south about an hour's ride west of the Ramp gates and hopefully blocking Valgene's diagonal path. They all believed, based on Count Mere's words and actions, that Valgene had not reached the gates yet. Being thus still many miles from them, it was hoped that any other force that came from Hesk would be too far away to assist Valgene. It was the best plan they could come up with for now.

What began as a breezy, clear dawn changed as the morning progressed. Heavy rain clouds appeared above promising a wet afternoon. Olaron, traveling fast with Count Ilmore and his knights, was lost in his thoughts. For the first time in his life, he was riding forth into a dangerous situation at the end of which might be the first real battle in a war. Solanto had not been at war for thirty years, not since the war with the Ice Tribes. As a young man from a heroic family, he felt excitement. Yet, too, he was nervous and hoped that, if it really came down to fighting, his training under his father's direction would be sufficient. As Ilmore had pointed out, he did have a sword and knew how to wield it...in training. But as he had been told many times by old warriors, a living battle was different. The hours seemed to go by as quickly as the movement of his horse's feet.

Great luck was with them. At mid-morning they found themselves climbing a rise. Looking down, there was a wide valley beyond. Clearly in the distance could be seen the movement of a large cavalry unit. They could even see Mere's smaller group a little eastward, moving to merge with the larger force.

"There they are!" said Olaron, pointing.

"They can see us here if they are looking!" said Ilmore. "Let us go back behind this hill, dismount and wait a little. If we watch over the rise, we might see your brother coming up in their rear."

They hunched over the edge of the rise and watched. After another half hour, Olaron began to lose hope. Valgene and Mere's forces, now merged, had disappeared eastwards, and Ilmore was suggesting they should probably follow now if they were to be present for the confrontation.

"We can still strike a blow from the back," he said.

Suddenly, one of Ilmore's knights called out. "Look!"

Visible to all, emerging from the woods westward, was a troupe of less than twenty horsemen, riding like the wind on Valgene's trail.

Quickly they mounted and charged down the hill to meet them. Soon they were spotted, and perhaps thinking they were sent by Lord Mere, the pursuers drew their swords.

"Lord Ilmore! You all stop here and let me ride forward!" offered Olaron. "Matteo will recognize me quick enough!"

Ilmore called his riders to a halt and Olaron raced. Soon, the pursuers slowed as the non-threatening single rider approached. Most sheathed their swords, and within moments, Olaron was facing his brother.

Matteo was stunned. "Whatever are you doing here?"

"Searching for you, of course!"

"You never do as you're told, do you?" Matteo asked, exasperated.

Olaron quickly explained, and shortly, Count Ilmore drew up alongside.

"My Lord Ilmore!" said Matteo, nodding.

"We have no time to linger, Lord Matteo, but your brother had a good idea, and so we should make haste together. We can strike them from behind when Captain Santher engages Valgene. Santher has a considerably larger force."

"So, we really do have a chance," said Matteo, breathing deeply. He offered a small smile to his brother.

"We do, but there is the possibility that more Hescians will come from the Ramp Gates to help Valgene," said Ilmore. "Let us go. We saw which way they went from yonder hill. We are about a half hour behind them. Yet they are forewarned now of Santher, considering Mere this morning. They may not know of us, though."

They could not rest, of course. Racing forward, the two brothers did not really have a chance to catch up on their adventures. Yet the mind of each was on the other now as they rode side by side.

Matteo was wishing Olaron had not come, but now he understood that Olaron was at that particular age when young men tended to start making their own decisions for themselves. Their father had warned Matteo it was coming soon: *He'll buck you...or me...one day soon. If he continues to resist, then that's when we have to let him go.* Recalling the words, Matteo smiled inwardly. Olaron had a level of bravado that, once it did begin to exert itself, needed to have space to expand. Often it was intense situations that allowed a boy to enlarge himself and join the world of manhood. Matteo decided the time had come. He no longer had the same authority over his younger brother he once did. He only wished the situation in which they found themselves were not so dangerous. Isatura needed to be his sole focus. He didn't want to have to worry about his brother, too.

Olaron could tell his brother was annoyed, yet he was aware something had changed within himself the last few days. Matteo would have to adjust. Not unlike his distant cousin Kodi—in many ways the two were alike—Olaron could no longer hold back. The world seemed much bigger and more complicated...and more perilous all of a sudden. And he found he wasn't afraid. As the world got bigger, he himself *felt* bigger. Come what may, he was capable, and he would do his part to help his brother rescue the princess. She wasn't just 'the princess,' either. The moment Isatura and Matteo pledged Bond-troth on the hilltop the other day, by the laws of most lands those two were in a connection that could not be broken except through intervention by the Matrimonial Order. In a way, Isatura was already a part of the family. Olaron knew if he himself were facing such a predicament, Matteo would come to his aid.

The rain began with frequent bursts. It slowed them only a little, however. They were determined. At long last they found themselves climbing out of the bowl-like valley in which they had been riding since early afternoon. They stopped momentarily and Olaron and Matteo together dismounted and walked to the top of the hill. They looked down.

The rain had divided into floating curtains and foggy clouds that drifted over the plain below. Less than five miles from the rise upon which they stood were the great bronze gates of the Grand Escarpment Ramp. Just beyond could be seen the west-flowing, North River and the Great Falls plunging in white torrents out of their cutting in the Escarpment. On any other day it would have been a spectacular panorama upon which to ponder the beauty of the northern world. Even the drifting wet clouds and rain sheets added to the spectacle of it.

But there was no time for the brothers to contemplate the view.

"Look!" Olaron pointed. Out on the fields below could be seen two cavalry forces facing one another across a half mile of flat, mist-filled terrain. Colors were difficult to discern in the gloom, but the nearer force, the one they had been following, appeared to suggest red and white, while the further force—that of Captain Santher's Kingsmen—hinted of blue and silver and blocked the straight path Valgene had been making for the Ramp. Santher certainly looked more formidable, for he had a contingent of lances in front, whereas Valgene had none of these. But was there any movement at the Ramp? It was difficult to tell.

A low cloud came up and blocked the view in the distance. For the moment, they could not see the Ramp or the river beyond.

Suddenly a small contingent went forth from Valgene's line and approached Santher's men.

"There will be an attempt at a parley, but it won't help. Valgene's only hope is to get Isatura behind that gate, otherwise all is lost for him. Let's go!"

The two raced back to the horses and quickly explained to Captain Cludder and Count Ilmore what they saw.

"Then let us do our part!" said the old man. "As soon as the battle begins, we will charge down the hill!"

The time had come. In fact, it came quickly. Almost as soon as Matteo's riders organized themselves at the top of the rise, they saw the Hescian force charge forward towards Santher's Kingsmen contingent. A trumpet was heard and Santher's men charged too.

Yet not all the Hescians charged. A group of fifty rode straight eastwards towards the Escarpment.

"Valgene is using his main force as a diversion!" called out Captain Cludder.

"He intends to run around the main battle with Isatura and make for the Gate!" said Matteo. "Let us move!"

"For the king and for the princess!" called out Lord Ilmore.

It did not need clarification or further planning. Matteo and Ilmore's contingent made a beeline to intercept the smaller force. That was where Isatura would be, still in the saddle with Valgene or maybe with one of his best riders.

They rode fast, Matteo in front, with Olaron just behind him. The downslope of the hillside gave them momentum and it seemed possible they might indeed catch up. Olaron looked ahead, and it appeared to him that Santher had foreseen Valgene's plan and had sent a large contingent as well in the direction of the smaller force. With luck, Olaron thought, they might surround Valgene. He wondered mightily what might happen at that point. Would Valgene threaten the princess's life in order to secure safe passage to the Gate? Would another force emerge from the Ramp?

Suddenly, he heard a call from Captain Cludder in the rear and looked back. Cludder and some of the others were pointing southwards. Matteo and Ilmore's troupe came to a quick halt and gathered closely.

"It's Mere!" yelled Lord Ilmore. "Dammit! He must have spotted us on that hill!"

It meant their effort to swell Matteo's contingent was all for naught. Mere was forcing them to split up again. Matteo was hot, but there was nothing for it. He had to go after Isatura.

Ilmore understood and yelled. "I'll hold off Mere and his men!" He and his knights veered off.

It was unfortunate that the group had to split, for neither now had an advantage in numbers. Nevertheless, without some means to slow Count Mere, they themselves would be intercepted before they could reach the princess. Though there was still a chance of success, particularly with Santher's splinter group attempting to create an anvil for Matteo's hammer.

Ilmore's group now charged off to meet Mere, and Matteo with Olaron, Cludder, and the Kingsmen continued in their race to catch Valgene.

A vast sheet of rain swept up from the west along with a strong wind. Olaron could not see the main battle which he knew must be taking place somewhere off to his left. All his thought now was on staying at his brother's side. It looked as though the Hescian contingent had slowed down, probably due to the separate force that Santher was also sending in their direction. All Olaron could hear was the rain and the sound of galloping hooves all around him.

At long last, they reached the Hescian force which had stopped and turned around. Plain for all to see upon a knoll was Valgene, shielded by a line of sword-wielding riders, with a distraught Princess Isatura before him in the saddle.

Matteo could not have stopped even if he had wanted to. The hammer struck.

Olaron's youth seemed to be no hindrance. Maybe his anger was not quite the intensity of his brother's, yet he was hot for a fight. He wielded his sword with serious efficiency, and within half a minute had defeated his first opponent, slicing his arm, causing the Hescian rider to fall from the saddle. Olaron, however, did not have time to see if he might have broken his neck. Immediately he was engaged by another rider, this one better protected with armor. Nevertheless, Olaron was agile and forceful and knocked the rider's sword out of his hand. Then, the Hescian made the unfortunate mistake of looking to see where it landed, when Olaron with a great movement swept out and sliced across the rider's uncovered face. If he survived, he'd be scarred for life, yet Olaron hardly cared. As the fight continued with the accompanying neighing of horses and yelling of men, he found himself yelling too with the rest. If his older brother had been paying attention, he would have presumed the young man was a seasoned rider, which he was, despite his youth, and an accomplished warrior, which he was not, and yet it appeared he was on his way to such a designation. The blood of the hero Bagarro strong in his veins, Olaron seemed almost charmed as he fought.

It was a slaughter. They had defeated most of Valgene's contingent, yet he himself still stood on the rise with his bodyguard around him.

"Let her go!" yelled Matteo. "Let the princess go, Valgene!"

"You fool!" replied Ultrech's son. "You think you can beat me? I'll slit her throat if you or your men come any closer!"

Isatura struggled, but all could see she was bound. Valgene pulled her head back by her hair and placed his sword close to her throat. There was terror in her eyes.

Matteo held up his hand, and all his riders came to a halt.

Valgene repeated. "You fool man! You thought you could force me to give her up, did you?"

"She's the king's daughter, Valgene! You would murder the king's daughter? I don't believe it! You're destroying almost five hundred years of alliance and friendship!"

"Friendship? Bah! Carlomen has had enough time to prove his friendship to Filiddor, but Amerro has him on a tight leash, doesn't he? Tolos will be ours, or the alliance ends, and you'll never see this one again! She can be my hostage, or she can be dead! Do not test me further! Which do you choose, Matteo?"

It was down to it. This had been the main fear from the beginning—that Valgene did have it in him, if pressed hard enough, to kill Isatura. All along,

Matteo and the rest had some hope that if they could just prevent Valgene from reaching the Ramp gates it would be enough to convince him to give back the princess so as to assure his own safe return to Hesk. But now it had come to it. The man was willing to die if he could not carry the princess alive back to his lord in Aster. Clearly, Filiddor had sent the right man for the job. With his sword to her throat, ultimately, what choice did they have?

"Her life is in your hands, Matteo," said Valgene with a vicious smirk, pressing the sword blade on Isatura's skin.

Matteo watched his betrothed as she barely shook her head and mouthed the word, *no!*

Matteo lowered his sword, and just as he did so, some two hundred more Hescian riders in red and white approached from the north. As Olaron and the rest could see, this new force from the Ramp Gates had ridden to Valgene's assistance.

No one said a word as the bodyguard and Valgene with the princess in tow moved slowly now to join the larger force where they would be better protected. Valgene spoke one last time.

"I could order them to run you down, Matteo, but I won't. You let us depart, now, and Carlomen can await my lord's messengers! There doesn't have to be a war if you stop right now!" Of course, Valgene's situation was still precarious, and he needed to get the princess behind the Gates. Even now, the main force with Santher leading, having defeated Valgene's bigger contingent was riding swiftly in their direction.

Finally, Matteo nodded. He had no real choice. "The war has started, Valgene. You and Filiddor began it, but for the princess's sake I'll yield. For now."

Olaron could see his brother's desperation, and he could still see the terror on Isatura's face. He had a quick wish that Kodi was there, for if he were, he reckoned his cousin, having seen him handle a bow on their outing together months before, could have shot Valgene in the face without any bodily danger to Isatura. He himself was a good shot, but he would not have risked it any more than any of the rest of them, even if he had brought his bow.

Matteo had one last comment to add as Valgene moved into the safety of the large Ramp force, allowing them to surround him. "If you harm her, Valgene, you won't live long, you hear me?"

Valgene laughed cruelly. "Like I said to you before, I don't think so!"

Santher's force was suddenly there, and the captain appeared unharmed. Matteo called out to him and raised his hand high. "Halt, Captain!"

Santher raised his own hand, and his force drew up and stopped. He himself could see it was hopeless. Valgene laughed cruelly one more time, and he and the Ramp force made their way unopposed. They all watched hopelessly for long minutes. Valgene entered at last into the cutting, and when every last man was inside, the great bronze Gates closed with a clang that echoed across the plain. There were several trading wains at the base ready to pay the toll, but no more were allowed through to the Ramp. Most of the traders were looking in the direction of Santher's troops, shocked by the battle they had just witnessed. The long peace was broken, and they surely thought the northern world had turned upside down. Some were turning around and heading back west, fearful the situation was still dangerous. However, it could be seen that several walkers were making their way towards the battle site.

"Monastics on Pilgrimage," said Santher. "They'll be a'wanting to help. Maybe some be Healers. We can sure use them."

He sent some of his men to go and meet them.

Olaron approached his brother only to see that his proud countenance had fallen. "So sorry, Brother."

Matteo looked at him. He attempted a smile. "You fought well, Brother. Very well. Father will be proud."

Before Olaron could reply, however, Ilmore's knights road up from the south. Their numbers were depleted. Only six returned from the diverted side battle with Count Lis of Mere.

"Lord Ilmore is dead!" called out the foremost rider. "Lis killed him and made off south!"

"No!" exclaimed Santher. Though there were virtually none remaining alive of Valgene's first force, many Kingsmen had died, and this news added to the horror of all that had transpired. They rode swiftly, following Ilmore's knights to the place where they had gone up against Mere's own, close to the Escarpment wall. Four knights stood kneeling at Ilmore's stricken body. Santher, Matteo, Olaron, and Cludder dismounted and walked up, and they too kneeled. Ilmore's face seemed peaceful.

"He be one o' Solanto's great heroes from the Tribal War," said Santher sadly.

"And the first hero of this war," added Matteo. "He sacrificed himself to save Isatura. Maybe he should not have come, as old as he is, and yet of course he would have had it no other way."

"No, that he would not," concluded Santher. "Methinks he seemed to know what migh' happen to him and told me before we left Thorune to bury him beside his father in the castle garden. There be too many good men here to be a'carryin' back, but we shall certainly take him. We'll send for help from the villages and have the others buried in the fields here. And tis only proper we be 'a buryin' the Hescians, as well. Obviously, they won't be comin' forth to do it themselves."

Olaron struggled with his grief, for he had grown fond of the old man in the few short days he had traveled with him.

"I cannot stay with you, Captain. I have other things to do." Matteo then looked at his brother. "Olaron, I want you to..."

"No! You need my help!"

Matteo appeared defeated, and he no longer had it in him to argue. He nodded. Then he looked up the Escarpment wall. It was sheer. "How the Guardian's Teeth am I going to get up that?"

"There be no way up the Escarpment, Lord Matteo," said Santher. "No way. And from the southern hills is the Durn Swamp. No way through it, they say."

And then a soft Voice unlocked a memory in Olaron, and it burst out of him like sunshine after rain. "But there is! There is!" he exclaimed excitedly.

And then the sun actually did come out, and the rain clouds dispersed.

Matteo looked at him. "What do you mean, Olaron! What are you saying?"

"And it's not even so far away, I reckon! In Tulesk! Kodi told me! There is a path up to the Highland from behind his home. Behind his town Felto and beyond the Wolf River. He used to hike up there and camp with his friends."

Quickly, he explained everything he remembered Kodi telling him about the obscure path. “His old grandfather can point it out to us, Matteo!”

Despite all, Matteo could not help but to grin at his brother, who was so beside himself with boyish cheer. And surely it inspired Matteo’s first hope.

“I’m going with you, Lord Matteo,” said Captain Cludder. “We could use a good map of the Principality, though. Santher?”

“I have me one in Thorune, Captain. Ye must take it. Ye must go that direction to get to Felto, anyways.”

It was more, really, than Matteo could possibly have wished for. He looked again up the Escarpment wall. “I’m coming for you, my love. Be brave, dear one.”

He looked at Olaron and smiled.

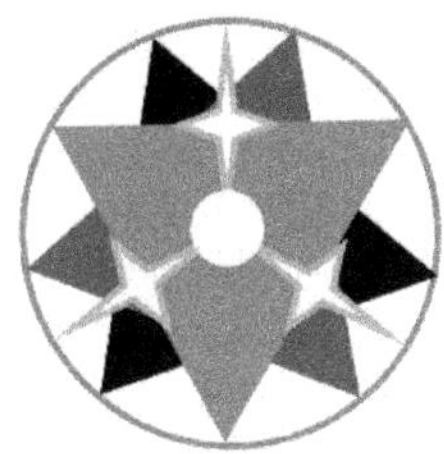

Chapter 3—The Staff Comes to Nant

The travelers disengaged the harness from the Pearl Colossal near to where Curdoz had first communicated with Vanaratu. In his farewell, Curdoz received the impression from the World God that they would encounter him again.

Curdoz relayed this to Nikal. "He said his task is not yet complete."

"It doesn't surprise me," said the prince.

Arriving in Sevarr's port a few days later at sunset they were greeted by Sage Ralle. Musca was with him, and the twins' reunion with the beast was joyful. They parted from Ulna and Maru who went straight to Father Kienne's manor. They had not dwelt on goodbyes, because it was understood that the Healer pair, having played such a crucial role on their journey, would be traveling with them to Tirilorin for the Installation Ceremony of Nikal and Kodi as War Wizards.

Among other news, Ralle revealed that a letter had been forwarded to him by Sage Enric in Tirilorin. They followed him to his home, and most dispersed for baths while Curdoz read the letter, already decoded by Ralle for his benefit. Nikal had gone off to the palace in order to take news directly to his father. After a late supper served by Monastic servants, Idamé begged off to bed, and Curdoz called the rest of the group together and informed them of the letter's contents.

It was from Grand Duke Mannago in Solanto. It contained news Curdoz had been suspecting, yet much that had been missing before was explained. At the Council of the Kingdom, Filiddor pressed again his father's claim to the Tolosian Peninsula, but this time he had brought with him a document which he said had only recently been discovered in palace archives. The centuries-old document was from Terianh himself and showed a change in the original border agreement. It gave T'vani, the first Prince of Hesk, jurisdiction, not only over Tolos, but also Stavenland once the Wingless dragons of Tolos were gone and Stavenland occupied. Filiddor claimed that before the document had been delivered to T'vani, it had been intercepted by the remnants of the Ralsheen, the progenitor peoples of the Ice Tribes who still dwelt, in those earliest years of their weakness, in Stavenland, unbothered by the peoples that settled in southern Solanto. Stavenland was more remote at the time from the more inhabited parts of Solanto, and the Solantines never tried wresting it from the Tribes until much later when the kingdom expanded in that direction, and by then the Ice Tribes had grown much stronger. In the last Ice Tribe war, when Stavenland was finally taken and the Tribal Chieftains were fleeing with their belongings over the Ice Mountains, quantities of documents were confiscated by the forces of Filiddor's father Lanwi.

They were brought to Aster, but their contents had never been translated, for nearly all were of the Tribal language. However, Filiddor had taken recently to looking through them when he discovered this older document.

Filiddor demanded now that based on the claims of his father for his assistance in the last war, reinforced by Terianh's document, that Amerro's right to the Peninsula be revoked. However, he assured the Council that in generosity he would otherwise honor the status quo on Tulesk, old Stavenland.

Curdoz had not finished explaining all the contents of the letter before Tiliruf interrupted.

"It isn't right, sir. It's fake. The document, that is. I've studied everything regarding Terianh's administration, and he clearly designated the imperial boundary in the north at your North River, the Escarpment from the old Ralsheen Ramp north to the Ice Mountains to include Hesk and did not even include the Tolosian Peninsula. He maintained that the dragons would likely remain there forever, and he stated that the remnants of the Ralsheen were sufficiently cowed, leaving them alone in Stavenland as a sort of tiny breadbasket in order to raise crops, and the Ice Mountains to the north coast of the continent. He said they would never become a threat to Solanto, Hesk, or the Empire. Of course, he turned out to be wrong on that, eh? Obviously, since he never even lay claim to Tolos or to Stavenland, he couldn't bloody give it to T'vani now, could he? He spoke highly of T'vani in the records, and gave him great credit, but T'vani was perfectly content with R'magdelos, which he renamed Aster, and the Hescian boundaries."

Everyone in Ralle's parlor looked at Tiliruf with surprise.

Curdoz blinked at him several times. "I...I..." He paused. "You can show me those records in Tirilorin?"

"'Course I can. And you can get Enric's scribes to make copies of it all and send it back to your Mannago friend. There's a lot there. Even Father hasn't looked at it, because most of that earliest stuff is in Ralsheen script before the Sages created the new Anterianhi language and script. Which, by the way, has an Elenite base, as that's what the slaves there like Terianh used to communicate with each other so the Ralsheen couldn't know what they were talking about."

Curdoz blinked again. "You knew all that? And you learned Ralsheen?"

"Eh, something wrong with that, sir?"

"Enric told me you were scholarly."

"Well, I'm kind of selective, eh? I, er, didn't mean to be rude and interrupt you on that letter. It just kind of broke out of me."

"I'm glad it did, Tiliruf. I appreciate your input. Why should I be surprised you know that much about Terianh? But it's a mystery to me you can ignore the Guardian Meical's relationship to him like you do."

"I reckon I can, though. I told you I know everything about imperial history; you just have never asked, eh? But that Filiddor bloke is duping you, sir."

"We know he's duping us. But he is clever."

Curdoz then explained from the letter that Mannago challenged Filiddor on the Ice Tribe delegation. However, King Carlomen had chosen to believe his excuses that it was only about the fur trade. Duke Snoffit of Ascanti and several of his barons spoke in favor of Filiddor's claims, though nobody else did, and Duke Amerro walked out angrily from the proceedings due to the king's indecisiveness. The king said he would issue a proclamation on the matter in three months' time.

Having now concluded this discourse, Kodi chimed in. "You don't think our father is in trouble, do you, sir?"

"Not based solely on the information from Mannago's letter, Kodi. There is time remaining, it seems. Your father might return home by then."

"But you still worry, don't you?" asked Lyndz.

"Yes, I admit I do, because the situation with the Ice Tribes is volatile, certainly, and the prince or even Duke Amerro might act without the king's approval. That is what Mannago fears, also."

"Well, it makes Lyndz and me anxious, but Father is resourceful and smart. I wish we could be sure he's received messages from Duke Amerro on the situation, but we can't."

The following morning, Monticu and his lords met in the council chamber with the two Sages, Tiliruf, and Kodi present, Prince Nikal with the Eagle Staff in tow. They would have allowed Rainwing to attend as she was a designated emissary from Berug, but she was still dealing with her anxiety over losing her wings and did not wish to be seen. Even so, she offered a jest before the men left from Ralle's home. *So, I suppose I'll just stay here with the rest of THE LADIES!*

Lekktor had left the capital two weeks before, returning to his palace and station in the southern port city of Hildred. He took Dira with him, of course. Thankfully he was not there to inject his poison on Nikal or to speak against his brother's position.

Not that Nikal would have allowed him to do so in any event.

As wielder of the Staff his position was assured. Granted supreme authority in war, he quickly went about undoing some of his brother's war-hesitant policies, and no one on the Council would go against him. Not that they would have, for most of them preferred Nikal and knew his worth, and the King himself placed his own military authority under that of his second son.

Kodi was regarded with great favor, and they looked at him as an able young lord. The tale of the quest to Modela, and his heroism during the Sea Serpent battle were related in full. When his descent from the hero Bagarro was made known, it seemed to them Bagarro himself had been resurrected, and because of it they were even more inclined to acknowledge his co-possession of the Eagle Staff. Yet to the minds of the lords, Nikal was its primary possessor.

Nikal chose not to argue the detail of this point, and Kodi wasn't going to press it. They accepted him, deeming him worthy of being Nikal's right hand, and affirmed the knighthood bestowed upon him. That they stopped short of giving him special authority suited Kodi. He wasn't ready for the command of armies. He felt energetic and capable, and he even had ideas, but he lacked experience. For the time being, it was best he remained free of specifically Nantian constraints. His Vision Called him to other purposes as well, in addition to the fact that soon he would be declared a War Wizard by the Sages and thus of the Orders of the Guardian. He needed a certain amount of independence from political complications.

The lords' meeting went on for hours, and the travelers gathered much news reflecting the war. Nikal had been out of touch for a month. It would give them much to discuss on the way to Tirilorin and for the few short days they were to stay in that city.

They remained three additional days in Sevarr, mostly in order to allow Nikal time to issue orders and to arrange a military command more to his liking. Kodi and Tiliruf remained with him as he went about the city, and they learned much about administration and planning.

Of key importance, Nikal sent a large delegation of naval officers along with five Council lords loyal to Nikal to the Crown Prince in Hildred, the main port in the southern part of the kingdom where Lekktor lived most of the time. They had an official letter with them from the newly instated War Wizard that required Lekktor to turn over most of the other half of the navy he controlled to these trusty officers. Lekktor was to keep only six warships to patrol home waters and was ordered to take personal command aboard the ship of his choice. Nikal knew Lekktor would be furious in having his command shrunk so enormously, but Nikal needed the ships for the eastern war—had in fact wanted them long ago—and, it had other purposes besides. One, Lekktor would not be on the island itself in order to scheme, and two, he would not take Dira with him on board a ship, and so between occasional dockings he would by necessity have to leave her alone. Though he would have her guarded, she would at least have a few more personal freedoms and be relieved of the presence of a hateful husband.

Nikal went often to the palace in order to communicate with his father and to handle business. Yet he did not stay there, preferring to sleep at night at Ralle's manor. He did, however, take Kodi and Tiliruf to his rooms at the palace to retrieve the promised archery gear for Kodi.

The bow was nicely carved, even with inlaid metalwork, and made of strong yew. The quiver was leather like the lost one, though not as ornately tooled. Both were in pristine condition, as Nikal had never used them much, and though neither bow nor quiver held the beauty and value of the old, Kodi acted very pleased. With him it was more than an act, for it was his nature to value any fine thing presented to him as a gift. As far as he was concerned it was a newly treasured possession; it had been presented to him by a prince who was his friend and mentor.

Something interesting happened while the three men were in Nikal's rooms. They were looking around for any other of Nikal's possessions that might be of value for the journey, for example a set of ivory kings and castles in a velvet-lined case, and two quality cloaks that the prince gave to each of the young men. They would be excellent on the ship during rains. There was even a tooled silver brandy flask that Nikal retrieved and handed to Tiliruf with a nod.

"You ought to have that," he said to Tiliruf's laugh and thanks.

It was with the laughter that a noise came from the parlor adjoining Nikal's bedroom, and when with curiosity they went to look, someone was walking out the door. Apparently, the intruder had not realized anyone was there until the mirthful outburst and was now swiftly retreating.

"Stop!" said Nikal firmly and strode forward. But he paused and caught his breath when he realized who it was.

It was Queen Gatha, his mother. She turned around, her eyes at first refusing to look into those of her son. "I am sorry, Your Highness. I meant not to intrude."

"Why have you come to my rooms, and since when have you ever addressed me as 'Your Highness?' I am your son, Mother. Although perhaps you had forgotten." He said this with firmness, though the sadness was apparent.

She looked up. The face seemed old and cold to Nikal, a far cry from the apparition of the younger and motherly Gatha portrayed by Modela on the island beach. “I had heard you were here, but I was not aware others were with you.”

“We will take our leave, Your Majesty,” said Kodi instantly. He bowed formally, as did Tiliruf, and the two made for the door.

“No!” Nikal commanded. The two stopped in their footsteps. “If there is something you wish to say to me, Mother, you may say it with Sir Kodi and Swordmaster Tiliruf present! I think I prefer witnesses. Let there be no...*misunderstandings* between us.”

There was an attempt not to sound cynical, but no doubt he was suspicious. Kodi and Tiliruf stood firmly and squelched their discomfort.

The queen looked at Tiliruf for a moment, and then her eyes lingered on Kodi’s face. Her eyebrows lifted slightly. “That one is an innocent.”

Kodi’s eyebrows puckered.

“Why do you say that, Mother? You think you know the depths of a man by looking at his face?”

“I can look into a man’s eyes, yes, and tell whether he has been the cause of others’ pain. He has not. Or if he has, he certainly didn’t mean to. Unlike most men.”

“What is the point you wish to make?”

Her face displayed northern Elenite features. It was evident where Lekktor got his fairer complexion, but the smile she now bore was not meant to be inviting. “My point is that I did not know there were any innocent men left. There certainly are not in Nant.”

She looked straight at Nikal as she said this.

He paused, thinking for a moment before replying slowly, “You are suggesting perhaps that the pains I endure now are repayment for a profligate youth?”

“These two do not know what you were like, do they? You attempt to hide from your past.”

Tiliruf was clueless, but Kodi had gleaned from Nikal’s occasional sharing when, at times they were alone, hints and old regrets came through. He had come to understand the prince had engaged in a period of debauchery in his youth, in part under the influence of his older brother. Of course, Nikal was too noble to ever place blame for his own choices on Lekktor.

Kodi could not help himself. Lekktor would not be the kind of brother Nikal deserved, but *he* would. He spoke in his strong, masculine voice. “I am aware, Your Majesty, that all men, even those you deem innocent, have secrets for which they are ashamed. Nikal received Absolution from Sage Antonin and is no longer a slave to the wrongdoings of a past for which he is repentant. He is not the same man he was then, and of all people you, his own mother, ought to know it.”

It was a sage-like choice of words, surely reflecting Curdoz’ influence. Kodi could never have offered up such profundity prior to leaving home.

She looked at him and sneered. “There is no such thing as forgiveness in Nant.”

“Of course there is! And if there isn’t, it’s only because fools refuse to seek it out and take it when given. You *prefer* holding onto regrets? I think it is *you*, Your Majesty, who is hiding from something in the past. Nikal is your son!

Why did you hurt him? For we all know what you did. What possible motive could you have?"

Tiliruf stared at his friend in wide-eyed shock. That Kodi would dare confront a queen, question her motives, and essentially call her a fool to her face, was beyond his experience.

"You are less innocent than I thought at first," she replied, coolly.

"Perhaps he's just smarter than you thought he was, for just 'cause Kodi's made out of gold like you said, doesn't mean he's stupid about the world, eh?" said Tiliruf, amazed his own lips were moving. "Kodi's right, eh? What *was* your motive to do what you did to Nikal? We'd all like to know, eh? How can you like that weasel Lekktor more than Nikal, eh? Eh?"

So many *eh's* reflected nervousness on his part; his heart was pounding at the tense encounter. He would, however, stand with Kodi, and Nikal, too. He did it with Sea Serpents, he could certainly do it with her.

"To hurt another by hurting Nikal," suggested Kodi, glaring at the queen. "Because you can't convince me, or anyone for that matter, that Nikal ever did anything to *you*."

It was unclear what Gatha intended or expected when she came looking for Nikal in his rooms, but what she discovered was more than she was apparently equipped to deal with. She went silent and had astonishment written on a now pale face.

For his part, Nikal was nearly as astonished. He really didn't expect the men to say anything at all—it was, after all, *his* mother, and she was the queen. If she wanted to, she could call the palace guards and have these two arrested for insolence and otherwise create a clamor. And even though Nikal could easily in his position overrule her, their words were nevertheless brave. He only intended them to stand by as witnesses in case she really did have something important she wanted to convey. He was amazed. He knew he shouldn't be surprised when it came to Kodi. The man was as brave as any he'd ever met; his coolness with the Sea Serpents was proof of that. Yet in front of his mother not even Aron would have proved a truer friend. Kodi was apparently undaunted by any challenge...whatever or whomever it was. He was even more amazed by Tiliruf.

Gatha's continued silence said something. "Suffice it to say, gentlemen, that Mother *does* like the 'weasel' more than me. But that is not news." Then he looked at Gatha and continued. "Yet your questioning, my friends, has enlightened me, I must say. You fear something, don't you, Mother? What is it? What is it that you fear? It cannot be me you fear, for you know me well enough to know that even now despite everything I would never hurt you, and as you well know, I still have said nothing to my father. You and Lekktor rightly expected I would keep silent. Yet, as you can see, I do have companions and will not walk alone in this world. What truths *are* you hiding?"

The queen didn't answer. She was ghostly pale now. With one final glance at Kodi, she turned around, whisked by them, and marched out the door.

The three stood there silent for a moment, looking at one another.

Tiliruf shook the silver flask in his hand. His heart was still pounding. "Damn, it's empty. I could sure use a nip after that."

A half-dozen thoughts went through Nikal's mind. Why precisely had his mother come in search of him? Had she had a change of heart and a wish to express regret for what she had done, encouraging Lekktor to take Dira away from him? Had she desired to seek forgiveness? Was it possible the presence of the others prevented this from occurring, and would it have been better if they had left the room and allowed them a private moment? Yet Nikal felt he was perfectly right to be wary and request witnesses, considering recent events. She could not be trusted. She could have sent him a sincere letter if she had wanted to or a note requesting a private meeting. There was good reason to believe she wanted to confront and goad just as Lekktor had done in these same rooms all those weeks ago. Certainly, her face showed no sign otherwise.

He considered her words. Why would she bother to allude to his youthful transgressions? What did she mean when she said *there is no such thing as forgiveness in Nant?* Why did she go pale when Kodi made his last statements? Perhaps he hit close to the mark? He *was* an archer, after all.

"What did you mean by your last, Kodi? The last you said to her?"

"Huh? Well, I really believe it, that you've done nothing to hurt her. I think she is angry at your father the king. Actually, I shouldn't take credit for that; that was Lyndz' conclusion, but I think she's right. You've admitted to us he ignores her, and I heard what Ralle said at his house and in your father's audience chamber before we went in search of the Staff. She was trying to do damage to you and in the process hurt the king somehow. He does like you best, that's obvious, and she likes Lekktor best. It's just piss poor that she's taken it out on you. It's not your fault you're the better man. She was deliberately trying to make your past into an excuse for what she did to you. Kind of fired me up, that did. She was being dishonest at least, and at most I simply despise it when people insist on holding others to old errors. It's nothing short of pathetic. The real question, in my opinion, is why *does* she like Lekktor?"

"Sorry I called him a weasel," said Tiliruf.

"Actually," continued Kodi, "what you said, Nikal, makes a little more sense—the idea she fears something. I mean, in a way, how could she hurt your father by what she did to you if he never finds out about it?"

Nikal was staring at Kodi, listening to all the wisdom and wondering much. When he finally processed Tiliruf's statement, he turned to him and harrumphed. "You're not sorry at all."

"Er, no. I guess I'm not at that. Besides, you repeated it, eh? But I say Kodi's right, eh? Find out exactly why she likes Lekktor so much better than you that she's willing to sell you out like she did, and you'll understand. 'Course now she could be mad at you for punching her favorite in the face and giving him a beaked nose."

"I almost forgot about that!" said Kodi, cheerily. "So that's where that blood stain in the carpet came from by the bed back there."

Nikal just shook his head and put on a smile for their benefit. Part of him wanted to laugh, and he couldn't help the surge of goodwill he felt towards the two who were so willing to demonstrate their loyalty; loyalty meant everything to him these days. But thinking of his mother and his brother...and Dira, destroyed any semblance of mirth he might have had at that moment. They grabbed the bow and the other things and left his rooms.

Nikal never saw those rooms, or his mother, ever again.

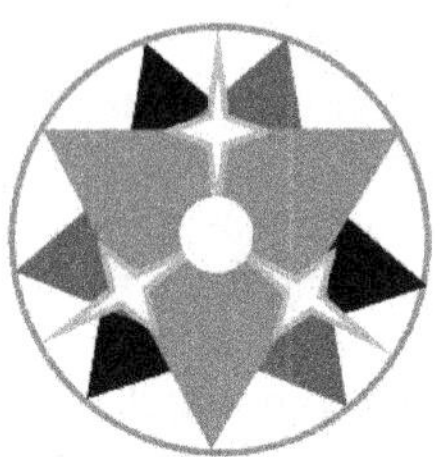

Chapter 4—Symbol

Not since the installation of the new republican government following the abdication of the emperor had the citizens of Tirilorin witnessed such an event, and none from the current generation. Under a bright sky full of puffy white clouds, they gathered on the vast lawn upon which stood the massive golden statue of Terianh on B'ulstread. Thirty thousand stood looking in the direction of the great flight of stairs where the activity surrounding the rite was to take place below the Palace doors. They were the lucky ones. There were as many more who delayed too long leaving their homes or their workshops and thronged the streets leading to the Palace. If the rich of Central City thought their privilege would allow them simply to ride up in their coaches just before the ceremony began, they found they were mistaken; the streets were blocked by the multitudes.

All the key players were present, having arrived much earlier in the day. High Master Naloro sat beside Madam Midianna, Master Yamin, and some forty Assembly Masters. The war ambassadors from Hralindi and Essemar sat not far away. War Marshall Jaden stood nearby with a large number of officers in the Brigades. Too, there were the high officials of the Orders of the Guardian in Tirilorin: Mother Superior Nastrumé, Father Garule of the Healers, various Heads of the three Monasteries in the city, and of course, Master Enric. He sat in the front with Curdoz on his right and Ralle on his left. All three Sages wore fine, well-preserved vestments retrieved from the basement archives of the Palace, these having been used in generations past during the coronation rites of the last emperors.

Sitting next to Master Genehbro in the front row were Tiliruf, Lyndz, Rainwing, Sister Hollina and Mother Idamé. Sisters Maru and Ulna were behind them. Not far away, near to the Brigade officers and, dressed in military garb, were all the men of Nikal's ship. Enric was insistent all who had been involved in the search for the Staff be present, and there were three empty chairs representing General Aron and also the men killed by the Sea Serpent. Enric wanted it understood that sacrifice had been required in gaining the Staff, and they should be honored.

At an angle facing the three Sages, several steps down on simple stools sat Prince Nikal and Kodi. Unlike the Sages and the high Order members, they did not wear robes, but rather they were outfitted in high military style as they had been in Sevarr when they went before Monticu's Council.

Kodi, with the sword of his great-great-grandfather at his side, was both excited and reserved. In a way, he felt out of place, pomp not being his strong suit.

On the other hand, he felt he was exactly where he should be. The Calling had come to fruition. Once upon a time he had received a dream-Vision as he slept in his bed in Felto, and that was where for a long time he believed this adventure had all begun. However, his meditations with Curdoz and Enric had at least made him think deeper. He knew now that the workings of the Guardian as they related to him had begun long ago, before even his birth.

He recalled Father Marco's private exposition to him as they sat at dinner at King Carlomen's table. Aura Bondings, and the offspring of such magic, were, Marco believed, calculated by the Guardian. *Planting Seeds,* is what the Healer Father called it. Kodi figured Tiliruf would probably say 'manipulated,' but he himself could never see it that way. He didn't feel as though he were being used or controlled, nor did he believe his sense of choice or free will was being compromised. Instead, he was part of a great movement in a universal drama that went back to the beginning of time when the Mind of the One fashioned the stars. Like Curdoz would say, that which was good and beautiful was, in some part, good and beautiful as it compared to that which was not. These conversations, and his own reflections upon the role of Meical as Guardian, and Meical as Taxiarch, had opened his mind to the likelihood that across the vastness—upon which he often looked out in the star-filled night as they crossed the sea—were numberless souls in countless worlds laboring to keep the good and beautiful paramount to the evils that threatened. Some were given particular qualities—Gifts, as it were—to be fighters, warriors in a battlefield against those evils. He was one of these. He was pleased to fight at Meical's side.

He did love. He did care. For him, the Principles were great driving forces, as Curdoz had explained. The cynicism of Tiliruf, and also of Nikal, did not come naturally to Kodi. Even with regard to his father he had cast away what little cynicism he had within a few weeks of leaving Felto. Leaving there had freed him, and the more he opened his mind, the more joy—contrary to cynicism—controlled his thinking, indeed controlled his whole being. Even in the worst danger, when the Serpents threatened, enemies representing purest wickedness, he fought with a smile on his face. He laughed to himself remembering that Tiliruf had noted it and later called him mad. He was not aware that Curdoz had noticed it too, having said nothing, as it only confirmed for the Sage that Kodi had been properly marked by Meical as exceptional.

Yet not all enemies are of pure wicked intent like Sea Serpents, which according to legend were spawned in the springs of the Dragon's Teeth beyond the Infested Jungle and nurtured by the tears of imprisoned and maddened rebel world gods. He had not encountered enemies that might also harbor a level of goodness in their souls. He had become aware of this in his quest to become a friend to Nikal, and so he had learned in part what made Nikal cynical and introverted. Nikal was a fighter because he was talented, and not because he enjoyed it. He was a great captain because he was needed, not due to a desire for conquest or fame. He followed Meical's Calling, not because he felt close to Meical like Kodi did, but rather out of a sense of obedience to something he believed had meaning and was higher and better than the indiscretions of his youth and the sadness and pains he had endured of late. He fought *because* of others' needs and hopes, not because he retained hopes for himself. Nikal had warned him of the sadness and actual anger he felt as he and his armies fought the Alkhan in the east. A great many of the Human men who fought on the enemy's side, he said, were not evil at heart, but were slaves to the will of another. In fact, many were descended from sea travelers and soldiers captured and enslaved by the southern powers in times past. Some were descended from Nantian sailors. Even the beasts the enemy used were under spells of madness.

This was just an example of the gray areas and the uncertainties of life. Things weren't, Kodi realized, as black or white as he had once presumed. He had not learned it quite so well from his twin sister who understood easily such subtleties, for in his case anyway, the teaching had to come from another man for it to have the desired impact. Kodi had always wished for a brother, though his image of such had always been of a little brother, someone like Olaron, his cousin with whom he got along so well and happily shared similar interests. Well, he thought, Meical chose to provide an older brother instead, and that was just as well.

Kodi knew he needed Nikal's talent and realism, and he hoped very much he was being the required good brother in return. As all this raced through his mind, he saw Nikal frowning, and so he reached and put a hand on his shoulder.

Nikal was keenly aware of Kodi's presence as the two sat, their backs at an angle to the multitude on the lawn. Without a doubt he gained much from Kodi. He had spoken of it to Idamé at the time she revealed the Aura to him. He had come to depend on Kodi—had in parallel to the younger man's need for a mentor gained much from Kodi's energy and innate joyfulness. When a man is despairing, anything of goodness that might draw his focus out of himself is—though it might be hard for him to label it thus—a gift. Kodi was Meical's great gift to Nikal: a 'genuine' brother spoken of in the Prophecy, the one who was to take Lekktor's place. All the friends did their part to keep Nikal's heart warm when it threatened to go cold, but it was Kodi who did the most to fill the void. Often Nikal found himself moved. The younger man was sturdy—rock-solid certainly in body and with strong moral underpinnings, but most importantly in loyalty. It meant everything to him after having lost his mother, brother, and lover, and lately his best friend—had indeed come to believe he had lost everything of value and would never again experience even a moment of respite from the gloom. He knew it wasn't just Kodi. Kodi held open a door to the others in the group, and so he had grown closer to all of them. They were all family, just like the Prophecy stated. He could not always hold onto his gloom when around them.

The others would, as time went on, keep him steady. The friends could without a doubt take the place of his mother and his brother and the friend he left on the island. They were doing a superior job of it, he knew. What might his life have been like had his actual mother been as warm as Idamé, his father wise like Curdoz, and what if he had grown up beside Kodi instead of Lekktor?

Yet surmounting all was the loss of Dira and the total helplessness he felt there. There were memories now he could never banish from his mind. There could be no complete healing. His new friends could not take her place. He was wounded. The most they could do in that regard was to try to staunch the flow.

What would it take? He pondered as his brow inevitably puckered and his shoulders sagged a little. Would he just bleed on, little by little, until the efforts of his friends no longer availed? The Staff had no real meaning for him.

Just as the despair, despite the grand pageantry around him, was beginning to weigh in for the thousandth time upon him, he felt Kodi's firm hand on his shoulder. He looked over to see the smile on his true brother's face.

Curdoz, as only a great Sage could, was reading the two men sitting before him on the lower steps of the Palace entry. This was one talent which had not left him when Modela took away his Gift. Apparently, his ability to discern mood and general thought patterns was innate. Or maybe it was simply the result of long practice. He smiled when Kodi put his hand on the prince's shoulder and saw Nikal's face relax. The boy, he thought, doesn't even need the magic of the Healers to work his own brand of healing.

Boy, he laughed to himself and shook his head, realizing he was carrying over a long-ago conversation with himself back in Thorune. And then he looked over to Lyndz. She was queenly, even as she sat next to the huge Etoppsi female. What a powerful mind she had for one so young, and how it had grown in so short a time.

Though strong minds intrigued him, there were other aspects of their personalities that actually stirred him. The twins had in the last few months filled a void in his heart he never even knew existed prior to his meeting them. His uncle's words had embedded themselves into his heart. What else could he do? They had become dear to him. A Sage takes on himself a father-like role in the country to which he is assigned, and Curdoz was careful to foster that relationship with the subjects of the king of Solanto. Yet his own unhappy connection with his father had imparted upon him a sort of wariness, so despite his efforts there was still a hint of distance. But as the tears fell beside his uncle's deathbed, so too dropped away the desire for distance.

The twins made it easy, and so his heart had latched onto the Fothemrys as though they were his own. He had become a surrogate for Hess. Curdoz hoped he was offering a side of a father's role that helped the twins grow, instead of holding them back. He realized in part he was trying to make up for what Hess lacked. He did it, yes, but tried to check this thought. He could too easily find himself likening Hess to Luvin, his own father. Hess held Kodi back, and Lyndz too to a lesser degree, but he had otherwise helped grow the twins into highly capable and moral individuals. Luvin in comparison was a hard father, and Curdoz had difficulty deciding whether he had learned anything of great value from the man short of how to ride a horse and grow potatoes. But he remembered Uncle Normene's words that Luvin was hard due to a hard life. Luvin loved Curdoz; he just didn't know how to show it. He had always allowed Curdoz' mother to do it instead. So, when she died untimely, Luvin was incapable of picking up the slack.

Curdoz hoped he had forgiven. It appeared, particularly now he had the twins and the others in his life, his subconscious dwelt far less upon the old hurts. It was more important now to love and work toward the benefit of those he cared about rather than dwelling on the old grudge that he himself had not likewise received such devoted care. And yet, from others such as his uncle, and from Ida, he *had* received it. He had become more attuned over time to these blessings. Maybe not as joyfully as Kodi, but he felt nevertheless now a sense of contentment he had long lacked, even now with the loss of his Gift. He wondered at the juxtaposition with the war and hardship that would surely test them in the months ahead.

He looked at Nikal again. He so wished the prince could also experience that contentment, for such could surely aid him and steady him in the times to come. Without Dira he knew it was elusive. Curdoz felt certain the two had been physically intimate, probably for quite a while, as it would explain somewhat the depth of the prince's depression. How awful it was to lose the feminine that gave such a man a sense of balance and a feeling of wholeness. He looked over at Ida, and his heart twanged. He again chuckled and shook his head. He would have to be content. He could not dwell upon the might-have-been. That choice had been made long ago. He had not gained from his Ida quite what Nikal had gained with Dira. On the other hand, he hadn't lost it, either.

"Master Tiliruf's mind is troubled," said Enric, bringing Curdoz around to another one of his charges.

The Solantine Sage turned to look at the son of Genehbro, sitting on the other side of Lyndz from Rainwing. "What Genehbro said when his son returned without the Sword was most unfortunate. I pressed the value of that blade upon Genehbro, and in retrospect..."

"Don't give up. On the meaning of that Sword or on its giving," said Enric. "It helped open the minds of many, if you ask me. Including Tiliruf's."

The young man who represented the last generation of the House of Terianh the Great stared into the distance. The great golden statue of his ancestor was all he could really see, and the crowd of thousands and the associated great murmuring thereof was lost. As his eyes pinpointed the image of the Sword in Terianh's left hand his thoughts expanded in a sea of resentment. He was infuriated with himself for having dared, after receiving the Sword in ceremony, to daydream and build up within himself hopes that he too could achieve a sense of high purpose.

Why the thumping shaft am I sitting here? He felt he was a great nobody compared to the ones around him. He didn't belong on this stage and felt foolish in the fancy clothes he donned. He wanted to abandon the quest altogether. Coming back to this thought again and again, he couldn't understand what it was that kept him from doing so.

'What do you mean you lost it? What was the point in you going with the others if you return with less than what you left with!'

It didn't matter anymore once it had been thoroughly explained by Nikal and Curdoz that his father apologized for his words—apologized profusely and even humbly. And then all Tiliruf could do was pretend all was well. The pretense made him snicker to himself with disgust.

...you return with less than what you left with!

The words stung, not only because they came from an angry and disappointed father, which was enough to dishearten any son despite the sincere apologies afterward, but also because it was precisely the truth as he himself saw it. He had gained nothing.

Yet he couldn't leave the group, because now the group was all he had left. It appeared he'd pinned all his hopes for himself on his acceptance of Kodi's friendship, the insistence upon joining the quest, and then his subjection to Nikal. If he abandoned them now there really was no hope he would *ever* return again with anything at all. He might as well go live in his favorite North Bend brothel and never come out. In his anger and angst, he'd gone there last night in secret, and it seemed a safe place. Always good for a bit of physical and emotional release. His body begged desperately after its six weeks' fast. Maybe he'd give Kodi the slip and go again tonight. He knew his best friend was onto him, though. Oh well, he thought, Kodi could use a good thump too if he wasn't so damned good and choosy.

But his thoughts didn't stay in North Bend. He kept thinking of the 'good and choosy' Kodi, who really was the best friend he'd ever had. But he'd become close to them all. Several images flashed through his mind: the scarf Idamé made for him that he always wore onboard ship, the swordplay with Aron on the open deck, the terrifying yet exhilarating flight over the waves with Rainwing, the conversations on historical topics and botany with Lyndz. His muscles were bigger, which he certainly approved of, and he spent a long time after his bath this morning flexing and staring into his tall gold mirror. Maybe he had gained a little something on the journey after all. And though the soothing words of some of them could at times seem empty, there were others that helped. He couldn't quite remember, in his current angry state, what Nikal had actually said to his father to mollify him for the loss of the Eagle Sword. The words themselves weren't so important. The fact it was Nikal, though. Here was a man who despite his hardness and reserve appeared to understand him. Or at least a particular part of him that even Kodi couldn't quite get. He looked over at the prince who was now looking with a friendly smile at Kodi, the latter with his hand on his shoulder.

Tiliruf sighed and tried to relax as he remembered Nikal's hand on his own shoulder at the very time his father was word-slamming him so unjustly. But thinking of his father's words made him angry again. Sitting beside his father right now only increased his anxiety. He unconsciously shifted away.

And so, from his other side, Lyndz, out of the blue, reached over and took hold of his hand. "Tiliruf, it's a grand day, isn't it? And good to be with those I care about, no matter what comes after."

As he looked into her deep brown eyes, his heart twanged. The thought of retreating again to North Bend left him. His anger abated. It was a natural sort of smile he returned and not his usual rascally smirk. He gripped her hand securely. He was unaware that two Sages had been watching him intently and that an eyebrow on each had suddenly risen sharply.

Mother Idamé's mind was in high pitch. That morning there had been no time to meditate. Of course, she could no longer, since her Gift had been taken, achieve the Mode, something that up until then had at least kept her sane.

She tried to brush it away, but aside from that, she felt overwhelmed with how fast everything was progressing. Curdoz and some of the others often spoke of how slow things were moving and their desire to make their way east, but for her it was as though the clock had sped up since she had run into Curdoz back in the inn in Thorune, and it looked only to be getting faster.

Part of it she knew was the stress of traveling by ship, something she hated, and which kept her on her back half the time and on her toes the other half. They were to leave again in two days. All she really wanted to do was go back to Enric's temple garden and lie for weeks on the bench cushions and listen to the birds sing in the pines, the sea breezes blow, and the little brook trickle over the stones. And read books. And drink tea in the afternoons with Hollina. Better yet retreat to the Valley for a year. Maybe by then, she thought, she'd have built up the courage she needed to face the tasks before her. Or maybe by some miracle, should she bathe in the waters of the Lake, her Gift would return, and she would feel more like herself.

She shifted in her seat and resettled the scarf on her shoulders, the new one made by Ulna, Maru, and Lyndz on the ship. They had used different colors in its making, appropriate for a Mother Matrimonial. She was gripping the end of it. The weather was warm, but the wind off the sea blew up the front steps of the Palace.

"Something troubling you, dear?" asked Hollina beside her.

"No, dear, I'm fine." But her smile quickly faded again. She was annoyed with herself and the self-absorption that seemed to rule her since that day her Gift was taken. She felt she was becoming petty and self-centered as she allowed Curdoz and others to pamper her. *I'm just a useless old fat lady,* she would sometimes say aloud in the presence of the others after she had lost her Gift.

Nonsense! Rainwing would scold her—at least for a few days until Rainwing herself lost her wings. At which point the Matrimonial was forced to scold herself: what was her loss to that of the Etoppsi woman?

I mean 'female,' she chuckled to herself, and for a brief moment was outside of herself again. She looked up and noticed how beautiful the sky was.

"I don't believe you," Hollina pressed.

"Really, dear, I'm fine!" It was a little less of a lie this time.

She looked over at Rainwing. She was amazed and even envious of the Etoppsis' ability to lift herself above her loss. Since they had left Nant and since there was little chance she would be seen by one of her own race on the short trip to Tirilorin, the Berugian had put upon herself once more a proud and confident demeanor.

Then she looked over at Kodi and Nikal, and for a moment thought she was looking at reincarnations of Terianh or Vanayisu-Modelo, or even Human incarnations of Meical Himself. How powerful and confident they looked, archetypes of masculine virility and strength. But how young Kodi appeared, even so.

Likewise, she thought, as her eyes found the daughter of Elisa, Lyndz was a model of feminine perfection. She appeared to be in friendly conversation with Tiliruf, innocently holding hands, as friends do—like she and Curdoz sometimes did. What was it like, she wondered, to be as stunningly beautiful as a full golden Orohmoon on a summer night, flanked by bright stars all around? Idamé thought of herself as a somewhat plain girl when she was Lyndz' age, and over the years she became plump. Yet it was much more than Lyndz' beauty that Idamé admired. The younger woman had an inner strength and drive that was as superior as that of Kodi's. Though different, for Lyndz' strength carried a more thoughtful strain, less hot and more *aware*. Deep. Though equally brave. At least that was what she saw in the young woman she had grown to cherish as a daughter. She had a difficult time seeing in what way she was benefiting Lyndz. She helped train her with meditation, achievement of the Mode, and with discernment, but other than companionship, the Matrimonial had her doubts. And even if she could count those things, as she considered it now, she believed she had done all she was capable of doing and wondered—not unlike Tiliruf had she known it—what further role she could possibly play. She no longer had her Gift, so what use was there? *Tagging along.* Then she remembered what Curdoz said the other day when she in private relayed these doubts to him.

You know better, Ida. Elisa would not have given the family blessing, and I would have been forced to use my authority. Then Lyndz would likely be in constant fetters, wondering always whether leaving was the right thing. Even her Vision later might not have overcome doubts. You have been a transitional figure at the very least, for a young woman to leave her mother after being by her side for over eighteen years cannot be easy. You've supplied a required role, but I say 'at the very least' because I know you have more to do. I think you're being dishonest with yourself, quite frankly, because I know you are holding something back. You had a Vision, for one, and for another you know what Lyndz' Vision was all about, and you were a part of that Vision, too, weren't you?

Then Idamé's cheeks flushed, and she felt an impulse to change the subject. It embarrassed her, for she did not like keeping secrets from him, particularly when it was plain he knew she was doing just that. He was too good at reading her. He always had been, even now when they could no longer share the emotional mind connection through the Gift. But overall, what she really knew she lacked and desperately needed was courage. From her vantage, the others had ten times—a hundred times—as much as she.

Lyndz sat regally in another dress borrowed from Linova, this one emerald green and with the green silk sash from Princess Isatura wrapped around and tied in her front. She had at least not lost the sash. Her Tirilorine friend had offered her a necklace and even a buckle for the sash, but surprisingly she found herself declining. She knew now why. It felt wrong to mimic even for a few hours the buckle the princess had presented her and the pendant her father at such cost and with such effort had had made for her. She felt the loss and their absence should remain on her mind. She was making a sacrifice necessary for the group to achieve the higher goal of having use of the Eagle Staff.

She laughed a little at herself for this, for she knew that in a way the others had acquired substitutes, or at least symbols thereof. She had even been in on the knitting of Curdoz' new stole and Idamé's shawl. And the prince had supplied her twin with a replacement bow and Tiliruf with Aron's sword. She was also quite aware of the obvious substitution of Kodi as the replacement friend and brother to Nikal. And in the case of the brother, anyway, it was much more than symbol, for it was even more real and good than the two brother princes' relationship had ever been.

These did not bother her in the least. It was perfectly appropriate for them to have these things, and all were gifts beautifully given and well-received.

Yet she felt her case was different in part for two reasons: one, because the jewelry did not define her as much as those things defined the others, and two, because there was one person who indeed could never acquire a substitute for her loss. Her dear friend Rainwing seemed to be recovering fairly well, but at the least Lyndz wanted to remain in symbolic mourning for Rainwing's loss, even if it was in her mind only.

Therefore...no necklace, no buckle. *Symbol is everything, isn't it?* It looked as if everything of late *was* symbol. She'd relayed this thought to Curdoz who fully agreed with her:

The impoverished soul is the one that disregards symbolism.

She looked around at the beautiful sky and at her twin with his hand on Nikal's shoulder. She looked to her left. Tiliruf was much too quiet, lately. She reached for his hand.

"Tiliruf, it's a grand day, isn't it?"

Rainwing was perfectly aware that nearby eyes were often on her, some glancing askance, unwilling to appear to offend, yet others staring. In her mind she was laughing at them, for she no longer had any hint of embarrassment in the presence of Humans. Too many of them were, to a large degree, odd, petty, and often concerned with the stupid side of things.

She knew she was using what her favorite philosopher, Seabreeze Stargazer, called *defensive mind techniques.* It didn't bother her. It was expounded in the treatise, *The Etoppsi Consciousness:*

'Though pride is the less-than-perfect undercurrent forcing the issue, such mechanisms are really an element of inner strength that allow the Etoppsi individual to cope with incongruence...'

She had lost her wings, but she had to force herself to deal with it. It helped that she was friends with Sundasher, the heroine Legionnaire, and now she understood her even better than ever. Sundasher was always cheerful whenever Rainwing visited. Rainwing had always expected she herself could never again be cheerful after such tragedy.

Yet there was a difference, and this was why she was not looking forward to when she might encounter other Etoppsi again. Humans were one thing. Etoppsi quite another. Sundasher still had *one* wing, and it was obvious to anyone she had made great sacrifice in order to protect her land and her people. The amputation scar was there from the top of her shoulder all the way down the right side of her back.

So, she couldn't help wondering what that idiot Modela was thinking. Did she really believe that leaving her scar-less, covering over the area on her back and shoulders where her beautiful wings had connected to her body, with skin and fur, was a good thing? It really annoyed her. Why could she not have scars? At least other Etoppsi would see that sacrifice had been made, right? Better had she lost them in the fight with the Serpents like Estader had his leg. She glanced over at him sitting there with the other sailors. He had a huge grin on his face. How bizarre it was that Modela had given him *back* his leg.

Instead, it was as though she'd never even *had* wings. All she was now was furry beast. It was as though she'd crawled out of the canyons like one of the great cats or a wolf or a bear. It was most infuriating, really. An Etoppsis would look at her and think she wasn't even Etoppsi! Wings were a critical part of who they were as a race, images of the Taxiarch in all His glory. In a way, her friend Sundasher still had that even if she couldn't fly.

The Humans, of course, were clueless to such a distinction. *They* probably thought she was lucky not to have two giant scars down her back. Kodi and Tiliruf, *idiot males*, had said something along those lines. It made her want to spit when they said that, just like when they would refer to her and the others as, 'the ladies.' Nikal understood, and Lyndz, of course. What great friends they were to her. She felt closer to them than anyone. But she liked them all. Even Kodi and Tiliruf were like having young topling siblings with all the teasing and banter that go along with family. She had grown up as an only topling. So, they had helped her to become a little less serious and more attuned to the playful. Though Tiliruf especially could be 'testy.' Anyway, she often thought, despite their silliness, she'd make a better Human than an Etoppsis. The thought brought her up short, however: without wings she really *was* more like a Human.

She was pretty sure she didn't really want that. Instead, she wished very much that there *were* wounds, red and swollen, and recently stitched. Maybe even a bit of soreness and pain. She'd have to talk to Ulna and Maru and see if maybe there was something they could do about that.

'...otherwise the individual is required to purge the underlying pride...'

Oh. Shaft your thumping logic, Seabreeze Stargazer! She mused this, laughing to herself, appreciative of having learned the meaning behind a couple of Tiliruf's expletives, even if his use of them reflected a sort of pure object coitus that was strange to her. Yes, she supposed deliberately creating scars would be too obvious and fake. And the Humans would think she'd lost her faculties.

Still, she thought, it wouldn't hurt to ask the Healers their opinion on the matter.

When it appeared to Enric that all was in order and the noon bell rang out in a nearby tower, he stood and raised high his right hand. No Sage of Tirilorin had been in front of his city's populace to offer a blessing in a hundred years at least. After a moment, the dim roaring of the great crowd fell away. Sister Hollina, who had in her lap an engraved copy of the *Book of Meicalian Histories and Prophecies,* came forward and presented it to Enric.

He opened it to a particular passage:

Entering into the secret realm of the Second Peoples, the Guardian appeared to the Qeterali in the land of Kel. At His direction they fashioned for Him a Staff. From a holly tree it was made. White was its color. At its head was carved the likeness of an eagle in flight, and in its talons was a perfect Solvermoon. In unknown sacrifice was its magic quickened.

To three of the Chosen, Lphai, Slomi, and C'nturi, the Guardian presented it. "Take this Staff to the north. Find the one called Terianh. A young captain is he. You shall find him in the rebel army near to the southern pass of the mountains on its eastern side. Handsome and tall he is with a bright complexion, for he comes from those lands east of the Mountains. He laughs much and his smile is one of joy. Lay your hands upon him, proclaim him My Brother, and give to him the Staff. For with it he shall continue the fight against the Ralsheen. Though much sacrifice is still to come, and much time may pass before the end of the war, for though the magic of Siriné is strong, have hope."

"And where will You be, Master? Will You not go with us and present the Staff Yourself?" asked Lphai.

"You are My servants, My Chosen, and you stand in My place in perfect fullness, for three is a goodly number. Mind, Messenger, Message. Creator, Emissary, Calling. I am the Messenger, the Emissary. Go as three to the one who is therefore Called. I have another task to hand, and into the sea I shall go. Farewell for now. You shall see Me again, for I do not yet ascend to the cosmos. I will find you in the North."

Then they watched as Meical the Guardian removed His garments, and His body enlarged itself to that of a god. From a high cliff near at hand, He dove headlong into the sea and was not seen again for nigh on a year.

Though the Chosen were perplexed by this, they had faith, and the three named by Meical did as they had been instructed. They found the young captain, Terianh, son of Moronia, the slave woman whom the Guardian had addressed in the crowd at M'gnani's palace many months before. As a youth he had been taken from his mother to serve as a soldier in the emperor's army, but now he led a force of former slaves in rebellion. In ceremony they laid hands upon him, proclaiming him Brother of Meical, and they set the Staff of the Eagle in his hand. Soon therefore, the other rebel armies flocked to him and in unity proclaimed him their high leader. Brother of Meical they called him, but also

Hand of the Taxiarch, and as a general he went forth on the great horse B'ulstread.

Curdoz and Ralle took turns reading as Enric held open the book. Their voices were strong and carried far. Enric returned the book into Hollina's care. War Marshall Jaden then brought the Eagle Staff to Enric who took it and stepped down five steps to where Nikal and Kodi stood.

He set the Staff upright before them. Nikal reached first and placed his left hand high, about a foot below the carved Solvermoon, and Kodi with his right hand gripped it just below Nikal's.

Enric spoke. "Your Highness Nikal of the Royal House of Nant, and Sir Kodi of the House of Fothemry of Solanto, you are Called by the Taxiarch Meical Beyond All Stars to be His strong arm in the fight against the evils that threaten the peace of our world. Have no fear of this Calling, for you are chosen Brethren of Meical Himself. By Calling you He has declared that you and you alone are the keepers of the keys to unlock the magic of the Staff. Yet always the choice is yours. Do you accept the Calling?"

"I accept the Calling of War Wizard from the Taxiarch Meical," said Nikal.

Kodi repeated Nikal's words.

Then Ralle and Curdoz also came close, and all three Sages placed one of his hands upon the head of the prince and the other upon the knight.

Enric spoke for the three. "As Sages of the Orders of Meical the Guardian, we proclaim the Message, that you are War Wizards, by way of the Messenger, by way of the Mind!"

Then the three removed their hands and together Nikal and Kodi, taking care not to detach their grips upon the Staff, turned around to face the great crowd. The Sages moved back several steps to flank them.

Instinctively, the two new War Wizards lifted the Staff high, and from it there came suddenly a great glow, bright white, bathing the two momentarily in light brighter than that which the noon sun cast upon them. The great crowd roared, and the people of the city of Tirilorin were united in common purpose.

Neither of the two men appeared visibly startled by the white glow. Kodi described it later to Lyndz, when pressed, that it simply 'felt right,' and certainly the magical connection between man and Staff came about in that moment. He left much out in his brevity with Lyndz, but he could not tell her all the truth, for it was not meant for her to know. There was more. Much more.

For to Kodi at long last the Voice came again into his mind. More obvious this time than when he made the offer to Onri in Thorune, and clearer than when he felt drawn to Bagarro's sword the first time he held it. The noise of the crowd diminished into nothingness as he heard it.

You have done well, Kodi, My Brother.

Meical! Kodi was glad. It was as Modela had promised, and yet he was so perfectly comfortable with the presence of the Voice, that he was already outside of his own sense of surprise and into his care for another. *Do You speak to Nikal, Meical? He needs You.*

I do speak to Nikal, for he is My Brother, as well as you, like Vanayisu and Berug and Terianh. I claim you as My brothers, for you are most like Me, and the Mind does not mind Me having favorites. But I know what you are really asking, and the best answer is that though I speak to him, he cannot hear Me clearly, for his heart is not as full of joy as yours. But that is of course why you stand beside him. Do not judge him, for it is not weakness that he does not hear well. Your world is a fallen one, not as corrupt as some, and more so than others, and so not all have the same heart as you. But have no doubt, Kodi, that I favor him as much as I do you, and that the choices he has made in the circumstances of his life have been the right ones since the days of his atonement under my wise Antonin. And you too have helped! Though he may not hear Me speak words, he hears yours. Yet his heart is broken. I cannot foresee his healing, but I do see hope for it. Don't ask Me more. I only see a little, and that which I do see, I cannot reveal all.

I would feel unhappy to think I am more blessed than others.

And I am not saying that. However, what I will say is there are tens of thousands here today, and they are blessed because of you. But I could say that of many others standing beside you.

Will You always talk to me like You are doing now?

There was then a mirthful laugh that set Kodi's soul sparkling like it did when he lay back in the Lake waters of his Vision, taking in the sunshine.

You have many to talk to, Brother. Such great friends, and more in your near future. Yet when you need Me, when you feel your choices are dependent on My judgment, then call for Me, Hand of the Taxiarch.

Please, Brother, one more question. Why do I not see Your face? Your body? Like others do. Like Lyndz did.

The merry laugh came yet again, causing the light of the sun to pierce Kodi's heart.

Not all need to see Me, and those who do see only an image I construct by which they can comprehend Me. But should my War Wizard Brothers wish to get such a glimpse for themselves, then they should do as you in Tiliruf's gold mirror! Yet in addition—for the mirror is but a reflection—is how others see them.

"Ha, ha!" Kodi laughed aloud, even as he stood there holding the Eagle Staff with Nikal. The roar of the crowd groaned in his ears again, and Nikal was glancing over at him with a bit of rare smirk.

"Tens of thousands stare at us! Whatever is so funny to you, Kodi? Straighten up. Stand tall now."

Kodi obeyed, though still with a grin on his face. "I, er...sorry, sir. It's good, though."

"I'm glad you think so, my friend. But I'm ready for this celebration to end."

"You felt it, though, didn't you? When the Staff shone white?"

"Yes, I did, but it doesn't make me so...gleeful."

"I know it doesn't. And I understand. I swear I do. It's terrifying, but if it's all the same to you, I'm going to do my best to smile when I can. I know it won't be easy, and I know how dangerous this thing is."

"And people will die."

"Yes. I realized that weeks ago as we took it from Modela's hands. And we ourselves might die because of it, because we'll be targeted by the enemy, and there may be times I'd almost rather die than use it against others. But if I prepare my mind a bit differently than you, you won't judge me for it."

"No. I trust you, Kodi. I have to. It is a burden we must share."

"The Guardian just spoke to me, Nikal."

Nikal glanced over at him again. "Like I said, I did sense something. I was reminded of the time Rainwing put her hand on my head and revealed the Prophecy. I could hear the echo of His Voice then. But oddly, there was something else I remembered, too: when I made love to Dira...which I know you have guessed about us, and so I will not hide that part of my past from you."

Kodi nodded. "The Staff is a male instrument. Curdoz said so. It has a potent energy to it that sort of makes me *want* to use it. It's meant to be entrusted in the hands of men who have loved. I think because it's supposed to balance the violence and cunning of the man who wields it. Curdoz is always cautioning us about balance, and so I've been thinking about it a lot. I haven't loved a woman like you have. But Meical seems to think I'm good enough for it anyway. He said that if you or I want to see His image, then to stand naked in front of a mirror."

"Meical said that?" Nikal's smile became full. Unforced. "Such a statement would certainly make one laugh."

"Yeah," Kodi said, grinning again. "But He said too it's how others see us. Nikal, He's saying to you that how you saw yourself and how Dira saw you when you and she made love is one of the images you should have when you bear the Staff. And I guess for me I'm just going to have to imagine it for myself, and the mirror reflection will have to do for now. And it's not only the physical, but rather it's the whole of our maleness. Tiliruf and I have talked of the art behind heroic nudes of the gods and other statuary and artwork of Classic times, the symbolism it represents. It's what's best about being a man on Dumhoni. I mean the sort of men like we are, 'cause I know everybody's different. But it's the strong, fighting warrior, the protective king, the wise Sage, the father, the brother, *and* the lover. All of that is represented in the art, and it is what you and I represent, too."

"That's pretty deep, Kodi. The ideals of those, you mean."

"Yeah, exactly."

"So, I should imagine, say, Terianh as the ideal warrior and king, Antonin or Curdoz as Sage and father...probably Aron as lover to Modela, don't you think? And you, Kodi, as the ideal brother."

"Thank you, Nikal. It's an honor, and you know I think the same of you. But all those things are who *you* are, too, when you wield the Staff."

"And for you, too."

"At nineteen I *am* young, like Curdoz says, so it's not going to be so easy for me to think of myself as some of those things yet like king and father. But everything's led to this day anyway, and I certainly feel the power of the Staff. So Meical is telling me it's all in me. Everything I need to use the Staff is in me. And you, too."

"So, there's no real training, is there? I understand, now. And like you, I feel a kind of compelling desire to test myself with it. It's nothing like the magic of other Gifted, is it? Like you suggest, it's more like the mating instinct, and it makes good sense that it might be like that considering that it is so dangerous, and so its use would otherwise come with much hesitancy."

"Only the best of brothers could talk like this to each other, Nikal. War Wizard brothers, and there's never been such a thing before, you know. We, you and I, are the first ever. It means something."

The crowd continued to cheer for many long minutes.

Nikal smiled. "I have been glad you have been by my side ever since our first private conversation at Genehbro's estate. You know that, and you sensed the need I had. We gain strength from one another; I no longer doubt that. But there is a big difference in how we look at the use of this Staff. I want it all to be over and done. I want the end of the war here and now, for good or ill. And you, I can tell, are looking forward to each and every day between now and then..."

"Because it's all hope to me."

"And there is no hope for me. Yet for your hope and for Rainwing's and everyone else's, I go forward. There is no other choice, in any event. Not anymore."

"But Meical told me there *is* hope for you. And the Prophecy spoke of hope."

"A Prophecy which likewise came from Him. And I suppose He said I am supposed to listen to you?" Nikal quipped.

"Um, hmm. He rather did say that, ha!"

Nikal had fallen into Kodi's orbit long before, as he admitted to the comfort of his presence from their time in the apple orchard. Kodi knew it, and yet he was not unwise to the contrast of his friend's ongoing depression revolving around the loss of Dira. Meical Himself admitted Nikal's heart was broken. His lover was lost. Brotherhood, it seemed, was all he had remaining. But Kodi felt that what Meical meant by hope for Nikal revolved around what was lost. He continued, "You've got to always picture in your mind your love for, and even making love to Dira. You can't let it go, despite the pain after. You hear me, Nikal? You can't shove it away just to help you get through the times before us. That's the wrong way of going about it. Mother Idamé says the Aura is a magical connection. You are still connected to Dira."

Nikal sighed, appearing close to breaking down, and Kodi worried he may have gone too far or said the wrong thing. But then the prince bucked up and said, "Oh. And my ability to connect to the Staff is proof of it?"

"Yeah, I think you're right. I hadn't realized that, but you're right."

"I...I didn't give up one for the other, did I? I did not really give up Dira for the Staff." The roar of the crowd had at last subsided, and their companions were making their way down the steps towards them. Nikal turned now and looked directly at Kodi and winked a big wink. "You and I need to get off, alone, with a brandy bottle. We'll do that tonight, I say. It may be a long while before we have such a chance again."

And such conversation did they have, as Nikal and Kodi with Musca sat in the sands on the beach, away from the city, with stars uncounted as the roof over their heads. Golden Orohmoon was quite bright in waning three-quarter phase, since Solvermoon as a sliver would set soon. The Staff lay near to them, though they would often pick it up and examine it, for it was connected to them in almost physical sense.

They spoke long, yet atypically, Nikal talked the most, and under the influence of his friend and of the brandy, he bared his soul to Kodi more even than he did to old Antonin long ago. Kodi listened as the other spoke of his many regrets. He detailed his debauchery and the shame of his teen years. He described his remorse and confession and of Antonin's forgiveness, and of his hopes afterward. He spoke in great detail of his love for Dira, and even of their strong passion: of the sheer joy of bodies connected, of swimming in the lake, of flower picking in the field, of cooking breakfast together, of lying naked under stars and moons, of conversations, of the needed healing of emotion and of body. Kodi was transported into a world he increasingly longed for at his core and told Nikal that the love he and Dira shared was exactly what he wished for himself. Nor did Nikal warn him against its pursuit and its unforeseen implications, as he might well have done only a day before.

Kodi revealed for only his second time ever his liaison with the stablemaster's daughter, how it had affected him, and of the subsequent guilt and shame that accompanied it. But then Nikal offered an entirely unique way of looking at it, implying that the connection with the Staff had in a way altered the affair, for though it was thoughtless in its execution, it was, even in its deficiency, a reaching out for the feminine balance. An imperfect symbol, yes, but a symbol nonetheless. That even that memory might aid Kodi in the use of the Staff. It felt good to Kodi to hear the words from a friend.

"She seduced you, Kodi. She overawed your instinctual nature. She was older. It was calculating entrapment, and she bears the greater brunt of responsibility for what occurred. Yes, you could have resisted. You are not guiltless, yet your actions were not atypical considering your youth and the male instinct you so wisely described to me earlier, seeking out as we do the need for the female. The point is you were repentant in your heart, you afterwards resisted entanglement, and changed your views of women, just as I did. You are in firm control of yourself, now, a man of the best quality. As you admitted, you learned things you needed to learn, and sounds like she did, too. I believe what you learned will be valuable when you find your eventual life-mate. Meical has Chosen you, and, as Antonin taught me, His forgiveness is eternal. None of the War Wizards were virginal, and that appears to be important, as you pointed out, and I think you're right about it, because something is different about us in comparison to Vow-takers. He doesn't choose Vow-takers as War Wizards. He chooses men who've learned to control that part of themselves yet retain the underlying passion and the capacity for that kind of love. I think your affair with her can have positive implications in how you make use of the Staff, like you said the same about me."

They picked up that instrument yet again, reexamining the imagery that Kodi had revealed earlier, and realized there was even more. The orb of Solvermoon was a prehistoric symbol of the Human world, as the stars were of the Etoppsi, and Orohmoon of the Qeteral. But it was also understood in love poetry that Orohmoon was the embodiment of the nubile female and Solvermoon of virile masculinity. They deduced that the Eagle was chosen deliberately by Meical to be carved into the Staff to represent Terianh, foreseeing it as a sign of his House. They contemplated its making, and though they could not discern how the Staff's quickening came to be, they did recognize that Meical had the Qeteral make it, and that it must have been formed by Qeteral magic, and not Meical's. It was of Dumhoni and not otherworldly. Despite their ignorance of the Qeteral race, Kodi suggested it had to be male Qeteral behind its making and its quickening.

"You think so? That makes sense, of course," said Nikal.

"And I'm guessing it was more than one bloke. It feels...what's the right word here? Multiplied? Plural?"

Nikal raised an eyebrow, but nodded.

They spoke on Meicalian philosophy. Neither was expert on Meicalian Mysticism, as neither had read the ancient texts or studied in the Valley. Yet they both had wise Sage mentors who took active roles in their spiritual development along with unique experiences of their own that connected them closely to Meical. Their understanding of Principles was the same, and their chosen Disciplines matched up almost precisely. Each discovered in the other a *'spiritual familiar.'* It was as though they shared the same blood and the same heart, differentiated only by environment and experience. Yet even here, Kodi could shed genuine tears for Nikal's struggles and pains, and Nikal could absorb into himself—and on occasion reflect—Kodi's uncompromising joy for life.

Much of the talk was strange, or it would have been in virtually any other company. Only the rarest breed of friends can commune at the level—so much of the personal, of the spiritual—that these two War Wizard brothers were doing. But maybe, not so unlike an Aura, these were connected by the magic of the Staff. It defined brotherhood in its purest form, whereby trust and fullest understanding between them would be, forever after, given constants in the bond they shared.

Long after midnight the two took a few more nips of their brandy, and hearkening to the call of the waves, stripped and swam. Musca sat by, guarding the Staff. Orohmoon missed her mate, for the remnant of Solvermoon had slipped over the western horizon, so instead she looked down lovingly on the forms of the two men. As they reveled in the crashing surf, Kodi proclaimed loudly that it was the Lake Vision all over again.

Even Nikal could feel the Presence, and the echo of the Voice seemed more than echo. For this night, Nikal felt healed and whole. He laughed, glorying like Kodi in the gift of his soul and of the power of his body as it splashed and fought the waves. For him, it was as good as any Vision.

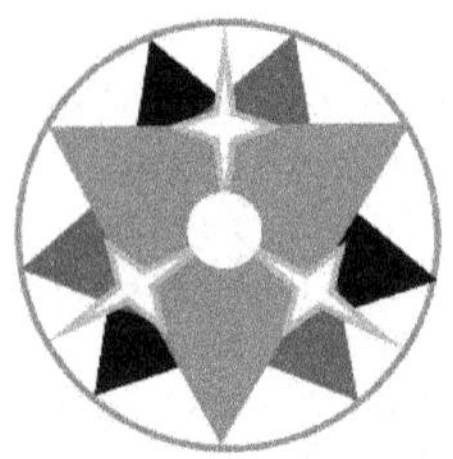

Chapter 5—Siriné

Accompanied by a contingent of guardsmen on horseback, the Alkhaness approached a city on the shores of the Sea of Siriné.

Dru had never been this far south. Most of his life had been spent closer to the smaller Khestadone Sea, the capital city, and once on an excursion to the northwest where he engaged in a skirmish with the Nantians of Fort Danzilet. Yet he had heard of this place. Men in the army did not like to be stationed here. Inundated with heavy rains and terrible lightning—Siriné would bounce from shore to shore—this city would often receive her winds and floods. They told of cohorts being struck dead in the streets by her lightning, a terrible roulette game of death, as the goddess's presence was not sufficient excuse for them to take a break from their patrol duties, burdened by heavy waxed cloaks to fend off the driving rains. At least the city's enslaved inhabitants could huddle inside huts whenever She approached.

There was a legend that the goddess was 'reborn' here, that She had been a beautiful being in feminine form who had walked the world but had chosen to become a Storm of Terror in order to demonstrate Her true power. A temple of worship was built on the edge of the cliff to mark the spot. Rites of sacrifice took place here, and from what Dru had heard, those men struck by Her lightning were Chosen. Their bodies were then taken into the temple by the priests. The details were sketchy, as only the priests were allowed access to this temple, but certainly the men never saw again the bodies of their compatriots.

The stories were few and hushed, undergirded by an element of fear. In any event, to be assigned to serve in this city was not a welcome proposition. The high priest of the temple, they said, was stark white of skin, terrible to look upon, and wielded magic over the mind. In his life Dru had seen a handful of the white-skinned. Some were temple priests. Others were trusted satraps that ruled provinces, and they would come to the capital to confer with the Alkhaness. One resided in the capital and governed the city. And, like here, there was a temple in the capital with a white-skinned priest. The white-skinned had a different language they used to speak to one another.

This was the first time Dru had been in the contingent to come here. He understood his mistress the Alkhaness would travel here from time to time to confer with the goddess Siriné. The word was she would go into the temple as the Great Storm approached, and she would always have someone with her. Sometimes it was a woman deemed beautiful by some, and sometimes it was a man, often a soldier in the prime of his life. Whoever it was would follow compliantly under her mind spells, enslaved to her will, and that slave, once inside the temple, never came out of it again.

On this journey, they had brought with them a guardsman from her own citadel, someone Dru had known for years by the name of Thurin. He was not unpopular, but none dared question the choice. Dru had liked him. He thought of him as a friend.

He looked at Thurin's naked figure pulled by an open wagon, as they all rode together into the city. The man was not bound, as his mind was no longer his own. A spell of enchantment had been placed on him. His eyes were glazed. He looked at no one and spoke to no one.

Dru was troubled.

Ever since the Alkhaness had returned from the Berugian border, the uncontrolled thoughts that had been intruding upon his mind had been doing so with more frequency and lasted for longer periods of time. Sometimes he was completely enthralled by his mistress, and this was the case whenever he was in her presence. Now, more often than not, whenever she would go somewhere or even enter into her chambers and close the doors, or now as she rode unseen inside her carriage, an imagined Voice in the recesses of his mind opened him to memories, and to regrets, and to worries. Again and again, he would be reminded of two people whom he was now convinced were his parents, from whom he had been taken by the soldiers as a small boy. He could see their faces ever more clearly. He would picture the brave Nantians from the skirmishes outside Fort Danzilet. And more than any other memory he would recall the Etoppsis he slew.

In his mind's eye, Dru could see the creature's face and unclothed sculpted body very clearly. The Etoppsis was huge and proud, delighting in their combat together, even as a warrior might. It was a fierce fight, more even than the great bear of the Alkhan Dru had slain in the tournaments. He had always thought of Etoppsi as animals, for that was what he had been taught. And this one was a spy who deserved what he got. Its wing was damaged. It could not escape. Yet, the words of the creature during that heated conflict came into his head.

'Defeat me you might, for you are strong—an image of the Taxiarch Meical in His glory, at least for a Human. You should be a king. Instead, you are but a slave, and defeating me will not gain you freedom. I feel sorry for you.'

Dru overcame the beast's vast might and stabbed him through the heart. At the time, he believed the creature's words were that of a beast and a fool, and for his heroic feat Dru was honored by the Khestadone army. It was one of his glorious moments, which until recently he looked back on with pride.

No more. His regret had become intense, and his sorrow for Thurin's upcoming fate seemed connected to it. After all this time he couldn't understand why he now cared about a dead Etoppsis. They were animals. But something about the beast's words haunted him: *the Taxiarch Meical.*

Why was he drawn to that name?

He also knew full well there was no one in all Khestadon whom he could ask. His senses told him that to mention the name aloud would be dangerous to his very life.

Riding through the city, the residents fell prostrate to the ground. They recognized the black, red, and gold carriage of the Alkhaness. They saw the man in the wagon. They knew what it meant. The procession made its way uphill towards the temple.

In the night, Dru was awakened by an immense peal of thunder. Siriné approached. He sat up, but all was dark. Another flash and by it Dru could make out the bunks where the rest of the guardsmen slept. A square, deeply inset window was open in the stone wall, but he saw no shutter and no means to close it. All was wet under the window.

The lightning came in more frequent flashes, yet it appeared despite the thunder the rest of the guardsmen were tired from the long journey and slept through it.

He had thrown off the musty blanket, the heat oppressive despite the rain outside. Lying back, his body exposed, his black eastern skin glistened with each lightning flash. He kept thinking of the words of the Etoppsis: *an image of the Taxiarch Meical in His glory*. He had never realized until now that somehow, despite not knowing what the creature was talking about, that it was offering up to Dru a compliment of some sort. He was, in a sense, honoring Dru and his *physical form*. Dru was indeed a giant, the largest man even among all the Alkhaness' champions. He was physically imposing beyond the measure of any other man. Dru knew it, and he felt some genuine self-pride in his size and strength. The Etoppsis was acknowledging this value, too. It was...something they shared.

Etoppsi are not just animals, he concluded. He took a deep breath and his face puckered. *What other lies have I been told?*

He imagined a whisper in his mind, though he could detect no words. He sat up on the edge of his bunk. With the next flash of lightning his eyes were drawn to the door.

He pulled on his trousers and boots, though he felt no need to don a shirt. His black skin might even help hide him, he thought. He strapped on a sheathed knife.

He didn't really know what he was about to do, but the thought of poor Thurin continued to haunt him. He could do nothing to save him, but he had a sudden and desperate need to understand clearly what his friend's fate was.

Between the next flashes of lightning, when all was momentarily dark, Dru slipped through the door and into the wet night.

A murky yellow glow filled all the sky in the direction of the sea. There was also the almost continual lightning, yet the sheets of rain and the general darkness acted as a glimmery and shadowy camouflage. He moved stealthily behind a series of columns and walls. His trousers were soon drenched but his boots were impervious to the wet, and he moved easily enough. The rain on his face and torso was sharp with the wind, but he was not troubled by it. Instead, it induced an inspiring element upon his consciousness, adding to his determination. The cooling rain on his skin seemed good despite the onslaught of wind-driven raindrops. With an element of defeat, by the thousands they steamed on his black hot flesh. Realizing his choices of the last half hour were truly by way of his own free will, he reveled in his powerful body, and the words of the Etoppsis repeated themselves in his mind: *An image of the Taxiarch Meical in His glory. You should be a king*. It was a sense of self-love he'd never experienced before.

An important corner had been turned in the life of Dru, and somehow, somehow, he knew it. Despite the gloom surrounding his thoughts of poor Thurin, despite the terror his mistress instilled in him, despite death itself, Dru knew in his soul he was not the same man he was when he fell into his musty-smelling bunk a few hours before.

An image of the Taxiarch Meical in His glory.

A particularly close blast of thunder caused him to pause. Then, he smiled. Why had his fear been displaced? He knew instinctively that the Alkhaness could detect the presence of people near her, and yet behind this fear, or rather replacing it, was a sort of awareness of himself that was more powerful. He felt free from her hold over his mind. The intruding Voice that had plagued him the last several months and which had never really spoken real words to him before was now an imagined whisper: *This is an evil place, yet you are not alone. I walk in your footsteps. I see through your eyes, Dru.* He knew he was just imagining the words, but with his renewed sense of bravery and daring, he trusted them anyway.

The main temple itself had a fearsome outline, like a spiked crown. It reminded him of the helm the Alkhan himself wore when he visited from the east at the time of the tournament years before. It perched at the edge of the last high cliff on the edge of the sea. He knew he would not be able to enter its front doors, for the temple priests would surely see him, but he was instead inspired to determine if he could get around to its back side.

The ground on which the temple stood was rocky, pock-marked, and nothing grew on it. He slipped himself over a low wall defining the perimeter of the complex and soon found himself climbing through crevices and over rocks. All was wet, and some spots were slippery and treacherous, yet he made good progress moving along the east side of the temple foundations. He didn't know it, but the winds and driving rain on the western side would likely have forced him to turn back. Unrealized, he had taken the path of least resistance, and against tall rocks he had momentary respites from the Storm's onslaught. He worked himself in this direction for a quarter hour and, looking up, he caught sight of what he knew must be the northeastern corner of the temple. The going was a little smoother here, but after another five minutes he came upon a pockmarked wall about twice his height. Looking this way and that, he realized he had little choice but to climb to the top and see what he could see.

The wall protruded out at an angle, and with his superior strength he gripped the wet but rough rock and climbed steadily. When he peered over the top, he realized he had arrived at his target. Before him could be seen the sea under the yellow glow and lightning flashes. Sounds of enormous shifting waves crashed two-hundred feet below. In the distance was the churning madness of the Great Storm, Siriné in all her supposed glory.

The sight sickened him. For years he'd never pondered the words of his Oath when he joined the army; they suddenly came back to him, and he felt shame:

Praise to you, Siriné, Mistress of the world.
Praise to you, Siriné, Mother of the Alkhaness.
To the Alkhaness we pledge our bodies,
To you, Great Goddess, we pledge our souls.

"I pledged my soul to *that?*" he asked himself.

No. You pledged yourself to something you believed was high and good. I felt it and became aware of you.

Dru was convinced he was talking to himself, and yet the words seemed to fit. But he now understood that the churning madness in front of him had no hold on him anymore. Though he knew the Alkhaness could still order him to do her bidding, and that he would be nearly powerless to stop himself, at a higher level of his being he was free. Beyond the Alkhaness supposedly was this fearsome storm goddess, who despite all the danger she might represent to the world, was little more than a rat in a dungeon of her own making. He now knew the goddess had not chosen by her own will such a form. She had been confined here by a Power beyond even herself. He had no vocabulary to explain to himself the spiritual or cosmic implications of what he felt, but he knew with all his heart he was no longer bound to the rat in the dungeon. A part of him now existed in a higher plane.

Even so, he also knew the rat carried disease and even poisoned teeth. And when he edged up a little higher on the wall and looked down, he could see for himself the disease and poison at work.

Below, about a hundred feet away, he saw her. He knew it despite the fact she had removed her mask and leather gloves. The yellow of her robes marked her. Her arms and face were white. She must be of the same sort of people as the temple high priests and the satraps, and Dru wondered their history. Her hair, typically white and bristly, hung dank and wet. He was shocked to realize what she truly looked like and believed he preferred her in her mask. He also realized that even though he was looking straight at her, his mind was still his own. A barrier separated them. He knew neither she, nor the Great Storm, could be aware of him. There was no sign of the temple priests. The Alkhaness must have ordered them to withdraw, or perhaps it was understood by them they were not to participate in her communications with Siriné.

She was not alone. Atop a large black block, surely an altar of sacrifice, stood Thurin. The block was set at the very edge of the cliff, the frothy sea below. Dru looked back at the temple. Dark and foreboding it stood.

It appeared the Alkhaness was in conversation with someone. Her lips moved, and her arms rose and fell. But there was far too much noise from the crashing waves, wind, rain, and thunder. Dru could not approach closer. Yet he remained anyway. For Thurin's sake.

You must not attempt a rescue. She will kill you. I need you.

Nor could he, even had he been close enough to hear, have understood the conversation. The language shared between the Great Storm and the Alkhaness was the same used by the white-skinned, of which Dru knew nothing:

"Another magic, Empress Mother. It moves against us. I have felt it."

The great water vortex at the center of the storm could not be seen in the distance. Yet the clouds above it swirled in a vast circle, highlighted by white flashes. The presence of the world goddess, dark spirit transformed—and trapped—spun outward through the wind and rain-filled airs.

She had arrived.

WIND AND WAVE, TOILING WATERS, SERPENT FLESH. COME! COME, DAUGHTER!

Ch'yad sighed. She tired of that spirit—impotent in so many ways, unable to expand its will, with power only within a confined orbit. Though that same spirit gave Ch'yad her own long life and magic. "You need me to walk the land, Siriné. I will not come. You know what it is, don't you, Empress Mother? This new magic that moves."

She felt a surge. The goddess was always angry, yet this was more intense. Full of hate.

THE GUARDIAN! WHO IS THAT? HOW DARE YOU SPEAK OF HIM! THERE IS NO GUARDIAN! I SHALL EAT YOU. I SHALL EAT HIM! A FEAST IT WILL BE. COME AND EAT WITH ME, DAUGHTER! TASTE! TASTE! THE YOUNG SERPENTS ARE SMALL AND DELECTABLE. YET THEY ARE NOT ENOUGH.

The howling winds threatened to lift Ch'yad off the ground. Her yellow robes were soaked from the pounding rains, her face and hair were dripping, but she held herself steady.

Of course, she had not mentioned the Guardian. To do so was blasphemous. Was that the answer, then? Did the old Cosmic Schemer plot against them? *He will not succeed this time*. "How does this magic work, Siriné?" she asked using careful words.

LIGHTNING, LIGHT, TERRIBLE LIGHT. EARTH AND WATER AND AIR. FIRE AND ICE. POWER IN THE HANDS OF...A MAN. STOP HIM.

Now she was getting somewhere. "A *Human* man?"

THE INNER STRENGTH AND WILL OF A HUMAN MAN WIELDING MAGIC DERIVED FROM QETERAL. MASCULINE POWERS AND EARTH FIRE. THAT IS WHAT IT IS. POWERFUL IT IS.

Ch'yad had no idea what she meant. Siriné often spoke in riddles. Or in madness. Humans had no threatening inner magic, unless, as with her and her twin, it was given them by Siriné herself. That of the so-called Valley of the Gifted was weak. That they should even call it magic—limited healing powers and bizarre Bonding Auras—was laughable. The ones called Sages were nothing like their predecessors and had no magic at all that she could discern. Feeble. The old priest in the temple behind her, descended from those who traveled with her and her brother from Tolos long ago, was strong in the magic the Alkhaness had transferred to him. And there were a few others like him in her realm she also trusted with some magic in order to instill obedience in the masses. But Siriné was not talking about any of them.

And Qeteral magic was limited to a few notable tricks. Though of course they successfully kept their land hidden for centuries. Even Siriné could not discover it in the days of her power. That was certainly something. Though Ch'yad had herself not pondered much the Qeteral over the centuries. They were not a threat to her ambitions. "It is not Ch'ain, Siriné, nor my warlock men Of the White."

CH'AIN? WARLOCK MEN? DON'T MAKE ME LAUGH, OR I WILL EAT YOU. YET CH'AIN KNOWS. HE SUSPECTED. CH'AIN SENT THEM LONG AGO TO BLOCK THE PATHS TO HER. THE WITCH. I TOLD HIM SHE HAD IT. FOR I HEARD HIM WHEN HE TOLD VANARATU. FOOL.

"Who told Vanaratu?"

VICIOUS GIRL! HOW DARE YOU SPEAK OF HIM! THE GUARDIAN IS A MYTH, I TELL YOU!"

There it was again. There were pieces of Siriné's history the Alkhaness would never understand. Most of it was not important to her. "Why will Ch'ain not tell me? What does Ch'ain know? Be plain, Siriné!"

WIND AND WAVE, TOILING WATERS, SERPENT FLESH! I HUNGER FOR OTHER. OTHER FLESH. FEED ME! FEED ME, MY DAUGHTER. FEED ME. OR COME YOURSELF!

Ch'yad looked at the one standing on the great stone. She had never learned his name. Names of slaves were not important, and she'd had so many over the centuries.

This one was unbound, docile, chained to her will. He had northern white skin. He might be descended from those she or her brother had captured in the shipping lanes or in the old wars with the Anterianhi long ago.

"The great goddess calls for thee. You have been chosen. Go. Fulfill your oath."

He nodded, unseeing. He said nothing, of course, for it was the rule that hers was always the last voice. Besides, he had no need to ever speak again.

The man limped to the edge, where below waters pounded the cliffs with unchecked violence. As the winds whipped in frenzy, he raised his arms high, and leapt.

The wind increased. A mighty wave like a giant gray-green tongue lifted high and crashed with lustful hunger across the cliff, splashing the altar and the platform behind.

Ch'yad raised her own arms high in anticipation. From the darkness above, a crooked serpent of blinding yellow light struck out. Her body convulsed and glowed white hot.

The sacrifice had been received. The Alkhaness felt the power of the world goddess flow through her like liquid hot iron in a weapon mold.

Ch'yad was that weapon.

Dru had seen all he could see, had taken in all he knew he could comprehend, and much he knew he never could. The lightning strike upon his mistress's body, and the deafening peal of thunder, was as much as he could bear. And yet she stood.

Go, now. Now!

"Farewell, Thurin," Dru said quietly to himself. He eased himself down from the rock wall and returned the way he had come.

Back at his bed—his cohorts still asleep—he stripped off his drenched trousers and lay on the bunk. Though wetness still patched his body, and his black hair hung damp, he appreciated the coolness generated upon him from the airs of the open window.

"I refuse to be the next one *Chosen.*"

Be wary, Dru. She is stronger than ever, now. She can still control your mind. Yet there is hope. Tonight, sleep in My peace.

Dru slept.

When the convulsions stopped, Ch'yad gasped. Sensing in the storm that the goddess's anger had withdrawn and the madness lessened, now was the time for clear answers. She would not stay satiated for long. "Tell me, Siriné! What did you hear? What...was told to Vanaratu?"

AH, YES, HE WAS A FOOL. HE HAD CHANGED ME, CHANGED ME, CHANGED MY BEAUTIFUL BODY. HE THOUGHT I COULD NOT HEAR HIS WORDS TO MY TREACHEROUS BROTHER. HE SAID TO VANARATU TO TAKE THE STAFF TO VANAYEMA'S ISLAND, FAR IN THE WEST. SHE WOULD GUARD IT.

Of the old records saved on the last ship Ch'yad had studied much. She knew who Vanayema was, an ancient enchantress of the time of the making of the three mortal kindred. She had not before believed in such a creature...but, "The Staff! Do you mean..."

YES, DAUGHTER! THE STAFF THAT DEFEATED YOUR FATHER LONG AGO. OH, HOW I MISS YOUR FATHER. HE WAS BEAUTIFUL! THE MOST BEAUTIFUL IN ALL THE WORLD! BLEACH WHITE HIS BODY, GOD-LIKE AND POWERFUL. LIKE SOLVERMOON HE SHONE AS HE LAY UPON MY BED. HIS EYES WERE GOLDEN YELLOW LIKE OROHMOON. OROHMOON, THAT I MADE. NO MAN COULD SATISFY MY DESIRES UNTIL HE CAME INTO THE WORLD."

The detail was making Ch'yad impatient. "The Staff of Terianh? Terianh the Rebel?"

IT HAS RETURNED, YES! LONG AGO, CH'AIN SENT SERPENTS THAT I GAVE HIM TO GUARD THE PATHS TO THE WITCH'S LAND, BUT THEY FAILED IN THEIR TASK. VANARATU MOVES AGAIN, HE DOES. HA, HA! I WILL DESTROY HIM WHEN HE COMES. AND HE *WILL* COME. HE WILL COME SOON. HIS END IS NEAR, I SENSE IT. I HAVE PROPHESIED IT, HAVE I NOT? AND I WILL CAST HIS TREACHEROUS SPIRIT INTO THE VOID. NO POWER ON EARTH WILL MATCH MINE...IN THE END.

"Who carries the Staff?"

I TOLD YOU!

"A Human man, yes." So Siriné did not know who it was. Goddesses were not omniscient. All in all, Ch'yad cared less for Siriné's cryptic knowledge than for her power. She wondered if Ch'ain might know who it was. Apparently, he already knew more than she concerning this matter. Always keeping secrets from her he was.

Of course, she kept secrets from him. One day he would have no more secrets. *I will be the mistress of all secrets.* It was time to get the information she needed most while Siriné was fully coherent. "I have news, Empress Mother! The land of Tolos has been cleared of the Dragons! Your prophecy has come true!"

The winds whipped high, and high gray waves weaved and rolled like fat creatures in an orgy of drunken excess.

THE CROWN OF CHARMS! YOU MUST RETRIEVE THE CROWN!

To be sure, Ch'yad thought. But she must block her mind from dwelling on it, or the goddess might read her thoughts. "Then you must tell me now exactly where to find it! You prophesied long ago that when the Dragons leave Tolos, the Crown of Charms would be found!"

AND YOU SHALL BRING IT TO ME! I SHALL RESUME MY FORM AND MY WILL SHALL NOT BE DENIED! ONCE I HAVE IT, VANARATU CANNOT HOLD ME HERE. I AM BEAUTIFUL! BEAUTIFUL BEYOND THE MOONS AND THE SUN! ALL SHALL BEHOLD ME AND LOVE ME! THEY SHALL BEHOLD ME AND THEY SHALL BOW BEFORE ME! ALL SHALL BEHOLD ME AND WORSHIP ME AS THEY ONCE DID. YOU MUST GO TO TOLOS, CHILD. YOU MUST RETRIEVE THE CROWN AND BRING IT TO ME! YOU SWORE TO ME YOU WOULD DO SO, CHILD. YOU AND CH'AIN SWORE TO ME. YET SO FAR YOU HAVE NOT DONE SO!

"So many Dragons could not be overcome, Empress Mother, and you know it. And Tolos is very far away."

DRAGONS! I DO NOT RECALL EVER EATING ONE. I EAT THEIR COUSINS. THE SERPENTS ARE DELICIOUS, THEIR FLESH SPICY, THEIR BLACK BLOOD SWEET.

"Yes. You are indeed powerful, Siriné. More powerful than any in the world today!" She must humor her.

BRING ME THE CROWN! IT IS MINE. YOU AND CH'AIN WERE LITTLE HUMAN CHILDREN. I BECAME YOUR MOTHER AND GAVE YOU PERPETUAL LIFE. YOU ARE STILL CHILDREN. YOU NEED YOUR MOTHER.

Ch'yad and her brother had debated this before, long ago when for years they lived together, before he left for the eastern land to form his own realm. It was one of the things they agreed on: Siriné had killed their Human mother. In a way, neither cared, for Siriné provided the two immortality and was the source of their inner magic. Yet Ch'yad had no intention whatsoever of returning here with the Crown should she gain it. And there was nothing Siriné could do about it. Yet always she must be indulged.

"The Dragons are gone from Tolos, Siriné! You promised when that happened you would tell me where to find the Crown of Charms. So I could bring it to you, of course. I cannot bring you the Crown if you do not tell me where it is hidden! Do you understand me, Siriné? Where is the Crown's hiding place?"

THE DRAGONS ARE GONE, YOU SAY? THE GATE! THE GATE! YOU MUST USE THE GATE! IT MUST BE HERE IN THE SOUTHERN LANDS, FOR THE DRAGONS, THEY CAME FROM THE SOUTH! THAT IS THEIR HOME! I EAT THEIR COUSINS, I DO.

Ch'yad could sense that the effects of the sacrifice were already beginning to wear off. So Siriné had heard of the Doorway. Ch'ain had finally told her his speculation that that was how the Dragons came to Tolos and destroyed their home. "You mean the Doorway? I hunt for it now, though Ch'ain nearly thwarted me. I am close to discovering it, I think. But you only mean it as a shortcut."

YES. A PASSAGE FOR ARMIES, BUT AS A QUICK WAY TO THE CROWN.

The Alkhaness wondered how much Siriné knew of the Doorway, if Vanaratu had made it perhaps, and why She had not mentioned it before. But she did not have enough time to question her on this. She already sensed the storm moving off east. Some things were more important than others. "When I get through the Gate and into Tolos, where do I go to find the Crown of Charms? Tell me now, Siriné!"

And as Ch'yad stood there in the howling tempest, Siriné told her. In vivid detail and with images cast into Ch'yad's mind the dark goddess revealed to her how to find it.

...YET IT MISSETH THE GREEN STONE CHARM. I DO NOT NEED IT FOR MY RESTORATION. IT SHALL BE FOUND LATER.

Ch'yad's face rarely demonstrated emotion, nor did it this time. Yet she was most puzzled by this new tidbit of information. "Your prophecies have never mentioned a green stone being missing from the Crown! What properties did this green charm possess?"

I SENT IT TO YOUR FATHER FOR HIS PROTECTION. IT DID NOT REACH HIM IN TIME.

So, its attribute was magical protection. Siriné apparently intended for the emperor, Ch'yad and Ch'ain's father, to have it before the last battle. Ch'yad could not help but wonder if events might have turned out differently had the stone reached him before Terianh the Rebel confronted him with the Staff.

"I will find your Crown, Siriné! I swear!" *But I won't be bringing it to you, and I will hunt the green stone myself. You will not touch it again.*

Ch'yad intended to place it on her own head, and when she did so, the whole world would be hers. She would no longer need to come to Siriné, for a permanent share of Siriné's power was in the Crown of Charms. Ch'ain could not properly wear it, for it held the divine powers of the female. She had learned that much from Siriné long ago. Even their father could not control it. It sat where Siriné placed it when at the last she went off to fight Vanaratu. Clearly that last didn't go as planned. Then the Dragons came, by the thousands, and overran all the land of Tolos and devoured the last of the great Ralsheen Empire, and Ch'yad and her brother as children escaped just in time. But the Dragons were now gone, likely starved out in competition for food. Ch'yad would find the Crown in the deep place where Siriné hid it and where no Dragons could get to it. As Alkhaness and Empress, she would rule all, and even Ch'ain would submit to her.

Was there time left for further inquiries? "You shall be queen of the world, Siriné. But tell me of the magic that brews. Tell me of the Staff if you can!"

HE CAME TO ME.

"Who?"

CH'AIN. I WILL EAT HIM AND YOU. I ALWAYS PREFERRED THE WHITE-SKINNED. THE MEAT IS SWEET.

Very little time remained. "Tell me what we face, Ch'ain and I. Tell me, Empress Mother."

HE IS RIGHT. CH'AIN YOUR BROTHER IS RIGHT. YOU MUST ENGAGE YOUR WAR NOW. YOU WAIT OVER LONG.

Surely, they sounded exactly like her brother's own words. So, he had tried to manipulate Siriné. *Or perhaps me, through her*? Yet the goddess must believe that indeed this Human man was a threat. Terianh killed the emperor with the Staff.

But the Alkhaness was far more powerful than her father ever was. Yet maybe it was indeed time to make her move.

"I will bring the Crown to you, Empress Mother," she lied, just as the spirit of the goddess slipped eastwards and out of consciousness.

I MADE IT. LONG AGO. IT IS MINE. BRING IT TO ME, AND I...WILL...EAT...YOU.

Exactly so. Which is why you must never have it, Stepmother. The rain stopped and the winds grew less. The Alkhaness raised her arms and mumbled some words. Her white hair and yellow robes drained of all water, and she returned the all-covering mask and donned the arm-length gloves. She turned from the violent waters of the Serpent Sea. She saw the high priest approach. He would wish to know, but she would tell him little. He would beg for a tiny share of the new magic.

She looked back at the sea. *If all goes well, I shall never have to come to you again, Siriné.*

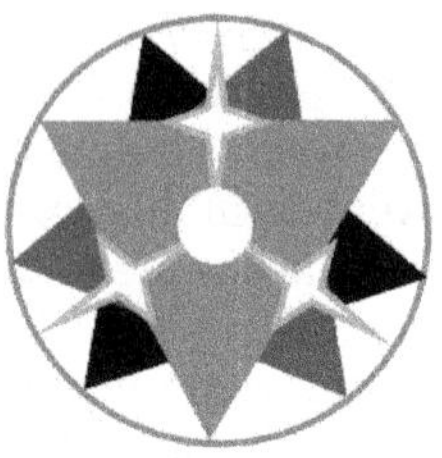

Chapter 6—Fort Danzilet

Fort Danzilet sat on the Southern Continent on a small peninsula which jutted northward into the Central Passage and overlooked a harbor. There were two fortresses, really. One commanded the harbor, near the tip of the peninsula, called North Fort, and about four miles inland South Fort was built at a point where a narrow pass between mountains connected the peninsula to the lands beyond under the control of the Alkhaness of West Khestadon.

It was a stronghold of the Nantians, built after the Lintiri War, but it was more than a fortress. Around the harbor and including North Fort was a large and beautiful, white-marbled city, called simply Danzilet. It had its own strong defensive wall that essentially cut across the peninsula, and Brigade units were responsible for this wall's defense. It had a specific purpose—a final line, should the enemy breach South Fort's defenses and threaten the city, giving the populace a last chance to escape by ship under the protection of North Fort.

The city operated under the control of merchants, they and most of the inhabitants being citizens of the Republic of Tirilorin. There were other cities and outposts of the Republic and of Nant along the shorelines of both the Northern and Southern continents, the sea being narrow here. It was the trade route that led hundreds of miles to the east in the direction of the Eastern Kingdoms.

This was its narrowest point, as the peninsula pointed to the Northern Continent to the lands of old Lintiri less than twenty miles away. If on a clear day one were to climb into the hills south of Danzilet and look off past the city and over the blue sea, the shores of old Lintiri could be sighted. That kingdom was mostly abandoned after the last war, with the exception of a few shoreline enclaves which then fell under the authority of Tirilorin. The entirety of the Lintiri royal family and its government were overcome and destroyed during that war. Many Lintiris had been captured by the khans and taken to Khestadon and enslaved, and most of the remainder moved west to Tirilorin. Reconstructing the Lintiri kingdom was no longer considered practical, especially as the imperium, too, soon collapsed.

From west to east on the Southern Continent was a mountain range, tall, narrow, and rocky. It offered superior protection from West Khestadon. The Alkhaness claimed all this land, but in her weakness following the last war, the narrow land at the base of the mountains and which fronted the sea had been cleared of her control, colonies had been established, and the Kingdom of Nant had no intention of allowing her to have it again.

Fort Danzilet was the largest city and most imposing of all the strongholds in this region, and it was a key to control all. It was, during normal times, the home of a quarter of the Nantian Royal Navy, its purpose to continually guard the entrance eastward that led south into the Khestadone Sea. This was done in attempt to block passage of the still dangerous navy of West Khestadon, and also to discourage piracy. When war began in the East with the Alkhan, it became more important than ever to ensure none of the West Khestadone ships emerged to assist East Khestadon against Essemar and Hralindi. The Nantians had built more ships and had doubled its Danzilet-based fleet. It was a major strategy of the Nantians in this war and surely kept the Alkhan from advancing faster than he had so far done. The Alkhan had no navy of consequence due to limited timber resources, and so he relied entirely upon land routes across desert terrain in order to get his armies to the war front.

South of Danzilet's defensive wall was a wide area of wealthy estates harboring vineyards, olive groves, and citrus orchards, wines and fruits being an important product in the trade route system. There was also a large acreage reserved by the Nantian military for cavalry and weaponry training. In the hilly area beyond were marble quarries and stands of cultivated forests used mostly for fuel, ship repair and for local construction. Between two monolithic peaks was the narrow pass southwards. Long ago this had been a major roadway for the khans during the Lintiri War. Nowadays it was blocked by a wall with ramparts and the building of South Fort like a great citadel behind, and these guarded against the Alkhaness' claims.

There had been skirmishes. The Nantian army would patrol the far side of the wall in order to keep the gap leading to it clear of her soldiers. Not too far beyond, on lowering slopes of the rocky hills leading to the plain behind it was a small city and fortress of West Khestadon. It and South Fort faced each other over the distance under a hostile peace of sorts, but occasionally there were encounters. It was no secret, really, that this was one of a number of training grounds for the Alkhaness' armies, and there was inevitable conflict. The Nantians always held their ground.

Yet the magic of the Alkhaness had undoubtedly grown, and it could be felt by some of the soldiers patrolling the rampart walls as a kind of fearful tension upon the air. It had become more dangerous to send troops in any real numbers to monitor the gap beyond, although stealthy spies would sometimes be sent in the night in the direction of her city in order to determine if she might be massing for some greater conflict. Since the war in the east between those kingdoms and the Alkhan, it was determined the Alkhaness had been enlarging her city and stationing more troops. To date, however, the peace had held, as she had not yet sent forces to try to take South Fort. Here, on the other side of the gap along sun-filled shores, the inhabitants of Danzilet felt safe, and the subtropical beauty and prosperity of the place did not lend itself to significant worry. But the Nantians would always warn them: *If war comes with the Alkhaness, this is where she will strike.* There were contingency plans in place for a withdrawal of the citizens and armies.

The worry had increased. Since the news of Tirilorin's decision to mobilize, and of the skirmish with the Etoppsi at the end of their Great Wall, the situation at Fort Danzilet appeared to be growing more precarious. Already, an addition of two-thousands of both Tirilorine Brigadiers and Nantian soldiers had been brought here to reinforce the defenses. Thousands more had passed through already on their journey to the east to reinforce the armies there. The increased military activity had spooked some of the richest citizens who then packed up and left for the relative safety of Tirilorin. Yet most remained, convinced Danzilet was as safe as it had ever been. Maybe it was, and maybe it wasn't.

Prince Nikal and the others had arrived by way of his ship some days before. They had led a large fleet of warships and transport vessels supplied by War Marshall Jaden and had docked here, though most had already moved on east. But for those who remained for now, it was not necessarily a respite. Almost immediately Nikal had taken Kodi, Tiliruf, Hadon, Manwul, and many knights in Nikal's service to the training grounds to work with the B'ulstread warhorses supplied by Genehbro and others for cavalry duty. Tindalle was here, Nikal's great stallion, silver-coated not so unlike Rainwing and Musca. Kodi's new horse, Scadyne, was a gorgeous, red-coated animal, and Kodi and he had taken to each other in perfect harmony back at Genehbro's estate. Too, Scadyne and Musca enjoyed one another, an odd pairing that, yet not so much considering the spirited nature of each.

Curdoz had come out to the training area, too. He had an important function, at least for the time being. He held in his possession the Eagle Staff of Terianh, determined by plan to always keep it handy in the near vicinity of Nikal and Kodi. He was not alone with it. That war was coming was better understood as six armored knights were assigned the duty of protecting Curdoz and the Staff. They followed Curdoz wherever he went with this.

Idamé was not seen very often by the men. She remained at a mansion in Danzilet belonging to a Mother Matrimonial and her accompanying Sisters who were assigned to live and work in the city. Rainwing and Lyndz stayed here, too, at least at night. Though all had grown very fond of Ulna and Maru, those two had chosen, with Sage Ralle's permission, to spend a month in Tirilorin studying in the Library and then to return to Nant.

Rainwing was not one to be left out of the fun of training. She might not have her wings anymore, but that did not diminish the fight in her. It may have been that her emotions had healed from the loss of her wings, or that the physical exertion helped her cope. The main point was she had moved past her loss, and her zest for life was still strong. She held forth near to the cavalry training ground in an area used for javelin throwing and spear casting. She was good. Very, very good. She seemed to have the strength of ten strong men and aimed with an accuracy that overawed the Human men watching her. Her lack of wings, though they couldn't help but wonder her story, seemed to make no difference in what she could otherwise do with that powerful body. Her muscles rippled silver in the sun.

Lyndz would come out too, sometimes, and had insisted upon learning archery. Idamé did not act pleased, but Lyndz had recently taken charge of herself, and when Kodi teased her, she retorted.

"What? Who do you really think I am, Ko? Quit treating me like some helpless damsel. I'm going to learn archery, and that's that! Quit sounding like Mother Idamé."

A bit shocked by her vehemence, as he had not in the least meant to seem discouraging, he replied, "I don't think of you as a helpless damsel, and you know it. It's just different, that's all, seeing you like this. Out here with all these men with their weapons. You've changed."

"And what do you mean by that, eh? And *men* are everywhere we go, doesn't matter where I am."

"It's not bad! I swear. Sorry."

"Well, then, give me my space, Brother. And on top of that, I want you to find me a proper knife, or give me yours and find another. I'm going to learn to throw. Rainwing's going to teach me. We're in dangerous places. I'm going to learn to protect myself. I'm grateful for what Nikal is doing by giving me a guard out here, but I'm tired of sitting back and knitting shawls! I'm a descendant of Bagarro, too, you know. And Grandfather Jugan. I've got their blood in me just like you. Well, you know. You're the true warrior, Ko, really. But I've got to learn a tidbit or two. I've just got to."

"It's just the novelty of seeing you this way. You look right sporty, actually. Wearing the lady-cut trousers all the time now, and boots. I think it's great. And looks like you're already good with the bow. You've got some good form."

"Learned by watching you, haven't I?"

"Yeah. But you're not throwing with my hunting knife. Father gave it to me, and I care for it perfect like he showed me. It's much too big for that anyway. I'll get you a trio of throwing knives; they're made different, you know."

Realizing now how determined she was, Kodi did better, not only sending the promised throwing knives but ordering a trusty Nantian trainer to work with her personally on her archery and chosen implements every morning for three hours. He could tell Rainwing really didn't want to break from her own routines. Besides, Rainwing's bulk, hand size, and other factors made it difficult for her to really demonstrate to Lyndz properly how she needed to handle what were to Rainwing small implements.

Lyndz' bow and quiver were very decent ones, given her back in Tirilorin by Steffia, Manwul's new wife. She was remaining in Tirilorin despite the fact she had a warrior impulse not so unlike her husband. She'd almost certainly have chosen to join the new female archery companies, except for one thing.

She was pregnant. It was early still, but she could tell, and it was confirmed by a Healer, who could sense the new life developing in her.

"*Thumping Thumpers Make Three,*" Tiliruf had joked to Manwul when he had heard this astonishing news upon their return to Tirilorin after the search for the Staff.

"Yeah, they damn well do!" Manwul had replied with a roguish grin.

"And this feat was probably achieved in my own bed at the estate, eh?"

"'S not your bed, scoundrel. We're in the guest cottage!"

"I've slept there lots of times, mate!"

"Shut up, Tiliruf! I don't want to think about that bed with *you* in it."

"Tut, tut, tut. You know you shouldn't call me a *scoundrel.* That's not nice coming from my *bodyguard*, eh?"

Upon their arrival in Danzilet, Manwul and Hadon certainly did follow Tiliruf everywhere he went. They wouldn't let him out of their sight, per Nikal's orders. Their continued presence put somewhat of a damper on the son of Genehbro. Brothels existed in Danzilet, and though they might not have actually stopped him from locating one and making use of its services had he been insistent—Nikal had not specifically forbidden it—being insistent just didn't work for Tiliruf on this. Part of the overall fun from his perspective was the delightful night-time sneakiness involved in pursuing this favored activity. He was not allowed 'sneakiness' anymore. Manwul and Hadon would have followed him right into the front door and stood outside the sofa rooms. He doubted, even if he'd paid for their own enjoyment, that they'd engage with the pleasure women. They'd given up their North Bend pursuits years ago under some dumb, *Discipline*-inspired mutual pact. Of course, Manwul was Bonded now, and Hadon would talk dreamily—and rather suspiciously—about that exotic, dark-skinned ambassador from Essemar.

Tirilorin had bathhouses in most parts of the city, yet since all the mansions in Central City had each their own running-water bathing rooms, Kodi and Lyndz and the rest never made use of the public ones. Danzilet, on the other hand, was particularly noted for its beautifully appointed public baths with elaborate heated water systems, and virtually everybody in the city used them. Fresh water was supplied by a combination of concrete aqueducts and underground piping from a reservoir in the southern hills. The pools, both warm ones and cool, were lovely, with falling waters and mosaic art depicting frolicking sea animals and fish. The city's girls and women could be found frequenting the baths in the mornings. Lyndz would often go early and met many interesting women much like the business class in Tirilorin. In fact, many of them knew Madam Arlay when she spoke of her. Men and boys dominated the baths in the evenings, the soldiers after their training or maybe after a round or two of ale at local pubs. In any event, the baths were stress-free places where all could immerse themselves in the soothing water pools and engage others in carefree conversation.

To newcomers it was all very luxurious. Servants employed by the city would provide hair-trimming services, offer oil body massages for tips, or otherwise serve by the bath pools with washing and shaving supplies and linen towels and robes. Even Order Healers would occasionally show, taking turns from their work at the Hospital. They would apply their green magical touches upon those who were stiff and achy. Afterwards, soldiers usually returned to their rooms in the North Fort barracks to rest up for the next day's training.

Tiliruf, Manwul, and Hadon shared a room in North Fort, off the hall of a tower containing also Curdoz' private quarters and the rooms Kodi and Nikal shared together. Sometimes Kodi would come to Tiliruf's room to indulge in some fun with the three Tirilorines, but more often than not, he remained holed up with Nikal. They always had strategies to discuss and histories of Terianh to read in order to glean all they could on how Terianh made use of the Eagle Staff.

Tonight, after a glorious hour at the baths—Tiliruf tipped generously for all their decadent oil massages—the three Tirilorines could be found by themselves in their room lazing about half dressed, expanding upon their relaxed state with a new bottle of brandy. Tiliruf smoked while the other two only drank. A lot.

Puffing on his pipe, Tiliruf, perhaps feeling thwarted again by a wish to slip out alone into the night, or maybe due to a very different and unacknowledged angst building within him the last few weeks, threw out a question that seemed reflective of the first idea or resistant to the second. "What's so great about monogamy, anyways, eh?"

"It's good," replied Manwul, who had readily started the *man game* by downing a quarter of the bottle, insisting he needed to test its quality.

"Damn good," repeated Hadon with a smile. He'd had three good-sized gulps himself after Manwul assured him it was 'passable.'

To that last, Tiliruf took the largest swig, half-empty now, sat up and looked at Hadon in wide-eyed shock. "You've been shafting the ambassador! I knew it! And when'd that start up exactly?"

"He likes the details," said Manwul, nodding at Hadon and pulling his chair closer so they could pass the bottle around. "Pretty normal, that. 'Spose I do, too. I'm good for the repeat, mate. Tiliruf could tell you're not just *courting* her."

Hadon's smile turned to a self-satisfied smirk. He grabbed the bottle from Tiliruf and took another large nip. "Night you left to look for the Staff. Ah, that first night...damn."

"Eh? That night! That very night? You only met her at the dance the night before! What is it with you men committing to life-mates just a day after meeting...and less than that in Manwul's case, eh? That was more like a minute-and-a-half. *Auras.*"

"Well, no Aura for me, but I took Lord Kodi's advice. Smart man, he. He made me realize I already knew what I wanted, and obviously so did she. And she's got a name, Tiliruf. It's Sturla, and maybe, like you, I never imagined real love for one woman could be so damned fun." He then leaned back and crossed his ankles, and his smirk grew a little smirkier. "I called on her that afternoon, and when she saw it was me...I don't know, but I got all grinny, 'cause she had that happy and inviting look in her eye. She'd obviously been thinking about me since we parted at the dance. So, she invited me to dinner, Eastern style, and yep, the *courting* phase ended about half-way through a night walk in the Palace garden. We were standing holding hands in that ironwork gazebo looking out above the hedge. Never seen so many stars in all my life. Maybe a moon peeked above the hedge, but something triggered, and we both felt a sudden need to release some pent-up energy. It was animal and wild, and we weren't quiet about it, either, and if anybody else was snooping around the garden that evening, they'd know exactly what we were about."

Manwul and Tiliruf chuckled merrily at this delight-filled description, while Hadon took another nip and continued his tale.

"Weren't willing to stop quite with just one go. First time's more like winding up the clock, you know. Just kind of makes you tick faster. So, she followed me home. Manwul was of course off that morn with Steffia, twinning what we were doing out at your father's country place." He winked at Manwul, who snickered with a *'yep'*. "I know our house ain't much to brag, but Sturla thought it was charming. 'Course she didn't really come for the house tour, did she? After removing a lot of *unnecessary garb,* we had better things to look at than old furniture. She's mesmerizing, she is, and the gold jewelry on her dark skin. I knew I'd landed right in one of those erotic Eastern love tales. She said I was 'the healthiest white-fleshed specimen' she'd ever seen and made me feel like a damn World God. The shadows we made on the wall in the lantern light—like a damn theater play! It was just fiery good and went on all night. Slept arm in arm till noon. Beautiful bath. Then she, uh, had her belongings brought over by her servants in the afternoon, and they and the cooks all settled right in. Cheery lot, they, and I could eat Eastern cooking the rest of my life, I swear. Anyway, night after night it repeated in perfect pitch."

"And you weren't going to stop her moving in, and who'd care anyways. Proud for you, I really am, but I got to know, mate. Is it real, eh? That magical *Eastern Squeeze?* I've always wished... Gi' me that bottle!"

"That and lots of other things. Shaft, Tiliruf. Talk's making me go all..." Hadon had to shift in his seat. "Oh well, I do miss her."

"Tiliruf's the one getting happy," stated Manwul, snatching the brandy away. A big man, he was a first-rate consumer.

"She pregnant, too? Shut up, Manwul." Tiliruf took a particularly large draw on his pipe. He then produced a perfect smoke ring and suggestively blew a series of rhythmic puffs right through the center of it, to the others' sniggers. "Horsey thoughts got to *go* somewhere, don't they?"

"Well, it's true we've kind of thrown caution to the wind. I, er, don't think she's in Steffia's state. But if she was to have my babe it'd be the best gift ever, and I'm ready to do my part. Anyway, she's thinking she'll leave and sail east soon. Sturla's main job was to argue for the mobilization, though she stayed to encourage Midianna and the promotion of women into archery companies. If we meet up, I'll probably get that Mother Idamé to do us up a little do. We want to make it official and all, but up till I sailed it was wonderful to feel all wild and frisky and not so settled. But she gave me this." He fingered a gold link chain on his neck which Tiliruf had seen several times on the journey from Tirilorin, as Hadon never took it off. "It's her claim on me. I gave her my grandmother's Nantian pearls. Been saving 'em for years. The love she made to me that night...um, um, um. She cracked open the Hralindi Oil."

"Shaft! Hralindi Oil! They get that sometimes in North Bend! The massages they do with that, stars! Sure different than the ones we got tonight at the baths by *male masseurs*, eh? And other good stuff, yeah. They sell that package for a right fortune. Silky. And that smell. Fires the senses."

"Sturla gets it by the quart." Hadon replied.

"And she had some delivered out to Steffy at the cottage. Was that ever a good night. Er...and a long one. Open another bottle, Ruffy. Or get me my own. You got tons in that trunk. *Hralindi Oil.* Why'd you have to go and bring that up, Hadon?"

"Steffia's got those strong hands, you see." Hadon said, leaning into Tiliruf.

"You know it. She's an archer, isn't she? She'd be right good at *Bow-and-Arrow*, eh?" He and Hadon laughed uproariously. Manwul put on that rogue grin of his, while, not waiting for Tiliruf to do it, he opened another bottle and started all up afresh.

By now they were exchanging sniggers and guffaws like nutcracker thirteen-year-olds around a campfire. They soon broke out a pack of Fifty-twos, and the camaraderie continued to grow between these three. There was an earthy quality to Manwul and Hadon that largely helped Tiliruf feel rooted despite some of his latest angst. Until recently he'd only seen their determined and gentlemanly public demeanor. They had not before been a part of his circle. Lukas and Colinn were a shared set of mutual friends, but he'd never really heard from them that these two had such playful private sides. He'd always thought them a bit aloof, a little too attached to the Meicalian Disciplines for comfort. He knew they went regularly to Sage Enric for the Affirmation, and of course they never allowed themselves anymore the bawdier temptations of North Bend and refused to gamble beyond coppers. Yet he'd never invited them to his rooms for games and brandy, though he realized now they enjoyed these pastimes as much as he did. They had trained together under Jaden and had commonalities there, too, along with mutual memories of their Tirilorine heritage.

Tiliruf was slowly coming to terms with his views on the Disciplines, or at least with the fact that others took them seriously. It seemed all those around him now were associated with Meicalian *mysticism* in some form or fashion. With their joint submission to Nikal and determination to do well by Kodi, they'd begun to treat one another with fraternal support. And all along Manwul and Hadon had high regard for the House of Terianh. Undeserved in Tiliruf's point-of-view, yet there it was. They showed him honor in public, calling him "Swordmaster" like they always did Jaden, and assisting him in all he did like esquires. And of course, they were the best to train with on the field and to keep his skills at their best. Then each evening behind closed doors they'd revert to the familiar, let loose with a sense of fun and shared humor, and rummage without asking through his trunk for their preferred spirits. Tiliruf could not possibly have realized how these particular relationships over time enlarged his appreciation for the people of the city of his ancestors. It was the beginning of a nostalgia that eventually grew into something beneficial despite torturous bumps in the road ahead.

Kodi wasn't so sure he liked his new designation. But *Lord Kodi* was how every man referred to him now since the Installation Ceremony. It took some getting used to, for sure. He'd never really gotten used to *Sir Kodi*, conferred upon him by Nikal's shipmen after his knighthood, and all of a sudden, he'd been raised even higher.

Nevertheless, he did look the part. Upon Scadyne in company with the Prince on Tindalle, those two were paragons. Nikal had appointed Kodi princely garb to wear. In addition, Sage Enric himself had ordered for both men gold medallions in the shape of the Symbol of the Orders of the Guardian, a circle within which was an unusual, many-rayed star with a large, white, round-cut crystal in the exact middle. All parts of the symbol had specific meaning to the way of life of Order Members. Each point of the star represented steps along a path to *wholeness,* according to Enric, a philosophical concept espoused by the Sages. Curdoz taught them the meaning of the symbol on the journey here from Tirilorin. To go with the medallions were blue, damasked short cloaks of fine make, though not so heavy in material like the vestments the Sages wore at the Installation. They did not wear these in training exercises, but otherwise, when they went about other duties—Curdoz insisted they don them. They were reminders to all that these two were War Wizards of the Taxiarch, Members of the Orders.

They had been one week in Danzilet when a rider came in from the citadel at South Fort.

"A messenger under truce has come from the Khestadone Witch Queen, Your Highness!" said the rider to Nikal. Kodi stood by. Curdoz, too.

"What!" Nikal stood up. "Let us go, now!"

In ten minutes, Nikal and Kodi with their knights, along with Curdoz, Tiliruf, Manwul and Hadon were galloping out of the city in the direction of the southern fortress. In a quarter hour of fast riding, they arrived. Quickly, they climbed to the top of the ramparts and looked down.

Symbol of the Meicalian Orders

The outer circle represents the path of a Calling, beginning with the Mind of the Creator responding to needs great or small (1). Cosmic Meical, in His role of Guardian or Taxiarch, acts as intermediator and issues the Calling (2 and 3). The individual responds and acts upon the Calling (4, 5, and 6). Outcome and Blessing are the result of inspired action and fulfill the original need (7 and 8). Joy results from a sense of purpose and represents closeness to the Mind of the Creator (9), hence a circle. Love, represented by the large clear disk in the background, is the driving force behind all, and a constant reminder of purpose at every step. Action is key, denoting willingness, and errors are seen less as failures than as a means to grow. The combination of Soul, Mind, and Body (the 3 triangles), in tandem with Cosmic (mystic) forces, and driven by love, represents a sense of spiritual wholeness. This is represented by the white center disk, a part of the larger disk of love. When designed in metal to be worn, commonly as a medallion, the center disk is represented by a diamond or a cut crystal meant to symbolically reflect outward the individual's inner faith in Meical, spiritual wholeness, and love for others. The symbol is also displayed on the green flag of the Orders, green representing the green light of Meicalian Gifted Magic.

The Orders symbol represents an ideal. Designed to train those Called to the Orders, it is sometimes taught to lay persons who choose to adopt a structured Discipline and then adapted with individually designed constructs. In such cases, wholeness can be defined in a variety of ways but should have both an inward and outward focus.

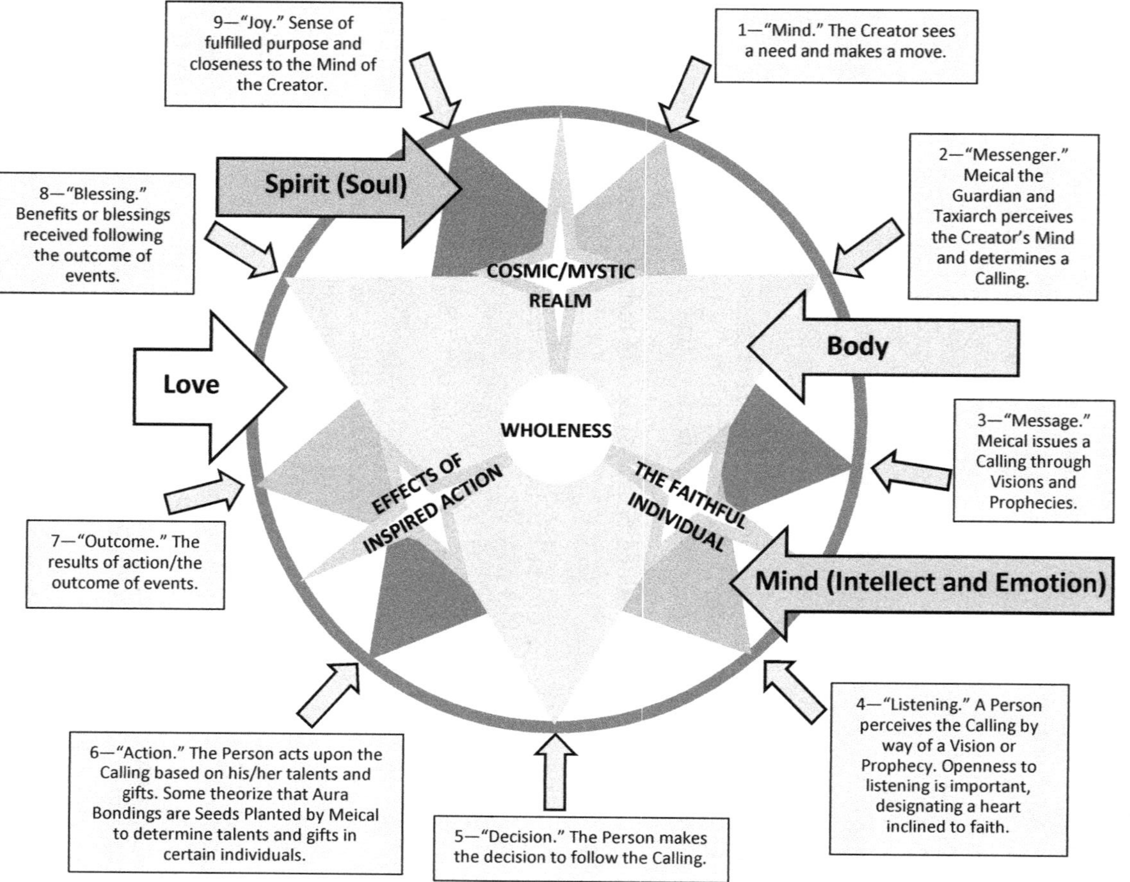

Below them on the Khestadone side waited a group of mostly black-garbed riders. But one man was in a red cape. He held forth a standard of white, denoting the truce.

"Does this happen often?" asked Tiliruf.

"No," Nikal said. "This never happens. Ever."

"We'll ride out to meet them, then," said Kodi. "You must carry the Staff, Nikal."

"Yes," agreed Curdoz. "We must witness what they have to say."

Nikal knew too they must do this, but he also knew something else. "They will make a demand. They are ready for war."

Kodi noticed a troubled look on Curdoz' face. "Curdoz?"

"We knew this day would come," Curdoz replied slowly. "I...I remember this. I saw this in my Vision."

Kodi had suspected Curdoz withheld details from his long-ago Vision. "Why have you held onto this?"

"I held onto hope, as I am required to do."

"What followed, Lord Curdoz?" asked Nikal.

Curdoz stared directly into the prince's stern eyes. He held steady for a moment. He then held forth the Staff for the prince to take.

"Battle. No, I did not see the Staff, but now I know. Now I know."

"This is where it begins for real, then," said Manwul.

"It began in the east some time ago," said Nikal grimly. "It is here, now."

The men rode out of a small steel gate and approached the riders.

The one holding the white flag handed it off to another, dismounted, and stood forward.

Nikal alone dismounted with the Staff in his hand.

The red-caped messenger nodded. He had black skin of Eastern origin. He looked long at the Staff. He then spoke in a heavy voice.

"Her Exalted Majesty, Alkhaness of Westrealm, has a message."

"What is it?"

The messenger then looked upon the detachment behind Nikal and spoke in louder voice.

"She requires your full withdrawal from the Southern Continent, as all the lands to the shore of the sea belong to her."

"Perhaps they once did. We took them from her after the Lintiri War, a war she and her cohort the Alkhan waged without cause upon our free peoples."

Unmoved by this, his eyes stoic, the herald retorted. "She wants them back. You are to abandon Fort Danzilet and the city within four weeks' time. If you do this, she will allow another four months for you to withdraw from the other outposts and towns you currently hold along the shoreline north of the mountains."

"Really? Does she offer something in return for such an extraordinary request?"

"She does. She desires a full peace should you withdraw fully from the Southern Continent."

"That, she does not," said Curdoz, now dismounting and stepping forward to stand by Nikal.

The messenger turned his attention to him, though there was no change in his dark eyes. "Those are her words. Take them as they are."

Nikal stepped closer to the man and held forth the Staff.

The man's eyes animated momentarily, and he very clearly swallowed hard.

"Do you know who I am?" asked Nikal.

"I...you.... The seagull and crown on your breastplate. I believe you to be Nikal of Nant."

"Very good. Do you know what this is?"

"I...I may have heard a legend once." The man definitely did not like what he was seeing.

"This is the War Wizard Staff of Terianh the Great. It is mine, now. And like Terianh long ago I am prepared to use it. You return and tell Her Majesty that I, Nikal of Nant, under orders of Great Meical, Guardian, Taxiarch on High, am to fight anyone who attempts to take possession of our lands and who wishes to enslave our people. Your Alkhaness is a witch with a desire to conquer all, and we all know she will not stop with possession of the Southern Continent. My counteroffer is this: the status quo, and she is to keep her armies within her currently defined realm. She is to refrain from assisting her cohort the Alkhan in the eastern war. She is to keep her navy within the Khestadone Sea and any piracy must end. She is to disengage from any further action against our allies the Etoppsi of Berug. Should she do these things, peace will reign, and she need not see the Power this Staff wields. As I hold this in my hands, I sense her. She holds forth nearby in your city yonder?"

The man swallowed again. "She...she is aware of many things."

"Of course, she is." said Curdoz curtly. "Return with the prince's message and return with her own answer in two days. What follows, of course, is up to her."

"May I ask who you are, old man?"

"Hmm. Perhaps I do appear a bit gray and scruffy today. I am Curdoz, High Sage of Solanto, of the Orders of the Guardian Meical on High. And you tell Her Majesty this, too. Meical, Taxiarch and Guardian, watches. He is aware of all that goes on here. She should not underestimate His determination to keep Dumhoni free for the Peoples of the Mold. The Ralsheen Slave Empire was destroyed long ago with the Staff His Highness now wields. We do not wish to return to Dark Times of domination and slavery."

Nikal then nodded to the man, who understood nothing more was to be said. The red-caped captain returned to the others, remounted, and they rode south in the direction of the distant city.

The men rode back through the gate.

"A bit 'scruffy today,' eh? You're cracking me up, Curdoz."

"Honestly," said Curdoz, ignoring this, "it was good you did not introduce everyone, Nikal. If we can keep her from knowing about Kodi, then all to the better. She does not need to know we actually have a backup War Wizard. I'm glad you didn't wear those medallions and capes today, as it would have denoted Kodi of equivalence to you. We've been too open in our actions. There have been black crows this morning, in little packs of three or so, flying to and fro. Probably spies to discern our numbers. She may already know more than we would wish."

"So you sensed her through the Staff?" asked Kodi.

"I did. And holding the Staff I believed she could sense me, too. That messenger was surely high up in command to know anything at all about the Staff.

Curdoz is right, Kodi. I don't want you touching the Staff while we are in Danzilet."

"Maybe not, but I will fight at your side."

"Yes, oh yes. You will."

"So, they will come back?" asked Hadon

"Absolutely. An army."

"With *her,* eh?"

"She will wish to test herself against the Staff," concluded Curdoz. "Something has changed, I think. She has somehow gathered new magic. I wish I understood how."

Idamé was in fetters.

"Oh, no! You cannot mean it, Curdoz!"

"An army resides in that city south of here, and Nikal believes, and my Vision showed, that a battle will take place here."

"And the outcome?" asked Rainwing.

"No, I didn't see it. Not really. I don't think...what I think is that this is a test of hers. A test against the newfound Staff. I don't know, Idamé. But it's plain the war doesn't *end* here. Our Visions showed tasks beyond this point, did they not? Clearly, she desires control of Fort Danzilet. It would bring the greatest possible advantage for her. It would loosen Nantian naval dominance and serve as a launching pad for further conquest. This is where they launched the Lintiri War. She has surely pondered an assault on Danzilet for years. Who wants to see war? Nobody. But this is the world we live in, Ida. This is our time."

Actually, the words did give Idamé some measurable sense of calm. "Yes, yes. You're right. There are other tasks before us. This battle must be fought; I see that now."

"Have faith in our young heroes, dear. In all the history of war I doubt there has been gathered such a group of men as what we have. The enemy is strong, but so are we, and the Staff must present itself. Would you feel safer upon the water in Nikal's ship, Ida?"

"Absolutely not," she stated emphatically. "I'm not moving an inch unless they breach the wall. I need a task. There is the Hospital of the Healers. I'll present myself."

"Oh, I will, too," said Lyndz, though a little annoyed with herself. She had been training hard with her archery and knife-throwing, and Rainwing's powerful fighting sense had been rubbing off hard on her of late. But she knew a battle front was not her place and hoped it never would be. "This is for Kodi and Tiliruf and Nikal and all the rest."

"Well, I'm fighting!" stated Rainwing emphatically. She went straight in search of Nikal for an assignment.

"But you can't fly, Rainwing!" said the unthinking Tiliruf, when the Etoppsis arrived at the men's headquarters, declaring her intent.

She puffed up massively and blasted him forthwith.

"DON'T REMIND ME, YOU SPIKE-SHAFTED HALF-GOAT! AND NEITHER CAN YOU, OR JUMP OFF A CLIFF AND PROVE OTHERWISE!" Her voice boomed like a battering ram on a bronze gate, and probably everybody within a mile could hear her. Kodi covered his ears. "And you think I haven't fought even Wingless Dragons on the ground? THAT'S HOW WE FIGHT THEM,

YOU STUPID DOLT! When's the last time *you* fought Wingless Dragons, tell me that? SPEAK UP, SHAFTMASTER!"

Tiliruf went a brilliant scarlet at this tirade and withdrew hurriedly, Manwul and Hadon following him out.

Nikal looked at her. "We'll find you some gear. I'll bet you anything there is something in the fortress for you. What weapons do you want?"

"Big ones."

Nikal nearly grinned. Kodi definitely did.

"And don't station me anywhere near Tiliruf. My hands might slip," she added with a grimace.

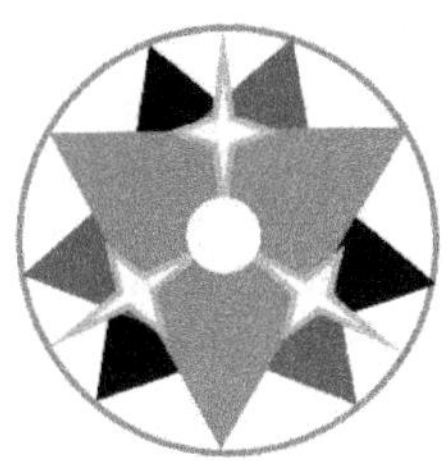

Chapter 7—The Alkhaness' Secret

As it was growing dark, Lyndz was surprised when Nikal himself came seeking her out. His request of her was shocking. He had brought a map with him.

"Bagarro's blood and more: Aura Bondings, Visions and Prophecies have marked you out," he said. "Kodi is the warrior, like you say, but you need to make use of your talents, just like he does."

Thankfully, Idamé was not present. She had gone to bed soon after supper.

Rainwing did her best to whisper. "I'll go with you. We need to do this, Lyndz. We need to test this out again."

Lyndz was wide-eyed. "Does Kodi know about this, Nikal?"

"No, er. I'd prefer he didn't."

"Good. He'd want to protect me. But it's too far away, their city! Five miles south of the wall? The magic doesn't work that far. Only about a half mile. Your wall isn't close enough."

"We'll manage it," said Rainwing. "I'll get you close enough. It should be a black night. All to the better."

"I can send specialty scouts with you."

"No," replied Rainwing. "Lyndz and I can and will do this alone. No Human will mark our passage. I know more of the geography than you might realize. And I've studied the maps on this region for twenty years. I've seen a copy of this one, too. And do I ever know the dark."

"I need black garb," Lyndz said, with a bit of excitement. "Trousers, not a dress. A short black cape with a hood."

"I'll meet you at the wall in an hour. You'll need most of the night," said Nikal. "I'll send word. The soldiers will not hinder your access to me."

"Where is Kodi, anyway?"

"The battle will not take place tomorrow. I *ordered* him to go have a little fun with Tiliruf and the others. And that means a lot of brandy and smokes. I want him out of the way for a little."

They had all arrived at the rampart, and Nikal had brought with him the requested black clothing for Lyndz. They were in a little side room within the wall itself, and Nikal turned his back while Lyndz changed.

"Honestly, Nikal. I'm not that squeamish. We've lived on a ship together, haven't we? It's *you*. It's not that pack of jokers Tiliruf plays coppers with back in Tirilorin. Though I don't think I'd even be bothered by their gaping anymore.

Maybe I was a modest sweet country lass upon a time, but I'd swear now that was years ago."

"To me you're a queen among queens to do this, you know, and queenlier than any queen I know, and I do know some. I hold you in highest honor, of course."

"Ha! And yet you're sending this queen on a dangerous mission in the dark of night in enemy territory. I thought queens sit in castles and move pawns around, drink tea and eat cakes."

"Bah! My Queen Silverwing, I assure you, does not drink tea and eat cakes!" Rainwing stated with emphasis. "Yet she does move pawns in such ways; most know not they are pawns being moved. Yet I believe myself to be one such pawn of hers, though I admit I do not mind. But also, a queen must endure hardship sometimes."

"Well, I'm ready as I'll ever be. I'm dressed now, Nikal. Turn around. You know, I could do with a good Human hug before I go. If you're Kodi's brother, you're mine too. That's just the way it is."

Nikal did of course grant the request. "Thanks, friend. I know I seem distant much of the time, but it's clear you understand how grateful I am for the joy and grounding you provide us all. You and Rainwing here really are like sisters, I think, and the Prophecy said so. But I don't think I've ever hugged Kodi."

"You don't have to. You're around each other constantly, and I'm not stupid to how that Staff connects the two of you. But he *is* the best hugger in the world, but he's not here to do it, though you're not so bad. A little more practice, maybe. Princes should be less stiff. At least this queen says so anyway. Let's go, Rainwing."

Outside the wall on the Khestadone side, Lyndz paused. "I'm going to do it now. I want to get my own lay of the land," she whispered in Rainwing's ear.

The Etoppsis nodded. It was, of course, only a moment of time for her.

"Did you see a green light?"

Rainwing shook her head.

"Good. I must have good control now on that. I don't think anyone is nearby. I'll let you lead."

They made good time. The moons had set early. The stars, patchworked by clouds, provided all the light Rainwing's eyes needed, sharper than that of eagles, or owls at night. Lyndz was light of foot, and Rainwing moved with the stealth of a jungle tiger. Lyndz had never really noticed before that her Etoppsi friend's silver-gray fur did not glisten in the dark. The two of them were undetectable shadows.

Every once in a while, Lyndz would pause again and enter into a Moment Mastering expedition. All in all, this was the best possible testing ground for her and would prove enormously beneficial upon their future quest assigned to them by the Guardian. No ordinary spy could have managed what these two were doing. Considering all, Lyndz wondered if Nikal might suspect something about that. Maybe his request was also meant as an opportunity for her to get some serious experience. If he did have suspicions, he clearly was not relaying them to Kodi. She was grateful for that. Despite all of Kodi's support, he still harbored a protective streak. She knew it was natural, and she loved him for it, yet he could prove an obstacle to her plans. The three females could not yet foresee how they were going to extract themselves from the men without trouble when the time came to do so.

The fourth time Lyndz entered the magic, still a good way from the city of the Khestadone, there was a hitch.

"Soldiers," she murmured in Rainwing's ear. "Very close."

Rainwing put her own mouth to Lyndz' ear. "Yes. We could walk right past them, I think, but let's not trust our good luck. Follow me up into that rocky wooded area." She pointed.

Under scrubby trees and around large boulders they moved. Lyndz entered into her magic more frequently, and along with Rainwing's uncanny instincts they determined a clear path. Within another hour they had managed their way quite close to the fortress city.

"They have dimmed the lights on the walls," Rainwing offered. "They do not want the Nantians to gauge the numbers they might be hiding."

Lyndz understood. "We'll have to get closer still. But let me enter the gates from here and see what I can see."

Closing her eyes yet again, Lyndz entered into the Mode and walked out of the Dome of Light. Eventually she came upon the gates. These were open at the end of a short drawbridge over a narrow, rocky ditch. Soldiers were walking in and out of the gates and over the drawbridge, all in black, with no torchlight, and of course, in the magic, were not actually walking but were perfectly unmoving. Nevertheless, she touched none of these apparitions, unreal Images though they were.

She walked past them all and into the gate.

There was a little more light here with a handful of torches. As Kodi had done in his experiment with Theneri, she noted the strange 'frozen' tongues of the torch flames. Returning to task, she didn't in the least like what she saw. Everywhere she looked were hundreds, nay, a thousand easily just in this space, of black-garbed soldiers. A few, likely officers, wore red capes or yellow ones. She looked all around, but she was near to the edge of her half mile, and there was only mist beyond that could not be penetrated.

She returned in only one second of Rainwing's time. She shook her head. "There are thousands, I'm sure. We've got to get in so I can take in more, but I don't know how to do that. I'll need help estimating the numbers, Nikal wanted a cavalry count, too, and we've got to try to find the Witch Queen if she's really here."

"How wide is the ravine, do you think?"

"Not too. Perhaps twenty feet."

"I can carry you and jump it. That's easy. Let's follow it east and see what we can see."

They did so, traveling east with the city's black walls in sight. Soon they came to a rocky incline that reached up within ten feet of the top of the wall itself.

"This city," offered Rainwing, "I don't think was built for a determined onslaught. I think even Humans could breach the walls here."

"But was there really any need to build it like an impregnable fortress? The Alkhaness probably understood all along that the Nantians never really wanted any of these lands. It's mostly an unprotected plain beyond, from what they've all been saying."

"Nor is it especially old. Older maps don't show this city. However, Berug has sent scouts this far, in the dark nights, of course, in order to spy out the land. Some years ago, one of our Eye Feathers had his wing clipped by a hail of arrows over this city. He flew too low. They captured him. No one knows whatever happened to him, though surely he was killed. Let me go into the Moment with you. I'll figure out a way over the top."

Lyndz had only one other time taken Rainwing into the Moment experience with her. The Dome of Green Light was a bit tight with Rainwing's size, but that was when she had her wings still. It was more manageable this time. Despite all the warnings old Brother Theneri had written into his little book, Rainwing simply had no qualm and no fear, and Lyndz had become adept at the magic.

Together within the Moment, all of course was perfectly still and perfectly silent. They could even talk in normal volume.

"This is the place. See? We jump this, and it's an easy climb up to the top of the wall. Pathetic design, but this is not the case at her capital nor her older cities on the Khestadone and Siriné shorelines. Those have high walls and strong gates they close at night. We'll have a harder time of it when we go there."

"I think Mother Idamé has strong memories of the capital and citadel of the Alkhaness. She hasn't been fully forthcoming on her Vision. Of course, she's scared. And who can blame her?"

"I agree. She's thrown out some remarkable tidbits in our conversations. You clearly see what I see. She knows more than she's telling. That female I bet will be written up in books as the greatest spy in Human history! It's up to you and me to get her past her fears, though."

"You bet. We can do this, Rainwing. I know we can. We can do all of it, I'm telling you. It'll be hard as the Dragon's Teeth when we go south, but somehow, we'll do it, and we'll do it together. The Guardian will be pleased!"

I already am.

"Did you hear something, just now, Rainwing?"

"No, what did you hear?"

"I thought it was a Voice, but honestly, I don't think so. Yet I feel good, all of a sudden. We're doing a good job. I shouldn't feel happy in such a terrible place, but I do. I think Kodi feels like this all the time. His attitude amazes me. Let's go."

Returning back to real time, they set out again and were soon over the wall. This section of the city was dark as pitch. Yet it was admittedly spooky. No soldiers were stationed here. Black walls of buildings with blacker windows overshadowed them. No one marked their presence.

"It's tense here."

"I feel it. Let's risk no more. We're close enough to nearly every area of the city, don't you think?"

"Yes."

"In one brief moment we'll actually be done and can leave."

When hours later they returned to a relieved Nikal at the Danzilet rampart, they discovered he was not alone.

Idamé was in tears.

"We're fine, Mother. I swear!" Lyndz could not hide her aggravation.

"I searched everywhere. I couldn't sleep! They brought me to Nikal upon my begging."

"Oh dear," said Rainwing.

"Well, I didn't cover that possibility," said Nikal, with a look at Lyndz that spoke of the deepest possible apology. "Truly, Mother Idamé, you must see the importance of my request of Lady Lyndz."

She burst into another round of tears.

"How long has she been like this?" asked Lyndz, doing her best to hold Idamé close and to pat her lovingly.

"Two hours at least. Sorry. And of course I didn't want Curdoz to know about this either and would not send for him."

"Don't apologize," declared Lyndz. "Mother Idamé, look at me. Look at me! Right now!"

The poor lady looked up with bloodshot eyes.

Despite her aggravation Lyndz smiled quite warmly. "We did it, Mother. Don't you realize what that means for us? Be brave, dear one."

Idamé sobbed. "But your mother. I promised."

"Listen, Mother. My mother is not a stupid woman. She knew. She knew. I swear she did. She knew there would be great danger for me, too, and not just for Kodi. She knew. Those conversations back in Felto were terrifying for her. But she knew she had to let me go, and that promise you made helped her get past her initial fears for me. But she's a thousand miles away, Mother Idamé. We have tasks to do, and you are a major part of it, and I'm a major part of it, and you need to save those tears for something genuinely awful, you hear me? Rainwing and I are perfectly fine! Aren't you so glad we have Rainwing with us!"

Idamé finally, after another moment, realized. She took the end of her shawl that Lyndz, Ulna and Maru had knitted for her, wiped her face one last time, and sat up. She held Lyndz' hand and reached out to touch Rainwing's large one.

"Yes. Yes, dear. I am very glad, indeed! Oh, thank the Guardian!"

It was a turning point for her. It took daring, compassion, and serious firmness on Lyndz' part. But there it was. The Matrimonial Mother had grown in those minutes. In future, most of her tears centered on joys and upon the worst of worsts, and yes, there were some of both ahead of them. But the anxieties and fears she carried inside her dutiful, loving heart were largely expelled, or at least mitigated by high wisdom, from that point forward for as long as she lived.

The portents were beyond the pale. Curdoz paced rapidly back and forth across the room of Nikal and Kodi's quarters. All had been summoned by Nikal after breakfast to hear the tale.

"Bright white skin! Bright white skin!" he repeated.

"You think she's one of those Ice Tribesmen, then, Kodi goes on about?"

"Tiliruf, don't you see?" offered Nikal in order to clarify. "We know the Alkhan and Alkhaness are at least three-hundred years old. Some legends put their existence in the Khestadone lands much further back than that, even. No one hardly ever traveled in that region due to Siriné. Not even the Berugians would explore that way. And so, the khans built up their power over time and largely in secret. There were many Humans living there, probably descendants of escaped slaves from the Ralsheen era. They lived primitively, and so they were overawed and overcome."

"She's Ralsheen, then," said Kodi, flatly. "And so is the Alkhan."

"Ralsheen!" exclaimed Idamé. "Lyndz! What did you see on those scrolls?"

"It was only the one parchment. I couldn't read it, but Rainwing could. And you're right. She's pure Ralsheen and worse."

"I know Ralsheen," said Rainwing. "Studied it for years. That parchment read just in this way. Listen!

I, Ch'yad, Alkhaness, on this day have seen through the eyes of my servants that the Staff of Terianh exists. I, by my recent conversation with Siriné, know her revelation to me is true. The Staff that by Terianh's hand destroyed my father, Emperor of Ralsheen, has been rediscovered, and is now in the possession of the Human man by the name of Nikal, known to be the second-born of Monticu of Nant. I am more powerful than my father, of course, and I will avenge him."

"Her...her *father!"* exclaimed Tiliruf. "You can't be serious!"

Rainwing glowered.

"Oh! Rainwing, no! I swear! Stop! Don't! Er, eh?" he pleaded.

Rainwing, looked at him intensely, but after a moment she relaxed. "It's fine, *Shaftmaster*. I realize that was not an insult."

Tiliruf smiled. But it was quite close to a nervous grimace. "Don't call me that."

"It fits," joked Manwul.

"Stop it!" Curdoz nearly shouted. "Stop the jests!"

Nikal glowered at all the men in the room. And at Rainwing, too.

They obeyed.

With resolute seriousness, Hadon spoke. "Tell us, Lord Sage. What does all of this mean?"

"Ch'yad," repeated Curdoz. "*Ch'yad*. Damn it all! What are the roots of that word? Child of *something*. I haven't read Ralsheen in years and years. It's on the tip of my tongue, but I don't remember!"

"Child of...fire," said Tiliruf. "I'm pretty good with Ralsheen, too, you know."

Rainwing looked at him. She nodded. "Tiliruf is mostly correct. *Child of Fire*. They didn't always use *Ch'*, but they often did. *Ch'* is like a suffix. 'Chagra' or 'Charo', could be feminine or masculine, and it made no difference in the names of the royalty and nobility. Of course, 'Ka' was used to denote male or the masculine and 'Li' for female or the feminine for virtually everything else and were commonly articles to denote masculine or feminine noun forms, like we use *a, an,* or *the*, nowadays. But again, not in the royal and noble family naming systems of the Ralsheen. 'Chagra' the feminine, clearly in the Alkhaness' case. 'Li yadri' is *fire* in Ralsheen like Tiliruf says. 'Li yadris' *flame*. 'Li yadrisa' *flames. Daughter of Fire* or *Daughter of Flame* or *Flames*. Well, come to think of it, 'Ka Y'drisi' is *lightning*. So, *Daughter of Lightning*. Take your pick. That is her true, ancient name. Probably no one in all her realm knows her true name, unless they knew it of old, that is, if they came from or descended from her time. There actually could be a few. Favorites, maybe. Some of the satraps and their families. Maybe even priests in their Siriné temples. Surely they came here, maybe on a ship, a remnant of escapees, as Tolos was overrun by the Dragons. The Ice Tribes of the north would surely understand the language. Yet the Khestadone slave peasants and soldiers do not speak Ralsheen. There were Humans living in that land long ago as Nikal alluded to, not under the sway of the Ralsheen, possibly escapees from the older Empire. But most today descend from Humans captured in piracy, both Eastern and Western, most from a couple hundred years ago, though a number in recent times, too. They do not use that language at all, then, only common Anterianhi. That parchment was meant as a *future* reading by those who know, or would come to know, Ralsheen. Their elite, if you will. She's keeping a record of events. Oh, if we could find journals! But she'd surely keep them in her chambers in her citadel." She eyed Lyndz momentarily. The latter raised an eyebrow.

Tiliruf did put on a serious tone. "Honestly. I'm not trying to argue. So, you believe her to be Ralsheen, and it's obvious she thinks she is, but tell me, eh? Why is the name important?"

"I can use it," said Nikal.

"Yes. You can," agreed Curdoz.

All were silent for a moment, but Hadon spoke up again. "The Alkhaness is the daughter of the last Ralsheen emperor. The Alkhan would be..."

"Her brother," Kodi concluded.

"Her brother." Curdoz agreed with emphatic conclusion. "He would be the last emperor's son...and heir."

Lyndz went wide-eyed with sudden revelation. "Twins! They're twins, too!"

Idamé's famous eyebrows hit the roof. "Oh! Oh! Oh!"

Curdoz looked at her. "You nearly got there first, didn't you, dear? Long ago in our conversation in Thorune. I should have seen it, too. The Guardian didn't tell Kodi, because He didn't know for sure, but almost certainly He suspected. And so Kodi's and Lyndz' genders, their entire pedigree up to and specifically including their shared birth...I should listen better to Marco. Maybe he was there before any of us. I don't know. We knew the 'twos' thing. We knew the male and the female. But not the *twin siblings* idea. Lyndz is surely correct. Twins."

Tiliruf looked quickly between Lyndz and Kodi, "You...you...you really are meant to...like a *counterpoise* or something! I can't believe it."

"Told you so, though you'd think the Staff and Lyndz' Gift would have been enough to prove it to you," said Kodi. "But there's more to it. I can't counter him without Nikal. Lyndz can't counter the Alkhaness without help. In a way, yes, we are..."

"Symbols," concluded Lyndz.

"That's the point of the Vision I had, I'm sure of it."

"You are far more than mere symbols," said Nikal.

"It's all *about* the two of you!" said Tiliruf. His eyes were wide in a realization he'd been resisting for a long time.

Manwul spoke. "Since when'd you start believing in Meicalian mysteries, Swordmaster?"

"I...I...shut up, Manwul. Shaft you."

"It's about all of us," Kodi proclaimed. "It's about you, too, friend. I've told you so, and I thought I'd made it plain to you, you were in my Vision. I saw you eating the apple under the statue."

"The statue of Terianh the Great," added Nikal.

"How'd you know, sir, eh? Oh, never mind. Kodi told you. Shaft you, too, Kodi."

"Tiliruf was in a Meicalian Vision you had, Lord Kodi?" asked Hadon in awe. Both he and Manwul looked intently in Kodi's direction.

"'Course he was. He sat under the golden statue of Terianh. He's the main reason we came to Tirilorin in the first place."

The two men's gaze turned to Tiliruf.

"Don't look at me like that."

Manwul almost whispered. "Lord Kodi's Vision really means something for you, Swordmaster. I've learned enough from old Enric to know that. Why don't you see it? You truly stand connected to a past I've always kind of wished for, as have a lot of other Tirilorines. I'm never letting you out of my sight."

"Me neither," said Hadon.

"You almost never do now, so what difference is that, eh? I'm just a man."

"Don't overdo it, fellows," said Nikal. "You know your job."

"We're all symbols of something. And more than symbols, it seems," said Lyndz.

"All because you found some damned witch is albino, yeah, sure," said Tiliruf.

"Don't go cynical on us again, dear," said Idamé. She reached over and patted Tiliruf on the cheek. He turned red, as he always did when she would do this.

"I don't know, though. Cynicism keeps me sane, eh? The rest of you are cracked. But hey. C'mon Lyndz. Rainwing. Tell us the details of all you saw. And you're braver than a lion, Lyndz, I swear. Doing what you did! That's the grittiest thing I ever did hear of, you going outside the south wall in the dead of night! The Witch's lair! Two women..."

"Females!" screeched Rainwing. "And what of it? You're as chauvinistic as Etoppsi male Feathers of the Wall Cyclone! Did you train under old General Heavywing? I think so."

"Maybe. Who's that, anyway? I want to meet him."

"He's being sweet, Rainwing," interrupted Lyndz, smiling at Tiliruf. "It's a compliment!"

"Humans," said Rainwing with disgust. "*Men!*"

Lyndz launched in.

"She was awful to look at, though not a wrinkle one on her face or arms. Her eyes were yellow like cats, just like Kodi described from his dream. Of course, he couldn't get a good look at her skin color because of her mask and gloves!"

"It's true. Since then I'd even thought she might be an Easterner. All you see with that mask is those yellow eyes!"

"Her hair was white bristles. She was looking out a window in the direction of South Fort. She was alone in a tower room. There was nothing else of significance in the room with her besides that parchment, except for her gloves and horrible mask. I bet she wears them all the time when she's out of her rooms in public view. Outside were the largest men. Champions, Rainwing says. Bodyguards."

"One was the biggest *man* I have ever seen," added Rainwing. "An eastern-derived, black-skinned paragon as big as me. I'm sure he's an efficient killer, and I don't have a clue why, but I liked him."

"You *liked* him?" Tiliruf's face showed puzzlement.

Rainwing opened her mouth to reply, but Lyndz went on.

"He stood alone, away from the others, but I think he's important somehow. It was just a passing thought, and obviously Rainwing thought so, too. But it makes no sense, of course. Like all, he was surely under mindspells under her strictest control, but his eyes seemed less glazed, more aware or thoughtful.

Perhaps he was an officer, though his garb was not distinctive. I don't know. Again, nothing of real importance, but there were a hundred or more of these giants, some Eastern black and some Western white and Nantian descent. We scoured everywhere. Rainwing and I believe there to be five thousand soldiers in the city. And about seven hundred horses."

"That's about what we've got here, though fewer horsemen, as most are off east," said Nikal. "Of course, she might have others on the way, but this is good information. Back to the writing. Lord Sage, how do you think she'd be in communication with Siriné?"

"Vanaratu told me it really wouldn't be so hard for someone with a powerful mind, perhaps little different than the link he and I share. I can only guess she sometimes travels to the Sea of Siriné and speaks to her from shore, and Vanaratu believed the Serpents we fought on our way to Modela's island came from Siriné, ones she did not devour, and were under spells of enchantment. It could have been either Ch'yad or her brother responsible for that. Vanaratu and I guessed her brother, since he is specifically known to have great control over the minds of animals like the bears and wolves he has used in his wars. We mustn't forget that, despite her entrapment, Siriné is a destructive force with World God magic, though confined by the Guardian to the Sea bearing her name. I suspect now she has, over centuries, transferred some of her magic to the Khans. Before, it had been tidbits of mind magic, but now their new magic is probably more destructive. Which is why the Guardian moves us now to counter them with the Staff. Considering what we've found out, Siriné would look upon them as her children. She was the emperor's consort. She can have no children of her own. They are fully Human, *Of the White* albinos like the Chieftain class of the Ice Tribes, but now with life forces of immortality derived from that of Siriné. It was said the last emperor himself was nearly a hundred years old, though still in the prime of life, and he derived long life through Siriné, it seems. If she loved anyone, it was he. But this is what I think, and that's that she would not readily transfer her destructive and mind powers to others unless she felt truly compelled to. She is maddened and has no means of escape. Shifting powers to these stepchildren of hers is almost like reaching out in order to try to escape. The Guardian might have suspected some of this, but He cannot see clearly in regions under the control of evil. He'd have to be here Himself. But this is a dangerous situation of the utmost gravity, for the emperor had no significant magic, but his children have been granted it by Siriné, and the Staff of Terianh will have its work cut out for it."

"You think *they*, the khans, could transfer magic to others? Could Vanaratu transfer magic like that, too?" asked Tiliruf.

"That's a really good question, Tiliruf. Good discernment there. Let me answer the last question. Yes and no. The Guardian surely forbade the gods from transferring their magic. Vanaratu could, I think, but he will not. Only the evil ones would perhaps consider it, and I'm suddenly reminded of the old legend of the Sea Serpents, that their evil natures are the result of the Tears of the rebel World Gods of the Dragon's Teeth. That, too, would be a sort of escape of evil. Vanaratu confirmed that to me, actually. So, to answer your first question, I think that could work. But surely transfer of magic is also a weakening of the one who first held it. Maybe the Alkhaness could do so, too, but she's not going to give up much to anyone, morsels of mind control, perhaps, to her satraps in order to maintain control over the population. Makes good sense to me. I'm glad you asked the question, Tiliruf. You've given me something to ponder. That's not the first time you've done that, either."

"Gee, thanks."

The conversation ended eventually, and they all dispersed. The next time Kodi had a private moment he reached into his mind and spoke.

"Brother Meical, are the enemies twins, too, like Lyndz and me?"

Think upon all my servant Curdoz has said. I believe much truth has indeed been revealed to us now. Encourage the others in the upcoming battle, My Brother.

"There will be a battle, then, for sure?"

Curdoz was not wrong to hope otherwise, as there was potential for the Alkhaness to refrain, perhaps even for years to come. But in the end, it was inevitable, and recent revelations proved it for me. Lyndz is not my only eye, though hers has proved the clearer. The Alkhaness has grown strong indeed, and she is about to test herself. Ask no more just now, Kodi. Much is clouded. Success depends upon faith, even if the free world should fall, for according to the Mind, Whom you and I serve, Effort is of spiritual value greater than its Result. Of course, you understand much of this already, My Brother.

Yet, the free world will not fall by way of this battle, Kodi. That much I see. Other battles are to come. Take them one at a time. I chose you and Nikal for all the right reasons, as you are symbols indeed. And I have great faith in My Brothers, for you are more than symbols. War Wizards of the Taxiarch. Polemarchi, as the Etoppsi would call you. Commanders under Me, as I serve the One. We fight evil. That is what we do.

For the remainder of that day Nikal and Kodi, along with Curdoz, considered their defense. North Fort was left with few men, as nearly all were sent to South Fort.

"We need to fight in front of the wall. It's what we have to do. I don't want to be stuck in a siege for weeks or months feeling the need to reinforce with the last armies coming from the west. I need them east, not here. I want a quicker resolution, or we'll never get off to the Qeteral, nor would I have the best knowledge as to how to proceed after. We can't stay here! I've got to go east, as I believe that is where I ultimately need to be."

"I agree fully," said Curdoz. "There are still the Berugians to counter the Alkhaness here in the west. Should we lose Danzilet, it would still be a long time before she could build a new navy here and challenge Tirilorin and Nant. But she'd have to challenge Berug first, before she could do that."

Nikal continued. "It isn't a perfect situation for my plan, as the wall gate is small, as that was deemed safest in the construction and of the wall's original purpose. We never have intended to send forth great forces into her realm. A full-scale retreat through the gates by foot soldiers, let alone cavalry, would be hard indeed."

"You could cut it open if you had to."

"What?"

Kodi nodded to the Staff in Curdoz' hands.

Nikal raised an eyebrow. "You mean like Terianh did at the Siege of R'lichi?"

"But only if you have to, like I said, to enable the retreat. Which might not even happen. You can block it up after. The Power doesn't drain. Terianh said so. You've felt it. I've felt it."

"But I can drain from using it. I will surely have used it much already in the battle, let alone a retreat."

"A powerful Healer, then? Of course! Would that Xeno were here from Solanto," said Curdoz. "He's the most powerful Healer in that country, according to Marco. But send for a pair from the Hospital. No. I'll go. I will choose them myself. Should have thought of it already. We're not used to this, are we? Though Terianh had the Sages at his back. They had healing powers and would heal his fatigue. Have Manwul take charge of the Staff while I'm gone."

Curdoz rode off to the Danzilet Hospital.

Nikal continued with Kodi after he left. "It'll be dangerous for anyone near the gate, of course."

"It'll work, you'll see. Don't stint Tiliruf, either. You promised me. He's the world's best swordsman and a rider of the first rank. He needs the fighting experience as much as me, at or near the front line, should you order a charge."

"He'll be with us. That has always been my plan. But we'll have to stand somewhat apart on that knoll yonder to work the Staff. Kodi, this is a real test for you. You've got to take control, though General Cruz commands the cavalry. I'm talking about my household of knights and Tiliruf and all. You keep it tight."

"And no beasts, you say?"

"Her brother has hundreds, bears and wolves of great size, as I've mentioned in the past, but all indications are she does not use them, and Lyndz saw none. I think their magical powers are different, as Curdoz implies. The Alkhan's mind expands outward, sees more, controls more, masculine power that is wild and hot, and his bears and wolves respond to it. Her mind in large measure is focused inward. Curdoz thinks so, too. I suspect he is the stronger magically and more dangerous of the two, though less cool and calculating perhaps. However, I'm guessing at more than I really know. What I do know is he controls from the back, and we have never seen him. It won't last, and he will come himself when he senses me going east with the Staff. I surely dread that day when I confront him. Yet she is here, now. She's going to be in control from the front. She'll want to inspire fear, as that is how she controls all in her realm. Some of what I'm implying here is really cryptic and guesswork, I know, but..."

"You believe we can do this. Me, too. We'll make her see the light and back off, at least for a while."

"I think so."

There was a pause, and then, as they were alone, Kodi said, "I spoke with Meical earlier this morning."

Nikal raised his eyebrow. "He confirmed some conclusions, I presume. I can understand you would want to know some of that."

"The forthcoming battle is less crucial than others ahead of us. He has faith in our talents."

"That is good to know. I hope His faith is well placed." Nikal smiled and put his hand on Kodi's shoulder.

"Some of Meical's words," said Kodi, "regarding faith and symbol make even better sense to me now. We are faith and symbol, you and I, and more than symbol. He said, '*We fight evil. That is what we do.*' "

The messenger did not return within the two days Curdoz had required.

The third morning dawned after a brief rain in the night. Rainwing stood on the rampart with her eyes intent upon the south and the distant city of the Alkhaness. She wore a large chain mail suit of Anterianhi steel, which undeniably had been fashioned ages ago for some oversized and wealthy Human nobleman, stored away in a dry dungeon in North Fort. There was not a rust spot on it. It was an amazing piece, as that quality of metal was rare. Rainwing had mixed feelings. "I'm not sure it won't slow me down. It's heavier than the dragon mail we wear in the Legion. I'll start with it, though." Against the rampart wall in front of her leaned an ancient Etoppsi mace so heavy that it took three men to carry it. Its history and how it got to Danzilet was unknown, and though she was hesitant about the mail, she thrilled with this. She also was given a huge shield and had a pile of casting spears.

She suddenly boomed. "They come!"

"Move it all out, General Fouch!" called out Nikal, coming up to see. "Get it in place!"

From the too small gate it took a long time to move out six hundred horses, most of what they had, but there wasn't much point in keeping many behind the wall except for messengers to the city. And some five hundred archers and three-and-a-half thousands of foot soldiers. Another thousand remained in the citadel and on the ramparts and towers of the wall, including artillery men operating a long row of fireball launchers. Most of the foot soldiers were Nantian strongmen, though there was a contingent of Tirilorine Brigadiers. Two hundred cavalry were also from Tirilorin, as were several brigades of archers. For the Tirilorines this was to be their first engagement, though they had many captains among them who had served in the east as Tirilorine mercenaries.

Nikal wasn't entirely pleased by the fact so many were inexperienced.

"It won't matter," Kodi said.

"It does matter," replied Nikal. "Your confidence is inspiring, Kodi, but don't ever undervalue the need for experience, and this is no ordinary situation by any measure, if one could ever call a battle 'ordinary.' You can't. Yet their training has been good, I'll admit. Jaden's the best there is, no doubt about it, and his officers are good. Wish he were here. I could use him. Cruz and Fouch are good. We ought to be at least as well-trained as any of hers. Probably better; that's my best hope. Let's go. The rest of us need to get in place ourselves. They should arrive late afternoon."

It wasn't as though the large contingent around Nikal would remain continually in place, yet in effect it was like a mini army within the larger army and was meant to operate somewhat independently from the rest. There promised to be plenty of action for all.

Tiliruf was of course in this group, and truth be known, this was surely his true place. Nikal strode up to him.

"I'm expecting to knight you after this, Swordmaster." Nikal smiled at him.

"Thanks, sir. But I'm a republican, eh? The Assembly doesn't approve Tirilorines receiving honors from the kingdoms."

"Well, guess what. War Marshall Jaden doesn't care, and he's in charge, now, *eh?*" And he winked. "And as War Wizard I'll do what I want. You stay tight. Manwul and Hadon watch you, but together I want your focus on Kodi."

"I know my job, sir. And stars knows, this is better than Sea Serpents, for me, anyways."

Curdoz was not allowed by the Order of Sages to be a part of any battle except in pure defense. Though hale, he wasn't fast, nor was he experienced with any weapon. He would observe from the ramparts. He had found for Nikal a pair of locally prominent male Healers by the names of Eliander and Shane. Shane, as a matter of fact, was a black-skinned Essemarian. It was more typical for Hralindis and Essemarians to be assigned to their own countries after their study in the Valley, mostly due to a wish to return to the cultural familiar. The same was true of Westerners. However, there were those from both East and West who desired to expand their horizons and requested assignments that, from their point of view, were exotic, and so immerse themselves in a new setting. Shane was one. Being on the trade routes, in Danzilet he could still commune with Eastern travelers almost whenever he wished. He would prove a most interesting individual. In his teens before his Calling Vision, he had trained as an archer with the Essemarian cavalry and so was not a novice to the military. Curdoz was extremely pleased. Eliander was from the countryside east of Tirilorin, a country farm boy like Curdoz, and he knew horses, too. Both men were of large build and muscularly fit compared to typical Order Members, both had superior reputations at the Hospital, and both were honored to be assigned to this new duty despite the dangers. Curdoz could hardly have wished for a better pair.

They had been outfitted in lightweight armor over leather and given short knives attached to belts. Kodi had spent a few minutes earlier in the day getting to know them. He reckoned, and was right, that he could speak good words to them in order to boost their confidence. He remembered Jaden's words long ago about leadership. He'd been practicing ever since he'd left Tirilorin the first time. He could inspire, and he did. He also knew Nikal didn't have the time for it.

The Healer pair were stationed to the left rear with their own contingent of horsed guardsmen around them for personal protection and could in a minute's time get to Nikal if the need required it.

Rainwing was on the other side of what was overall a relatively narrow field. She was in a group of foot soldiers. A few were assigned to her as retinue to carry her many casting spears. Curdoz could make her out from the rampart wall. She was a giant in that heavy mail and carrying that massive shield. She was under the captaincy of nobody per her own request to Nikal, and she would operate independently.

They all watched as the enemy approached.

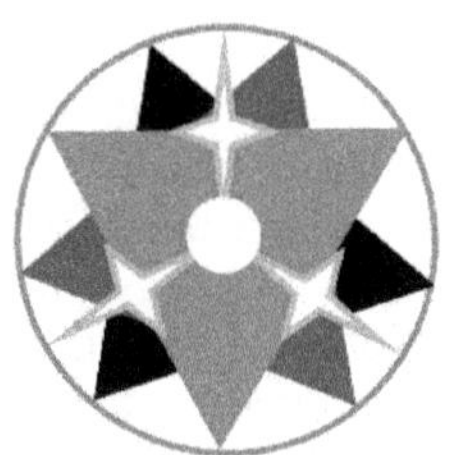

Chapter 8—Battle at South Fort

"Where is she?" asked Tiliruf. It was late afternoon. He'd been watching intently for an hour. Nor was he the only one getting bored from sitting in position. Even the horses were getting shifty.

The army of West Khestadon had arrived. Still some distance beyond bowshot, they could be seen maneuvering into place. Lyndz and Rainwing had apparently counted accurately. It was larger than Nikal's army, considering he had left many to defend Danzilet in case of disaster. His primary hope was that superior training would prove more effective than sheer numbers. Aside from the skirmish at the Berugian Tower months before, the Witch Queen's forces he knew had not engaged in battle before. His Tirilorine units were green, but no more so than the black-garbed army in front of them, yet most from his Nantian troops had experience that should prove valuable. His cavalry was experienced. Mounted around him were many knights, some two hundred, in full armor.

"She is here," said Nikal. "I feel her close. Keep watch."

After a time, it appeared as though the enemy had finished positioning itself. Their cavalry had split into two groups, flanking an army of five thousand.

"They have fireball launchers. All ours are on the ramparts. The height advantage is good," said Manwul. He sat mounted on Tiliruf's right side, Hadon on the other. Kodi was behind the three, by Nikal.

Nikal did not respond to this but continued to gaze forward. *It shouldn't be long, now,* he mused.

The sun was westering to their right. In the wide space between the two armies, suddenly there was movement. Out of a mist that seemed to rise from the ground, a large contingent of men appeared.

"Magic," said Kodi.

"Concealment," said Nikal. "She used it in the last war to hide her brother in order for him to escape. It has to be a pretty powerful magic, I would think, to cover so many. I wonder how quickly she is able to apply it. Quickly, I deem."

The men were giants. There was no other word to describe them, as they were Rainwing's size. There were a hundred of these at least, in a wide array. Most carried heavy maces, yet some held massive swords. And in the middle of them, upon a chariot of red pulled by black horses and driven by a giant charioteer was a figure.

She was slight in comparison to the giants surrounding her. Yet she stood out plain in black leather and wore a red and gold cape. On her head was a helm and mask of silver metal that covered her face completely. Long white, bristled hair hung below the helm, surrounding her shoulders like a mane. She bore no instrument or weapon in her hands, yet appeared commanding, and surely at that moment all eyes on that field and on the ramparts behind Nikal were on her. A silence reigned on all.

In that silence, Nikal lifted the Eagle Staff. It glowed white. From him came a deep voice, magnified by magic. It was powerful and inspiring in its intensity. The late sun shone brightly as he spoke.

"You should not have come, Alkhaness. Our army is strong, and so are our walls. Does it not denote something upon you that here we stand ready? Here I stand, and held by me is a relic of the past. One relic that defeated an empire, five hundred years ago. The emperor's army opposed it with numbers ten times what you have here, and it made no difference. I assure you this talisman has not lost an iota of its power in all the centuries between. Go back, and let us retain the peace. Even at this moment you can turn back and not begin. For once it begins, you cannot win. Meical, Taxiarch on High, will not allow it. I, Nikal of Nant, War Wizard, will not allow it."

Nikal's voice disappeared into the distance. The Alkhaness then raised her hand, and in a thickly accented voice, also magnified, that seemed to echo all around, she replied. And as she did, a coldness dawned in the hearts of all those who heard it.

"You are a fool, Nikal of Nant. That which you bear is not powerful enough to defeat me. The emperor was weak. He had no magic to oppose the Staff. I am not stupid to history, no. I will have Danzilet. These lands are mine. Your chance to depart was offered already. You do not get another. Such a shame that many will die now due to your lack of wisdom. In my hands lie the power of Mighty Siriné herself, Goddess of the World."

"Imprisoned by Meical Himself in a torrent of storm in the little sea to the south of your lands. What does she do but threaten your fishing fleets and devour baby serpents fed to her by the Jungle rivers?"

Tiliruf, among others, stared at Nikal. *He taunts her. I wouldn't. What a bitch.*

"Your information is limited," she replied.

Nikal nodded.

His nod was a signal. He and Kodi had determined beforehand to be on aggressive offense as much as they could. Kodi stood in his saddle and lifted his hands high in the signal he had learned.

'Volley!' shouted General Cruz in the distance. The bulk of the cavalry in which the Nantian general had taken position, stood in the center.

With that, a massive hail of arrows was launched from every archer on the field in the direction of the Witch and the giants around her. Those around Nikal shifted in anticipation. They watched as the giants lifted their massive shields.

The defensive movement proved unnecessary. All watched as the Alkhaness raised a hand once more. A hot charge blasted forth from it in the direction of the hail of arrows. They incinerated by the hundreds in a white blaze and disintegrated. Only a few ashes fell from the sky.

Damn, said Tiliruf to himself. *Just damn! I knew it wouldn't be easy.*

The enemy army behind the witch's contingent moved forward as one.

"And here comes their own volley," yelled Kodi.

Nikal sat forward and from the Eagle Staff he sent forth his own magic. It was different than that of the Witch. Upon the airs could be seen a vision of visible wind, swirling clouds of wavy light, and the arrows of the enemy blew aside, reaching not a single target. A breeze blew across Kodi and the rest.

Kodi raised an arm and indicated another signal. It was picked up immediately by the other officers on the field.

"Advance!" General Cruz's voice could be heard, and the main army moved forward. In time, the two armies drew quite close.

Suddenly, a shadowy darkness crossed the field. The witch had again moved her hands. A great blast of thunder could be heard. Smoke appeared on a now dead and blackened spot on the western flank.

"She just struck down thirty men at least with that, Nikal!" Manwul shouted and pointed across the field.

"Do it, Nikal!" Kodi shouted. "Meical is with you!"

Nikal seemed to grow large as he sat upon Tindalle. His eyes blazed. He lifted the Staff which flamed white again. And from it white lightning burst out straight for the Alkhaness herself. To those standing near, the sound it produced was momentarily deafening.

She blocked it, though it surely killed a few of the giants closest to her. She stood tall, her arms stretched wide. A yellow shield of light blew out around her. She and the horses and her chariot were not harmed. She then seemed to give her own signal.

The enemy charged.

Kodi signaled a third time. The combined Nantian and Tirilorine army charged forward to meet the onslaught.

Behind them the wall guard had come to life. Great fireballs were launched from on high. Some of these were blocked by the witch's forceful magic and burst asunder in the air, but not all. Some landed and enveloped many in the enemy's ranks in flame as they charged.

The giants of the Alkhaness, who had stood steady, had now been outflanked by the two units of their own cavalry who poured toward the center to engage General Cruz's own. From a neutral observer's perspective, it was extraordinary to watch.

For many long minutes, more magic flowed as War Wizard and Witch each did their best to inflict as much harm on the enemy as they could before the two armies were so mixed. Yet always there were concentrations of each other's forces here and there that seemed to offer particular targets.

Magic in lightning bursts with accompanying thunder rolls, followed by waves of not-quite invisible shields, were the order for the two opposing magics. Many lives were extinguished on both sides, those caught by the blasts destroyed in a mere moment. Nikal's face showed a deadly sternness and cold focus. Kodi occasionally called out suggestions or offered encouragement. Obviously, the face of the Alkhaness could not be made out. Yet the movements of her arms and hands and total stiffness of her body as she stood in place on her chariot, inspired a sort of mesmerizing fear.

Blood. Death. Not only the cavalry contingents, but also the armies of foot soldiers had for long now engaged each other with ferocity. The sounds of battle—yelling, angry men, neighing horses, and swords clanging upon shields—were at their maximum.

It seemed the Witch was capable of pulling elements out of the air itself. When the sky grew dark again, and a black cloud condensed out of the winds, Nikal was prepared this time. When the lightning blasted from on high, he had the staff pointed out and blocked it. Like a bronze gong two hundred feet across, the witch's lightning clanged upon a shield of electric heat and burst up and outwards. The sound was deafening and made some of the horses skittish, but then it was over.

"Keep it up, brother!" called Kodi. "We're moving forward! Somebody's got to challenge her bodyguard. Cruz can't get to them on his own!"

The large unit around Nikal moved. A series of the enemy's fireballs suddenly appeared. Nikal whipped up the Staff. In an amazing feat of new magic, he seemed to capture them all with grasping white tongues and slung them down straight on the enemy itself. There were bursts of fire. Hundreds fell. It was the single most devastating piece of magic used so far.

Nikal frowned.

"I know it!" yelled Kodi. "I feel your pain, Nikal, but don't let up."

"I'm not going to let up, but I hate it."

The witch was surely infuriated by this on Nikal's part as it caused her forces to lose momentum. This time she aimed low. From both hands a broad beam of yellow-fired pulses came forth. The air seemed to grow cold all around. A large contingent, some two hundred at least, froze suddenly in place. Covered in rock-hard ice, they could not move. And then, in a scene horrible to watch, every one of them shattered in vicious carnage.

"DRAGON'S TEETH!" shouted Tiliruf at the top of his lungs. "SPIKESHAFTED WITCH!"

Kodi's smile that seemed often to appear, and to which he clung in order to keep up his own spirits and those around him, faltered. "Those were mostly new Tirilorine volunteers," he said in a voice barely above a whisper.

Nikal's face displayed shock at first, but then he let out a howl of rage. Kodi watched his eyes blaze as his War Wizard brother lifted the Staff with both hands above his head. In the near distance was a massive boulder the size of a mansion, a rock cast off in some avalanche of the hills in millennia past. Magic from the Staff poured forth into the earth below this feature—seemingly embedded forever in the landscape—and it moved. With utter amazement in the eyes of all, the War Wizard lifted the object of many tons out of the hard ground and dragged it fifty feet into the air. The power emanating from the Staff was a thick pulsating arm of white hot, unstoppable light, which then wrapped itself around the rock like an enormous hand. Then Nikal swung the Staff with his left hand and slung the immense object with unimaginable fury at the enemy. It slammed down, crushing hundreds.

The ground shook at the impact, and many hundreds more, all around, fell to the ground. Many horsemen and their terrorized beasts fell too in the near vicinity.

The crash and the quake having caused a sort of pause in the battle, Kodi saw that the Witch Queen appeared also to have fallen. He could see that her chariot had turned over, and the horses that pulled it lay stunned or dead.

Yet Nikal, too, had fallen. Tindalle was skipping around, riderless but unharmed.

"NIKAL!" Kodi yelled. He himself was one of the few, along with Tiliruf, Manwul and Hadon, who had somehow managed not to fall in the miniature earthquake. He jumped down from Scadyne and raced to his friend. Keeping his head, he raised his hands and issued an unused signal. The Healers should arrive shortly. He then bent down and lifted Nikal's head.

"I...I think I'm okay, Kodi. That took a lot out of me. Take it. Take the Staff, right now. Go after her while you have a chance!"

True to their purpose, Shane and Eliander arrived and promptly took charge of Nikal. Green pulses moved rhythmically from their hands into his head and into his body. Kodi then took the Staff and jumped back on Scadyne. Tiliruf, Hadon, and Manwul closed ranks around him, as did most of the rest of Nikal's own cavalry contingent. They advanced in the direction of the witch's downed chariot and of the giants who had now regained their footing from the earthquake. These were picking up their arms again. Battle sounds slowly resumed all around the field after the momentary lapse due to the falling boulder. Horsemen were quickly remounting, the ones not hurt.

Upon the rampart wall, Curdoz watched gravely as the battle unfolded. So far, the wall was safe. Two enemy fireballs had landed behind, but their fires were soon put out and no one as yet had been hurt. The artillery men working the launchers atop the wall were admirable to watch, capable and disciplined. They had their own signal system, and they were able to launch with regular precision. They were greatly effective in reducing the enemy's ranks. Eventually, however, the two armies on the field were fighting in such close quarters, that the launching of fireballs had ceased in order not to do damage to their own men.

Unlike Nikal's group, focused as they were on the magical battle between War Wizard and Witch Queen, Curdoz was able to see more of the fighting going on between the great armies as they engaged each other. In particular he could see Rainwing. She was amazing, and he watched her for quite some time. Every spear she threw skewered its intended target. For a time, she and her assistants were able to retrieve a few and cast again, but finally she discarded the tactic and resorted to her mace, and her assistants drew their swords and blended into other units. Yet even alone now, no enemy could withstand her, and surely a number of friendly foot soldiers hung near her in order to take advantage of the terror she inspired in the enemy combatants nearby. They made headway, always advancing to the enemy's center in the direction of the giant men around the Witch.

"What is she doing?"

Rainwing had paused again. To the Sage's astonishment, she cast off her chain mail.

"She can't swing so well with it on! It's a hindrance. May the Powers protect her!" It certainly appeared now as if she were moving much faster and even more gracefully than she already was. "She's a goddess if ever I saw one!"

The giants themselves were virtually unassailable, and none seemed to get close enough to inflict any real harm upon them. Horsemen had quickly learned they were in danger if they got too near to the Alkhaness, for she would blast them off their mounts. Only the foot soldiers could get near, but they had little impact on the giants. Like Rainwing, many of the giants had heavy maces, though others wielded broadswords of great size which they wielded unmercifully as they protected the area around the queen.

Archers had mostly returned in the direction of the wall, for they were vulnerable. Occasionally they could send out volleys in the direction of concentrated groups of enemy soldiers or at the enemy's cavalry. Sometimes the queen was able to stop the arrow clouds like she did at the beginning of the battle, but occasionally they had success. The problem was that the enemy too had success. The battle was, at the moment, in neither's clear advantage.

He saw when Nikal moved his cavalry unit forward in order to approach. He realized they were going to try to get to the giants around the Witch Queen.

Suddenly, to his enormous surprise, Musca the dog stood at his side.

"Musca! What the blazes are you doing here?"

The beast's eyes then glowed bright green and he stood unmoving for a moment. "Great balls of fire!" Curdoz stated with uttermost shock. Musca then left him abruptly and raced down a stone stairway towards the gates. Curdoz ran to the inner side of the wall to look down. The dog was barking animatedly. The men there were perplexed.

"Let him through!" Curdoz called down. "Listen to me and let him through! Now!"

Curdoz was of course not an officer, but the gatemen had no intentions of not obeying the Sage. They seemed to understand his urgency.

They moved to open the gate, and Musca charged through. Curdoz sprinted back to the other side and watched as the big silver beast raced like the fastest wolf in the world towards the battlefield. He disappeared in the melee.

Incredible blasts of magic infused the air. There were terrible screams of dismay, and Curdoz felt a great cold gust across his face. He couldn't make out right away what it portended, but when he shortly afterwards saw the great, megalithic boulder lifted into the air, he cried aloud, "Guardian, have mercy!"

When the thing dropped atop the enemy—mostly enemy he hoped—even the wall he stood on shook some from the impact. There was a pause in the battle as many near the rock fell from the quake. He had lost track of Nikal and Kodi, but soon he saw Kodi and his knights astride their horses advancing upon the giants. Enemy horsemen charged at them. The Sage stood rigid, his eyes wide. "Oh, Meical! He has the Staff! He has the Staff! Whatever has happened to Nikal?"

He watched as Kodi with Staff in hand, along with all his knights, engage the enemy's cavalry, and they were only a mere stone's throw from the giants, who also moved in their direction to attack.

"Where is she? Where is the Alkhaness?" He could see her chariot was down but could not pinpoint her bright yellow and red cape. He saw also that Rainwing was approaching the giants, and out of nowhere, there was Musca, his fur gleaming in a little ray of sunshine, an arrow flash of speed.

Curdoz took in his breath, his eyes suddenly wide. "Of course! She's...she's Ralsheen! But that's just Ice Tribe to him! He senses her!"

Suddenly, there were calls off to his right, and men pointing to the sky. Along the blocky ridgeline, against a setting sun, could be seen perhaps ten dark figures, great-winged giants. They were rapidly approaching on a westerly wind.

"Upon my word! Ah, I hope they can help! We need everything we can get!"

Kodi was not afraid of the Staff, not by any means whatsoever. Yet he felt a keen sense of caution. He knew he couldn't fight with his sword just now, holding the Staff as he was. He was alert. But what unfolded before him now was a scene of the most extraordinary inspiration.

A strong contingent of the enemy's cavalry crashed into his own unit, and the most splendid fighting he'd ever imagined was taking place all around him. Keen upon protecting him, their War Wizard just like Nikal, they broke upon the Khestadone knights in stunning assault. It was glorious.

But it wasn't these Nantian knights of Nikal's he found himself awestruck by, though they were impressive to say the least.

It was Tiliruf.

His friend stood forward on his own magnificent B'ulstread stallion, a shiny, deepest brown—nearly black—beast whom Tiliruf had named long ago the simple, but to Tiliruf, very meaningful name, "Apple."

Outfitted in shiny mail, Tiliruf upon Apple advanced like a king. And as the young man lifted his sword—in his left hand—something seemed to click in the scion of Terianh.

As if blessed with some unknown magic of his own, Tiliruf swung Aron's old blade with a precision and skill that seemed to go well beyond all the training he'd ever had. The enemy knights were of course trying to kill him, unlike all the many friends Tiliruf had sparred with in his life. But they were all around him dropping from their horses like flies. With a speed unmatched almost by Kodi's very eyes, Tiliruf's blade swung in extraordinary fury. It was utterly uncanny. Already, on his own, the son of emperors had dispatched twenty enemies in a mere minute. Here he was, then he was there, and even Apple the stallion was ablaze, bounding about with his own sense of meticulousness among the many other mounts that attempted to approach them.

And Tiliruf was not even holding the reins.

And nearly as beautifully, Manwul and Hadon had done their own dead-level best in the melee. That they were not yet titled Swordmasters, this was, Kodi realized, due to only one possibility—Jaden's undue perfectionism. It was clear now to Kodi the only reason he had not offered them the honor was the mere fact they were, in his mind, not as good as Tiliruf and Nikal. But Kodi knew instinctively that there were probably only some twenty Swordmasters in all the Human world, and most were not as good as what he could see demonstrated by these two Tirilorines. He had a thought suddenly, and he buried it for later.

With the realization his mind was wandering a little, he grew immediately alert again.

There had been no sign of the Witch Queen now for several minutes. It was plain she had not been crushed by the giant boulder, for though the close impact had overturned her chariot and killed her horses, these could be seen even now just a little way off. The giant bodyguard had shifted their position in Kodi's direction, and he then realized something.

She's hiding in her concealment magic!

And he deduced she probably was, just like Nikal was doing, recovering from a shock. He turned his mind to the Staff.

She is here.

And she was almost certainly observing him. That she hadn't attempted already to blast him was due to two possibilities, or both. She was still recovering and was rebuilding her magic. Or she was curious to see why he, a stranger she had not yet encountered or knew anything about, was carrying the Eagle Staff with such a sense of unassuming familiarity.

That the good mind logic, inherited from his mother's side and demonstrated early by his twin, had been emerging rapidly over the last couple months in Kodi himself, Kodi didn't yet quite admit to himself. Nevertheless, the logic was indeed there, now. His mind was working.

He doubted he could do precisely what Nikal did with that boulder without losing strength like Nikal, but he was quickly working in his mind something entirely different.

The Staff was connected to him, just as it was Nikal. And it had a spirit, he knew. An actual soul.

It also, he realized suddenly, had a mind.

It can think like me if I open my mind to it. It...it knows me by my touch of it.

He then made the Eagle Staff of Terianh the Great work a magic that came straight from his knowledge, and as importantly, from his deep emotion.

The Staff glowed white hot in his hand. He climbed down from Scadyne. He then closed his eyes for a moment only, then sent forth a beam of white light into the ground at his feet. Suddenly, in a perimeter of perhaps a hundred feet, a shell of opaque white light burst out of the ground in a circle and blew up over them in a sort of bubble, not so unlike the green dome of light he had experienced in the Moment Master session with Brother Theneri. It surrounded everything within that hundred-foot perimeter and, upon Kodi's direction, expelled every enemy within it, blasting them high and outward as if they had been picked up by an imaginary hill giant and thrown. Tiliruf, Manwul, Hadon, and most of his knightly contingent were safe within a protected sphere of watery white light.

"Shaft, Kodi! Shaft! What the shafting Dragon's Teeth did you just pull off with that thing? Blazes almighty!"

The magic was actually so specific that the horses of the enemy, whom Kodi had no desire whatsoever to harm, were unhurt. Yet most of these did indeed...and quite surprisingly...march on their own, right out of the bubble in search of their blasted-away masters. Though they were all dead he knew. He'd never killed a man before. Only sea monsters. He now understood better what Nikal felt.

For all practical purposes the greater part of the enemy's cavalry was finished. Kodi stood for some moments unmoving and didn't respond to Tiliruf. Within the perimeter, obviously, the fighting had ended, and as they watched, a few others of their contingent nearby raced inside it for protection.

The giant bodyguard of the Witch was suddenly there. They were the most formidable force left to the Alkhaness.

But they could not penetrate the barrier.

Maybe Tiliruf wanted wordy explanations from his friend, but the magic was explaining itself. That within the barrier was a friends-only club.

This helped Kodi settle a little. He felt the Witch near, but plainly, she was not within that hundred-foot perimeter.

And the moment he realized that, she struck.

A burst of yellow lightning crashed upon Kodi's magical barrier. It had no effect upon it. He looked all around, trying desperately to find her, but he still couldn't see where she was. Still hidden.

That's, er, pretty effective, you damned piece of hideous female nastiness. Show yourself.

Rainwing had fought with fury. She gloried in every slain enemy. Maybe there was indeed a piece of the Etoppsi subconscious that was more animal-like and wild than that of most Humans. There almost had to be such differences in the races of the Mold. They had planted in them, by Meical Himself, upon Vanayisu and Vanayema's children in the Molding, some innate differences. Etoppsi were by nature ruthless to their enemies. They had an anger inside them that boiled hot at insult and injury and invasion of their space. They had control, too. Which might explain why she could blast Tiliruf when he said stupid things, yet not take him by the throat and throttle him. She knew instinctively that Tiliruf was a friend, despite the chauvinistic things he sometimes said that seemed insulting of her or of other females. She understood he never really meant anything by it.

But that control did not apply, of course, to the Khestadone. The Human soldiers under the control of the Alkhaness had implanted in them mindspells that displaced their humanity. Silverwing had taught her this long ago. Did she have a sense of sorrow for their slavery? Probably. A tiny part of her, particularly since she studied and attempted in part to adhere to some of the old Monastic Disciplines, she knew of the Guardian's sense of care for all people. Yet it did not blind her to the threat the Khestadone posed. A sort of logic told her those slaves, upon their death, went to the Stars, and believed fully that they would be released from all the evils imposed upon them in this world.

Yet she had family back home, friends all around her, a country, and even a world, in the here and now, which she was required to defend. Toplings and Human children appeared before her in her mind's eye. They must grow up in a free world. She had little space in her mind, then, for any sense of mercy.

She had finally reached the giant men, the Witch's bodyguard, and upon them she broke with the fury of...a Dragon Hunter.

They might be nearly as big as she, but they still did not have the strength nor the speed to match her. Nor the eyesight, the instinct, the stamina, the ferocity, nor really any sense of having been wronged to the level she had. They obeyed the Alkhaness out of fear and by way of magic imposed within them. But that magic was not based on any sort of genuine loyalty, but rather they were as automated machines working off the energy provided by a watermill. If they had it within them to actually express their truest feelings for the Alkhaness, these would have been fear...and hate.

So, unlike Rainwing, they didn't have such wonderful reasons for which to fight and to which to attach their own sense of fury.

Aside from their very lives, of course. But that was defense.

Rainwing was purest offense.

While the invisible Alkhaness was concentrating on Kodi and his amazing shield wall, the famous *Rainwing Dragonfighter, Rainwing Serpentslayer,* was smashing her bodyguard to pieces.

Tiliruf was peering steadily into Kodi's face. The War Wizard's keen brown eyes were not at all blank, but they were indeed staring. Tiliruf understood that his friend was concentrating with all his might, which he had come to realize over their time together was formidable. Kodi was a fun and funny friend. But he was also a power to be reckoned with. An extraordinary power, Tiliruf believed, for all the genuine good in the world.

When Kodi whispered a command to him, Tiliruf nodded and did not argue.

He turned to the others and yelled, "Form up! Form up!"

With renewed vigor the cavalry contingent charged forward. They easily broke out of the barrier like water and crashed into the giant bodyguard.

Some of them fell, but the large-sized enemy could do more damage to the horses than normal foot soldiers or cavalry. Tiliruf was infuriated when a mace came within an inch of Apple's nose. He yelled at Manwul and Hadon. "Dismount! Send the horses back to Lord Kodi's shield!"

If Tiliruf was a swift killer on Apple, he was a whirlwind on the ground.

He simply could not be caught. He slashed and slew men thrice his size, moving with the speed of a World God. And Manwul and Hadon were right beside him the whole time.

All of a sudden, there was a pause, and Rainwing stood before him.

"Thought you didn't want to get near me," he quipped.

"Who got near who, *eh?*" she mocked. But then she smiled. "You're a sublime warrior, Tiliruf. I'm impressed. I've certainly never seen a Human—or an Etoppsis—move like you."

"Except maybe yourself."

"Well, yes. I didn't mean to compare you to me!" She laughed raucously.

And so did Tiliruf.

Yet the fight continued, and the two soon drifted apart again.

The Witch Queen was concentrating every magic she could think of at Kodi's shield. Lightning blasts. They were fully absorbed by the power of the shield. Freeze beams. They coated the shield with layers of ice and then with a bursting pulse from the shield they cracked off in loud explosions. She hurled missiles of stone and cast-off shields by the dozens, but nothing worked.

Yet Kodi was getting tired. Many Nantians and Tirilorines, overcome or hurt, had managed to get themselves into the shield between the Witch's blasts. Already there were a hundred or more, and they were depending on Kodi to save their lives. Horses, too, had taken cover. There was Apple, and Manwul and Hadon's mounts. Kodi was not worried, though. As long as the witch was focusing on him, he knew those three were fine.

Meical, I...I'm sorry. I...I can't keep this up.

There could not be more than thirty left of the giant bodyguard. Yet they fought on. Rainwing battled like a monstrous jungle tiger, and if she could have breathed fire like a Dragon, it would not have surprised anyone. She shifted in and out among them, downing several from behind, when all of a sudden there was a pause again. A wide space seemed to have opened out around her, and standing before her was the biggest Human man she had ever seen.

Yet she *had* seen him. Quite recently. It was the man she and Lyndz had marked as somehow different in their spy mission.

He held his mighty sword before him, but despite her hesitation, he did not take advantage. Rather—shockingly—he stared at her.

His dark eyes then darted all over her. Those eyes. Those different, unclouded eyes. Rainwing lowered her mace and stared back. The fury that drove her gave way to that piece of her mind that, instead, exerted control. And she spoke.

"Before me stands an image of the Taxiarch Meical in all His glory."

He started. His eyes focused wide on her own. "What? What did you say to me?" He spoke in a rotund voice, in modern Anterianhi, but with a flavorful accent. "Who is Taxiarch Meical? Tell me, *who* is he? I must know!"

She paused. There was desperation in the question. "He...Meical is the Guardian of the World, of course. Of our world. Of Dumhoni. And others, according to what we understand. As Taxiarch He fights against evil in the worlds He knows and loves."

She was amazed with herself, standing there as she was, having a conversation of mystical matters with her Khestadone enemy. Why was she hesitating...to kill him?

All of a sudden, and before she could respond, the man puffed up, and with the speed of lightning, he cast that massive sword in her direction.

Rainwing for a moment thought she was dead, but to her shock the sword crashed just past her into another of the enemy giants who had come up from behind.

She glared in shock at the huge black man who had just murdered one of his own in order to save her life. His eyes began to roll horribly, and he fell forward on his arms and knees and looked up at her in anguish.

An enormous sense of pity overwhelmed Rainwing. Yet, with some gumption, she turned, withdrew the sword from the dead man's body and, wiping it on the dead man's clothes as best she could, she then presented it to the prostrated man.

"You are a mighty Human warrior. You should have your sword back."

He stood again, but he was still anguished. Tears flooded his eyes. Human tears seemed always to move Rainwing for the emotive passion they exhibited. And on a Human male especially they seemed extraordinarily expressive to her. They were typically rarer than a female's. He took the sword from her, touching her furred hands in the action. The black of his skin matched that under her fur and on her palms.

Through the tears he forced a question. "What...what happened to your beautiful wings? You are a...woman from Berug?"

Her eyes in a constant wide state from the beginning of this whole affair actually grew wider.

"Er, a female Etoppsis, yes." She had no heart just then to expound upon a full-fledged explanation of terminology. An image of a patient Idamé found its way in. "I...I lost my wings. They were taken from me, in sacrifice for my friends. And...and yes. They were very beautiful."

The tears stopped. He wiped them away and looked at her. His eyes were no longer shifting around. He seemed more himself. "I...I think not as beautiful as what I see before me. I am so sorry."

Rainwing nodded, but the look he bore as he spoke such words to her created a tremendous struggle in her mind, and it was almost more than she could stand. "You bear a terrible pain, I think. I must go. My friends need me. You will be in danger if your queen sees you speaking with the enemy. May Meical the Guardian watch after you."

She turned around to go, paused, and spoke with her back to him. "Thank you for saving my life just now. I'll never forget it. Tell me your name."

"I am called Dru."

"I am called Rainwing."

Then, leaving him, she ran back to the battle.

Meical, I...I'm sorry. I...I can't keep this up.

"That's impressive magic, Kodi. Now give it back to me."

Unbelievably, Nikal stood before him, and he appeared perfectly well again, though he had an unhappy frown on his face. While Kodi still held the Staff, Nikal took hold of it and, in perfect accord with Kodi's own deep emotion, kept the magic intact. Kodi collapsed onto the ground and immediately perceived a dark face close to his own, and green light.

"Shane! Bless you, man! But where is Eliander? Shane?"

Shane looked with seriousness into Kodi's face, a fire in his dark eyes. "I killed the bastard Khestadone who stabbed him. I couldn't save my friend. I tried. You're exhausted, Lord Kodi. Be still now. I'll fix you."

Ch'yad was incensed at the presence of the second man. From the safety of her Concealment charm, she did everything she could to burst that barrier of his, but nothing worked. When she saw that Nikal of Nant had retaken control of the Staff from the other, she began to doubt herself. That there were two of the so-called War Wizards who could so casually take turns with it seemed unfair. She decided, however, to show more of what she was capable of.

She turned in the direction of South Fort. She didn't need one so big as the boulder Nikal moved, but she found what she sought. With both hands lifted, she applied a yellow beam of Siriné's earth magic and lifted the object from the ground. Waving her arms in the direction of the distant gate, she cast it forward with all her might.

"GET OFF! GET OUT!" shouted the Sage at the top of his lungs.

Everyone atop the wall ran away from the center as the great boulder came hurtling. With a colossal boom it crashed upon the gate, blasting it and a section of the wall around and above into rubble.

Curdoz fell stunned and saw no more.

Nikal discarded Kodi's defensive barrier and magnified his voice. "Turn it on me, Ch'yad Alkhaness!"

All grew totally still in the near vicinity, and Nikal actually smiled. "Yes. I know who you are. Daughter of the Emperor. Child of Flame. Show yourself!"

"NO! HOW...HOW *DARE* YOU USE MY NAME!"

She was so distracted she jumped as a massive arrow penetrated the ground at her feet. Looking up, she saw another sight that unnerved her. Etoppsi Wingfeathers, fully armored and wielding enormous bows, were shooting spear-sized arrows at her position. Though they could not see her, she put upon her invisible body a barrier. She aimed up and blasted two Feathers out of the sky. The rest withdrew eastward.

Still invisible, she dropped her barrier.

It was, for her, a terrible mistake.

An image of massive silver slammed into her. Snarling and biting, the wolf-like beast knocked her full onto the ground. She was visible again and her helm and mask went flying, revealing to all her white face. Stunned, she was unable at first to stop the attacking beast as it snapped upon her leathered left forearm and bit down with jaws of steel. It yanked and thrashed, and the pain she experienced was unbearable. But as it came for her face, she gained some traction with her mind and threw up her block again and the beast bounced back from it, snarling viciously. She automatically applied magic to her bleeding stump and staunched the flow. Then with her remaining hand she threw a bolt of power at the animal but missed. The beast was fast, and she was in too much agony to put up a controlled fight. And from her right, just a little way off, a blast of enormous power struck her.

If she had not had up her block, she would have been killed. Her mind went cold, and she vanished once more.

She'd had enough. She knew, now.

The Staff of Terianh could not be overcome by the power within her. If the Staff moved east to engage her brother, she could, if she wished, bring up a much larger army from the south and conquer Danzilet. Yet what good would it be in the end should the Staff return? To utterly defeat it she needed something more. The Crown of Charms. As she now had a moment to work a magic easing her pain, her other plans worked upon her mind.

The beast had moved off. She stood, walked away, unseen by anyone.

Nikal blasted at enemies left and right. Khestadone soldiers and the few remaining horsemen flew into the air in bloody bits, and before another minute had gone by, the remainder of the army of the Witch Queen disengaged and retreated in shambles southwards. This had all been way, way too close, he thought to himself. He would order no pursuit.

He looked up grimly at one of his knights. "Ride immediately and retrieve all the Healers from Danzilet. Have the remaining horsemen in the city bring them out here at once."

The sun set upon a bloody day.

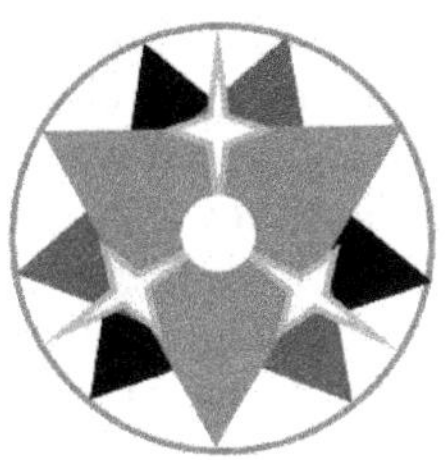

Chapter 9—Aftermath

"Where are they, Ida?" asked a weak Curdoz. He sported a large bruise on his forehead and others all over his body. His right arm was wrapped in heavy cloths. "You must tell me."

Weak, but improving by the minute.

Shane himself stood at the Sage's bedside in the Hospital at Danzilet applying rapid green pulses into his body, and it was he who answered. Idamé was actually washing caked blood and dust from the Sage's body with a warm cloth.

"We held the day. You're lucky not to have been hurt worse or killed, Lord Sage. You fell far. Don't move, and I will tell you. Give me a moment. I'm working on your pain and blood flow. The other Healers kept you in sleep while they attended to worse cases."

"He knows more than I, dear," said Idamé reaching for Curdoz' hand and holding it for a moment. "He was there. Our friends will be fine, dear. Yet we lost Brother Eliander."

"Oh, Shane. Oh, bless you, Brother."

Shane nodded. "He Dances the Stars now. All his friends here will honor his memory. Shh, shh, shh. Another moment. Be still now."

Two more minutes passed, and Shane indicated it was okay for him to talk again.

The sage's voice was much stronger. "He was your close friend. You worked together for years. I'll do the death rite myself, Brother Shane. They have retrieved his body?"

"Yes. That...that would be a great honor to his memory and sacrifice, Lord Sage. I'll tell the other Healers and Monastics. We would all be so pleased."

"Have the burial place and time arranged and I will be there."

Shane nodded. For another minute he had Curdoz remain perfectly still as he focused on the arm. "All right. That should do well. You'll have some tiny discomfort in that arm for a few days, but Mother Idamé can remove those wraps. I'm somewhat of an expert at bones." He then moved his hand to Curdoz' head and applied the green light. The Sage was feeling greatly better than when he awakened five minutes before. Shane then offered a quick summary of events. "I never imagined in all my life I would experience anything remotely like what I did yesterday. The Witch Queen withdrew to the south, as I think you understand. They say she was maimed by the great silver dog belonging to Lord Kodi."

"Ah, I knew there was something extraordinary about that dog!"

"Yes. They found a bloodied white hand in the remnants of a black leather glove. Perhaps a thousand of hers survived the battle. She lost nearly all her cavalry and maybe all but ten of her giant bodyguards. Prince Nikal would not order a pursuit. The sun was setting, and it was quickly growing dark. We have many prisoners. They are dangerous, however. Their minds are spellbound, and we have many guards over them. I think Healers may remove the spells if given time. I must get a good sleep tonight, but as soon as I get a chance, I plan to spend a little time with them and see what I can achieve. It'll be magic against magic, a new challenge. Prince Nikal and Lord Kodi are surely tired, yet they push themselves. Not so unlike us Healers, I suppose. I will be looking in on them after I leave here. The Swordmaster Tiliruf a' Terianh sleeps late this morning in the barracks along with his bodyguards. All witnesses say his swordsmanship skills were beyond heroic. General Cruz is dead."

"I am sorry to hear it."

"Prince Nikal ordered an honor guard around his and Eliander's bodies at the meditation chapel of the Monastics. Many hundreds of ours died, many of horrible means inflicted by the Witch. Her freezing spells were nightmarish to witness. I'm sure you saw some of it from the rampart before she broke the gate with that boulder, and you fell. That killed several at the gate level, for unlike some of you on top of the wall, they could not see it coming. That was her last large-scale attack, as it was shortly afterwards that she herself was savaged by Lord Kodi's dog. She went invisible again and withdrew at that point. Healers were at the field afterwards for much of the night and saved many hurt men. Sadly, some were beyond healing, and we put them to sleep to end their pain and lend them comfort as they departed the world. Monastics from the city have gone out to Bless the dead and the burials. Did you see the Etoppsi who arrived before you fell?"

"Yes. Tell me more."

"Two were struck dead by the Witch after they shot bolts at her from the sky. The other eight took their bodies this morning to the high hills and built cairns, yet I think the eight met with the prince this morning. They were sent by the King of Berug to submit themselves to the authority of the War Wizards."

"And what of Rainwing? You know, the wingless female?"

"She and the Swordmaster were largely responsible for breaking the giant bodyguard of the Witch. She appeared physically fine after the battle but left the field almost the instant the enemy retreated."

"She's secluding herself, dear, with Lyndz," explained Idamé. "I think they may have gone up into the hills. At the moment she wishes to see no one else. But she is unhurt, like Brother Shane says. I'm sure she wishes for some peace after yesterday."

"What I could see of her on the field was nothing short of something out of the Great War in the Deeps of Time, when the gods of goodwill fought the Rebellious Ones. I will write that in the histories when I get a chance."

"I saw some of it too, at least until I was called to attend Prince Nikal. It was just as you say. I have read those histories," said Shane. He stopped applying green light. "All right. You will do quite well now, Lord Sage. I will leave you with Mother Idamé. She is a most excellent nurse. She has you cleaned up. I've assured there will be no dangerous clotting from your bruises, and the bruises should be gone quite soon. None of your cuts were deep enough to be of much concern, yet I fully mended them anyway, and you will not be scarred. You can go to the baths for a hot soothe whenever you feel up to it. It is only men at the baths today. We've instigated rules due to the filth from the battle. Full soapy washes in the running pools before any are allowed time soaking in the hot ones, as those waters are not replenished as rapidly."

"I am feeling very well now, Brother Shane. You are a powerful Healer."

"He looks worlds better, Brother Shane. I was so worried."

"Thank you for the kind compliments, Mother Idamé. Lord Sage."

"You will call me Brother Curdoz." Curdoz reached out and grabbed Shane's arm. "I want you to go east with us, Shane, yes! Take a day or two to consider. I see the need now for someone to organize Healing aid for all who surround Prince Nikal and myself, including during battle. You're in Sage Enric's jurisdiction, but he would sanction my authority in this. Being from Essemar you could provide additional guidance for some of us who aren't as familiar. Nikal has Healers with the armies in the east, but you could bring two or three others of your choice, and a helpful Monastic or two. In fact, I want Scribes. They would prove useful servants for me and help me chronicle events. Enric can send replacements to Danzilet."

Shane raised an eyebrow. "Hmm. I rather find that a compelling offer, Brother Curdoz."

Idamé agreed with Curdoz. "Do consider Curdoz' proposal."

"I am always grateful to be needed, of course. To travel among such heroes..."

"It'll be dangerous, as Eliander has proven," said Curdoz. "Yet we must have Healers handy."

"I understand, of course. I will let you know upon the morrow my decision whether or not to travel with you and will send word this afternoon on my arrangements for Brother Eliander. I will go to the lords now."

Curdoz leaned up on his other arm. "Tell Nikal and Kodi I am commanding you to put them to sleep. And if either resists, do it anyway. Apply the charm sneakily if you have to. They won't buck me."

Shane seemed to think this an excellent idea. He smiled warmly at the Sage and walked away.

"His language demonstrates a high scholar," said Idamé. "And a disciplined mind, if you ask me. And warm bedside manners. Discerning dark eyes. Good-looking."

"Ida," said Curdoz in a low tone. "I believe his magic to be extremely potent. Like Marco tells me of Xeno back home. I feel as good as a dream after his touch. Something's happening, I think."

"What do you mean?"

"The depth of new magic is what I mean. And heroes. As though the Guardian is ushering in an era similar to that of the days of the Great Sages."

"I just wish He'd give me back my Matrimonial Gift."

He took her hand, held it, and leaned back into the pillow. "It was Modela who took it, not Meical. We gave in order to have the Staff, and I can't imagine how yesterday would have turned out without it, can you? I'm still holding out hope, though. Yet I don't know what it is, really, that I'm hoping for."

"Well, dear. As long as you hope, then so will I."

He grinned at her. "Er, how long are you going to make me lie here?"

Her own smile spoke of affection. "Let me get you some food, dear, and send for fresh clothes from your bags at North Fort. I'll remove those arm wraps, and we'll go pay our respects at the monastic's chapel."

"You won't breathe a word of it to anyone, Lyndz."

"Definitely not, Rainwing. It's very personal. Extraordinary, though. He chose to save your life! If you were to ask me, I would say he...that he is attempting to cast off the Alkhaness' mindspells."

"That's precisely what I'm thinking too. The eyes. The eyes."

The two 'females' had climbed up behind an olive tree estate into the rocky hillside. They sat together on a large boulder, and from here they had a pretty view of the city and harbor. Numerous ships could be seen sailing the routes east and west or into and out of the harbor. Overhead, all was clear and blue. No stranger would have imagined that only the afternoon before a major battle took place nearby that threatened that prosperous picture.

"Intent on the *identity* of the Guardian? And why would he be so interested? What you said ought to have been nothing to him but jargon."

"When I said the name, he was startled. I believe he'd heard Meical's name before and been dwelling on it. It captured him, who knows how long ago, and his curiosity of it was making an inroad on his whole way of thinking."

"And why did you say it to him at all?"

"I don't know! I don't know! I was moved! He was huge. He was muscular. His skin was black and shiny. In that first moment in which I saw him there, his face was male Etoppsi-like. A severe but captivating quality not so unlike Hawking's, if you know what I mean."

"I do. The fur on your faces covers nothing, Rainwing. Nikal's face takes on that same quality sometime."

"Yes! And when I saw the Guardian's face in my Vision, though it was Etoppsi for me, it was like what I saw in Dru. An air of nobility, and that's what caused me to pause in the first place, I'm sure. And then...and then it grew expressive, of course, as I described; when he broke out in tears, I was even more moved. But that was later."

"After you'd said that about the Guardian, right. But it wasn't as though you would never expect his face, Dru's face, to achieve a level of emotion. He's Human, after all."

"No, you're right. The entire encounter had an emotional quality, like that Vision. Everything seemed to go quiet. I lost track of the battle going on all around us."

"It was incredible, Rainwing, truly. You felt pity and compassion, and clearly, he felt those same things for you when he understood you had lost your wings."

Songbirds twittered, flying between the scrubby trees and amongst the rocks. Rainwing watched their play for a minute. "He called them 'beautiful.'"

Lyndz was observing Rainwing's thoughtful expression. "And he'd never seen them, I know. Yet it is *possible*, don't you think, that he'd seen Berugians before?"

"Yes. Definitely possible. Though only in the sky—male Eyefeathers from the Sky Front."

"Even so, he'd of course presume them to be beautiful."

"Except they are taught we are no more than foul animals. The Khestadone despise us. They become almost livid when they encounter us."

"Well. This one didn't. And that's just the mindspells, if you ask me. And we've determined he's breaking out of them. At least we hope he will."

"I hope he will. But Lyndz! How dangerous that will be for him if he does break through! It's probably already dangerous. This...this *transition* sometimes *shows*. The rolling eyes, remember? There's a loss of control."

"That's terrifying, Rainwing. Horrifying to think what could happen. Let's hope the Alkhaness is so distracted by events she doesn't notice changes taking place in one bodyguard."

"I wanted so badly to help him."

"I know you did. I would have wanted to, too."

"Could I have done more yesterday, do you think?"

"No. There was nothing more you could have done for him yesterday. It wasn't the time. He wasn't ready. It could have damaged..." she paused. "Rainwing! I think I see something! I'm thinking back on what you and I felt when we first saw his image in the Mind Mastering the other day. Maybe Meical Himself is *working* on Dru's mind! Directly! He's *chosen* Dru. Picked him out of all that slavery horror in Khestadon. Maybe for Dru's own personal need to know of something higher than the Alkhaness and that horrid Siriné whom they've been made to worship. Or maybe for another purpose in order to achieve something."

"Or...or both." Rainwing's eyes grew bright as she looked at her friend. "Oh, Lyndz. I almost chose to tell you nothing, but you have so helped. I am often full of self-pride and keep so much hidden. But I've never had a friend like you."

"Nor me either, Rainwing. You inspire me. We're damned good for each other. That's just the way it is. We're not a whit different than Nikal and Kodi. We're sisters in a sort of mystic realm, just like they're brothers. It's a quest we're on together, you and me. Now." She turned to her pack. "You ready for my little picnic? I brought you plenty of lamb."

They set everything out.

"The oranges they grow here are divine. What are you doing, Lyndz? You don't have to peel them for me!"

"You want my loose peels, then?"

"No. It's a texture combination with the juicy insides that makes them so tasty."

It is true Rainwing described every word for Lyndz, and much of what she sensed and felt. She was being as honest as she could, and the sharing between the two expanded on their closeness. Even so, the female Etoppsis did not express to her friend the depth of every emotion in her encounter with the man called Dru. She didn't quite know how to do so, as those unlabeled feelings were beyond her experience.

Thoughts of Dru would trouble Rainwing for a long time to come.

"Spikeshafts, I can't move."

Hadon came over to him. "Have a couple swigs, Tiliruf. We'll get ourselves off to the soaks as soon as Manwul wakes up, and that'll help us all heaps. We all smell of blood and horse, dirt and sweat. I'll take your money bag, and we'll give the masseurs gold if we have to. And if they're not there I'll go fetch them. I could use a good rubdown. Here. Lean up."

He helped Tiliruf take a couple of mouthfuls of sweet rum and took a couple for himself. Knowing he needed other, he forced Tiliruf to drink fresh water from a large goblet he filled three times.

"Thanks, mate. Were you ever something, yesterday. Kodi threw out a thought to me last night. I've got a surprise for both of you when we're feeling better, eh?"

"Praise Nikal for giving us our private space here. The silence. It's a tonic. I've had servants take all our things to be scrubbed and polished, by the way. Our horses are being attended to. All I want right now is to be clean. To have everything about me, clean."

"It was nasty work, Hadon. But we do what we got to do. I...I've never felt so good, actually. Er, not my body, though. It feels like I've been beaten by clubs."

"You and Rainwing are heroes, Swordmaster. You broke that blasted bodyguard to pieces. I get it that it's been a burden to you to have that bloodline you do, but what I saw would make your ancestors proud. And it sure made me proud. Proud to witness, and proud to fight at your side."

"I'll take that, thanks. But you and Manwul just being there made it easier for me, eh? None of my ancestors rode into a battle alone. I was stupid to act the way I did back at the estate when Nikal charged you to watch after me. Thumpin' shafts, it's you that's got the real burden putting up with my horseshit. When I think about it, that's what I didn't want you or anybody else to have to do."

Hadon smiled. "I've got us some food from the kitchens. Sit up now. You can do it."

It was hard for Tiliruf to sit up; he was painfully stiff. Yet he managed it and took to the proffered food with a relish.

"You're amazing, eh? I'm starving. Surprised you can move any better than me, mate."

"We do what we got to do, like you said."

They ate much of what Hadon acquired but left enough for Manwul. They didn't have to wait long before the big man finally roused himself. He sat up on the side of his bunk. He was naked, having thrown off all his bloody garb when they arrived late in the night and crashed onto the bed.

He took in a big whiff through his nose. "It's me, isn't it."

"We're all pretty nasty. I'll get us clean bed clothes later. I've sent off most of our things already for a good scrub. Eat a little. We've been plotting our own scrubdown at the baths. We're just waiting for you. We'll stick to the ones here by North Fort."

"Why, that'll feel right nice, I reckon." He yawned but grabbed hungrily at the food Hadon offered. After a minute he was feeling more awake and looked at Tiliruf. "I'll fetch you a Healer, Tiliruf. Can't have you looking like a bedraggled hen. We got to get you spiffy and show off our little hero."

"You're cracking me up, mate. And who's little? Just 'cause you're a damn horse."

"I was no horse compared to those blokes yesterday. I didn't know men could grow that big. Cover 'em with fur and give 'em wings and they'd almost be Etoppsi. They're as big as Etoppsi *females*, anyway."

"Yeah, well there ain't many of 'em left. You took out your share."

"Rainwing, though. Speaking of Etoppsi females. You *really* need to be more careful around her, Swordmaster. She's going to knock your block off one day, if you keep saying dumb stuff."

"She asks for half of it, anyways."

"She don't ask for the other half, and that's the half you need to be wary of, Ruffy."

"Put on something, Manwul, and let's go," said Hadon, impatient to get to the baths.

The big man stood and wrapped a blanket around himself. They looked at him with smiles on their faces. "What? There's none o' my clothes that have it in their mind just now to grace my filthy body."

They chuckled mightily, though the movement made Tiliruf wince in pain. He finally stood, very stiffly, leaned over Hadon's shoulder, and they were all off to what they hoped was going to be the most glorious bath they'd ever taken in all their lives.

"You cracked a rib, 'a Terianh. A swift hard blow you might not even remember in the thick of battle. No hot soak or rubdown until I fix it. Don't move a muscle," said the patient but firm Shane.

"Well, that explains a lot," said Manwul. "We thought at first it was just muscle pain from his level of exertion."

"It was both, really," said Shane, studying Tiliruf carefully. He would move his hands here and there, close his eyes and apply the green light. "It's conceivable he performed a movement where the armor didn't give well and cracked it himself. There's deep bruising here."

The baths had been crowded when they arrived, but no one denied the three spaces in the cool pools for washing. All the men there were praising them, slapping them on the back, many having heard of their extraordinary prowess of the afternoon before. A number of Nikal's knights who had been a part of the action against the witch's bodyguard were there describing it for others. Manwul and Hadon had to fend them off Tiliruf because he'd flinch when anybody touched him. After they had managed to get thoroughly clean—Hadon had to wash Tiliruf's lower legs and feet as it hurt him to bend that far—they wrapped towels around their waists and lay Tiliruf carefully down on one of the benches used for body massages. He seemed spent from the exertion of the bath. He was panting, and his pain seemed worse rather than better. Manwul had determined to hunt down a Healer when Shane miraculously turned up just at that moment. He could tell quickly something was wrong by the young man's breathing and hesitant movements.

Hadon apologized. "None of us are used to this, quite. Sorry, Brother Shane. I see now we should have been more alert to his pain and sent for a Healer much earlier. Perhaps we think we're all young and invincible. We managed fine getting back here and into our beds last night. But this morning...especially for him."

"I'll have him well soon, gentlemen."

"How do..."

"Shhh. Hush, a' Terianh. Barely breathe for a few more seconds. Be still. Ribs are tricky."

Tiliruf complied.

"I think he's wishing to know more how Healing works. He's never made use of it before."

Shane nodded as he now began to pump big waves of green light straight at Tiliruf's bared right side. "The body is made up of things called cells, millions and millions of them. And Healers have the Gift to concentrate and sense the damage done to them and make repairs. That's the simplest explanation I can give you just now. We can see in our minds the damage done. Healers often work faster in pairs, but it isn't necessary, of course. So, the rib and all the muscles and tendons in this area of his back and side must be repaired. And a bruised kidney. I am especially good at these particular systems."

"You're good at all of them, aren't you?"

"I...have been told so by other Healers. Thank you. Perhaps I am, yet a Healer should never raise himself above others, as he is a servant of the Guardian. I'll readily ease your own discomforts when I'm done with him. The ministrations of the masseurs will also be of benefit, but in his case only after the Healing, otherwise they'd only worsen it." He then spoke to Tiliruf. "That's good, Swordmaster. It knitted well. The rib bone, that is. I'm getting most of your tendons and muscles now in your torso and that kidney. You don't seem to have any bruising of note in your limbs." He then folded back Tiliruf's towel and examined with magic. He put on a slight smirk for Tiliruf's benefit. "No worries for your...*critical components*."

Without comment, Tiliruf smiled back. He appreciated the Healer's hint of humor and Manwul's and Hadon's chuckles. His face noticeably relaxed after another few minutes of magical ministrations. Finally, Shane stopped.

"Oh, stars praise you, Shane." Tiliruf sat up without the slightest hesitation, rubbed his chest and sides, and stretched to his fullest.

"Feeling a little more yourself, I hope, 'a Terianh?"

"Thumping thumpers, yes."

"He's an *Order Brother*, Tiliruf," admonished Manwul. "Drop the crude expressions."

Shane laughed. "No pretenses, please. Brother Curdoz has asked me to join up with you, and I'm considering. We may be seeing much more of each other."

"If that's the case, then just call me *Tiliruf*, Shane. I ought to be more mannerly with my language, they tell me."

"I will continue to call you *'a Terianh* sometimes, as it reflects well, I think, upon much I detect about you."

Acknowledging the respect offered him by a man himself deserving of his own high respect, Tiliruf chose not to protest. He looked at the Healer and nodded. "We are terribly sorry about Brother Eliander. He's a hero to all of us."

"Assuredly, he is," agreed Hadon.

"Aye, we'll remember always his sacrifice," said Manwul. "Meical's Blessings to you, Brother Shane. 'Twas a wrench to lose your friend. You seem to be taking the loss well."

Shane's dark eyes glistened slightly at this, and he shook his head. "Say rather I've had little time to think on it. I think I've been forcing myself to stay busy in order to fend off a sadness, though I have strong faith in life beyond death and know my friend experiences now joy beyond measure. I keep getting sidetracked and was on my way to Prince Nikal and Lord Kodi, but after I check on them, I'll give myself a respite and meditate upon my lost friend, and then make arrangements. Brother Curdoz has kindly offered to perform the death rite."

He then placed his hands on Hadon's shoulders, and likewise Manwul's, healing most of their muscle aches. They expressed gratitude and promised also to attend Eliander's death rite. "Now, go sink yourselves into those lovely hot water pools, all three of you." He nodded and left them.

"I'll never make fun of the work of Order Healers again as long as I live. I feel like a miracle after that, eh? Ah, ah!" Tiliruf sighed royally as he slipped down into the hot pool.

"They often work wonders. I don't know how you could possibly be so skeptical."

Tiliruf had been skeptical. Though he wasn't likely to tell anyone why. Healers had attended his mother following his birth, but they were not able to save her, dying as she did a few days later. He understood logically that often times there was too much blood loss and trauma, and he knew the facts from his father. Childbirth was dangerous and tricky for some Human women. Yet this bit of his history carried difficult thoughts for Tiliruf, and so he'd had a hard time giving Healers their due respect. Besides, they always said their Gift came from the Guardian, and he'd never believed in Meical, and this unbelief didn't help his attitude towards them. Witnessing the work of Ulna and Maru had opened his mind somewhat, yet something in Shane's physical touch touched more than just his body.

"Well, I'm not anymore. I feel good as gold, nearly."

"I suspect Shane is more powerful than the ordinary Healer. And he has a practiced, cool-headed disposition, doesn't he?" Hadon observed.

"Aye," agreed Manwul, splashing warm water on his face. "He'd never hurt a soul before in his life, I'm sure. Yet Flynce was part of the group fighting off the enemy around Nikal when he was down, and he told me Shane whipped around and stabbed Eliander's killer with barely a grimace. He was intent upon the need to get Nikal back into action as fast as possible, and that's the professionalism of an experienced officer, not what you might expect of a hospital Healer who's just seen his best friend stabbed through the neck. We're lucky to have someone like him come along with us."

"Really handsome for an *Order* chap," offered Hadon. "I've met many Easterners, and they're all superior in comportment, but he may be one of the best looking."

"Aye," agreed Manwul. "And fills out his shirt, too. Probably mid-thirties, but still prime. Which strikes me even odder than the handsome face for an Order bloke. Most Valley folk are more bookish and plain, and often scrawny or the opposite, fat. That man takes a keen interest in his body."

"True. He is easy to look at. I don't know about him calling me *'a Terianh,* though."

"Half the Brigade volunteers with us from Tirilorin refer to you that way, Tiliruf," said Manwul.

"They do?" He'd been oblivious to this.

"It's a title of honor, really, 'Son of Terianh,' even if it is your ordinary surname. It's not ordinary to them. Promise me you'll accept it and not be a noodle about it." Manwul looked at Tiliruf seriously.

"I won't be a noodle, since they insist on it, eh? But I'm nothing like Terianh," he said with some annoyance.

"You heard the good Healer, just now. Brother Shane says it reflects well on what he sees in you."

"Yeah." Tiliruf dunked himself under the hot water for a second and came back up. "And what do you *see in me*, Hadon, mate?"

"A great Swordmaster. Yet if we were drinking your brandy in our room, then I would say, 'Wet-curly-haired-Ruffy-scoundrel!"

The three laughed heartily and soon waved down the masseurs, paying a hefty sum, considering they were in much demand today.

Despite the laughter, the origins of his various names and titles began for the first time to play upon Tiliruf's thinking. The vast difference in application of Brother Shane's *'a Terianh* on the one end, and the Library Girls' *Ruffy* on the opposite, seemed to reflect thoughts he struggled with and kept mostly to himself. But the themes of contrast and comparison were not new. In some form or another, he'd been struggling with them all his life. Many young men—and some old—struggle with the same sorts of themes. Obligations. Expectations. Desires in opposition to these, along with cold realities of the limits of a man's psyche, his actual abilities, and his sense of self-worth. Compared to others, however, Tiliruf was the only man in all Dumhoni who was regularly referred to or addressed as *'a Terianh*, probably the most famous name in the history of the world. And there wasn't a single Human, Etoppsi, or Qeteral in all Dumhoni who didn't have some idea in their mind as to what that name meant.

Including Tiliruf himself. To him it meant a gargantuan golden equestrian statue of a historic world hero with a magic Staff in one hand and the world's most famous sword in the other. Well, five centuries later, that magic Staff was in the hands of two other men, not he. He told himself he was not jealous. The love he had for those particular two was more robust than any conscious love he had for anyone. The sword he once did indeed hold in his possession, but it was ripped away from him just as he was finally beginning to appreciate its significance and claim it for his own. Sometimes he felt all he had left were borrowed things, like Aron's sword, and even the *'a Terianh* name. He would do as Manwul said and not be a 'noodle' when people addressed him with it, yet much of the time he put on a false graciousness at its use. He was not conscious of his real fear that a day would come when nobody would associate the name with him at all, that they might even forget *Tiliruf* and *Swordmaster*. That he would be left sad and alone with only *Ruffy,* an alias he made up for prostitutes of North Bend ignorant of his pedigree, and now turned into a joke nickname by Kodi, Manwul and others. He found it funny coming from them, and he was more comfortable with it than *'a Terianh...*depending on who used it. He would, on the other hand, feel quite different about *Ruffy* if it were used by say, Nikal or Mother Idamé. Or Lyndz. He had a feeling he would quite hate it. And how would he feel if prostitutes should discover his identity and call him '*a Terianh?* On the occasions in which these thoughts surfaced in his mind his stomach would go sour.

"Only one thousand more are to be stationed here, Governor Surring. It will be as strong a presence as before the battle, but it is the most we can afford."

"But we were hoping, since you yourselves must go and take away the Staff..."

"Larger numbers would make little difference should the Alkhaness return."

This information did not make the city governor of Danzilet any happier. "And do you think she will, Your Highness?"

"She may. But not for a few months it is to be hoped. She was maimed, as you may have heard. She will have to heal and reorganize."

"She has larger armies than what she brought to Danzilet, we think," said the male Etoppsis who was present, a reddish-furred giant, armored, and with black wings folded behind him. He went by the name of Flamefur. Not unlike Royal Hawking, his voice was big and boomy, yet far younger, a Sky Front officer in his prime.

"Lord Curdoz, the Sage who came with us, certainly thinks so," agreed Kodi. "The Alkhaness came in order to test herself against the Staff. She'd convinced herself she'd overcome us easily. She'll think twice before coming back here, yet she probably has other plans. But Danzilet is a target as long as this war lasts."

"More of our citizens are likely to sail west, particularly after you depart," stated Surring.

"You need to ensure commerce and the flow of supplies remain smooth," Nikal reminded him. "War Marshall Jaden has given you authority to require any to stay in order to maintain the war effort and to service the military, both Nantian and Tirilorine, stationed here. You've got a good plan for a quick abandonment of the city, so make sure everyone remembers it. Encourage those who live outside the city's walls to find lodgings in the city and go out only in the daytime to work the estates. This will ensure that most are near to the harbor should escape be required. We will do this, and it should be a help. It was Lord Kodi's idea. We will use the Staff's magic to move boulders and block the area just on the far side of South Fort, particularly now that the wall has been damaged. It will hopefully discourage, or at least slow down, any other army she might send. With her magic, I think she could with much effort blast it away, but it should prove formidable. I want your city's engineers to assist the garrison in rebuilding South Fort's wall as quickly as possible. If it is only her armies that return, you'll stand a great chance, and you should defend yourselves..."

"But if she comes herself, you need to abandon the city. Do not hesitate. If she starts to breach South Fort, issue the signal."

"Lord Kodi is correct. Now we've experienced what she's capable of, without the Staff we don't think that any place could stand against her for very long."

"Yet you said she was maimed?"

Kodi looked in the corner at a perfectly content, snoozing silver dog. "Musca, we think, ended the battle for us yesterday, but it will not weaken her magic. The Guardian made that clear to me."

"If only we had an army of Elentine Nobles." Nikal winked at Kodi as an aside.

"The Guardian!" exclaimed the Governor with a badly concealed chuckle under his breath.

Nikal looked at the governor with serious expression. "Lord Kodi has a unique closeness with Meical the Guardian. It would be unwise of you to be skeptical of the information, Governor."

"He and His Highness are the Polemarchi!" boomed Flamefur with pride. "The High Commanders sent to us in our need by the Taxiarch Meical!"

The governor was startled by the Berugian's vehemence. He looked at Kodi. No doubt he thought him handsome and lordly, yet young. He then looked at Nikal. "I will do my duty to the city and follow yours and Jaden's orders, of course. I may send mothers with small children west."

"I concur with that idea, Governor," said Nikal. "But only on ships already bound for the west as they come through port. No special transports. Should any choose to travel to Nant, I assure you my father will welcome them."

"Yes, Your Highness, and thank you." He bowed low, indicating he had no more to discuss. Yet before he left, he turned to Kodi. "Do you have *Visions*, then, Lord Kodi?"

"It is different than that, Governor."

The governor raised his eyebrows. "You actually *speak* with...*the Guardian?* From afar? The tales say Terianh the Great did so. And you...?"

Kodi nodded.

The man stared into Kodi's eyes for a moment, his eyebrows still raised. "I am most sorry, m'lord, if I appeared rude. You and His Highness saved our city yesterday, and I will not forget."

He bowed respectfully before Kodi and left their chambers.

Sighing with a sense of exhaustion, Nikal nevertheless turned his attention to Flamefur. "We, Kodi and I, as Polemarchi, accept His Majesty Eagleron's submission. It is more than symbolic, yes, but from our point of view, we only expect His Majesty to continue his war effort against the Alkhaness as he sees fit."

"Yes, Polemarch. This is presumed, yes, and there is no need for any of us to return just now with your reply. And yet the king sends us as his emissaries in his place. We are to follow the orders of the Polemarchi."

"I understand. You will prove useful to us, absolutely. Do the others feel rested?"

"Certainly. Do you already have a task for us?"

"Choose two. Have them fly the shipping lanes west and find Marshall Jaden's last fleet which should be heading this way. Find him and give him a full report of yesterday's battle, and of our conversation just now with the city's governor. Tell him everything you told me of the earlier action at Eye-tower Fifty-five, of the Qeteral Dragon rider and of Berug's current state of readiness. He may already know some of it. Clearly there have been messages in the last couple weeks between Tirilorin and Berug, or you wouldn't be here. Return to me with his numbers and remind him that I and our comrades will have left on our search for the Qeteral of Ulakel before he arrives. After stopping in Danzilet, he is to continue east with the last armies, yet he already knows this. I'm sure I will have another task quite soon, messages for my generals in the east and the Queen of Essemar. Lord Kodi and I need to discuss further, but we may choose to divide the eight of you into various teams and send you to work in different directions."

"That is perfectly well, Polemarch."

Nikal smiled. "On etiquette we would ask you address us by our Human titles and names, Lord Kodi and Prince Nikal, or as 'Sir' like everyone else. There are subtleties, but 'Sir' works well for addressing most Human men, and 'Lady' or 'M'Lady' for most Human women, 'Madam' works but only really if they are Bonded. Most Nantians and many others will address me as 'Your Highness,' but I do not favor it. In announcing or referring to us, use 'Polemarch' in communication with, and in reference to, our alliance with Berug. But use 'War

Wizard' in communication with Human governments and command structures. Any questions on that?"

"No, sir. That matches reasonably well with what I have studied of Human culture. Royal Hawking also tutored and tested us for an entire day before we flew here."

"Excellent. Your current military rank is...?"

"A commissioned Rainstorm-major, sir, or *Storm-major* is the short form. Cloud-captain Windsdown, the brown on brown, is my next in command. The others are trained Feathers, three of whom have experience as Eyefeather spies. All of us are from the King's Guard."

"Brown on brown?"

"Brown fur and brown wings, sir."

"Oh, of course. King's Guard? Excellent. On a different note, now, you understand Rainwing of Green Isle is one of my close companions?"

"Yes, sir. I know Professor Rainwing. She taught Windsdown and me. Trust me, sir. Our Queen remonstrated with us to set aside all prejudice as to her choice of old Monastic abstinence, yet for myself I never found issue with it and always liked her quite well at the Institute."

"You have heard of her great loss? You must understand it has been a terrible blow for her, and for all of us, really."

"Absolutely, sir. In me she will find only respect and sympathy. In fact, I have messages for her from Queen Silverwing. She and the king honor her for her sacrifice."

"She will be glad to know it. Approach her with some caution, Storm-major, as she will presume prejudice and pity, neither of which she wants from other Berugians, most especially Skyfront males. She might seem cold towards you at first, until she understands your sincerity."

"Windsdown and I were contemplating using some humor."

"Definitely," said Kodi, interjecting himself. "That's what you should do, Storm-major, especially if you say you know her and are familiar with her."

"Thank you, sir!"

Nikal nodded, though he drew in his brow. "That will be all, then."

Flamefur bowed. He opened the door and squeezed his way through it. Nikal turned to Kodi.

"Humor? She has serious demeanor."

"She does, but she's also funny as heck."

"Funny?"

"All that chatter between her and Tiliruf—you all think she's mad as a hornet, and on the surface, she sort of is, but it's more like brother and sister bantering. I should know. Anyway, they needle each other, 'cause they think it's funny. Some of the stuff Tiliruf says is sort of dumber and chauvinistic. But honestly, if there's such a thing as *female chauvinism* then Rainwing's guilty. So yeah, I know it could prove thorny, but I think humor can work, 'specially if Flamefur knows what she can be like..."

Though they were tired, they might have discussed more, for they liked talking about personality, including delving into each other's thoughts. Since their night of commune on the beach outside Tirilorin they'd come to understand how much alike they were at a deep level. Yet they did harbor different experiences which colored their perspective. To converse with one another this way had become a welcome distraction from the demands upon them.

However, just then, Shane walked in.

Both Kodi and Nikal stood and proceeded to welcome Shane warmly. Musca too got up and skipped over as the Healer sat down, licking his hand and getting into his face as with the loving affection of a devoted pet.

"Superior animal," said Shane, running his fingers through Musca's silver fur. He even examined him with some bursts of green magic. "Not a blemish. Not a scratch. Muscular. Pretty green eyes, which I imagine are quite rare. Who would have imagined a dog would prove so heroic in such a critical battle, and against such an evil foe? He's one for the chronicles."

"He is that, for sure. Shane, we can never thank you enough for your devoted sense of duty to us yesterday," said Kodi. "Losing Eliander was not at all what we'd expected. We believed the guard would..."

"It is war, Lord Kodi. Have no regrets. He and I volunteered, as we knew we were the best from the hospital to do so. The whole situation unfolded in shocking sequence, impossible to predict. Yet, considering his sacrifice it is my hope you, or at least one of you, will be present at the death rite. I attended to Brother Curdoz earlier today, and bring word he is doing well, now. He offered to preside over the rite."

"We will both be there, Brother Shane," said Nikal. "You send me information on where I can send a letter describing his heroism and sacrifice. Do his parents still live?"

"They are elderly, but yes. He took me to meet them years ago. East of Tirilorin in the country. I will supply the information. Brother Curdoz, by the way, has asked me to join your group."

"Really!" said Kodi. "You should do that, Shane."

"I am thinking on it and promised him an answer tomorrow. And he also required something rather shocking." He paused for the drama. "He commands me to put you both to sleep, as he knows you have not rested. And as he has placed your health into my care..."

Kodi winked at Nikal. "Sleep? What is that, Shane?"

Nikal rubbed his face. "We've got so much still to do. I was thinking we should ride back out to South Fort and..."

"General Fouch assures me he has had several good hours of sleep. I spoke to him a few moments ago. He will take charge while you rest."

Nikal sighed. After a pause he admitted, "Fouch is proficient and efficient. I'll be giving him Cruz's command anyway. Well, then. Especially for Kodi's sake, I'll give in to Curdoz' *order*."

"I'll set guards at your doors to keep everyone out. Now, if you please. Prepare for bed and get into your cots. I want to do a thorough examination on each of you before I put you to sleep."

Despite being comparatively young, Shane had an aura of authoritative seriousness. A kind warmth accompanied a deep, rolling voice. Tiliruf had felt it, and so did these two. His dark eyes displayed a level of sincere caring, and the touch of his strong hands had a depth of meaning behind it. As long as their relationship during this war lasted, they would not deny his Calling as Healer.

He explored their bodies, mostly bared now for sleep, with the green magical light, healing this little bruise and that minor scrape. He took damp rags and washed away the worst of their grime. Their minds settled finally, and tension dissipated. They yawned as they watched him work.

"You've got healing hands, Shane," offered Kodi. "No doubt about it. You're my first Eastern friend, by the way."

Shane nodded. "As you are a provincial from Solanto, I should not be surprised. Differences are of the Divine Mind, of course."

"Absolutely, Shane. And I know we're more the same than different. And we share faith in the Guardian. And most importantly, we're both good-looking bucks."

"Ha!" Shane laughed greatly. "Thank you for the compliment, m'lord."

"My friends do not call me 'Lord' anything. Though I keep meaning to tell Manwul and Hadon the same. Did I not just claim you as a friend?"

"Likewise, me, Shane," agreed Nikal.

On a stool just between their two bunks, Shane swiveled around back to Nikal. "Understood....my friends."

After a half minute, Nikal asked a question. "What're you thinking about, Shane? You're an observer. I see your mind working as you look over us."

Shane's voice typically exhibited an unemotional, steady cadence. "Kodi's compliment is not so distant from my thoughts. I tend to use the term 'specimen' when acknowledging men with exceptional physical traits, and you two are superior. The bodies of strong men like those of the two of you are always remarkable to me. You don't see what I see when I probe with the magic, the difference in the levels of energetic elements in your blood compared to the ordinary man. They're heightened considerably. And the movement of such enriched blood in your body, causing muscle, brain, heart, and organs to work with great efficiency and so drive you with a sort of animal intensity. The Peoples of the Mold of course are more than animals. Divine Purpose in the Creator's Creation. That interplay of the animal body and higher spirit of the Mold Creature I find fascinating. Which is why the Guardian Called me to be a Healer, I'm sure. Yet it's usually the middle-aged and older folk I come into contact with at the hospital. I have to try to ease pains and correct imbalances within their systems growing slowly more fragile from aging or other factors. Or children with fevers, bad scrapes, or broken arms. All you young knights are superior specimens who rarely need the deeper magic of a Healer unless you're actually damaged. Though it's men like yourselves they illustrate in the Healer compendia on anatomy in the Valley. The artists like to demonstrate the ideal forms of the male and the female, for example, in labeling the parts of the body or naming the muscles."

"That's interesting, Shane. You're also a deep and strong man. It showed on the field yesterday," said Kodi. "Curdoz told me you trained as a youth with the Essemarian cavalry. There's a fire in you, too."

"Maybe so. A'Terianh and his guards are like you, too. Though he actually was hurt quite badly. I had to work on him pretty diligently at the baths."

"Really? Didn't know he was hurt. He seemed fine before he left the field. We had conversation."

"What happened to him?" Nikal leaned up to ask. "I worry about Tiliruf."

"The A'Terianh is worth worrying about. The pain didn't manifest until after awakening from sleep. Cracked a rib and bruised a kidney. He's fine now, he...ah, look at your hands!" He said this last to Kodi, who flinched, and then reached over to Nikal's. "Both of you!"

"Ow! Spikeshafts dammit that hurts, Shane!"

Kodi chuckled. "He's at ease with you, Shane. He doesn't loosen his tongue like that, unless it's to me about...er, stuff we talk about to get off our chests."

Nikal, with an introspective look of shock on his face and staring at the palms of his hands, turned to Shane. "Sorry, Brother Shane. I swear I didn't realize they were hurting so much until you touched them. Kodi's right. I didn't mean to come across so snappy and uncouth. What's the matter with me? Sorry."

"Nothing is the matter. Being keyed up so tightly causes us to set aside pain, and you're just now relaxing. It was the same with Tiliruf. I'm not surprised you didn't notice it. Now you're relaxed—yet also exhausted and deprived of sleep—you're dropping your social guard. But really, sir, have no worries about stray words with me. Passionate men speaking their minds seem more real to me than the reserve of most Monastics and many of my Healer friends. Yesterday was tough on everyone. You most of all. You navigate a world with great demands, Nikal. Kodi, too. So much depends on you. And you have your own desires and needs in conflict with that. I'm not aloof to the emotional dichotomy of a good man being forced to fight and kill. And...and now I know that piece of it firsthand in myself." Shane paused briefly. "Yet let us focus on the physical. Did the Staff vibrate, then, as you employed the magic?"

"Yeah. Yeah, it did," said Kodi. "And like you saw, we held it with both hands a lot of the time. That old statue of Terianh holding it in one hand and the sword in the other don't work for me. Working the Staff holds all your attention. So, yeah, it's like it's alive. And it gets really hot."

"Hmm, that's probably an important part of what creates the fatigue while using it. The Healing I applied at the battle was to the mind—to return energy to your power of will. We were not thinking of the physical fatigue to the hands and arms."

Their palms were red, almost raw, and though they were just now realizing it as Shane had drawn their attention to them, altogether their hands ached dreadfully and were curled with stiffness. They did not recognize how intensely they had been gripping the Staff during the battle. Though this was nothing compared to the deeper hurts of Curdoz or Tiliruf or others, Shane applied the Healing touch to their palms, watched the redness and felt the inflamed heat disappear. He then massaged them and the wrist muscles up to the elbow, applying additional deep muscle Healing. Nikal grinned Kodi-like when the pain went away. "Thank you, Brother Shane. Kodi's right. You've got kind hands."

And when it was Kodi's turn, "Ah, that, yeah, Shane. My mother or Lyndz'll rub 'em for me sometimes at night, after I've done a lot of stonework and they're hurting."

"He's attuned to much of our unspoken needs and discerns our hearts as much as our bodies," said Nikal. "A brother along with the rest of us. Stick close, Shane. I admit it's dangerous. But you've lost Eliander, and so I wonder if perhaps you might need us now as we need you. What about it? No more living with Monastics in a monastery. You've got the heart of a Healer but a connection to the soldier. That you chose to immerse yourself into the fearful demands of yesterday speaks to that inner fire Kodi mentioned. And talk about 'specimen.' Clearly you push yourself physically, and that also speaks to that inner fire. I know you can face what comes. Go with us like Lord Curdoz asks."

Shane looked at him with raised eyebrow. "I had not thought of it in quite that way. Perhaps life does call us into a number of dichotomies, War Wizard of Meical."

Recognizing this massaging action really did speak to a sense of sleepy relaxation they seemed to need, Shane spent a good minute or two on each of their four hands. And there was mutual connection in it, for before he let go of each of them, they gripped him with the soldier's grip. It wasn't a movement he was used to, as Brothers in Orders tended to lift palm up to each other in Affirmation. Yet the grip came naturally to Shane.

"You will not awaken for some time. Drink plenty of water when you awaken. Baths following, of course. Then a solid meal."

He applied the green light across their foreheads. They fell promptly into a restorative sleep.

Musca followed Shane out the door. Fouch had sent guards, and the Healer reiterated the order that the War Wizards were not to be disturbed. He then looked down at the dog.

"Wish to keep me company?"

Musca wagged his tail.

"They call you *Musca*, do they? Come along, then. We're going to the Monastics chapel. And I wish to see Lord Curdoz again. I've made up my mind."

"Shafts, I don't want to see them! Not yet. Damn it all!"

"They're your own people, Rainwing. You have nothing to be ashamed of around them."

Returning from their picnic through fields to the city in early afternoon, Rainwing and Lyndz watched as two of the Etoppsi Feathers landed in the space before them. The two males walked towards the females, and when they got close, they surprisingly bowed.

"Since when have Skyfront Feathers worn armor?" asked Rainwing.

Lyndz thought her tone a bit rude but said nothing.

"Our Queen issued the command, Professor Rainwing, so that we have better protection against fighting Humans on the ground." The red-furred male actually winked. Rainwing started at his choice of address. "Didn't recognize me with all this on, did you, Professor?"

"Flamefur! Is that you? And Windsdown, too? I can't believe my eyes!" Then all of a sudden Rainwing's bright eyes grew sad and she turned away. "I don't want you seeing me like this."

To her shock both males actually fell to their knees.

"Our King and Queen offer greetings." Flamefur held forth a scroll. "Shall I read it aloud?"

Since Rainwing didn't answer right away, Lyndz answered for her. "Yes, good sirs! Do the honor! She wants to hear it, of course. She's just being bashful."

"I'm not being bash..."

"Then here it is," boomed Flamefur, with somewhat of a playful grin on his face.

To Rainwing of Green Isle our sincerest greetings. News has reached us of your heroism in the fight against the great Sea Serpents and of your sacrifice in order for the Eagle Staff to be returned, thus allowing the Human Polemarchi great and necessary magic in the fight against our enemies. You are noted as a national hero in the annals. A plaque commemorating your deeds shall be installed in the Hall of Heroes at the Institute. You are henceforth awarded Noble rank, the honorary title of Dragonhunter Legion Master, and for the remainder of your life a position on the Sky Council of the Kingdom. It is our wish at present that you continue your current service to your Human comrades. Yet when you choose to return to Berug you shall take up your position on the Sky Council and honor us with your wisdom, advice and consent. While abroad, you are assigned as High Emissary and are to represent the interests of your king and queen in all matters to all governments in the lands in which you travel. This commission is to last until the end of the current war. These honors and commissions are awarded to you, yet it is understood by us that your Calling to the Taxiarch is paramount and that you are not to perceive these as restrictions upon your choices. Use them, yet follow foremost your High Calling to the Taxiarch.

"And a further message from Our Queen..."

"Wait!" said Windsdown, punching his cohort. "You said I get to read that one!"

They struggled like toplings for a few seconds, causing Rainwing to chuckle, and Windsdown finally yanked it out of Flamefur's hand.

To my dear friend, Rainwing. Understand I ponder the pain of your great loss and believe you to be the greatest heroine of Berug of the current age. My thoughts are always with you. In honor of our friendship and of your sacrifice, I am bestowing upon you one of the two Flame of the Sun Rubies in my possession, this to be made into a golden necklace as a symbol of your nobility. I have sent the stone in presentation along with resolutions to your mother and father to symbolize your possession, yet I look forward to the opportunity in future of presenting it to you in person. The next time one of my messengers is sent to us, please send with him a letter describing everything. I am eternally grateful for you and for our friendship and thank you for all you have done for me and for your country. May Meical, Guardian and Taxiarch, Affirm you. Silverwing.

"Now, see, Rainwing!" said Lyndz. "Everybody in Berug knows what a hero you are, whether you have wings or not!"

"We certainly do," said Windsdown.

"Oh, get up! I can't stand it, you kneeling like that! *Human* ridiculousness!" said Rainwing, smiling.

"Whatever Noble Professor Rainwing commands," said Flamefur, with added chortle, and of course both males stood.

"These were your geography students."

"Seven years back, m'lady. And we were her *favorite* students," answered Windsdown, jokingly.

"And her smartest," added Flamefur.

"Oh, listen to you two!" said Rainwing, in an admonishing tone not unlike Mother Idamé and trying to hold back a laugh, though she wasn't doing a very good job of it.

Rainwing's ice was obviously broken, she introduced them to Lyndz, and they all continued to chatter happily for quite some time. As it turned out, they really were some of Rainwing's favorites, some of the few *males* who held no prejudice about her choice of chastity. Nor had they ever fallen under the particularly chauvinistic command of old General Heavywing of the Wall Cyclone, having served instead in the Island Cyclone before being chosen for King's Guard. It was plain Queen Silverwing chose them personally for these reasons in addition to their ranks and abilities. Eventually, Rainwing made a request of the two. Helping them set aside their armor, as this would be uncomfortable otherwise, and knowing no Human would dare touch it while they were away, the two males lifted the two females gracefully into the sky. Rainwing felt great joy at being airborne, and Lyndz felt joyful for her. Before long, they descended to the top of a stony hill several miles westward of the city where the seashore abutted the rocky range. Rainwing wished to see the cairns and to honor the two Feathers who had been killed by the Alkhaness. They remained a quarter hour. Though Lyndz endured, Rainwing finally realized it was cool and windy for her, so they left and returned to the field to retrieve the discarded armor and the picnic things. They walked and talked their way back to the city.

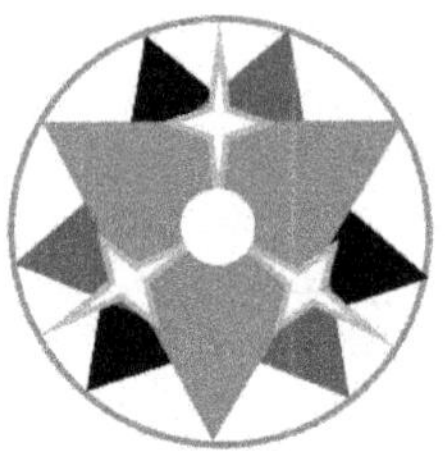

Chapter 10—The Etoppsi Males Come for Supper

It was some two hours past ordinary dinner time, and the kitchens at North Fort were still active. Cooks churned out quantities of food for a mess hall half full of soldiers, many who had slept the day away in recovery from the battle and its aftermath. Conversations were subdued throughout the evening as men came for supper and left. Many had lost friends, and there was a general gloom over the death of General Cruz who was well-liked by all who had served under him.

The atmosphere in the mess hall would soon change in a most interesting way.

Having bathed after a restful, Healer-induced sleep, the two refreshed War Wizards were now carried off to the messes by a boisterous threesome, Tiliruf, Manwul, and Hadon. They brought with them an assortment of liquors out of Tiliruf's bottomless trunk. By coincidence, Rainwing and Lyndz showed up at the same time. Lyndz had received reports as to their safety yet seen none of the men since the morning before the battle. Joyful hugs ensued between her and her brother and the others, and even Nikal joined in on the pleasure inspired by the gathering. Despite the sadness for the many who had died, they had much to be thankful for. The other soldiers and officers in the mess found themselves refilling their mugs and gathering near in order to feed off the inspiration of these heroes and listen in on their versions of the battle tales as they related them to Lyndz and clarified various points with one another.

As they were eating and drinking and telling their tales, other 'guests' arrived. Two of the Berugian Feathers had been sent off on the communication mission to War Marshall Jaden, but the remaining six, also being hungry at this time, marched in.

All eyes naturally shifted in their direction, and the large room grew quiet. Their armor was gone. In the lead and tallest of all, Storm-major Flamefur and Cloud-captain Windsdown alone wore broad necklaces—more like collars—made of many antler points interwoven in silver chain.

Something about six unclothed, giant, winged, perfect-specimen Etoppsi males in their young prime walking into a room of Humans was overpowering. It was, to say the least, not a regular occurrence. Aside from the Meicalian Feast in Sevarr, the presence of Etoppsi in the Human World had not been a common thing since the first century of the Empire when their race helped build Tirilorin, Guardian's Gate, and other world wonders. As has been mentioned before, Etoppsi exhibited a muskiness. It cannot at all be defined as unpleasant. When that aroma was ever described by the few Humans who experienced it, words such as 'keen,' and 'captivating,' were used. The friends were used to Rainwing's scent, like meadow flowers and strongly herbal. It definitely had a captivating quality, energizing at times, relaxing at others. Yet there was something quite different in that coming from the six males. Old Royal Hawking's scent had been subdued in comparison. Etoppsi musk was strongest and most compelling in males in their virile prime, and here it was multiplied by six.

Written accounts existed by Human philosophers and other observers from the past as to the emotions produced by Etoppsi contact. They had additional words to describe how that race affected Humans, and they had concluded that their musk was a large part of what triggered these emotions: "commanding," "god-like," "erotic."

It was heightened by the vast size, exotic form, and enhanced muscular physique of the glossy, tight-furred, unclothed Etoppsi body, folded wings framing it majestically from behind. Humans would find themselves putting up barriers in their minds in order to confront the impact on their senses. Yet truth be known, when these six males walked in, it was as if it were cold midwinter and six World Gods of prehistory had entered and brought with them a hot, steamy summer sun, inviting everyone to bask in it and draw from its raw energy.

Considering their scent and their awe-inspiring presence, many of the Humans put on interesting smirks, some others displaying almost embarrassed grins. Nikal understood it. He'd had more experience with Etoppsi and had witnessed the impact their presence could have. He'd also made effort years ago to read some of those older philosophical writings and books on Etoppsi. Rainwing understood it, though she herself had resisted it since her teens due to her choices, training herself nearly to be immune. Lyndz had earlier in the day experienced the compelling aroma and muscular feel of Windsdown when he flew her to and from the rocky hilltop. She smiled then, jokingly telling herself she was never going to wash his scent off her clothing, and she smiled now. The six giants oozed, with both their looks and with their aroma, a hot, raw quality.

Etoppsi with a bit more age (such as Rainwing) were often annoyed by the stares of Humans. These six, on the other hand, took it in stride. They didn't especially mind they were being observed as paragons of virility. Rainwing suspected they knew this precisely, and that was why she, too, snickered. The suave demeanor in their walk and on their faces reflected accurately the two former students she knew well back at the Institute. With other students gathered around them before class, Flamefur and Windsdown would boast of their athletic feats and competitions, and their multiple experiences at the most recent Star Revel. They'd started that rite of passage young, and they'd never stopped, and they were still unbonded. They had a few years remaining before their unbonded status would begin to be scrutinized by their peers and to feel more urgently the call to find finally the monogamous mate. In the meantime, each would dance the dance of the most self-assured male Etoppsis. It wasn't just their erotic quality. It was equally the warrior image and the sense of massive muscular strength and raw power of a huge fit body. That piece of it was something Rainwing connected to, being a former member of the Dragon Legion. She did not resist that value like she did the erotic.

Rainwing earlier had said to Lyndz when her friend commented so positively of the two male Skyfront officers. "You need to understand, Lyndz, Windsdown and Flamefur are of an elite caste. They've always been exceptional since they were toplings. You might compare them to your brother in that way. They stand out in Berug. They're some of the biggest Etoppsi, a trait especially envied. Flamefur's red fur is rare, and that sheen on Windsdown makes his brown fur especially rich. I admit they are gorgeous. They're looked on as exemplars of Meicalian Taxiarchan masculinity, yet these two don't have the level of male chauvinism common in the Sky Front. Which is why I liked them so well back then. They boasted of their escapades and sexual prowess, yet were funny about it, and never at the expense of a female's dignity. That sort of boasting is not considered uncouth as it might be with Humans. Flamefur is quickly working his way up the command structure. He can be charming and subtle when he wants. Someday he'll be Cyclone-general, you watch."

"If I didn't know I was so good-looking and admirable in so many ways, I could be intimidated by that, eh?" Tiliruf joked in a whisper and elbowed Kodi.

"They really are something to look at without armor. Idamé talks about how Hawking was 'striking,' but these blokes look..."

"Ready to 'strike!' I wish I could bottle that scent and make a smelly soap out of it for my baths. Every woman ten miles around would pounce."

"You'd like that, wouldn't you?"

"'Specially since the boys don't let me out at night. It'd be great if they'd come to me, instead!"

"Hadon," whispered Manwul likewise to his friend on the other side of the table. "You see the size of their damned *penis* pouches?"

Hadon chuckled. "And that red one's arm muscle is bigger than your thigh, big man. And a chest like that he could just *twitch* and crush our bones."

"I'm not going to argue with that. I've decided I want to be an Etoppsis when I grow up."

"Me, too. I want to look just like that, fly with big wings like that, and always smell like that. The collars on the big ones. They look like damned kings!"

"Sit with us, Storm-major Flamefur. Cloud-captain Windsdown," said Nikal, piercing rather loudly through the room whispers. "And have the Feathers sit behind us just here, so they can be a part of our conversation if they wish. We'd all like to get to know our furred and feathered friends! I'll have the servants bring out plenty; have a seat. Meats, potatoes, nuts and fruits are what you like, of course. There is plenty of ale for the Feathers. You men over there by the barrels, bring full mugs out for them. They like ale as much as you do. Introduce yourselves and make them feel at home. Swordmaster Tiliruf, pour Flamefur and Windsdown a couple of your own special bottles; it's almost as if you knew they were coming!"

"I do seem to anticipate special occasions, eh?"

"So," boomed Flamefur, sitting down on the bench opposite the table from Nikal and beside Rainwing. "You're the scion son of Imperial Terianh, they say?"

Tiliruf nodded appropriately. He got up and with the charm of a host poured out two bottles of his finest Nantian vintage into two beer tankards and handed them to the rusty red giant and across the table to his shiny brown partner. "Swordmaster Tiliruf defines me well enough."

"And an inspiring one. I caught a good view from above of you and Professor Rainwing yesterday. Devastating performance, and I mean that of course in the most positive way. The speed. The grace. The instinct. All warriors can learn from this one."

"Oh, he's turning on the charm," said Rainwing chuckling.

"Ha!" burst out Windsdown, who sat beside Nikal. "Does she ever remember *you!*"

"Rusty here is loaded with compliments, though they're usually for himself," Rainwing said, and everyone laughed.

Flamefur grinned hugely. "And so, they are compliments well-placed, I'd say." Great mirth ensued all around at this fine joke. He looked at Tiliruf, "And what is it you Humans say when you lift the first drink?"

"Cheers!" said the Swordmaster winking, lifting his bottle to his mouth. All in the room said *aye*, and proceeded to drink whatever they were drinking, mostly ale from the barrels against the wall.

"Good stuff, Nantian Brandy. You're a Human male after my own heart, Swordmaster! Thank you for the treat!"

"I'm sure you and I are already friends, mate."

"Flamefur," said Lyndz, "tell them about Rainwing's honors. She deserves all the compliments, for sure."

Flamefur used a big boomy voice that filled the room and grandly summarized. All were impressed.

"That's remarkable, Rainwing!" said Hadon.

"Extraordinary!" agreed Manwul.

"Sky Council of the Kingdom of Berug!" said Kodi. "Well-deserved."

"Congratulations, my friend," said Nikal with a pleased expression. He stood up. "Here's to Noble Professor Rainwing of the House of Green Isle, Dragon Legion Master!"

All cheered loudly and drank. Food was brought out for the big guests on large platters. The conversation grew a little quieter for a while as they allowed the Berugians to eat. Lyndz and several others also went to the kitchens to retrieve more food or beverage. A few soldiers left the mess at this time, but most remained, drinking beer. Several, including Tiliruf—he brought a pipe for Kodi, too—proceeded to kick back and smoke. Others played *rounds-on-squares* from several sets on the tables.

"Had you seen Humans before yesterday, Storm-major?" asked Manwul a little later after introducing himself.

"Khestadone only. Though I have certainly spotted sailors on Nantian ships before. I spent two years as an Eyefeather. They are specialty spies. Several of us here have had Eyefeather experience. Stormgale, there, has several commendations. And we were at the retaking of Eye Tower Fifty-five. That reminds me. Professor, do you remember Greengul of the Legion? She heard I was being sent to find you and offered a greeting and well wishes."

"Certainly, I remember Greengul! I worked with her. We overlapped a year on the River Legion before I left to teach at the Institute. Superior piece of work. She's as hefty as some males and with what I would call a piercing intelligence. Was she at Fifty-five?"

"She led the sneak assault through the Jungle, and her team overcame the one Wingless and discovered the Qeteral rider. She's been promoted to a new position. They've made the Legion command structure more military due to the crisis."

"More military? Hmm, that doesn't make me happy, but I can understand. Yet I'm certainly proud for her."

"She's called *Dragon-colonel*, and she's in charge of the southern Jungle border in the vicinity of Fifty-five. I agree she's remarkably capable. Her mate is Bronzemight."

"The sheepherder? Interesting pairing, that. But he was a pretty one. He would often host bonfire gatherings and feast our unit with mutton. Those were fun times. Thank you for relaying her greeting. It's good to hear from home."

Before long they finished eating and shoved their benches back.

"You were not wearing those antler-point collars this morning," observed Kodi. "Do they signify you being officers in the Sky Front?"

The two officers looked at each other. Flamefur replied, "No, Lord Kodi. Not really. Though many officers do own one."

"I'll tell you," said Rainwing, snatching from Tiliruf a bottle of rum he just opened, and pouring half the contents into her mug. "They are recognized in Berug and don't have to be explained there to anyone. I'm sure they've never had to do so before. They're not allowed by the Sky Front while on duty, but at meals and other times they will wear them. It represents their membership in a kingdom-wide caste or male elite called the *Soaring Stags*. Members are called *Stags*."

Kodi got it immediately. "Ah! You're the biggest and the best at everything, is that it? But with a sort of code of conduct?"

"You may describe it in just that way, Lord Kodi," replied Flamefur.

Rainwing further explained. "The Soaring Stags developed informally among Etoppsi males following the demise of most feudalistic elements in our society. Though feudalism has largely dropped away, what you Human men might call knightly chivalry has remained and is strong with our males. The warrior image is strong, and virtually all Stags are or have been either in the Sky Front or the Dragon Legion. With their codes of conduct, the Stags are considered well-disciplined and respected. Understand, though, that it is physical attributes and displays of prowess that define chivalry among Etoppsi males. To get in the Soaring Stags, a male has to prove himself in wrestling, lifting, speed-flying, and other competitions in order to be invited by others to join. And yes, it's often the biggest who have the advantage. But Stags have developed additional reputation, and it isn't just physical sports and competitions..."

At this she paused and chuckled. The Etoppsi males at the other table also seemed mirthful.

That's when Tiliruf's senses kicked in. "It's your *experience with the females*, eh? The *elite*, yeah, we get it. Ha!"

The two males chuckled bigly, with no especial hint of embarrassment. There were murmurings of delight all around the room. The other Etoppsi were laughing. Yet Kodi noted the one called Stormgale, a stately tan specimen with black wings, only grinned and folded his enormous arms.

"And just how does that particular piece of it work with you blokes, eh?" asked Tiliruf.

"Yes," added Hadon. "You have to understand, Storm-major, we men are curious about...about...well, what the Swordmaster said."

"Oh, no," said Nikal, raising his eyebrows high. "I think I see where you're leading this conversation. C'mon, men. Read books."

Kodi, with his sense of the social, overruled him. "Yes, Flamefur. Rainwing'll have long conversations with the women, but she won't tell us men anything about..."

"Etoppsi *reproduction*, eh?" concluded Tiliruf. "The *science* of it, you see!"

"And these *Star Revels* and such we all hear about," said Manwul more bluntly.

There were affirmative murmurings all around the room at this.

"Oh, listen, Rainwing," said Lyndz. "Do I need to stay here for this?"

"If you want the *male* perspective, eh? Rainwing avoids the topic, anyways, so delightful to the rest of us who haven't made a vow like she has."

Rainwing gave Tiliruf that eye. "You have a problem with my choices?"

"Er, eh, no. 'Course not." His face twitched.

Rainwing wasn't too much annoyed. Since the battle yesterday, she'd begun to feel more tolerance for Tiliruf. They'd survived a brutal battle together, and she'd been quite impressed by him. "I probably do avoid the subject, though I've explained a little to Lyndz and the females," she admitted. "Why would you want to leave, Lyndz? You're not one of those squeamish teacup 'ladies' of Tirilorin, embarrassed by topics like *mating*."

"No. But my mother would be pulling me out of here right now, if she were here. She thinks it uncouth to speak of these things with males present, what she would call 'mixed company.'"

Flamefur and Windsdown were chuckling through all of this as they chewed contentedly on unpeeled oranges.

"You all, I'm beginning to gather, wish to be educated on the matter of...Etoppsi mating culture?" asked Flamefur in a nonchalant sort of way, plopping another whole orange into his mouth.

"Yes!"

"Exactly so!"

"Who doesn't?"

Every soldier in the room was particularly keen on this topic and drew in closer. Nikal rolled his eyes, shook his head, and reached over to snatch the remaining half bottle of rum Rainwing had begun. He took a large healthy gulp.

"And who better to teach an animal pack like this crowd," said Rainwing. "Rusty, you are such a piece of work and always were."

"Why, thank you, Professor," he winked. "And of course, I've always honored your choice. That one female wouldn't turn up at the local Star Revel was never a hindrance, of course, for me."

Even Nikal burst with mirth at this boast and drank some more, settling in for the ride.

"Let me start, Rusty," said Windsdown. "You know they're going to need some biology before they listen to you brag! There are a number of differences with Humans."

Flamefur nodded and sipped on his brandy.

Windsdown was an excellent teacher. From a professorial point of view, Rainwing was quite pleased with his style and objective approach to the subject. He'd studied more on Humans than most Etoppsi and could make comparisons. All the men and Lyndz listened in rapt attention.

He first described male maturation. As they heard him tell it, Etoppsi males began to grow huge beginning around 13 years. By 15 their mating drive kicked in, but it could for about two years be controlled through *"self-release practices."* This elicited chuckles of understanding among the Human men. Windsdown and Flamefur both admitted, however, that they practically skipped this stage. By 17, the mating impulse was uncontrollable for males. For about eight days every month based on the Solvermoon cycle—and the timing was essentially the same for all—Etoppsi males had to mate females at least a few times during that period or suffer body and emotional trauma. They would become violently ill and suffer from a terrible anxiety. Self-stimulation simply did not work anymore by this stage. The bodily union with the female was required. Rainwing wanted to qualify this last statement, as she noted that there had been males in the distant past who could take the Monastic Vow of chastity. Respectfully acknowledging his old professor's point-of-view, Windsdown chose not to address it and went on.

Etoppsi could, he said, mate like Humans on the ground or in their beds, and this was preferred as they aged. But among the young there was a near-universal love for mating while in flight. Most listening knew Etoppsi made love while flying; it was widespread legend, and some had heard the phrase *Star Revel.*

He took some time to describe female maturation. Females matured at the same general age as males. He made it plain, and Rainwing agreed, that females did not have that overpowering drive to mate until they actually experienced mating the first time. He said that though abstinence did not cause illness in females, once a female experienced mating, her inner fire was triggered, and she began to desire it nearly as much as males.

"So, you're saying the virgin female in a way makes societal sacrifice to aid males through the cycle?" asked Lyndz for clarification.

Windsdown was confused by the question. "M'lady, where is the sacrifice, and what do you mean by *virgin?"*

Many chuckled at that, of course, but most were respectful of Lyndz—the only lady in the room—asking what certainly seemed a fair question for a woman to ask.

Rainwing answered. "Virginity with its Human concept of sexual purity is not really an understood theme with the Etoppsi race, Lyndz. Which is why many give me grief for my choice. But like many of your Human clothing items, most don't even know the words *virginity* or *chastity,* unless they've studied Human culture or the Orders of the Guardian in more depth. Your understanding is partly correct, however, that Etoppsi society, including its females, understands well the need to help males especially get through the cycle. There can be initial hesitations with the inexperienced, more so on the female side, that do speak of strong emotion. Yet it's more anticipation than angst. So, the Etoppsi female would not perceive it in the manner of being "used" for her body like the Human female who might feel put upon by a particularly insensitive Human man or unkind Bondmate. The Etoppsi female would never feel undue pressure to mate with a male she didn't really want to. Under ordinary circumstances, Lyndz, an Etoppsi male meets his needs for mating without desire building so strongly to ever force himself on an unwilling female. Does that make sense?"

"She wouldn't really look at it as a sacrifice, yes. You've tried to explain that before to me, but I think I understand better."

"I assure you, Lady Lyndz, the females like what we do for them." Windsdown winked, and she and everyone laughed uproariously.

Then Windsdown finally broached the subject all the men seemed so keen on: Etoppsi Star Revel. Star Revel was the collective name given to the night-time mating parties scheduled regularly for the unbonded young during the fertile cycle each month. What occurred during Star Revel was quite shocking for Humans, though of course the Human men present in the mess hall indicated various levels of envy. Throughout the night of a scheduled Star Revel, males and females would make the rounds and mate with as many others as they wished.

When this sparked an immediate round of questioning, Windsdown realized he'd left out a key difference that separated Etoppsi males from their Human and Qeteral counterparts. He then explained. Unbonded Etoppsi males did not release seed during the climactic moment. There was no risk of impregnating his Star Revel partner. This revelation produced a sort of amazed wonder among the bucks in the hall, and the reactions were hilarious, causing many in the room to laugh loudly. Men were downing their mugs and going for refills. Windsdown also clarified that yes, Etoppsi could experience a great many climactic episodes in a given night and not really grow tired of them. He knew this was also different for Humans. All the men now were overcome with envy. Rainwing was chuckling merrily through all of this, as was Lyndz, who was getting such a kick out of the envious or laughing faces on her brother, Tiliruf, Hadon, and the others.

Eventually, years later for some, and at their very first Star Revel for others, a male and a female would realize a strong connection. Typically at that point, the couple would begin courtship and mate often. Once they agreed to commit to one another, they would then be Bonded and remain monogamous the rest of their lives. Windsdown explained that it was only at commitment that the female would trigger in the male's organ a specialized gland that then allowed for the production and release of his seed. At which point it would be released with every mating act, no different than the other two races. However, precisely like the Qeteral, a female Etoppsis could never be impregnated by a different male other than her chosen Bondmate, as her body would reject seed from another, producing offspring only from her Bondmate. Windsdown also made it plain there was a difference in mating following Bonding, as it was more controlled, creating greater emotional attachment between the Bonded couple. He then asked Rainwing if she would be willing to take over for a little and describe actual reproduction. He sat back and downed a few swigs of brandy.

The female Etoppsis described reproduction. Lyndz had learned much of it from her already, but almost none of the men had. A female's eggs within her body would be impregnated by the male's seed, but she could choose the timing to gestate. She said it could be anywhere from right away to several years before a mother would choose to gestate, and pregnancy lasted eleven months. Not only that, but the mother could also sense the gender of her fertilized eggs and choose the one she wished to gestate. Culturally it was typical, but not universal, that a couple would wish to have both a male and a female topling. She said in royal and noble families, since it was still a cultural norm for males to inherit titles, that in those families they nearly always chose to first produce a male topling and often another. She said that Royal Hawking would be an example of a second male commonly desired in such high families. She said in her own family she was an only topling, and Flamefur interjected that he was the only male topling in his family but had two sisters. Windsdown said his family was more typical, as he was an older male topling with one younger sister.

Since the 'lecture' was somewhat 'scientific' at this point, Manwul asked if adultery were common. Windsdown patiently explained that adultery was almost unheard of among Etoppsi. He said that there was a strongly addictive quality to the contact between Bondmates, and that though there were old myths and stories about adulterous affairs in Etoppsi history, all the characters in those tales were seen as villains and had frightful endings. The temptation of adultery wasn't much of an issue.

As that seemed to end the scientific part of the lecture, the others began to take on the curious envy in the quality of their questions.

"Just how many of these Star Revel events have you been to, eh, *Rusty?*" Tiliruf looked at Flamefur with a wicked grin.

Flamefur took to Tiliruf's informal use of his nickname with a sort of relish. "Oh," he said casually. "Four-hundred and seven."

He plopped another orange into his mouth.

Lyndz' eyes bulged out of her head.

Rainwing laughed. "He's a counter. You males can be such boasters. And Stags are the worst of the worst!"

"And just how many different females have you mated, eh?" Tiliruf was always perfectly at ease asking questions like this. Nikal just shook his head and sipped more rum.

"Five-hundred or so is an average," Rusty teased. "Would you care to share a little more of your brandy?"

Laughing at the grinning male's obvious pretense at deflection, he nevertheless poured out another bottle into his new friend's mug. "You're not *average*, Rusty! That's why you wear that collar! You were itching for us to ask, so quit playin'. How many?"

He pretended to count on his gigantic fingers. "Four-thousand, six-hundred and twenty different females. There were a handful of times I didn't quite reach my goal. I travel all over Berug for these, you see. Some of them have kingdom-wide reputations."

"And just who is it that gives them their reputations but other Stags like *you?"* Rainwing laughed gleefully.

Men were going berserk all around the room, groaning and grunting, beating the tables and laughing at these incomparable statistics. The other Feathers were also bursting with joviality.

"Believe every word," continued Rainwing. "They had a reputation even before they were my students and plainly have kept it going all these years! They've worn Stag collars since they were seventeen."

Both Windsdown and Flamefur chuckled grandly.

"That's funny as heck. And you're how old now?" asked Kodi.

"They're 26," said Rainwing. "Stags are notorious for putting off finding the monogamous mate and Bonding until about 30."

There was a bit of break in the conversation at this point, and Rainwing and Lyndz took the opportunity to leave. Rainwing had not slept well the previous night following the battle, and Lyndz was getting sleepy. Several of the tired men left as well. But most stayed on, and after a bit, the conversation picked up again among some of the leaders.

Upon questioning, some of the Human men opened a little about their own experiences to the Etoppsi, who, it must be admitted, were equally curious to learn of Human nature.

As the Etoppsi listened, to them Human mating seemed complicated and hugely variant. Etoppsi sexuality was comparatively straightforward with relatively universal norms. Monogamy was the understood rule for Humans, like it would be for the Qeteral race, at least insofar as it was promoted by the Orders, particularly by the Matrimonial Order. But the Human drive and experience seemed to the Etoppsi much like their own. Therefore, a pure monogamy like that of the Qeteral, whereby one man and one woman only ever mated for life, was hard to achieve by young Humans, desirous of giving in to their mating impulses. Clearly, it created for Humans dissonances and difficulties. The Etoppsi learned about prostitution, orphanages, and unwanted babies, Bondings of obligation due to unintended pregnancy, deliberate 'entrapment' on the part of some women, more about the prevalence of adultery, and mistresses used by wealthy men. It was an eye-opener for them.

Nikal tried to explain. "Men don't have a monthly cycle. We can engage the impulse at almost any time. Essemarians and Hralindi do a better job than we Westerners in being respectful of the woman's cycle. They usually allow young women to lead in the relationship. And so, they experiment with better care before Bonding, as entrapment is taboo. They have few unwanted children in their orphanages, and limited prostitution in some of their biggest cities. Humans in the west tend to be more demanding and selfish, with poor role-modeling. Yet many do make a strong effort. You shouldn't think entrapment by females is greatly prevalent, nor is every western man cavalier in the ways described. Male desire is not so unlike your own as you have deduced. It's hardest for males from the mid-teen years into their twenties. The greater bulk of men and women Bond during those years with the express moral code of containing their mating impulses within monogamy. And by the late twenties most of the rest have gained the maturity and control required to meet the monogamy Discipline. Upon finally Bonding, just like Etoppsi, the connection with one's Bondmate becomes quite powerful. Yet unlike Etoppsi, adultery does occur with some. Often, wealth and status will give one a sense of power to do whatever they wish, whether it is outside the Human Disciplines or not."

"Interesting," observed the one called Stormgale. He didn't seem to approach the subject with quite the level of humor as others had been. That Nikal was being more serious just now possibly caused this one to feel freer in speaking up. "Why doesn't every Human man bond young in order to contain more properly his mating drive? It seems your race, like the Qeteral, were designed in the Molding for a sort of definitive monogamy."

Kodi seemed attuned to this one's depth. He did not have the boastful flair of Flamefur and the others, and he had a guess as to why. "You're already Bonded, then, Eyefeather? All the rest of you are still not Bonded?"

"Yes, sir. My Bondmate is Yellowtips, and we Bonded following our fourth Star Revel after just two months. We kept looking for each other after the first one, you see, and so it began to dawn on us what that meant. Wild Star Revel and *Stag* stories are great fun to hear, but our tales of early love are just as common if not more so. It's true that perhaps I look at it differently, as I am comfortable within a happy Bonding. Even so, based on everything I've ever heard of or studied of Human culture, in the case of Humans the risk of impregnating the female would, in my opinion, establish a definitive monogamous principle like it does with the Qeteral."

"Maybe, Stormgale," said Kodi. "Maybe. You heard how Nikal described our Eastern neighbors who adhere more carefully to the woman's cycle, and that might allow for a little more leeway than what you're suggesting. There's no excuse for some of it, you're right, like unwanted babies and treating women disrespectfully. Those are against the Disciplines, for sure. But we're careful judging. We're all so different. The desire to mate doesn't match up with the timing of falling in love. Waiting until we know we're truly in love with someone is hard. Some of us succeed okay at the waiting, yet some of us give in, and some can be pretty caddish about it. I'm not trying to make excuses for Human men, but if it weren't for the caddishness of many of them, much of it wouldn't be seen that way, but more like Star Revel for you Etoppsi. Though we tend to be more private about it all. There's another difference between us, it seems to me. Etoppsi mating is open."

"Oh, Yellowtips and I very much enjoy flying off to the hills or the canyonlands to be alone. Bonded couples don't attend Star Revel."

"Stormy is right, and there are certainly a few more subtleties to Etoppsi mating culture than I have described," added Windsdown, nodding respectfully to Stormgale. "The early love tales are quite common, like Stormy says, and he represents the greater number of Etoppsi males at our age. Like with Humans, Etoppsi can also be different from each other, with the mating drive and finding one's true love not aligning so neatly. The rest of us here are wound up somewhat acutely, whereby we look at Star Revel as a sort of high point of our youth. We look forward to the cycle kicking in each month, pushing us to action with the females. It can be intoxicating. All the senses are aroused. In the day we meet up in groups with the females at the sky taverns for drinks, play coy, flirt, and make little promises. Then at night there is a powerful aroma as we all gather in flight. Our own mingles with the enticing scent of the females and keeps us highly stimulated."

"You're joking," Tiliruf joked.

Windsdown looked at him and lifted his arm to his nose. "Hmm. Do you detect our musk? It's true it's strongest on males who haven't yet Bonded."

"*Detect* it?"

"So, it's strong, then, for Human noses," concluded Flamefur, automatically sniffing his arm, too. "I don't think Windy and I understood that before."

Nikal laughed. "Don't misunderstand what Tiliruf is saying, Storm-major."

Manwul chimed in. "I'll make it plainer. Every man here wishes he smelled like you and Windsdown and your Feathers back here. It's like no other smell. It's like Hralindi Oil, maybe, but there's more to it. I'm sure you fellows don't know what that is, but it's an expensive oil some of us can get every now and again for erotic massages, which feels and smells really good rubbed on our skin by our women and kind of fires us, if you know what I mean. But there's more to your musk that flavors it all golden and hot and sunny. I don't remember it being quite so strong on Royal Hawking back in Tirilorin."

"No, it wouldn't be. That's something we didn't mention before that I know is different in Humans. If our Bondmate dies, mating desire evaporates and never returns."

"Really, eh? That's not happy."

"So, you see, there are stages of our musk, too. It's strongest from the time we begin mating until we Bond, and it's strongest of all during that ten-day monthly mating cycle. After Bonding, the scent contracts and the mating drive settles out and is more controlled. Bonded couples can be away from each other for months if they have to. And then when one's mate dies, the scent contracts yet again and the mating drive shuts down. Musk is definitely reflective of the mating drive and impacts desire. I suppose it could be strong for your noses just now. Royal Hawking didn't warn us..."

"We *like* it, Rusty," reassured Tiliruf. "Humans get greasy and rank without regular washing, eh? But we'd take fewer baths if we smelled like you!"

There were chuckles in the room.

"Hmm. If you say. I've often wondered why you take so many baths. We only do so if we get dusty or dirty. Here's something else you will not know. And it's happening for nearly all of us in the Sky Front right now and hasn't done so in ages, at least not in such a universal way. During war the mating drive gives way to our fighting instincts."

"Explain more on that," requested Kodi.

"We males are in the monthly cycle right now, but as you see, we are here rather than seeking out Star Revel back home. When our country is threatened, males can put it off. Bonded males like Stormy can do that anyway. It's often those already Bonded who visit Nant or Tirilorin. Or in Hawking's case, widowed. We unbonded males can't be so far away from Star Revel if the cycle is approaching. Or females must also travel as part of such a delegation. But in war there is the theory that elements in our body and scent alter slightly, driving us harder to fight our enemies. The country and our families must be protected, and that protective instinct overpowers the mating impulse. The loyalty response, too, kicks in harder, and obedience to authority. Some of that is theory espoused by our philosophers and scientists, but it is widely believed, and no doubt the mating drive is stifled when we're under threat. We've been warned we may feel a little anxious without mating during the cycle, and I think we all are feeling it, but it isn't making us ill like it would during peaceful times."

"That's intriguing, Storm-major," admitted Nikal. He'd never heard of or read about these subtleties. "The good of the whole in place of the individual need."

"We believe it to be a part of the Taxiarchan Disciplines for warriors, designed for Etoppsi males by Meical Himself. Professor Rainwing would regularly go off topic in geography class and talk on this subject. She believes that the fighting drive is just as strong for females. I believe she's probably right, based on the individual. But that's not the common view of the Skyfront Command. They have a strong male bent and male hierarchy. Stag code and culture admittedly has some chauvinistic elements, and the officer corps is heavy with Stags or Bonded former Stags. Yet everyone admires the Dragon Legion which has many females who are extraordinary fighters, of course. And they are considered elite. Factually speaking, except during war, Legionnaires do far more fighting than Skyfront Feathers, as Dragons are a constant threat. Rainwing herself is strong evidence for the Discipline in females. No one would dare argue with her in class." He ended, and there was a short pause. Then, looking all around, Flamefur sniffed his arm again and put on a grin. "Pardon what may seem a bit of self-consciousness, but do all of you others standing further away *smell* us? Even through all that fragrant *tobacco* smoking you Humans do?"

There were universal confirmations.

"But you say you like it, and you're not just following some sort of polite etiquette by saying so? And you'd agree with what Manwul and Tiliruf here say about it?"

There were additional universal confirmations.

"Hmm. Fascinating. Does it have some sort of *effect* on you?"

There were winks, murmurings, and chuckles.

"Put it this way," said Nikal, diplomatically. "It's safe to say it inspires us in the same manner as it triggers yourselves: thoughts of erotic prowess but also the powerful warrior sense. When they tell you they like it, they mean it. Manwul and Tiliruf got it right. All the focus on this sort of talk makes a little more sense now to me if, as you say, your musk is right now at its most robust. I suggest this encounter between yourselves and us just now is probably quite unique, as you are, with the exception of Stormgale here, unbonded males..."

"And you're *in rut*," winked Kodi. Everyone laughed.

"And making us all right *bucky*," added Manwul. "Like I'm a Stag with real antlers instead of a collar and want to butt heads against some other buck in order to keep all the *does* for myself. Hadon, mate, feel up to a boxing match?"

Everybody chuckled.

"We want to *be* you, Rusty, get it? And fly off to Star Revel, eh?"

"Or go fight Sea Serpents," said Kodi.

"Yeah, that. Actually, both."

"You can't really do that at the same time, Tiliruf," said the Etoppsis.

"I know, Rusty, but like Kodi implies, if we had those big bodies and those giant wings and smelled that *healthy*, that's what we'd be trying hard to do just now. Thumping frisky females in the sky under the moon, fighting our friends for dominance, and slaying Dragons."

"Aye, aye!" was the common response around the mess hall.

Flamefur raised a furry eyebrow and looked at Nikal.

"It's also strongly related to the amount of drink they've had, Storm-major. But trust me. We're all reaching out for playful diversion from the horrors of yesterday. It's been an enlightening few hours."

"We've been restrained, if you ask me, eh?" said Tiliruf.

"Definitely," agreed Kodi. "Manwul's right. I suddenly feel like punching somebody. Tiliruf, mate, feel up to a boxing round after Manwul and Hadon have their go?"

"Prince Nikal, promise us you'll keep the Eagle Staff under your bed tonight and away from Lord Kodi," Hadon joked. "He might get a hankering to eliminate the competition and blow North Fort to bits while we sleep!"

"I'll put Musca the dog on guard duty." Nikal chuckled.

All laughed heartily. It seemed a good point to end the general discussion, and most now left including two of the Feathers and Prince Nikal. A few others lingered for a little. Stormgale and Kodi drew off to discuss mating Discipline philosophy; it seemed they shared overlapping thoughts on the matter. Tiliruf and Flamefur proceeded to open and taste one of Tiliruf's other bottles and talked about the pros and cons of various liquor imports and Nantian Brandy vintages. Manwul, Hadon, and a couple others were in a corner with Windsdown joking more about Stag culture and Star Revel and with amusement would take in great whiffs of his scent trying to describe it more accurately. A Nantian officer sat with the remaining fourth Etoppsis and taught him the game of rounds-on-squares. Amity was established between the males of both races and also bonds between some of them, a few of which grew strong and more important over time. Finally, a half-hour later, after exchanging a great many bows, slaps on backs and thumps on shoulders, they all left the mess, leaving the sleepy kitchen crews alone at last to scrub things down.

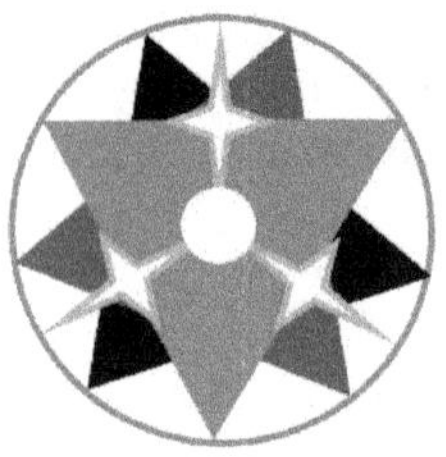

Chapter 11—Disturbance at North Fort

Mid-morning the next day, Eliander's burial took place. Shane chose a secluded spot near to a cypress tree in a large garden attached to the monastery where they lived. A monument designed by the local chapter of the Healing Orders, with words chosen by Shane, would in time be installed over his grave. Tiliruf sought out the Head Father of the monastery and, requesting him to keep it secret, gave him gold to pay for the monument. Tiliruf assuredly honored Eliander's sacrifice, but though he said nothing to anyone, the gift correlated with his new-found appreciation for the role of Healers in general. He looked back respectfully on the dutiful work of Ulna and Maru following the Sea Serpent attack, but he had Shane on his mind in particular, the level of warmth and quiet respect the man had shown when he Healed him the day before.

Honors continued in late afternoon by the citadel at South Fort with hundreds present. Firstly, Kodi brought out Musca and showed him off to the crowd. All roared with delight at their hero dog who had savaged the Alkhaness and consequently brought the battle to a quicker end. Rainwing stood forward and bowed, and her recent honors were listed by Flamefur, and her heroics on the battlefield were noted by Prince Nikal. Everyone cheered. She still had that loyal rooting section of sailor-soldiers from Nikal's ship who regarded her with such great respect. They were especially loud and boisterous, making her smile, yet she kept a cool demeanor. General Fouch read a short speech in honor of General Cruz, whose body was to be transported back to Nant for burial. This ended with a salute by the whole of the military present. Then the prince, based on his own observations and the advice of Kodi, General Fouch, and others, conferred knighthoods on several who had proven their heroics. Among them included not only Tiliruf as expected, but also Manwul and Hadon.

For the latter two, it wasn't their only honor. Upon Kodi's earlier suggestion to Tiliruf, it was determined that Manwul and Hadon should be promoted as Swordmasters. It was plain that in their duty to Tiliruf, in the life-and-death struggle against the enemy cavalry and bodyguard, their skills put them on the level with those of other known Swordmasters of recent times such as Aron and Jaden.

It was unexpected, and neither could disguise how moved by it he was. They'd been wanting this for themselves for years and been working hard for it. Nikal stood by and assisted, Curdoz blessed their swords, but it was Tiliruf himself who presided over the short rite to honor his two devoted bodyguards.

"But what would Jaden say?" asked a watery-eyed Manwul when all the honors were over, and the friends had all gathered to congratulate them. "He didn't think we were ready."

Lyndz thought the feeling shown by the big man was sweet. She produced a handkerchief and reached up to wipe his eyes. Hadon was grinning, yet also had to wipe his face with his sleeve.

"If he had been here and witnessed your effort the other day, he'd have no argument," said the prince with a level of adamant reassurance. "Yet you are sworn protectors of the House of Terianh, and it was Tiliruf's place to make the decision and perform the rite. As a Swordmaster he had the authority to make the call, and it was a smart one and the right one, and as a Swordmaster myself I agreed with him. Jaden will be pleased; don't you worry."

A newly minted *Sir Tiliruf* was floating on clouds this afternoon. His angst seemed to have withdrawn for a time. Being honored as a knight by Nikal had great meaning for him. No doubt he felt some of the brotherly affection for the prince that defined the relationship between Kodi and Nikal, but he looked at Nikal also in quite a different way. Rather like a father figure, Nikal had worked to mold him into a different man, one with a sense of responsibility to others and to himself. It was almost certainly for this connection to Nikal that he preferred now being called *Sir Tiliruf* over *Swordmaster Tiliruf,* even though Swordmasters, considering their expertise and rarity, were perceived by convention as ranking much higher than knights. *Sir Tiliruf* carried with it more happiness for him, whereas his loss of the Eagle Sword subconsciously tainted the other. And a great many of the soldiers took to it, as it was quick to the tongue and less of a mouthful.

Even so, it was gratifying for him to be in his position as Swordmaster and, admittedly also, *Of the High House of Terianh,* if mostly for the purpose of designating honors to others. Today was the first day, and Manwul and Hadon were the first two (and secretly also Eliander by way of the monument donation) to whom he was able to show such honor based on his position and social standing.

Tiliruf's understanding of men had changed beginning with Kodi's arrival in Tirilorin back in the spring. Tiliruf before had friends whose company he enjoyed. Yet he lived with the view that all centered on him. He played around. He spoiled himself. He was the focus of attention, the center of an all-male social circle. He still continued a little in his desire to be the center, drawing attention by way of his gregariousness and humor.

What had changed was his realization that all these other men had important worlds of their own centered on them. This *other person* shift in thinking had been almost foreign to him before. Part of it assuredly was the *quality* of the new men in comparison to some of those such as Yakob, Spens, and Cawlbert, who were knuckleheads. Part of it had to do with the additional few years these others had on him and their maturity, particularly as they displayed responsibility in a now dangerous world. Kodi was an exception to the age difference, but not on any of the other. They shared the common body and social animal nature of two, nineteen-year-old strong, outgoing, good-looking men. By way of these real and familiar things, Kodi then served as a key that opened the door to other pieces of men's souls, things Tiliruf longed for but didn't know how to get past his cynicism in order to find. Kodi and the other men had hearts open to a belief in the Guardian. Tiliruf didn't even now give a lot of credit to the term "spiritual," but he could tell that these men had a certain 'quality of being' and attitude towards living that was different than anything he was used to. Without Kodi having come into his life, he may not have ever noticed.

Had Tiliruf come then to believe in Meical the Guardian? It was beyond him to actually label any of the pieces of this spiritual journey he was on. But the answer if he were honest with himself, had to be yes. He had come to believe by way of the experience of these other men, the reality of the Staff, the realized predictions of the Prophecy, Kodi's Vision containing him, and now by way of a new belief in the genuine origins of Healing magic by way of Shane's touch. There was much in Shane's power aside from mere pain relief.

Based on his personality, it had to be from men that Tiliruf gained belief. That the Prophecy came from the twins' great-grandmother and expanded through Rainwing, that Lyndz had her Vision and become Gifted, and that the Healer Gift belonged to Ulna and Maru, though perhaps these facts assisted, he needed to see by way of the reaction of other men to the Guardian. Otherwise, he might still have resisted belief based on some old chauvinism. He would in time grow beyond this—was doing so even now, particularly as he engaged with Lyndz and Rainwing and valued their intellect, on par with his own. In the meantime, he was still drawn to wisdom by the wisdom of other men. In some measure he was lucky it was, as Jaden would say, *the best of men* with whom he now journeyed. None other could have gotten him past himself. It wasn't just luck, of course, and old Enric could have told him so. Even so, the full value of the Guardian *to him* at a personal level, and his realization of his value to the Guardian, would still be a long time in coming.

Thus, he was beginning to hold these other men in very high regard. They were genuinely good men, each a sort of treasure chest, full, itself crafted of fine material. What was important to them, such as the relationships they valued, the work they did, the honors they received, and the joys or the sufferings they experienced, were becoming important to him. At times, like today, he felt a certain concord with them. It was unfortunate he couldn't always hold on to that connection in his mind and grow into the strength it offered him. Unlike Kodi, who, supremely self-assured, gained only strength from his male comrades, Tiliruf, who if he dwelt on it much, instead grew confused. His desire to connect would give way to comparison. They were givers. Despite his talents, despite his growing sense of responsibility, and despite his connections to them, he would look back and visualize his life as that of a taker. No matter how much true companionship, high honor, and fraternal affection these men showed for him, though he unknowingly needed and craved it, it was never enough to overcome self-doubt and seemed instead to delineate his growing angst.

Again, though, not today. Today, he was *Sir Tiliruf*, and he felt a temporary contentment.

Upon confirming that the large group of friends would gather later for supper at North Fort, the three new knights, in high spirits, rode back first.

Leaving their mounts with attendants, the three made their way through one of the halls of the North Fort tower wing containing the rooms used by themselves, Nikal and Kodi, and Curdoz. Approaching a corner turn, with Tiliruf walking in front, suddenly before them on the floor was a black crow which cawed loudly and fluttered noisily up to a window ledge.

"Must've flown in the window," said Manwul in the rear, without much thought at first.

Hadon, on the other hand, puckered his eyebrows. Then, out of the corner of his eye he detected a shadowy movement. Instinctively he dived in front of Tiliruf, just as the latter, who like Manwul had his eyes only on the bird, rounded the corner blindly. Just as Hadon reached for his blade, he was struck through the right collar region by a thin knife and staggered back into Tiliruf.

Manwul drew his blade in less than a heartbeat, and suddenly before them were several men in Nantian soldier garb bearing down upon them. Nikal and Kodi's doorway stood open behind them.

Tiliruf's mind caught up instantly, as in one movement he lay a bleeding Hadon down and drew his own weapon. He immediately noticed three of the soldiers were black skinned. There were no Easterners among Nikal's forces in Danzilet. "Prisoners escaped!" he yelled.

It was a furious charge. Hadon was down, of course, leaving only Tiliruf and Manwul to fight. But they were not Swordmasters for nothing. Manwul dealt death blows to two in less than six seconds, and Tiliruf's lightning speed overcame three more. Two of the escapees remained, and they fought hard. Nevertheless, in another half-minute it was over. Seven dead or dying Khestadone prisoners lay in the hall.

Nikal and Kodi's room appeared to be empty. Manwul stood guard as Tiliruf raced back to Hadon.

"They...they were trying to steal the Staff," Hadon gasped through his pain.

"Nikal has it back at South Fort. Don't talk, mate. I got you." He tried applying pressure to the bleeding.

The crow cawed and flew out the window.

Moments before, the next set of friends had also arrived at North Fort. These included Kodi, Lyndz, Curdoz, and Shane. Musca, too, had trotted up with them. As the Humans dismounted, Flamefur flew down and landed with Rainwing in tow.

Suddenly, Lyndz noticed Musca's eyes flash bright green. They faded and he growled viciously. Lyndz' eyes bulged, and she caught her breath, and the beast did it again. Kodi half imagined a green light around Lyndz, but then she practically screamed.

"Musca's a Moment Master!"

"What!" yelled Kodi after a pause.

"Great Meical on High, are you sure?" exclaimed Curdoz at the same time.

"I'll explain, but listen!" said Lyndz rapidly, "Tiliruf and the men are under attack up by your rooms! Some of the Khestadone have escaped and put on Nantian gear! One of the prisoner rooms is emptied, and the guards are dead! Hadon's been hurt bad!"

A crow flew out a tower window, and they could hear it caw.

"Go after that bird, Flamefur!" yelled Kodi. "Kill it! If you see any more, eliminate them. They're spies!"

The Etoppsis flew off. Kodi drew his sword and tossed his hunting knife to Rainwing and, along with Musca, they ran like the wind into the fortress. Kodi yelled at other guards along the way to follow. Curdoz, Shane, and Lyndz followed last. Lyndz drew out her throwing knives and gave one each to Curdoz and Shane.

"I spent several minutes in the Moment," she said as they hurried along. "Seven or eight prisoners escaped and killed about that many Nantian guards and took their clothes. It was one of the guarded rooms away from the others. The rest appear to still be in place and don't seem to suspect a breakout. Looks like they were trying to get into Nikal and Kodi's room."

"To try to steal the Staff. Nikal has it," said Curdoz. "Or maybe to commit a murder. Go into the Moment again. What's happening now?"

Lyndz seemed to go still for a split second and returned. "They've been killed by Tiliruf and Manwul! It's over! But like I said, Hadon's hurt. He's bleeding badly."

"It's safe now, Shane. Go!" Curdoz said to the Healer.

Shane ran on ahead. Lyndz and Curdoz paused.

"Musca's a Moment Master, Curdoz! I saw his eyes flash like you've mentioned before, and I just saw it for myself and knew it was Magic and what it meant. His eyes went green a second time. I reacted instantly and 'followed,' if you understand my meaning."

"I think I do, yes."

"And he was there! I found him there, in the Moment! With me! We were in the Moment *together*, Curdoz! He had his own dome of green light that he entered through, right beside mine. He and I searched through the fortress together! His eyes were glowing green the entire time. I can't believe it!"

"That explains a hundred things about that beast."

Tiliruf cradled a still-bleeding Hadon. Kodi and Rainwing, along with Manwul and some of the guards that had followed Kodi were racing in and out of the rooms and down the halls searching. Shane arrived and immediately set to work on Hadon. Tiliruf, himself covered in Hadon's blood, looked at Shane with desperation.

"The bleeding won't stop! The cut went through him!"

After a few moments of applying the green light, Shane opened his eyes. "You'll be alright, Sir Hadon. Relax. Relax. Be still. Try to keep him still, a' Terianh."

"He was quicker than me, eh? Knowing what that damned crow meant, jumped in front of me and took that blow in my place. He saved my life he did, I swear."

Manwul, allowing Kodi and Rainwing to manage the hallway search, now bent down to his best friend and gripped his hand. "Shane says you'll be alright. You're a hero, buddy. You did your duty to Tiliruf."

Hadon tried to smile but didn't speak. Shane was pouring green light into the shoulder. Tiliruf spoke kind words as he continued to hold him. The bleeding stopped, and unbelievably, just as Curdoz and Lyndz arrived, the ripped skin healed over, leaving behind a bloody mess. Nevertheless, the Healer continued pouring magic into the area. There was a lot of damage to fix. He spoke to Hadon in a gentle voice. "You're going to be weak for a few days. You lost a good deal of blood. Must build up your strength over time. It was very close. If it had severed one more blood vessel or been closer to the heart, I doubt I could have saved you." He looked at Manwul and Tiliruf, raised an eyebrow, and gave them a no-nonsense look. "We can take him to the hospital, or he can stay in his room here if you're willing to play nurse. No spirits of any sort for him until I say so, not even a smidgen, you hear me?"

"Yes, sir," they both said, looking a little guilty. "But yeah, we want to keep him ourselves," Tiliruf added firmly.

"Send word to the kitchens. Water. And cow or goat milk. All the food he wants to eat, especially meats and cheeses. Leafy vegetables like spinach and turnip greens. Don't let him fall asleep until you've fed him a good solid meal and drunk lots of milk." He stopped applying the green magic finally and seemed pleased. "Good as new. Or will be. I'll come check on him again. Tomorrow let him walk about a little if he feels like it, but still plenty of rest. In two days he should be feeling a little more himself again."

"Nikal plans for us to set sail that afternoon," said Curdoz.

"He'll be good for it. But no strenuous activity, again until I say so."

"Thank the Guardian for your Gift, Shane," said Lyndz.

"Manwul and I will clean him up and watch after him," said Tiliruf. He turned to Hadon whom he was still cradling. "Not going to leave you, eh, mate? I owe you one."

"That...that sounds good," said Hadon, still weak, but breathing steadily and no longer in any pain. He was smiling contentedly now and gripped Shane's hand in gratitude. Rainwing picked him up with ease. Their room was only a little way down the hall. Manwul and Tiliruf followed.

Kodi sent guards off to get word to Nikal and General Fouch what had taken place. He and Shane along with the rest of the guards went off in the direction of the room from where the prisoners escaped to see if by chance any of the overthrown guards survived and were in need. From Lyndz' information, it didn't sound hopeful.

When the other Etoppsi saw Flamefur in the sky curiously chasing a crow, they went after him. He yelled orders, and they all flew off in different directions hunting for any others. Flamefur caught the one crow quickly and ripped its head off like a farmer might yank off the head of a chicken he's about to pluck and cook for dinner. Over the next two hours, the Berugians did indeed spot and kill three other crows, all of which seemed to have emerged from the direction of North Fort. Upon a further order from Kodi, they remained on sky patrol until nightfall.

"Good work," said Nikal. "You handled it all well."

He arrived at North Fort himself, along with many of his knights and the Staff in his hand. He'd now heard all the stories. Kodi could tell he was unhappy. It pained him that eight of his guards had been killed by the prisoners, although the prince always hid such feelings behind grim determination. On the other hand, he was, like everyone, immensely intrigued by the discovery of Musca's apparent magical Gift.

"Anything in history, Curdoz, on an animal having Meicalian Magic?"

"It's a complicated answer. Magic derived from the elements of Dumhoni, yes. Like your Staff. Like much of the innate magic of the Qeteral. Yes, there are animals that have such magic and come into many stories. But Meicalian Gifted Magic? Not that I have heard of or read about. But we learn in the Valley that the different kinds of magic are related and interact with each other, as ultimately, they derive from the Mind of the One. What we call Meicalian Gifted

Magic, some postulate is innate elemental magic which is then *unlocked in Gift* by the Guardian. Certainly that is the common viewpoint among the Order of Healers. Clearly, though, Moment Mastering is the most rare of Meicalian Gifted Magic."

"I have to admit," Kodi said, "I'd never mentioned it before, because I just thought I was imagining it. But I've seen Musca's eyes go green before. It's plain to me he used Moment Mastering back in Aster when he made me get out of bed to follow him to witness the Ice Tribesmen on their arrival to the city that night. I saw his eyes flash green once."

General Fouch doubled the already heavy guard on the Khestadone prisoners. It was obvious they were still under spells of enchantment and very dangerous. Curdoz and Lyndz deduced the crow had been used by the Alkhaness to trigger an order, still under her magical control.

"She may know more of our movements than we would wish," said Nikal. "She knew which rooms were ours."

Curdoz agreed. "Have the governor issue a decree to the Danzilet populace to do their best to eliminate any crows. Won't be easy, but it should be tried. It's a shame. Up north I like them, the way they strut about acting all cocksure, and cawing in the early mornings while I sit in the garden. But these here could be spies, and we're unable to distinguish between innocent and enchanted."

The next day, Shane, and all the Healers he could gather, set about trying to remove the spells from the minds of the captured prisoners. The Khestadone were forceful and violent when they realized what was about to happen to them, and the guards had to hold each in place while two Healers together applied a particular form of Meicalian Healing Magic. Shane explained that it hadn't been used in centuries since the time of Terianh and the Great Sages in order to counter the magic of Siriné. It targeted, he said, an area at the base of the brain. The prisoners writhed and cursed as green light penetrated their skulls. It was a difficult undertaking, each attempt was time consuming, and yet it appeared to work. By the end of the day, they had removed the mindspells from almost thirty prisoners. As soon as he was released from the mindspells, each prisoner seemed almost a new man. His anger and hatred for his captors dissipated. Curdoz monitored this activity for a while, and he was greatly pleased. He hoped at some point they could be released and experience a better future. He would talk with the Monastery Head and arrange some basic education for them on what to expect in the free world they would someday enter. They would have to be taught who the Alkhaness really was and the truth behind the goddess Siriné whom they had been taught to worship. They still had many more prisoners to work with, but Shane had to leave early and turned the job over to others. He was busy, along with the friends, with other tasks.

Hadon healed rapidly under the determined ministrations of Tiliruf and Manwul. They had, the afternoon before, washed and fed him. His gold necklace from Sturla had been slathered in blood, and they thoroughly cleaned it and put it back on him. Upon awakening from a long nap, they made him eat again. Then, they chose one of the short stories in a book of erotic Eastern romances they had borrowed from an officer. They had great fun together as Tiliruf and Manwul read it aloud, replacing the names of the lovers in the story with those of Hadon and Sturla. The next morning, Idamé came for several hours and applied her good-natured motherly care. She loved hearing Hadon's sweet talk of Sturla, though he refrained in Idamé's case describing their most intimate activities. She guessed this about them anyway. It was plain from his words Sturla had moved into his house, and if that was less the norm in Tirilorin, it was typical in Solanto and other places, including Essemar from where Sturla hailed. As always, the Matrimonial was much moved by true love and of course promised to do the Bonding rite should the opportunity present itself. With fun she predicted their first child would be a son who would have darker skin like his mother, but would otherwise look just like Hadon, and would grow up to be a Swordmaster like his father. Lying on his cot, Hadon had joy written all over his face playing Idamé's image in his mind.

While she was chatting and giving him another careful sponge bath, Tiliruf and Manwul were able to attend to all their packing for the journey. Reassured she would stay with Hadon, they went into the city to buy him new white linen shirts and a vest to replace those slashed and bloodied in the attack. Tiliruf bought him the most expensive vest he could find, made of a heavy, damasked, dark red linen. For good measure he bought one for Manwul, too, who liked it so well he wore it out of the shop. Not so unlike Tiliruf, his two bodyguards always wished to look dapper when they were out and about. They also bought more spirits in order to resupply Tiliruf's trunk. It had been getting too lightweight.

It was impossible to be sneaky when they brought it all back to the room.

Idamé tsked. "You understand Curdoz isn't allowing you to drink when we get to Ulakel? The only strong beverage Qeteral drink is honey mead. The old accounts say they look with disfavor on heavy states of drunkenness."

"Mead hardly qualifies as a strong beverage, Mother Idamé. How would you know if we drink that much anyways, eh?" asked Tiliruf, who was carrying a heavy sack containing many bottles of fine Nantian Brandy. *"Heavy states of drunkenness...*I don't have the slightest clue what you're talking about. This ain't much, and I share away most of it, don't I, Manwul?"

Manwul was holding a large basket containing at least ten bottles of a variety of other imported liquors. Though Tiliruf had a big smile on his face, Manwul, who didn't know Idamé quite as well, definitely looked sheepish in front of her. Averting his eyes, he quickly packed away the incriminating evidence into Tiliruf's open trunk and kept his mouth shut.

"Don't you be getting clever with me," Idamé admonished. "I've never understood why it is men enjoy drinking as much as they do."

Nevertheless, she couldn't maintain her annoyance. Tiliruf put his bottles into his trunk. Fully aware her eyes were still on him, he pulled out the carefully folded scarf she had knitted for him on the earlier ship journey. He kissed it like it was a sacred thing and proceeded to put it around his neck.

He displayed his most fetching grin and looked sweetly into her eyes. "I love this you made me, eh, Mother Idamé? It's my favorite thing in the world."

It wasn't really a lie. He cherished that scarf from her, even if he was using it in the moment as a mollifying method of changing the subject. Idamé's raised eyebrow appeared to relax a little, and she made no more mention of drinking. Instead, she offered up a report on Hadon, who was quietly snoring. And while she did so, with the scarf still on his neck and without the slightest hesitation, Tiliruf filled anew the silver flask Nikal had given him back in Sevarr. There being a quarter inch remaining in the bottom of the bottle, with a wink at

Manwul he upturned it into his mouth and set the empty bottle next to a little waste bin already full of empty bottles.

Idamé went on talking about Hadon.

While all this was going on at North Fort, Nikal and Kodi, along with Curdoz and the Berugians, set out for South Fort. Shane went with them. It took several hours of strange work and determination. Taking turns, the two War Wizards set about blocking the narrow valley just in front of South Fort's walls on the Khestadone side. They moved massive boulders one at a time that they either lifted out of the ground nearby or actually broke off with powerful magic from the cliff faces. Soldiers on the walls and those beginning the repairs stopped what they were doing in order to watch. It was strenuous and mentally demanding for Nikal and Kodi. Between turns, Shane would apply his Healing magic and restore each War Wizard to his full strength. It was an extraordinary operation that Curdoz would describe in his journals. By the end of the afternoon, the way from West Khestadon was blocked. No army was likely to come that way again unless the Witch Queen chose to come again and test herself. But they all believed that was unlikely at least for many weeks, if not many months.

Something quite astonishing occurred later in the evening. The two Berugian Feathers who had been sent to report to War Marshal Jaden returned. But they were not alone. Each carried with him a Human woman and her bag of belongings.

Idamé was beside herself when she saw who it was.

"Haven't been away from you more than a few weeks, but you have been on my mind constantly! I missed you both so much!"

"We just couldn't stay away!" said a beaming Ulna kissing the Matrimonial on both cheeks. "Maru and I found ourselves getting antsy in Tirilorin! Sister Hollina sends you a big box of tea!"

"That's just splendid!" Idamé replied, taking possession of the gift.

"The idea of going back to Nant was weighing heavily on us," explained Maru. "We kept feeling a nudge, and after talking with Brother Enric and Sister Hollina, they helped us understand that, perhaps all along, our true Calling was to travel with you! We jumped on board with Marshal Jaden just before they set sail. We were so hoping that somehow...somehow, we'd cross paths with you before your next stage of the journey! How opportune those Etoppsi messengers proved, and we love to fly! And so here we are!"

"Oh, Maru!" exclaimed Lyndz, giving both Healers loving hugs. "I can't tell you how encouraging it is to hear that! This is perfect, I tell you. Perfect! Do we ever have a lot to catch you up on!"

Rainwing, too, was most pleased. "We definitely needed more females. And Curdoz and Nikal were becoming anxious about having too few Healers with us. Brother Shane found three other Healers and two Monastic Scribes willing to travel with us, but they are all men. We'll be in a fleet of three ships when we sail for Ulakel, but we'll get Nikal to make sure all us females stay together."

Nikal was delighted by the return of Ulna and Maru. "You two are some of the bravest women I've ever known and naturals in managing hardship. Of course, the females can travel together."

"Put us on our own ship if it can be managed," said Lyndz. "Away from Kodi and Tiliruf and the rest."

Nikal raised an eyebrow, but he, possibly more than anyone, understood Lyndz was turning into a strong leader with ideas of her own. If she gained strength from other females around her, then it was no different than how he and Kodi related to each other. He decided that her request was fair enough. It may have seemed a little odd for Kodi not to travel with his sister or for Curdoz not to be with Idamé, but Nikal ensured that the females had everything they asked for.

So it was that the friends were split into three groups, one to travel on each of three ships. On Nikal's ship with him were Kodi, Curdoz, two of the other male Healers chosen by Shane, and also the two Scribes. Curdoz intended to work with the Valley-trained Order members in establishing journals of the times, so that records would be available for future historians. Those five would share what had before been the females' cabin. On the second ship were the five females and Musca. There was no need to worry for their safety, considering the discipline of Nantian sailors. Even if any were to press unwanted attention on any of the 'ladies,' there was always Rainwing to provide intimidating protection. It would not prove to be an issue. And Rainwing was considered by all the sailors to be fascinating company, as she was such a great storyteller. Finally, on the third ship were the three Swordmaster-knights, along with Shane and the final Healer. Shane wanted to monitor Hadon's recovery. He would also prove a strong influence on this set. It must be said, Shane, though a determined and disciplined man, harbored a contemplative streak. He would himself gain greatly from the engaging camaraderie of these men. In any event, there were two Healers on each ship as Nikal wished, and everyone had favored comrades with whom to travel.

Kodi had felt that making use of the Berugians for a message system outweighed their usefulness as a fighting force. He even recommended they only wear their special armor during conflict. This order was certainly well-received, as all eight Feathers naturally disliked it. They had as difficult a time making themselves wear it as Rainwing did herself during the battle. And so, they were divided into four units of two Feathers each. Windsdown and one Feather were to fly at once to the East and take messages to the Queen of Essemar and the allied army currently keeping the Alkhan's army at bay. Once War Marshal Jaden arrived, they would take orders from him. Two with Eyefeather experience were to remain in Danzilet and work as spies for General Fouch. He would use them regularly to patrol over the adjacent region of West Khestadon to monitor any troop movements of the Witch Queen. Two with the least Eyefeather experience were to station themselves in Tirilorin, and travel between that place and Sevarr in Nant or even to Berug, carrying messages between the capitals. Finally, Flamefur and Stormgale, whom everyone now called *Rusty* and *Stormy,* would travel with the friends on the journey to Ulakel. All eight Feathers were subject to being sent on flights to various points in order to maintain communications, and even to carry Humans with them as needed, just as they did with Ulna and Maru. Though they did not have to wear their armor while performing patrol duties, they were required to carry it to their assignments and keep it handy. Yet even on patrol duty they strapped their huge bows and quivers to themselves to be used if needed, but this was no different from regular duty on the Sky Front back in Berug.

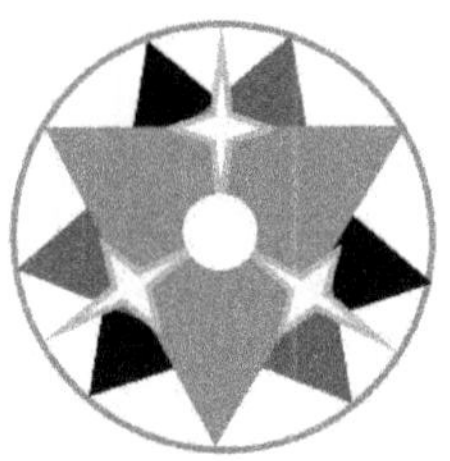

Chapter 12—Sailing for the Land of Ulakel

The three ships set sail in the direction of the great Lintiri Sea. Due to countless islands, reefs, and rocks, it was dangerous to the uninitiated, but these ship captains were familiar with the waters. If a storm were to brew, it could be treacherous indeed, but storms like those they experienced on the way to Modela's island were rare in these waters.

It had been Nantian policy to guard the outlets of the sea, and there was a route used to get to those shores that led to the Great Plateau upon which it was understood was the land of Ulakel and the people of the Qeteral. In the past, Nantians had made attempts to contact the Qeteral, but their border was guarded by powerful magic. No Humans had been to Ulakel since the Qeteral closed off their border after the abdication of Emperor Zarelio. For a century now, none had been allowed through. The Qeteral clearly did not wish afterwards to have contact with Humans. What limited trade had occurred in the days of the emperors had ended altogether.

They had been sailing two days when Curdoz entered Nikal and Kodi's cabin one morning with interesting news.

"Vanaratu is nearby."

Their eyebrows shot up.

"Really?" replied Nikal. "What does he tell you?"

"Some of what he tells me is plain and other less so. He is aware of the battle and aware of the retreat of the Alkhaness. He reads things through the waters and sky, and the ocean creatures and seabirds tell him things, and I explained other things. He did not know she and the Alkhan were Ralsheen but had long wondered their origins. He believes as we do, that they must be drawing magic from Siriné and suspects it is much greater than in the time of the Lintiri War. He was contemplative. He says his time is soon coming."

"And what does that mean?" asked Kodi. He and Nikal both had puzzled expressions.

Curdoz shook his head. "I don't know. He did make it plain he believes the path of the Guardian is to be followed and that we are doing that. He won't be following us much further, as the form he has been given is too large to navigate the rocky sea where we are traveling. He remembers from long ago it being a beautiful and strange sea, sometimes gray and misty, haunting and lonely, sometimes alive and sunny with many birds, many fish, and dolphins. Sea Serpents never go there, as it is too shallow and rock-strewn for their preference. He will be on the watch for our return from the land of Ulakel. I felt tension in his mind as he said that last, and upon questioning, he said only then would we know more. In the meantime, he promised to keep watch."

"So, he will be a part of another *adventure* with us, come then."

"Yes. His contemplativeness tells me it is to be a dangerous one. I would almost describe him as anxious."

"I believe so, too, and I am also anxious," said Nikal. "Let us hope at least for no dangers before then. At the least the Qeteral will not harm us, should we even be allowed to find them."

"We'll find them," Kodi replied with assuredness. "I'll explain to the Etoppsi somewhat of our history with Vanaratu and then send Rusty over to the other ships to tell them the latest," said Kodi. "I'll have Stormy do a bit of reconnaissance, then Rusty can join with him in a flight further afield."

After a few moments, Nikal turned to the Sage and asked, "How are the Monastic Scribes Shane chose for you working out?"

"Fast writers. I can dictate at normal voice speed, and they get it all down. They will be able to recreate it all in standard script later. The regular meditations they do I follow right along, and it's helpful in clearing my mind. They seem a bit overwhelmed by my office. They act expectant sometimes, and when I light my pipe, they can't believe I'd do something so everyday and ordinary. Even so, they have a strong sense of servanthood and attend to my every need and comfort. I admit I've missed having a servant staff like at Island Saundry. Perhaps I've been spoiled a little." He winked. After a moment or two of silence, Curdoz looked around the cabin and breathed in deeply and chuckled. "Those boys keep it strong in here."

"It's more Rusty than Stormy," offered Kodi. "Though it adds up. Lucky it's a good smell. Can get tiresome in cramped quarters, but this is the only space big enough for both of 'em to lie down and be out of the way. And they're fun to talk to, even if their voices are loud. They're different from each other, and I'm not so sure they're friendly back home. They speak *proper* to each other, see. Nothing like the way Rusty and Windy were."

"Stormy gets impatient with Rusty's forward personality," offered Nikal, "and believes he pushes the boundary on his mating nature and that it's past time he should settle down with a life-mate. Stormy thinks the Flying Stag order promotes unhealthy male culture of female sexual conquest beyond the meaning and moral norms of Star Revel, and that it leads to misogynistic attitudes in the Sky Front. You may have heard Rainwing comment before on those same attitudes. Rusty insists it isn't like that and defends Stag values, but Stormy challenges him on it with some solid logic. He's certainly more intellectual and reminds me of Hawking."

"Rusty's all right, though," said Kodi. "You see how he honors Rainwing. I admit Stormy makes good points, and I sort of agree with what he has to say, considering what little I know of their culture. But guess what, Curdoz? Did you know Etoppsi kind of cuddle in their sleep when there's more than one? In little groups of two or three or more, like puppies. We realized it when they lodged all together at North Fort. They were almost in a pile. And it's the same for these two here. They're most of the time on their bellies, their arms folded under their heads for pillows, but their two big bodies are pressed together, wings relaxed and sort of covering each other like blankets. There's got to be some attachment there, despite their being so different when awake."

"Interesting. There is probably an underlying connection between them. As Etoppsi military males they exist in their own understood camaraderie. Consider how they so quickly lost two of their own at South Fort. If you don't count Rainwing, there're really only the two of them here with us in a new world of Humans—ships and sailing and other strangeness they're not used to. They may not be fearful, but they probably do feel protective of each other. During sleep there is vulnerability."

"That makes a great deal of sense," said Nikal. "It is well-known dangers can increase our sensitivities to our comrades."

Kodi nodded. "You're right. Anyway, we unseal and open the window when it's not too splashy outside. We've figured out that breathing their scent at night gives us, er...interesting dreams." Kodi winked at Nikal.

Nikal concurred with a return wink towards Kodi and a most un-Nikal-like, guilty grin in Curdoz' direction.

Curdoz puckered his brows. "I am always concerned with your emotional state as War Wizards. Night dreams can affect us in positive or negative ways."

Had Curdoz known what was coming, he might not have pressed. Kodi plunged in, though he'd never before used quite such frankness with the Sage.

"One hour I'm having a wild dream, *bucky* if you must know, uninhibited like ole rake Tanksen back home, with crazy fool women I'd never get near in waking life, including some of that flouncy crowd in Tirilorin! Then next hour I'm reliving a version of the Sea Serpent battle, fightin' all mad and happy-like. Killing hundreds of 'em left and right. Then it's back to the bucky. Well, not all the women are the type. Let's say I've had a stray thought for a few of 'em that're kind of pretty...or so. Just kind of surprises me my mind can go all damned horsey and 'experimental' in my sleep the way it has the past couple nights. I admit lusty dreams come to me every once in a while, but nothing so over-the-top as these. My own Star Revel like an Etoppsis. Nikal's dreams are right sweet though."

Curdoz blinked, suppressing a sense of shock as he processed Kodi's information. Recovering half a moment later, he turned to the prince. "The Lady Dira? You're less anxious about reliving your memories, Nikal?"

Nikal breathed in deeply. "Kodi has helped me see a little straighter. Repressing the past is not helpful in connecting to the Staff, to the Guardian's purpose, or to Kodi here who deserves my honesty. Most importantly, it isn't fair to Dira. And they were very good memories. I think you deduced the true level of our relationship some time ago, did you not?"

He nodded. "You would meet in secret rendezvous?"

"At her father's hunting lodge on Lake Gwinnett. For about a ten-month period. I would anchor off Noess upon return from the east. Three times we met...and loved. Happiest days. Yet all too few of them. Of course, I still get sad."

In his mind, Curdoz cursed Prince Lekktor for being the cause of this. "Understandable. Yet the Aura connects you always. Your dreams aren't as 'experimental' as Kodi's, I take it?"

"One fetching big man, with his one willing and exceptionally beautiful woman, quite, er, shapely," said Kodi with Tilirufian silliness and a big grin at Nikal. "But just as *expressive* as mine, as it turns out, if you know what I mean. It really does sort of prove the Etoppsi male musk, at least during their monthly rut, has its *effects* on sleeping men. I think it's *scientifically interesting*, as Tiliruf might say. I wonder what it would do to sleeping Human women, ha!"

"Well, I guess I did ask," the Sage admitted with a hint of grin as Kodi continued to chortle. "Aside from it, what Kodi says about the particularly *monogamous* nature of your dreams with Dira would be the Magic of the Aura, of a certainty." With some vehemence he added, "Which made all of your encounters with her *perfectly rightful,* and don't ever forget that. You will never dream of another but her, Nikal, I don't think it would be possible, despite the extravagant influence of Etoppsi musk. Kodi, on the other hand..."

"I swear it's not going to mess with me, Curdoz. You should know me well enough by now; I ain't the scalawag type. I admit the dreams are intense, but I feel right happy when I wake up, don't I?"

"Well, listen, if they become a problem, we'll get Brother Gustus or Brother Luwiss to do the Healer sleep, and that would avoid..."

"It's not a problem, I'm good. Real good," he grinned roguishly like Manwul might.

"He means..."

"I know what he means. I just don't want him developing a sort of second personality that muddles with his waking mind. We need only the clear-willed, self-disciplined Kodi."

Kodi spoke seriously and rather philosophically. "That wilder boy in the dreams has always been a part of me, Curdoz. I've met him there other times before now. Awake, too. It's true he's not an innocent, but he's got good instincts, and he's the one doing the fighting, too, you know."

Curdoz nodded and pondered the truths there. "Well, I suppose he is at that. And you always seem to know what pieces of yourself to draw upon at key moments."

"I need him, but *Wild Boy* don't dictate all I do as *Meical's Man.* Though he does, er, offer up some suggestions for the future." He winked.

The Sage tried hopelessly to suppress a smile and raised his eyebrow. "Hmm, yes. I suppose as I've made clear before, the Vow wasn't meant for War Wizards."

"You are so very wise, *Lord Sage!"* Kodi teased.

Curdoz chuckled. "I'm pleased you trust me with the intimacies. I don't know I'm much of one for advice on the subject aside from my strong promotion of monogamy. It's critical as War Wizards to be faithful in love to one's life-mate. But considering everything, to remind either of *you* to keep it in check strikes me as unnecessary."

"You once told me to..."

"Back in Aster, I know, before I knew you quite so well, and you had made me angry about something."

"Yeah, probably did," admitted Kodi with a great grin.

On the second ship, the females held forth in the cabin with the door shut.

After Lyndz and the rest shared all the news, in addition to Lyndz' Vision in Tirilorin and Idamé sharing somewhat of her deep fears, Maru and Ulna were in a state of utter wonderment.

"Well, we're going with you all the way," said Ulna.

"It's terrifying, but Ulna speaks for me," added Maru. "You can count on us. It's plain as day we're to be some of the *females* meant to help you! Never thought in a thousand years I'd do anything so dangerous. And then those Sea

Serpents attacked, and right after a raging storm! And my whole world turned upside down. I'll face anything. You could have told us ages ago, but I can understand, of course. Not blaming you at all for wariness. Be confident, Lyndz, that the Guardian moved us, too, in our desire to find you again. He wants us to be a part of this. We learn in the Valley He doesn't always make things perfectly plain, as He wants to ensure we feel our choices are free and not determined. It's exactly what He's done here."

"Every day, you hear me, Mother Idamé? I'm going to put your mind into the Mode," said Ulna, turning her attention to the Matrimonial. "You can find peace there. I know this must be making you nutty inside. I'm quite good at the magic. But let's be reasonable about it, dear. What's a minimal amount of time to help you achieve good relaxation?"

Idamé had given up her tear-dabbing back when Lyndz chastised her at South Fort. She expressed a more logical sort of gratitude instead of her typical emotional sort. "Is thirty minutes too much, dear? Just after supper, I think."

"Not at all. That's about what I would have suggested. We'll get you in a better-focused state to face your fears. And you'll sleep better, too. But if you or any of you find you can't sleep, tell one of us. That's a quick mend."

"I'll be monitoring your health every day," said Maru. "You and Lyndz and Rainwing. Shane ordered us to monitor the crew, too. And Ulna and I will start it on each other. Shane's smart to order a daily Healer's examination routine. Should have thought of it myself. He's right. The mental and the physical are closely connected. Always liked that boy back at the Valley. He'd do lectures. Despite how young he was, they'd let him teach. The Body in Nature, and the Human Male Body are his expertise, but that man can do a Healing touch on a woman like no other. We'd almost line up and beg, wouldn't we, Ulna?"

The other Sister chuckled. "She's exaggerating, but she's referring to private gatherings where we'd all of us chat over wine and be sort of affectionate, leaning against each other on sofas or laying our heads on our friends' laps and relaxing. Offering up personal Healing touches on each other, you see, as practice. Converse about the week's lectures. Shane was often with us. He was a quiet, warm-hearted sweetie and just kind of make us melt with that voice of his, even when he'd put on that no-nonsense demeanor and use his serious look and extrapolate on one of his theories. I say he's quiet by nature, and he is, but he can get passionate about his philosophies. I believe him to have a genuine Meicalian aura."

"And a pretty frame. I really think Easterners as a whole make more of an effort to stay fit. He'd go running and get all sweaty and shiny, then go dive in the Lake! Come to the gatherings smelling all Lake water and manly! He's preserved that healthy fresh look, too."

"Listen to you, Maru!" Lyndz laughed.

"Yet again, Eastern skin...doesn't seem to age so fast! Well, Lyndz, it was just that he cared about the body in nature. Engaging with some animal-like impulse in the natural world can rejuvenate the spirit. That was one of the topics he'd lecture on. Opened the minds of some of us who were focused on intellectual and meditation routines. I actually learned a lot from him, even though he was so young. Of course, we all were, then. He and I were close." Maru's eyes shifted a little at this. She looked at Mother Idamé, then at Ulna who shook her head. Lyndz raised an eyebrow. "Anyway, the point Shane is making is we all need to help each other with both mental and physical pieces of our nature. Quit worrying about your age and weight, Mother Idamé! You get a bit seasick, but you keep me informed the instant you feel woozy, and we can fend that off. Nothing stops you when you're on solid ground. You're a horse if ever I saw one. You walk and move as strongly as any of us."

It was actually Lyndz who expressed some emotion as Maru said this to Idamé. "I don't know how I could have possibly thought we'd get far without Healing Magic. What a relief to have you two in on this! I admit I've been largely relying on Rainwing's incomparable courage. She's built me up."

Rainwing nodded and spoke as softly as she could in order for her voice to remain in the confines of the cabin. "Yes, but I won't deny Healing Magic can keep us moving forward foot by foot, day by day."

When Maru realized how careful Rainwing was trying to be with her voice, she exclaimed, "Oh! What a nuisance, dear. You shouldn't have to hold back every time you want to say something. We can do the Privacy Magic. Encompass all our speech in the confines of this cabin. No *male* will hear a word we say."

"Curdoz and I used to do that all the time, of course," said Idamé. "That's excellent, Sister Maru! Do it now and show them how it works. This is splendid. We called them Voice Blocks, in other words, blocking the voice from escape."

Rainwing actually chuckled. "There were times on the voyage to Modela's Island we should have done this!"

They talked together under Maru's Voice Block for a long time before going about some chores.

It was maybe an hour later when Lyndz cornered Maru privately out on deck. Maru realized Lyndz was about to ask her something personal and demonstrated the Voice Block again. "Yes, dear Lyndz?"

"You and Shane, hmm?" Lyndz nodded. "Back in the Valley."

Maru grinned. "You caught that, did you? I almost wanted to bring it up but thought better of it. It was exactly two encounters when we were both a bit tipsy. I was the one who initiated it. I thought him exotic and was enamored. And he was willing. Very. But we're just good friends, Lyndz. Ulna knows all about it. But I decided it's best Mother Idamé not know!"

"Of course! I think it's sweet to think about it, Maru."

"It *was* sweet, Lyndz. But it was also kind of moving. It's hard to explain the feelings involved. Maybe we weren't using our best judgment, and yet I think it's affected me in positive ways. He's dear to me, that man is, but that sort of thing is off limits for me now. But I know him well, and though I know he values the Vow, in his case, I suspect he takes it with a grain of salt. He's too much a sexual creature to discard it entirely. It's like we have discussed before; Easterners' views are different. Most of them—actually nearly all of them—have had sexual experiences before they come to the Valley. I've known other Healers, especially men, not just Eastern men, but Western, too, who struggle with whether the Vow has much relevance to their Calling. I think Healers in general think of the body differently than Monastics. But I can assure you Shane's experiences are limited and careful, even warm and thoughtful, towards whatever woman he might find himself with. Just like he was with me. Eastern men have great respect for women. You once said to me your impressions of Meical the Guardian and His face from your Vision were of your brother and father, but also had erotic elements. Well, for me, it's Shane's face—and body—that come to mind when I remember my own Vision and think about the Guardian."

"I can see that!"

"He's the prettiest man in the entire Order of Healers! We all thought so back then, and seeing him again now a dozen years later, it's still true. That short black beard he's grown makes him prettier than ever."

"I'm rationing your intake," said Shane, holding his hand out.

"Ah, Shane, damn it to the Dragon's Teeth, eh! We thought without Nikal or Mother Idamé here we'd do what the heck we wanted on our own ship!" Tiliruf turned sort of pink. Yet he didn't have it in him to push back against Shane's rules. He didn't even take a determined 'last swig' but rather handed over his silver flask. Truth be told, he had quickly developed deep respect for the good Healer, as did they all.

"It's a matter of good health, and I want you to triple your water intake. It doesn't mean you can't enjoy your rum and brandy, but you go through me. Evenings only, after supper. A few swigs to enjoy games over. And I like to partake...a little, and I will skewer you all at Kings and Castles. I'll trust you not to get at the bottom of that trunk of yours."

"He won't," said Manwul firmly, handing his own rum bottle to Shane, who promptly corked it. Manwul then took it and stuffed it carefully in the bottom of the trunk.

"Well, doesn't sound so bad, I guess," said Tiliruf, realizing he wasn't being asked to totally teetotal.

"Spirits become an easy crutch for the soldier or sailor under stress. Gentlemen of your caliber need to have more of a care and be examples to the common soldier. You need to be a little more deliberate about it, and not so whimsical. 'Time and place' is the most universally taught Discipline, though in willfulness too many don't pay attention to it. Men are the worst. Maybe once per week you fellows can imbibe with a little more fervor, privately in the cabin or wherever. Though nothing whatsoever in Ulakel except the mead they will surely offer."

"Yeah, Idamé's already warned us."

"We cannot offend them with drinking Human spirits, as we must consider our seeking them out as somewhat of a diplomatic mission, considering how long it has been since we've had contact with their race. You're to return to your sword play on deck the days the swell isn't too strong. You've been slack since South Fort. You three are very strong, I can't deny it, but let's get back to your routines. The Nantian exercise equipment below decks...excellent. That's where we're going to get our Hadon back up to snuff. Manwul, I want you to work with him. A little more push each day until he's back to his old strength."

"I feel pretty good, but I'm surprised how quickly fatigued I still get."

"Be proud your body was strong enough to cope with the trauma. Your endurance will come back. You'll be strong as an ox again by the time they choose a landing site. Like yesterday, Brother Labert and I will do a daily examination, using magic to determine your physical and mental states and make adjustments where we can. It'll help you relax in the evenings. Maybe you won't even wish so hard for a liquor bottle."

"Not likely, but yeah, I'm happy for you to work on me. Who could complain about that? You think it could just be you, eh? I...er...trust *you*."

"I'm fine with either," said Hadon. "And I'm sure Manwul is, too. I think Tiliruf has a point, Brother Shane. You're powerful, and I think he could really use the insight expressed in your abilities. Focus extra on him and let Labert work on us."

"His body does contain unusual differences," admitted Shane, nodding in Tiliruf's direction. "I think there really is something in the Terianh blood, and it's fiery. I think it's what gives him his determined speed. I wish I could examine Master Genehbro for comparison. I agree to it, of course. I'll be your personal Healer, Tiliruf a'Terianh, whenever we're together. There may be times when my focus will have to be on the War Wizards. Every other day I'm going to have one of the Etoppsi take me to their ship so I can observe and examine them myself. And Father Curdoz, too. And during any battle, my purpose is to keep the War Wizards from becoming overly fatigued from using the Staff."

"I understand, eh? Of course. Nothing against Labert, by the way, I swear. Why'd you call Curdoz *Father* just now, eh?"

"Hmm? I didn't realize I did, although I know I use it in my writings. It's the older form for addressing Sages, and some of us in the Valley made use of it when approaching members of the High Synod. It's still valid, but the use of the term *Brother* came more in favor some fifty years ago. Of course, *Father* is still used for Heads of Healing and Monastic Orders. I think either form has value and is just a matter of how one perceives the relationship. Certainly, I have come to appreciate Lord Curdoz' role as I've learned more of the facts of what has taken place the last several months, not to mention all the good he has done in Solanto over the years. He has a superior reputation in the Orders. But he told me specifically to address him as *Brother* or only by his given name, so I have done so."

Shane walked over to the little desk and began writing. The other men continued in some chit-chat for a while. Brother Labert was out and about elsewhere on the ship. It was mid-morning. They were slow about getting dressed for the day. It was warm and none of them donned shirts. Hadon wore his gold chain from Sturla, and Shane wore an elaborate silver Order medallion, prominent on his dark chest. Hadon was playing esquire, polishing Tiliruf's boots. Manwul was refolding clothes into his trunk. Tiliruf was fingering Aron's sword for the hundredth time since it came into his possession, though he soon set it aside and with some special tools began cleaning out thoroughly his and Kodi's pipes. After some time, Manwul looked over at Shane and asked what he was working on. The Healer brother was certainly intent.

"Hmm?" Shane looked up. The pucker in his brow relaxed. "Well, I'm adding to a set of observation journals I began years ago. This isn't the narrative that Father, er, *Brother* Curdoz requested of my witness at the battle, but it reflects my own personal studies on masculinity and males. It's naturally more on Human men, but I intend to make comparisons and contrasts with Etoppsi males now that I actually know some, and Qeteral men, too, when we meet them, if they're willing—I hope they are. But I'm using all of you as subjects. I haven't had specimens like you to study in such depth."

"*Specimens,* eh? Our great looks and impressive physical attributes? Ha!"

"Certainly those!" he chuckled. "But I really mean qualities on top of the physical ones: War Wizards and Swordmasters—you are a kind of elite in the *man world.* I wish to try explaining to the curious thinker what that means, and the sort of extraordinary men that fill such roles. What is it about Lord Kodi, for example, that makes him favored by the Guardian, so much so that they actually speak to one another in the spiritual mind realm? I think we have to deduce their two minds work somewhat similarly, youthful yet wise, serious but playful. There is a joy that surrounds Kodi, and joy defines the Guardian. The prince feels the presence of the Guardian, too, but from what I gather he rarely hears His Voice. Lord Kodi fulfills the Voice role for the prince in Meical's place providing that mind balance a War Wizard surely needs. Sir Hadon and you, Sir Manwul, are powerfully driven by love for your new life-mates—you yourself have a child on the way—and now a committed sense of duty to the House of Terianh. And you...," he looked at Tiliruf. "The *A'Terianh,* the latest son of the emperors' line, have a talent both on a horse and with the sword that is supernatural. You have a blood composition that boils hot in a figurative sense. A raw maleness, both animal and spiritual, that in my mind's eye when I examine you is as a bright orange lava described in volcanism. Does it come down directly from your great ancestor? Father to son through the years? I'm convinced it does. The male seed has dominated, with few daughters, and the male line has never been broken in your family, a most interesting fact. Imperial History has always been of great interest to me. Though not all your forefathers were as great. Generations were often skipped it seems, and yet to me it is plainly there in you. The specifically *male* material of Terianh the Great dwells inside of you. Those who read my writings in the future I hope will find my observations valuable."

"Which means you're planning to write with honesty, aren't you?" asked the perceptive Hadon.

"I am. Honesty is important, or the reader only sees abstracts. There is biography here, certainly, along with my own philosophical extrapolation and analysis."

"Biography? I don't want to read it, then," said Tiliruf, displaying his typical skepticism.

"You might in a few years, 'a Terianh. You did say you trusted me."

"That's what I heard, mate," said Manwul. "You want him as your personal Healer, and that's already pretty deep, if you ask me. You never ask much of any man."

"His touch is restful, eh? There's good...I don't know...'stuff' in it, what can I say?"

"I don't really want any of you reading it, anyway," said Shane, chuckling. "Not for a long time, maybe not until the book itself is finished. An author wants to get his words exactly right before he allows others to read what he has written. Right now, it's just the compilation of observations."

"Well, I'm fine you doing what you want. You have your own potential to fill, mate."

Shane nodded. Looking at each of them as if gauging their desire to really know more, he seemed to decide they did and continued. "There are themes of which I will be exploring. There is a theme of brotherhood. You all represent it. The prince claimed me as a part of it, which meant a good deal to me. I felt a connection with all of you the moment he said it. It's the main reason I made up my mind to come. I wish to explore how that theme plays on masculinity and manhood. I believe it to be a powerful driver, men lifting up and inspiring their friends, if you will. A positive force, as it were."

"I agree with that, mate," said Manwul. "I like that idea a lot."

"Won't deny bits of that," agreed Tiliruf. "Men are the best company if you ask me. Can't talk horseshit with women present. Er, Lyndz ain't *too* bad."

"Though there is more to it, that freedom of being able to drop one's guard in conversation among favored male companions is definitely an important piece of it. There are other themes, of course, which drive laymen like you," said Shane. "Sex especially."

"Damn right," said Manwul. They all chuckled.

"The need for what some philosophers call the *Feminine Balance* is powerful," Shane continued. "And it certainly includes physical intimacy and mating, but also emotional need and attachment. Bonding love, that is. Most especially in those of you who do not take the Vow."

"You'll be exploring that *side* of us?" asked Hadon with a chuckle.

"Observation, Sir Hadon. Share what you're willing. You've been open about the Ambassador, of course. Yes, I've written down some of it. Why should such a fine story not be told?"

"He hasn't expounded to you the *raw* version, eh?"

"Er, maybe it'll come out again on one of those rare nights he lets us drink a wee more," said Hadon with a wink.

Shane chuckled. "The philosophical thinkers that have access to such books tend largely to be Members of the Orders, Vow-takers. As a means to distance thoughts from sexual need, many tend to discredit, in a subtle way, the needs of the layman. This is wrong, in my opinion, even if it is subtle. And some of the older writers were downright dismissive of it as if it were a flaw in the Mold design. A greater understanding is required. Not much has been written on the subject in the last two centuries, and it's all ill-informed. I tossed that thought to Brother Curdoz. He knows what I'm doing and says he is supportive of my writing on the matter."

Manwul laughed. "Not so sure even years out you finishing your book is far enough away, mate. To protect the innocent! I'm kind of ashamed of what I was five, six, seven years ago. If I mention names of some of those women, or the North Bend pleasure girls, don't put them in a book! I was unfeeling and cared only for my own wishes. And back beyond that, too. I kind of took advantage of my size and was a genuine bully when I was a boy and teen. Hadon, too; we were terrors to some of those poor blokes."

"Yeah, we were," agreed Hadon who put on a powerful red face. "Hate thinking back to then. What bastards we were. Master Enric was close to our folks and found out and reprimanded us pretty regular. He'd even make us apologize to some of the boys we terrorized. Probably started making us think a little deeper, even if it didn't stop our wildness altogether until much later. Nowadays I love that old man, even though I was resentful of him for a long time. Swordmaster Jaden's the one who really formed us into good men later."

"I'll write down that thought if you don't mind. I'm sure Jaden uses some Taxiarchan-derived Disciplines in his training. Males of strong body must, when necessary, fight against threats. It doesn't deny the female willing to train and fight, but in our world, where we believe Meical is its *male* Guardian, it's especially natural that males step forward when the community is threatened. It's an important part, I believe, of how our world works. Other worlds may work differently. Anyhow, there is value in honesty to the curious future. You speak of errors or embarrassments in your past, and I'm not an idiot. Of course I'm not going to identify tertiary individuals in my book; that would be unfair to them. However, the facts of earlier experiences give the reader an understanding of where you came from and how you have changed and grown. Yet I make it plain you are now of the highest value to the Guardian Himself, and of the world. Manwul the boy bully and pleasure seeker experienced a life change, a spiritual turn-around, and became the good man he is today. Likewise, Hadon. You began young abetting each other in unsavory ways, but over time helped each other grow up. It is not uncommon among boys who remain good friends into their adult years. Study yourselves, and you may find you helped each other grow more than Brother Enric or Swordmaster Jaden did, though they may have unearthed the underlying goodness in you and given you necessary focus. But the beginnings of obedience to their teachings and training began from you pushing each other into that required mindset."

"That's probably all true," admitted Hadon. He and Manwul looked at each other and nodded. "Master Jaden may have once said something similar."

"I know it is a gargantuan concept, but despite earlier errors, can you really deny the Guardian's Called you two specifically to great purpose? Just as He has the War Wizards? And probably from a young age."

"No, sir," said Hadon. "I know He has. Sometimes I feel it pretty strongly."

"I agree, Brother Shane," agreed Manwul. "I think you're saying past error is a valid part of my story. I suppose it is. Even Steffy knew something of my old reputation, but she don't care. It's not important to her. Rather just who I am now."

"Past error is also a driver of men. It's your entire story that has made you who you are. In the future you will be looked upon as exemplars and today's historical heroes."

"Not so sure I agree with all that, Shane, eh?" said Tiliruf, who wasn't willing to let the conversation settle there. "I've never been one to accept the idea of *determination* which you imply by the term *Calling*."

"We are free always to make choices."

"Kodi says the same thing, but it doesn't always seem so. Found out I was in his Vision. And was in some dumb *Prophecy*, too. I feel sometimes I'm being pushed—shoved, really—in a direction, and I don't like it much, eh?"

Shane looked keenly at Tiliruf. "There is a level of determination in the Mind of the One Who did the Creating in the beginning, and I believe the typical laws of science prove it. The One did not intend the universe to be haphazard anarchy. Likewise, the Mind of His Chosen Servant, Meical the Divine. But little gods we are, with enormous power of choice, as genuine love cannot exist outside of choice. And love is key to joy. Remember that. *Determination,* then, and only if you *must* label it so, is in the paths of goodness that are there before us should we open our minds to them. And there are so many paths of goodness. Take Kodi as an example, shall we? He is on a clear and determined path. Yet almost any path he may have chosen for himself would have led to much good. He accepted a given and specific and rare Call, yet the Mind would have worked on him through most any other choice he might have made. Kodi is a good person. An innate joy that's compelling."

"I agree with that last. He's the best man of all of us. Knew it in my first real conversation with him. Not that I believe the rest of what you say as you present it, but assuming for the sake of argument it's true, you're implying I too may have a number of good paths I could choose. Is one *bester* than the rest? You seem assured Kodi has chosen the *bestest* one from the choices he had, and I'm inclined, sort of, to agree, but it still *feels* confining, that is, if I were to put myself in his shoes and consider it. Speaking for myself, you understand. He doesn't feel that way at all, eh? It's as though he's happy as a lark, even through the worst, like those damned Sea Serpents. Though I've never understood quite why."

"My answer would be to simply make a choice, whatever it is. Worry over discovering a 'bestest' path is error. Stagnation results from resisting *all* choices, as we would be denying the divinity instilled into us in our Creation."

"It seems to me any such choice becomes then a determination."

"I see what you mean, but only, as in a science experiment, a choice to action leads to a result, yet then more choices and then more results. Yet *always* choice, then, at every stage along a path. Does that make sense? Always freedom."

"A little. You speak of obedience, though. Does that not limit freedom? Not trying to be an ass questioning you this way, Shane, I swear. But this topic of freedom and determination has always kind of fired me. Kodi and I argue about it. Curdoz gets pissy when I bring it up."

Shane nodded. "Hard questions don't make one an ass, Tiliruf. I'm sure Curdoz has much on his mind in his focus on the War Wizards and Lady Lyndz. Talk to me about serious topics anytime you like, day or night. But here it is. All you men, and I too, have submitted essentially to Prince Nikal's authority. It would be wrong of me to say that obedience does not limit one's choices, for it does. At the moment we're stuck on a ship and are not the captain of the ship. Although, we could each of us go back or refuse further compliance. That choice is always there, too, and the prince is not one to put us in prison for noncompliance. I suggest you chose to be obedient due to some level of foreseeing the goodness in doing so. Did he threaten you with the sword?"

"Of course not. It's just that Kodi was standing with me and submitted first, and I didn't want to be detached from him so soon after getting to know him. He'd become my best friend, the best I've ever had. I really thought at the time Nikal was being kind of arrogant and presumptive. I can't say we got along especially well at first. But yeah. Maybe if I'm honest and gauge it, I guess what you say is mostly true as there was a split second I might have done differently. I certainly believed Nikal to be a great and worthy man. And still do, very much so."

"And nothing has stopped any of us from instead crossing the borders and submitting to the khans."

"Would never do that, of course," said Manwul.

"No, I would never do that," agreed Tiliruf. "I'm an ass, but not that much of one, eh?"

"And I meant it obviously only as an extreme. So, obedience to that which is good and higher than ourselves has high value, though there be risk in it. Yes, it can often create a narrower range of further choices, true. I submit that we chose obedience out of love, whether it be love for Nikal or for the good he represents in his fight against the enemy. I submit that a concept of genuine manliness comes through obedience. Obedience to that which is good. I have espoused that view many times in the lectures I presented in the Valley. Do you see it differently?"

Tiliruf was silent for a time. "You believe then the better men are both obedient and, shaft it all, *disciplined*. I hate that word, I swear."

Shane answered slowly. "Maybe you hate what you think the word means, as you believe it confines you to a cage?"

"Yes. Just so."

"Honest enough. Yet I think in a world such as ours, where there indeed is evil to be confronted, that obedience to that which is good, and the resulting discipline, go a long way in confronting evil successfully. Thinking back, Tiliruf of the High House of Terianh, would you have preferred being *absent* at the Battle of South Fort?"

Tiliruf raised his eyebrow. It was plain that last from Shane struck a chord. After a long, thoughtful moment he said, "No. But parts of me do not wish to be obedient and *disciplined* except to myself and what I want *for* myself. Playful freedom. Including regular trips to North Bend." He winked. The others chuckled.

"It is hard," Manwul said. "Why the shaft is it so hard? Tiliruf's point is valid. There is the common phrase, *doing your own thing*, and likewise, *being my own man*, essentially unencumbered by too much responsibility, and the idea is given a lot of positive credence. We men want things that make us feel as if we control our own destiny and that make us feel *happy*. Mating is only a piece of that bigger concept."

"Yeah, but for me an important piece, eh? But Manwul's absolutely on target overall with what I mean."

"I could lecture on that concept, and have before, as it is wrought with certain flaws, but we would be going off on a tangent. So let us focus more specifically on sexual desire as Tiliruf has expressed, and as he admits rightly is often in the forefront of our minds when we're young men. And as I have said, sex is a powerful driver of men; it can even be seen by the Healer in the man's blood composition and is acutely stronger in the young. We were created in animal form with animal bodies and animal needs. It is meant to be a good thing. No doubt our animal selves do create in the good man dichotomies and dilemmas. Though we are more than animals. To believe we are *only* animals diminishes our value in Creation. And so, we are each *spirit*, connected eternally to a mystical realm. Yet I have always been one to promote the animal needs, for I believe they *symbolize* much in the spiritual. Good food and drink, play and competition, socializing, exercise, sex, fighting when necessary. When it comes to a boy or young man's sexual drive, or of a woman's for that matter, the most I can say is that, from observation, it appears eventual Bonded love and monogamy work well for this world of Dumhoni. You all three admit to having or having had a strong and experimental sexual drive, yet not all men feel such need to experiment. It varies greatly from one man to the next. Ultimate monogamy seems to be the proper rule, and almost all Males of the Three Races comply, eventually."

"I can't explain it, except I grew sick of being a rake," said Manwul. "Don't know if my body changed or my mind changed, but it did. And now I can't imagine loving another besides Steffia."

"But you and she were of an Aura, eh? *Determination* again," said Tiliruf.

Shane replied, "The Matrimonials teach us that the Aura creates the strongest bond through the quality of lovemaking and locks the pair reproductively as they cannot produce or sire offspring outside that bond. It is close to impossible also for the fantasy mind to stray to others once they begin lovemaking. So, there is determination there, true, in the magic. Yet choice to love initially and to continue loving each other is always there, and that's not really controlled by the magic. Do you agree, Manwul?"

"Absolutely. Steffy and I look back and believe we fell in love the instant we met, even in that minute before the Aura. The way she first looked at me hooked me. I wanted to love her and she me. The Aura had nothing to do with it. It doesn't control us. However, it made it easy, as we could move past a longer courting phase! She admitted she probably would have taken time getting to know me, even though she really liked what she saw! Big handsome chap that I am, you know."

"I don't doubt your love for each other is real, eh?" Tiliruf felt a need to clarify. "Shouldn't've called it *determination* in front of you like that. But I still think Auras are really presumptive on Somebody's part and don't think much of 'em. Like Somebody's actively stirring the pot and adding random ingredients."

"Auras are not random," said Shane. "Yet even Auras can be resisted, and on the rarest occasions are, though the reproductive lock on production of offspring is magic and cannot be changed unless there is a second Aura after the death of one of the partners. But back to what I'm getting at, no less than in any other bonding commitment, it reflects again on the idea of obedience. In this case to one's life-mate or to a sense that monogamy really is best. I'm not sure when we are young, we really know that yet, even if we are taught it. The young can be bull-headed and often don't look beyond the current moment. Compare also to the Etoppsi who desire wide experience. Yet our Human bodies do work differently, and mating makes children without adherence to the woman's clockwork cycle. And so, we eventually understand, sooner for some and later for others, the truest value of monogamy demonstrated by the needs of children, the stability of family, and for a most-valued companion. Yet the sexual drive is there before we really understand those things. No, it isn't easy to navigate that. The thoughtful Vow-taker, even Matrimonials who naturally value monogamy, are hesitant to judge the one who engages in experimental young sex. Yet the costs of it can be quite serious, and we truly are cads when we dismiss altogether the possible consequences. Western men are the worst."

Tiliruf opened his mouth, but it was Hadon who spoke the words, probably with more couth. "As you acknowledge mating is so important, how do you manage your Vow of Chastity, Brother Shane? And you're an Easterner. You grew up in a different culture."

Shane hesitated. His eyes shifted and he repositioned himself in his chair. A corner of his mouth lifted in a half smile. They'd never seen that expression on his face before.

And it was no less an Eastern man's look than a Western's.

Tiliruf saw through it. "Eh? Ha! None of that abstract jargon we get from other Order blokes about *submission to servanthood unencumbered by romantic love.* They sound like prissy neuters when they talk like that! Sex isn't always about *love*. *We* should know! You're not as *chaste* as you might let on, are you?"

"Put it this way, a'Terianh. I try. I think the Vow has value for most Order Members, and I take mine seriously. I've breached it on occasion in...rare situations. I never press myself on a woman. The problem for me, if you call it a problem, is, well..."

"When a woman presses *you,* ha!"

"Something about me certain women like. They find me 'safe' and 'comfortable,' I think."

"A gentleman lover!" exclaimed Hadon. Mild shock showed on his face.

Shane paused, as if evaluating Hadon's phrase. "It's rare I let myself fall into it."

"Numbers, here, Shane," demanded Tiliruf.

"Geesh, Tiliruf!" exclaimed Manwul. "You're always pressing for juvenile details!"

"I admit I'm a nosy pecker, eh? But listen to him. He certainly isn't being self-deprecating. '*If* you call it a problem!' he says. Obviously, he doesn't think it a problem. '*Falls* into it!' He *lets* himself '*fall* into it,' because he likes it!"

"It's all right, Manwul," said Shane. "I've made it plain that honesty is valuable. This journey has opened my eyes to the value of honesty. Life has taken a dramatic turn, not just for me, but for all of us. If we're part of a brotherhood, then we're meant to share and care and affirm. You three aren't going to judge me any more than I would judge you. Also, if I want future readers of my books to understand the realities of men, and if I'm using observation and evidence to back up my analyses, then I should be factual. I *have* to be one of the examples I use. I intend to be. I've written down a great deal about myself. Honestly, I don't believe a rigid taker of the Vow of Chastity would have credibility to even write a book on this subject. But for now, I need you to keep it quiet. It'll be in my books, eventually, but for now I don't need Curdoz knowing quite that much truth about me.

"I theorize a great deal about sexual nature and culture and believe wholeheartedly in the value of monogamy, as I've made plain. That is, once the couple bonds in commitment. But for Humans, if you respect the woman's cycle, occasional mating before commitment can take place, er, for fun. It can be a healthy, happy thing. Even if you have no expectation of ever Bonding, that doesn't necessarily insist on chastity. It is how most of us Easterners look at it, both men and women. I'm not speaking for the Orders, you must realize, and my opinions don't match their teachings.

"Tiliruf's right. The truth is I'd had a lot of experience before I went to the Valley for my studies. It's typical of youth in Hralindi and Essemar. You might even say it's encouraged. But compared to the West, where men dominate and cads tend to cajole women into mating, in the East the emphasis is on the young woman having control over it. He might flirt and make known his attraction, but she is the one to make the determination to share the gift of pleasure. And it is assumed always she is aware of the details of her cycle. Mothers teach this to their daughters before they reach puberty. Unexpected pregnancy is rare in the East, as you may know.

"But I grew more reserved about it over time, especially during my time in the Valley. My Calling Vision was a powerful spiritual experience, and it really transformed me. I feel my relationship with the Guardian is a deep one. I turned my focus on my studies, of course, but also beauty and nature, and started thinking of my body in a different way. More than just a sort of mechanical thing built for mating. I felt it was a part of my Calling as a Healer Novitiate to build up muscular strength, greater self-control, and strength of will and purpose, to match with a new kind of self-love due to Meical's faith in choosing me. I wished to emulate Meical with the strength and talent within me. To me, it all goes together as part of my spiritual Discipline. Overall, these foci have really worked for me."

"I look on you as a strong-bodied and strong-willed man, Brother Shane," said Manwul.

"You're a powerful and devoted Healer; I agree," added Hadon.

"My time in the Valley was the happiest of my life. It was the most beautiful, green-growing place, with waterfalls and rivers, and the Sapphire Lake. Not going to lie, the professors could tell I was brilliant. After just two years they trusted me to teach my own classes, the first Novice to do so in a century. I taught a class on the Body and Nature, which I crafted myself, and I also taught the primary course for Healer Novitiates on the Human Male Body, and those subjects have ever been my expertise, on top of Intuitive Healing. The High Sage of the Synod was practically my personal mentor. I got away with much that others couldn't. I refused to wear woolen monastic robes in the summer, for example. I hate them. I now refuse them altogether."

"You can't show off that artful body in those, can you?" teased Manwul.

"You're giving me many compliments, this morning, Manwul. Nowadays I really believe their old symbolism of poverty and denial are lost, but they still carry meaning for many Monastics and Healers, and so I try to avoid the topic. Back then, however, I mostly just felt like they suffocated me. I exercised all the time, and you can't do it in robes. I'd go hiking, come back and dive in the waters to wash. There was a group of women, Western women, who thought me good-looking, exotic probably, due to being a black man. Although there were many of us Easterners, but...I don't know..."

"Admit you have great looks, Shane!" said Manwul. "You're a shafting pretty bloke! You stand out!"

Shane put on a subtle smile and continued, "...and when they found out where I was, they'd come sit on the banks and watch. They'd stare and call out teasers while I soaped up and swam, but I didn't care. Wasn't going to change my favorite swimming spot out of a false sense of modesty. And knowing they thought me attractive just boosted my ego. Their compliments encouraged me to maintain a strong body. I admit, though, I had a couple of too-tempting encounters with one or two. You boys shouldn't ask Maru too many questions about me!"

"You and Sister Maru!" Tiliruf gasped. "Sister Maru? You're joking! Sister Maru?"

"You keep it quiet, a'Terianh! Let that particular one for sure be a secret between us three, not even Kodi and Nikal. I don't think she'd be embarrassed, but I'm familiar with East and West, and I know Western women tend to be more wary of others knowing of their encounters, if they've even had them, that is. Not to mention the fact she's a Sister and took the Vow like the rest of us did. Eastern women don't actually brag, but they're not at all ruffled when an old relationship is revealed in casual conversation. Anyway, there was a bit of nostalgic shock when Maru and I saw each other the other day when she arrived in Danzilet. *I know that face, Brother Shane, even under that sweet black beard!* She called out when she saw me, about twenty feet away. *You still fill out a shirt quite nicely!* She gave me a big hug. *I always liked the way you smell!*"

"The way you *smell?*" said Tiliruf laughing.

"It's what she said! It was good to see her, and I returned the compliments, if less flirty. Back in the Valley, she got me to drop my guard a couple times when we'd each had a little too much wine. Passionate moments for both of us. I'm revealing this to you about her because it was transformative. It was the first time I really felt strong emotion in the encounter beyond just the physical that dominated my action in my teens. But mostly we were just good friends, she and I. She and Ulna were part of that passel of women that liked spying on me. I couldn't help but like that crowd. They were generally brilliant and great conversationalists. They took my classes, were serious-minded, and engaged in conversation with me on my theories. They were my best friends. Since then, most of my better friends have been men. But those women helped me mature, and I think I helped them. I'm not the least surprised Maru and Ulna have been a big part of all that has happened lately. They're brave, adventurous, and like I said, brilliant and disciplined."

"Well, seven years to go without is a damned long time! Imagine that!" Tiliruf said. "Since you left the Valley, what's it been like, eh?"

"It's women that have met me somewhere, like at the art museum or sitting by them at a play. They find me attractive, intelligent, softspoken, and safe. Nor does it really bother me if they perceive my black skin as interesting and exotic. And two or three have in fact been Essemarian. Women traveling through on their way to Tirilorin, though I promise you, Hadon, I've never met Cee Amirah, Ambassador Sturla Keen! Unlike you, rich noblewomen tend to ignore me. Perhaps I don't dance as well as you!"

The men all laughed.

"The rest have naturally all been of Danzilet or Tirilorin. It happens often that women flirt with me, even patients, but there has to be something attractive and special about a woman for me to pay attention. And so, I'll find myself a little overcome by her chosen words, something we share in common like a favorite painter or playwright, or maybe depth I see in her eyes. She'll be sophisticated and independent and has put off Bonding. We'll have dinner, or find a garden to walk in, and wonderful conversation. It gets more wonderful from there. A Healer can tell if a woman is at her infertile time, although it has never been of issue, but I am careful, and she has never minded me making certain with magic. A night or two at an inn, then, or her own place if she lives alone. All mutual and giving on both our parts, incredibly satisfying and beautiful, but short-term. Fun stories I shared only with Eliander afterwards. He was like me that way. He wasn't one to pass up when a perfect situation presented itself. If either of us hadn't returned to the monastery at the likely time, we each knew what was going on and covered for the other. That was one of the similarities we shared. We each needed a secret-keeping 'confessor' who really understood what it was like..." Shane paused and chuckled.

"Eh? What? You *know* you want to tell us!"

"We teased each other for ages, he and I. We took a ship to see the sights in Tirilorin. About five years ago. I went on my own one morning to one of the art museums and encountered a young woman. She was lovely and brilliant. We shared a meal, conversation, and a walk through the city. Then we spent an incredible night together at an inn. Well, the next morning we entered the dining room for breakfast, and there was Eliander sitting at a table eating breakfast with a woman he had discovered at the theater the night before!"

Manwul, Hadon, and Tiliruf laughed hugely.

"We saw each other across the room," Shane continued. "That image of his face—sharing a smug 'aha!' moment with me—is one that will stay with me forever. And there are other Healer pairs like Eliander and me, more in the East.

"Like I said, though, I try. And most of the time I'm able to avoid being drawn in. Too much of that sort of thing is addictive and can interfere with a Healer's Calling. I don't want to *use* women. It would be easy to slip into indulgent selfishness, but it isn't supposed to be that way. It's meant to be giving and rewarding for both.

"When I've had those encounters, for me—and Eliander was the same way—it was the most perfectly natural thing. The best word for it is 'healing.' It was physical and spiritual at the same time. Really spiritual. That's what I mean about it being hard to explain and very different from my early experiences as a teen boy. I do a better job describing it in my journals.

"Anyway, as you know, in the Orders, sex and romance are taught to be distractions. But if it were all up to me, I would put reforms on the Vow. For the seven years of Valley life, and for the first year or so afterwards, the Vow makes sense, as it builds character and self-discipline and allows the Order Member to focus on Obedience to the Guardian and their Calling. And many of those Called to the Valley are very young, some as young as thirteen and fourteen. But the emotional and the spiritual life *change* for many. Every second year after leaving the Valley, I say the individual's Vows should be reevaluated. All of them, the Vows of Poverty and Obedience, too. It isn't necessary that every Healer or Matrimonial remain under the Vows. And a separate Order could be established for Monastic men and women who wish for a new way of serving outside of typical monastery life. Outlooks change, Disciplines change, spiritual needs change, emotional needs change. Even our relationship to the Guardian takes on new meaning. The Vow of Chastity in particular has value only while it still works. I say it works for me, even if I set it aside on occasion. I don't need a bonding relationship. I don't want a wife. If I had a wife and family in Danzilet, I don't believe I would have come on this journey. I know now this journey is my Calling from the Guardian, and I'm determined to do my best for you men and the others. *You* are the 'family' I need to focus on—your good health, mending your wounds and pains when needed, a friend, I hope, when you need an ear. But for others, the Vow can turn into emotional confinement that is decidedly unhappy and so can create a spiritual malaise. Falling in love or giving in to the draw of a sexual encounter can cause guilt and shame for an Order Member, and the hierarchy doesn't look too keenly on those who confess, even though we're supposed to. For me, elaborating to Eliander was my confession, ha! Yet even for the ones who are subject to Auras, some in the leadership often act as though the couple did something backhanded and wrong! If guilt and shame depress you, then, it makes it harder to live up to your Calling. As times change, and the Vow becomes a burden and a focus of guilt and shame, then its effectiveness needs to be reconsidered. It has short-term benefits; I really believe that. But as a life-long commitment it is untenable to expect it of every Order Member. Just like it was for Etoppsi and Qeteral, and that's part of why they quit the Valley ages ago. The expectations placed on them by Human Sages and Synod members was too much. It's an argument I intend to present in my books, too. A lot of them aren't going to like it, and it might damage me a little, which is why I don't really want Curdoz knowing all this until I can gauge better his own feelings on the matter. But I'm determined to get it done, and if they won't approve it in the Valley, I'll get my book made in Tirilorin and find a benefactor to pay for copies made. Er, it's going to be a really big book."

"If the Order's too rigid to do it, I'll pay for it, Shane, eh? Why wouldn't I?"

"Well, thank you. But the Scribes who make the copies are going to be shocked by it all!"

The intensity of the War Wizards' dreams did not go on endlessly. The Etoppsi male rutting cycle quickly came to its end, and after Flamefur and Stormgale had for fun splashed in the salty waves one afternoon, a large measure of their pheromones that had affected the men's sleep were either neutralized or washed away. Their scent was always 'engaging' rather like Rainwing's, just a little muskier and more animal, and would still encourage 'interesting' thoughts. In a way, these realistic dreams had given Nikal especially a measure of daytime ease as he recalled more clearly than ever Dira's face and their joy together. It was surely Kodi, with his insistent humor, who helped Nikal appreciate their value, instead of dwelling again upon separation from her and so descend into gloom.

The closeness among the female set grew, as the two Healer Sisters were now a major part of it. On the journey to and from Modela's island, Lyndz, Rainwing, and Idamé had to retain some guardedness, as Lyndz had chosen not to share her Vision with the women Healers, and the Matrimonial had shared little of hers. That was now no longer the case. Some of that Valley closeness that Ulna described began to display itself. Ulna would often lie back on the bunk with Idamé as the latter knitted, and sitting back against the bunk would be Maru throwing bursts of green probing light and Healing touches on Lyndz lying with her head in Maru's lap. Rainwing would be close beside them. Delighting in the ability to talk in her own normal volume under Maru's privacy spell, she seemed remarkably comfortable considering her usual intensity. Musca would often lie against her or snooze with his head resting on her lap.

The three Swordmaster knights rapidly grew close to Shane. To them, as Manwul had said, he was the most 'real' Vow-taker they'd ever met. They'd engaged with other Easterners over the years in Tirilorin—sailors and tradesmen. But, not counting Hadon's Sturla, Shane was the first Easterner they could claim as a friend. He had a different perspective, and with an obviously deep spiritual nature, he was also a man close enough to their own age who keenly related to the minds of young men. He was all the time willing to engage and share his inner thoughts, and they with him. Beforehand, though Manwul and Hadon liked talking mysticism and philosophies, they would rarely do so with skeptical Tiliruf, as the latter was, in a way, too smart for them and too able to discredit some of their disjointed logic. In addition, there was a certain impatient emotional streak on Tiliruf's part when such topics were brought up which didn't make it any easier. With his greater degree of education, Shane could express better in words ideas that Manwul or Hadon never quite could before. Those two learned heaps from him they never did from old Enric. Tiliruf was willing to engage in these topics now, even if he did not always agree with what Shane had to say. He had come to believe in the reality of Meical the Guardian and yet still pushed back on mysticism and Shane's logic as the Healer connected spiritual matters to the physical realm. Shane could go one-on-one with him on strange tangential discussions and was far more patient than Curdoz could be, both with Tiliruf's skepticism and also with what Curdoz might have called his 'juvenile streak,' but what Shane better understood as 'uncensored,' reflecting an underlying level of realism.

As noted, Shane had a muscular frame. He, Tiliruf, and Hadon were of comparable size. He did not funnily boast about his own great looks like some of the others, but his self-pride was otherwise obvious to his new friends. And so he enjoyed physical movement and exercise and involved himself closely with what the men did including all the exercising routines and sword play. Already good with archery, Shane wished to be better in close quarter combat if he were to be near to the War Wizards in battle as Curdoz had asked of him. Healer Labert they understood was a decent horseback rider, but otherwise had not had much physical training, although he was willing to learn. He was pudgy in the belly but had good strength in his legs, arms, and shoulders. And he did learn and over time gained great stamina, and it was plain he had a brave streak. He was not a bad companion and could be fun at Fifty-twos, happily smoked his pipe alongside Tiliruf, but the men did not share with him in the manner they did with Shane. Labert was a methodical Healer and would go about providing examinations to the officers and crew of the ship. The four tended to talk more when he was out of the cabin, which was often, as he did not like feeling cooped up in it.

Tiliruf began to look forward to Shane's regular evening examinations and Healing magic. He'd lie back on his bunk, either close his eyes or look into Shane's interesting dark face as he worked and welcome every burst of green light. Shane provided Tiliruf with a measured sense of calm and learned more of Tiliruf by way of his magic, through their conversations, and also stray words, than Tiliruf realized.

Many days later, having now made a great many observations, Shane wrote this about Tiliruf in his private journals:

...and so he trusts me. The relationship we have is a good one. It seems I can communicate at a level with him that no other has so far done. The young man is as keen of mind as any I ever knew, with perfect memory, too. His knowledge is encyclopedic. He knows Ralsheen better than I do, and certainly High Anterianhi. He's absorbed hundreds of books, if not always the most edifying. Some of them were. He's the best scholar of Anterianhi imperial history in the world today, I am certain of it. Even though he resists Meicalian Mysticism, he nevertheless has touched on spiritual matters to a degree many Order Members have not. I can certainly understand Lord Curdoz' impatience due to the cynical values applied to Tiliruf's many questions, but I find him to be a subtle intellect despite the casual worldliness. He is one of the great men of our times yet refuses to believe so.

He is troubled by much, and I have discovered it is partly in the makeup of his body's elemental fluids, beyond the cure of any herb. There is royalty in his blood, like Nikal's, yet tainted by strange elements pressing upon his psyche, and on his body, and I worry for him. It isn't madness, and they are not poisons. I don't know what each represents, and I suspect not another Healer could detect them aside from myself. Within the hot orange in my mind are crimson, purple, and black. But it is not an evil empty black, which I've seen before in those under the mindspells of the Alkhaness, and which can be eradicated by concentrated Healing Magic. Instead, it is "solid," if that's the right word. Like black iron. It glows hot just as do the other colors and cannot be removed by Magic, not that I would even try, as it is part of who he is. But it isn't normal for any typical Human. I think they are Cosmic-spiritual elements, possibly unknown magical components which I presume must be derived and manipulated by Meical through generations of Aura Bondings in the Terianh line, and largely male. That's my best guess, anyway, as War Wizard theory contrives charmed bloodlines, and certainly so in the Terianh, and possibly also the Berugian royal line. They might explain Tiliruf's uncanny speed when he fights, and also his fighting brilliance and godlike handling of his mount during battle, but they are not what one might call 'natural' outside such a bloodline. I was surprised when I saw them in Tiliruf only by the novelty. Otherwise, it makes some sense considering Terianh the Great, and the male line remained intact. Even so, my instinct tells me those elements are concentrated strongly in Tiliruf, and what should be his innate ability to balance them properly isn't working. I suspect the Guardian knows this, as He has focused His attention on him, proven by being in a Vision and in a Prophecy. But I think they may be taking a harsh toll on Tiliruf the older he gets, as they manifest themselves in his spirit. As I say, it isn't madness, and they are not poisons, but they are 'intense,' and unchecked they could lead to unhealthy effects both physically and mentally and, based on my observations, are probably already doing so. Their movement through his body and brain seems too haphazard and just beyond natural control.

Tiliruf needs me, and that the Guardian saw fit to bring us together makes all the sense in the world. I think I can help him. If Meical has given me the power to see those colors, then somehow I can help in modifying their effects. When I lay my hands on him and concentrate on the colors, they realign. It's like a reverse of the rainbow effect of white light split into colors by a prism. He refers to it as restful, and it surely has that effect, but it is mentally stabilizing, too. What I'm doing for him is not ordinary Healing and includes Mode magic. I'm sure someday I will explain to him some of this, but for now I believe such knowledge would not be helpful.

Yet he will need more than me to achieve what he is capable of. Should he live through this war he will outshine most of his ancestors, but survival will not be sufficient. He could still be overcome by the self-doubts that have plagued him his whole life. His greatest defect comes from the motherlove he didn't get, and a self-absorbed father indifferent to his escapades. Curdoz suggested that to me, and I agree with his assessment. Therefore, Tiliruf is somewhat indifferent to women aside from the physical release they provide him, though he has a kind heart towards the Lady Lyndz and Mother Idamé, which is certainly something, an important step in growth. One of his strengths is the realization of the greatness of the men with whom he now keeps company. He honors them. In fact, he loves them, though he may not use that verb to describe the emotion he feels. How he bodily held and even spoke to Hadon following the latter's stabbing at North Fort was tender. Soaked through by his friend's blood and fearing he would surely die, he spoke only kind and thought-filled words, as gracious as any trained Healer at the deathbed of a patient. And his mindset towards the prince is deep, like the father he should have had, though they are only ten years apart. My hope is that relationship is never broken, for if any individual can grow Tiliruf into a strong and confident man it is Nikal. Nikal seems to know it, and that is good. He pushes through his own impatience and makes efforts with the younger man.

Yet war carries with it many uncertainties. The loss of the Eagle Sword was no less than a trauma and still affects Tiliruf deeply. It seems to have set his spiritual growth back, as it were. It was a symbol he needed for himself, and, as an object, it has no substitute. He won't speak of it unless I make him do so with a Voice Block during my ministrations. We need to work through that loss. He needs to see that the symbolism attached to his bloodline is not in an object but rather in himself. His heroic feats at South Fort prove it. It was sheer glory, as from Classic times. In each their own way, all the men tell him that very thing, and they honor him, as he does them. But he is resistant.

He's happiest when Kodi is around. And no doubt Kodi's inherent joy is something that easily rubs off on anyone he's with. Sometimes I do wonder if Tiliruf resents the unusual closeness and privacy between Kodi and Nikal, a relationship very different than their own, as if it is something Tiliruf wishes for himself. Hadon and Manwul are excellent companions, however, and they read his mind almost as well as I do for not having Intuitive Healing Magic. They serve and steady him quite well and exercise him with the superior qualities of the Swordmaster skills they share. Tiliruf has apparently been quite generous to them with his money and has paid for everything for those two since they left Tirilorin. I provide the deeper level of private discussion Tiliruf needs. Maybe I help make up a little for what he does not get from Kodi and Nikal. I hope so. And I've certainly shared with him some of my own personal stories. I do so not because I need it, but because I think he does, for to see where we were similar as boys and as men, how our minds progressed in this and that sort of way as we grew up, and all in order to maintain that level of trust. If it weren't for his self-doubts, we otherwise are similar in certain ways. Our intellectual level is similar, our physicality is similar, my sexual nature in my teen years was indulgent and exploratory like his, among other things.

Yet his emotional needs are great, like a lost child. I would never tell him that in those words; he would resent me. And I would, too, if someone said such to me. He senses his neediness. It disturbs him. And so, he tries to ignore it. When I chat privately with him through Voice Block, I make effort to focus on one topic at a time, working through his cynicism. It would be cruel to illuminate to him all at once all his many issues and the probability of interconnection. He hates anything smacking of determinism. He isn't ready to believe the Guardian has Called him as He has the rest. Not yet. I play him carefully, and more than any man I have ever met he deserves such care. Should we survive this war, I will follow him as needed. I will never give up on him. If I have to provide specialized Healing Magic thirty times a day to keep him steady, I will do it. My Calling to aid the War Wizards is logical, considering my strengths, but if we survive this war into a future of peace, Tiliruf will be my long-time charge. I'll have to explain some of this to Curdoz or Enric without divulging all. Those strange elements in Tiliruf's blood cannot be 'purged,' as they are a part of who Meical made him into, and so they will have to be... the best word I can think of is 'managed.' And so, Meical willing, I will 'manage' him. I will have to make him understand that he needs this long-term, probably life-long management, and that is not going to be easy.

Though in the long run, as I have implied, he may need more than me. A greater influence than me would be a loving woman. He needs female sexual release and a lot of it, but from a woman who loves and understands him, and one whom he can love with his deep heart and not one he pays. In his case, she will be hard to find. His history with women works against him. He seems to know it, too, and pretends not to care. I think he cares a great deal. He seems almost jealous of what Hadon and Manwul have with their new life-mates, and it isn't just their mating tales. Yet he flamboyantly estimates he has mated some one-hundred women, many of them a great many times over, and mostly prostitutes of North Bend with the exception when he was younger of a handful of ladies of class, though of a manipulative sort. Far be it from me to recommend any man seek out prostitution over mutual sex with willing women, but in his particular case I'm glad he threw off that earlier set, as they could have destroyed him through entrapment and manipulation. It bothers me to know there is such a set, and it seems such women can be just as guilty of wealth and privilege as barons and rich merchants in the Western kingdoms who keep mistresses. I think they could have done horrible damage to Tiliruf, and casting them aside was possibly one of the smartest things he did in those years. A wisdom of sorts had to have penetrated his mind. I will have to consider how to reproduce some of these thoughts in my book on males. Tiliruf's case is surely enigmatic, possibly with some valid components in the choices he's made. When the men and I talk about the sexual nature I really want to express my strongly negative views on prostitution but feel it unwise to appear as if I target him in judgment. It's not the purpose of a Healer to craft guilt in anyone. In any event, I worry it has damaged his ability to love a woman properly. He may actually believe the same thing. But what would that mean for the House of Terianh should Tiliruf never seek a life-mate? The word is that Genehbro, like most of that line, was subject to an Aura. Not surprising to consider Tiliruf was the sole subject of that Bonding. And so Genehbro cannot sire anymore children. There are some very distant cousins who descend from the imperial house, and most of the royal houses have some Terianh blood, but not in a direct male line. The male material, I deem, both from my magical probing of his body and also by way of the Aura Bondings, to be critical to the Guardian's wishes for the Terianh line. Some of that is only a guess, though, on my part...

It wasn't long before Hadon and Manwul noticed a difference in Tiliruf. He had taken on a calmer mood. Less anxious. Less self-involved and more other thinking. These were just the beginning of what would turn out to be for all the friends some of their most enjoyable weeks and least worrisome. In this adventure to the Qeteral there would be some moments of intensity and a great many thought-provoking situations, conversations, and learning experiences, but generally they were to experience some kinder times in relative peace. For a few they would qualify as some of the most critically important days of their lives, and others as major turning points. They were memorable days that in future they would reminisce about regularly.

Beyond them would be darker, more dangerous roads.

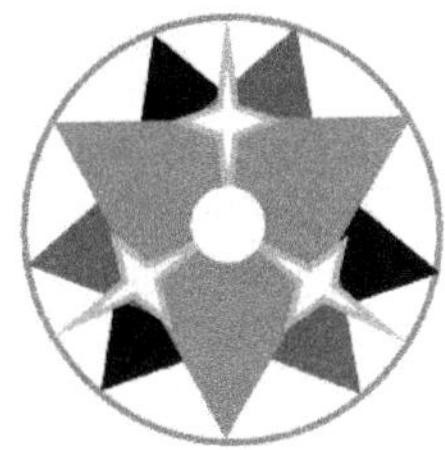

Chapter 13—Mixed Welcome

It had not been easy to find the anchorage, as the green forest grew densely to the shores of the sea. At one point, however, a sort of beach opened out, and then beyond this a high spit followed shortly after by a well-protected small harbor. They were able to anchor quite close to shore. Captain Avantrees, of the ship carrying the females, was pleased. Leading the rest, he had been, with his navigator, the most experienced in these waters. It was a place he had been hoping to pinpoint again. Having then disembarked, Nikal ordered all the ships' crews to remain seaside for the duration. The three Healers chosen by Shane—Labert, Gustus, and Luwiss—remained with the crews. Deens and Findun, the two Scribes now employed by Curdoz, followed through the forest with the rest of the party. Thick growth marked the forest line with the beach and harbor, but only a few feet beyond, the forest floor opened up, and it was easy to walk amongst the virgin trees.

"They have only small pack ponies, which they use as beasts of burden for farm use and pulling carts. Theirs was never a horseback riding culture. They did learn shipbuilding from Humans, but had only a few, using them to explore in the Lintiri Sea, a limited fishing industry, and for trade with old Lintiri. They abandoned their use when they secluded themselves following the emperor's abdication. Except you saw that curious pile of rotted lumber back there Nikal thinks is only about twenty years old or so. No explanation for that." As they walked through the forest, Lyndz was expounding on the many things she had learned in books about the Qeteral while in Tirilorin. "Their houses are built entirely out of wood on stone foundations, with brick or stone fireplaces, but decorative, like hunting lodges of the Human merchant class. They have no large cities, but rather innumerable villages scattered throughout their land. They engage in most every kind of art, including sculpture, painting, mosaic, tapestry, and other weaving. They do fine woodwork and hand-carving. Though they don't at all wear the amount of clothing common to Humans, what they do wear is beautifully made from linen, often dyed and with elaborate embroidery. Some of their clothing is fancier for formal occasions. They don't wear wool, though they weave wool carpets and tapestries. They evidently have a unique gardening style which includes a great deal of stonework sculpture designed to mimic nature, such as little mountains and waterfalls. They're most famous in the Human world for..."

"Ceramics." Tiliruf concluded.

"Yes," agreed Lyndz. "I've seen some of it in Tirilorin, and it is exquisite. There are various styles of it. Some of it is pottery of strong make and reasonably practical in that regard, though it's expensive enough, but the more valuable product is the finer art ceramics. All of it is beautifully painted, often with birds as a motif, though sometimes with other animals like deer. It was virtually the only thing they traded, and Humans paid handsomely for it. To have a piece of Ulaki ceramic is a sign of wealth in Central City. Madam Arlay had a glass-encased cabinet full of it next to the main fireplace in her largest parlor. She had inherited it all from her grandfolk who collected it back in imperial times. You remember, Mother Idamé?"

"I do. It was wonderful! Hollina and I oohed and aahed."

"I've got a pair of matching Qeteral vases on my mantle," offered Tiliruf.

"Of course, you do," kidded Kodi.

"Servants put fresh flowers or greenery in them every week."

"Of course, they do."

Tiliruf looked over at his friend. "You just like teasing me for being rich."

"Of course, I do. Actually, I like teasing you for all sorts of reasons. But yeah, I remember them being kind of fancy. And colorful. Mostly blues."

"They were mostly greens."

"Of course, they were. I was too busy sampling from your cabinet, which I found more impressive."

"Gosh, Tiliruf. I can't believe you let him within thirty feet of it!"

"Of the liquor cabinet? That was the main point, I thought," said Tiliruf, with a wink in Kodi's direction.

"No! Of the mantle, you ninny! I'd love to get the opportunity to send a piece of painted Ulaki ceramic back to Mother in Tulesk. I know she'd treasure it. I wonder..."

Though the general northwestern direction was presumed based on maps indicating the Great Plateau and the land of Ulakel, it seemed that Musca the dog had chosen to lead them. As the lead group continued in a sort of line, if Musca chose to veer off slightly, Kodi, with Curdoz and Nikal's agreement, ordered them all to follow the dog.

"I don't know what he senses. His nose is working hard. He's determined."

"It is almost like a trail," Nikal agreed. "Worn places between hillocks, stones seemingly shoved aside making the walking a little easier than elsewhere. But like that rotted pile of lumber, my guess is it has been at least twenty years since anyone came this way. It is a little more northerly than I might have led us, but that beast knows things. Lyndz, have you sensed anything or noted his eyes flash?"

"Not yet. Kind of hard to do considering how he stamps on ahead of us."

"Stormgale and I could fly above the trees."

"No, Rusty," said Kodi. "And half-mile reconnaissance on Lyndz' part with her Gift isn't going to do us much good here. I believe we should all stay together. Let Musca be our guide. At least you saw the distant line of the Plateau's ridge when you flew a little as we landed. That's good enough for now."

"What little information we have over the long years describes people getting lost, not so much by entanglement, but instead by direction," said Nikal. "They would be making a virtual beeline in the direction of the Ridge, only to find themselves approaching a point they'd recognized and been to already. As if they were going in circles."

"It is a powerful magic that can alter the thinking mind in such a way," said Curdoz. "Even the most stubborn Nantian explorers would again and again return to the same earlier point, upon which they would finally give up and return to their ship. There was never any hindrance at all if they returned in the direction of the sea and their ships. All sense of direction would return to normal."

"But did they have an Elentine Noble with them?" asked Kodi.

"No dogs of any sort, as far as I recall. That is a curious observation," said Nikal. "It would be interesting if an Etoppsis in flight would experience the same dilemma as Humans walking, but I suspect strongly they would. The old information does not speak of Etoppsi ever finding them, either, when their Barrier is in place."

"Regular contact between Etoppsi and Qeteral has not taken place since before the Ralsheen Dark Times," said Rainwing. "Long ago, before that period, there was no Barrier. Again, just after the Anterianhi Conquest, there was some contact, and we have Ulaki ceramics on display at the Institute, and a handful of Qeteral books. The two races share a deep love of nature. Tall, old trees, for example. But, yes. They are the Gardeners. We are the Builders of Stone."

"What are Humans, then?" asked Tiliruf.

"The Shipbuilders, of course. But also, *The Prolific* or sometimes *The Fruitful*. You populate the world more rapidly and have many ethnicities and countries."

"We like mating more, eh?"

Flamefur snorted.

"Oh, Tiliruf!" exclaimed Idamé.

"There are fertility differences, of course, but generally speaking, passion is equal among the races. However, our lives are shorter," put in Shane. "Yes, we tend to have more children, whereas the other two races' females can choose pregnancy at will. And as there are more Human generations, too, in a given time frame, the increase in numbers is accelerated. Considering length of lives, I believe there is something none of you have considered."

"What is that?" asked Curdoz.

"There may be older generations of Qeteral who remember when Zarelio was still on the throne in Tirilorin. They will remember a time when there was more coming and going, and some will have seen Humans in the past."

"You have a job to do, Tiliruf," added Curdoz, out of the blue and curtly.

"You've said so already, and so did Father," said Tiliruf, somewhat hotly and turning to face Curdoz. "I've worn my Eagle embroiders, as you see. Saved 'em special for the occasion."

"Don't be flippant about the Eagle, a'Terianh," said Shane, though in soft tones, pondering the sudden interaction between the Sage and Tiliruf and looking between the two of them. He didn't like Curdoz' tone at all. "They're a real part of you, and you wear them well. But Brother Curdoz, he doesn't bear the brunt of diplomacy. It was the triple Visions, and that's mostly you and Lord Kodi. I hope you're not expecting Tiliruf to *be* emperor when he isn't."

"No, I am not. The point of course is a hope the Qeteral see that we value the peace and intercourse, and the *symbolism*, of imperial days. I am hoping Tiliruf's presence will be seen as symbolic and," he added vehemently, "*serious* gesture."

Nikal also looked at Tiliruf and said in calm demeanor. "You are not an emperor, but you are the Eagle you wear, as I think you understand me, do you not, Swordmaster? You really do wear it well. It suits your looks and the battle hero that I know from South Fort. Many of the Qeteral will see you as the *A'Terianh*, as Brother Shane so wisely refers to you, and for which you are becoming more greatly known by our armies."

Tiliruf's face turned to serious composure. He ignored Curdoz, but he looked at Shane, and then he looked back at Nikal. "I hope for times to feel at ease while we visit them, eh? But I promise I will not let you down, sir."

"I believe you," said Nikal. To Curdoz he smiled and said, "No more warnings needed, Your Grace."

Curdoz blinked several times and nodded. "I apologize. Tiliruf has proven his value many times, of course. Suffice it to say as I have so often done with the twins on our journey been reminded of youth, and so I have found myself mistaken as the particulars present themselves."

But that evening when they camped, Nikal took Curdoz aside and spoke again to him. "Unless absolutely necessary, Curdoz, I would ask you create a new Discipline for yourself whereby you make your wishes for Tiliruf known through me. You are a true father to Kodi and the Lady Lyndz, and even to me, and the warmth shows. But you are lacking in much patience with him. Your attitude towards the fall of the imperial house is being taken out on him. I too was greatly impatient with him when we first met but soon realized the error. I still get impatient with him sometimes, but I fight it. Consider, then, the man who broke the Alkhaness' bodyguard the next time you engage Tiliruf. Did you ever say a word of praise to him for that? The great man who achieved highest accolades, without the use of any magical Staff?"

Curdoz' face, had there still been enough light, would have shone crimson. "Oh, my. Enric would be disappointed in me. I only commended Rainwing."

"I thought not. And I want you to review your battle chronicle with your servants. And fix it."

"I...I will do that."

"You and I know of his initial immaturities, Curdoz, but he has advanced greatly on this journey. Isn't that what we all wished for him? And who of us isn't flawed in some way? So, to act upon impatience with a kind of random curtness is no good. He'll just be curt back. And he had done nothing this afternoon to justify you drawing attention to him as you did. Shane saw it immediately. In any event, to tell Tiliruf he has a job to do is my job to do. Your impatience is damaging your credibility with him. This venture to the Qeteral is surely under your authority, because of your Vision, and as a Sage they will look to you as the Messenger they trust. But consider a bit of officer ranking. When it comes to the military *males*, use your War Wizards as your generals, Kodi and I, and then let us handle."

The Sage nodded. "This man is feeling old right now. Everything you say is perfectly right."

"You speak from wisdom, of course, but not always by way of tact when it comes to Tiliruf. But I'll tell you the best thing you ever did for Tiliruf, though you may not have understood it when you did so, was to invite Shane aboard."

"I'm beginning to see that. For all of us, really."

"He spoke to me about a concern or two, and it appears he's becoming attached to Tiliruf and will protect him, even from you. He has a powerful and deeply attuned mind; you can feel it when he's close, in his perceptive words, and certainly when he lays his hands on you. It isn't just the extraordinary Healing Magic. He was a little vulnerable following Eliander's death, but has come back into his strength, probably even stronger than before, now with new high mission. Shane will have his own ways of handling Tiliruf, I think. Let's observe more than intervene, shall we?"

Curdoz nodded. "Considering all your many cares, Nikal, your insight is acute. I believe you hear the Guardian's Voice more strongly than you admit."

"Every now and then, when Kodi speaks to me, I hear a doubled voice, not too different than when Rainwing laid her hands on me and spoke the Prophecy the first time."

The summer was growing late, but the weather was still warm. There were no incidents in their travels in this charming but lonely land. Hadon had fully recovered from his injuries and was strong again just as Shane had promised. This first night of camping he and Manwul took the first watch, followed by Rainwing and Maru, and finally by the two Etoppsi males who then awakened all as the sun rose.

"The dog beast is ready to move," said Stormgale. "We have not such creatures in Berug."

"They wouldn't like living in your stone towers, anyway," said Kodi. "But dogs are great workers. There are retrievers who help bow hunters retrieve small game, and shepherd breeds who work for sheep farmers, and hounds who help in big hunts locate prey, and the breeds are all different looking from each other. Shepherds have long hair, and the others have shorter hair. Some have long ears that flop down. Musca's breed are thick-coated, powerful war dogs from Eleni. They're bred specially to sniff out Ice Tribesmen and attack them in battle, and they can hunt like wolves do. You have wolves?"

"We do have wolves in the wilder parts of Berug."

They packed up quickly, stamped out their campfire and followed the Elentine Noble. Kodi and Stormgale marched together, and the Human explained much to the Etoppsis of dogs and horses and even cats kept for killing mice on farms and on ships. Certainly, Etoppsi were familiar with herd animals such as sheep and goats. There were also many large exotic creatures on the savannah lands of Berug. But they did not keep any furred animals as pets. Many did keep tropical birds as pets that originated from their southerly islands.

Flamefur flew above the trees twice that day, just to ensure they were still headed in the direction of the Ridge. But Kodi would not let him go any distance.

"It is much closer. There are a great many birds, too, flying in flocks to and fro. I have also seen raptors."

"Could you see the mountains beyond?" asked Curdoz.

"I could."

"They're haunted, they say," said Tiliruf. "That's what some really ancient tales tell, anyway."

"Haunted?" asked Lyndz. "In what way?"

"Ghosts," he replied with spooky emphasis.

Lyndz turned to Curdoz. "I don't really believe in ghosts. Do you know, Curdoz?"

He nodded. "It is the land of the mountains towards the west and northwest more particularly. It is the land of the gods. I have spoken to you of it before when we sailed on Guardian Lake. That land that leads beyond to Guardian Lake is difficult to approach, but explorers in the ancient past, and some Qeteral accounts too, describe what one might call 'apparitions.' Perhaps remnants of the gods' creative souls that appear and confuse. They can be terrifying, and so it is best avoided. Yet I believe they have no real power aside from how they may affect the minds of mortals..."

Shane interrupted. "Brother Curdoz, true. But there is also a theory that the gods are truly present there, as behind transparent, unbreachable veils. More, then, than remnants or apparitions."

"I have heard of that theory. But we must admit the evidence is limited. In any event, in the times before the Great War, their high city was located there. No one has ever found such a place, and I'm sure all is ruin, if not dust. I wonder what Vanaratu might say of it. But do you recall me telling you of Noromoray as we left Saundry? That is the northernmost point of that section of the Corellyan Mountains. And they are sometimes called the Haunted Mountains. And so again, that land is the land where upon a time long ago the gods dwelled, before the Great Rebellion, and before Meical's Second Coming when he entrapped the evil ones beyond the Dragon's Teeth and created a realm for the good ones beyond the Great Barrier in the Sea. To separate the gods from the Peoples of the Mold He came to understand was necessary. As we know, Siriné and Vanaratu disobeyed."

"I want to go there, and see these apparitions of the gods," said Kodi.

"You're mad," said Tiliruf.

"He is a naturally adventurous sort, isn't he? But be careful what you wish for," said Nikal, winking at Kodi. "Of course, we don't have any kind of time and won't be going so far."

"And then more northeasterly," continued Curdoz, "is the arm of the Imperial Range that leads to the Valley of the Gifted. Though one really cannot separate the Corellyan from the Imperial, as they connect. It's just that the Corellyan head off west, whereas most consider the Imperial as the north-south divide of the Northern Continent. Anyway, following the Conquest, some few Qeteral would travel on a path through the mountains and study in the Valley with Humans. Eventually, however, they grew disenchanted with Valley interpretations of the ancient writings in favor of granting the Guardian greater divinity and also struggled with the need for the Vows. And so, some three-hundred years ago they stopped traveling to the Valley and sending new Gifted. Yet they do continue their own Orders that include a Matrimonial and a Healer class, though they follow no Vows and are allowed to Bond. Yet Healing for Qeteral is more limited than it is for Humans. They never get sick, unless they be accidently poisoned, and their bodies heal rapidly on their own from the ordinary hurts of life. Healing is largely confined to those involved in more severe accidents. No doubt their bodies are charmed and more magical than that of either of the other two races. It may be that Qeteral and Humans more resemble each other in size and physical traits, but in other ways Etoppsi and Humans share more similarities of disposition and adventurousness. And as Shane pointed out yesterday, Humans average from seventy to ninety years, Etoppsi to a hundred or so, and the Qeteral to a hundred-sixty. What is interesting, according to legend, is that average range of death for Qeteral is extremely slim, within a handful of years of that hundred-sixty mark. They can tell when they will die within a year of doing so. Of course, they can be killed in battle, and many died in the Great War of the World God Rebellion. They afterwards learned their Barrier magic, and Siriné could not get to them centuries later during the Ralsheen Dark Times."

Lyndz had more to add. "And most have few children, one or two being the general rule. Yet they are capable of having as many as they wish, and some few couples do have more. Sometimes four generations or even five might live in the same home. The transition into adolescence and adulthood can vary but is usually several years later than in Humans. Humans in most cultures are considered adults at sixteen. But that's not the case for Qeteral, as it is more commonly twenty-nine, thirty or more before they are considered to be of independent age. Their men by tradition choose the moment of their manhood by proclaiming it to their family, and Bonding occurs only after this, usually in their thirties. There's much less variation in physical forms compared to Humans, and so their men are taller and stronger almost always, and do the harder labor, but when it comes to their art, both women and men do much of it together. Archery is common for both, and both hunt, and both garden. Their skin tone is copper brown, and their hair is black or brown, usually long, though it can be of various curl or straightness. Eye color can vary, but blue is most common."

"You learned a lot in those books," said Tiliruf. "What about the different classes?"

"They have noble families, and they have servants, but accumulation of wealth is not a strong value. Aside from a level of society engagement, nobles and commonfolk live quite similarly and commune readily without a big sense of privilege. Inter-Bonding of the classes is a little more common, as there is much interaction, more so than with Human noble families with commoners. The royal couple reign together as they do in Berug, though one specifically is elected from the royal family by the nobility, so it isn't always the oldest son. If he or she is a son, daughter, granddaughter, or grandson of an earlier reigning couple they are eligible for election. They choose whom they perceive to be the wisest and best leader. Then the spouse reigns in partnership. At least that's the way they used to do it long ago."

"It will not have changed," said Curdoz. "Qeteral live as they have lived for the last thousand years and rarely does tradition change among them. They are not noted for experimenting with the new. As a race, they do not like change. It's one reason why they did not often allow Humans to visit them. They do not like their pot being stirred."

"Some will not appreciate our coming," said Shane. "Yet many will be curious. Some will be wary of us and keep a distance and may not even speak to us, whereas I suspect curiosity will get the better of most and will demonstrate welcome."

"I agree," said Curdoz. "Curiosity is common of all the races, even if the Qeteral inherit much skepticism of Humans. They will also be immensely curious of our Etoppsi friends."

"As I am of the Qeteral," said Rainwing.

"Which reminds me," said Nikal, "the presence of the Qeteral dragon rider in Berug and the presence of enslaved Qeteral at all...that information is to be divulged only through the talks with their leadership. Do not speak of it otherwise, as it will be a great shock, I believe. Flamefur will surely be called upon to describe what he saw and what he learned at Eye Tower Fifty-Five. A big reason we chose him to come, of course."

"Yes, sir."

"And because he's funny, eh? That's why I would've picked him, anyways."

"That's true, too," said Kodi.

"And just why did you pick me as the other, Polemarch?" asked Stormgale, displaying interest in his furred face.

"Because your Eyefeather experience was the best, and because I like you and your strong values, that's why."

"Thank you, sir."

"The two of you make a contrasting pair, I must say," said Shane. "Lord Kodi was smart in his thinking."

"Is that true," asked Flamefur, "that our perceived 'differences'..."

"...influenced my choice, absolutely," concluded Kodi. "You represent different perspectives on living as Etoppsi males, and it's a good thing. And Rainwing's the scholarly female, though I didn't have to choose her. She was part of the package."

"Part of the package?" said Rainwing with annoyance.

"Just a phrase, Rainy," said Kodi.

"RAINY!"

"Stormy, Rusty, Rainy, what of it, eh?" said Tiliruf.

"Uh," mouthed Kodi, perceiving a sudden strong need to backtrack. "Will drop that nickname in your case as of this instant."

"Have you been calling me *Rainy* in your private conversations?" Her face turned severe.

"What makes you think we talk about you at all, eh?" goaded Tiliruf.

"Shut up, Tiliruf, buddy. And the only right answer is 'heck no, Rainwing.'" Kodi winked at Tiliruf but made sure Rainwing didn't see that.

Still skeptical, she addressed Tiliruf's bodyguards. "You there, Manwul and Hadon, do you call me that when you chat?"

"Heck no, Rainwing," they replied in unison, displaying upon their faces what could be seen as a good rendition of shock at being so wrongfully accused.

"Do we have to add back in, *Of Green Isle?"* pressed Tiliruf.

Before Nikal could speak, Shane did.

"Why press the issue when she clearly doesn't like it, 'a Terianh?" he asked softly.

"I...I wouldn't tease her if I didn't like her. Honestly, that's the truth." Tiliruf then blinked several times as Shane continued to look at him. "But maybe it's wrong to expect everyone to respond to humor the same. Sorry, Rainwing. I don't think I understood how needling it must seem when I do it."

Curdoz raised an eyebrow.

Rainwing in her turn also blinked. "I know there can be fun in a certain amount of banter. It doesn't always bother me. It's just that dropping the 'wing' part of my name is kind of hurtful, because it's the only wing I have left. Mother chose my name with much thought. Why should I expect you to think as an Etoppsis does?"

"Oh! Of course, eh? It would be hurtful, I see now." In fact, Tiliruf did a short bow.

"And it was Kodi who said it first," added Rainwing with a puckered brow in Kodi's direction.

"Yeah, trust me, I'm fifty times sorrier 'n Tiliruf, just now," said he.

Nikal, Manwul, Lyndz, and Hadon chuckled quietly under their collective breath. But nary a soul, as long as Rainwing lived, entertained that short-lived nickname ever again.

The land changed as late afternoon approached. Rocky brooks were crossed. Along the brooks were broad-leaved azaleas. Boulders and low-lying rock shelters defined more of the landscape. The great trees, however, continued.

"I've seen more birds the last half hour," offered Maru.

She wasn't the only one who noticed the birds. They would drop down from the heights of the trees and flutter and sing in the undergrowth. Then they would fly back into the heights and disappear.

"I would speculate the Qeteral know we are here," said Curdoz. "It is well-known birds are used as scouts by the Qeteral. I have often wondered how far afield they go to gather information."

"And they haven't stopped us with that Barrier Magic, and we're nearly at the ridge of the Plateau. Musca still has a trail, though," said Kodi.

One more night they camped, and Kodi and Nikal stayed awake with Curdoz debating the signs back at shore from two days previously.

"I believe strongly it was Qeteral," said Nikal. "It's as though they had tried to build a ship maybe two decades past. But I can't imagine it would be for the purposes of revamping a fishing industry as in centuries past."

"What types of ships could they build?"

"Combination sailing, rowing. Galleys and the like, not so unlike the Khestadone and older Anterianhi make. They learned from Humans in Lintiri who traded with them. It is a less-advanced method, of course, compared to modern caravels and galleons, but still useful, all-in-all."

As morning approached, they were surrounded by the sounds of many songbirds.

"It's lovely," offered Ulna. "It reminds me of the Island."

"For my part, I don't like being reminded of that place, eh?"

"Neither do I, Tiliruf," said Rainwing. "We agree on that one. But we should not fault the birds."

"No, we shouldn't," said Nikal. "Let us pack and go. Manwul, what is your estimation as to how far we've traveled from the shore?"

"Fourteen leagues, sir."

"Not counting the birds, we've seen no animals aside from squirrels," said Kodi. "I'm having to give Musca some of the store. Otherwise, in this kind of setting he'd be night-hunting. He's been sleeping like a log next to Nikal and me."

But the beast was again raring to go, and they followed for a third day. And he paid no attention to any birds.

Nevertheless, the amount of twittering, whistling, and calling amongst the undergrowth and trees increased greatly. It made the forest feel alive, almost magical. None could walk with a frown.

Sometime in the early afternoon, Musca, oddly, stopped and sat upon his haunches. He whimpered.

Kodi called a halt. "He's curious about something."

"I see nothing, eh?"

"Be still, everyone," said Nikal. "The birds have stopped singing. Draw no weapons unless I say."

In fact, all around them was a stony silence.

Suddenly, Musca barked loudly. Then, a sound like soft singing was audible. It began somewhere from the left of where they stood. It was warm. It included variations in a low pitch, melodic, yet without rhythmic cadence. It traveled as if on a breeze among the trees. Musca lay down. He whimpered again. His tail wagged a little. The singing stopped.

"That's his friendly whimper. When someone he knows comes for a visit."

"You know the communication of animals, Human?" said a masculine voice in front of them. "I find that difficult to believe."

Most jumped out of their skin, as there was no indication otherwise than direction whence the voice came.

Fearless Kodi spoke out. "I know this animal, as he has been a companion for some years, and so I am used to his manner."

"You are the Human called Kodi?" The voice was deep, but it seemed accusing and skeptical in tone.

All were surprised.

"And how do you know my name, sir? Do you hide behind a tree?"

"As for your name, the queen my mother has told me of it. She imprinted an image of your Human face into my mind. I do not hide. You just cannot see me. Because you are a Human."

"As a matter of fact, yes, I am," said Kodi, undaunted. "And I presume by your words you are a prince of the land of Ulakel, but I have no need to tell you that you are a Qeteral, four times now. As I presume from all you say, it was your mother the queen whom I saw in my Vision in the spring. We have been taught that you have magic of invisibility. Yet we have come, as you well must know, in peace. I charge the queen's son to show himself."

"You choose to be rude, Hurlin," said another softer voice, also distinctly male. "Be not so. Honor our mother's wishes. It is to greet them and lead them home for which reason we have come."

Just then this second man who was speaking showed himself, as the last of his words could be seen coming forth from his mouth. Immediately to his left another man appeared. Then, remarkably, all around the acre in front of the party many individuals, both male and female appeared. As they did so, forest birds would land on arm or shoulder of some of them and perch, as if tamed to do so. At least twenty persons stood before them. All held bows with arrows ready, though none were aimed.

Every individual had smooth, rich brown skin. All had dark hair, shoulder-length or longer, of varying thickness, straightness, or curl. The men were fully exposed above the waist and below the knee, and not a one was less than six feet in height with well-formed muscle from calf to shoulder. The women were uniformly shorter by some inches, though also fit in build, and in addition to a half pant of different cut than the men, each wore a loose, linen, open shirt that exposed their curves. Every individual was...

"They are beautiful to behold," said Maru.

"Damned good-looking bunch," said Manwul.

"Most gorgeous lot I ever saw," agreed Hadon.

Kodi blinked, and then stood forward, took a knee, and bowed. "I am Kodi of the House of Fothemry from the Kingdom of Solanto. We have come to seek the woman from my Vision from Meical the Guardian."

"They pronounce His name, Myghal, Lord Kodi," spoke Curdoz, who also stepped forward and introduced himself. "Myghal the Divine. I am called Curdoz, High Sage of the Guardian of the Orders of...Myghal, to the Kingdom of Solanto. I too had a Vision in the winter in which many of your people appeared to me, and so our coming to you is directed by the Guardian on High."

"You are a Sage of the Guardian? A Messenger from the Valley of the Gifted? I've always wanted to go there!"

It had been, according to Lyndz' observation, the second man to drop his invisibility magic, standing next to the first. Along with that little detail, she also recorded the following:

He was gorgeous. His face was youthful, expressive, with inviting blue eyes. He was younger than the others who greeted us. He could on occasion demonstrate a flirtatious quality: a cheeky half-smile and the sort of knowing, raised eyebrow. A confident charm, but he was nothing more nor less than polite to everyone, the perfect gentleman. His black hair was shoulder-length and wavy. His exposed shoulders, chest and abdomen were of statuesque perfection, and as I almost immediately noticed, sported faint lines of dark hair on his torso. A hint of fine dark hair created sideburns almost on his face. Though all present were exotic and lovely, he stood out. It was plain to me, and shocking to realize, he was...

"He's part Human!" she came up and whispered quietly in Curdoz' ear. "And I suspect young compared to the others."

Curdoz stared for a moment, awestruck at the truth of the observation, and then replied. "Yes, young man. And what is your name."

"I am Lumin. It is my brother Hurlin who spoke to you first, and then my brother Olin here."

"Your mother is the queen and has three sons?"

"Yes, exactly! And a daughter, my sister. She is not here, though. We have a bigger family than anyone I know!"

"You provide too much information, young brother," said the first voice, that of Hurlin. He stood a little apart from his brothers. Though handsome, tall and lordly, Hurlin's face was less friendly than almost all the other faces there.

Olin, the other brother, the one who showed himself first of all, was also handsome. His face was not unfriendly, nor did it contain the eager and friendly smile of that of the youngest brother. He spoke again. "He has given no secrets, Hurlin. Be patient."

Hurlin did not respond but instead turned his focus in the direction of the giant Etoppsi males. He actually bowed to them, though he had not done so to anyone else. "We are honored that you seek us out, Sky Kings. Our scouts relayed to us your coming."

"We are grateful for your greeting," offered Flamefur in a loud, rumbling voice. "I am Flamefur, and this is Stormgale, of the Berugian Sky Front. Allow me also to introduce my teacher, Noble Rainwing of Green Isle, friend and advisor to our Queen Silverwing. She has ambassadorial status and represents our kingdom."

When Rainwing stood forward, there was a gasp among the Qeteral.

"You...you..." said Hurlin, clearly stunned.

"Have no wings. It is true. Yet I am an Etoppsi female, nonetheless." Though she didn't do so, she might easily have added *and don't ever forget it, you young cock.*

"Noble Rainwing lost her wings in great sacrifice," said Nikal. He stood forward. "She and others were required to sacrifice something of great value in order that we might gain this."

When he uncloaked the Eagle Staff, all faces among the Qeteral displayed various levels of shock, and there was much murmuring among them.

"The Staff!" exclaimed Lumin excitedly. "The Eagle Staff of Terianh the Great! Can you believe it?"

"It comes home!" said Olin. "Mother did not speak of it to us!"

"She may not have known, as it did not appear in my Vision," said Kodi.

"Its seeking came by way of Myghalian Prophecy," said Curdoz. "Another tale."

"Who, then, wields the Great Staff?" asked Hurlin.

"Two of us do," said Kodi, plainly. "Prince Nikal and myself."

"You are the Prince Nikal of Nant?" Hurlin then bowed to Nikal, who was holding the Staff. "We have heard of you, yes! But...but *two* War Wizards? Are...are you certain of this?"

"Yes," said Nikal simply. "We both wield the magic of the Staff."

Hurlin looked back and forth between Kodi and Nikal. He stepped forward. "I wish to touch it."

Nikal nodded and held out the Staff.

"Come, Olin. Come Lumin. Such a strange thing, that a Staff should return to Ulakel. Though we knew, of course, that it still existed." He glanced in Curdoz' direction. "Another tale. That is if the queen chooses to tell it."

The three brothers came forward, and all watched as they handled the Staff, its eagle, moon, and rod.

"It breathes," said Olin after a few moments.

"Of course, it does," said Hurlin.

"What do you mean?" asked Kodi.

"If you are a wielder of the Staff then you would know."

"It is alive, if that's what you mean, yes. It grows hot and vibrates at my touch and speaks to my innermost thoughts when I wield it."

Hurlin looked at him with a sort of patronizing smile but said nothing more. After a few moments his eyes shifted left. He plainly noticed Shane's black skin and eyed him closely for a moment. Then just beyond Shane, he noticed Tiliruf for the first time. As he eyed Tiliruf's eagle medallions and embroiders, his face went to surprise. And then it seemed almost to curl into a sneer. Abruptly he pivoted to his brother Olin. "You will offer all the courtesies. I find I need to step back a little. If you wish to continue the greetings and answer questions, I will not interfere. I've seen enough."

And to everyone's great shock, Hurlin stalked off to a point somewhat beyond the other waiting Qeteral, and he too, waited.

Olin frowned in the direction of his brother but then turned around and took charge. Yet he offered no apologies.

"In my mother's name, I welcome you," he said in a quiet voice. "Lord Kodi, you are correct that it was my mother who saw you in a Vision from the Divine Myghal. Prince Nikal, your name has been heard among us, for we gather some news of the world through the birds and other means. We are aware of your policy to protect the waters that lead to our home. I'm sure my mother will have gracious words for you. Lord Sage, a time may come when I would like to sit with you over a cup of mead and question you on...theological matters?"

"I would be most honored to engage in such conversation, with the understanding we may enjoy the mead and be friendly to one another and yet possibly not agree on all points?"

"Surely."

"How should we properly address you, the princes?"

"Spare us the Human phrase, 'Your Highness,' but otherwise address us according to other custom."

"The same likewise to me, Prince Olin," said Nikal.

"That is a gracious enough address, and yet feel free to call us by our names alone when we gather for friendly conversation."

He turned to Shane. "Your name, sir?"

Shane nodded deeply. "I am Essav Shanna Soor, but am known by my diminutive, *Shane,* or *Brother Shane*. I am a Healer in the Orders, sir."

"I admit I was not expecting to meet an Eastern Human. Your appearance is indeed striking. Of course, the appearance of any Human or Etoppsi in Ulakel is, shall we say, out of the ordinary. Welcome, Healer Shane. We have one Healer in our village, Solone, who will be most intrigued to meet a Human Healer. I will ensure the two of you meet."

"Thank you, Prince Olin. That is very kind."

Olin then turned to Tiliruf and bowed deeply. "My brother is not impressed, but I say your signs are worthy ones, son of the emperor. My mother will be greatly pleased to meet you, as am I. May I grip your hand in greeting, *A' Terianh,* of the High House of the Eagle?"

"Thank you for the gracious words, yet the honor is mine to meet a prince of Ulakel." Tiliruf said this with perfect unforced grace. "I am known as Tiliruf. The last emperor was my great-grandfather."

"If you will permit me to indulge a viewpoint, Zarelio's abdication was a grave mistake and has done great damage to the intercourse between our two peoples. You, of course, cannot be blamed. Your presence, however, will provide much thought amongst many, Lord Tiliruf. I presume since you wear the Eagle that you are truly the heir to his legacy? To that of Terianh the Great, whom all honor? And yet it is not you who bears his Staff, I see."

Shane spoke, "His father, Master Genehbro of the High House of Terianh, dwells still in Tirilorin. Tiliruf is his only son and indeed the last heir and designated so by his father. I can assure you the blood of imperial Terianh flows through this one's veins. It should not be presumed he would bear the Staff, as Myghal took the Staff from Terianh at the end of the Anterianhi Conquest and had it hidden away."

Olin nodded. "You are correct. I should not be presumptive, as Myghal the Divine makes His own choices, and always the right ones. The Staff did not belong to Terianh but was a temporary gift. In a way, the Staff cannot be owned, as it truly is alive."

"Tiliruf, Prince Olin, is the greatest swordsman and knight of the modern era, of talent directly descended from Terianh himself. He is a hero, though he is not a boastful one. A description of our recent battle with the Alkhaness can wait."

At the mention of the Alkhaness, Olin's face grew dark. "Give her not her self-imposed title. She is but a witch who enslaves and murders."

"I agree," said Tiliruf.

Olin's face returned to calm. He then faced Nikal. "You will find I am typically the quiet one of the three brothers." He winked at Lumin. "Should a rapport develop between you and Hurlin, I suggest that would be...wise. He has a strong following among the nobles. He will respect *you,* Prince Nikal. That is certain."

"You...are making to me a suggestion of sorts."

"I am. And of the Etoppsi, whom it is difficult not to admire with their strongly disciplined culture. Engage him, do. You should understand that Hurlin's, shall we call it 'attitude,' towards you as Humans is not atypical. Like him I myself am not impressed with much of Human history, and much of Human nature I find...disconcerting. There is no reason to suspect anything less than graciousness on my mother's part. Myghal is the Divine Mover of events. We wish not to hinder Him. It seems He obliges you to a task? And so, therefore, we will do all as He requires. Perhaps I say too much, however."

"What you say and imply is not far from what we expected," said Curdoz. "Your self-imposed protection has had its effectiveness over the many centuries. We have not come with any ill intentions whatsoever, but, as you say, are following what we believe to be the will of Myghal."

"My mother certainly believes that, and therefore so do I."

"You mention only your mother. What of your father, the king?"

At that, Olin paused and breathed deeply. Lumin looked down.

"Our father was king for a short time alongside my elected mother. Now he dances the stars. It is a tale of sadness you must learn, but my mother should be the one to make it known to you. It seems likely his tale is closely connected to your coming, but allow that to be determined in council."

Curdoz bowed, then lifted his hand in blessing. "May all his children prosper."

Both Olin and Lumin nodded.

"Thank you, Messenger of Myghal," said Olin. "Now I believe I have presented sufficiently certain expectations. We will treat you honorably while you remain among us, of course. Let us indulge a little more in...mutual curiosity. My brother Lumin and I wish to meet all of your party!"

Kodi nodded and next introduced Lyndz.

"Twins!" exclaimed Lumin with surprise. "Humans have litters?"

Kodi and Lyndz both chuckled.

Curdoz spoke. "What an extraordinary observation, young Prince Lumin. It would truly be odd should either the Etoppsi or the Qeteral have more than one topling or child at a time. It simply does not happen in your world. Twins and even triplets do occur among Humans, but they are not so common as to not be of some interest. Certainly, as twins they are special."

"I see! Lord Kodi, would you mind showing me that hand grip Lord Tiliruf did with Olin?" Lumin certainly seemed intrigued by Kodi, and his eyes shifted often towards him.

Kodi, with a great big smile on his face complied. "There! And be a brother to me, as in the spirit of Myghal!"

"Yes! I want to get to know you and Lord Tiliruf and all the rest of you, if I may!"

It wasn't that Lumin was a child, as he was not. He was tall and handsome as described, with a fully formed man's body. His movements were graceful. The smile on his face wasn't remotely silly or overly playful. He was generally soft-spoken. He did not demand to be humored. In some ways his curiosity was on the level of Kodi's, and plucky in social manner likewise. He was young and not young. Sometimes he displayed the excitement of a boy, but as a man often subtle. His blue eyes held much depth.

"Of course!" said Kodi. "And we want to get to know you. I don't think I will call you anything but Lumin, and I don't ever want you calling me anything but Kodi."

"Drop titles for me, too, Lumin, eh?"

"Well, that's easy!"

"Prince Lumin, how old are you, if you don't mind me asking," said Lyndz.

"I am twenty-four. And you, m'lady?"

"Kodi and I are nineteen."

"That seems strange to me," said Lumin. "You seem older than I. Like thirty or so! But yes, Humans are so young. Your names are easy ones, too, Kodi and Lyndz. They could even be Ulaki."

Kodi felt confident to ask the unasked question. "Lyndz and I reckon you have Human blood in you, Lumin. Is it true?"

"It is! You can tell! Olin, they can tell!"

Olin nodded. "His father's father was Human. No doubt he will tell you that story."

"He was your grandfather, too!"

Olin again winked at Lumin. It was plain there was a bond between the two. "Of course, my brother. But his features show more in you, as you know quite well."

"It must be the hair, Lumin," said Tiliruf with his own wink and a nod, pointing to the dark line down Lumin's torso and then rubbing his own cheeks as if demonstrating whiskers.

"Others refuse to tease me for it, you know," said Lumin with some wittiness and a grin.

"That would be because you are the son of the queen," said Tiliruf. "Kodi and I'll tease you for it, if it's all the same to you. You'll have to tell us all about your family."

"You're very handsome, Lumin."

"Thank you, m'lady. That is very kind of you. As are you. You're one of the most beautiful women I ever saw."

"Thank you, Lumin. What a kind compliment," said Lyndz.

"Yet you do wear a lot of clothing. Though I knew it from books. Are Humans so cold-natured?"

Kodi laughed. "Trust me, Lumin. We are not cold just now. It has been a hot hike!"

It was true no hair was visible on Olin or Hurlin, nor on any other Qeteral in the party. Yet the Human maleness was quite plain in Lumin. And as they all understood as they grew to know the Qeteral over the next many days...

Lumin was both very, very Qeteral, and very, very Human.

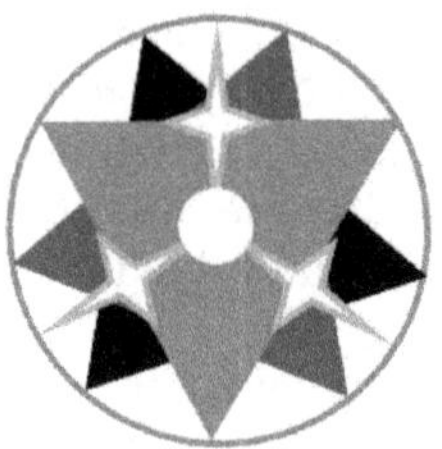

Chapter 14—First Impressions

They were to camp one more night, near to a small stream that plunged down in a series of cataracts from the heights of the Plateau. The Qeteral had created a camp here in advance for the purpose of providing hospitality for the guests. A troupe of ponies, untied and unconcerned, wandered nearby. These had brought all the accouterments for the camp and were meant also to carry the visitors' baggage up to the Plateau the next day. Prepared campfires were now lit, foods were unwrapped, and containers of fresh water and mead were made available. The stream paused here in a pool of clean water, and the Human men were particularly eager to wash and present themselves to their hosts in the best light possible. None had bathed properly since Danzilet.

"You hesitate to bathe alongside your men?" asked a Qeteral woman by the name of Mishoo. "I have read this of your people, but it seems odd."

She, along with two others, Halta and Frith, had attached themselves as escorts to Lyndz, Rainwing, and Mother Idamé. Mishoo especially had the aura of a leader. Others had walked and talked alongside Ulna and Maru. All these women were now camped close together, warming foods on little fires and sharing with one another. The men were separate, though nearby, a little closer to the river.

Before Idamé could reply through her obvious shock at the question, Lyndz spoke.

"It's true we could use a good bath, too, friend Mishoo! But we will wait for the men to finish and then go ourselves before it gets too dark. Interesting you should bring up the subject, as we've discussed some of these same cultural expectations with Rainwing in the past. It's common for Human men and women to swim and bathe separately, as it's considered cultural modesty to avoid nakedness in mixed-gender company. There are subtleties, as men tend to be less modest than women," she chuckled, "particularly in packs. I understand this is not the case among your kind, am I right?"

"It is natural to enjoy the company of one's own gender, and we often separate for a variety of social activities, or talk, just as we are doing now, or work tasks," said Frith. "But not always for swimming. All swim together beginning when we're children. We have many swimming places and swim or bathe together most days. Yet there are certain constraints, too, for us. A lone man and woman would not do so together unless they are committed to Bonding."

"Of course, and that's certainly the same for us. So perhaps when we come to your village and are at ease we should do differently?"

"Lyndz, dear..."

"Now, Mother Idamé!" interrupted Maru. "If you say 'it isn't seemly' one more time, I swear! If Lady Lyndz wishes to join with them in their ways of doing things, you must not interfere. You promised her you wouldn't. So, Frith and Mishoo, if I understand what you mean, there's little concern at the swimming places? The erotic element is absent?"

"No concern," said Mishoo. "We only enjoy the pleasure of the water and the sun on our skin, of the company, and can admire the physical qualities of both men and women without the sort of embarrassment that you imply. I would not say the erotic is entirely absent from the mind, and a young woman might see a man whose physical form appeals to her, which may lead later to introductions and courting. But such thoughts are largely tertiary, as there are children and elderly at the village bathing places, too. It is meant to be an informal social occasion with an element of play, especially so when many children are about. It is not the proper place or time for displaying erotic intentions."

"That men and women can bathe in such company together and largely dismiss erotic thoughts is probably easier than Human propriety would admit," said Ulna, matter-of-factly.

"So, the tradition of separation during bathing has evolved for you Humans? Perhaps it was not that way in the ancient past?" suggested Halta.

"Yes, I think that to be the case," said Lyndz. "In the western countries, I know, anyway. Yet in some measure, that the tradition is retained in our culture today has some value. Though it varies greatly from one Human country to another, men are more dominant in the social and political structure in the western countries and largely act with a greater sense of privilege. Some Human men can be too forward in how they view women and might allow their minds to be inflamed by the uncovered body. Trust me that I do not mean any of the men in our company would dare act without deep thought. They are disciplined among ladies. Only my brother Kodi and Tiliruf are, as Humans might say, 'eligible' anyway, as Manwul and Hadon have life-mates, and the rest have taken the Vow of Chastity for the Orders."

"The Nantian prince, too? He has taken a Vow as have the Valley-trained?"

Lyndz struggled with the answer and looked at Idamé.

Who took the cue. "Of a certain kind, dear Halta. He is subject to certain constraints that will not allow him to... consider a stray woman at a swimming hole." And in order to veer the subject away, she added, "You know, that sweet Manwul has a child on the way. Hadon will Bond his life-mate soon, I think. Such dears."

Halta looked at Idamé with a kind smile. "You have a warm demeanor, m'lady. It is appropriate, then, to call you *Mother?*"

"Please, dear. It is a title, but for many in my position it is also an endearment."

"I will, then! Yet I must admit you remind me a little of my grandmother. She is a Bondswoman, as are you."

"Oh, you must introduce us, Halta. I would so like to learn the traditions of your Bondswomen! Do you think she would allow me to attend a Bonding Ceremony?"

"I know she would. Her name is Vitalle. I look forward to introducing you!"

"Lady Lyndz," said Mishoo, who regarded Lyndz with deep interest. As were the other Qeteral women, Mishoo was leaning back on the ground with her shirt untied. The linen fabric lay idly across her mostly exposed brown breasts. None could truly be bothered by Qeteral exposure, for their beauty was so natural, in a way not so unlike Etoppsi. Their superb bodies fit into the natural order of the woods and rivers, sky and earth. Mishoo also had wisdom written in her face. They later discovered she was of noble blood with connections to the royal family. "This...*dominance* of the Human men. Do you feel as though you are being manipulated by their sense of privilege? Are they...dragging you along?"

"No, not at all. It is true that up to this point in our journey we have been in more of a role of following. Yet understand, we all of us believe we are following the will of Myghal. But we have contributed in our adventures according to our talents." She then looked at Maru and the others as they listened to her explanation. Maru nodded encouragingly to her. Lyndz looked about, then lowered her voice. "As has my brother and the Lord Curdoz, Mother Idamé and myself have each of us had our own unique Visions from Myghal, and Rainwing has received a Prophecy. There will come a time soon in which...there may be a parting of the ladies from the group, based on Myghal's instructions."

"You could use more training, then, in the arts of defense?" Mishoo suggested with great discernment. "There will be danger involved in your task?"

Even Rainwing raised an eyebrow. "She could use more training, true. My ways of movement and fighting are not the ways of the smaller races."

Ulna spoke. "Mishoo, what is needed is a level of secrecy. Lyndz has received some good training back in Danzilet based on her insistence. But none of our men need to know the particulars as to why she presses for it, as they would act protectively and question us. They are not in the know as to the elements of Lyndz' Vision, as she was directed by the Divine not to tell the men. Mother Idamé has not told all of her Vision to the men, either. And Maru and I could use a bit of training, too."

Mishoo's eyes puckered as she took this in. She then leaned up and with determined expression looked around at the group. "I can make that happen. I detect for me a Calling from the Divine in this. Your presence among us speaks to me keenly, Lady Lyndz. This has all happened for a purpose based on the workings of the Divine. The Matriarch intends for all you ladies to be housed at the palace, while your menfolk will have a pavilion at the edge of our village. The separation by space and activities could work to our advantage, I think. I shall speak to the Matriarch and to Princess Ryn on the matter. They'll keep it close."

All those in the circle nodded as though they were acknowledging a new secret pact between them.

There was some laughter and commotion at the riverside.

"The men appear to be finished, ladies. Let us go down to our own delightful bathe, shall we?"

"We will join you, Lady Lyndz!" exclaimed Frith.

"Oh, yes! Let us have a bit of our own fun, ladies. Maru, can you find the lavender oil soaps we bought in Danzilet? Isn't Solvermoon bright this eve?"

Rainwing tssked at the renewal of the use of the word, *ladies*. "I prefer the term *females.*"

Mishoo nodded, regarding Rainwing and her words. "I like the philosophy behind your thinking, Noble Rainwing. The word represents better the powers and prowess of the Cosmic Feminine. Let it be so among us."

Rainwing smiled hugely. "I knew I would like your kind very much."

Most stayed awake well into the night as Solvermoon did his weaving dance between the stars and wispy clouds. The three races, Human, Etoppsi, and Qeteral, made strides in communicating with one another. It was surely a rare moment not witnessed for centuries.

Only Prince Hurlin retained a kind of aloofness, and together with two or three other Qeteral men they set their own camp at the outer edge of the larger group. Nikal decided now was as good a time as any; he took Olin's advice and approached the eldest brother prince, sat by him on the ground, and created conversation. Hurlin demonstrated some graciousness by having one of the others pour out for them some golden mead into two silver cups, who at a nod from Hurlin then left the two princes alone in their conversation.

Hurlin often skirted directly answering questions as if there were need to retain secretiveness, yet he did not pursue additional distance in mannerism. He respectfully nodded to Nikal as the latter offered information as to the current war and recent battle with the Alkhaness. It was plain the Qeteral prince was absorbing this news. He finally offered a compliment of sorts aimed in Nikal's direction.

"It seems of the Human countries, Nant alone retains somewhat the discipline of the former empire, an attempt, at least, at retaining a semblance of strength that the Divine Myghal expected of Humans when he established Terianh on the imperial throne."

"I would agree that our policies of a strong military and protection of the trade routes from the southern threat are meant to fill a void, with the resulting trade networks maintaining a level of social unity among the Human constituents of the former empire. There is still the connection also to the Orders of the Guardian, and each country retains a Sage. Barant, however, went its own way long ago, even before Zarelio's Abdication."

"Yes, and Barant will present itself as a threat in your future I strongly suspect. And in the resulting weakness from the Abdication, even Nant has not yet been able to restrain the southern Human powers, your Alkhan and Alkhaness."

"I'm not so sure we have ever considered those two as mere Humans." Nikal was bothered by Hurlin so deliberately oversimplifying the history.

"I understand they have dark magic, of course, but what other race of being did you expect them to be, Nikal?"

Nikal looked intently at Hurlin. He did not respond to this bit of baiting but took a sip from the silver cup and veered the subject. "In what way, Prince Hurlin, have you heard my name? Your brother gives me specific credit for the policy of protecting the routes to the Lintiri Sea. Nantians have attempted to reach you before, as I'm sure you must be aware, with the hopes of coordinating policy and retaining good relations with your people."

"There is no need for such coordination. For your oversight of the Bay and for keeping most at a distance from our borders, we thank you." After a short pause, maybe Hurlin realized his words were too dismissive, because he then modified. "Though the Human beard seems strange to look upon, you have sincerity behind it and depth in your eyes, Prince Nikal, and I am, for my part, honored to meet *you*. Suffice it to say that by way of the flora, fauna, and airs and waters and earth, the leadership of my people are able with our gifts to discover certain generalities beyond our borders and a few details as well. The simple answer is that your name is known in the world. As the Divine chooses only Humans, or in the case of Berug the Magnificent, Etoppsi, to wield the magic of a Staff, made by my people, it makes sense to me He chose one such as yourself. For my part I am indeed sorry that the evils of your Human world have led to the current need for a War Wizard. The Empire had a chance to press its advantage after the defeat of the southern powers following your Lintiri War but did not do so. The khans' magic was more limited then than it is now. Yet, I detect much honor in you, Nikal, and what history we know of you seems to prove it."

There were compliments and non-compliments in the Qeteral prince's words. It was plain he adhered to a philosophy that each race was solely responsible for itself, a sort of universalized separation, a degree to which Nikal doubted the Molding of the three races was ever meant to go. Nikal believed rather that Ulakel's isolation was itself error. Maintenance of the magical Barrier made sense when under threat, as the Qeteral especially, with their slow reproduction rates, could ill afford the loss of life associated with a big war. A few major battles would nearly wipe out their whole race. Of course, they should use magic to defend themselves. Absolutely. But Nikal also took strongly to old imperial notions that the more numerous Humans, with their fighting instincts and stronger military should strive to protect their Qeteral brethren, hence his own policy to guard the routes into the Lintiri Sea from both the curious and also the pirates in the employ of the southern khans. For the Qeteral to avoid all contact then with the peaceful Human countries appeared to be a form of racist pride. The fact the empire divided into its constituent realms and the emperor's Abdication were just excuses used for isolationism by a conservative people. Were they all like Hurlin, though?

Possibly, Hurlin represented older ways, because at least here and now, based on their queen's Vision, he and his people were attempting a welcome. In a time of genuine war, too, for that matter. It seemed likely as not that Hurlin was letting off a bit of steam due to prejudices challenged by new action under his mother. Therefore, Nikal was determined not to argue the politics and took deliberate hold of the good pieces. He raised his cup. "Then I look forward to you and I getting to know one another in the short time we are here among you and your good people. What is your mother the queen's name?"

"She is the Matriarch Gwyn. It is appropriate for you and your people to address her as 'Madam Matriarch' or as 'Queen Gwyn.' She is the granddaughter of the former monarchs, and daughter of Prince Hakonn and Princess Linea, my grandparents. All of them still live and provide much counsel to my mother. My great-grandparents abdicated around the time of Lumin's birth, as that is more our custom in comparison to Human kingdoms where it is more typical for your monarch to rule until death. Hakonn is focused on scholarly pursuits, and his art, and was not interested in ruling, though he trained and educated my mother should she be elected from among the royal kin, which she was. I, and my brothers, too, study with him."

"And your mother Bonded the half-Human."

Hurlin paused, drank a little from his cup, then nodded. "I'm sure the bloodline must seem curious to you, yes. He was born to a noblewoman, my paternal grandmother who still lives. Knowing of your imminent arrival, my mother sent for her to come stay a while at court. She will tell you the story of the Human to whom she Bonded, and my mother will relay to you that of their son my father."

"Do you remember them well, your Human forebears?"

"The Human died years before I was born. I was fifteen, Lumin the youngest, four, when our half-Human father left Ulakel. He...attempted a mission. He died in his failure."

"You imply the mission was hopeless?"

"No. I make plain the mission failed because of my father."

Nikal raised a high eyebrow. He suspected something. "Do all agree with your interpretation of those events?"

A snide smile showed on Hurlin's otherwise handsome face. "I'm sure young Lumin might interpret the story as one of heroism, and perhaps he is not the only one, so, no. You do have some discerning shrewdness, Nikal. The Divine Guardian must think highly of you, of course. I myself am not so keen on my Human bloodline and consider it error for the different races to Bond."

"Stories say there is other Human blood in your history."

The snide look left Hurlin, but he did not smile. "It is not denied, that is true. Most of the noble families have a Human in their ancestral lines. Always a Human man. An adventurer who was welcomed into our land. Never has a Qeteral man Bonded a Human woman."

"Interesting. There was genuine love in those Bondings, I would think, or they would not have come to pass."

Hurlin looked unhappily at Nikal. "Maybe."

"It is not my desire to make you uncomfortable, Hurlin, only to discover a little more of the history of your peoples and your culture. We are considered Brethren races, slightly apart from our Etoppsi kin, due to our many similarities in looks and body structure. Our two peoples share so much, and you took on Anterianhi language from Humans centuries ago as part of the unity following the Ralsheen Downfall. I think that says a lot. In far ancient times your people taught us much about agriculture. You helped stabilize and civilize our wandering, nomadic race. But particularly, recent history may play into the reason behind which we have come? Do you not think that is a possibility?"

"My mother and good Olin do indeed think so, as they believe it relates to my father's failed mission. I will retain my viewpoint until we all meet in council with my mother. Until now she has admittedly kept much to herself. That, of course, is her prerogative."

Nikal nodded. In the near distance he heard Kodi's laughter as he, along with Tiliruf and the rest, were engaging with Lumin, Olin and others. He decided to change the subject a little. "It is plain you and your brothers are close."

There was a hint of unforced smile. "Surely. Family. Our sister is Ryn. Her birth falls after mine and Olin's. Lumin was born years later. Yes, of course, we have great love between us. Lumin both annoys and charms. He is young. I hope he isn't...I hope he doesn't..." He paused and looked up in the direction of the laughter.

"Have no worries where any of us are concerned," said Nikal. "We sense his youth and will have a care. He will be greatly liked and appreciated by my friends. Is it his Human characteristics that annoy you?"

Hurlin half chuckled. "Probably. But then, as I say, he charms. That, of course, is his Qeteral side."

"You are capable of a rare joke, I see." Nikal chuckled, too. "Perhaps it is the Human side that charms. He is a remarkably good-looking man."

"I admit his telltale Human features probably do give him exotic appeal, as the young women in our village will hardly leave him alone. He has matured more rapidly than is typical, as you see he has caught up with Olin and me. Though he still has much of the boyish nature and is years from a declaration of full manhood. What of yourself? We understand the king your father has another son, your brother. What is his name? Does he grow his beard, too?"

"Um, no." It was all Nikal could do to hide his feelings. And yet, he also wished Hurlin to understand a tidbit. "Lekktor will follow upon my father to the throne of Nant. Yet, I have discovered that brotherhood can take other, more meaningful form, and the Staff and its magic, along with our mutual love apart from the Staff, have connected the Lord Kodi and myself very powerfully in strong bond. He is the brother I am most close to, then, and many of the others with us on this journey are my family, and we believe the Guardian Himself has established this through His words to that effect in a Prophecy."

Hurlin nodded. "There is much in what you say and don't say. There is friction between yourself and this Lekktor. I am sorry but will not press for detail. On the other I surely believe, Nikal, the fact you and this Lord Kodi carry the burden of the Staff's magic together tells me a great deal. For I may know more than you on the magic and on the creation of that talisman. It is more than magic. It is spirit. Though he seems young for a War Wizard, even for a Human. Surely, he is only shortly beyond boyhood in your culture?"

"Actually, by three years, whereby he has grown much in wisdom and body, is a natural leader and universally admired. Kodi suggested to me, and I believe him, that the Staff is made by Qeteral *men* alone, at least two."

Hurlin stared long at Nikal before replying. "He discovered that? From what source? It is not in *The Histories*; I know for a fact."

"It's true, then."

After another long pause and another drink of his mead, Hurlin replied. "It does contain the power of men beyond the simple masculine symbolism of a staff. I suppose it would be possible for the bearer to realize it. When did you...he...discover this?"

"The day of the War Wizard Installation Ceremony when the power of the Staff fell in white light upon us."

Hurlin sat up. "Even before you wielded it in battle? The Divine was spiritually present in the ceremony and established the magical connection? For all to see? Astonishing!"

"I hope you will come to understand that the Lord Kodi, despite his youth, is truly the center of much, along with the sister, the Lady Lyndz. Kodi especially is very close to Myghal, and Myghal is very close to Kodi."

"If you say. Though you, Nikal, seem to me more on the level, one who approaches the heroism of past days. Vanayisu, Berug, and Terianh were all great leaders before a Staff was provided them."

"I accept that Myghal has chosen me and values my talents, but again, Kodi and Lyndz are central to His purposes. I have come to believe they are the best hope for ultimate victory. There is more to Kodi and Lyndz than you may realize: receivers of Visions, descendants of imperial heroes, brave adventurers, and even a Seeress. You value blood?"

"I...tend to, yes. You imply, then, Myghalian Auras? Or perhaps the theory of the Divine Planting Seeds?"

Nikal smiled knowingly. "You have not really considered it much in regard to Humans, have you?"

"I..." There was the slimmest hint of a guilty look on Hurlin's part.

"Auras are prominent in their family, including their parents and grandparents, and Sage Curdoz suspects for many generations previously. Have faith, good Hurlin, in the maneuverings of Myghal the Divine."

"I do try. Do you?"

Nikal winked. "I do try. Let us not pretend, my brother prince, we who honor the High One as we do and who are committed to the protection of our people, that we find that to be an easy task."

"No. That it is not. Much is enigma." Hurlin nodded. He didn't smile, but he did raise his cup to Nikal and drank.

Interestingly, it was at this moment that Musca ambled over from the central part of the camp. He looked at Hurlin and wagged his tale. Then, he proceeded to sit just between Nikal and Hurlin.

"May I examine your animal?"

Nikal indicated in the affirmative, and Hurlin reached out to place his hand on the dog's head. He then proceeded in the quietest voice to sing in deep tune with what seemed like words but were certainly of no words Nikal knew. Nikal did not interrupt. Musca looked intelligently into Hurlin's face as he did this. There was a moment or two when Hurlin paused and quickly took his hands away as if startled by something. He looked up at Nikal briefly but then returned his hands to the beast's head and sang in different tune. In another minute, he was done. Musca flapped his tail once and then lay his head down for a relaxed snooze.

"We have dogs," he said. "The name of this breed?"

"He is called Musca. His kind is the Elentine Noble, a war dog from Eleni."

"This is the one who, as you say, bit off the witch's hand in battle?"

"It is."

"I am not so sure that his kind is not related to one of ours which we call the Mountain Hunter, though we only have a few in these hither parts of the country. Most are in the northern part. Yet we do have one breeder of the type in our village. They certainly look quite similar, though this one is heavier. Are you aware that this one has magic? I have never known of magic in any dog, only in some birds. Though of course there are fairy tales and legends of magical animals from the past."

"Yes, he has demonstrated this magic to us. He belongs to Kodi and the Lady Lyndz. Allow one of them to describe his magic in forthcoming councils."

"It is with the birds we have the best communication, though certainly we retain intelligent pets such as Musca. I must admit this one to be an intriguing animal. He has permission to wander freely. I have read in his mind that he is most disciplined. I have explained to him to avoid our farm animals. Yet I can tell he is a hunter. He is free to explore a bit of his wild side while he is with us. I told him just that, and he understands."

"I shall relay it to Kodi. I know he will be grateful. Thank you."

The two princes continued in some further discussion pertaining to Ulakel's geography and the distance of the hike the next day. Yet it wasn't long before Nikal took his leave of Hurlin in order to retire for the night.

It cannot be said that Nikal grew close to Hurlin. The Qeteral prince continued to retain certain attitudes about Humans, and so getting to know him was a difficult task. These attitudes manifested over the next several days in disdain for Tiliruf, which quickly became mutual (though Tiliruf to his credit tried not to show it in front of Hurlin), and a dislike of Kodi, who tried diligently to be friendly but who nevertheless stood his ground when they couldn't agree. Hurlin didn't like that. He grew jealous of Kodi's influence among the Qeteral and the relationships he established with others in the royal family. And Hurlin virtually ignored all the other Humans, with Nikal being the main exception along with a mild regard for Curdoz. Nikal found the relationship tiresome as he found himself occasionally paired with Hurlin during dinners or activities or felt required to communicate with him when no one else would. Nevertheless, he dutifully persisted. He sensed Olin was right when he implied that Hurlin was powerful and perhaps a key to future cooperation between the races. In the long run it paid off, as Nikal's deep nobility and sense of sacrificial duty was something Hurlin was indeed drawn to. Their conversations would ultimately impact Hurlin's choices when the future grew dark.

Like the trek Curdoz and Kodi took to the top of the faraway Escarpment to Hesk, it was a many-hour hike to reach the Great Plateau. Yet here the wall was far more broken and less sheer, leaning back in a series of cliffs. As opposed to the stark, rocky walls of the Ramp, here was much green growth. The trail was winding, following along natural formations such as creek beds and cliff walls. Perhaps long ago it accommodated cart traffic. Yet now it appeared to be only used, and rarely, by the occasional Qeteral scout.

When they reached the top in late afternoon, they realized the land was not as flat as some had expected. It was varied, flat with grain fields in many places, yet also rolling and pocked with many cuttings into its surface. Water proved to be a significant feature with many brooks and streams. It was a charmed place with trees of fantastic height in scattered groves or those of large girth with shady canopies in park-like settings. The ears of the Humans were entertained lavishly by uncounted birds of many colors and kinds performing enchanting tunes in contrast or in harmonies as a symphony. Late summer flowers bloomed colorfully in glades. It was as if the whole of the land was a garden of ingenious design, whereby every which way they looked they were treated to a splendid view.

Meical. What is it about this place?

All were moved by the beauty of Ulakel, though none so much as Kodi. Unlike any other place he had ever visited, this land captured—enraptured—all his senses. In ways he was reminded of his deep knowledge of his home sites such as the Wolf River valley where he knew every tree, every boulder, every path. He felt that same sense of ownership now. In other ways he was reminded of the sunny warmth and exotic feelings inspired by their arrival and first day on Modela's Island. Here he could imagine himself—his own young, handsome, and healthy body—as the exotic animal in its original, most natural setting. And finally, he could recall the movement of his soul as he explored the Valley of the Gifted in his Vision and the long moments as he rose into the golden air out of the depths of the Sapphire Lake and heard plainly and clearly the life-breathing, spirit-affirming Voice.

Magic permeates here in the rocks, trees, soil, water, and even the maneuvers of the deep places far below the ground. This was the playground of the gods before the birth of the Three Peoples. And because of its magical undercurrents, it became the natural home to the Qeteral when they left the Valley in the years following their Molding. And so, due to their strong magic instilled into them by the One and through Me, it remains a blessed land. The Qeteral are a blessed people. I would encourage you then, My Brother, to allow your heart to expand as the land and its people speak to you. Tell my Brother Nikal, my servant Curdoz, and the Matriarch, that you are to remain here three weeks. Your task will soon be known.

The village where the queen resided was surprisingly close. It was not necessary, despite it being a large and populated land, to trek for days to a more centralized capital. Traffic increased as they approached the village. Stout ponies pulled carts on roads paved of stone and brick. None rode horseback as Lyndz rightly suspected. Most walked or were cart drivers.

Yet all moved aside and gazed on the guests as they passed. Surely the Humans drew many looks, particularly those men who sported beards on their faces, a feature the men understood made them appear more animal-like or mythical in comparison to the beardless Qeteral. But the Etoppsi drew the most astonished gazes. As the giants passed by, most bowed towards them. However, some children were so amazed that if one of the Berugians looked at them they would use their magic and disappear from view.

Mishoo reassured Rainwing and the others. “It isn’t fear, but rather astonishment. All those living near were made aware you would be coming. Very little of our art or books contains images of your kind, though you may be described not so unlike the gods in children’s tales.”

“You must fly for them later, Flamefur. Stormgale,” said Rainwing. “They should witness the splendor of our kind in flight.”

At a point, Musca looked at Kodi, wagged his tail and ran off through a field. In the tall grass he scattered a flock of grouse or some such similar ground-dwelling bird and ran on.

“Let him be,” said Hurlin, who had spoken to none but Nikal since their meeting the day before.

Kodi looked at him. “Thank you, Prince Hurlin. Nikal told me what you said. I am glad you like...my dog.”

Hurlin might have harrumphed, or he might not have. He did not speak again. A few may have noticed the odd interchange, but most did not. Only Tiliruf and Kodi looked at one another with raised eyebrows. With regards to Musca, they would not see him every day, yet Kodi was not concerned. It was essentially the first time since they trained at Genehbro’s estate outside Tirilorin that the beast was entirely free to disappear at his own will. And plainly, he sensed Kodi and Lyndz to be perfectly safe here, or he would have stuck close.

They came to a path that veered from the main road. Following this as it dipped into a secluded hollow, they soon encountered a huge red and yellow pavilion on a great green lawn. Only a few yards away, a spring of crystal water splashed outward from a rocky wall into a large inviting pool. Rhododendrons draped over the far sides of the water, flanked beyond by the pines, hemlocks, and hollies that surrounded the hollow. There was even a privy built like an enclosed wooden gazebo about a hundred feet away. It was a private and appealing setting.

As Mishoo had explained already, the men and male Etoppsi were to be housed here during their stay.

The pavilion itself was more like a grandiose traveling palace. Shane said later it was reminiscent of pavilions used by the royalty of Essemar and Hralindi when they would travel in great retinue about their countries in times of peace. The great entrance flaps were tied back revealing inside a plush, inviting space, every square foot covered in carpets, with beautifully carved tables, and chairs which leaned back as lounges, these covered in animal pelts and furs. Even the interior canvas walls and ceiling were painted with natural scenes by mural artists not so unlike the great wall painting Enric had done in his parlor. Here it was hunting scenes with Qeteral archers and deer in wildflower meadows at sunset. The sunset segued overhead into a nighttime scene of shooting stars, renditions of the two moons and mythical constellations.

Servants were already here, gathering water in silver pitchers, placing baked breads, fruits, and other morsels on sideboards, and making up actual beds behind additional interior draperies. There were four of these interior "bedroom" divisions, three with four individual beds each as if to give the men choices, and the last for the two Etoppsi males. Even they were given huge plush beds side by side. All these spaces had additional tables and chairs, dressing mirrors, and heavy benches for the Etoppsi. All around were open window flaps to allow in the daylight and the breezes. There were lamps on the tables or hanging from poles which could be lit in the evenings as needed. Another servant carried a large stack of towels to a table by the outdoor bathing pool under a canopy. It was all quite luxurious, and at the same time it had a hunting lodge atmosphere.

Olin explained all. "...and so you are to relax the next two hours, and then dress for a reception and dinner with the queen and representatives of the nobility at the palace. These servants will shortly leave you, but others will come and escort you at the proper time. It will be a great affair with many guests to honor your coming to us. I wish for you to bring the Eagle Staff when you come. Leave all other weaponry here, but dress in what you consider your proper Human clothing for presenting yourselves this evening. However, in the morning, you will find clothing of our own kind, and if you so wish, you are welcome to be comfortable and dress in the manner of our own people for the remainder of your stay. We encourage you to feel at home. All in the village are aware of your coming to us. Beginning tomorrow, feel free to engage with the villagers, and come and go as you like. My mother will establish a schedule for council meetings and dinners. She may wish at times to meet with some of you individually or in smaller groups. There will be servants coming and going often between here and the palace. If you need anything at all, please let them know."

They left the men and male Etoppsi and led the women and Rainwing out of the hollow. Soon the servants were done with the setup of the pavilion and its accoutrements and left them alone in their new arrangements.

"Comfort," said Hadon with a sigh. "I hate military barracks and camps. And ships. I like nice things."

"You've always liked nice things. You're like Tiliruf, mate," said Manwul.

The men were exploring all around and throwing off boots and opening up their packs, setting their spare clothes out to air, and choosing which beds they wanted to sleep in.

"I need to lay my head down for a quick nap," said Findun, "unless you need me for something, Brother Curdoz."

"Not at all. I am going to sit in one of these glorious lounge chairs and smoke my pipe," said Curdoz. "I might even doze a little, myself."

"There are books here!" said Deens. "Look, Brother Curdoz."

"Really?" said Curdoz. As he started puffing on his pipe, he took one of these from Deens, leaned back and began thumbing through it. "It's High Anterianhi but in the florid Qeteral script. Thankfully, we're familiar with it from the Valley, aren't we, Deens? *The Tale of Vanaratu and the Diamond Pool.* How intriguing! I wonder if it has to do with...hmm."

"I'm going to plunge into that water pool and swim for like an hour, and shave," said Kodi. "C'mon, Ruffy. C'mon, Nikal. Get your damned boots off. It's all peace here. And magic. Meical told me he wants us to take in the blessings of this land, so that's what we're going to do. For now, it's as if you're thousands of leagues away from the war, so let it leave our minds for a while. Manwul, Hadon, Shane, let's go."

"You bet," said Manwul. "This place makes me feel like a king. Come, Nikal. Listen to Kodi."

"I'm coming. I sense the life here. Pull this tight boot off for me, Manwul."

"They have treated us most royally," said Stormgale boomily. "I'll sit by the waterside and drink my own pitcher of this cool mead they brought."

"I'm in full agreement," said Flamefur. "Pour me a jug of that, Stormy."

"Gorgeous carving on these tables. Polished silver. The art on these canvas walls!" Shane was taking it all in. "I want to read that book, Brother Curdoz, when you're done. But I'm coming, Kodi. I'm like you. These first hours I want to bask in water and the late afternoon sunshine and lie on the cool green grass and listen to the birds. Let me lay Healing hands on each of you before you get into the water. We need these moments of freedom. They are becoming rarer."

"I'm coming, eh? One second." Tiliruf grabbed Curdoz' pipe and took three deep puffs. He handed it back to Curdoz with a wink and ran to catch up with Kodi.

As the rest entered the village proper, the female visitors were taking in the architecture. Charming. Detailed. Exquisite craftsmanship. Plainly, the idea of beautifully constructed wooden complications was meant to display itself as an art form. There were towers and upper rooms with verandahs, many glass-paned windows of mullioned pattern, awnings and dormers and wide eaves, along with carved patterns in the highly decorated trim work. Walls and roofs were covered in dark shingles, and all was left to age naturally. Only were the door and window framings painted. These, like the bridge railings they had crossed over, were bright colors, typically red or yellow and stood in architectural contrast to the dark shingles.

In contrast to the darkness of the shingles were planters hanging off the edges of balconies or just outside the windows. These were overflowing with bright-colored flowers, green and silver herbs. In front of each house were small, bright green lawns with trimmed, rounded boxwoods as foundation plantings. In the lawns were flagstone or brick walkways, these winding also down the sides of the many houses through vine-covered archways leading to what promised to be, behind each and every house, more gardens. These could not be seen well from their vantage, but Lyndz later described her impressions once she discovered more:

There were no fences or tall hedges that separated these backyard gardens. Instead, it was open, allowing for walk-betweens through archways or between pleached fruit trees. To create barriers by way of dark hedges or walls was not the Qeteral way. One might find these in the much larger palace garden, but village life of the Qeteral involved much going and coming between neighbors, in addition to a strong wish to be able to allow for vista of the countryside. Neighbors commonly entered each other's gardens, not only with the wish to see how well their neighbors' gardens were growing, but also to help one another in the vegetable and herb patches. There was much sharing, you see. One might have the potato patch, whereas another was growing tomatoes and onions, while a third was growing beans on tall stalks. Mixed in all were melons and squashes. But everywhere were patches of flowers, many with little or no culinary value, but were simply there for their beauty. Yet some of the flowers were indeed edible and appeared in many of their foods, such as nasturtiums and lavender and the petals of roses. Also, further behind on the edges of the fields were uncounted beehives for the making of honey and mead. In any event, this describes somewhat the theme behind the village house gardens. The palace gardens and those more public, meant for sheer art and pleasure, entertained entirely different themes, of course...

And then they approached the palace.

It was incredible, and all entirely of wood just as were the village houses. But on huge scale. Thousands of trees were used to create a magnificent palace. It could be called a palace, despite the material used in construction. Stone blocks were used in the foundation and in its many fireplaces and chimneys, but otherwise it was crafted of magnificent logs. Eaves were covered in dark shingles. The windows were often doorways that opened onto verandahs at various levels, up to four stories! It was of the most fantastical design all around. Logs were used at angles and vertical to create designs. Shingles, too, were applied to create patterns. Roof beams extended beyond the eaves, and the ends were carved in the likeness of birds or animals. It reminisced a Human hunting lodge in a way, but was otherwise more massive and much more detailed and contained hundreds of rooms. The interior was as luxurious as any stone palace in Human countries. Tapestries and carpets, not imported from the East, but of their own ingenious handicraft. Furniture, all of beautiful hardwoods and all of it detailed in carving. All of it as detailed as that which Grandfather Jugan was once noted for. The Qeteral did not use gold leaf, yet gold was apparent in the threads of the tapestries, and silver candelabra and silver table furnishings were everywhere.

A great many servants were on hand, not so unlike at the Imperial Palace in Tirilorin, and these were joyful, happy personages, all as regal as royals, gracious and accommodating. Were they simply curious of us as outsiders of a different race? I do not think so. Instead, the servant class was self-assured and most friendly, and we became friends with several of them. And as all their race, they were beautiful to look upon. They looked like princes and princesses. Nor did the servants adhere to a uniform style of dress as would servants in Human lands, but each displayed individuality in the colors and embroidery on their garb. Even Mother Idamé, despite her conservative attitudes on dress, could admire their beautiful bodies and faces and never made the remotest comment regarding their limited clothing. She would complement each as to the embroidery and colors, and they would tell stories regarding their make, that their mother embroidered this or that or that the linen weave was done by someone they knew. They were wonderfully receptive of her continuous compliments. Yes, there were subtleties in the differences between servants and the rest. The men servants always wore a sleeveless, open, vest-like shirt, just as did the women. This set them apart, for most Qeteral men, except the elderly, did not wear shirts in the routine of the day, but only for dinners and councils. The female servants did not wear hair garlands or necklaces. Otherwise, they were all as lovely as princesses. However, I came to understand that the servants had days when they did not work, in which they spent time with their families, and on these days they would dress in the same manner as everyone else. Out in the village, one could not tell the difference between those employed as servants and those who were not. Surely, Human noblemen could learn much from the Qeteral in how they allowed their servants to be themselves, as important within their own families and situations as were those who did not work as servants. For the Qeteral, to be a servant was simply a form of work they chose, just as shopkeepers or other trade. Quite often, the servants were young, and to work as a servant was something they did for a period of years until they chose a different means of livelihood. However, a few of the highest-level servants were ones who had been working for the royal family for years, deeply devoted and loyal. In any event, if I were to ever be a lady over many servants, I would work to help them achieve their goals for eventual independence just as the Matriarch does for hers.

Kodi, Tiliruf, and Curdoz shaved fully, whereas Nikal, Hadon, Manwul and Shane shaved to better define the borders of their beards and trimmed them short. Deens and Findun sported long beards, though they did trim them to be less scraggly. The men had brought with them certain finery in which to dress for the purpose of introduction to the Qeteral. All wore clean white linen shirts, ruffled at the cuff. Over these, Manwul and Hadon wore the fine red vests Tiliruf had bought for them. Tiliruf dressed as the A'Terianh with a completely clean set of eagle embroiders. He always stood out princely and dapper in any regard. Curdoz wore his knitted stole and had the War Wizards wear their golden Order medallions over their shirts and their blue damasked short cloaks. Shane wore his silver medallion. Deens and Findun had, at Nikal's orders, set aside their monastic robes back on the ship in favor of ordinary men's clothing of good quality, and they also had silver Order medallions, less ornate than Shane's. They were not used to presenting themselves in this manner, and like Idamé resisting a fine dress for the Dance in Tirilorin, they worried a little as to whether they were being perceived as the servant-Monastics required by their Calling. Curdoz assured them that their brown robes would be entirely out of place.

"That show of servanthood is valuable to Humans familiar with the role of Monastics, but would be lost on the Qeteral, I think."

"And they're ugly and uncomfortable," said Shane. "You look like real men, now."

Kodi chuckled.

"I have come to see you have progressive views, Brother Shane," said Curdoz.

"That is true, Brother Curdoz. I may be the most progressive duck in the Order's pond."

"I am not bothered by it, of course. If this journey has taught me anything it is to question pieces of the Order's traditions. They are not suited in every locale."

"Likewise, I question the Synod's restrictions on Bonding of Order Members. People change. Auras should not be the only element they consider."

"Actually, I agree fully."

Shane raised an eyebrow.

The two Etoppsi, as always, wore nothing, except Kodi had Flamefur wear his antler collar. He was always pleased to do this. His reddish fur was gorgeous, and Stormgale's shimmery tan amplified his incredible physique. Both were stallion-esque. Their wings framed them regally, and they always looked like great sky kings, just as Hurlin had greeted them the day before. And as Tiliruf noted, they just smelled damn good.

"I wonder if they know we Etoppsi cannot eat bread and most vegetables," said Stormgale, with a concerned eye at the stack of baked breads on the table in the pavilion. There had also been nuts and fruits, so they had not gone hungry that afternoon.

"They know; I heard Lyndz tell them so," said Curdoz. "They seemed aware of the fact anyway. Fear not. They are great meat eaters like the rest of us."

Servants arrived at the expected time. These were all men, and they wore open-fronted vests, beautifully embroidered. They came to understand, as did Lyndz, that servant men always wore vests, but also that even those who were not servants wore them at meals, council meetings and parties, this to lend an element of decoration or formality in such settings.

It had begun to grow dark, and yet they found on their walk to the palace that torches had been placed to light the way. All the villagers stood in front of their houses to greet the guests with bows and friendly hails.

"Welcome, Humans!"

"Welcome, great Berugians!"

"Welcome, great Sage from the Valley! We are honored to have you!"

Curdoz would smile and lift his hand in his standard blessing. Whether they really knew this sign or not, he didn't know, yet they probably understood the meaning behind it as they bowed their heads to him in response.

Occasionally, some would step out and grip arms with some of the men, usually Kodi or Nikal. Some were curious of the Staff being carried by Nikal.

"War Wizards, just as Prince Lumin told us!" said some of the children.

"Come and visit our workshops soon and converse with us, m'lords!" said some adults. "We wish to know you better!"

"We will do that!" said Kodi, graciously. "I am a woodworker, myself. And a stonecutter. I want to see your own craft."

"Will you fly for us, Sky Kings?" asked a brave youngster. "Lumin said you might! We want to see it!"

"Perhaps we will do that, my young topling," said Stormgale. "Perhaps in the morning early!"

"That one wears Terianh's Eagle! Lumin was right!"

Clearly, Lumin had gone about the village that afternoon and relayed much of the news.

Yet, there were some who seemed to offer skeptical glances and would turn and whisper to their neighbors.

"Some fear your presence speaks of the war to the south," offered one of the servants. "None wish to be a part of Human wars."

"No one of good heart likes war," said Nikal. "Yet even your own train in the arts of defense, do you not?"

"We do, of course. Prince Hurlin is responsible for the training of men, and Lady Mishoo for women. They have been more diligent of this the last year. My years as a servant end soon, and I wish to train in defense with the prince."

Nikal nodded. "That is most noble of you, good man. I wish you well." He understood that Hurlin had a certain skeptical wisdom, but this tidbit implied a more worldly wisdom he had not quite gotten from him in their conversation the night before. Obviously, the prince had been acting on the increased dangers in the world and was not merely relying on their magical Barrier. That was good to know. Of course, it was possible it was his mother behind it.

One thing Nikal had learned over the years was, if you really wanted to know something, ask the servants directly. "Did the Matriarch order the uptick in training?"

"I believe it was the prince himself, m'lord. He is believed to have the greatest magic in the land and sees much beyond the borders. And he is responsible for the Barrier."

Nikal raised an eyebrow. However, the Barrier magic was likely a matter of some delicacy, and he did not question the servant further. Yet even the idea that certain Qeteral were more magically powerful than others was a concept he had not considered before. He wondered if Curdoz might know more of this and decided to question him later.

A hundred windows and doorways streamed golden light. It went without saying the men were as astonished by the palace as were the women. Torches by the dozens were arranged in the wide lawn in a semicircle and lit the palace from the outside. As they were led to the large, open front doors, they found the women and Rainwing waiting for them. The women were dressed as handsomely as the men. Lyndz had brought a light blue dress and navy sash. Her hair was hanging long and elegantly. Idamé was wearing her colorful knit shawl, and Ulna and Maru were also wearing lovely dresses.

"They wish us to enter into the reception line with you," offered Lyndz. She reached up and felt Kodi's newly shaven face. "You are so handsome, Kodi! Walk in with me."

"And you are as beautiful as any princess, sister of mine! Have you met the queen?"

"No, this will be the first time. It is meant to happen in formalities. Our rooms are most splendid, by the way. They open onto balconies that witnesses the sunset over the most incredible garden!"

They were greeted inside by brighter light. Overhead, suspended from the tall ceiling was a massive chandelier sporting a hundred thick candles. It was made of hammered silver and enormous stag antlers. Everywhere were gleaming golden walls of wood, beautifully shellacked with almost mirror-like sheen. Carved sideboards carried silver candelabras. More lanterns of silver hung from columns and as sconces on the walls.

And there were a hundred Qeteral at least; nobles from many miles around had been invited by the Matriarch to greet the guests. Every woman wore a lovely, draping long pant cut at angles with one side draping over to the other and a short-sleeved blouse, which opened at the front. These were tied loosely with ribbons across or with large loops to accompanying buttons. Even though their breasts were mostly covered, their sensual cleavage showed. The linen was consistent in color on each woman, with pant and blouse matching, these trimmed with embroidered silk in contrast. Some wore blue, some pink, some yellow, and some light green. They also wore necklaces of various kinds, typically of polished colorful stones. Many wore garlands of flowers in their flowing dark hair. The men wore a loose short pant that tapered in a cuff slightly below the knee, their sandal straps wrapped high around their calves and shins, little different than what they had seen already on the men. Yet here, being a formal occasion, they wore the sleeveless, open-fronted vest, whereby their musculature was still fully apparent, the vest merely something that decorated their physique. The colors of their clothing were more muted in comparison to that of the women. Their pant was white or cream, and their vest was of olive, brown, or cream, a few were black, and yet these also were embroidered. Some of the men wore collars or necklaces of mixed light and dark wooden beads.

As Maru noted later,

They were all so lovely. That a whole race is so gifted with beauty that to cover them nearly head to toe in bolts of Human cloth would be a disgrace to them. In the Human world we have the fat, the not-so-pretty, the downright ugly, the skinny, the wrinkled old, the pock-marked faces of the poor souls who had such bad pimples as youth, the overly hairy, and so on and so forth...of course Humans feel this need to cover their flaws when they are in public. At great occasions we wear the most elaborate clothing we can afford. It simply is not to be considered for this flawless, beautiful, healthy, lovely, brown-skinned race of the Qeteral. For them, clothing is to highlight what is already a superb figure. And though some of their old take on more weight, they are nevertheless unwrinkled, with lovely skin, hair that does not gray, and wise faces. Envy, envy, envy, that is all I can say for myself.

They stood all around the great, octagonal entrance hall, with space between, though Bonded couples stood together, in order to greet the visitors. There were a handful of younger lords and ladies similar in age to Lumin. There was no announcer as at the great Dance in Tirilorin. Instead, each was to introduce himself or herself. And though this did indeed take quite a long time, it was nevertheless a gracious and memorable undertaking. Lords and ladies of the Qeteral received and welcomed each of the guests. Even Deens and Findun, with their less notable roles, were graciously received.

Tiliruf heard himself called *a'Terianh,* or *High One*, many times. He never wished for such titles, and yet he fell in line with expectations and replied with all grace. That he was something of a cad and a flirt, a youth who sought out prostitutes for release, drank like a sailor, and cussed up a storm in other company, he could do none of these things here, nor did he feel particularly the need to disappear and go do any of these preferred activities. Instead, under the strong influence of Shane's magic, whereby his mind could maneuver with more ease, he countered with the most appropriate grace to each individual, memorizing names, titles, and details by the dozens. His imperial forebears would have been pleased with his unassuming comportment. Not every Qeteral noble displayed warmth. A handful he encountered acted like Hurlin, with hints of skepticism. These performed pleasantries, even if they may not have been pleased with his presence. He was gracious to them anyway. He did not allow himself to be bothered by strangers not liking him. He understood they were not pleased by his great-grandfather's abdication. It had had political repercussions and upset the four-century balance of the imperial unity. Yet there were some here who were pleased to know him and went out of their way to invite him to visit them at their estates should he find the time to do so during his stay.

Curdoz received willing bows. It was true Qeteral views had veered from Valley teachings centuries before. Even so, as has been noted, Human Sages were looked upon as Myghalian Prophets. Until the Abdication, it was only Sages and their minimal retinue that were allowed access to Ulakel and were always highly regarded. That regard still showed. He blessed all with raised palm and a blessing in High Anterianhi, "Ela mor Tuna Myghal Enamoros Ien Olloray!"

Nikal and Kodi kissed so many ladies' hands and gripped so many men's they lost count. Not that they were really counting. Yet it was plain they were looked upon with a certain astonishment. That a War Wizard—two War Wizards—men who were Gifted by the Divine with the magic to control a Staff, and who had brought the famed Eagle Staff itself with them to the country where it was made, was to the Qeteral a most unexpected occasion. Though they had heard bits and rumors of an upcoming visit, countenanced by the Matriarch, more than her cryptic words this denoted to them that Myghal was indeed moving events in extraordinary ways. And so, the two were each referred to as *Brother of Myghal*. Though it applied to Nikal, the title came to stick more fully with Kodi in the following days even outside the palace. Nikal was more readily referred to as High Prince, or simply Prince Nikal. In any event, Nikal and Kodi did not quite understand in the greeting line the level of high reverence behind such a greeting. As it turned out, the title carried certain political and even religious weight. To be a *Brother of Myghal the Divine* was to be at a level barely short of divinity itself. It took the two a little time to become aware of this.

Lyndz was often addressed with a title that, technically speaking, she did not genuinely hold. *Princess of the North* is what they often called her. She could not act dumbfounded, but she quickly understood it was offered based on her exceptional beauty. Most were mesmerized by her stunning looks, even as Humans were in other lands. Though she was honored, she couldn't help later in private but to complain a little to Idamé.

"But I am not a princess! And honestly, Mother, I am grateful they think I am beautiful, but am I not more than that?"

"Of course, you are, dear. You have the intelligence of a queen, and Gifted, too. Yet consider how handsome Kodi is and how beautiful you are has helped how they have perceived our race and our visit here. It is because of the two of you, I think, that they feel more connected to Humans than they might have if a bunch of grizzly drunken sailors or gaudy prostitutes from North Bend slipped into their country!"

"Ha! Oh, Mother! I know you must be right, but as I have matured, I have grown beyond my girlish wishes to simply be attractive to the eye."

"Mishoo and the others see it, dear. They haven't said a word about your beauty and do not refer to you as a princess. They see your talents and your drive to excel and to do your duty in the troubles ahead. Consider then, that when most first look at you, they do indeed see how lovely you are. Most of us are not so lucky and must make up the difference in how we are perceived with a tad more effort."

"Oh, you're so sweet, Mother. Honestly, that does make sense, I see. It's not that I don't wish to be beautiful, but I find I care more that I am beautiful for those whom I love and don't give a damn what strangers think of me."

"That has some wisdom behind it, dear, yet also note that your beauty is a gift, and so it graces us all and gives us something to enjoy!"

Ulna, Maru, and Shane were honored as Healers and therefore Gifted by the Divine.

Similarly to Human greetings in other places, the Etoppsi, having such large countenance and platter-sized hands, were the subject of many bows rather than handgrips and kissed hands. Rainwing probably would have pummeled anyone who tried to kiss her hand in any regard. She alone 'endured' the greetings, whereas everyone else was enjoying themselves. Ever since she lost her wings, she felt she was the subject of stares and unasked questions. She had since lost her taste for grand affairs. Nevertheless, she persisted and introduced herself as Ambassador Rainwing. Nor was there, had she known it, a single Qeteral who was not intrigued by her, her commanding presence and gracious greetings in the names of King Eagleron and Queen Silverwing. In future days, as it became more generally known her wings were given in sacrifice for the Staff, their positive perceptions of her increased even more.

Idamé was regarded as a kind of odd grandmother, yet all were as friendly to her as they were to anyone else. Some of the noblewomen invited her to take teatime with them if she could manage it with her time. She was ecstatic to know that Qeteral ladies had teatime.

This line of greeting continued slowly about the room, Lyndz and Kodi leading all. They then came to a part of the great hall whereupon they stepped up to a higher level like a dais. On the other side of elaborately carved wooden screens the twins found the royal family, standing in wait to greet them.

The Matriarch, Queen Gwyn of the Qeteral, was flanked on one side by Hurlin and Olin, and on the other by Lumin. Tonight, the princes wore sleeveless, open-fronted vests as did all the Qeteral men.

And to Lumin's side stood his sister, the Princess Ryn.

To say that Kodi did a double take is an understatement. He did indeed do a double take, but a great many things went through his mind at once.

His only thoughts had been on the queen. He understood the day before from Hurlin and Olin that it was the Matriarch who was the one who shared his Vision all those months before. Essentially, she was the only Qeteral whom he knew, sort of, in advance of coming here. He understandably looked forward to meeting her in person and to share a special word or two with her. And there she was, in the center of the royal family, as beautiful and as regal as he had perceived of her in the Dream. To find her was his Calling as he understood from Meical, in order to determine something regarding an important task he had been Chosen for. What they shared from the Vision was unique, as explained by Curdoz.

Yet to the other side of young Lumin, there before him was another woman, young, of exquisite beauty, with the most piercing blue eyes in a most stunning face. This was surrounded by jet black, waving hair that fell long down her back. Atop her head was a ringlet of white flowers, a crown to grace her mesmerizing loveliness. Her white damasked linen blouse was unbuttoned, exposing the full curves on a body that could only be described as uttermost perfection.

When her eyes met his, Kodi's whole being, mind, body, and soul, was enamored. Unequivocally his body responded, his heartbeat throbbed in his ears, and with uttermost will he squelched the surge in his groin that threatened to carry him off into uncontrolled fantasy. Here before him was something much more than a Vision.

He swallowed hard and forced himself to look fully at the queen her mother, who at that moment stepped forward with hands out to greet him.

With a warm, enveloping smile, she took both his hands into hers.

"Kodi! At last, we meet!"

He nodded, returned the smile, and recovered full composure.

"It is my great honor, Matriarch. How often you have reappeared in my mind as I sought you out. How glad I am to be here, now. It is our hope that now we can determine this task that my brother Myghal has set us on."

"I know the task, yes, though I have felt the need to retain mostly my own counsel until you came, and as was instructed in the Vision. Tomorrow we will hold a council, yet tonight, let us enjoy the company! Though at another time you will meet more of my family. Please, introduce me to your sister."

Lyndz stepped forward and curtsied. Kodi took her hand and placed it in Gwyn's hand.

"This is Lyndz, my twin."

"Madam," said Lyndz.

"And do the two of you look so much alike! You are both most beautiful people. And of your parents?"

"We are the only son and daughter of Hess and Elisa, Count and Countess Fothemry in the duchy of Tulesk in the Kingdom of Solanto."

"Of Solanto, that much I knew, of course. Lady Lyndz, you are to be close to me in council while you are here! I see great wisdom in you, I do!"

"I am most pleased to serve, Matriarch."

"I sense the deep magic of the War Wizard in Kodi, yet I detect something powerful in you, too, lady. It is much different than Healing and beyond the Aura-magic of Bondswomen. Are you Gifted with other magic?"

"I am, Madam. I will be glad to describe it to you more fully sometime."

The Matriarch smiled kindly and nodded. "You have met my three sons, of course! Meet now my daughter, Ryn!"

As Kodi had placed Lyndz' hand into that of the queen, Gwyn now reached and placed her daughter's hand, first into that of Lyndz.

"You and I are great friends, Lyndz, I know!"

To Kodi her voice was song.

"Thank you so very much, m'lady!"

"Call me Ryn always, Lyndz!"

"I will do that!"

"Lady Mishoo is my friend and cousin and gave us particular report of you." She said this with knowing smile. "Whatever we can provide you while you are here among us, consider it done."

"Thank you, Ryn." Lyndz nodded and seemed most pleased for some reason.

And then, finally. Irrevocably. She, on her own volition, reached out and took Kodi's hand, and he kissed it.

If he retained his lips on her skin for a moment longer than he might have...

...it was likely.

She then spoke clear words he would never forget.

"A great young lord stands before me. I shall never be so blessed, I think, as to know you. Kodi."

Oh, the words and the subtleties of words. Kodi beamed.

"It is a great lady who graces me with such words, and it is my highest honor to know you. Ryn."

She backed slowly away as to allow her brothers to come forward and offer their own greetings. Yet she nodded at Kodi and retained a most stunning smile on her face.

It was only Olin and Lumin who came forward. Hurlin retained his distance from them, focusing instead on Prince Nikal who now stepped around the wooden screen.

If Hurlin did not appreciate the greeting his sister had given to Kodi, and he to her...

...it was likely.

Gracious words continued to be offered as the remainder of the visitors made their way to where the royal family stood. All these words were memorable, and even Deens and Findun felt as though they were most honored guests.

To the Sage the Matriarch said, "I wish to meet with you and the Lord Kodi early, before the council I have arranged."

"Of course, Madam."

It was Rainwing with whom the Matriarch had the most memorable exchange. She reached up and placed her hand on the Etoppsis' shoulder. "I have been told you offered the greatest possible sacrifice in order to take the Staff. Tell me where it was bestowed."

"With Vanayema of the Mold, Madam. In her secret island in the Great Western Ocean."

Even the Matriarch could not hold back her own Idamé-like high eyebrow.

"Oh, my! That highest of all females presents herself, does she? Her magic moves through this world and knows almost no bounds, except those she imposes upon herself. Mother of all of us she may be and queen of queens, yet she acts the mad sprite sometimes!" She stood there amazed for a long moment, looking into Rainwing's eyes. Finally, she squeezed into Rainwing's shoulder. "Yet one must have faith she retains a mother's heart, and I believe she does. It will not be the last we see of her. However, the greatest heroine of our times stands before me tonight. Sit beside me at the council meetings, Ambassador."

The great feast was splendid, and, probably to his relief, Kodi was not placed next to the princess, or he might have clammed up. Rather, the queen wished to have him beside her, and Lyndz was at her other side. The princess sat beside Lyndz, then, on her far side. Not unlike her time with Princess Isatura, those two engaged in most friendly conversation. Kodi and the queen spoke much to one another. However, it is true Kodi occasionally stole a glance down the table at the princess. And if there was a time or two in which their eyes briefly met, and smiles exchanged...

It was likely.

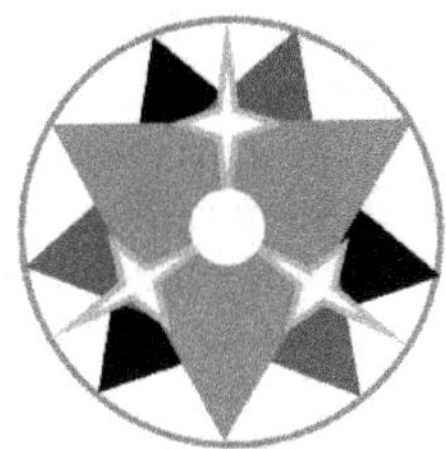

Chapter 15—Lovestruck

Late in the night Kodi lay on his bed in the pavilion. On one side of him in the next bed Nikal was in restful slumber. Outside in the near distance a bird sang in melodious tunes.

"Shane, I need you," he whispered to the figure in the bed on his other side. "And do a Voice Block, please."

Shane sat up and turned to him. There was a burst of mild green light.

"You're in a sweat, Kodi. Whatever is the matter?"

"I can't sleep."

"That is odd for you, isn't it? Tiliruf tells me you're a great sleeper. I was beginning to sense your restlessness next to me. I was awake listening to the nightingale. What troubles you?"

"I think I just wish you to put me to sleep. The Matriarch wants to meet with me and Curdoz early."

Shane did not immediately do this but began a more thorough examination. "Oh. Your body and mind are...Kodi, I know those elements moving in your blood. Are they ever strong in you just now. And you're...er...well, ha!"

"Yeah. Sorry."

"That's not going to embarrass me, Kodi. I know everything about how young men's bodies work, and yours plainly works. But I'd say something is stirring in you beyond...er, *urges*. You haven't spoken to Meical in your mind of this, have you? But I believe you were wishing to talk to someone."

"I can't help it, Shane. I've never felt like this for anyone, ever. Never, ever. I didn't know it would overwhelm me so totally. She's a princess! She's a Qeteral!" He looked at Shane in some desperation.

"The Princess Ryn?" Shane's raised eyebrow could be seen in the half-light. Many thoughts now went around in his keen mind. After a moment his expression turned to friendly concern, and he leaned forward. "You're anxious. You've lost control. I'm a man; I understand. Though it's been a while and...well, never mind. Hold on, be still."

He worked his magic to settle him. The relief, when it came, manifested in the drip of a tear from Kodi's eye.

"Listen to me, Kodi. You will be all right. So. I suspect it would be a mistake in your case to deny you may be in love. Because from what I hear, you rarely look at the same woman twice."

"Tiliruf's exaggerating. Er...but maybe only a little. This is sure different, though."

"Yes, I'd say it is. Two things, then. One, it was bound to happen. You are a War Wizard, a man of passion with a big heart capable of great love. A great big, good heart, Kodi. And that part of you is why Meical chose you. Two, and I know you know it, you mustn't pursue a princess. It is beyond all manners and all protocol. Royals initiate relationships, not the other way around. I doubt it's any different with the Qeteral than it is in Human kingdoms. The key then, here, is if she feels likewise."

"I think she might. I really think she might. Those incredible, intelligent blue eyes just kind of bore into me. And her smile when she would speak to me was, oh, wow." A dreamy smile came across Kodi's own face...

...causing Shane to chuckle. "All right. If so, then allow her to open a relationship on her own volition. If she invites you to partake in some sort of event or activity with her, then you follow her lead. And isn't that usually best, Kodi? When the woman displays favor first? You have become a powerful man, in the Human world at least. And already here in Ulakel, you and Nikal are being shown great reverence because of the Staff. I think that matters. It would be a mistake for you to be the one to press. What you might think is just subtle flirtation on your part before she makes a move could have consequences."

"Yes, I believe what you say. I really do."

"Because you are most gentlemanly."

"I just can't talk to Meical about it right now."

"Because?"

"Because He has always made it plain I should follow my heart and make my choices. I don't wish to act dependent and reach out to Him too often. And He reminded me I have great friends to talk to. Though I didn't know you, yet, when He said that."

"Then I'm honored to be your confidante on this, Kodi. I can deduce several reasons why you'd hesitate to speak of this to Nikal or Tiliruf. I can help steady you. That's why I'm here."

Kodi felt much more at ease, now, after Shane's magic. He sighed and wiped his face. "Boy, do I feel better. I really am drenched."

Shane grabbed a towel on the nightstand and like a nurse began wiping him down. He went and retrieved some quality oil from his pack and had Kodi turn over for a massage. Many Healers made use of massage in their work, and Shane was one who knew its benefits. He'd done it for Tiliruf more than once on the ship journey. Kodi's gratefulness, too, was apparent, and just as for Tiliruf, they became a welcome if irregular treat as long as Shane was around. From their perspective, his hands on their skin carried elements of the protective brother, even of a caring father, and certainly of a friend who understood. Tiliruf, who often hired master masseurs, claimed he was even better, because he would add in bursts of calming magic as he went along.

He spoke softly as he worked Kodi's back.

"You were fighting and not fighting. A mix of emotions and body reactions. You just needed a bit of steadying. You were naturally responding to seeing...not just a beautiful woman, but a woman of your dreams, for the first time. Some sexual fantasy thrown in, of course. I've been there more often than I'd care to admit."

"Yeah, *you* are the fantasy, from what I've heard tell."

Shane chuckled. "It's true I'm not your typical Healer. But never more than fantasy, if you understand me. I'm not going to say I don't have an inkling what genuine love for a woman might be like, because one or two of those women really moved me. You'll need to hear it from my perspective rather than secondhand from Tiliruf. No telling how he's embellished some of it! Anyway, I almost hate to remove some of that out of your system, even if it is just temporary, ha! Yes, it's sexual, but really, it symbolizes Human joy. Animal-like it might be in the way the body reacts but driven by an inner longing of the soul. And that longing is meant to be a good thing. You understand me?"

"I do now. She's *exquisite*, Shane. And that's a word I never use."

"Indeed, she is. What man is not moved by such beauty? You heard the others talk of her as we came back after dinner. Even my eyes went to her many times this evening. And honestly, Kodi, it can be hard on a Human young man especially for his eyes to have access to such a woman's skin and revealing shape. You're not as used to it as Qeteral men. Particularly Westerners with their expectations of cross-gender modesty. We Easterners are less reserved regarding the exposed body, a little more like the Qeteral. We don't separate for swimming, for example. Yet you handled yourself at the feast with grace, from what I saw. The Matriarch and you were engaged, and clearly you maintained your charm. Back here in bed you could let your mind wander. Have faith in your own self-discipline. Meical does. I foresee you are not going to act the fool. I am telling you your feelings for Ryn are valid, and you should acknowledge that validity yourself and label your emotions positively but then control them with an overarching logic and caution. I suspect you're quite good with that, really. I'm sure you understand, as do the best of men, that a woman is so much more than how our bodies might react to their bodies. They offer balance to the man's being. I'm trying to teach that to Tiliruf, but I'm not sure he believes it. In any event, you know it naturally, or you learned it over time, and that truly is why Meical chose you."

"I learned it after...after a mistake."

"It was a mistake because..."

"Because I let the girl seduce me. I wasn't careful, and I came to understand she was trying to trap me with a baby and guilt me into Bonding her."

"Ah, yes. I know some Western women are motivated differently than their Eastern counterparts. My experiences were never like that. I'm sorry they were for you. No baby, I presume."

"Lucky me. But I was angry with myself for having been such a fool, and for realizing how I absolutely didn't care for her at all. And then I started focusing more on what Father has with Mother and knew that's what I really wanted for myself. But it was hard to keep focus and avoid women. Really hard. Times I came close to buckling. Easily could have been like Tanksen. Bluuter. Local rascals."

"And if you had?"

"I think Meical might not have given me the Vision, or at least not the way it happened. Eventually the shame would have caught up with me, and I think I would have had a terrible time getting past it. In other words, I wouldn't have been ready. I would have felt unworthy of the Calling."

"You have strong moral underpinnings. That Vision was not meant for a self-indulgent cad. I know you are right. Avoiding young women was a smart choice for you. And so these new feelings you have for Ryn are therefore clearer and sharper."

"You don't seem worried much over this, Shane." Kodi turned back over, as Shane was now finished with his ministrations.

"Maybe a little. It creates an unexpected complication to our visit here." Shane looked him in the eye. "Yet I am required to have faith, and so are you. In part it's faith in Meical, but at least as much as that, it's faith in the individuals in this fellowship of ours to aid each other in making good choices. But I have no doubts Meical made a great choice in you."

He then placed his hands on Kodi's head. "Sleep now, Kodi."

Early next morning Stormgale and Flamefur went for a fly. Surely the village children were out and about watching and cheering, and probably many of their folks, too.

And just as Olin had said, servants had supplied for the Humans quantities of Qeteral men's clothing.

Kodi was fully recovered. That he had struggled with emotions the night before, only Shane knew of it.

"This is great. I'm all for this," he said. He had bathed again and put on a cream-colored linen pant and one of the open-fronted, sleeveless vests. "Cool comfort. I could go like this all the time, er, except fighting in a battle. That wouldn't do."

"I can't do the sandals," said Tiliruf. "They don't feel right."

"Me, neither," said Manwul.

"I don't think our boots look too odd," said Hadon.

"Has a rugged appeal," said Shane. "But I like sandals. I'm quite used to them."

However, it was only those who still qualified as young and had such excellent physiques that were willing to wear such minimal garb. Curdoz and the two Monastic Scribes were totally uncomfortable with the very idea and refused.

"They won't mind, of course," said Shane. "It was merely a suggestion thinking we might be more comfortable, although I think it's diplomatically important that at least some of us have taken to their suggestion and shows how we honor their way of life. But don't wear the stole, Brother Curdoz. It's too much. Deens and Findun, you're fine in the Human clothing. If you're not comfortable with the other, don't worry about it. It has been hard enough for you after Monastic robes to adjust to ordinary *Human* clothing, let alone Qeteral."

In fact, the six younger men, Kodi, Tiliruf, Hadon, Manwul, Shane, and Nikal looked quite studly. Only Kodi and Shane wore the Qeteral sandals. The rest wore their boots for now, though most would successfully try harder with the sandals after a few more days. For the time being they wore the vests, too, as they understood they would be in council meetings that day. However, there would be many hours and whole days whereby they would discard these and would walk about shirtless in the village like any prime Qeteral stallion.

Kodi looked most the part with his smooth, brown, young skin and with his dark hair having grown long the last months. Nor did he have as much hair on his body as the other two who had the same coloring as he, Nikal and Manwul. And for now, he kept his face shaved. Tiliruf and Hadon were not especially hairy, either. Shane in his blackness, and Tiliruf with his blond hair and freckles, stood out the most. They all kidded each other as they elaborated on these comparisons. The point was they all knew they represented different ideals of the Human Male, even if one or two, namely Nikal and Shane, did not openly brag about their good looks.

"It's a part of the Qeteral male experience, too," said Shane. "They like their own cocky display. And the limited dress isn't remotely thought of as primitive. Only Western Humans could think so. It's a little more deliberate based on how perfect and artful they consider the gift of their bodies. There is nothing whatsoever wrong with a bit of vanity, in my opinion. We Eastern men also dress in more limited clothing back home. The pant we prefer is longer and billowing, but otherwise it's much the same look, even the open vest and sandals. We will dress more elaborately in long saris for formal gatherings, and certainly our warriors, both men and women, dress logically with protective clothing, boots, and other gear."

"Qeteral seem to smell better, though," said Tiliruf.

"That's because they barely sweat."

"I didn't notice, eh?"

"I tend to observe, but I had read it somewhere and was paying attention. Lumin carries a Human scent and sweats more than the others. Just bathe regularly and we'll be fine."

"The water thing."

"It *is* the water thing, as it's always healing. But being clean is of value as to how one is perceived."

"I don't deny it. Who doesn't like to be clean?"

"I like getting dirty, but then I like the contrast of getting clean, being all relaxed and happy after a hard workday," said Kodi.

"I'm sure the Qeteral men are the same. All the ones we've seen are clean, though. I reckon they have to get dirty sometimes, eh?"

"They swim or bathe two or three times a day from what I gather."

"I would if it were convenient. And it seems to be here. The after-lunch swim is when they mix with the women, eh?"

"And children and the old. Maintain a grip, Tiliruf," said Manwul.

"Like Aron might say, 'it's all good.' I'm not going for a Qeteral woman anyways. But shafts, they're gorgeous."

Findun and Deens looked shocked. "I'll keep taking my baths here in the hollow, I think," said the latter.

"Of course, we will," said Curdoz. "Let the younger men express themselves at the swimming holes, if they wish. Just have a care..."

"And don't stare," concluded Shane with a chuckle.

"You fellows are actually making me laugh," said Nikal, his muscular arms folded across his broad chest in a beautifully embroidered white open vest. He looked like a great king from ancient times. He wasn't really laughing, but he did have a smile on his face.

"That's our job, mate," said Tiliruf.

"It's Lumin coming, look." Kodi nodded to the lip of the hollow where the path emerged. "Must be here to get Curdoz and me. What's he carrying?"

"Looks like a drawing pad," said Findun.

"Damn, he's a fine-looking man," said Hadon.

"Genuine stud," said Manwul.

"True, eh? He's prettier 'n Kodi, even. If I had a face and body like that, I'd want to live on a southern island surrounded by voluptuous young sirens to wrap me up in warm arms and legs and rub me all over with oil."

"He's a boy to the Qeteral," said Shane.

"That body is not a boy's body," said Manwul. "He's as big as his brothers with muscles big enough to flip them both over. Another few years he'll flip Rusty over."

"He's full grown, I think, though I'd like to examine him. It's partly from his Human blood," said Shane. "His grandfather and father must have been large, tall men."

"You men will keep an innocent demeanor around him, all the same," said Nikal. "I promised Hurlin."

"Of course, eh? He's a heart. He can drink a ton of mead, though, like Rusty drinks brandy. Gives me headaches, that too-sweet mead. I hate that stuff."

With that, Lumin was among them. "Mother wishes to see you, now, Lord Curdoz and Kodi. She's decided she wants you to come, too, Nikal."

"She wants to hear the Prophecy for herself," said Nikal, his face a little pale.

"Of course, Lumin," said Kodi, soldier gripping Lumin's arm, who liked it so well. "We'll go. Come down here and see us often, won't you?"

"May I stay some of the nights? Mother says I can. Teach me that Kings and Castles game?"

"Certainly," said Nikal. His face changed to warmth. "Stay with us whenever you wish."

Curdoz, Kodi, and Nikal made their way, but Lumin remained.

"Look, Tiliruf! I drew you!"

"You drew me?" said Tiliruf with a friendly pat on Lumin's shoulder.

"Lumin!" exclaimed Shane. "That's...that's extraordinary!"

Lumin had quickly turned his pad to the first page, displaying a rendition in charcoal pencil of Tiliruf's face. It was a stunning resemblance: cheeky grin, and freckles, framed in detailed curly hair. In the bottom corner he had drawn in the Terianh Eagle.

Tiliruf stood there aghast. In a good way. "Oh, gosh, Lumin. It's amazing! You did this from memory, eh?"

"Sure. We sat together at dinner, and I memorized your face. I drew it this morning."

"That is impressive," said Hadon.

"I want to draw all of you while you're here. Ryn said it'd be real smart to have a record of your visit."

"So, you're an artist," said Shane.

"I'm the best around, everyone says. Grandfather Hakonn arranged for me an art teacher years ago, and I've been doing it all the time. He's had carvers make woodblocks of my art and has printed much of it into books. Er, I don't really need a teacher anymore."

"You're better than the teacher."

Lumin smiled big. "Sir Manwul and Sir Hadon, can I draw you next? Together?"

"We'd be honored, Lumin. And we've been best buddies since we were little boys, see? That'd be great to put us together! Where do you want us to be?"

"Go sit by the water, just there, I think. Oh, no, don't take off your boots! I want them in the drawing, too. I think Human boots are interesting. Grandmother gave me my grandfather's boots, and they even fit me now. I wear them sometimes. Hurlin thinks they're dumb, but I don't care. Olin thinks they're kind of neat."

“Hurlin wouldn’t think they’re dumb if he had to plod through bloody battlefields or tend in the mire of horseshit,” whispered Tiliruf to Shane and the scribes, as the others marched over to the waterside.

“You don’t like Hurlin,” whispered Shane.

“Is it obvious? He’s an ass.”

“I don’t disagree, but he is powerful. I sense his magic when he’s near.”

“You can do that? Then warn me when he’s coming, so I can put on my fake smile, eh?”

“Don’t cross him.”

“No? Maybe you should tell him the same. Aron’s sword’s right over there in the pavilion.”

Shane glared.

“I’m not going to mess with him, Shane. He utterly refuses to grip my hand, though. He turns his face from me. Did you see that last night?”

“I did. It was calculated rudeness. He didn’t greet Kodi, either, if it makes you feel any better. Your bows and pleasantries were fair ones anyway, so no, you’re not obvious. I am proud of you. The queen was gracious.”

“Oh! She’s a great one. The only other queen I ever met was Nikal’s mother, and she’s a right fright, that one is. I wanted to punch her for being snotty to Kodi and Nikal. Not that I would ever punch a woman, except the Alkhaness.”

“Should I be recording this conversation?” asked Deens with a smile.

“Er, no,” said Shane.

They then walked over to where Lumin was drawing.

Suddenly, Shane held out his arm as if to hold them back. “It’s magic! Look! Look at his hand! And his eyes close sometimes!”

Tiliruf and the Scribes were awestruck. Lumin’s left hand was moving faster than even Tiliruf wielding a sword at South Fort. His eyes would indeed close for long seconds, yet his hand did not stop.

Manwul and Hadon were oblivious to this. They sat several feet away by the waterside and, as instructed by Lumin, they were chatting relaxed with one another, telling jokes and laughing.

“You mean individual Qeteral might have special magic, eh? Aside from disappearing and talking to birds?”

“Definitely. And as I said, Hurlin’s magic almost exudes from the pores of his skin. It’s palatable. Olin’s strong, too. The Matriarch commented to me upon the strength of my Healing magic. She could detect it.”

“I think pieces of that are in some of the books in the Valley,” said Findun. “There was the Qeteral novice, can’t remember her name. She studied there ages ago, back when Qeteral would study in the Valley. They say she could make trees grow mature from saplings over the course of a summer. There was another who could create flame for a campfire by placing his hand on a stack of sticks.”

“There’s also the tale of one,” offered Deens, “who could memorize a whole book in High Anterianhi in one reading and then write it all out in Qeteral script from memory.”

“Some of that is remarkable. Tiliruf has that kind of visual word memory.”

“Yeah, I do. Lyndz does, too.”

“But we shouldn’t deny the magic of it in a Qeteral. Plainly, we are witnessing it right now in young Lumin.”

And then, amazingly, the young prince had completed his drawing. It had not been ten minutes.

"Come! I'm done! See!"

"What?" said Manwul. He stopped laughing at Hadon's joke and jumped up.

All came to look at Lumin's creation.

Before them on the drawing parchment was a scene. Trees, shrubbery, grass, water that seemed to reflect. All in astonishing detail. And two jovial Human friends sitting on the grass, laughter on their faces.

Wearing boots.

Hadon spoke. "It carries emotion, Lumin. That's high art! That's my friend Manwul and me. That's us!"

"It's just who we are most of the time!" exclaimed Manwul. He reached around Lumin's neck in a bearish hug. "Er, except the Qeteral clothes! And yet it's more us than ever. You even made me hairy. Damn, I'm a handsome thing."

Manwul laughed at his own silliness but then a few tears fell. Hadon, too, was wiping his own face.

"I..." Lumin was perplexed.

Shane explained. "Lumin, Hadon was nearly killed only a short time ago by one of the Alkhaness' soldiers. I saved him. Consider that Manwul nearly lost his longtime mate. What you've depicted here is life itself, forever displayed in a most realistic sketch. I think it apropos you chose to put those two together in your drawing. They are very much brothers."

Lumin looked at Shane. His eyes changed from boy to man. His chin lifted.

"You shall have it, then," he said, matter-of-factly. He carefully tore the page out of the drawing pad and handed it to Manwul. And his words were that of a man. "One does not deny such a bond. It makes me happy to have created a moment of joy for you."

It was a royal gift, no doubt. Manwul plunked down on the grass and held the incredible drawing. He wiped his face. "Thank you, young Lumin. I will treasure it. In fact, Hadon and I will share possession. We'll pass it off to each other over the years, we will."

"I'll have it framed in northern ambernut under glass," said Hadon. "Won't Sturla be amazed? She thinks Manwul's a sweet big bear cub. And his Steffia'll love it, too."

"I will do one or two for all of you to keep, then," Lumin said with a fun smile more boy than man.

"Lumin," said Shane, "would you mind if I laid my hands on you as a Healer and explored the makeup of your body? It is most interesting to me you're part Human."

"Sure! My left arm is tired. It always does that when I draw."

"Easy mend! Come lie down in the pavilion. Deens, bring our young prince one of those apples and a loaf."

One reason Matriarch Gwyn wished to see the three men first was to gain as much knowledge as she could prior to the council meeting planned for later in the morning. She had Curdoz and Kodi recount their Visions (though Curdoz withheld somewhat, and Kodi left out some of the emotion in his). As anticipated, from Nikal she wished to hear the Prophecy. He didn't leave out verses but hated recounting it. Curdoz was also asked to recount what he could of Vanaratu and his story. She had already heard somewhat from Kodi and Lyndz the evening before at dinner as to some of the particulars of the journey to Modela's island.

She had only one counselor present for this early meeting, and that was her father, Prince Hakonn.

He, nor any of the other royal relations, had been at the dinner. They would be meeting them for the first time at the council later. Yet Gwyn also had intentions of more dinners to take place over the next several days whereby they would mingle in a different setting and with more open conversation. So, they had not yet met either her grandparents, the former Matriarch and Patriarch, nor her mother-in-law, the "grandmother" who had Bonded the Human. The dinner the night before was meant mostly for noblemen and noblewomen to participate in a high reception.

Hakonn, her father, was someone she trusted in close counsel, an ally in all things. And yet the first impression the three Human men had when they lay eyes on him and experienced the severe quality of his face was that here was another Prince Hurlin. They looked much alike. Though he was well over a hundred years old, he looked younger by several years than the fifty-something Curdoz, and still with a muscularly fit physique. No Human would have thought he had grown grandchildren in their thirties.

As it turned out, the man was most like his middle grandson, Olin. Quieter, less unfriendly than Hurlin, but with vague hints of skepticism, rarely worded. He was gracious enough in the initial greetings. What they eventually discovered about Hakonn was that in large measure he had conservative views, attuned as he was to attitudes prevailing among many regarding isolation and the damage done by the Abdication of the last emperor. He was one of those who had little to say to Tiliruf, for example. He acted as a kind of counter to his daughter who was generally more progressive. She desired this kind of counter—a check to decisions on her part that might push the Ulaki nation too uncomfortably.

Hakonn was one who always distanced himself from political power. He could have been king had he wanted it. He didn't, preferring the role skip a generation in favor of his daughter. His passion was in scholarly pursuits, and years ago he had been a highly sought-after teacher of the noble classes. That was before his son-in-law died. In the absence of the dead king, Hakonn took upon himself the fatherly role in the family. He and his wife Linea largely ordered the royal household and the education of their grandchildren in order to take these burdens away from their busy daughter.

It was hard to read his reactions to this or that news, as he retained always a face of dispassion. He did more listening than questioning. Usually, he waited for his daughter to turn to him and ask his views before he would comment.

He nearly always used 'lord' and a higher-level address with butler-like formality. And though he may have distanced himself from direct political power, he nevertheless expressed certain unreserved authority.

"Lord Prince, you will bring the Eagle Staff to me and allow me to examine it. If you and the Lord Fothemry will permit it, I would like to examine your minds as you each hold the Staff. It is...similar to your understanding of Healer magic."

"May our Healer Shane participate?" asked Nikal.

"That is permissible."

With Curdoz he offered graciousness. "High Lord Sage, would you please accompany me and my wife on a day soon to my study whereby we would like to show you certain volumes and gauge your council on a few particulars regarding Myghalian philosophy? At a special luncheon, too, we would like to introduce you to some scholarly friends who have come many miles in order to meet a Sage from the Valley. Invite the Mother Matrimonial Idamé. Some of these friends of ours are themselves Bondswomen."

"That is a most gracious invitation, Prince Hakonn. Thank you."

And he would address his own daughter always as 'Matriarch.'

"Yes, Matriarch. I concur the full value behind the Lord Prince's Prophecy. However, I do not believe there is anything in it that directly affects the Qeteral. It pertains to the Nantian royal family, new relationships, and choice-making on the part of the Lord Prince. Yet it is enigmatic. I have little more to offer as to its full interpretation. It is most intriguing that portions of it by the Human Seeress, the Lord Fothemry's great-grandmother, match that of the Berugian Ambassador. I do suspect one thing, however. When the more limited version was first given to the Human Seeress, I would say the Divine had not yet established that it was to apply to the future Lord Prince."

"You do not think then the Divine foresaw the future?"

"As you are aware, I do not like to question His Divinity. Suffice it to say a great man had to demonstrate high virtue."

"I do not know that I am so virtuous," said Nikal, "and felt required to accept the Calling as Rainwing presented it whether or not I appreciated its contents. Even so, though parts of the Prophecy proved painful, other pieces of it have come to have great meaning, particularly in the relationship between Kodi and me."

"Certainly. And this dual control of the Staff is unique and unprecedented. High Berug was intimate with his lord Vanayisu, Father of All, yet it was only following the latter's death that the first Staff's power then came into High Berug's possession, and he concluded the war."

"Whatever happened to that first Staff?" asked Kodi.

"It is unknown. However, what is known, among the Qeteral anyway, is that its magic was broken at the end of the war of the gods. If it exists in the world, it is only a piece of wood with no magic. That first was made of black ebony from wood brought to us from southern islands by the World God, Torovúr. The Eagle Staff, of course, is white holly from Ulakel."

"Who made it?"

Hakonn hesitated. It was the Matriarch who spoke.

"Kodi, that is a great secret, and yet my father and I have much debated this. Give us a few more days to ponder whether to share it. Father thinks not, as do Hurlin and Olin. I think maybe. Yet even Terianh himself knew nothing of this matter. To do so could have implications."

"Yes, Matriarch." He nodded.

"Yet we understand," said Hakonn, "from Lord Prince Hurlin, that you are keen to the knowledge it was made by men alone, and that you discovered this. That much cannot be kept from you, it seems. It lends itself to why I would like to examine you as you hold the Staff. I promise then I will be open with you as to my discoveries. The Matriarch considers you worthy."

The Matriarch looked kindly at Kodi. "I was able to probe your mind a little in our shared Dream. The Guardian told me your name. It was enlightening to know that a Human man had such goodness in his heart."

"And of your father-in-law?"

"Oh, Kodi. He was a very good man. My mother-in-law will soon tell you his story. She is looking forward to meeting you. He was held in regard by many, a great traveler from Eleni. I meant mostly that you are Chosen by Myghal, and I see why. What we did not know at the time of the Vision, and neither did you it seems, was that the Eagle Staff would rise again and that you and Nikal would wield it."

"I have pondered it much," said Curdoz. "It was to not overwhelm Kodi with too much knowledge in the beginning."

"That makes much sense, of course. And though I had hope as given to me by the Divine in the Dream, I admit to much uncertainty that the task, as is known to me, could have been achieved. Yet with the Staff, and as Vanaratu has returned, there is indeed great hope. But we will lay out more in council later."

With regard to Kodi's Vision, the Matriarch did make one comment.

"It speaks highly of Tiliruf a'Terianh that the Divine singled him out to be a key part in this. Surely greatness is still to be found in the Imperial House, and for my part I find that to be hopeful for our world's future should peace be gained again. He bears himself with grace. Many were skeptical when we received word from Olin of his presence among you. I was not."

Of Curdoz' Vision she also spoke to her father, "Do you agree there is more here to affirm the appointed task?"

"Yes, Matriarch. I admit having been skeptical. Yet I see nothing here that decreases the exceptional danger."

She looked at the men. "This has all been most enlightening."

They were given another two hours before the council was to take place. As servants led them to the palace doors, Kodi made known he would like to find and speak to Lyndz. One servant then led Nikal and Curdoz on, whereas the other led Kodi to a portion of the palace on the second level where Lyndz and the others were staying. Upon arriving at her rooms, however, he discovered she was not alone. In a wood-paneled parlor she sat with the Princess Ryn herself. They were engaged in conversation.

If Kodi was hoping for another opportunity to see the princess, there was a good chance of it. He may not have wished quite that his sister would be witness, yet the circumstance was without choice just then.

Ryn was wearing an open-fronted green, short-sleeved shirt. Much skin and curve showed. A garland of flowers draped down her neck accentuating her breasts.

She stood.

Kodi swallowed.

Yet it all turned out as good as he could have conceivably hoped.

"Kodi," she said. Her blue eyes shone. She stood forward, and he kissed her hand for the second time.

"M'lady Ryn."

"I shall leave presently so you and your sister can exchange news. It is fine to see you again. I have been wondering, Kodi...would you accommodate me, perhaps tomorrow, as a kind of favor?"

Kodi's world turned upside down, and yet it seemed so very right-side up.

"I would be more than delighted, m'lady," he said with all grace and a twinkle in his brown eyes. He probably wanted to say, 'gyah, yeah!'

"Accompany me tomorrow morning to the potteries, just you and I. I would like to show you some of the craft I most enjoy. Perhaps we'll do a piece together on the wheel."

And though he probably wanted to say, 'heck, yeah, you bet I would,' what came out was, "There is nothing I would rather do than to spend the morning with you, m'lady."

"I shall send for you, then!" Her smile was infectious.

Kodi was nearly overcome. His grin showed extra big, but he otherwise held firm. "Thank you...Ryn."

She then spoke a goodbye word to Lyndz, yet before she left, she spoke to Kodi one last time.

"Our Qeteral attire is most becoming on you, Kodi." Her eyes were bright stars. "I anticipated it would be."

The servant shut the door behind them as they left.

Totally forgetting where he was, he made a step forward as if to follow.

"Kodi!" yelped Lyndz.

He turned around and blinked.

She whistled. "Oh, my. I, er, don't think I expected what I just saw. Oh, my. That has come out of the blue."

Kodi couldn't speak.

"You were hoping for it, I see," she said with a knowing grin.

"I...I..."

"She's extraordinary, Kodi. How could you not be charmed? Sit, Kodi."

He complied.

They didn't speak for a few moments. Finally, Lyndz spoke again.

"She's Qeteral, Kodi."

"Does it matter?"

"Yes, and no. Yes, because all craziness is running around in my mind. Seeing things that might not even be there. But here goes. She's already in her thirties, though she's really the same as us in Human years. She's going to live to be around a hundred and sixty. She will remain young for many long decades while you age the Human way. She's a princess, and you're the son of a count. Though really, you're now a high lord and *Brother of Myghal*, which is almost godlike to some of them. I'm sorry I'm seeing all this; it's just part of what I do is anticipate. But ultimately, no, Kodi. If this leads to something bigger it doesn't matter, and their family is already part Human. For the moment as I saw the two of you standing together, and as you looked in each other's faces, it was the most gorgeous-looking couple I've ever seen in my life. You're a hunky piece of superior flesh, brother-of-mine, looking like that! With a perfectly handsome, almost Qeteral face to go with it. She is attracted to you, Kodi. She *'anticipated'* you being...being *half bared*, and she got an eyeful, didn't she? Er, you really didn't come to see me! You were hoping you might catch a glimpse of her again, and that she might just catch sight of *pretty-boy Kodi* showing off his big muscles and well-turned legs in Qeteral garb. Don't hem and haw! It's perfectly fine, of course. I'd do the very same, I'm sure. Of course, she's absolutely stunning, Kodi. What woman doesn't want to look like her, I might add?"

"You're as incredible as she is, Lyndz. Why do you think my sights are set so high, if not because I've been looking at you for years? Nobody's ever compared, er, until now. And it's the smarts, too. I want a woman like you."

It was surely the greatest, most complimentary thing any brother could ever say to his sister, and Lyndz beamed hugely.

"Well, I'll tell you this. She's smart as a whip. She certainly qualifies, and I've come to admire you so much, Kodi. You're a great hero, and certainly good enough for her. But, gosh, be careful, Kodi! Her mother! Her brothers! This is royalty we're talking about here."

"Yeah, so Shane reminded me last night when I couldn't sleep."

She paused before she spoke again. "Well, you outgrew what bit of fool you had in you a few years ago. I know you're smart, and I know you're careful—to a degree. You're also a risk-taker, though. But as long as she's doing the leading here, you cannot fall into error."

"Shane said that, too."

"Shane's the smartest man of the lot of you. He out-wises good old Curdoz, if you ask me. Now, listen. It's interesting when you think about Ryn's invitation. Clearly, compared to certain Human cultures, a Qeteral princess must have some freedom over her own activities and choices and can entertain and communicate with whomever she pleases. But don't assume too much. We're still guests here."

They chatted a little more on this until a pause.

"You're looking superior yourself, Lyndz."

She in fact was wearing clothing much like to what Ryn was. They had given the women clothing just as they had the men, and she and the Healer women chose to wear it. She also wore a flowered necklace Ryn had brought as a little gift for her to wear for the day until it faded.

"Mishoo and Ryn have been most encouraging, and it feels right, here in Ulakel. I only keep the loops drawn because they're there. It feels good to get out of dresses and long-sleeved shirts and lady trousers."

As it was, she wouldn't always have the loops drawn or the bows tied, and her curves would be even more visible. She had discarded old modesty for now. She wanted to live as the Qeteral at least while she was in Ulakel, and that's what she did, and Kodi and the other men wouldn't dare tease. Yet it was hard not to stare. She'd turned into a princess of the forest, sufficiently Qeteral in her own looks, walking high and proud, and even Idamé could not fault her. She was simply too lovely, a kind of sunshine goddess who stepped out of the woods into even more sunshine.

Kodi had not intended to stay long, but he and his sister hadn't had close conversation in quite a while. He remained, ate some of the fruit and bread that was in the room and drank some tea, and they spoke together until time for the council meeting. The best of what came of this was a renewal of their faith in one another, strong support, and encouragement in all matters as pertaining to their emotional and mental growth since they left Tulesk, and as to their hopes for the future. Probably the one sad thing was that Lyndz still was required to keep certain secrets from him.

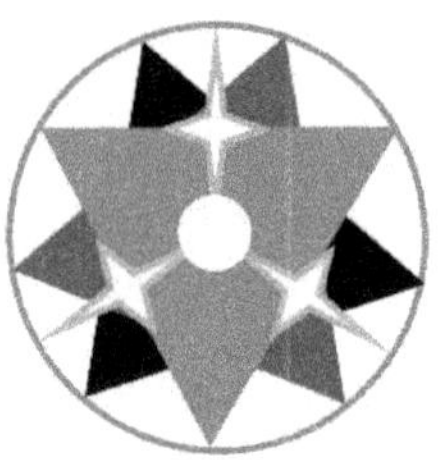

Chapter 16—Revelations in Council

The council began in the fourth hour of the morning. Human and Etoppsi visitors were led in flights of stairs to a high broad balcony which looked out westward on a picturesque countryside. The sun went in and out behind puffy clouds for the remainder of the day. Half the verandah was shaded by a massive pergola, this covered in great shady vines which climbed heavy wooden columns from the ground three stories below. At the forward edge of the decking were huge terracotta planters of flowering shrubs, herbs, geraniums of red, and other vibrant flowers. Birds flitted about and sang among the shrubbery and the pergola vines. A series of wooden chairs with cushions were arranged for conversation, though there were small tables interspersed as well and benches for the Etoppsi. Refreshing cool drinks were available in pitchers.

They discovered that only members of the greater royal family were present. There was no one, then, among the nobility from the reception the evening before. They would come to discover that, though the nobility engaged regularly and offered council in private discussions, they were not involved much in decision-making, ruling only their own estates. A high trust pervaded the general government of the land.

In a way, society was a little more ordered from the top, and the Ulaki people were ruled in an enlightened manner by the Matriarch and her functionaries. It was less democratic than the Republic of Tirilorin, but even in comparison to the Human kingdoms or Berug it did not demand a good deal of political debate. The truth of the matter was that the Qeteral race was largely unified in a land where peace reigned supreme. Was there difference of opinion among them? Certainly. But a balance of collective mind pervaded. The proverbial "boat" was rarely "rocked," and even if it ever was rocked, cool headedness tended to dictate outcomes. Theirs was a race of strong emotion, yet also serene and reflective, tending towards intellect and the aesthetic of nature, art and craft.

In some ways it was a model society, almost utopian. Yet there were pressures of a sort. The population of the land was nearing the limits of sustainability without serious changes to the manner in which the land was used. It was an estate, family-farmstead, and village-centered society requiring a great deal of wide-open space, in addition to a landscape they cherished and which they always hesitated to modify. It might be another hundred years or so until it truly became a pressing issue, but already Qeteral families had been moving into the more remote mountain valleys in order to sustain this sort of life. But these areas, though also beautiful, were more challenging with regards to productivity.

A more natural pattern might have been to shift new settlement southward, south of the Plateau into the forested lands that separated the Qeteral from old Lintiri or even into Lintiri itself, largely abandoned except for some coastal trading enclaves. Yet the idea carried uncertainties, for to carry the Barrier magic beyond the current border was a doubtful proposition. Its power was in part based on space. It would weaken if it moved south away from the majority of the people and away from the Plateau where a certain magic underlay the land itself. And no one was willing to attempt any sort of colony, as their racial isolationism would surely become more difficult to uphold. The flaw in the Qeteral was in racial pride, in isolationism, in resistance to the new, a refusal to take risks, and a presumption that the Qeteral way of life could continue forever unchanged. They needed something to change them, to open them, to fear Humans less, and it was really something in their mindset and collective unconscious that made such change difficult for them. However, as long as the khans of the southern continent were a threat, such change could not even be risked even if some could be found who were willing to colonize.

The Guardian was not unaware of these problems. He understood the Qeteral mind. In large measure He loved how Qeteral thought and lived, and morally they were the least Fallen of the three races. But they needed to shift the workings of their minds whereby they could engage more readily and more equally with the other races and nations, to contribute to their betterment and them to theirs. He had His plan, and He had chosen a certain few to help in the regaining of a balance for all the races, but winning the war was key, and also subtlety.

A piece of the subtlety was in the coming of the group to Ulakel. He wanted the Qeteral to see and know some good people from the other two races, Humans in particular. It may be that the Matriarch herself was wise to this. Maybe not to the fullest depths of Myghalian Design for the world of Dumhoni, to all the subtleties on His part, but she understood from her Vision, that at the least, the coming of Kodi and the others had meaning behind it that was extraordinary, and it had something to do with a future beyond current events.

And so, she *controlled* accordingly the interaction between the races, so as to garner that unity of purpose from her family and people for future change. She believed the Guardian had trust in her, and like Kodi, she had trust in the Guardian. She also trusted Kodi. When he spoke, she absorbed his words and pondered them closely.

Her grandparents, the former Matriarch and Patriarch were present, as was Hakonn her father, and Linea, her mother. Present, too, was her mother-in-law, Manoo. All most handsome people. Even the former Matriarch and Patriarch, now close to a hundred-fifty years, though less muscular and sensual in comparison to the younger generations, retained beautiful skin, un-grayed hair, and faces of deep wisdom. Also present, of course, were the Matriarch's four children. Though Lumin was considered to be young, what mattered most to Gwyn was that Lumin plainly liked the Humans a great deal. Though they would speak very little, Manoo and Lumin were important due to their unqualified openness to the sister race of Humans.

That three Etoppsi were also present added significance to the entire affair. As the Matriarch had requested of Rainwing the evening before, the Berugian ambassador sat beside her. The Eagle Staff was placed upright in a stand between Kodi and Nikal, and many were attuned to the fact that the absence of Rainwing's wings allowed that historic implement to be there in the first place.

As Curdoz had gained permission beforehand, Deens and Findun were present to take notes. They looked odd with their long beards, sitting to the side at a table with their parchment, and they never spoke. Yet they did feel important.

It isn't necessary to relay the whole of the conversation, but to summarize. This is what took place, and this was what was learned.

After all had been introduced to one another, Matriarch Gwyn had Hakonn tell a background story. The facts, heretofore unknown to anyone aside from the Matriarch and Hakonn, astounded everyone.

In the time of the Anterianhi Rebellion, when the Guardian had come to make Terianh into a War Wizard, there came a point where it was understood that the Ralsheen, still with a sizeable and powerful navy, would be able to hold out indefinitely in the Tolosian Peninsula. There were no easy ways for Terianh's armies to gain access to it. Another means had to be used in order to finally destroy the evil Ralsheen and bring peace again. The Guardian then came a second time to the land of Ulakel, the first being when he commissioned the Eagle Staff. He chose forty, men and women, taking them in a ship to the Southern Continent. They traveled even to the Serpent Sea, and upon disembarking they traveled westward. He took them to a point not so far from the settled lands of the Berugians on the borders of the Infested Jungle.

Being of great magic, and with the Guardian's presence, the forty Qeteral were able to counter the poisons of the Jungle and travel about it with ease. Here, the Guardian, with unprecedented power, opened a Doorway—a kind of magical gateway—connecting the Infested Jungle with the Tolosian Peninsula far to the north. Travel from one to the other could take place in a matter of minutes. No World God nor magical Qeteral have such power to alter the dimensions of space, but Myghal, being of the Cosmic Mind of the Creator, He alone had such power. Along with the commissioning of Terianh, this would be His great contribution to the war. The Qeteral with their magic could communicate with the Wingless Dragons of the Jungle. Gathering two thousands of the ferocious beasts into a great army, they released the Dragons through the Doorway into Tolos.

It was also at this time that the last Ralsheen emperor was engaged in his final battle against Terianh the Great in present day Ascanti whereby the emperor was defeated and killed. And then the Wingless Dragons came through the Doorway into Tolos, ravaging unchallenged, destroying the last of the Ralsheen armies and cities, and Siriné, having been challenged by Vanaratu, was not present to fight them.

Having assured the Guardian they could return to Ulakel on their own, Myghal left the forty Qeteral a magical key in order to close the Gateway and alone to make their way home. He left them in order to find Vanaratu so they could deal with Siriné.

However, when the Qeteral came to the shore of the Serpent Sea to retrieve their ship, to their great distress it had been blown away and destroyed in a storm. All that was left to them were the little skiffs with which they had landed. Being then their only means of transport, in the four small boats they rowed, following the western shoreline. They did this with the hopes of reaching a point around the rocky land in those parts whereby they could then walk to the north. There were some Humans living in those lands, progenitors of those eventually enslaved by the khans, and maybe they could receive some help from them. They hoped then to be able to send birds as messengers to Ulakel for assistance in returning home.

But the Serpent Sea is a strange sea and unpredictable, and those southern places are subject to many brief storms, and so, such a storm appeared and carried three of the boats into the deeper waters.

They were never seen again, and from the remaining boat only ten despairing Qeteral ever returned to the land of Ulakel. It was presumed the remaining thirty were lost in the Serpent Sea.

Hakonn then extrapolated from the tale of Vanaratu as told to them by Curdoz that morning.

It was not long thereafter that Vanaratu entrapped Siriné in the Serpent Sea, as instructed by the Guardian. The Guardian crowned Terianh as First Emperor of the new Empire, granting him authority over all Humans and designating him High Protector in a union with the Qeteral, and then went Himself to the Serpent Sea. Having then transformed those two World Gods into their different forms, being Called by the One to the challenges of another world, Myghal bade farewell to Vanaratu and departed into the heavens. He did not know of the lost Qeteral.

It was here that the Matriarch herself took up the tale.

But as was discovered only twenty-five years ago, the thirty Qeteral were not drowned in the sea in the storm but were carried to its eastern shore. Trapped, however, by the furies of the storm of Siriné and her raging whirlpool, escape was impossible. Nor could the thirty discover a means to overcome the jagged mountains that separated them from what later became East Khestadon. The birds that dwelled in this land were not great flyers, being rather heavy and eaters of fruit. They could not be used for great flights north in order to send messages, and gulls and their relations do not like the Serpent Sea. So, the Qeteral were confined in a small land on the eastern shore. Luckily, the land was one of tropical beauty, for it did not contain the horrors of the Infested Jungle. It was a flourishing place of many birds, other wildlife, and many lush fruits. They built for themselves new lives in this rich place, and though they missed dreadfully their own land of Ulakel, nevertheless over time children were born to them, as most had been un-Bonded beforehand, and they were able to achieve a level of prosperity. As the original thirty died, the new generations were largely content to continue here. Though the shore itself was sometimes ravaged by Siriné as she bounced from coast to coast, the Qeteral established their villages inland and were safe.

They were content then for four long centuries, bearing many children, until the coming of the Alkhan to his new realm of East Khestadon. And in time, as the Alkhan sent out his minions to explore the lands southward; these found rugged ways across the jagged mountains.

The Qeteral were discovered. Sending troops and savage beasts, the Alkhan ravaged their villages and took away some of them. For though they had their magic to disappear from view, his spell-bound beasts could sniff them out. Some twenty or more were taken in this raid, and what became of them was not known, yet it was presumed they were enslaved.

It was at this time that a juvenile albatross was found along the shore having been carried a long distance in a great storm from seas further north. This bird was nursed back to full health by the Qeteral, growing strong and with great pride. It was a brave and magnificent creature. They instilled magic into it whereby they could communicate their need. They sent it therefore on a desperate mission to deliver messages to their kin in the north. It succeeded in making the journey. It was by way of this bird that the Ulaki people found out that there were refugees in the far south, descendants of the thirty lost Qeteral, and that they were in difficult straits, unknowing when the Alkhan might yet send another raiding party in order to discover them all and enslave them to his will.

Having grown weary of ruling, and with so many great decisions to be made, the former Matriarch and Patriarch abdicated their rule in favor of their granddaughter Gwyn and her brave half-Human husband, Mabelin. Lumin was a little child at the time. Being of great engineering skill and understanding the books in their possession on shipbuilding, King Mabelin took many men to the Lintiri Sea shore and built a ship for the purposes of traveling to the South with the mission of finding the refugees and bringing them home. High though his purpose and strong his determination, it was a mission doomed from the beginning, and yet many believed at the time it was the only choice they had.

To reach out to the Nantians for help was strongly opposed by all, and in their pride the Ulaki attempted the fateful journey. For a period of a week, messages were exchanged, but as their ship, too new, too small, and with inexperienced sailors, entered into the waters beyond the quiet Lintiri Sea, it foundered and sank. This information was delivered by the birds. All were in great mourning, and it seemed the decision to attempt the rescue was not sufficiently planned. One small ship was never enough in the first place. More and larger ships would be needed, not to mention the likelihood of encountering the West Khestadone navy. Some thought the king a half-Human fool, though some thought him at the least, willing and brave, when no others among them had the knowledge or the courage to help their lost southern brethren.

The Matriarch despaired. It was then, however, that she received the first of two Visions from the Guardian. Myghal came to her in a Dream and told her to have hope, for there were now Humans born in the world, whom He believed could be of great help in time. He told her to have patience and allow them to grow and mature until in time they would come with the knowledge and help she needed to save the southern Qeteral. And in the Dream, the Guardian Himself expressed sorrow for His choice in leaving the forty Qeteral to their own devices at the time of the making of the Doorway and promised to do what He could from a distance to effect their eventual return.

In the following years, messages were sent back and forth to the south by way of a kind of bird that only dwelled in the land of Ulakel, the white ravens. Some of these would be lost in the dangers of the passage, yet others would succeed, and by way of these messengers the southern Qeteral were encouraged. They were to hide themselves the best they could from the Alkhan and await the years. And though they indeed did so, they continued to express a certain hopelessness, for all now understood the extraordinary dangers involved in any rescue or journey.

The second Vision Gwyn received from the Guardian was in the last winter. An experienced white raven of great wisdom and bravery had achieved the return journey from the South. Yet the news was bad. Yet another raid by the Alkhan and his beasts had come and taken away more of their people. They were growing more desperate and had little hope that they could remain safe. Some six hundred remained who had not been taken and enslaved. The land was small and there were few more places whereby they could hide and yet maintain the production of food. Sad and fearful of the future, it was then that Gwyn received the second Vision, and in it she perceived Kodi. Myghal spoke to her and explained what He had in mind.

This was the task, now, as Gwyn in the midday sun explained to them all. Only her father Hakonn had been privy to it. But now she told all present what was to be done.

Great ships were to be provided by Human Nantians, seven great ships. Led by the World God Vanaratu, they were to journey with Qeteral among them, to the south, through the Khestadone Sea, and through the narrow straights to the Sea of Siriné itself. They would find the land on the eastern shore where the southern Qeteral were hidden, find them, and bring them home to Ulakel.

Throughout the telling of the tale, there were a great many interruptions, questions, jaw-dropping exclamations, and a certain amount of argument. The former Patriarch found much to question, as did Hurlin. Both men were skeptical, but the former Patriarch ultimately grew quiet, for he knew he was no longer in the position to make the decisions and trusted his granddaughter. To deny the Visions from the Guardian was something he could not do. Hurlin, plainly, was not convinced, yet even he could not go against his mother's will.

Suggestions were made. Nikal offered assurances. Curdoz and Idamé reaffirmed all by way of their own Visions. Kodi expressed willingness and brave words, and Curdoz was privately very proud of him and his manner, as was Lyndz.

Then, Rainwing suggested it might be possible with other planning for Berug to get involved and for Etoppsi to seek out the refugees and fly them home. Hurlin offered his approval of such an idea. However, though the Matriarch was quick to offer high thanks for the suggestion, what was understood now from the Vision was that, with Vanaratu's magic, secrecy of a kind could only be achieved in the waters, otherwise the khans would perceive the plan should Etoppsi be discovered in flights east and then north and fight them with magic. It was then that Kodi also concurred.

"Myghal has spoken to me now. He says the plan He gave to the Matriarch is the one to be followed."

"*He* says so to *you?*" said Hurlin. It was the first he had spoken to Kodi since telling him to let Musca romp freely through the fields. It was almost as if he were looking for an opportunity to jump at Kodi. It seemed to have little to do with the value of the plans being considered. "Why does He do so? How do we know you did not make this up? I find it hard to believe the Divine speaks to you so clearly despite being a War Wizard. I do not deny you control the Eagle Staff, but this seems unprecedented to me to claim the Divine speaks to you in words. Telling you to do this or to do that. Lord Nikal, is this what you meant when you said Kodi is close to the Divine? I understood you to mean in spirit."

"And why would not that be sufficient, Lord Hurlin? You and I agreed that faith in the Divine is of high value, and we have these Visions and Prophecies to tell us something of His determination in this matter. I explained certain things to you regarding Kodi, and Lyndz, too. But yes, Myghal speaks to Kodi, and sometimes I hear the echoes myself in my own mind."

"They are the Brothers of Myghal," said the queen's mother-in-law, Manoo. "Do you deny this, Grandson?"

"It is meant of course as a symbol, Grandmother, the War Wizard who fights for the Divine."

"It is more," said his other grandmother, Linea. "To be a Brother of Myghal is to be connected in spiritual union with the Divine. I met with Mother Idamé this morning, and she has spoken to me of Kodi's Gift of being able to speak with the Divine. I asked her this because of the myth attached to War Wizards that they can speak with Myghal. I wished to know for myself. Berug and Terianh, it is said, could speak to Him, as of course could also Vanayisu, Father of All. Mother Idamé is of great heart. There is no desire to deceive on her part, or by Lord Kodi and the others."

"Thank you, Lady Linea," said Idamé.

Gwyn nodded at Kodi, who took that as a cue to explain.

"The reason, good Hurlin, that Myghal said what he did to me just now was in order that Vanaratu's skills and magic were not to be circumvented, and also that there is more to this journey than meets the eye. It is part of His plan, and it has been a long time in the making. He was gracious, actually, to Rainwing's suggestion, but what He is saying is that there is more to all of this beyond the attempted rescue."

"You understood all of that from such few words?"

"I did, for I have come to know the manner of his communication with me."

"And just what else is there besides rescuing our brethren from the South?"

"He would not say. I did not ask, and I won't."

Hurlin pshawed.

"I am not attempting to be difficult, good Hurlin. The point is that my Brother Myghal will not tell me all. Where His plan involves others is not meant to be my concern unless he deliberately makes it known. Rainwing's plan was a good one, and its possibilities began immediately to play in my mind. That Myghal then intervened in those thoughts was important to Him. He doesn't typically communicate with me in the way you suggest, telling me to do this or to do that. But in this case, He did not wish the idea to be carried through, and I felt it had something to do with Vanaratu. But He's not going to tell me what He expects of Vanaratu, as that is between them. And Myghal may have other reasons besides even these."

"He is being gracious explaining these intricacies in their communication, Lord Prince Hurlin," said Hakonn quietly, "for he does not have to do so."

Hurlin looked at his grandfather and nodded. It was plain he respected him greatly. He then looked at Kodi and also nodded. "I grant it."

It was not an apology, but it was an acknowledgment. Yet it was not likely that the exchange really improved Hurlin's attitude towards Kodi.

"What I am strongly opposed to, Mother," Hurlin continued, "is that any of our people should leave the protection of the Barrier in order to go south with the Humans."

Olin, who had not yet said a word then spoke in his normally quiet tones. "That concern did come to my mind. However, I concluded for my part that our people must make common cause with the Humans, for it is our own people we are wishing to bring home."

"I don't wish them to be corrupted by..." Hurlin started, and then his voice faltered.

"Corrupted by what?" asked Maru and Ulna at the same time. It was never stated by anyone, as they hid it well, but the two women Healers were nearly as annoyed by Hurlin as was Tiliruf.

Tiliruf never said a word during this entire conversation, though he shook his head about a hundred different times at all the pieces of information as they presented themselves.

"Our people," said Ryn, "will not be corrupted. They would be on a mission of high purpose. Be not so skeptical, my good brother. I have great faith in our Human brethren. They are little different from us, really. What joy our grandmother has when speaking of our Human grandfather, such a strong and good man. Those who have come among us even now are of the highest and best nature."

She looked at Lyndz first as she said this, then to Kodi, and smiled.

Hurlin frowned.

"I think I understand a little of what concerns Hurlin," offered Nikal. "Let it be admitted that not all Human and Qeteral values, outlooks, and actions align. Too, the Etoppsi. Our peoples are each different in sundry ways. Hurlin, I understand you may fear Human strangeness and actions you may consider uncouth. Yet my shipmen are the best, or they wouldn't be on my ships. Wherever we might be required to disembark in the places we rule, your people will be graciously received. Do you have faith in me, Hurlin? It's important to me to know that you do."

"I...I guess I do." Hurlin nodded to Nikal. His face was marginally softer when looking at Nikal.

"It is sufficient," said Gwyn. "I admire my son's concern for our people, of course. His mind is where it naturally lies, in the protection of his people. Hurlin, you understand how greatly your family reveres you and your great strength of purpose, the Gift bestowed in faith by the Divine upon you at birth to take control of the magical Barrier in your maturity. Our country is well-protected because of you, with your strong brother Olin at your side, he nearly as powerful as yourself, and others.

"Yet Olin is right, too, for our own must share in the sacrifice of regaining our own. Our own people, lost to us for centuries, now numbering some six hundred, are in desperate straits and need us. Your offer to help us, Lord Nikal, gives me such high hope. Of course, we are grateful beyond measure and trust you."

"Lord Sage and Mother Matrimonial Idamé," began Hakonn, "there is a magic I can employ whereby I can determine the Qeteral faces you saw in your Visions, those whom you saw on the ships as you described and who are meant to go with you on the journey. It is an important detail we have overlooked in our discussion. It would be helpful for Lord Prince Hurlin and myself to have the information. It will be mostly he who chooses who is to go."

Hurlin was looking grim, yet he nodded in compliance.

"Of course, Prince Hakonn," said Idamé.

"That is remarkable, of course," said Curdoz, "if you can determine such specifics in our memories."

There was a short pause.

"Oh, no!" exclaimed Lyndz loudly, startling everyone. "Oh, no!"

All looked at her.

"What is it?" asked Rainwing, great concern on her face.

"I see something! I see something! Oh, no!" Lyndz looked wide-eyed at Kodi.

"What do you see, Lyndz?"

"That's what the khans are trying to find at the Berugian border! The Doorway!"

As it dawned on them all that she was right, a great many jaws dropped in horror.

"That's it! They wish to find the Doorway and send an army into Tolos!" Curdoz exclaimed in rapid words.

There was long pause.

"Another warfront? But they would be stuck there without ships, wouldn't they?" asked Kodi. "Lyndz, our father could still be there!"

The Matriarch acted confused and requested more information, and this was when Flamefur was at last called upon by Curdoz to describe the recent incident at Eye Tower Fifty-five.

When he then at the end of his tale spoke of the Qeteral Dragon Rider, the Matriarch, among some of the other Qeteral, stood from their seats.

"The Alkhan has indeed enslaved Qeteral to his will, just as feared!" she proclaimed. "He is using them to control the Dragons!"

"Unthinkable!" exclaimed the former Patriarch and Matriarch together.

There was another long pause.

"And yet, as you have told us, your kind can communicate with and control the Wingless," said Nikal. He looked at Flamefur. "You are to depart tomorrow in flight to Berug, Storm-Major. Matriarch, is there any other information you can provide? Did the ten Qeteral who returned provide maps or any other records as to their time there? We must send all the information we can to King Eagleron. That region must be protected. Did...did they have this *'key'* to the Doorway with them, the ten?"

"No, they did not. I presume it must be among the refugees even now, unless..."

"Unless the Alkhan has already confiscated it from them," concluded Rainwing. "Flamefur should make all speed. I will write everything, and you will present it to King Eagleron and Queen Silverwing."

"Certainly, Ambassador. I can make the flight in less than a week, Nikal."

"I concur with Kodi and do not understand the value of sending an army to Tolos, for as you say, they would be confined there unless one of the khans was to go also," said Nikal. "That is a possibility, but then he or she would be absent from the South. It might have made more sense prior to the Alkhaness engaging us."

"It is possible something may be wanted from Tolos other than establishing another warfront," said Shane. "Yet even if it were to establish a foothold in the north, it would be a major blow. They could then with time build boats to land on the Ascanti shore. Brother Curdoz! They could make common cause with the Ice Tribes!"

Curdoz raised a high eyebrow. "Ralsheen descendants! I have worried if there have somehow been communications between the khans and the Ice Tribes, though I have no evidence. Except of course now we know the Ice Tribes have opened dialog with the Prince of Hesk, whom we cannot trust. It was mostly the coincidence of these events which made me wonder."

"Your thinking is surely right," said Shane. "Could they have used birds? Black crows like those we found spying at Danzilet? Difficult yet conceivable. Should we send messages to Solanto?"

"I think we will have to," said Curdoz. "Stormgale, do you know the way?"

"I know the direction."

"I know it all," said Rainwing. "Geography, even of the Human kingdoms, is my forte. I can provide the information..."

"But not first to the king in Ferostro," said Curdoz. "Rather to Grand Duke Mannago, and then he may send you to Duke Amerro in Tulesk, but then you must immediately return and find us, Stormgale. And bring back all the news from there. Kodi and Lyndz, Amerro would know if your father has returned safely from Tolos."

"There may be records," said the former Patriarch, "and it may be that the whereabouts of the southern Doorway can be discovered. I shall go myself and look for the information in our archives as soon as we dismiss. However, the northern terminus was not known to those who aided the Guardian."

"Tolos is a huge place, as big as a large dukedom or principality," said Curdoz. "It makes sense He might have opened it into their last capital city. It is presumed that that was far in the interior, yet its location is unknown. The Dragons have at last died out only recently, and the twins' father has been exploring the peninsula under the duke's orders to find their lost city and any treasure, but whether he has yet found it is uncertain."

They were in council for another hour, and during that time the battle at South Fort was discussed, and Lyndz described her Gift of Moment Mastering and in that of Musca. She also described her earlier spy mission with Rainwing and what they had discovered, or rather *how* all was discovered, as Curdoz had already made plain the khans' being the twin children of the last Ralsheen emperor. The Qeteral agreed Lyndz' and Musca's magic was a most extraordinary Gift and not something that had ever occurred among their own kind. In addition, the earlier journey to Vanayema was recounted, and it was made known all the sacrifices the company made in order to gain the Eagle Staff. The Qeteral were moved by this, and following Hakonn's initiative, they all stood and bowed to Rainwing, and Gwyn offered kind words especially to Tiliruf for the loss of Terianh's Sword.

"Why does everyone call him *Good Hurlin*, eh?"

"I respect him, that's why," said Kodi. "I want to demonstrate that though I disagree with him, I still respect his views."

"Even when he's wrong?"

"You heard the Matriarch," said Shane. "Hurlin is the most magically powerful Qeteral alive, and it seems his brother Olin is next. I told you I could sense their potency. That is because the magic itself is emanating from their bodies at all times to maintain the Barrier."

"Even while they sleep?"

"I suspect so. Remarkable. That is power nearly at the level of the World Gods. The two were chosen by Meical, no less than Nikal and Kodi, to be the ones to protect their kingdom."

"But it doesn't mean he has to act so unfriendly."

"He distrusts Humans, and based on history, he has good reason," said Nikal. "Ours is the race most prone to violence, most prone to sexual license, most prone to mistreatment of women, most prone to adultery, murder, and a hundred other evils. The Qeteral? None of these things, though they still suffer from pride and prejudice. Hurlin doesn't know any of us well enough yet to counter his views. Though it is true he resists getting to know us. He loves his family. He is loyal. And they plainly value him highly, and it isn't just because of his magic. There is pride when they look on him. He will surely be the next king when his mother abdicates."

"Well, let's hope she doesn't do that anytime soon, eh?"

The Etoppsi had gone with the former Patriarch to the archives to assist him in looking for histories or journals that might reflect on the ten Qeteral who had returned from helping the Guardian all those centuries before. Curdoz was writing at a table in the pavilion. He had numerous messages and all sorts of details he wished to send both south and north with the two Etoppsi.

"Hurlin is not our problem," he said bluntly. "He is no enemy, Tiliruf. He eventually came around as you saw. Could somebody go to the palace and ask Rainwing if she's finished with her letters to Queen Silverwing? We need to package them when we're all done. Nikal, I think you should have Flamefur fly first to our ships and give the news to the captains."

"Yes, I will. I've also decided that for us to sail to Danzilet as first destination when we leave here would only waste valuable time. I'm going to have Flamefur fly to Danzilet rather than all the way to Berug as I had first intended. I want him back with us as soon as may be, and one of the other Etoppsi can take the messages on to Eagleron and Silverwing. I've decided that the four additional ships should prepare and then meet us in the open waters north of the Khestadone Sea. A large fleet is there already, patrolling those waters, but I want fresh sailors and supplies from Danzilet. It might help if Hurlin knows we won't have to stop in Danzilet and his people be 'corrupted' by the immoral citizens of a Human city. I'm exaggerating of course, but any tidbit that might ease his mind is good, but more importantly it could save us two weeks' time or more not to sail there first to retrieve the four ships. I can send Flamefur yet again when we leave here when it is time for those four ships to sail out of Danzilet for the rendezvous."

"Shane and I'll go to Rainwing," said Kodi.

"Yes," said Shane. "I need to confer for a few minutes with Ulna and Maru anyway."

Those two left. The others remained in conversation. The Scribes were assisting Curdoz.

"That Lyndz is something," said Nikal.

"She truly is," agreed Curdoz. "I think it would have hit us eventually about the Doorway, but she is quick. Very quick."

"Her logic has caused me to think. I realize now I should send word by another Etoppsis at Danzilet to the east to warn Jaden of the potential for more Dragons on the part of the Alkhan. It wouldn't hurt to put in a request to King Eagleron for a troupe of Dragon Legionnaires to go east."

"As you are Polemarch, he will likely grant the request."

"I'll speak to Rainwing, Rusty, and Stormy and gauge their opinion on the matter. It would be wrong of me to call for Legionnaires if it would make them shorthanded. But even a few could be helpful."

At some point, Manwul and Hadon returned from where they had been. Lumin was with them.

He was grinning.

"After lunch at the palace he had us watch him in a village race full of young Qeteral stallions," explained Hadon.

"He won it, of course!" exclaimed Manwul, patting Lumin on the shoulder. "Never seen anything like it. No Human could possibly run that fast!"

Nikal smiled at the Qeteral prince. "That's excellent, Lumin. And I saw the drawing you did of Manwul and Hadon. Fine talent! Why don't you, Tiliruf, Manwul, and Hadon go for a little swim there? Curdoz and I are busy here just now, but I'll be freer tonight. Are you going to stay with us? I'll teach you Kings and Castles. I'm the best, except maybe Shane."

"I'm better than Nikal, Lumin, don't believe him!" said Tiliruf laughing.

Those four marched off for a playful swim, as Tiliruf, Manwul, and Hadon had nothing else to do, and Lumin was enjoyable company.

"The warmth you have in your heart is plain, Nikal," said Curdoz nodding in Lumin's direction.

"He is similar to Kodi in some ways."

"I have come to realize over long years that a happy self-confidence and joy define certain individuals. As an older man, I mark it keenly when I see it in young people. Kodi certainly. Lumin, it seems, is the same in that regard. The rest of us—we who struggle with rougher pieces inside our souls—are blessed to know them. For my part it is envy, but it is also inspiration."

Nikal looked at Curdoz and smiled. "I wholeheartedly understand. Did you happen to notice how Lumin was chuckling during Hurlin's gloomiest drama? And Manwul and Hadon were sitting either side of him and almost were laughing themselves. Thankfully, they were behind where Hurlin could not see them well.

"But back to what I was telling you earlier, Curdoz, I'm not happy taking only seven ships. We believe the Alkhaness has at least two hundred galleys that ply those waters, back and forth west to east as she supplies the Alkhan with foodstuffs. And most are armed. They don't compare to my ships of the line, but even so, we're sunk if we should encounter a fleet of just thirty or so; they'll overwhelm us. You believe Vanaratu is willing to engage them? I thought it was against his rules to kill people, even if they are enemies."

"It's true, he isn't allowed, but I doubt it's his purpose. If we encounter the Khestadone, it'll be up to us to engage them, and we will have to make use of our ships' firepower and the Staff. Whatever Vanaratu is doing will be related to magic and secrecy. I'm sure it will be extraordinary and beyond anything we may imagine. That's what the Matriarch is saying. The fullest scope of Vanaratu's power as a World God is less than it was, yes. But where he still has it, it is surely formidable, beyond even what we saw when he savaged those Sea Serpents. You're right he cannot use that kind of destructive power against people, but he likely has more up the proverbial sleeve."

Soon, Kodi and Shane returned.

"She says she'll bring her letters in another hour, Curdoz," said Shane. "She says she had been instructed by Queen Silverwing to give all detail of your journeys to and from Modela's island. It's taking her extra time. But the old Patriarch did find a five-hundred-year-old log in the library from one of the Qeteral who returned from the Guardian's assignment. There isn't much there, however, as to location. It was a three-week journey on foot from where they landed on the Serpent Sea. They crossed three small rivers that led into the Jungle and skirted a lake before they arrived in the location the Guardian chose to make the Doorway for the Dragons. It was down in a ravine against a cliff wall, in the Jungle itself. The descriptions were otherwise vague. But he's copying it all out to go in Rusty's package for King Eagleron."

"The Etoppsi may get much even from such limited information. Better than nothing," said Nikal.

"Well, I can begin getting Stormgale's package in order," said Curdoz.

"Maru, Ulna, and Lyndz were not there," said Kodi. "We asked where they were, but none of the servants seemed to know. We asked Rainwing, and she said, 'off and about, keep to yourself' and glowered at us! On our way back, guess what? We saw Musca. He was hanging around the village. And then a man saw us and hailed. He's that breeder of that mountain dog Hurlin told you about. Well, he begged me to let him breed Musca to one or two of his own. I said, yeah, I know Musca would like that a lot, go ahead! So, I whistled, and Musca came charging, and he went right inside the house with the breeder! We followed out the back door, and there's tremendous space back there. His dogs are beautiful animals, very similar to Nobles in looks. The two bitches came charging and sniffing and Musca got all playful. It was a lark. I explained to the man what I know of Nobles, and he was beside himself with thanks."

"Musca will be busy for a while!" said Nikal with a laugh.

Kodi and Shane marched off to join the others for a swim.

There was some additional coming and going between the pavilion and the palace that afternoon, particularly involving Curdoz, the Etoppsi males, Rainwing, and Nikal. They were finalizing preparations and messages for the Etoppsi males for their morning flights. Then, Manwul and Hadon, when they understood Rusty was flying to Danzilet instead of to Berug, asked Curdoz if he'd be willing to add letters from them to Steffia and Ambassador Sturla hopefully to reach them eventually through the shipping channels. It was even possible Sturla might receive hers in Danzilet, as she intended soon to go back east to Essemar and would surely stop there on the way. The Sage agreed to add their letters to the package. Curdoz and Rainwing spent much time describing directions and specific locales for Stormgale. Lumin walked around the village with the other men and introduced them to many villagers. Kodi discovered where the potteries were located, but he only told Shane about Ryn's invitation. The Healer was encouraging. Along about supper time, all the men had returned to the pavilion, and Lumin sent servants to bring them dinner provisions.

"The women are all having their own dinner in the palace garden," he said.

Despite the portents of the day, the magic of the land of Ulakel allowed them to set their ruminations aside by evening. They had a grand time together, and there was much laughter, and they wanted to be cheerful for Rusty and Stormy on their last night before being sent on their journeys. Nikal and Tiliruf together taught Lumin how to play Kings and Castles, and he achieved great success, even beating Manwul. Much mead was consumed, yet Tiliruf had none. He didn't want another headache from it. None of course allowed themselves to reach more than the mildest tipsy state. Lumin could drink mead like water, and it seemed not to affect him at all. They built a campfire, and Manwul and Hadon sang sailor songs.

When some of the others grew sleepy and retired, Lumin asked Kodi to go for a walk in the fields. Kodi willingly complied. They gazed out on the multitude of stars and spent a good three hours in commune, sitting alone together in a field of summer wheat. Some of their talk was fun and lighthearted and other more serious. Lumin plainly needed a friend, someone dissociated from his family, who would take him seriously and not look on him as a prince or as a boy. He seemed to know instinctively that Kodi would understand him rather as a young man with hopes and dreams.

Kodi did. He saw much of himself in Lumin, particularly of himself up until he left home. Their relationship grew rapidly into a powerful bond.

They returned to the pavilion to find them all asleep except for Shane, who was sitting reading the book about Vanaratu by lamplight. Shane let Lumin stay in the bed he had used the night before next to Kodi. Shane was going to sleep near Tiliruf that night. But he would not allow them to linger awake and so put both to sleep with his magical touch.

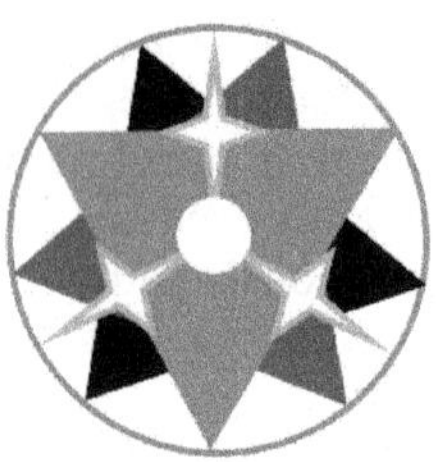

Chapter 17—A Morning in Ulakel

The following morning the men and male Etoppsi made their way up to the palace where they found Rainwing, Lyndz, Ulna, Maru, Idamé, Mishoo, and Prince Hakonn in the front courtyard. Here they wished goodbye and good flights to Flamefur and Stormgale. It was understood now that Flamefur might return to them within a few days after passing off his messages to the Etoppsi at Danzilet. Though he didn't explain, Hakonn made it understood that the magic of the Barrier would allow Flamefur to return without any hindrance.

It had been briefly pondered whether one of the Human men, such as Manwul, ought to travel with Stormgale. The Etoppsis could have carried him by the usual bodily grip method or better in a kind of harness that could have been quickly made from rope and canvas. A Human could have made the shocking appearance of an Etoppsis in Solanto work a little smoother. Most believed the existence of their race was a legend. The problem of carrying a man, of course, was the Corellyan Mountains. The bodies of Etoppsi were designed to survive the deep freeze, lack of good air and the extraordinary heights needed to clear the great heights of the mountains. Otherwise, a much longer journey involving the search for valleys and ravines through which to travel would have been required for a Human to breathe sufficiently and not freeze. There was too much risk in that and going southwest and around the mountain range would take too much time. Traveling alone, it was believed Stormgale might return to them with perhaps a few days remaining before they left Ulakel allowing them time to mull any news from the north.

After they flew off, as the men were returning to the pavilion, Tiliruf, joking with Lumin, realized he had lost track of someone.

"Where'd Kodi go, eh?"

Shane replied. "Umm, royal business. Don't worry about him. I want to do a Healer's examination on you this morning, Tiliruf."

Tiliruf complied.

When Kodi, clean, shirtless, and physically impressive, entered into the potteries, he found perhaps ten persons working. Most were women, but there were a couple of men, one with his young son. Two of the women had young daughters with them. There was some talking among two or three, yet the others were quiet and focused on their work. Some were at pottery wheels, whereas another seemed to be arranging newly finished pieces on shelves and making a list. Others were painting fine porcelain. These were superior artists. Most nodded cordially in his direction as if they were expecting him. It was a large place with much sunlight coming from opened doors and windows, the wooden walls and ceiling had been painted white, and each worker had a big space of his or her own, set up as wished with favored tools and other implements.

"Good morning, Kodi," said Ryn. She had entered from a rear door. She stepped up to Kodi, and to his surprise, she reached up and felt his right cheek. "You call it 'stubble,' do you not? Hmm, it is rough and curious, isn't it?"

Today her shirt was light yellow and sleeveless, bordered in a wide blue ribbon. It opened down the front, hung long, nearly down to the bottom of her matching knee-length pant, and contained no ties or loops. Her firm breasts were occasionally revealed by the movement of the loose drape of linen. She did not wear a garland of flowers today; instead, a few daisies decorated her hair. The scent of wild ginger could be detected on the air. Her ebony tresses flowed down her back in soft waves. Her skin as always was smooth and brown, and her eyes were brilliant blue. Her touch to his face was electrifying, her form alluring. Yet Kodi was reasonably controlled, in part due to self-discipline, in part due to having become more used to the revealing way Qeteral women dressed, but perhaps also due to a Healing session with Shane early that morning before anyone else had awakened. At Kodi's wishful request, the Healer chuckled but then applied special magic meant to help his body not overreact in the princess's stimulating presence. It seemed to be working.

"It grows a little each day, you see, but it is bothersome to shave that often, and so, yes, I do skip the chore sometimes. Mother Idamé seems to prefer it when it's cleanshaven and smooth."

"I think I would find it interesting to watch it grow a little while you're here."

He nodded and his smile was pure charm. He did not likewise touch Ryn on her cheek, as it might have seemed a little presumptuous on his part. This was still her play, and he recalled Lyndz' and Shane's advice. "All is well this morning with you, Ryn?"

"It is, thank you." Ryn seemed very much at ease, and her own smile was one of such warmth towards him, he felt almost compelled to kiss her face. Rather, he innocently kissed her hand, now for the third time. "Let me show you our work here, Kodi, shall I?"

Every time she spoke his name he wanted to melt. But he held firm, retained his charming smile, which under the circumstances was easy to do, and followed along as she showed him about the place. If he were nervous or felt out of his element with a princess, it did not show. He possibly did not hear every single word she spoke, despite being attentive. Maybe his thoughts would skip a beat, wandering back to something she previously said, or admittedly being mesmerized by how the linen molded itself over her curves, or by the song in her voice, or her scent.

He asked questions and commented politely as she explained the differences in stoneware and fine porcelains, the kilns in the backyard and the differences in firing, salt and ash glazes, among others, and diverse painting techniques. It really was interesting, for despite many other talents on his part, Kodi knew little about pottery. Upon approaching one of those painting a large, fine urn, the artist stood from his stool and nodded. Other stunning, finished pieces were on a table beside him. Kodi complimented his work.

"Thank you, Brother of Myghal. I am honored." The man bowed regally and then went back to his work.

The three children present were intrigued by Kodi and by this point had ganged together in a group of whisperers. Since Qeteral children typically mimicked their elders in dress, the boy was shirtless, and the girls wore short-sleeved linen. Even as children they had a handsome and noble quality about them. They approached him and the princess.

"Our lady," they said politely in a bow to the princess.

She looked down at them and smiled. "You wish to meet the Lord Kodi? He comes from the faraway kingdom of Solanto."

They bowed to him politely, and Kodi squatted down to be closer to their level.

"You look a lot like me," said the little boy.

Kodi winked at him and ruffled the top of his head. "I was just about to say you look a lot like me!"

The boy grinned.

Kodi added, "Humans and Qeteral don't always look so different from each other, do they? But did you get to see my Etoppsi friends fly about yesterday?"

"Yes, they're very different!"

"Yet noble with great hearts. They like showing off their big wings, you know."

"Are you a Human prince, too, like the Prince Nikal?" asked the younger of the two girls.

"No. In Solanto I was the son of a count. My father administers an area called County Fothemry. Fothemry is our surname. It contains a few villages, many farms, and a large amount of forest land. But it's only a small part of the kingdom."

"But now you're a War Wizard!" said the little boy, excitedly.

"It's true things are different now. Now they say I'm a high lord. But I answer to the Guardian, and Sage Curdoz and Prince Nikal are my mentors."

"Prince Nikal looks strong and kingly," the girl stated.

"Prince Nikal is very much those things. He is a great war hero in the Human world, and my Brother in the Order of War Wizards. I'm going to tell him what you said. I think it would make him happy to know you see him that way."

"They say you can speak to the Guardian. Can you explain it to us?" asked the older girl.

"Myghal and I do talk to one another. I hear Him speak in my mind, you see. He has a kind, friendly Voice, and He even laughs! Right now, He is far away from our world, for He tells me He has many worlds to watch after. I'm trying to help Him the best I can while He is away. With the war going on, He is depending on Prince Nikal and me to fight for Him with the Eagle Staff."

"How does He know what is happening here?"

"He doesn't explain to me everything, but I know that when He wants to, He can see by way of the minds of those who believe in and honor Him. He is proud of our world of Dumhoni and loves it and the people very much. He tells me it is one of His favorite worlds."

"Will you bless us?"

It was a most interesting request to Kodi, as it had never before been posed to him. It was odd for a child to ask, and yet maybe not so much for being

Qeteral. Qeteral children seemed to have more mature perspectives in comparison to their Human counterparts. A few quick facts presented themselves to his mind. It was usually Curdoz who "did" blessings. Yet he had seen Shane and Mother Idamé offer blessings before, too. Shane did so for Manwul and Hadon every morning, as it was part of a spiritual discipline they ascribed to. This gave the impression that though it was a regular function of Sages, any Order member had the authority to offer a blessing in the name of Meical. He himself was an Order member, but he was also different in the sense he was a warrior. He could be the subject of rage and killing. The idea of offering blessings, especially to children, appeared in conflict with pieces of who he was as a War Wizard.

Though maybe not so much with other pieces. For he was also *Brother of Myghal*, proclaimed so not only by the people, but by Meical Himself in a Vision and in intimate conversation. Kodi was himself blessed. Himself favored. The Brother, then, can surely offer blessings.

He felt drawn to be a little more personal than Curdoz' method of lifting a hand up and pronouncing. "Put your hands in mine, then."

Their hands were small and sweet as he enveloped all six of them in his own, and then the princess herself bent down and placed her own hand on top. For Kodi it added to the oddity, as her touch affected him with different emotions. Nevertheless, he found it reassuring in a way.

"My Brother Myghal the Divine Affirms you always, little ones."

It may have been the first time Kodi had ever done this, but it would not be the last. Most of the time it would be children like these who asked. He looked more like them wearing Qeteral clothing, younger and more approachable perhaps than the Sage. Having been taught patience by Curdoz, in addition to his own willingness to have a connection with the children, Kodi would offer golden smiles and big, warm hands, gather them to him like a playful father and speak the words. Occasionally they would then hug him or kiss him on his cheek. Or, like the little boy now, they might be bold enough to run their little hands across the Human hair on his arm and smile at him as if it were interesting rather than alien. His heart for the Qeteral people grew.

He may not have realized it, but a certain princess was endeared by his patient warmth.

This unexpected interaction—this blessing of the children—also impacted Kodi just then. It seemed to add another dimension to his being. As the children walked happily away, he stood and considered Ryn. His eyes traced every part of her face in a slow, complete way they had not done before. The smile he then bore her was not so much that of male-on-female charm, but more a happy expression of familiar contentment. It was as though he and she had known one another for years, like a boy and girl who had grown up as neighbors and played together, now seeing one another again after years of being apart. It seemed so right, a charmed moment.

Kodi was, in comparison to many of the other men in his set, lucky. He had grown up in a home with a level of familial joy. With Kodi, his father could have a severe streak, though these disciplinary talks and arguments with his son were always private and carried on away from everyone, usually far from the house. But within the household itself, and in the presence of Kodi's mother, the family dynamic was one of happiness. His father cherished his mother and had great pride in his family. There was teasing, joking, and laughter, along with adoration and pride among all of them for one another. Kodi was particularly lucky then to be around such loving, intelligent, and enjoyable women. And so, he understood and valued women differently than did many men and had a heart for the idea of family unknown to most of the others. Tiliruf grew up with a hands-off father and no mother. Nikal had a cold mother, and a father and brother who treated women awfully. Manwul and Hadon had no siblings and were troublemakers growing up, having been somewhat rebellious. Shane's early life approached most closely, for he had told them of his family; he came from a pack of five brothers and apparently two fun-loving parents. But aside from their mother, theirs was a male-dominant clan. For Kodi, women were a key part of his life growing up—his mother, his sister, Ansy the servant, memories told of Jugan's first wife, a series of village women who acted like doting aunts and grandmothers—all playing on his subconscious, coloring his perspective on life, even as he otherwise lived in a male-oriented world. No doubt he throve in that world, and male companions were crucial to his emotional and even his spiritual growth. That deep-seated sense of brotherhood bonds with men would never leave him.

But it wasn't his only world.

For Ryn's part, she had been greatly attracted to Kodi the moment she saw him at the reception. Having grown up hearing tales about the loving and adventurous nature of her Human grandfather, realizing from some of her loved-ones that Humans had within them emotional traits little different than themselves, she was open to—and intrigued by—the fact Kodi was Human. Being especially handsome with physical features that were similar to men she had known, Kodi's face and form were especially appealing to her. So, at the reception she had introduced herself warmly, and through a particular set of words between them, along with the accompanying body and facial language, she understood he...was unbonded. That was a first step.

The second step was the sister. Kodi, a touch embarrassed that Lyndz was privy to how he felt about Ryn, never properly knew how valuable Lyndz really was to him just now. In opening up a woman-to-woman friendship with Lyndz, in three or four good conversations Ryn of course valued Lyndz and her intelligence and talent. Those two would always be on the best of terms. But it was through her conversations with Lyndz whereby Ryn learned all about Kodi: his background and family, the respect and love within that family, his obedience to his parents, his reverence for his mother, and for his sister. Through Lyndz' obvious pride in her brother, Ryn could tell that Kodi was worthy of her attention. He was a War Wizard, yes, a role which contained certain elements including that of the warrior life: danger, cunning, and the willingness to kill in battle as part of a higher demand to make the world safe again. Yet Ryn hoped and was correct that Kodi was more than a warrior. He was a man of warmth, compassion, and deep love. She had learned in her studies that Humans were capable of deception, manipulation, and sexual promiscuity. Through Lyndz, Ryn understood that Kodi was kind, other-thinking, and self-disciplined. Positive perception was also gained by way of the obvious warm feelings her favorite brother, Lumin, had towards Kodi. She could tell already that Kodi had a big heart for Lumin who was so desirous to know more about Humans. That was important to her. And finally, to be a Brother of Myghal connected him in spirit with the Guardian. The Guardian would not have proclaimed the relationship had Kodi been unworthy.

Even so, she understood she was taking a risk, reaching out to Kodi in the manner she was. She doubted her grandfather Hakonn, or her other brothers,

Hurlin and Olin, would be approving. She could already tell that Hurlin had observed an interchange or two and was mistrusting. Nor was she certain of her mother. Though her mother highly valued and trusted Kodi, for her daughter to pursue a relationship with a Human man would likely create a dilemma of sorts, with certain political ramifications. The family already had strong Human blood, and not every Qeteral looked at this as good. Even some in the family, Hurlin obviously, were not keen on their own bloodline and looked upon it almost as a taint. *Humans are prone to sinful ways. Humans are aggressive. Humans should not be trusted.* Ryn had heard these things said many times, even from some close to her.

But her mother never said those things. Her paternal grandmother of course never said such things. Many others she knew actually believed Humans were interesting and passionate beings, adventurous and exotic. This visitation by the Humans had reignited some of that talk. Certainly, most of the villagers, and also the nobility who had attended the reception, were quite enthusiastic about their presence and acknowledged the visitors acted with graciousness.

Ryn had made a decision for herself the moment she laid eyes on Kodi. She had set out on a quest to know him. She had always been encouraged to make her own decisions. The love affair of her grandmother and Human grandfather was a story that intrigued her always, playing on her mind as she matured. To her, Kodi seemed like he might be well worth the risk. Their obvious attraction for one another could not be denied, so could there be even more between them?

To say then that each hour which she spent with him only increased her interest and attraction goes without saying. And in that moment following his blessing of the children, in which he, without any averting of the eyes due to worries over her high station, looked all about her face with familiar warmth, she almost certainly made another decision then.

There was a reason Ryn had chosen the potteries. Here at her pottery wheel, she was able to touch him. Reaching out to guide him, holding his hands sometimes as he experimented with clay for the first time, the two could laugh and talk closely and quietly. Though their hands were quickly coated in wetness and clay, it was a mutual thing that seemed to connect them, and an amount of emotion carried in the skin-to-skin contact. It was playful and sensual. With their hands they shaped a simple vase. She would later fire and glaze it. And keep it. This creation of something together was surely representative of something that was happening between them.

For Kodi's part, he could have sat at that pottery wheel with her every day, all day, for eternity.

If Mishoo had sympathy for the women, she didn't act on it. Except for maybe Idamé due to her age. Not so unlike Shane could be with the men, Mishoo was a pusher. Yet she was an encourager, too.

Today was the first day in which the Human women would train—in secret—with the Qeteral women. She had taken them the afternoon previously to show them the fields she had set up already for their training.

Rainwing was off on her own in a distant field. She did not of course need any extra training from a Qeteral. There was, however, a change in the routine she had set for herself. Since Etoppsi tended to fly when speed was needed, it wasn't really typical for their race to run. They might on occasion run a short way in order to help them take flight, depending on the movement of the airs around them. But they never really ran to get from one place to another. Their big wings on their back would actually slow down such an effort. Since Rainwing no longer had her wings, she realized she could run faster and further. But she wasn't used to it and would sometimes get off balance and stumble. And so her focus was on learning to run with more efficient, Human-Qeteral-like, leg movement. She would always be able to move quicker than any Human or Qeteral could, even without much running involved on her part. She'd proven that to herself at the Battle of South Fort. But she knew there might come a time in which a burst of super speed might prove useful.

She was improving by the hour. And had she thought about it, she was probably already the fastest-running person of the Three Races in all Dumhoni. What she *did* think about was that it was still ever so much slower than flying.

Idamé's routine would not change for three or four days. She was assigned to Halta, and Halta was a young, energetic woman. And with Halta, the Mother Matrimonial was to walk. And walk. And walk briskly, up hills and down, into the woods, across wide fields and little streams. All with a pack on her back containing food and water.

The best word to describe how Idamé managed the speed and push by Halta was just that—managed. And really, that was pretty good for a Human woman in her fifties who was inclined to be dumpy. Curdoz had often in the past complimented Idamé's legs. She had strong ones. Maru had noted it, too. As a Matrimonial required to travel everywhere on foot, she could go all day of ordinary walking at her own speed. But Mishoo and Halta were determined she improve that speed. And so, for these first days that was the goal: make Idamé move faster, build up stamina, and maybe lose a few pounds.

Lucky for her, the country through which she and Halta hiked was gorgeous. Also a blessing was the fact the two got along beautifully. Though there were times when Idamé was winded, there were moments too when they would stop, allowing her a sip of water and to catch her breath and then be able to remark upon the beauty of a little waterfall or a magnificent view, the aroma of late-summer honeysuckle, or the cacophonous melodies of songbirds that seemed to follow them.

Halta had a bird. It was a golden-winged blackbird with a delightful trill in its song. It would come and go, landing on Halta's shoulder from time-to-time as they hiked along. She would sing to it, and then it would fly off again.

Idamé was able to huff out a question. "Halta dear, tell me in what ways your people can make use of birds."

"Not all of us have our own favorite bird, though all Qeteral can talk to them. Some think about a third of women and perhaps a fifth of our men keep birds as familiars. We of course love their company. I've had Multy here for two years, now. Although we do not necessarily look upon them as pets, for much of the time they do their own thing and live their own lives apart from us. Nevertheless, they tend to remain near at hand, and if we call for them, they will come to us. The greatest use we put them to is to relay messages across distances. With our familiar bird we can impress messages into their minds by way of magic. Sometimes we sing the message, but it isn't always necessary. We can connect to their minds even without singing to them. For instance, if I wanted my Aunt Lemnui to know I wanted to come for a visit, she lives about two leagues north of here. I can impress that message into Multy's mind, and he would fly off to my aunt and deliver the message—or rather she could perceive the message with magic and send a return reply.

"Not all birds are suited, as some are less receptive to the magic. Sparrows and starlings are not much good. Or robins. Chickens and gamebirds we almost never talk to as that would be quite rude, now, wouldn't it? And often the larger the bird the more receptive it is in the manner in which we Qeteral can communicate with them, and the bigger birds are willing to fly longer distances to take messages. Night birds are useful, too, like nighthawks, whippoorwills, nightingales, and owls. Of the daytime birds, the best are white ravens. But crows, blackbirds, mockingbirds, jays are all good, though jays can have an angry streak. And all raptors are especially good, falcons and hawks particularly. Men tend to prefer raptors, including owls. Mishoo has a wonderful hawk, too. Of water birds, geese and swans and gulls of all sorts are good for really long distances, though not many keep those sorts of birds nearby. Gulls don't live on the Plateau. Water birds are not especially popular, then, as familiars. Although the Matriarch's grandmother kept a swan from what I've been told. It lived in the palace garden. I think it might still be there, very old, though the Matriarch herself uses white ravens for sending messages throughout our land. There are a few people who have a special magic by which they can see through the eyes of their familiar bird while in flight. Although, that magic only works for short distances, ten, twenty miles. Anyway, the raptors are the best for that sort of thing, as they have the best eyesight. It was by way of this magic we were able to count your party on your approach to our country and make ready for your visit. After we made contact with you in the forest, we then sent messages to the palace by way of the birds, giving them your names and so forth."

"And what about other animals?"

"We can, with varying levels of the gifts within us, communicate with other animals. I'm not good with it aside from being able to calm a growling dog. Mishoo is quite good. She can talk with many kinds of animals. But they are not as good as birds for the delivery of messages, since not every Qeteral can communicate with them. It isn't often there is need to communicate with animals anyway except for pets. For farm animals meant for food, and for the deer we hunt, just like for gamebirds and fowl, it would be quite rude to talk to them, wouldn't it!"

They'd been going briskly uphill in the sunshine, and Idamé struggled to laugh.

"There is a creek at the bottom with good water and shade. We'll take a break there, Mother Idamé."

Idamé nodded and with another deep breath plunged onward.

Ulna and Maru, in their thirties, were relatively lean and strong and had always been outdoorsy and adventurous. Those two were assigned to work with Frith, although they were not far away from Mishoo with Lyndz, sometimes gathering together for a quick break and a word. In any event, the two Healer women were made to run, take a brief break, then switch to archery, then another run, and then a switch to knife-throwing, and then to run again. Both women were half decent with archery, for they at least knew how to handle a bow. But they were bad at knife-throwing.

"Do I really need to learn that?" asked Ulna, who had just thrown another clunker.

"It can be quicker than archery if surprised by an attacker, so yes, you must, Sister Ulna," said a patient Frith.

Maru never complained. Nevertheless, by lunchtime she was getting shaky. Frith went to speak with nearby Mishoo, who called a halt to all their work. She had been working with Lyndz with running or crawling through obstacle courses, and between runs, knife-throwing and even long-knife moves. Mishoo was greatly pleased with her.

"You are a strong woman, Lyndz, quick to learn and talented. You're learning to anticipate with your Gift you described to me?"

"Yes. It's coming instantly as I need it. The moment I release an arrow or throw a knife I can use the Gift and, ha, actually see if it is aimed well, and then, if I'm unhappy, I can immediately prepare for another shoot or throw, and so move altogether more rapidly. I can also see where I'm going when I crawl through your obstacle courses and not waste any real time. I'll have to tell Rainwing."

"It's excellent you push with whatever skills or Gifts you have. Let's go to the palace for a lunch and a swim, shall we? The Matriarch wants us for tea later."

Ulna provided Healing magic to Maru, who returned the favor. When she went for Lyndz, however, Mishoo stopped her.

"She doesn't need it. Let her body heal itself. And after another couple days, the same for you two. You need to grow more used to body pains and muscle aches, and in time you will be able to push yourselves to even greater extremes. Save Healing magic for actual damage done. Although, you can always examine for the steadying of the mind, and always keep Mother Idamé Healed when you can. Her body can't take quite what yours can, but Halta's blackbird keeps telling me she's doing well this morning. I've relayed a message for them to return to the palace, too."

"She's stronger than she lets on," said Maru.

"And she's grown in courage, too," offered Ulna. "I'm proud of her."

"But she doesn't want to handle weapons. You have to understand that we Members of the Orders are supposed to avoid being a part of any fighting. Sage Curdoz is essentially our superior, and he understands the value of self-preservation, of course, considering the war and the danger. So, Shane is learning to fight and so will we. Our Calling to serve Myghal has changed us all. But Mother Idamé is still resistant to the possibility of having to hurt another, even an enemy."

"Well," said Mishoo as they walked along, "her belief is no different than that of any Qeteral or any other good person. We haven't fought in centuries, but we understand evil is present in the world. We have depended upon the other two races to protect us apart from our defensive Barrier, and we tend to blame Humans for most conflicts. It isn't fair to do so, in my opinion, either to lay blame on Humans as a whole or to presume they and the Etoppsi be the ones to sacrifice in war. I sympathize with the Matrimonial, of course, but she's going to have to get past that view. It recalls that of our more conservative people, including many in the leadership. I'll talk to her. And of course, on the mission, if it is possible to keep from bloody work, that's to be desired, especially for her. But defense is necessary, I think. I don't think we've got time to train her at archery if she's never had any experience with it, but she's going to have a brace of throwing knives and a hunting knife on her. She needs to learn how to use them.

"You know, an idea has come to me. I think we shall all go together on an outing for a night or two next week in a remote area we can get to in a day's hike. We'll take some basics with us and train in the night. You need to get used to moving and working in the dark."

"Rainwing will like that," said Lyndz. "She would agree with you."

"The rest of you walk on ahead. I want to hold back and talk with Lyndz alone for a little."

Firth, Ulna, and Maru walked on, while Lyndz and Mishoo slowed their steps.

"Now, your news the khans are Ralsheen makes me wonder. What about the Ralsheen language? I am unlearned on that."

"Rainwing knows it. Certainly how to read it. Hopefully we won't have to ever speak it," said Lyndz. "It's only the Alkhaness' highest officials that use it with one another anyway. Not even her bodyguards know it. They all use common Anterianhi. We surmise Ralsheen is maintained as a secret language among their elite, her satraps and so forth, at least in West Khestadon."

"We would not be able to pose as elites in any regard."

Lyndz stopped walking and looked at her with big eyes. "We? Mishoo! You never said you were going with us! I thought..."

"Ha! That's why I wanted to speak to you alone! I didn't actually tell you, but I intended to go with you almost at the moment you said you had been given a special mission by the Divine!"

Lyndz was ecstatic.

"But I certainly wanted to gain your agreement. And it's true I must get the Matriarch's permission," Mishoo continued, "but she and Hurlin will have to send trained Qeteral on the journey. Hurlin and Olin cannot go, as their magic undergirds the Barrier. I essentially follow them in the leadership among those who are trained with defense and for watching the boundaries. It's only natural I should go."

"They would actually send women?"

"Why would they not send women? Oh! Because you are basing it on what your Human leaders might do? Trust me, Lyndz. You want me, and you want other Qeteral women. It says so in your Vision; that's how I interpreted it when you entrusted us with it at dinner with Ryn last night."

Lyndz was beside herself with glee. She'd been considering directly asking Mishoo to go with them, and now she didn't have to. But she was also a little confused, as her mind kept playing with itself. She had been anxious about the details of her Vision.

"But you're presuming it will be at some point during the upcoming journey that our mission will be triggered by Myghal."

"Yes, I admit I am."

Lyndz nodded. "Rainwing and I believe so, too, as the sea route south puts us close to their land and closer to the Alkhaness' citadel than at any other point so far."

"Precisely. But you were never meant to go there without Qeteral women."

"You're that confident from my description of the Vision? How many are you considering should go, Mishoo? The bigger our group the harder it will be to be secretive."

"Frith, Halta, and myself. Maybe one to two more. I agree the group needs to remain small. But I want to think on it. For some unexplained reason the number five keeps rotating in my thoughts. But some of my thinking will depend on Hakonn determining those in Sage Curdoz' and Mother Idamé's Dreams. But I'm thinking how valuable it might be that we have enough for two or three teams, you see. Foraging for food. Reconnaissance missions. Backup team to call for as needed. Protection of supplies at a home base. I'll have my hawk, and Frith has a swift falcon. If each team has a Qeteral, then we can use the birds to send messages."

"Gosh, Mishoo! You really have thought about logistics already! You're excellent!"

"And we each have different skills. Now, I am very concerned about the idea of enslaved Qeteral in West Khestadon. There was only the one so-called Dragon rider seen by the Etoppsi?"

"Yes, although there were reports beforehand of two. The Alkhaness will not have been the one who initially enslaved and trained them with Wingless Dragons. That would be the Alkhan. Even so, it does seem plausible that by now he has sent some to work entirely for her, especially if she attempts again to find that magical Doorway near the Berugian border. It seems she needs them for jungle work based on what Flamefur said."

"Enslaved Qeteral worry me. Because it would be they who might more readily notice any Qeteral magic being used by us. They would decipher messages from the birds, and when we use invisibility, it doesn't hide us from other Qeteral. But I believe it will all be worth the risk."

"I see." After a pause, Lyndz spoke again. "Mishoo, you still understand that this must remain secretive? Rainwing and I will be watching for the opportunity to separate from the men, waiting possibly for a sign or new Vision from Myghal. We don't know yet how we will do that without causing a good deal of resistance and heartache. The Guardian may foresee something, but we don't, yet. It's going to be awful for everyone."

The Qeteral woman reached for Lyndz' arm and replied with a warm tone she hadn't used before. "I understand, Lyndz. It will altogether be difficult and dangerous. We will help you maintain secrecy. I'm sure it has been difficult not to share even with your brother. Know, Lyndz, I am going because I want to help you, not because I am seeking an opportunity for heroism. If I seem sharp or talk with a level of confidence, don't think I'm taking this task lightly. I'm not. But I do feel determined to help you succeed. I think the time has come for Qeteral to do more in the wider world. I'm tired of our people hiding behind the Barrier. This is a goal many of our women have, particularly the ones I'm close to like Frith and Halta. The Matriarch and Princess Ryn, though they may not speak openly, share this view. They are my cousins through Linea, Gwyn's mother, and we are good friends and talk much. Whereas many of our men are more reserved and conservative, wary of the outside world, both the dangers and corruptive influences. And so, I speak with a desire to cast off naivety and embrace my new relationships with you and Rainwing and the rest. I want to share in the dangers with my Human and Etoppsi sisters. I feel as though your Vision creates an opportunity for me and a handful of us to make a difference. It could be a catalyst for change, do you see?"

Lyndz was of course thrilled Mishoo was going with them. As were the others.

From the morning in which her Vision came to her in the statue garden in Tirilorin, Lyndz had been willing to try her best for Meical. The power of the Divine love He demonstrated to her had reached her deeply. Though He did not speak with her like He did with Kodi, like any dedicated Order Member she had faith in His Presence and gained much comfort from it. She understood from the beginning the task was dangerous, but she also told herself that Meical would not have appointed it to her if He believed it was hopeless. Plainly He did not think it was hopeless. What Mishoo now helped her to understand was that there was greater meaning in the Vision than she initially thought. Before, she believed it was simply a necessary task, and that for some reason Meical believed she could do it because of her Gift. It had not really occurred to her that there were broader implications beyond the fact it might somehow help the war effort. Yes, there was also the symbolism of *twins*, brother and sister, in opposition—she and Kodi against Ch'yad and the Alkhan. But Mishoo was suggesting that Meical was envisioning something even greater, beyond the war—a real change in the world. A change for women maybe? A change for the Qeteral? A change in how the three races interacted?

Maybe some or all of those things, in addition to others still hidden. Lyndz understood even now she did not need to know all the implications behind her Vision. But the possibilities did embolden her. She at this point began to feel a little more like Kodi did—that there was meaning in the effort, even if success wasn't guaranteed. This idea essentially underlay why Kodi retained a level of unqualified joy. As long as he continued to try to do what he believed Meical wanted him to do, then there would be good to come out of it, even if it should turn out he wasn't the beneficiary of his own effort. Meical's ideas and plans contained bigger, broader goals than what might be perceived initially.

Likewise, Lyndz now. The Vision she realized wasn't only meant for her.

She may not have realized the vast change in herself since the evening she sat by the fireside at home in Felto when Curdoz and Idamé turned up. There was a big contrast then as to her feelings compared to Kodi's at the time. He was ready for major changes and to leave home, and she was not. He had had a Vision, and she had not. There was finally a moment of overawing emotion when she, her brother, and Curdoz stood atop the pinnacle of Guardian's Gate. She was leaving Solanto behind and she was required to embrace change or perhaps go crazy resisting it. She would not do the latter. With the decision to embrace the future, then, she had grown. She grew more as she watched the maneuverings of the female politicians and tradeswomen of Tirilorin work in full measure alongside men. They inspired her. The Vision then came to her at the same time as did her new Gift of Moment Mastering, these adding a deeper connection to the Cosmic movements of the Guardian as He attempted to help the world resist the growing threat of evil. Now finally, others wished to aid her, and this added additional value to her purpose. She would have attempted all with just Idamé and Rainwing, but with Maru and Ulna adding themselves, along with Mishoo now, it all felt more 'right' just as that rightness was felt by Kodi when Meical engaged the magical connection with the Eagle Staff at the Installation Ceremony. The Guardian had now also given Lyndz the tools she needed.

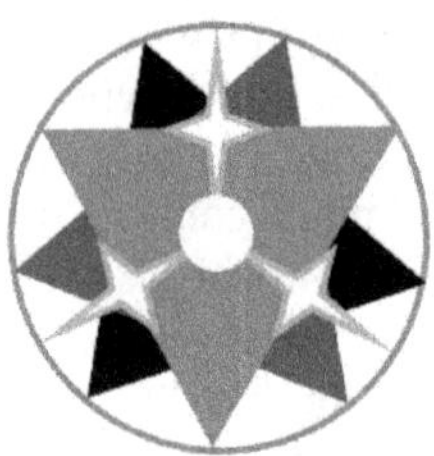

Chapter 18—Afternoon Swim

Considering they had been received generally well since their arrival, their own self-assuredness of their physical fitness, and also due to Lumin's direct invitation and encouragement, they could not be embarrassed in their bare skin among the likewise naked Qeteral at the village bathing hole after lunch. The six younger Human men, including Kodi, who had returned to his friends from his morning with Ryn (telling them nothing, by the way), Tiliruf, Manwul, Hadon, Nikal, and Shane, were the kind of extroverts who just were not self-conscious in such a setting. Under the surface, the exception would have been Nikal. He was generally more reserved overall. However, reticence wouldn't work when Kodi, Lumin and the rest were keeping him so cheered. They made him feel almost boyish sometimes. His presence among them was desired, and he didn't want to appear a curmudgeon or give in to gloominess. He complied and came along. Ulakel was such a beautiful place that it enhanced the senses and created a generally easy-going atmosphere. The day was gorgeous. The early afternoon sun shone welcoming and hot. And the water...

Oh, the water. The bathing hole was in a geological depression not unlike that of their pavilion and private pool. Like their private pool, somewhere downstream the water disappeared softly and casually through cracks into underground streams. Otherwise, it was bigger by far, and the flowing water and landscape was grander, creating one of the prettiest and most inviting river-water holes any of them had ever experienced. Little cascades flowed outward from rock faces into the pool. There was even a fantasy waterfall around and behind which one could swim and hide and play, along with a relatively dry cliff wall that people enjoyed climbing.

Great rocks, perfect for sitting half under water, could be found out in the middle of the river, and along with some Qeteral fathers, here could be found five of the Human men playing like big brothers with the children. There were balls made of waterproofed animal skins that had been inflated and were being tossed about. Little children would swim up to both Nikal and Kodi especially, who would pick them up out of the water and toss them back into it. Or in the case of the bigger children, the two men would lower themselves, allowing them to stand up and balance on their shoulders. Then, as the men stood up tall, they would jump off. And they would swim back to do it all over again. There was much fun and laughter. Plainly, the two War Wizards were looked upon as visiting heroes by the children. They wanted to touch the *'Brothers of Myghal'* (as their parents would refer to them), to feel the powerful strength in their Human bodies and see their faces up close and hear what their voices sounded like. They wanted to be 'in their world,' so to speak, to connect with the two Chosen by the Divine as their protectors from the world's evils. Human children might have been intimidated by the implied lordliness of such persons, but these Qeteral children had no hesitations. To them the men's warm smiles or eye winks in their direction were invitations to engage. And so that's what they did.

Kodi ate it up. He'd always been great with children back home. He never lost patience, and he treated every child as if he or she were favored little brothers or sisters. Nikal too would imitate Kodi's child-friendly manner and found it easy and more natural than he might have expected had he pondered it. For now, however, he was, simply speaking, happy. The Voice of Meical moving themes of compassion towards him within his mind seemed clearer and warmed his heart, and it transferred in a love for the children. Nikal would come back here many times while they stayed in Ulakel; the others didn't have to press the invitation on him again. In the water and among the eager and laughing children he felt close to true goodness and could forget his troubles. In fact, he'd probably never smiled so consistently in his whole life. He learned many of the children's names and recalled their faces in the future as he fought and wielded the Staff, giving him added reason for the fight and a certain amount of hope.

Young men, some fathers of these children, were sitting next to Manwul, Hadon, and Tiliruf on the big rocks talking and getting to know them. All of them also engaged occasionally in playing with the children or throwing the balls about. Manwul was almost as popular with the children as the War Wizards, a great playful bear, and surely the largest man any of the Qeteral had ever seen. He'd have three or four little ones hanging on his neck. He'd then stand up on the rock, pulling them up with him out of the water, and then others would start tugging and pushing to see how many it would take to topple his huge body, at which point he'd collapse with a dramatic "arrrrgh!" and a great splash.

"There can be no doubt your people are no different than our own when it comes to the love and attention of children," offered a Qeteral Healer by the name of Solone.

"Certainly," replied Shane who sat on the bank beside him in the sun. Olin had also come for a swim that afternoon and introduced the two Healers to one another. Solone had been eager to communicate with the Human Healer and share knowledge. Of course, Shane was equally eager. "Not all Human men have great fatherly instincts, and not all are playful, but many are. They may be warriors, but these have great hearts, all of them."

"I can see that."

Women were mixed in with men on the pool's banks, though the two genders tended to separate into pairs or little groups for conversation. In the water, the Qeteral women were mostly swimming in another part of the great pool, some with babies or toddlers, teaching them how to float and swim. Teens and those in their twenties were gathered in yet another part, jumping or diving off rocks. Old people bathed in shallows near the banks.

Solone had interesting observations.

"The hair on your bodies. It is inconsistent from one man to the next. We sometimes say in our tales that your men look like bears. Or goats! Especially because of beards!" He chuckled. "I am sorry to admit we have such preconceptions and prejudices. I admired the late king and his father, of course."

Shane laughed. "Perhaps we do appear more animal-like because of it. Body hair separates the mature man from the prepubescent boy. Yet the differences are often celebrated. Consider the Molding of the Three Races and how differently we were formed. In general, your race is more consistent in looks. Most of your men are tall, your women shorter, and all have dark hair. Your skin hovers around a brown theme, whereas Human skin varies markedly as you can see in us. There are Easterners even darker than me, and white or ruddy skin is typical in the northern kingdoms. Nantians are a genuine mix, typically of olive, tan, or even a dark tan. Your differences are in your faces, the curl or straightness and length of your hair, eye colors, and yes, some are more muscular than others. Though all of you, to our Human eyes, have unflawed beauty."

"As we age beyond 120, we lose some of our firmness and gain weight. So, you see us as *exotic,* do you? Many see your race the same way. We have fantasy tales that explore that theme based on the few cross-racial romances in our past. Which, by the way, have always been of a Human man and a Qeteral woman. But, too, from the other end, your Lady Lyndz is a stunning beauty, to be sure, and I have heard other men and some of the women speak so about her. Though many remember the late king and his father, and we even have Prince Lumin to demonstrate to us somewhat of the look of Human men, few of us alive today have ever seen a Human woman before your group came to us. Maybe a handful of the oldest among us who were part of the trade that went on during the end of the imperial days might remember a Human woman. Yet in her case particularly she looks quite like one of our own, as lovely as Princess Ryn. She is not Bonded?"

"She is not, nor is the Lord Kodi her brother or the A'Terianh."

"Nor yourself. This Vow of Chastity you people in the Orders take. You understand some of your Orders' restrictions are not well-understood."

"Ha! The Etoppsi don't even know the word 'chastity' unless like Rainwing they've studied it about us Human Order members who have taken the Vow. Consider it, for Humans in the Orders, a Discipline that helps us focus on spiritual contemplation and the needs of others. But I do not believe you would find our High Synod to be judgmental in its application to the other two races. At least not today. In the past they were more severe about it, I know. As neither Qeteral nor Etoppsi have been active in the Orders for centuries, I do not believe the Synod would ever again perceive..."

"Brother Shane," Solone interrupted, "are you envisioning a...a *future?*"

Shane blinked. "I...I apologize. It must seem as though I was placing higher value on the way in which we do things in the Valley, as if it is up to us to set the standard. I do not wish to be perceived as projecting Valley norms or to be so presumptive."

"No, not at all. You misunderstand. The Valley is the birthplace of all the races and is a place all Qeteral revere, and some of your party as you have stated have actually seen our common Mother, Vanayema Modela, who birthed our forebears in that Valley! There is admiration for the Valley's Orders, then, even if we are no longer a part of them. We still revere your Human Sages, I think you know. They are the Divine's prophets, directly connected to the Great Sages Chosen by the Divine in the time of Terianh the Great. You must understand I am not opposed to a future whereby all the Gifted from the three races share commune and high-level education with one another."

"Why, that's remarkable, Solone! How grand that would surely be! I wish Rainwing, the Etoppsi female, could hear you. She would find this most interesting. Trust me, and I believe Sage Curdoz would agree with me, that should such reunion in the Orders ever take place, much would have to change, and the Orders would have to be reworked to accommodate. Humans need more structured Disciplines, as our sexual transgressions, among other traits such as misplaced aggression, and the seeking after power and riches, are greater than yours. The Vow of Chastity is just one Discipline that works well for most of us Humans in the Orders." Shane paused, breathed in, and looked Solone in the eye. "Some of us do struggle with its necessity and cannot follow it rigidly. I cannot myself admit to you, Solone, that I am not one of them."

"I see. It is certainly understood by us that Humans are not always chaste till commitment. In comparison to us it is puzzling, but among us Healers we conclude that the nature of Humans is perhaps more experimental, in some measure more like that of the Etoppsi. Be not troubled by any judgment on my part."

"The 'experimental' varies widely among us, and many laypersons are chaste before bonding. The measure, then, is in respect for the other and not in self-centeredness."

"You cannot be a Healer, Brother Shane, and not be respectful. No doubt you act on your nature with care and reason."

"I do. I am glad you choose to understand."

"Brother Shane, I am beyond curiosity. Your presence and openness to me is a gift and allows me almost to indulge in *obsession* in my desire to know about your race and that of the Etoppsi! In addition to understanding how the Human Orders function and all their work in your Human world. Please, hold nothing back! I realize now this Vow of Chastity must in large measure be one of *example* to your laypeople in the area of self-control, even as you think it need not be complied with with perfect rigidity. Now, continue what you were saying about the Vows. There are others, yes?"

"Yes. The Monastics also follow a Vow of Poverty, whereby they do not build up wealth and so share most things in common. Many Healers and most Matrimonials also follow that Vow. I myself, for example, keep only some favored books, good clothes, and some family mementos and live with Monastics and other Healers at a monastery. Though Sages and the Heads of Orders tend to live in great houses with many fine things and Monastic servants to help them. In part that is in order to provide hospitality, administration, and helps with their diplomatic functions in the various governments. We also follow a Vow of Obedience to the Heads of our Orders, though currently my loyalty is transferred to Sage Curdoz. He has me also follow the will of the War Wizards at the warfront. That is expected, as War Wizards are an Order in and of themselves and during war outrank all others. I stand out in a way, for Lord Curdoz has assigned the health and well-being of our entire party over to me, and so I've been given my own level of independent authority even over them if it pertains to my expertise, though I've delegated somewhat to other Healers. Sister Ulna I have placed in charge of the health of all the females, and there are others back at our ships with Prince Nikal's knights and the ships' crews. I stray a little, but anyway, if there were to be a reunion with the other races' Orders, Disciplines and any related Vows would have to be reconsidered based on the differences of the three races but also, at least in my opinion, based on individuality."

"I agree. A more thorough evaluation of the individual's first Vision and Calling from the Divine Myghal and regular conversations regarding their expectations of the roles they play."

"Yes, precisely. And authority would have to be shared, whereas in the past it was nearly always the Human Sages and those of the Synod who took authority upon themselves and imposed the Disciplines on novices from the other races. Definitely ill-conceived."

"And there should be education by scholar-professors from all the races at a common university."

"Absolutely!"

"I very much favor your seven-year program..."

It soon became obvious that Solone and Shane had found in one another cross-racial soulmates. The two soon took a swim together, but then continued their conversation as they sat in the water on a rock. After a time, however, Solone took leave to attend to his wife and family but invited Shane for dinner and evening conversation over mead. Shane, grateful to have a new friend among the Qeteral, gladly accepted.

Tiliruf was having a good time in the swimming hole with his friends. He threw the ball about, 'tossed' a few children, had conversations, and got to know some of the Qeteral who likewise wanted to meet *the A'Terianh*. He felt it was productive and hoped they viewed him and his presence positively. Between these conversations he would swim about with some vigor, finally settling on another underwater rock. He would then look around again and take in the pleasant scene. He could not totally ignore the bodies of the young Qeteral women. They were certainly attractive and sensuous. Yet to him they were but a kind of candy. In his case, he was able to discard any need to 'taste' it. In part he was, unknown to him, still under some magic of Shane's, whereby it was a little easier for him to do this. He also had read enough of Qeteral anatomy to understand he could never have a tryst with a Qeteral anyway, as it presumed bonding and commitment. That was a definite no. He wasn't such a cad that he would knock up a Qeteral virgin and leave her with his 'seed' perpetually preserved in her body and then disappear from the country. Nor would any other means of sexual 'expressiveness' work here, considering his diplomatic role. He didn't even know if the unbonded young 'played around a bit' with each other and engaged in such forms of exploration.

Nor really did the specifics of any of these considerations intrude much upon his mind just now. He would only look, imagine a dash of fantasy, and then let it go. He was not aware that Shane's magic helped him with this, as Shane never explained any of the magic he used on him, and Tiliruf never really asked. He thought he was just in a better spot these days. Less anxious about himself. Less easily triggered by his inner hungers.

And then *she* arrived at the poolside and, casually, disrobed in the sunshine.

His were not the only young male eyes that beheld her as she stood at the banks. Yet he had become instantly oblivious to such other men. No other men, nor women, Qeteral or Human, existed just then.

Gazing upon her with his own eyes, mesmerized by her body's utter perfection which he had never before seen in its fullest feminine grandeur, his mind went wild. Beyond wild. He was transformed into the very heavens, the Cosmic Dance of interweaving planets and shooting stars. And from that moment forward, for as long as he lived, Tiliruf would never be the same.

He realized his mouth was agape. He felt his face burn red and hot, and, though half submerged as he was, he had gone stone hard in mere seconds.

Suddenly a ball was tossed at him by Manwul from a distant rock and landed with a splash on his face. Tiliruf cursed under his breath, grabbed it, and tossed it then to Lumin at another rock. Then he sank full under the water and swam resolutely in the direction of the waterfall behind which he could, possibly, calm down.

To his great fortune, there he found Shane working his muscles by climbing about on a reasonably dry but challenging rock face.

"Shane!" he called out to the Healer.

A few Qeteral were also swimming about under and behind the curtain of the fall and likewise climbing about on the rocks.

Shane, attuned as he was by now to Tiliruf's expressions and voice, understood the young man was in some sort of need. He let go of the rock face and fell into the water. He swam over. Tiliruf was looking at him with a most awkward smile on his face.

"You're hiding something. What is it?"

"You could say that." Tiliruf whispered in order for others near not to overhear. Although with the falling water, Shane had to get really close. "Er. Would you have a Healer's magic that could calm a bloke who's turned horsey? I can't seem to relax myself. All these women have kind of thrown me overboard, you know?"

"I, um, might."

Shane was determined for now not to let Tiliruf in on the knowledge that he had been manipulating Tiliruf's body and mind with magic meant to keep him, among other things, free of some of the anxiety he suffered. It was deeper than just relaxing Tiliruf at evening. It was magic that worked in Tiliruf's brain and affected him positively, usually for a full day, until the next application. Though sometimes he had to apply it more often. He had implored Kodi not to tell Tiliruf, using as he was some of the same magic occasionally on Kodi and even Nikal. They, of course, didn't mind the help. Tiliruf was a different matter, and the magic Shane used on him also contained other enchantments meant specifically for him. Manwul and Hadon guessed somewhat what Shane was doing for Tiliruf but kept their mouths shut, as they trusted Shane. They, too, understood that Tiliruf would not like to believe he was being magically manipulated, even if it was for his own good.

In the immediate moment, however, Tiliruf was desperate. Yet Shane had already applied the body-calming magic on Tiliruf before they came to the water pool, just as he had done with Kodi early that morning. He had suspected it wouldn't hurt Tiliruf coming here, and all it took was a firm shoulder grasp of friendship in order to inconspicuously transfer the magic. The thing was, both Tiliruf and Kodi, at nineteen, struggled harder than the older men in controlling their bodies' reactions to...*stimuli.* The revealing way Qeteral women dressed, and now of course as they gathered all around the swimming hole, their gorgeous bodies fully exposed, Shane suspected, from experience, that they could use a little help. In Kodi's secretive case, he was falling in love and was even more predisposed to the allure offered that morning by the Princess Ryn's close bodily presence and reciprocal attraction.

With Tiliruf now, Shane was somewhat surprised. Yes, the calming magic could be overcome deliberately. He had warned Kodi not to "press it" with

Ryn, or he'd find the magic would wear off quickly. It wasn't really designed to create even a temporary impotence, but helped control reaction. Well, for some reason, the magic had been overcome in Tiliruf just now.

"Don't ask me questions, eh?" Tiliruf blurted. "Just help me out, Shane."

"Of course," said Shane with a chuckle. "Come over here and sit on this rock. It's underwater, Tiliruf. Stop your worrying."

It worked. In moments, while other Qeteral were swimming about unconcerned and unaware, Shane could sense a near-full calmness restored to Tiliruf's mind...and body.

"Gosh, thanks, Shane. It's like when you Healed my broken rib, eh! What a wash of relief, I swear. But I'm going back to the pavilion now. I don't want to risk this happening again today. I actually think I could use a good nap. Want to go back with me?"

"Yes, I might have overcompensated with the magic and made you a hint sleepy. I suspect the revelry will end shortly anyway. From what I gather, this after-lunch swim lasts about an hour until it's time for most to go back to their work, though some of the mothers will stick around with their little children."

Luckily for Tiliruf his clothing was a good hundred feet away from where Lyndz was with Mishoo, Frith, Halta, and the Healer Sisters. He slipped out of the water just as those women were getting in the water after having lain in the sun for a little while.

"What do you know?" said Shane, obliviously. "It's Lyndz and the women."

With the quickest possible glance, Tiliruf was able to determine she was fully in the water and so could look for another second and cover his discomfort. "Yes. Well, good for her! I'm sure Kodi's glad she's enjoying herself, too!"

The two soon dressed in their Qeteral pants, Shane in his sandals and Tiliruf in his socks and boots. The two marched back in the direction of the pavilion.

"Anything you want to tell me now, a'Terianh?" Shane asked on the road.

"Huh?" Tiliruf seemed distracted. But then he looked at Shane and smiled. "Oh, that! Like I said, I think I was just overwhelmed by all those gorgeous Qeteral goddesses, you know? Pretty brown skin. Firm breasts, eh? Made me forget myself."

Shane would not press it. It may have been one of the few times in which his astuteness and accompanying logic did not work as well as it usually did. Had he made a stronger comparison to Kodi's situation, he might have considered there was indeed something specific—or perhaps someone—affecting Tiliruf in the same overpowering way in which Ryn affected Kodi. On the other hand, to presume Tiliruf might have strong emotion for one particular woman, considering his history with women, might have been farfetched. So, he took Tiliruf at his word. It appeared to be the logical answer, particularly if Tiliruf did allow his mind to wander deep into a fantasy while at the swimming hole. He was, after all, nineteen, typically indulged his strong sex drive back home with little qualm, and had gone without for several weeks now, ages for him. He often joked of an island fantasy, surrounded by nude women in a sort of orgy of carnal delight. The situation at the swimming hole could certainly lend itself to such imagery. "It is a bit overwhelming. We Easterners commonly swim in mixed-gender company, hardly any different than Qeteral. Just not so much in the West. I'm glad I was there to help you out. But you'd better try harder to get past it, Tiliruf, and not let your mind go like that. Can't say the same didn't use to happen to me sometimes way back during swims. Especially if a girl touched me; that could fire me pretty rapidly, even if she wasn't meaning to be sexual about it. Nobody much cared; it's just Human nature. A laugh or two. But here, of course, we're trying to be disciplined and diplomatic in our interactions with the Qeteral. Let me, uh, apply a charm I know before you go again. And if you don't fantasize so heavy, you should be all right."

"I will. I swear." In fact, Tiliruf did sound determined. "I shouldn't've let my mind go there. It just kind of bit me and made me a little crazed. Thanks for calming me down, eh? I'll just play with the kiddies or talk to the lads. Hadon and I should try climbing that rock wall like you were doing."

"If you fall, it's in the deep water. It's fun. When we get back to the pavilion, I'll put you on to sleep for your nap."

"Thanks, Shane. Some peace and quiet is just what I need, eh?"

"I'll read a book in the lounge chair and make sure the others are quiet and let you nap when they get back."

Tiliruf did seem better, or at least pretended to be. "Tell me about the bloke you were talking to, Shane, eh? Who was he?"

And for the few more minutes it took to reach their pavilion, Shane happily told Tiliruf about his new friend, Solone.

Despite his effort, Tiliruf wasn't really focusing that closely on Shane. Even during his magical nap, his dreams struggled with his need for peace. Eventually, even before he left Ulakel, he jotted out a poem that expressed his emotions of that day. But he shared it with no one. He folded the parchment into a minute square and stuffed it away into the bottom of his pack:

Having fun and feeling fresh
All naked in the water delish.
Friends old and new
And children too,
We all were playful river fish.

It was the general custom there
That everyone sunned and swam about bare.
Women and blokes,
The kids and old folks,
And no one at all seemed to care.

Off our shoulders jumped little boys
And little girls with splashing noise.
Talking with dads,
Throwing balls with the lads,
Simple, playful, afternoon joys.

Pretty women everywhere,
Lovely figures and faces fair.
Though some of us took
A closer look
I swear I didn't really stare!

The lassies would look at us too, you know,
Our muscular forms and manly show.
The old would admire
Our youthful attire
And remember their own fun long ago.

I had no struggles just then in my mind.
All anxious thoughts were left behind.
Good times we were having
My friends we were laughing.
The summer sun was bright and kind.

Then...laughing bathers seemed to pause.
I noticed several dropping jaws.
I turned to see,
And there before me
I finally understood the cause.

For there your feminine beauty's fame
Stood radiant in the sun's bright flame.
Your robe fell away.
And from that day
I would never ever be the same.

You wore all that nothing like a crown,
A queen in her invisible gown.
That long hair black
Loose down your back,
Your gorgeous skin all golden brown.

Though I knew well your stunning face
And seen you dressed in linen and lace,
No dress could compare
To your body bare
Or match your dazzling naked grace.

Before, I had resisted well
Your charms that caused my heart to swell.
Now a surge of desire
Set my loins on fire.
My heart beat like a clanging bell.

Though half underwater my body grew hot.
My stomach tied up in a knot.
With no control
Of the fire in my soul,
I swam to hide at the waterfall grot.

There I found my wise Healer friend,

His magic touch I begged to lend.
He quickly calmed down
This flustered clown.
My roused body he did amend.

I told my friend a little lie
"I guess I let my fantasies fly!
Those voluptuous women
Around me were swimmin'!"
I couldn't tell him the true reason why:

That there was really only one
Who caused this young man to be so undone.
Overcame my defenses,
I lost my senses,
And all my emotions overrun.

My friend determined to put me at ease.
In his brotherly way he tries to please.
Though it was absurd
He believed my word.
He chuckled a bit but didn't tease.

Afraid I'd lose my newfound cool
My friend and I dressed and left the pool.
But I took a chance
Stole one last glance
And then felt like a stupid fool.

For you are pure without any blame.
I've been a cad without much shame.
I know it's true
I don't deserve you.
But I'm telling you all the same,

I'll never look upon another.
I swear that there can be no other.
My heart will break.
But for your sake
I'll be for you just as a brother.

Or...is it possible to purge my sin?
The dissolute rascal that lives within?
And make me whole,
Purify my soul,
And maybe start all over again?

Is there a future which I can't see?
From my scalawag past I could be set free?
And come to deserve

Your virtuous reserve
And love you with the whole of me?

Dare I hope you would still be there?
Those perfect curves and face so fair?
With inviting eyes
And welcoming thighs
You'd love my own with your body bare?

As we left the water and walked ahead,
I heeded my friend and did what he said.
He put me deep
In enchanted sleep
On my little lonely bachelor bed.

That afternoon I know I slept,
My friend's healing magic so adept.
Yet for me, for you,
Which could never be two,
My lonesome soul wept.

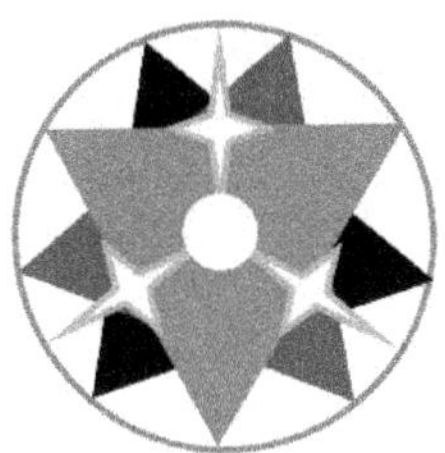

Chapter 19—Tiliruf's Discovery

It was late in the night and Tiliruf was wide awake. Maybe his long afternoon nap had undone his need for sleep.

Not unlike the previous evening, the men had gathered at the pavilion for games and talk. This time, not only Lumin but also Olin and a handful of other Qeteral men whom they had met in the last couple days had been a part of the gathering. Tonight, Curdoz had been somewhat the center of attention as they questioned him much about the Orders' views on the nature of the Guardian, and of the One, and of Human Order Disciplines. Shane was part of the conversation for a short while until leaving for dinner at Healer Solone's.

Tiliruf had not talked a great deal, although he did engage in a game or two of Kings and Castles with Lumin. Lumin was also quieter than usual.

All had been quiet now for some two hours, except of course for the cacophony of night creatures. Crickets by the millions chirped. Whippoorwills and owls called. There was also the return of the nightingale.

This place is nearly as 'birdy' at night as it is in the day.

The others were clearly asleep, and it felt a little emptier without the Etoppsi. Any hints of their strong scent were absent. Shane had not yet returned.

His mind still troubled from the onslaught of emotions earlier in the day, Tiliruf rose quietly and looked about. It was odd, for looking behind the curtained partition where Nikal and Kodi slept, he noticed Lumin wasn't there. He had told Olin he was going to stay again at the pavilion, but maybe he had changed his mind and returned to the palace.

Slipping quietly back into his Qeteral pant, Tiliruf grabbed up his socks and boots and headed outside. He needed to be alone. He determined now to take a walk in the night and try to gather his thoughts.

He made his way out of the hollow then turned from the road into a grassy field. Stars shone brightly and Solvermoon provided much light. In the distance he observed a large copse and made his way towards it. Upon finally reaching it, he discovered it contained many great-sized trees along with an undergrowth of rhododendrons and ferns.

Casually, he strode in. It smelled nice. Some of the trees were pines. He stopped occasionally and felt the trunks of the trees, observed their girth, and even felt the long leaves of the rhododendrons. He was familiar with plants, and botany was a science of which he knew more than the average man. But this sort of nature exploration was not especially typical of him, and yet what was going through his mind now was not typical, either. He needed. He didn't know what he needed. Maybe he guessed pieces, but he resisted putting words to these thoughts even in the confines of his own mind.

Continuing into the woods he was surprised when he came upon a couple of blankets laid flat upon a bed of moss. Sitting atop them was an unlit lantern. A strong beam of moonlight shone here, like anticipatory stage lighting before the opening of a play.

Just as he was about to explore this curious scene further, he heard a voice coming his way. His mind worked quickly, and he began to have a suspicion as to the purpose of those blankets. He considered backtracking. He hesitated too long, and now suddenly the voice was quite near. He deduced if he ran, he would create far too much noise. There was no time to retreat carefully and quietly. With no other choice he quickly hid himself under a thick cover of drooping rhododendrons and lay prostrate on his stomach. The ferns against his torso felt strange but were soft. He was a mere twenty feet from the spread-out blankets.

He then realized he knew that voice. A young man's voice. And then there was another voice, that of a young woman.

"Oh, dear one! You made it ready for us! Let me light the lantern. I want you to show me what you've drawn for me!"

It appeared all the woman did was touch her hand to the lantern and within it a soft, warm glow appeared. That, mixed with the moonlight, created a sublime radiance upon the couple. The forest behind and around seemed to disappear in a black backdrop.

The two embraced in a passionate kiss.

Oh, damn! Damn, damn, damn! Why am I here, eh?

Tiliruf was stuck. He was wise enough to understand that what was happening before him was deeply secretive. As he was out of the moonlit stage and concealed in blackness, though he felt guilty, to reveal himself now would have been both unnecessary and a horror.

The play had already begun, the actors and even the title of the play were revealed instantly to the only one in the audience:

Young Prince Lumin and His Secret Lover.

"Fal! You are so incredible. I have missed you."

Staring raptly through an opening in the foliage, Tiliruf could not help but admit Fal really was gorgeous. Resembling Lumin in age, but considering he was mature for a Qeteral, Tiliruf suspected she was older than he.

They sat upon the blankets, and in the lantern light Lumin unfurled a large parchment. "How do you like it?"

"It's wonderful. You and I making love! The realism is exceptional, love. I will look on it every night and dream of you. It shows your Giftedness, Lumin, the detail. Passion mixed with fun on our faces!"

Blazing thumpers! He drew her an erotic portrait of themselves! Lumin, I never would've thunk it.

Tiliruf couldn't make out much of the drawing from his vantage, but he could not help but to be intrigued. He had already seen some of Lumin's art and knew it was superior. Tiliruf was schooled in Human art, and from that vantage, for Lumin to be willing to draw himself making love to a woman would, in Tirilorin, have placed him in a rare subset of modern artists of eroticism, both portraitists and sculptors, who produced their art with an aloof rebelliousness to propriety. Yet they were truly interesting people, often young, often using themselves and their bondmates or their friends as models, and their art commanded gold among certain collecting circles in the cities. Such collectors also tended to be young. Though Tiliruf was not so familiar with Qeteral art, based on Fal's words he suspected erotic art was not so out of the ordinary. Sensualism in part defined their race. Even so, Lumin's work was surely demonstrative of a strongly sexual man, one with a level of sensual maturity beyond what Tiliruf expected of him.

Beyond even himself, Tiliruf thought. Tiliruf did not buy such art, as it inevitably showed two people in love. Since he had always resisted romance, it did not reflect his interests. Was he embarrassed by the reality of true love? But he would observe it in others' collections and in the museums. Did that reflect something subconscious beyond his connoisseur's eye?

Lumin, you continue to surprise. You harbor secrets, and buddy, I swear to the uttermost stars I will keep your secrets. Not Kodi, not nobody. I wonder if you've told Kodi about her. I damn well know you haven't told your brothers. They think you're just a Qeteral boy. You really are part Human, eh? More mature than you let on.

"No, don't put out the lantern, Fal. I want to see you. I want to see all of you in the light."

Lumin reached to remove Fal's shirt.

Oh, shafts! It's really happening!

Tiliruf was entranced now. The pucker in his face softened. What he was about to witness was something he had never before seen. True young love at its most innocent and intense, not in clay or marble, not in charcoals or oils. In genuine, ever-moving, sensual flesh.

Fal was as voluptuous as any goddess could be. She leaned back, Lumin unstrapped her sandals for her and then removed her pant. In her full nudity she was an extraordinary creature. He bent over her and fondled her breasts, and then for a long minute he enveloped with his lips one of her nipples and then the other, stimulating each with his tongue. She groaned softly. He smiled at her and then sat up. He'd been wearing his Human grandfather's boots. He removed them and stood. Slipping now out of his own pant, he revealed his full male body in a state of obvious readiness.

Damn, Lumin, you're nothing less than a muscled, frisky stallion.

When Fal leaned up on her knees and enveloped the last few inches with her lips, Lumin's face went all happy. "Ah, love. Ah!"

Yah. Blokes. We never say no to that, do we, Lumin?

She obliged him this way for a happy minute or two. She backed off and he then dropped down beside her in playful laughter. She rolled herself over him, and they again engaged in a passionate kiss. There were delightful sighs and vocals as they lay together on the blankets. For a time, they continued to stroke and kiss one another, their hands moving over curve and muscle, fingers teasing intimate parts. He rolled her over and lay half atop. Naked bodies, man and woman pressed together, to touch and be touched was pleasure in and of itself.

And then he moved himself down her body and returned the earlier favor. Her vocalisms grew intense quickly.

Qeteral ain't no damn different than us, that's for sure. You know exactly what...How long you been doing this, boy? There I go again. Boy...horseshit.

After a time, this preliminary fun gave way to the greatly anticipated connection. He lay beside her, positioning himself behind her back. He took hold of her breast. Her curvaceous form enfolded by his muscular frame, she turned her neck to kiss him. She guided him in.

"This is what I've wanted since I saw you at the water today." As he began his movements, his expression was joyous.

"I have, too, dear one. Oh!" She exclaimed. Her smile came close to laughter. "This is the portrait you drew!"

From holding her breast, one hand then moved down to play again on her most pleasurable spot. She groaned with gratefulness in her eyes, still looking up into his face, as he looked into hers and continued his deep thrusting.

It was the superior happiness on both their faces that caused a profound shift in Tiliruf's thinking. It went from a kind of admiring clandestine intrigue to that of intense longing. The feeling came so suddenly and powerfully the muscles in his face contorted, and he almost shed a tear. He found himself moved by the artful beauty of what he was seeing and of the natural groans and soft *aahs* he was hearing. How the light from moon and lantern played on their skin, the background night noises, nature's music...nothing was contrived. Nothing was fake. This position appeared incredibly intimate to Tiliruf. The two together were blissful. It was remote from his own experiences with the Library Girls. As if it were happening on another world entirely.

Their movement was slower than what Tiliruf expected in comparison to what in his case with the pleasure girls back home was more frantic. Nor was he the only one. Sometimes in orgy there would be other men and prostitutes in the same room. The men, wearing masks on their faces to hide their identities—though Tiliruf knew some of them—would make rounds among the fake-squealing women like the revolving child's game of chairs. Men desperate to express a fierce, privileged misogyny upon poor women who, Tiliruf seemed to understand now, only wanted their money. They didn't give a damn about the men's pleasures. Or their own. It was all pretense. It made him sick inside now as he considered it.

Yet here, the fully committed and grateful Fal could express her own grand, female desire, clearly enjoying her own likewise committed lover's body. She felt the same level of ecstasy as did Lumin.

Maybe, just maybe, Tiliruf had sometimes wished for this same kind of mutuality in his escapades, but typically the girl was just a receptacle for his own lust and, usually, quick release. Most often, he was alone with the girl in a private suite which he paid handsomely for, and he had at times made some effort after his own to create pleasure for her. Sometimes it worked and sometimes it didn't. One might warm to his efforts whereas another would be cool to them. But what he was witnessing here between the two, deeply-in-love pair, was oneness of purpose.

Two or three other positions the lovers used over the next several minutes, and then variations on these. Each beautiful to see, each enjoyed with its subtle differences in feeling. Tiliruf could not have removed his eyes even if he had wanted to. It was a dance. Eventually they settled into what was surely, like the first, another favored one. Lumin lay himself on his back with his hands behind his head and a contented expression on his face. Fal lowered herself onto him and, looking at him lovingly, began yet again the slow rhythm. Lumin would look with a kind of gratefulness at his own stiffness as she lifted herself high and then lowered rhythmically back down. Then his eyes would meet her own. She understood him and how powerfully she, with the whole of her body, fired the whole of his body, how much he craved it, and how much it meant to him to have her to express his need. Her long hair tickled his torso, increasing his overall level of physical thrill.

Tiliruf's memories of North Bend receded into the far regions of his mind.

That is the prettiest picture I ever did see, damn, Lumin! Aren't you a lucky bloke, eh? To have someone like her! I wish I...

As North Bend thoughts receded, his mind filled with a new vision. He hesitated, and then, with an uncontrollable surge of pent-up desire, Tiliruf went rock hard. The transfer of sexual heat across those twenty feet, paired with this new image in his head, was finally more than he could resist. Even if Shane's magic was meant to last this long, it was gone. He found himself palming his rod, pulling it free out of his pant. He couldn't help it. He felt guilty and horrible on the inside. But he needed. He just needed. And as he watched the lovers before him, Tiliruf imagined. He imagined himself like Lumin, with someone he loved...

Someone whose gorgeous, desirable body he had only seen in full in the sunshine that previous afternoon.

But I cannot tell you. I do not deserve you.

But he could not stop the vision. Before him on the stage his body replaced that of Lumin's. Lyndz' body replaced that of Fal's. The blankets were ones Tiliruf had brought under his own furtive plan earlier. The rolled-up portrait lying to the side, Tiliruf had drawn with magical hand by lantern light one night in the privacy of his rooms.

Over several minutes the groans of the lovers intensified and grew louder. Happy and playful. They had no hesitations. The village was a mile away. No one could overhear. Lumin reached up and fondled Fal's firm breasts, and again played his fingers on her nipples. Sometimes he lifted his torso and enveloped one in his mouth. At this, her calls grew more intense. After a time, she straddled him more widely and arched over him at a sharper angle. Lumin lifted his knees, and, with his heels braced against the ground he gripped her rump and began pumping more rapidly up into her. Soon, inevitably, her whole body shuddered wildly. She called out in rhythmic intensity, and then he, too, with his last powerful thrusts exploded in his own joy. A series of throaty masculine triumphs echoed one after another through the woods into the distance.

Tiliruf struggled mightily to keep his own intensity quiet. He buried his hot face in the cool ferns and, biting his tongue, released himself onto the ground below him.

He knew what he needed. He needed what he had just witnessed of the lovers before him. Not only the beautiful dance of the bodies, but also what those two plainly represented in their committed pairing. Their love was what made the accompanying body dance so incredible. But he couldn't have it. He just couldn't. He doubted he ever would. He suspected he would be stuck forever in an unrealized fantasy.

He took a deep breath and looked up. The two lovers lay wrapped together and spoke quietly.

"I want to stay and do this again in a little while. I could love you hour after hour for days on end!" Lumin's tone was mannish, confident, and funny. It caused Tiliruf to get out of himself again and found himself smiling at his young friend's boasting. He knew it wasn't entirely fabrication, as Lumin was energetic and potent, assuredly capable of great lovemaking feats if given the opportunity. Undoubtedly, he had experienced more fruitful nights with Fal before. Again, Tiliruf wondered how long this had been going on for them.

She giggled. "Me, too, my love. But we must get back, of course. We began so late. But a week is too long when I know you are so near. And just as you, when I see you at the water, I ache for you. Let it not be so long."

"Maybe even tomorrow night! Staying with the Humans at the pavilion makes it easier to get away than from the palace..."

Tiliruf raised an eyebrow.

You are a calculating dog, Lumin!

"...I will send a message to you with your little owl. And soon I hope I can declare for you, but I first must go with the Humans on the journey. It's important to me. I've explained it to him, our plan. Kodi said he'd help convince Mother and Hurlin."

"I know it's important to you. It will make all the difference. I will miss you while you are gone."

"When I return, I can proclaim manhood, of course. I will have met the requirements, gone way beyond them, even if I am young. And even Hurlin cannot stop me."

"We will make our love and commitment known, and I will declare for you. We will Bond and be together, and then I will bear you a child, Lumin."

"It is all that I wish, really. To be with you forever, Fal."

To Tiliruf's enormous relief, the two then stood and dressed. Following another passionate kiss, Lumin grabbed up the blankets and the lantern, and together they made their way out of the woods.

Quieter than a mouse, Tiliruf rose and followed. He soon saw the lamp go out. At the edge of the woods, he watched them in the moonlight make their way in the direction of the village. When they were far enough away, he emerged from the woods himself and made more to the right, in the direction of the hollow.

When he descended into the hollow, he felt tired. Yet he was not ready to go back to his bed. His mind was churning. Still with bits of dirt and fern plastered to his sweaty body, he walked over to the pool and lowered himself into the water. Attuned suddenly again to nature, he felt relief. Shane was right about water. It felt like cool heaven. Though still troubled, enough of his anxiety dissipated so that he felt a little more himself, a little more controlled. He didn't know it, but Shane had applied a whole new sweep of powerful enchantments on him as he slept in the afternoon, and now, after the inescapable rawness of the previous hour, the magic was reasserting itself. He swam about quietly for a while and listened to the night sounds.

He then noticed another descend from the pathway into the hollow. At first, he thought it might be Shane.

It was Lumin. He carried the blankets and the lantern. He suddenly vanished in the strong moonlight, along with all he carried. Momentarily startled, Tiliruf then realized he was trying to hide his return from any Humans who might notice.

Damned good trick I must admit.

He reappeared. He had seen Tiliruf. He came over and set the blankets and lantern down on the table containing the bathing supplies.

"That's you, isn't it, Tiliruf?"

"Come swim, eh?"

"Yes, I could use a wash."

That's what I always want to do after a good sticky romp.

Lumin dipped and soaped himself, then swam and rinsed, dunked his whole head under the water, then made his way to Tiliruf sitting half underwater on a rock and sat beside him.

"You have a smile on your face," said Tiliruf, secretly playing with him. "Where have you been, eh?"

"I, uh, just wanted to get out alone for a while. I lay on some blankets out in the field, you know, and looked at the stars."

With a lantern. Right. "I should do that myself sometimes, eh? It is beautiful and peaceful here in your land. I live in the big city, but we do have a pretty estate in the countryside."

Lumin was silent for a time. His smile wouldn't leave his face.

The envy Tiliruf had was internally laughable, and so internally he laughed at himself. Stupid thoughts ran through his mind about sitting next to a man whose thumper was bigger than his own, who could yell loudly and unhesitant in orgasmic triumph, who had a woman with whom he would, maybe the next night, be able to romp royally yet again. *Royal sex, yep, fit for a fit, young, potent prince.* And yet *for* Lumin's sense of joy, Tiliruf was proud. It was little different than both the envy and pride he felt towards Manwul with Steffia and for Hadon with Sturla.

"I, uh...Can I share a secret with you, Tiliruf?" His voice was not remotely boyish. It was mannish. He even slung his head and long wet hair with a sense of confidence. He seemed so very different from the innocent, curious boy they had met in the woods the other day. Tiliruf again realized that Lumin's initial demeanor did not match up with his man's body.

Tiliruf swallowed. "I'm your friend, Lumin. Of course. I think very highly of you, eh? What would you like to tell me?"

"Well...I lied a little. Sorry. I was not alone tonight."

Tiliruf held firm and said nothing.

After a moment, Lumin continued. "Her name is Fal. She lives in a farmhouse at the far edge of the village."

Tiliruf took several long moments before replying. He looked at him with a cocky smile. "You made love to her, eh? You planned it. With the blankets. The lantern. A secret night tryst."

Lumin looked guiltily down, though still with a smirk. "Trust me. The moons have come to know us well."

Tiliruf laughed almost too loudly and stifled it. "Eh? Listen to you being braggy about it! So, how long *have* you been seeing her like this?"

"Two years. We have been careful to keep it quiet. Yes, Fal carries my seed."

Yeah.

Tiliruf remembered when he first read about Qeteral reproductive differences from an old book in the Library and how incredibly weird he thought them. If it were the same for Human women, there would be a hundred and more, mostly prostitutes, carrying Tiliruf's "seed." Then he remembered it only really worked on virgins, as a Qeteral woman only preserved the seed of the first man with whom she made love. Her body rejected that of others. Tiliruf doubted he ever deflowered a virgin. He couldn't remember. Maybe one or two from Stri

Itruvi's set, a long time ago. Certainly not Itruvi. If he remembered correctly, she had deflowered him. He never did tell Kodi that.

What he now understood from Lumin's statement was that Fal was not capable of bearing another man's child. Only his. And the *way* he said it was surely a proclamation—odd, yes, but honest—of Qeteral male sexual pride. It was definitely that, though Tiliruf and the others came to understand the phrases, '*she carries my seed*' and '*I carry his seed,*' conveyed a whole creative philosophy for a young Qeteral couple, deeply meaningful, and a powerful statement of commitment. As it was, Tiliruf realized Lumin and Fal had been connected for life as a committed, monogamous pair from the first time they made love those two years before. She was his and he was hers. The thought was scary to Tiliruf. He realized now it must have been Qeteral-like sensitivities that caused certain men like Kodi and Nikal to look back and feel guilty about their pre-commitment experiences with women they knew they could not love—whom they really at the time didn't care about at all. Tiliruf was now feeling a little of that, too. He would never again tease Kodi about ole Jonell. He doubted he could ever again remind Manwul or Hadon about their old North Bend escapades as he attempted to excuse his own such escapades in brandy-driven conversations. They would laugh, but they also really no longer considered themselves to be the same such men as they were before, now that they had life-mates whom they loved.

He turned his focus back on Lumin.

"It's not the norm for your kind, I know, to choose a mate so young. More like 30 or even older, right? And you're just 24 what you told us. But Lumin. You're *Human,* too. It makes a lot of sense. You matured like a Human, you've had a man's body for years, and maybe it sounds dumb me saying it, because I'm not a good example. Kodi's the better man. You are a lot like Kodi, I think. But since you're really in love, and she's in love with you, you haven't done anything wrong. You and she are supposed to be together. I am really sorry you're made to feel like a boy, because that's not what I see. Maybe some of us did at first because of the kind of youthful curiosity you have and sense of fun. But now we know more about you. You're a Human man, I say. In fact, we all say you're a damned, good-looking buck. Like me, eh?" Tiliruf elbowed him on his arm, and Lumin grinned. "Like Kodi, eh? You're one of us as much as you are one of the Qeteral. Seriously, Lumin, many—most—Human men are Bonded and have children by 24. Heck, Kodi's dad Bonded his mum at 16 just before Kodi and Lyndz were born! Don't feel guilty."

"I try not to feel guilty, because my love for her is strong and true. The secrecy of it all has been exciting, like an adventure, really, and we've been happy. But it is hard to keep the secret and to be away from her for so much of the time. I can never speak to her or demonstrate my love to her in public. Hurlin questions and warns me all the time, and I feel like I'm always trying to cover myself." He looked straight at Tiliruf. "I don't know if I've ever thought of it before, but maybe I act as a boy sometimes also as a kind of cover. What do you think?"

"Yeah, could be, Lumin. Even the tone of your voice changes and the way you phrase your words. That's probably a pretty smart self-reflection."

"But this can't get out, or our families would be angry with us. She is older than I by four years, but still a little shy of what is considered proper for proclaiming a bondmate, and she's a farm girl, not from the nobility."

"Your Human grandfather wasn't a nobleman. He was a traveler."

Lumin nodded. He clearly liked that comparison. "Sometimes I want to proclaim it to the world. I did tell Kodi about it the other night. Now you."

Tiliruf felt relief to understand he was not the only one. "I'm glad you trust us, Lumin. I won't tell a soul, and I know Kodi won't either. But it's only a matter of time, Lumin. And then you really can proclaim to the world. Since she, er, carries your seed, they will have to accept your choice, and I think you realize that. But especially as a prince I can understand why you're having to be careful. You need certain pieces in place first."

Lumin looked at him. "You make me feel confident. I feel like you Humans understand me so much better than my friends or my own brothers."

"Well, maybe we do. Kodi talks a lot about it—this brotherhood we all share even though we're not related. He says we *need* it to help us be better men. I know he thinks of you as part of us, and now I do, too. So it's something maybe even the Guardian anticipated when we came here, eh? That we would become your friends. That you would have a way to express yourself more genuinely."

"I like that idea. Very much. I certainly would never have been allowed to leave Ulakel in order to seek you out. Though I've greatly wished to visit Human lands. I've wanted to go to Eleni, to where my grandfather came from."

"That's understandable. Yours is a big kingdom, and even though it's peaceful and beautiful here, you've still been caged in, in a way. You especially, with your Human background and wanting to know what we Humans must be like. Many of my foremothers came from Eleni, you know?"

Tiliruf had a reasonable level of astuteness, really. Yet, he had rarely talked to anyone before with such care. To actually bring the Guardian into it was uncharacteristic and reflected changed thinking. But Lumin was in need of encouragement, and Tiliruf hoped he was doing a good job. His own thoughts had been erratic. If comparisons could be made, he himself was in much greater emotional difficulty than Lumin was. Lumin had just come from making secret love with his girlfriend and between some of his musings maintained a natural, healthy smile on his face. Tiliruf's smiles right now were a little forced. He'd experienced some things that day, and that night, that would change him forever. He was not the same man he was when he awakened that previous morning. He felt a lot of guilt of his own and shame on top of it. Much of it revolved around his hidden feelings for Lyndz. Feelings that only that night he'd admitted to himself for the first time. And he still felt guilty to have witnessed what he did an hour ago. It was meant to be private and special. Memories of North Bend intruded upon his mind, challenged by many new thoughts. Those memories used to not involve guilt. He was also quite ashamed of using Lumin and Fal to enhance his own fantasy only twenty feet away from them.

The night wasn't over. To their surprise, they soon noticed another enter into the hollow.

Shane saw them in the water and walked over.

"Long night with Healer Solone, eh?"

"I have rarely had such extraordinary conversation. He reminds me of my lost dear friend, Eliander. What in blazes are you two doing out here?"

Tiliruf had an answer. "Well, if you must know, I had a hankering to take a couple blankets and sleep out under the stars, eh? But apparently Lumin was awake too and followed me out. Instead, we decided to take a swim and chat. Seems he needed a buddy to talk to. Come join us."

"I think I will, at that. What better than to be in the water under the stars and a bright Solvermoon. Everything around here is about water, isn't it? It's beautiful. Like the Valley of the Gifted. But the water's warmer here and even more compelling."

The Healer soon joined them at the big rock.

"Young Lumin and I were having a discussion about himself. A kind of contrast between his Humanness and his Qeteral-ness, eh? Perhaps you have an observation yourself you'd like to share, *Brother Shane?*"

It wasn't Tiliruf's style to address him formally as *Brother*, except in jest. Shane perked up and realized Tiliruf was, in a subtle way, attuning him to the realization that the conversation was indeed meant to be serious. It seemed Lumin was requiring some encouragement. He looked at the Qeteral.

Lumin spoke first. "Healer Shane, tell me what you really think of me from your observations. How Human am I?"

Tiliruf dropped down into the water and tread it, remaining close. Shane hunched over and splashed some water up on his face and then looked again at Lumin. "You know, maybe my conversation this night with Healer Solone has confirmed many of my thoughts about some of our races' differences. I would say, Lumin, in all honesty, from what I observed when I probed your body and questioned you the other day, is that you are at least as much Human as you are Qeteral, possibly more so. Because it's not simply an equality of material from your mother and from your father, but rather what each contributes unknowingly in seed and egg, what is activated in the womb before your birth, and which characteristics then dominate after your birth. I think the hair on your body is a strong outward sign of your Humanness. You sweat more than Qeteral and smell like a Human. In addition, your body matured at the rate of Humans, much faster than that of Qeteral boys. You are fully grown like a Human man at eighteen or twenty. I do not believe you will grow any taller. I detected all of that in your blood and cell structure. For all practical purposes, you are half Human or more, and even the makeup of your brain and fluids in your system resemble more so young men like Kodi and Tiliruf than they do even your own brother Olin, who graciously let me examine him too. You are a mature young Human, plainly and strongly your Human grandfather's grandson. There can be no doubt about it. You might as well have been his full son, like your father, as far as your body and brain are concerned."

Lumin nodded. He was smiling.

"Is that what you wanted to hear from this Human Healer?"

"It is, good sir. It makes me happy to know."

"I suspect it does, to know you fit within all Human norms. I suspect there is much Humanness in you that wishes strongly to exert itself. Perhaps an adventurous streak. There is a passion in you, hard to suppress. And certainly an openness to the new. But let me remind you, my young friend. You are still also very Qeteral. Particularly so in key ways. Your cells demonstrate the likelihood of the long Qeteral lifespan ahead of you. You're magical with all the typical Qeteral magic. You're especially Gifted in art by Myghal—an expression of the Divine Himself in this organic world. That sort of gift might occur in Humans, but not in the magical way it does in the application in which you demonstrate it. Aside from that interesting hint of Human sideburn on your face and that Human-like grin, your face and long hair demonstrate the serene, regal quality of the Qeteral. The hint of point on your ears, such a giveaway to your Qeteral heritage. And don't forget, you are a prince of the kingdom. You are subject to your mother."

Lumin swallowed big, and his smile faltered. Tiliruf felt kind of bad as he witnessed this. It signaled an abrupt end to the young man's post-coital bliss. *Never remind a young bloke of his mum just after he's had a secret sex romp,* he wanted to say but didn't.

"I...you are wise to remind me," said Lumin, thoughtfully. "Though I have contemplated some of this and cannot forget it, Healer Shane. But..."

"Lumin. Listen." Shane spoke more softly. "Now we Humans have come to your land and so much is happening, perhaps you wonder whether or not you should choose this or that, based on the new things you have learned about yourself. In a way, though, you are all of those things, and you don't have to choose one or another. You are capable of being all that you are: Human, Qeteral, Prince, Man. You still have a bit of the Qeteral boy in you, but mostly Human Man. Let me tell you something. Your mother is of such wise stock, Bonded as she was to a half-Human, she is not, I repeat NOT, unaware of her son and who he is. I've noticed the way she looks at you and speaks to you. She always touches you tenderly. It is different than the way she interacts with her other sons. In comparison to Qeteral, I've observed we Humans display our feelings and affections a little more obviously, which you do, too, and so your mother responds accordingly with extra warmth. Solone has confirmed a few of these things, for we spoke a little of you. He knows your family quite well. And I think it's more than just the fact you are her youngest adored child. She sees your father in you, beyond just the physical appearance; for Solone told me you look much like him, more than your brothers do. And importantly, she is attuned to the Divine, as she has had Visions. She knows."

Lumin looked at him long. His eyes were wide. "I think I see now all of those things. But...but Grandfather Hakonn...Hurlin..."

"Yes, of course. But...*they* are not your mother. They are not your deceased father, a brave king, whom you seem to know by instinct better than they do, even if they remember him better. And they are not you. You, Lumin, are you."

"I still feel I need help."

"I do understand, as they are powerful men. They care for you and have taught you everything you know, and so you feel you owe them all respect. Well then, in my opinion, continue to look on Kodi as a good guide, as I perceive you are doing. He will help you. He is the one of all of us who knows best the mind of the Guardian. But we are all of us on your side, Lumin. You're connected to us in your Humanness; we see that, and we want to affirm you in that." Shane then looked at Tiliruf floating in the water. "I haven't contradicted anything from your earlier conversation I hope."

"Not at all, eh? What you said goes pretty well with what I said. Er, better."

"Good. Now, can I encourage you fellows to go back to bed? It seems every day here is busy and full of activity, and we need good rest. I will put you both immediately to sleep. Let's get out and dry off."

As they walked toward the pavilion, Shane ahead of them, Lumin whispered to Tiliruf.

"You lied to cover those blankets."

"Eh? Human men lie a lot, brother. But I swear we don't mean anything wicked by it. Sometimes the truth creates unnecessary trouble, you know? Er, particularly for blokes. We can get in a lot of trouble and cause lots of it, ha! But most of it is kind of innocent, if you ask me. Just how many times have you lied when they caught you out of bed to and from those lovely trysts with Fal, eh?"

"Maybe I'll tell you more sometime."

"I'm all ears, eh?"

Tiliruf put his arm over Lumin's shoulder as they made their way behind Shane into the pavilion.

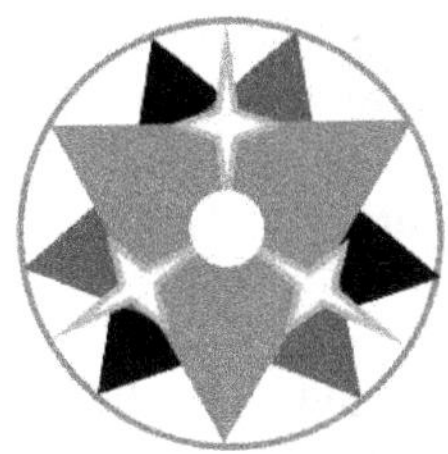

Chapter 20—The Truth of the Staff

"It is remarkable the power," said Prince Hakonn without much emotion.

"I think I'd have to describe it as raw, untamed. Wild," offered Shane. "Yet incredibly Dumhoni at the same time. Of this world and different than typical Myghalian magic. That comes to us by Cosmic spirit from the Guardian. This does not."

"The connection is there between them," added Hakonn. "The Staff contains latent power but is useless without them. No other could make use of it except that the Divine chooses them, just as He did at the Installation Ceremony Lord Curdoz described. It is useless in other hands."

"There is that piece of the Myghalian element, true. But I would say that part is mostly in the mystical relationship between the Guardian and the War Wizard, not in the actual magic," said Shane.

"Yes, it seems so," agreed Hakonn. He seemed disappointed. "In the choosing."

Nikal had of course asked. But Shane, when he'd heard what Hakonn intended, had also been insistent he be allowed to place his hands on each of Nikal and Kodi simultaneously with Hakonn as the latter examined the connection between them and the Eagle Staff. It wasn't that he distrusted Hakonn doing it alone. Instead, it was a combination of two things. Shane felt he himself was granted responsibility to monitor their health and minds, especially if magic were to be used on them. The sorts of magic Qeteral were capable of was still somewhat of an enigma to the Humans, even to Shane, who as a strong Healer was as magically powerful and knowledgeable as any Human could be. Secondly, the request to examine them in the first place seemed odd, and he suspected Hakonn had other motives and wanted to figure out what they were.

Shane was no pushover.

"Prince Hakonn, I believe you largely wish to understand why it is that Human men are Chosen as War Wizards and not your own kind."

Hakonn stared into Shane's face. He blinked once, then replied, "It is."

Nikal and Kodi both raised eyebrows. However, Kodi replied quickly. "I am not bothered, sir. I'm sure if I were you, I would wish to know the same thing. The magic of the Staff is derived from the Qeteral, and yet Humans and Etoppsi are the only ones ever chosen to wield it."

Nikal agreed. "And you want to understand why Qeteral are never so Chosen."

"I think I must apologize to your lordships for not making my full intentions known."

"Accepted," said Kodi, bluntly. "But you could've just asked, because I think I know. I'm sure there is more than one answer, but I believe mainly Myghal wants us all to cooperate. To fight the evils in this world is not the purview of just one race. The Qeteral are not meant to wield the magic alone. Or at least not this kind as it's concentrated in the Staff."

"Kodi's correct," said Shane. "This has been an interesting experiment, and I learned much from it. The power comes from the magic of the Qeteral, but the passion and intensity to make use of it is in the other two races. Not that passion is absent in the Qeteral by any means, but the Divine prefers it be wielded at this level by the two other races who are, as one might say, more used to fighting, anger, aggression. The Guardian..."

Nikal interrupted. "The Guardian doesn't wish for your kind to be corrupted by such an instrument of killing and destruction."

Hakonn turned away for a moment and looked out the window. While doing so he responded. "Because our race cannot handle such power."

"You weren't made for it," said Shane. "Your race is capable of being fighters, and you have so proven in the past. You also continue to train some of your own for war, even though you've experienced no aggression since the time of the Ralsheen. Plainly, you realize how important it is and do not wish to be caught off your guard. It demonstrates your wisdom. But generally, killing is not normally the Qeteral way and I suspect upsets a spiritual and emotional balance. Your kind represses that sort of emotion, though it is strong, and like Kodi says, it is concentrated—not repressed, or rather not well-tamed—in the Staff. I'm extrapolating a little, but I'm not so sure it could never happen that Myghal might choose a Qeteral as a War Wizard. He might if it is the right sort of man. But leading great armies against great foes is not what He had in mind for your race at the Molding. Yours is the race, I think, that balances the rest of us with a semblance of high love for all life and all beauty in the world. You are more teachers of peace and protectors of life."

"It isn't a defect," said Kodi. "Is that what you're thinking, sir?"

"Before you answer that one, m'lord," said Shane, "answer this one. Would you want your grandson Hurlin to be a War Wizard? You all have said he is the most powerful of all your people."

Hakonn turned around immediately, and for the first time they saw powerful emotion in his face. It was almost horror. "No!"

"And that is because you know in your heart how easily corrupted by this sort of power he *could* be."

"Yes. He will be king someday, I know. I think the Human phrase is *it's in the cards*. A reference, I believe, to your Fifty-twos games. None of his siblings is interested in ruling. Hurlin will be elected without question. I want him to be a good man and king, and we his family are all determined to ensure it."

"That Staff could destroy him. Have no fears, then," said Shane. "Your grandson has been granted great Gifts, in the measure the Divine saw fit. Based on protection not destruction. The greatest kind of king is the one who protects his people. But as you can extrapolate, it wouldn't be good for the souls of any of your men, not just Hurlin, to be the wielders of a Staff. And yet, the Staff's magic and such power derive from the Qeteral."

"Yet your people," said Nikal, "must see that it is because of the talents of all the Three Races, that great evil is resisted in this world when it comes about. Humans can't do it alone without you, and Qeteral can't do it without Humans. And the Etoppsi likewise."

"It's the cooperation of the races, as I said," said Kodi. "The Staff symbolizes it in a way. The Etoppsi appear to understand it, too, with their sense of a military authority deriving from Myghal as Taxiarch and proclaiming us as Polemarchi."

"You understood this always, did you? About the Staff?" asked Hakonn.

"I'm not going to pretend I knew that much right away, but once I learned more history I suspected. Think of it from a naive man's perspective. I only learned in winter that Qeteral and Etoppsi even existed. I considered it exciting to know of it. I presumed from the beginning we were all friendly with one another. I never felt of us as antagonists in any way. I sensed your daughter in the Vision, as you know. I knew her immediately as a good person. Meeting Rainwing and Royal Hawking the first time, I felt they were akin to me in a way. Beautiful, strong. The Molding only separated us races out of joy in the Creative process, different in incredibly wonderful ways, yet always akin to one another. Not enemies. Cousins, rather. Understanding that the Staff was made by Qeteral, it made sense to me, since I knew Terianh wielded it, that cooperation was a piece of Myghal's motivation. And there were choices there. Your people could have said no to the Divine when He requested you make Staffs. You chose to help."

Nikal added, "But you didn't always choose to help when you could have. I believe, Prince Hakonn, that though your people rightly fault the Abdication on us Humans, your own people could have inserted themselves diplomatically into those last years after the Lintiri War as the Empire was beginning to crumble. The Human countries would have listened and looked up to you for your cool-headed wisdom. Zarelio was not a good leader, but had he had sound advice from you and others, the Empire could have been saved. Strengthened with better cooperation with the steady heads of your people. There was too much harsh judgment at the time, but your people could have done something about it. Your father and mother could have done something about it. Instead, you isolated yourselves even further and broke off all contact after the Abdication. Many of your people resist cooperation, but you cannot find wisdom in isolation. I wished I could have expressed that to Hurlin."

"Hurlin hears, but he doesn't always listen," admitted Hakonn. "He comes by his views naturally."

"'Cause he learned from a hardnosed you," said Kodi.

As so often before, Nikal was amazed at how blunt Kodi could be towards powerful people.

Shane was less surprised. "Some of the traits you fear in Humans are the very ones that may save you someday. They've saved you in the past. More than once."

Hakonn paused long before replying. He eyed the three Humans one at a time.

"I realize now that a sort of resistance I have felt towards you and your visit here has been in error. Lord Kodi, your words are lovely and wise, and certainly reflect ancient understandings of the Molding of the Races. The word *cousins* to describe the races is in the *Ancient Book*, and the Divine Himself renews the wording as recorded by the Sages in the *Histories and Prophecies*.

Lord Prince Nikal, you are not wrong in your assessment. My father has often regretted doing nothing during those times, though I am probably the only one with whom he has ever shared such thoughts. He began, as a matter of fact, to put together a delegation to travel to Tirilorin himself after the Lintiri War. He had word that Hralindi and Essemar were about to separate from the empire. He was young and inexperienced and influenced by those who disliked Humans, blaming them for wars. So, he abandoned the attempt. You yourselves and your particular peoples were not the cause of that war nor this current war. They began with the khans, these remnants as you have discovered of the Ralsheen, corrupted by the wicked Siriné, and deriving their magic from her. For the first time you have caused me to feel pity even for their Human slaves. You didn't ask for this war any more than we did. I will bring Hurlin around."

"Well, guess what, sir," said Kodi. "Hurlin's harder-nosed than you are. Good luck."

"Olin will help me, I think. Perhaps I can even employ my father in this."

"Oh. Well, that's a plan, then."

"Yes," said Shane. "Work on Olin first, m'lord."

"So," said Kodi, pushing it, "now you see us differently, you mind telling us more about how the Staff was made?"

Hakonn paused. After a moment he replied.

"You are a bold one, Lord Kodi. The Matriarch left the decision to me, and so now I have decided. Yet it requires showing you. Not just telling you. We have a long hike to get there and back. It will be dark when we return. Meet me and my grandsons here in one hour. Eat a big meal. Bring the Staff. I'll provide small waist packs for all of us with food and water for the rest of the day. There are many streams to fill the water bottles. Just you, and invite Lord Curdoz. Hurlin will be angry with me on this, but I will insist he come."

"And Tiliruf?" asked Shane. "I think he should come."

Hakonn paused yet again. "Why?"

"Like the rest of us, he is on a spiritual journey. Could it help him to connect to his ancestor Terianh? This is important, I believe."

Hakonn thought for a minute.

"Yes, I imagine it might. I will permit the A'Terianh to join us, too. I have decided I must not resist your requests any longer. You are wise, determined men, just as the Matriarch has said."

"Perhaps your truer instincts about Humans are asserting themselves."

"Maybe. I admit I did not wish my daughter to Bond Mabelin, him being half-Human. I was most unhappy about it. But on that I was wrong. You are a wise and magically powerful Healer, Brother Shane. And insightful. Considering the tales you all have told, I have no doubt the Divine Chose you. Lord Curdoz likely discerned such a Calling when he requested you join them."

"Thank you, sir. I know now it is assuredly my Calling."

"I don't want to go, eh?"

"You're going," said Shane and Kodi together.

"It'll be good for you," added Kodi.

"Not so sure everything you blokes have led me into has been good for me," Tiliruf stated philosophically. "What's there to see, anyways? A holly tree grove? Where they got the wood from to make the Staff?"

"I don't know," said Nikal. "I have certain hesitations, too. But it's like Shane says. It's a spiritual journey. Kodi, too, if he has taught me anything it's to act with boldness and courage in this journey. There are secrets here the Qeteral have kept hidden but now feel called to share with us few men. I insist you come along, Swordmaster. And Shane went out of his way to press for your invitation."

"Oh, he did, eh?" He eyed Shane. "Damn you, Shane."

"You weren't supposed to tell him that, Nikal," said Shane smiling.

"Well, I'll go, eh? Better not be Sea Serpents," Tiliruf said with a wink.

"One doesn't find them in holly groves."

"Well, but if anybody *can* find them in holly groves, it's Kodi."

"Maybe," said Kodi unconcerned. "Courage, buddy. You're as important to this whole thing as we are. Have faith in yourself. The rest of us do."

It was indeed a long trek. The afternoon turned cloudy and windy. Hurlin, walking with Nikal, led. Olin and Kodi followed behind. Lumin and Tiliruf walked side by side next in the line, followed some distance behind by Shane. Curdoz and Hakonn were in the rear. On occasion, Lumin and Kodi or Lumin and Tiliruf shared an amusing pleasantry. Or Shane might call out with a question. Curdoz and Hakonn probably did engage in a reflection or two on Meicalian Mysticism. Yet, the weather seemed to reflect somewhat the seriousness and secretiveness of what they were about.

Except Tiliruf didn't feel quite like being serious.

"I hope it doesn't rain, eh?" he called out, mostly just to garner a reaction.

"It will in the middle of the night, but not before we return," said Hurlin.

"How do you know that?"

Hurlin refused to reply. It was Olin who did.

"We can tell, a'Terianh. We who work the Barrier magic. The skies speak to us."

"Oh. Thanks for explaining," said Tiliruf. "I completely understand now."

Kodi looked back at him and grinned and shook his head at the same time.

What seemed to be understood was that the Humans should not ask questions about their destination. Tiliruf felt sure Lumin knew where they were headed, but even he would offer no real hints. Though, when there was greater distance between the walkers, the two did once have a private interchange, on an unrelated subject.

"So," Tiliruf said in a low voice towards his ear and teased. "Two years, eh?"

Lumin looked at him oddly for a second, but after a moment he grinned his Human grin, and his blue eyes sparkled. He looked ahead and behind to make sure no one was close enough to hear them.

"Yes."

"Good, eh?"

Lumin chuckled.

"And you Qeteral wouldn't really have comparisons, eh?" Tiliruf added.

The grin disappeared, but he kept a friendly tone. "Not as a Human might be thinking, of course, no."

This led to a question Tiliruf had been wishing to know the answer to. What did it really mean when it was said that all Qeteral were devotedly monogamous?

"Experiment before with, er, other *sorts* of...?"

"You're really funny, Tiliruf." Lumin chuckled.

"It's true I've been accused of being obsessed with the subject matter, eh? I think I know you, Lumin. It's as fun a topic to you as it is to me."

"I guess I questioned you all the other night, didn't I? Manwul and Hadon, er, well. So...yes, I did. Many young people like myself do."

"Eh? Elaborate, buddy. I want to know."

"We get together in groups on hikes or at remote swimming holes to picnic and swim, and then flirty pairs might sneak away. And get to know each other."

Tiliruf grinned.

Lumin chuckled and continued, "I was bigger and more mature and tended to attach to that set in their late twenties. We did everything short of actually mating. That's what you're wanting to know, isn't it? I presume young Humans do? Or you wouldn't be questioning me about it."

"It is common, yeah, and was for me, eh? Not all, though. Kodi and I have talked about this some. Shane, too. It really varies."

Lumin nodded. "Just like it can with Qeteral. Some are more reserved about that until bonding. But others of us aren't so hesitant. I had those kinds of encounters with quite a few, Tiliruf. Does that shock you?"

"It makes me think of Qeteral as more like us, frankly."

"And they were older than I. But then in time it was always Fal and I singling each other out and separating from the rest. She was different. Our focus became each other." A self-satisfied look developed on Lumin's face. "Then together we went beyond one day."

"I see."

"We'd had many talks. We understood each other. I guess you could say I ached for the full experience and gave in to the desire."

"The Human in you?"

"It was out of step with what I had been taught was right and what seemed instinctive to my friends—that is to wait till proclaiming adulthood and formal commitment."

"But it wasn't just you, as you said."

"She would have waited, for years. But the moment was so excellent. It was an amazing place we'd found. It was a cliff overhang that overlooked a sparkling river. We knew we had a few perfect hours alone. She did not discourage me, not at all. She was ready for commitment and so she let me. Even so, I was overeager and could hardly stop myself, and I really think it was my Human side..." Lumin paused and breathed deeply.

"You are hesitant. Don't say more. I..."

"No. I don't think I need hold back with you, Tiliruf. But I'm not telling you the whole truth, because I had planned that whole day in advance. I knew exactly where I was going to take her and the amount of time we had. I was determined about it, if you understand me, and it all happened exactly as I was hoping it would."

“Of course. I’ve come to the conclusion you’re a superior sneak!” This caused Lumin to chuckle a bit loudly and turn about to make sure still that no one could hear them. Tiliruf added, “But then afterwards?”

“We said our words of commitment to one another. Then and there. There was no question about that. What happened with us does happen with some others, Tiliruf, that sort of moment that’s either planned or catches you by surprise, and...and you act on it before you’ve committed, though in your hearts you realize afterwards you’ve been very much in love with never any doubt about your future together; you just hadn’t said the words yet. It’s just that they’re many years older than what we were, nearly always after the man has claimed publicly his adulthood and been recognized so by his family. Then the two say their vows of commitment and later are Bonded in formalities by a Bondswoman in a ceremony.

“But I made sure it was wonderful for her, too. Fal loves the fun of it as much as I do. I’m thinking it has to be different for you Humans, but when a Qeteral woman carries your seed, it sets her aflame for you. And she made me feel so good about myself as a man, large and strong, and liked my Human looks. She’s intelligent and artistic, and I always thought her the most perfect girl around, with the most incredible skin and shape. I’ve written poems that describe more of my feelings, but mostly I wanted her like I wanted nothing else.”

“You were in love, eh? And like I told you before, you were already older than most Humans who, er, make love the first time. It makes more sense to me the fact your women can only carry one man’s seed for life, it would have a big impact on the connection between you. Like you said, that piece of it isn’t there with Humans. Maybe Qeteral would question your self-discipline in the matter since they think of you as too young, but no Humans would, eh? Even those of us who are damned cads know an honorable man when we meet one.”

“What is a *cad?*”

“You’ve turned this around on me,” Tiliruf chuckled. “But I’ll be honest. It means a Human bloke who mates many women and doesn’t...doesn’t much consider the relationship or the consequences. Please, don’t...”

“I think I understand, Tiliruf. I can...imagine...even if it seems strange to me.”

“Er...I’m glad it is strange to you.”

Tiliruf had been cheery at the beginning of the conversation, but his chuckling served now to hide a new discomfort. It had cost him some of his ego to express some of this. Especially since he, until recently, assumed all young men were cads (or “Vow-taking neuters” which he considered “fake” and therefore worse) with little genuine desire for a relationship based on true mutual love. He effectively ignored all examples to the contrary, and quite a few of his friends back in Tirilorin were cads just like him. He used their example and his natural cynicism as a means to justify his own shenanigans. There was more to this, too, relating to his low opinion of most women, as most of the few women of social standing that he knew, like Stri Itruvi, were manipulators. Again, until recently.

But meeting Kodi was a kind of turnaround. He came along at a critical juncture in Tiliruf’s life and began questioning his mindset about sex as pure object coitus. As Tiliruf had expressed honorable admiration for Kodi back at Zhock’s place in his desire, following his Jonell encounter, to avoid using women for mere pleasure and wait to express himself in faithfulness with one future woman, Tiliruf was likewise moved to honor Lumin’s commitment. Qeteral displayed some emotional differences, but unlike Etoppsi with their monthly mating cycles and Star Revel culture, Qeteral bodies, pleasures, and sexual function were comparable to Humans. In fact, they were exactly like Humans. Tiliruf was a first-hand witness to that fact the night before as he hid in the rhododendrons. A sort of 'what if' ran briefly through his mind as to what Lumin would have been like if the internal Qeteral female body functioned like that of their Human counterparts—if no magic were involved and preservation of seed were not at issue. Would Lumin have played around?

And yet he knew it was a really stupid sort of speculation, as the only piece of Lumin's sexual nature that was important anymore was confined in a union to the lovely and deserving Fal. Whom he obviously adored. The pre-commitment sexual exploration of Qeteral youth was commonplace, always mutual, designed as a means of learning about bodies and pleasures, eased sexual tensions, gauged compatibility, preserved the essential chastity of the Qeteral female, and also preserved both the male's and the female's sexual psyche in favor of a more mature relationship in the future with his or her eventual bondmate. This was what was meant by Qeteral monogamy. Tiliruf may not have outlined all that detail in his mind, but what he did understand even more fully now was that Lumin followed all the *Qeteral* rules and Qeteral nature regarding his sexual self, with the one exception of his age—obviously the result of his *Human* side.

And though his feelings had moved to the uncomfortable, he knew Lumin had nothing to do with it. He went on. "Lumin, understand I am only curious about you Qeteral, all the ways you're the same and different from us. And I really honor you and what you have with Fal."

"Thank you, Tiliruf. She makes me so happy. After that day was when I stopped going to those youth gatherings. Her, too."

"But you didn't really give up anything, eh?"

"I love her." He winked at Tiliruf and grinned. "It's all good, eh? And I can be a frisky bloke."

Tiliruf almost burst but kept it to a chuckle. He felt really close to Lumin just then. The young man was swiftly taking on Human phrases and expressions. Tiliruf had never, the way Kodi had, wished for a 'little brother,' but he'd got one without wishing. It opened his heart in a way he'd not expected.

Was it simply the worldly man seeing and valuing a level of innocence in the other? Often the worldly man wants to teach, train, and protect his innocent friend. But here, the worldly man was doing more of the learning, the innocent man more of the teaching. In any event, this sharing with Lumin would help focus Tiliruf's mind—that piece of it that allowed him to focus outward of himself—for a period of time.

Finally, in mid-afternoon, the nine approached a quaint village. People came out to greet them and were very surprised.

"It is the lord princes and the Human visitors!"

"We did not expect a visit, Lord Hurlin," said one. "It is an honor."

Hurlin nodded. "These are the War Wizards, Prince Nikal of Nant and Lord Kodi Fothemry of Solanto. Healer Shane from Essemar, and the Lord Sage Curdoz, also of Solanto. And the A'Terianh, Tiliruf of Tirilorin."

All were looked upon with the greatest astonishment, and there were many murmurings.

"The Eagle Staff!"

Yet Hurlin was not inclined to explain further. There were a few more greetings, but Hurlin, though he acted with some graciousness, would not linger. "We shall be going to the Sanctum."

This seemed to garner even more astonishment, yet they bowed their heads as the party continued through the village.

What the blazes is the Sanctum? thought Tiliruf.

Now could be seen a low and solitary hill. It was an odd landscape feature that stood ominous and alone.

"What is that? Just a hill?" asked Tiliruf.

Finally, Hakonn called for a halt, and they all gathered in a tight group.

"Explain now, Prince Hurlin."

Hurlin sighed, still displaying some annoyance. Yet he obeyed his grandfather.

"It is volcanic. It emerged here some thousand years ago. There are others like it in Ulakel, as this region sits on a caldera, that is an area where the heats and magma of the inner planet reach closer to the surface. It is still active, but grows no more, subject to Qeteral magic. We are going in it. Grandfather, I do not believe the Humans will be able to endure the heat."

"It will be intense, but they will endure," said Hakonn.

"It is why we sweat," offered Shane, "to dissipate the heat in our bodies. Men, be smart and drink your water."

Hurlin did not respond to this. He pointed in the direction of a tree grove. "That is where the holly wood was taken to make the Eagle Staff. This is its home. The tree itself is still deep within that wood and very ancient, for it was a great and straight branch that was used to create the Staff, not the trunk. Only men of the royal house know which tree it is. We will not be showing that to you. We revere this place. None may cut wood from there except with royal permission. It is sacred to us."

"A tree grove, eh?" Tiliruf looked at Kodi as if to say, *I told you so.* "Very interesting, of course. So why must we go inside the hill?"

"You will see," said Olin. He turned to Hakonn. "Grandfather, the messages were sent by Mother's white raven. They know we are coming."

"Very good. Lead on."

It took, however, another half hour, and the hill grew greater as they approached, dominating the view before them. At last, they came to a large path of flagstones lined with obelisks of dark gray stone. They were plain, uncarved, and ominous. This led to what appeared to be a cave with a strong bronze gate across its entrance. At the gate stood six men.

They wore the typical Qeteral male garb, including the vest, though powerful muscle showed, and all matched in red. They'd not seen Qeteral men wear red. But that was not the most unusual thing about them.

"They carry great swords!" Shane said with astonishment.

"It is true," said Hurlin, "that most of us who train use only our archery gear and long knives."

"These are your elite?"

"They are the only such who do so, and those who take their turns who live in the village, trained for the purposes of protecting the cave and its contents. Some two hundred are prepared to protect this site at a moment's notice. If necessary, they could seal themselves inside with many outlets for air and escape routes and many provisions."

But only if the Great Barrier were breached, said Shane to himself. *What in the name of Meical!* But he was not the only Human man who was thinking the same way. Nikal's face puckered greatly. He and Shane looked at each other with raised eyebrows.

The large *knights,* because they almost had to be called so, bowed to their knees.

"Your lordships," greeted one, a leader. Hurlin proceeded then to introduce everyone. They were awestruck, yet the leader spoke with more bluntness. "Lord Hurlin, this is most unusual. The messages by the raven...The Matriarch approved this, then?"

Hurlin's face turned stony.

Instead, Hakonn spoke. "She determined that the War Wizards and their compatriots should be granted this great favor. She trusts they will gain useful knowledge as they fight—for all of us—against the khans of the south. We believe them of the greatest character, our brethren in the Guardian Myghal Whom we revere."

The swordsman leader bowed. "The inner fires have settled somewhat of late. Pass in, then, great lords."

And so they did.

The heat increased as they traveled through a carved and winding tunnel. Torches of a different kind, presumably created of some Qeteral magic, lined the way. There were other tunnels leading off the main one, yet they followed Hurlin.

It was not to Tiliruf's liking. He looked at the walls and side tunnels in trepidation.

"Do not fear, my friend," whispered Lumin to him. He was smiling.

Tiliruf looked steadily at him. He said nothing, but in a way did feel reassured. Dragons were not about to jump out at them. Though it seemed the sort of place Dragons might like.

In fact, none of the Human men felt especially comfortable. Only Kodi now had stepped up unhesitant to walk beside Hurlin. If Hurlin was annoyed at Kodi being so close, he did not demonstrate it. Nevertheless, after a moment or two, Hurlin spoke to him.

"I did not advise this. I am not happy."

"I'm not a bad man, Hurlin. I'm a good bloke. What would you fear in me and Nikal coming here?"

Kodi. There are certain things he fears about himself. Not all Qeteral know of this place, only a few in the royal family, some of the villagers and the guards. They revere this place, but to them it is not a happy place and sparks much tension, particularly among men.

Yes, Meical. "Never mind, Hurlin. You don't need to answer my questions. But know I am grateful you brought us here."

"I cannot think of you as a bad man, Lord Kodi. I just..." Hurlin paused. After a moment he shook his head. He was annoyed with himself for even speaking.

Don't draw him out. It is not the time or place. I will tell you. He not only fears himself; he fears you.

Whatever for?

You are young and powerful, and he is jealous. He doesn't feel threatened by Nikal. But you are an enigma to him. For he sees something many of us see in you, goodness that defines you, and he cannot justify that with what he has learned of Humans. You even look like a Qeteral and are very handsome. In his case that is not helpful. He wishes you were something he could justify his dislike. He keeps searching for fault but cannot find it. When you display your boldness, it both annoys him and causes him envy. Mostly, he fears change, and your coming has changed much.

I see. "Again, I thank you, Hurlin. And I honor you. I'm sure my eagerness to come here today does not reflect your own feelings about this place. I did not understand that until now. Forgive me if you do not think that, as a Human, I feel proper reverence for whatever it is you are about to show me. But I do. I promise you I really do."

His whispered voice created echoes behind them, but generally, the others did not really pick up on the conversation.

Suddenly it grew very hot. The Humans had been sweating quite profusely and drank much from their water bottles. The Qeteral seemed oblivious to the heat. Lumin drank water and sweated lightly, but he otherwise was comfortable.

They entered a large chamber. It was surely the hottest place any of the Humans had ever been, though still they endured for now. In the far distance was a crevasse from which an orange glow emerged.

Before them on two stone slabs side by side lay two unclothed figures.

Nikal and Kodi stepped forward. Nikal held the Staff.

Their jaws dropped.

"Oh, Kodi. Two. Exactly two Qeteral men."

The other Humans came forward as well. Tiliruf was speechless.

"Oh, my," said Curdoz quietly. "Meical on High!"

Shane stared for a moment, then asked, "May I examine them, Prince Hakonn?"

"You may."

Shane stepped forward, and the other Humans followed him. They all looked down on two handsome young men, each with long ebony hair, motionless, with eyes closed.

"The Staff vibrates," whispered Nikal. "It is hot."

Kodi felt it and acknowledged it, looking intently into Nikal's eyes. "I did not expect this at all."

Shane then reached for the arm of one of the reposed bodies. After a time then the other.

"They have a pulse. They breathe." He put his hands on each of their foreheads. "Yet there is nothing in their minds aside from the functions that keep their bodies living. How is that possible?"

Hakonn spoke. "Their bodies are preserved in the heat and by magic."

It was Tiliruf who actually said the words that the rest hesitated to speak. "Their souls are in the Staff!"

They looked at Hakonn with faces of astonishment and questioning.

"Tell us," said Kodi. "Tell us, Hakonn."

Hakonn breathed deeply, then spoke. "These are the princes Velus and Strom. The Guardian came to them during the Anterianhi War and begged their sacrifice in creating the Staff for Terianh. They were the most powerful Qeteral men who had lived since the time of the Great War. They obeyed the Will of the Divine. Over a period of some days the two together carved the Staff, for both were woodworkers. Strom made the main shaft and carved Solvermoon, and

Velus carved the eagle as The Guardian directed, as we now know a symbol of Terianh himself. When they were finished, they bid farewell in ceremony to the royal family. Then, laying themselves down, the King their father set the Staff across their chests. With magic they transferred their souls and minds into the Staff, and all the power within them. In that way it was quickened with their two life forces. Their eyes closed. Their bodies were brought here in a great procession and laid upon these stones to be preserved. The Guardian ordered the three Humans with him, those who later became some of the first Sages, to take the new Staff to Terianh in Eleni. You must know that Velus had recently Bonded. His wife later bore for him one son, who became a good and noble king, a great friend to Terianh, and we, my father, my daughter, my grandchildren and I, are descended from Velus. My wife Linea also descends from him through a noble line."

"I will stay here no longer," said Hurlin abruptly.

Surprisingly, Hurlin retreated into the tunnel, and Olin followed wordlessly. Lumin and Hakonn remained with the Humans.

"Go ahead and touch them, War Wizards, and understand what it is you bear," said Hakonn.

"Hold the Staff for a little, Curdoz," said Nikal.

"Yes," agreed Kodi. "Meical says so."

Curdoz raised a slight eyebrow but did not hesitate to take the Staff. He, of course, could feel no heat or vibration in the talisman, yet he found himself staring at it intently.

Kodi and Nikal stepped forward and lay their hands first on the chests of the figures, and then on their heads and stroked their hair. Often the two War Wizards would look into each other's eyes as if speaking without words. At one point, Kodi nodded to Tiliruf, and so did Nikal.

Tiliruf squelched his discomfort. He too then touched each of the faces. With a strange understanding he said, "Terianh, you never knew this, did you?"

"He did not," said Hakonn. "It is believed the Guardian did not wish him to know."

"Yes," agreed Kodi, though he did not explain further.

"And so, the secret," continued Hakonn, "has been maintained by the Qeteral, mostly through the royal family, though also by the handful of others who are charged to guard their bodies. The village was built to house the families of the guards, of course."

"I guess," said Tiliruf, "that the secret had to be maintained, although I do not understand why. But, I do not have to understand why, eh?"

Shane smiled at him. "The Staff works only because their bodies are preserved here. Mostly because of enemies, Tiliruf. Should their bodies be discovered and destroyed..."

"The Staff will...will also die," said Kodi. "Their souls in the Staff and their bodies are still connected..."

"...in the realm of the world's magic," agreed Hakonn. "And so, you know what I am about to charge you all. You must preserve the secret and tell no one. No others alive must know what you have seen here today, or the power in the Staff could be endangered should an enemy learn the secret and the whereabouts of their bodies."

All nodded to him.

Lumin also came forward to touch the bodies. He bowed in reverence to them, though he had spoken nothing the whole time. Then, the Humans too, bowed.

"We have seen, then, what there is to see," said Curdoz, wiping the heavy sweat off his forehead. "Thank you, Prince Hakonn."

"It really is becoming too hot for us here," added Shane. "Another few minutes we might be overcome."

"Let us go, then," said Hakonn.

The Humans were relieved to be in the outside airs again.

Kodi alone walked briskly over to where Hurlin and Olin sat upon a stone. They looked up, a little startled, as he approached them. Kodi paused when he saw their faces. They wiped them quickly with their hands.

They've been crying, Meical.

Say nothing of it.

He continued his approach as they stood. He bowed reverentially to them.

"Again, I express our gratitude. Thank you, m'lords. Would there be a place where we could take a dip and cool off?"

Hurlin's face had returned to its sterner composition, though his eyes displayed the slightest redness.

"It is a reasonable request. And we shall take a bite before we begin the journey home. Follow along then."

Hurlin did soon lead them to a stream where they could bathe and cool down. All were grateful and remained in the cool water for quite a long time. Most remained quiet. There was one notable private conversation between the two War Wizards as they sat alone on a distant rock.

"...but it's a destructive magic, though not totally," said Kodi.

"I believe, then, that we underestimate Qeteral emotions. Yes, anger, destruction. All there, but the general personae of the Qeteral have so altered, or were perhaps designed so, that they cannot channel that level of it. But released in freedom into the Staff, there is no limitation."

"They live through us when we hold the Staff. I feel them, Nikal. I know those men, now. Strom and Velus. I have felt them when I hold it. I have heard them speak in my mind!"

"Me, too. You suspected, and you were right. But they are not apart from us in the sense the control is by way of *our* own minds."

"Yes. But I'd swear they give me ideas of their own. Ideas I would not consider alone. What's the word?"

"A kind of symbiosis."

"Yes, exactly. When I performed that magic at South Fort, it was what they suggested to me, remember? The 'bubble' you all called it after, whereby friends and even the enemies' innocent horses were safe, but enemies themselves...were not. So strange and yet so Qeteral. They knew it would work, Velus and Strom. I can't admit—that distinguishment—was what *I* was thinking. I just wanted to kill the other and protect my own. But...but I contrived the magic as...as it was *suggested* to me. It was as if they *ordered* me to do it that way."

"I felt it when I took the Staff back from you."

Kodi nodded. "I feel like a powerful World God when I wield it, I swear I do. My whole being is tripled! Me, Strom, and Velus together with the intensity of all our feelings mixed. I wonder how different it worked with Berug as an

Etoppsis in the first Staff he received after Modelo was killed. But probably not a whole lot different."

"You heard Shane say that in some ways the Etoppsi and Humans are closer in our mindsets. We look more like Qeteral, but we think and act a little more like Etoppsi. Much more assertive in our personalities, certainly more warrior-like. Qeteral know how to fight, but they hate it. It hurts them. I imagine it can damage them. We were speculating a little when we spoke to Haakon earlier today, but I believe it now more fully."

"Are you glad you came here, Nikal?"

"Glad and sad. In a way, Strom and Velus are forever trapped. They have been for five-hundred years. All for the preservation of the Staff, in order that it still works for us today in our need. But I think it was good you pressed for this. Shane was also wise to press for Tiliruf to come. It will increase his belief."

"It was upsetting for Hurlin and Olin. Velus, their own ancestor! Of course, they've seen them before, but obviously do not like..."

"...to see them trapped there. The sacrifice that was made. They gave up everything in obedience. Everything."

"I wonder why Hakonn made the princes come this time."

"Hmm. To keep them from repressing their emotions regarding? You were the one who taught me the value of keeping hold of my memories and my emotions. It is what Hakonn is doing for them. It does honor Velus and Strom, however, that they should visit on occasion."

"I feel more keenly for Hurlin."

"He is a deep-thinking, yet also an emotional man. We certainly should honor his self-discipline. These are collective memories and emotions for the men, princes in the royal house who descend from Velus, I think."

"I wonder if they are alike. Velus and Hurlin. I feel maybe so."

"Secretive family journals I'm sure have been kept. No doubt Hurlin and Olin have read them. Lumin honors them, but seemed less..."

"Lumin lives in the today, and his mind truly is more on his Human side. He is younger, too. He really doesn't care, you know, that he is a prince. He just wants to be a man, Nikal, and independent. He wants to live into the now and his dreams of his future."

Nikal shifted, and a subtle smile appeared. "You're keeping some close secrets about him."

"At his request, of course. He's been sharing with Tiliruf, too."

"His mind is that of the artist, less the philosopher."

"It is a different mindset than that of his brothers, you're absolutely right. And he is not burdened by responsibilities as they are. He is the youngest and they spoil him a little. He is not as magically powerful, of course, but he certainly is Gifted. He's much freer, and his mind can focus more on fun. And that's what Meical wants for him. He has self-involved traits, but no different than mine or Tiliruf's. You know, I'm an artist. A craftsman. Wood and stone. I'm good, too. Tiliruf knows art and would you believe, gardens? And he's a great design sketcher. He has drawn ships. He knows languages. Shane, of course, and Curdoz..."

"...are the philosophers. What am I?"

"You, my great brother, are the leader of men! The Human hero. Even the Qeteral knew who you were."

"I'd prefer to be an artist. Yet you remind me where my talents lie." Nikal paused and breathed deeply. "Kodi, I have decided upon something. My heart tells me I should do so. I intend not to go with you to the Deep South. You will take the Staff. I intend to hold back with the fleet near to the entrance of the Khestadone Sea and be on guard from a distance. We need some Human plans, too, on top of the others, and that's what I'm going to do. I feel as though Meical is in agreement with me."

"Then I will not question you on it."

They gripped hands.

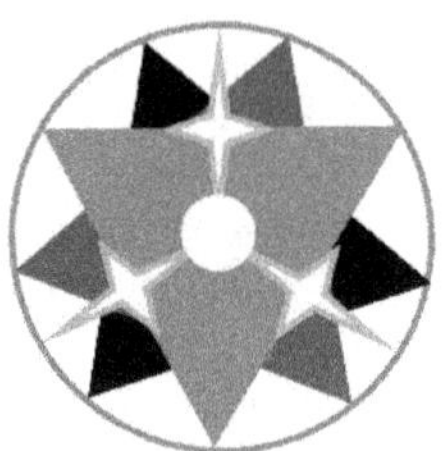

Chapter 21—Pleasant Days

The next few days in Ulakel were filled with many happenings. Hakonn and his wife Linea hosted a luncheon and afternoon tea, and much conversation between, which included Sage Curdoz and Mother Idamé along with a number of regional scholars who had traveled there for the purpose of meeting the Humans. The archival library of the palace where much of the conversation took place was surely impressive. There were histories here from the Qeteral perspective that did not exist anywhere in the world, though there were indeed many others that in long-ago times had been copied and were also found in the Valley of the Gifted. Hakonn had decided to change a little the informal scope of the planned gathering. Four "formal" speeches were presented. He had asked earlier if Curdoz would present a brief lecture on the Valley's interpretation of events surrounding the years leading up to the time when the Qeteral abandoned study in the Valley. Curdoz retained much memory of his studies of those times, as this was specific to classes required by those who were expected to become members of the Order of Sages.

He spoke of the resistance of the Human leadership of the Synod during those times to Qeteral interpretations of the Nature of Myghal and of the One and of Qeteral questioning of the need for the Vows of Chastity and Poverty. For many decades afterwards the Synodical leadership expressed only mild-level regret in the decision of the Qeteral to abandon training in the Valley. Yet in time with new leadership there was much soul-searching. Delegations would come to Ulakel in the attempt to invite the Qeteral to rejoin them in the Valley with shared educational leadership, but these were rebuffed as the Qeteral grew ever more isolated.

Then, Hakonn himself performed a half-hour speech that framed events from the Qeteral point-of-view. He admitted also to stubbornness on the part of Qeteral leadership but applied more blame for the rebuffed attempts to rejoin the Valley on political elements (his own royal ancestors) more so than on the thinking of Healer and Matrimonial elements in Ulakel. It seemed that the latter elements may well have attempted a rapprochement had the political class been more open to it, but they were not. This fact was really interesting to Curdoz and Idamé.

Then, a set of two speeches were presented that were focused less on division and more on light-hearted comparison and contrast. The Qeteral had their two Orders, of Matrimonial Bondswomen and of Healers, but these were much less bureaucratic than in Human lands. There was not a Mother Superior nor a Head of the Orders of Healers. All members of these two elements were considered equals. Hakonn invited a scholarly and notable local Bondswoman, actually Halta's grandmother, Vitalle, to speak on Matrimonial training and implementation in Ulakel, and then Idamé was asked to describe how the Matrimonial bureaucracy worked in Human countries.

Quite honestly, this sort of intellectual engagement among professionals was rare for Idamé. Yet she actually loved this sort of thing and had been much honored that Prince Hakonn had invited her to present. (She was also pleased to have a day of rest from the secretive training of the females!) She had prepared long into the previous nights a set of notes for her lecture. It was well received by all present.

"Idamé, that was splendid!" whispered a delighted Curdoz just afterwards as everyone stood up to stretch. "The Mother Superior could not possibly have lectured with such enthusiasm and made it so interesting!"

"She's a boring, gloomy sort; I should know! It did go well, didn't it?"

These speeches lasted altogether about an hour-and-a-half. And then there was mingling in the library whereby little groups split off in conversation before teatime. One group centered on Hakonn showing Curdoz some valuable volumes of Qeteral Myghalian theology. He pointed out passages of thinking and asked Curdoz' views. Curdoz was both wary and yet quite encouraged by the reception of his views. The greatest difference in belief was in the *omniscience* of the Divine Myghal. Whereas the majority of Qeteral believed Myghal's knowledge encompassed all past, present, and future, leading to a stronger belief in fate, the Valley-trained view was that He did not know all of the future and was capable of error. He pointed out for example (as these recent revelations had become widely disseminated following the Council meeting) Myghal being unaware for a long time of the Lost Qeteral in the South, and His actual apology in the Vision he presented to the Matriarch, and also of His not realizing that key elements of the Ralsheen, namely the khans, had somehow escaped the Dragon conflagration in Tolos. What Curdoz wished for them to understand was that Myghal, being entirely of the good (something they agreed upon) could not always know of that which was NOT good and seemed to be dependent upon learning of events and seeing through the eyes of some of His truest followers on Dumhoni. Myghal appeared to be both a spiritual and also a physical being, but the physical being was subject to time and space in the physical Cosmos, and because of this the term "Messenger" of the One was best felt to apply to Him. Curdoz argued that the word "Divine" could with some degree be applied to all that is Created and which held in spirit to the Mind of the One. He said he had no qualms applying the word "Divine" to Myghal, for he believed it to be true, but that it might (and he emphasized *might*) be applied also to others. Some seemed to disagree and offer alternative, more Qeteral-based viewpoints, thinking that even these "errors" were but part of a Larger Plan. Curdoz then emphasized that he too believed, with reservation, in the idea of a "Larger Plan" but only directly within the Mind of the One, based on the One's Love in the Creation of the Cosmos. The concept of Free Will was necessary for Love to be genuine. Though he was confident in the maneuverings of Myghal and admitted Myghal could indeed see somewhat of events in the future, Curdoz believed Myghal could only know a part and not all.

Hakonn kept the conversation centered on the intellectual rather than allowing emotion to interfere. And there was also the almost unexplained reverence shown by all of them for Curdoz as a Sage and "prophet" of the

Guardian even though he was Human. They listened to him, some with furrowed brows, but would also nod. Curdoz could not know if he "changed any minds" but felt, rightly, that the conversation and communication among them all was of greater value than coming to complete agreement on such matters. This conversation would give him encouraging thoughts and ideas. It almost certainly did also for Hakonn and some of the Qeteral. Not unlike the ongoing—and quite similar—conversations going on between Shane and Solone, it created a kind of vision for a different future among a few.

Vitalle and a set of Bondswomen, along with Linea, gathered with Idamé. Among their conversations she learned something of tremendous interest. Qeteral retained stories and myths surrounding Modela. Many believed that Vanayema actually appeared in Ulakel from time to time in the guise of a Qeteral woman. In these tales, a strange woman would appear, and through both simple and sometimes intricate webs she weaved relationships between various men and women. For example, a man might be walking alone in the woods, turn around, only to come across this personage who would then lead him back the other way in conversation. Then, surprisingly, they would come upon a young lady also walking in the woods. The man and the young lady would engage a little in disinterested conversation only to discover a few minutes later that the strange woman had disappeared. In great curiosity the couple would converse about the strange woman and then find they shared commonalities and interests in one another. Always, the couple would then establish a courtship, fall in love, and eventually be Bonded. And they would always make plain that had it not been for the appearance of the strange woman, the couple would never have met. There were many of these interesting tales, always involving the strange matchmaker. Some of them even claimed that they would once again see the strange woman at their Bonding Ceremony, she with a happy smile on her face as she watched the exchange of nuptials, but afterwards when they would look for her in order to speak again, again she was gone. Idamé was intrigued to say the least. And yet, too, she began to consider similar matchmaking stories that she herself had heard from some of the Human couples she had performed Bondings for in the past.

Sharing these stories later with Ulna and Maru, the three women began to wonder very much if Vanayema was more active in the world than any Humans had previously believed.

"And you heard, didn't you," said Ulna, "what Rainwing said the Matriarch said to her at the reception. She clearly believes Vanayema is active in the world."

"And the Matriarch is powerfully magical herself and probably is aware of things many are not," agreed Maru. "Altogether, the Qeteral know more how magic presents itself in the world. Rainwing believed her, I know."

"It would suggest," said Idamé, "that Modela plays her own role in Bondings, just as we know Meical is the one who creates Auras."

"It's fascinating," said Maru. "But don't tell Tiliruf. It'll just add to his assumption she's just a manipulating witch!"

"Well," said Ulna, "She is manipulating, and that piece of it cannot be denied."

"The Matriarch called her a *mad sprite,*" agreed Idamé.

Lumin took up a sort of permanent residency at the men's pavilion and spent nearly all his hours with the Human men. To say every single man liked him and his company goes without saying. But he had definitely changed.

As Qeteral boys grew into adulthood, they displayed fewer physical forms of friendly communication with each other aside from handgrips. In fact, they nodded heads more than anything, certainly a meaningful sign of mutual respect. In contrast, several of the Human men engaged in a good deal of jocularity with their soldier-grip handshakes, joking arm-punches, shoulder-gripping, arm-over-shoulder hugs, deliberate knocking into one another, dunking each other in the water pool, wrestling, pretenses at boxing and comical fighting and arguments. Lumin had by now joined in on these more playful methods of comradeship, and they came to him perfectly naturally. Qeteral rarely engaged in teasing or told jokes, yet Lumin had learned quickly these subtleties.

Even his manner of speaking had changed. His voice had assumed its deeper tones. He always spoke now like a confident man. It no longer appeared to come and go. His mannerisms altogether were those of belonging fully within this set of men instead of as a boy with big eyes looking in. When one of his brothers would come by with messages from the Matriarch for the Humans, or even when Olin would stay awhile at mealtimes, Lumin retained his self-assuredness, discarding the subtle hints of little-brother-like meekness he once showed when he or Hurlin were about.

When in a playful archery competition with Kodi—the two were equally talented with the bow—even his own laughter had altered. It was of a *broader* sound—a joviality of the man rather than the uncertain qualifying laughter of a boy out of his league. And the movement and form of his perfect muscular body as he performed his archery feats was compelling to watch. He even seemed taller to them.

"All the Qeteral are damned good-looking, but if I were to picture a World God, say, Torovúr the Hunter in physical form," offered Hadon to the others while they watched, "that's what Lumin looks like to me."

"Aye," said Manwul. "Like the model a sculptor might use, but better than any sculpture I've ever seen. I would venture it is the combination of Human and Qeteral material that makes him achieve such a superior look about him."

"I've noted the combination of traits," said Shane. "But I think I've been focused on his Human and Qeteral pieces and less the whole product. That is an excellent observation, Manwul. I'm going to write that down in my journal."

"A return to the first children of Modelo and Modela before the Molding nearly," offered Findun.

"What excellent reference to the mythology, Findun. I shall write that down too, but I think Manwul is most onto it. The combination of material has created a physically lookable man."

"But the manner, too. Is it possible for a boy to become a man in mere days?" asked Deens, thoughtfully fingering his beard. "He seems so different than when we met him and his brothers in the woods."

"Yes," said Shane emphatically. "Certainly, the male psyche can mature rapidly, though often more so under duress, such as fighting in a battle. Or the oldest boy in the family when the father dies. Or discovering he has impregnated a girlfriend and now must step up and act as provider. Or a revelation, such as a Vision from the Guardian. What about your Vision from Meical, Deens? Did that not change you, and rapidly? I think you told me you were fourteen? That is quite young for a Vision."

"Well, yes. I suppose I did take upon myself a more mature manner. It was a life change. I had been shy but was now forced to communicate my needs to others on my journey to the Valley, as I did not have anyone to provide for and escort me. My parents were much too poor to give me but a few coppers. That system is better now than it used to be."

"Yes. Now one only needs to travel to a monastery, and then the novitiate is well-advised and cared for at that point. However, in Lumin's particular case," Shane went on, "I would say his manlier side has been *unlocked* by our Human presence. It was not due to stressors, but rather encouragement and example. Kodi has become the example Lumin emulates—ha, and some Human vocabulary from Tiliruf—although it's more naturally himself than perhaps I am expressing. But I'm glad you all are also seeing something some of the rest of us are seeing. It confirms the change in our perceptions of him. Let there be no doubt Lumin is different than the day we met him."

"This is the genuine Lumin."

"Oh, yes, I say so. That World God that Manwul sees right there. Yet he can still be boy-like, but so can many of us. I suspect even World Gods could be boyish on occasion. Playful. Why not?"

And almost every night now, Lumin, who slept next to Kodi, disappeared for a few hours in the middle of the night when, it seemed, all were asleep.

Shane, night owl that he was, who often lay awake pondering ideas, grew curious. One time, as Lumin stood up and walked out, Shane got up to follow. As he was just about to head out the tent flap, he found Kodi's hand gripping his shoulder, shaking his head, and wearing a stern look.

"Never follow him, Shane. You will wish you hadn't. He'll use his magic and vanish from you, anyway."

"I've been worried he may be troubled about something, seeking solitude, but wishing to aid him if I can."

Kodi pondered for a long moment. "And of course, you're an excellent advisor. Lumin might be troubled about some things, but that's not why he leaves at night. He is doing nothing wrong and only what he wants to do. It is secretive, but I will not break my promise. But, for your sake, I will ask Lumin to tell you himself tomorrow. But if he doesn't, he doesn't."

And upon the morrow when Lumin did, in Kodi's presence, choose to tell Shane, Shane was wide-eyed.

"But you were beginning to guess, Shane," said Kodi, chuckling. He was not in the stern mood he had used with Shane at midnight. He was acting cheerful, as though this were fun.

Shane looked at Lumin. Almost whispering, although it wasn't necessary at the moment, he said, "You are secretly bonded, then, but not yet Bonded."

"I may in time choose to tell the others. But my family cannot know. You understand me?"

Shane did a bow. "Yes, lord prince. I apologize for my curiosity in your affairs. Forgive me."

"I consider you a friend. Don't revert to formality or apologize, eh? It isn't necessary. I love Fal. All my thoughts are on her. I am using these weeks away from the palace to see her more often. In the night, as you know. We've been...occupied." He winked.

Kodi chuckled.

"I, um," said Shane, "I suppose I might do the same. Actually, I know I would. It is, um, very Human."

Lumin winked again. "Yes. Yes, it is. But it is not *not* Qeteral, either."

"I honor your love for her, of course."

"Thank you, Shane. It means much to me that you do."

But in private later again with Kodi, Shane said this to him.

"He hasn't proclaimed manhood, and he is considered too young. I worry something I said a few days ago may have been encouraging, or...you didn't...or maybe Tiliruf..."

"It wasn't anything we said or did, Shane. He's been bonded to her for two years."

"Oh!" Shane was amazed. He'd not picked up on that tidbit on the length of the relationship. "He's...he's..."

"...made love more than any of us, almost. Except Tiliruf. And with Tiliruf it's not lovemaking; it's just shafting. Anyway, he sneaks off from the palace whenever he can to romp with her in the night; it's just easier for him to do so from here, 'cause the servants and his brothers aren't about. What's too young, Shane? He's twenty-four. My folks were fifteen and romped like rabbits! The point, of course, is they're devoted to each other. It's wrong they feel they have to keep their love secret, but I can't do anything about it. Just like my father resisting me leaving home and blessing me with manhood and my independence—my mother had to do it, because he wouldn't! Geesh, this hurts to think back on that..."

Kodi's eyes turned watery, though he wiped his face quickly. "But I'm not teary for me, Shane. I'm teary for Lumin. Because this same thing is happening to him. He is more a Human man than a Qeteral when it comes right down to it, and you know it, better than most. He wants to create a happy life for himself and Fal and raise a family. It's all he thinks about. Well, you know, then there's the romp. What young bloke doesn't think about that!"

Kodi paused, and both he and Shane smiled the same smile. Kodi's emotional moment had dissipated.

"He told me that lately he's on fire for her. Guardian's Nuts. Not in those words, ha! He's all sweet about it. But considering what you say, you may be right that our presence and encouragement has had an effect, making him more relaxed about their relationship. We've added legitimacy to it for him. He's proudly embracing his Human side with us here. Even Tiliruf makes him feel good about it.

"She's from a farmer family, but she apparently has a reputation for artistic endeavors, like Lumin does. She's three or four years older than he is. Shane," he paused and breathed deeply, "he wants to go with us to the south."

Shane stared. "I knew something else was brewing here with him."

"But don't you see? It's the method he wishes to use to return and proclaim his manhood publicly. It will prove his bravery and manhood, allowing him to jump past Qeteral social restraints for one of his age and of his family looking on him as a boy. It's a method that does happen sometimes. They have stories of brave boys who achieve something notable and proclaim manhood young. And then he will Bond Fal in Ceremony. He really is trying, Shane, to work within Qeteral expectations, particularly as a prince. He is trying to honor his family. But it isn't only that, because he could, in my opinion, come up with a less dramatic plan. The thing is, he really wants to go with us and learn and be away from home. His love for me and all of us is strong. He's never had such close friendships aside from his brothers, and with them he can't be fully himself. Going on this journey and being with us he thinks will grow him in helpful ways, possibly the only opportunity he will ever have to learn about the outside world. Ships and oceans and sea creatures and other places. He really has a dream about sailing."

"And you think Meical approves?"

Kodi shook his head. "As you understand, I try not to ask Meical about others. I can assure you He is not resisting my thoughts involving Lumin, and He would if they veer too far from what He considers good."

Shane nodded. "I believe you, I do, Kodi. But it's deadly dangerous."

"It is. Shane, you know I have thought on it ever since Lumin elaborated these secrets to me. I think it was the second night we were here. Boy, did he open up his whole heart to me. He was desperate for a trusting friend. And my love for him is fierce. I loved him the minute we first met him in the forest. I don't want him to be endangered any more than anyone else. But it isn't always about my choices. This is a journey, I think, of many dimensions. The women are up to something, too; I think we all know that. And Lumin has made his choice with Fal's blessing. Will we all act protective of him? Will his presence distract sometimes? Yes. But it's the right choice, and I see some strong positives in his presence being from the royal family with those lost Qeteral. I will be requesting an audience with the Matriarch and Hurlin together and request Lumin be allowed to go with us on the journey."

Shane shifted out of his general level of shock and then chuckled. "*Request?* I know you better now. You will insist."

"I will request at first." He winked.

"You will infuriate Hurlin."

Kodi chuckled himself. "I imagine so."

"You will be acting on your authority as a War Wizard!"

"Oh? You think it will be that easy? I suggest you not be there. Peace-loving Healer of the Orders."

Shane glared. "Hurlin's a big strong man. And taller than you."

Kodi winked and flexed his bicep. "Who's got prettier muscles?"

Shane couldn't stop himself from laughter. "You and Tiliruf are such cocky bastards. I'm not the one who will argue against your muscles. I'm sure you'd give Nikal or even Manwul a tough go. Speaking of Nikal, have you told him?"

Kodi laughed. "I'm going to tell Nikal *after*. Or better yet, I'll let Lumin tell him. He might have a fun story to tell."

Shane abruptly changed the subject. "And just how are you and the princess doing?"

Kodi put on a proud smirk.

For at least every other day, sometimes more often, Ryn provided an invitation to her Human male interest. Typically, it was long hikes to beautiful places and a picnic. The first of these was at a wide, meadow-like overlook at the edge of the Plateau. Kodi believed it might have been the very place he had seen the Matriarch in the Vision, when the white raven landed on her shoulder. Ryn was intrigued and confirmed that her mother did indeed enjoy coming out here. On this outing, it was Kodi who shared of himself in some detail. As they sat on the ground and lunched on sandwiches, at her encouragement he told her somewhat of his boyhood. He described Felto and the Wolf River and many other things. He then shared with her in great detail his Vision from Meical. What he did this time, which he had rarely done before, was to tell her plainly of the emotions he experienced in the end portion of the Dream.

She was in awe. She reached for and held his hand.

"What is your favorite sort of bird, Kodi?" she asked.

"Blue-tailed hawk."

After several similar outings of this kind, she took him to her paternal grandmother's woodland cottage. This was not Manoo's regular home now. She lived in another part of the country. But the place had long been in her mother's family, and it was where Manoo lived with her Human husband and raised their son Mabelin. She liked writing poetry and would sometimes come here to gather inspiration for her writing and when present was usually invited to court by Linea or Gwyn.

Two female servants bustled about providing refreshments and tea.

Manoo approached a hundred-and-twenty years old, and yet she still was beautiful. She had only begun to put on some weight common to Qeteral as they aged. Yet she retained a kind and youthful face, like Idamé, though a little more regal and of course of darker complexion.

"I would have to say he looked much more like the A'Terianh, for his skin was white," she said of her Human husband. "Or actually more your friend Hadon, for his hair was dark and with a beard. He was a large man, and he had green eyes that were lovely."

"And just how did he make his way to Ulakel?" asked Kodi. "Would not your Barrier have prevented his coming?"

"The magic is focused more on the southern border," she explained. "For that is where the danger lies. For the passages through the northern mountains, the one to the Valley of the Gifted, and the ones in the direction of Eleni, are much too difficult and rugged, even for a determined enemy. Though there are those who work the Barrier in the north, a lone man could slip through, though certainly not an army. I do not believe my grandson Hurlin would approve of me telling you such details, but I will tell you no more on that."

"What was his name?"

"His name was Feleep Pickerman!"

"And Grandmother always called him that, Kodi!" said Ryn. "Both his given and his Human surname together as a kind of playful endearing thing."

"It's true. 'Feleep Pickerman, listen to me! Feleep Pickerman, come help in the kitchen! Feleep Pickerman, it is time you come to bed!'"

Kodi laughed heartily. In a way, Ryn's grandmother reminded him a little of Ansy back home and the manner she used towards his grandfather.

Manoo continued. "He was first apprehended and brought to the village where my family lived. Do not fear that he was treated unkindly, for he was not. My father was lord of that territory and brought him into our home and treated him as a guest. Guess what Feleep Pickerman had brought with him to offer as a gift?"

"I can't imagine!"

"Apples, dear Kodi!" she exclaimed. "Apples! A large pack full of the most delicious red fruit any of us had ever laid eyes on! He carried them a hundred miles through the mountain passage!"

There was a good deal of laughter among everyone, including the two servants who had not left the room.

"She was smitten," said Ryn with a doting smile at her grandmother. "She had never tasted that fruit before!"

Kodi was laughing. "That's so wonderful, Madam. Tell me more of the story!"

"Well, my father was such a wonderful man. He did indeed send quick word here to the court by way of a raven, that a Human from Eleni had come. But in the meantime, Feleep Pickerman and I became quite acquainted with one another! My father and mother too were so delighted by his looks—for we had believed Humans were not so good-looking! He had a beard, like I said, yet was always determined to keep it trim, and it gave him a wise and striking appearance. And of his manner, of course, for he was most gentlemanly. They allowed our little flirtation to blossom!"

"But he was not of noble stock, as some have said," said Kodi.

"No. His family were hired pickers in apple orchards. They were really quite poor. He left home in order to seek out a new fortune for himself. He had been over passes to your Principality of Hesk but did not like the place."

"It is an awful place, Madam. I assure you Hesk does not represent the values of the Kingdom of Solanto."

"Of course, I believe what you say, dear Kodi. They almost enslaved him as a part of their army, yet he quickly escaped when he understood what they were discussing about him. He was smart, you see! He promptly returned to Eleni. But soon he set out again through the mountains southwestward of his home. He used much of his savings from his own labor to purchase traveling gear."

"The boots Lumin wears!" said Kodi with delight.

"Yes, of course! I had nearly forgotten I gave those to dear Lumin! He begged me for them when he was still a little boy!"

"You know he loves them so, Grandmother," said Ryn.

"He wears them around us a great deal," said Kodi.

"I am so pleased to know! Ryn, tell him to wear them next time he comes to see me."

"A lovely idea, Grandmother. We'll bring him over here and spend a whole day with you. Perhaps Olin will come. Hurlin is so busy these days."

"I understand, dear. The country depends upon him."

"Tell me, though," said Kodi, "what happened when the Matriarch and Patriarch learned of Feleep being here?"

"They sent for him to come here to explain himself to the court. But my family escorted him as a way of helping to speak for him and establish a friendly rapport. We did not wish him to be without a friendly presence. Now, it was a struggle, for they were quite unhappy when they understood he was not even a messenger from officials in Eleni but was merely a curious adventurer. They were ready to escort him back to the borders and put an enchantment on him so he would not remember the way back here. However, my father was close to the Patriarch, for they had attended lessons together years before. And through much maneuvering on Father's part, they allowed him to remain."

"But Grandmother, you're not telling the best reason," said Ryn.

Manoo giggled. "It was because I declared for Feleep Pickerman in their presence!"

Kodi was so delighted in all this tale.

“And so, Kodi,” said Ryn, “it was my great-grandparents who were ruling. You have met them, of course. My great-grandmother as Matriarch declared that their love for one another should be considered in their judgment.”

“Had you...had you...? Oh, sorry. I am forgetting myself,” said Kodi, looking at Ryn embarrassedly.

“I think I know what you are wishing to know, dear Kodi!” said her grandmother. “I must admit that yes indeed we had by then engaged in a secretive affair. It was a surprise to everyone, but the truth had to be made plain, for there was still resistance on the part of the Patriarch. And so, with permission we settled together here and were quickly Bonded in Ceremony. We were the first Human-Qeteral pair in two-hundred years. Some thought of us as strange. Some would not even speak to us. Yet some thought of us as interesting. We had an extraordinary set of friends, all open-minded. Feleep Pickerman acted with gentle demeanor and became well-liked by many in the village. He became a builder and designed and built many of the houses in the village. Our only son Mabelin was born near to the time Gwyn was born to Lady Linea and Prince Hakonn. Now, Mabelin took after both myself in his dark complexion and Qeteral face, but he was otherwise quite like his Human father, tall and strong, and had a most Human grin. Dearest Lumin takes many traits from Mabelin, very much so, though Lumin’s hair is even darker than Mabelin’s.”

“Lumin is proud to be part Human,” said Kodi.

“I know he is, and I adore that boy. And anytime I see him, I think strongly of his father and grandfather.”

“I do not think of Lumin as a boy, Madam. He is much the Human young man, little different than myself.”

She looked at Kodi for a moment and then nodded her head. “I must agree. He has matured as rapidly as did Mabelin, just as a Human man might. He is large and strong for his age. I am proud of all of my grandchildren, of course.”

She reached for Ryn’s hand and held it. She looked at Ryn, and then she looked at Kodi and smiled. She took his hand, too.

“I am honored to know you, Kodi,” she added. “I honor you as the Brother of Myghal, but my feelings I think must run deeper. Humans are little different than us. How can one not think so? When I look at you, I see such great goodness. And what a pretty man you are, dear! Are you sure you don’t have Qeteral blood?”

Kodi grinned. But then he attempted a question that he had been wondering about.

“Madam. When Feleep began to age in the Human way...” he didn’t know how to complete his question.

“Love is love, dear Kodi. We had many wonderful years together. It was only troubling, dear, as he so many times apologized to me for growing old and did not wish to leave me. It has now been close to forty years. Yet I will see Feleep Pickerman again among the Stars one day and Dance with him again! I cannot say it did not cause me much sadness at the time, and the loss of Mabelin brought also much sorrow. Yet, Kodi, you are the Brother of Myghal, and so I know you know. For though we are of the Mold and made for Dumhoni, we are also of spirit and made for the Stars.”

“Yes, Madam. That much I know.”

“For true love endures beyond what we know,” Manoo added.

She looked at Ryn as she said this and nodded.

Whether others were aware of this new relationship developing between Kodi and Ryn was unclear. Lyndz certainly knew. Shane of course knew. Hurlin was suspicious. None of the rest of the Humans were in the know, the men believing that Kodi was simply attending to meetings or responding to invitations. Plainly here, Manoo saw deeply and understood the look in her granddaughter's eyes and of those of Kodi as they often gazed on each other as they sat in her parlor.

Manoo was happy with what she was witnessing. She prophesied, "Young Kodi, should you live through these dangerous times, I foresee you will have a long and prosperous life."

"Thank you, Madam. What a grand thing that would be. Who would not wish for that?"

"And many children."

"Really?" He winked at Ryn. "I like that idea. It has...happy implications."

Ryn's smile was slightly on the grin side.

These little forward hints and charms would become more regular. Yet Kodi still maintained a level of discretion, allowing the princess to guide the relationship at her own will and speed.

That was only the previous day, and now he was relating it to the curious Shane.

"She wanted you to get to know 'Grandma' Manoo?"

Kodi beamed. "Yep. And old ladies always like me, you see."

Shane chuckled. "I don't think you need any further warnings from me on this subject."

"I appreciate them, actually. What I don't want is anymore of your special magic, buddy. I'm good to go."

"Really?"

"It, er, messes with the night dreams I've been experiencing lately, if you must know."

In a few days, Flamefur returned from his journey to Danzilet. He was able to catch up Nikal on much of the news, although there was not a whole lot to tell. All was silent at South Fort, and there had been no indication of a renewal of conflict in that sector. Things had settled, and the city was operating close to normal. The captive Khestadone soldiers had all now been released from their mindspells. Still under guard, Monastics were teaching them history. Most had taken well to the change in their circumstances. Many were begging to be allowed to join the army as that was the only sort of life they knew. They wished to fight back against the forces that had enslaved them. For now, General Fouch was exercising and training them under guard, but he was not yet putting them into any of his units. But they were being as cooperative as they could. Some were giving all the information they knew of the Khestadone army and of interior movements, but none were high-level officers that might know somewhat of the Alkaness' plans or even much regarding her numbers. In a general way their education and sense of geography were extremely limited. None of them knew how to read.

There were a few, however, who despite the removal of their mindspells, retained powerful beliefs in Siriné as the religion instilled in them since they had been taken into the Alkhaness' armies. They resisted thinking of Siriné as evil. And the history lessons given by the Monastics were not yet having an impact.

"That is because," Shane offered when he heard this, "they had never heard of Meical. They wish to believe in a powerful entity, a god of *worship,* and Siriné is the only such being they know. It is to be hoped that the example and belief of the Monastics will in time have an impact more so than the history lessons they are giving. I can certainly imagine resistance believing in Meical over Siriné if I had never in my life heard of His existence, and if I had assigned all higher notions to Siriné."

"Let us have hope in the work of the Monastics, then," Curdoz said.

"Nikal, if messages are sent again, have these who resist spend more time among the Monastics as they go about their daily work tending the gardens and during their meditations. And also with the Healers and the work in the hospitals. Allow them to see faith in action apart from mere lessons and lectures."

Nikal agreed.

It seemed there had been a halt in new advances in the East. The Alkhan appeared to be holding back on a new attack. War Marshal Jaden had arrived there and was for the moment holding the line. The Eastern leadership was expressing confidence with their greatly increased forces, but Jaden kept them grounded. He would lead no counterattack for the present.

General Fouch had been informed of the request for additional ships to be prepared for the southern journey. He was not, however, given much information, as Nikal had believed that for now it should remain secretive. What he was told, however, was to provide the stoutest Nantian navy personnel with the understanding the secret mission was of immense danger. Yet Rusty did say to Fouch that once the journey was underway, Nikal would send him further details. Curious, Fouch nevertheless would follow the prince's orders to the letter.

All the new information about the magical southern Gateway into Tolos had been sent by an Etoppsi flyer to Berug. It would be a few days more before any reply would be forthcoming to Danzilet, but Rusty had no doubts Eagleron would send Dragon Legionnaires to the East at the Polemarch's request.

Rusty was now given an additional duty. Every other morning he was tasked with flying supplies for the forthcoming journey to the awaiting ships at the Lintiri Sea. Enormous amounts of food stuffs were packaged and then placed atop a large canvas. Incredibly strong, Rusty could gather together the corners of the canvas in his gripping great hands and lift the great loads skywards. In this way, he was able over ten days to deliver five shipments, returning each evening long before sundown.

Tiliruf was often occupied. As anticipated, nobility who lived on nearby estates issued invitations to him for luncheons. Shane often accompanied him, although once or twice it was Prince Lumin who would. The nobility, though they had little power in the government, were nevertheless influential upon the general thinking among the populace and conferred regularly with the royal family. Those who actually invited *the A'Terianh* were ones who viewed him with reasonable favor, part of a progressive element close to the Matriarch. He was dutiful to Curdoz' and Nikal's wishes regarding the importance of this informal sort of diplomacy. But he was always kind of wary.

"What do they really want of me, Shane? Honestly."

"You should hire me as your counselor, don't you think?" They laughed, and Shane was surely trying to shift Tiliruf out of some anxious thoughts regarding this. "They feel a connection to your House. Keep in mind the Empire was established by the Divine through Terianh. The alliance with the Qeteral was a personal one with the emperors, and you are the only connection they have to that. They have questions. Your coming here has become more important than we initially expected. Curdoz says so. Don't you see it?"

"Yes, I guess. It certainly wasn't what *I* wanted."

"I understand. It has had symbolic meaning for many that you are an important part of this Human group who came, particularly that you are a close companion of the 'Brothers of Myghal.' In particular, they wish to understand from your perspective the new order of the Republic and what status and influence the House of Terianh still wields. Here's my advice. It may not be necessary always to offer opinions, Tiliruf, or express your feelings regarding the Abdication of Zarelio or anything of the sort. Focus on factual information. You know Republican history as well as Imperial history. Explain how the Republic operates. Enjoy the good food and the beauty of their estates and comment politely on everything."

Tiliruf always did put on a high-level charm. He was quite a natural at it, despite misgivings. Never for a moment would anyone have thought he was uncomfortable or ill-pleased with anything.

Following some of these luncheons, Shane would offer congratulations.

"Curdoz and Genehbro would be proud of your demeanor, a'Terianh. You demonstrated the grace of a high-level diplomat. That is a supreme talent. At nineteen-years-old it's just genius."

The compliments from Shane, Nikal, and Curdoz were encouraging for Tiliruf and made him feel good about the role he was playing as an important part of the group. Even so, he was always relieved to return to the pavilion after these luncheons. He would throw off his clothes and jump in the water pool as if to 'wash off the taint.' And if Lumin and Kodi were there, those three would play in the water like boys. Then afterwards as the night drew in, Tiliruf would sit shirtless and barefoot in the pavilion (as most of them did), smoke his pipe and play Kings and Castles with one of the mates or challenge some of them in a round of Fifty-twos.

Among other activities taking place during those wonderful days, Nikal, with Hadon and Manwul, would go on long day hikes, usually as guests of Olin, who would take them to some lovely places, or visit in the village and spend time with the inhabitants. They were always warmly received. The women and Rainwing were rarely to be seen by the men unless there was an activity or meeting at the palace. Rusty would fly often within a twenty-mile radius of the capital village and delight all those who saw him from the ground. He would land in scattered villages and greet and be greeted sometimes with great fanfare. Of all Etoppsi, Rusty learned the most about the Qeteral people. The Scribes and Curdoz had now begun to regularly visit the library at the palace and meet often with Prince Hakonn in his study and have intellectual conversation. Shane was doing essentially the same with Solone. Those two had become great friends, and Solone introduced him to other Healers who lived in the area. Shane was able to involve Ulna and Maru occasionally, who also enjoyed this give and take discussion among those who understood Meicalian Healing magic.

And on most days, there were the after-lunch swims. A strong rapport had quickly developed among most of the Qeteral villagers and the Human visitors. To Tiliruf's relief, he did not again see Lyndz at the water. It came to be understood that most of the time the females would swim and bathe at a pool in the palace gardens with their female Qeteral friends, this mostly in order to involve Idamé who would not go to the more public swimming places. Musca would on occasion turn up to check on Kodi but would soon disappear again to return to the home of the Mountain Hunter breeder.

"Strong male instincts, huh?" said Tiliruf one time. "I never could watch dogs thump, though."

"I always thought they're funny to watch," admitted Kodi.

"Difference between the city boy and the country boy," said Shane.

"Dogs don't know how to take it slow," kidded Lumin.

"I'm sure it's great while it lasts, though," said Kodi winking. "Breeder man's going to have puppies out his ears. Musca knows what he's doin'."

"You boys are too full of yourselves," said Shane.

"We're just talking about dogs, eh?" quipped Tiliruf.

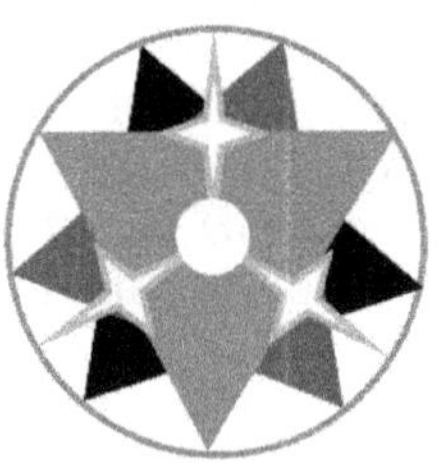

Chapter 22—Hurlin Says What He Thinks

"I admit it is an intimate magic, Mother Idamé, Lord Curdoz," said Hakonn. They were in his study in the palace. "Were it not for the nature of your Dreams being from the Divine Himself, I would of course not press for it. However, details could be critical in the planning."

"I agree," said Idamé.

"If you can determine individuals you know, Hakonn, of those that were among the Qeteral on the Nantian ships, I also agree it is especially relevant."

"Each individual has essentially been Chosen by the Divine for this mission. Let me reassure you, however, I will be searching entirely for the Dream in each of your minds, and once I find it, I will not stray into additional memories."

"That is good to know," said Shane, who as before when Hakonn wished to examine the War Wizards, also requested to be present for this exercise. "Brother Curdoz, Mother Idamé, try focusing on the memory of your Vision as Prince Hakonn begins the magic."

Hurlin was also present. He spoke little. He would write names.

Hakonn then proceeded with his powerful mind magic. He first explored Curdoz' mind. Laying his hands on Curdoz head, he closed his eyes.

It didn't take long.

"The Dream is clear. You foresaw the battle at South Fort."

"Some of it, yes. Although I did not know where it was until it came to pass, you understand. I imagined it was in the far east if anywhere."

When he was finished with Curdoz, he did the same for Idamé.

"I think the Divine sees great strength in you, lady."

"That is most kind of you to say," she replied hesitantly.

"You have a strong mind. You blocked much of the Dream from me and only allowed me to see those on the ships."

"I may have tried," admitted Idamé.

"You succeeded. I will not question you further, of course. The will of the Divine is working through you."

It was a curious interchange, yet she would say no more.

As Hakonn relayed to Hurlin the names of the faces of those in the Dream memories, altogether there were some thirty. It was remarkable he knew everyone presented to him from their minds, yet it showed the degree to which he was involved in so much, in this case in those trained in the border patrol. And among them were several women. These included Frith, Halta, and Lady Mishoo.

Upon completion of the magic, Hurlin spoke. "These are all well-trained, Grandfather. All live near and I will have them ready for the journey. I am not so happy to allow Mishoo to go, for I need her here."

"We will not deny the Divine's Calling," said Hakonn. "They will be lucky to have her. She is very magically powerful."

"What is her specialty, Prince Hakonn?" asked Idamé.

"There is not an animal that lives that she cannot speak to and even turn to her bidding. She doesn't have to sing in order to do it. She reaches their minds through her own powerful thought. She is gifted in other ways, as well."

Shane asked a bold question. "Lord Hurlin, if you had been among those in the Dreams, would you have left Ulakel to go on the journey?"

Idamé's eyebrow shot high. Curdoz stifled a grimace. He would have ordered Shane not to ask it if he had known in advance.

Hurlin, who almost never spoke to any of the Humans except Nikal and Curdoz, looked darkly. "I..."

He seemed about to say one thing then looked at his grandfather.

"...I would be one who wishes always to follow the will of the Divine."

Shane would remember Hurlin's answer.

There was one disturbing episode. It did not last but a half-hour, and it was in the middle of the night. Nikal was the subject.

It was around midnight in the middle of their stay when Kodi awakened to hear Nikal calling out loudly in his sleep.

"Ahhh!!!! No! Strom! Velus! I am so sorry! I never wanted this for you! Oh, the pain! OHH!!!"

Shane was almost there quicker than Kodi.

The Eagle Staff, which Nikal had leaned against the head of his bed when he fell asleep had slipped. It had a glow of white light about it.

Kodi pointed.

"It's against his skin! I should have realized!" Shane exclaimed.

Kodi grabbed the Staff. For a split second he felt a shock, a quick vision of two Qeteral faces, but the instant he removed it from Nikal's skin the pain was gone, though he still felt a tremor of power. He set it on the floor and the white light went out. "Nikal! Nikal! Wake up!"

He had to shake him. "NIKAL!"

Nikal's eyes opened wide, and he sat up screaming. "NOOOOO!!!!"

"NIKAL! It's me! Kodi! Your brother Kodi!"

Shane immediately placed his hands on Nikal's torso and strong green light appeared.

Nikal was wet with heavy sweat. Tiliruf, Curdoz and the others came over quickly. Rusty, too.

"What has happened!" asked Curdoz.

"I should have realized!" repeated Shane. "The Staff was against his skin as he dreamt. That cannot be a helpful thing!"

"Oh, no!" said Curdoz. "You're right! It's too powerful an object!"

"Nikal!" Kodi spoke loudly in Nikal's face. "It's your brother, Kodi!"

Finally, as Shane continued to apply magical Healing powers, Nikal's eyes came into focus. He looked into the face before him. "Kodi!"

He grasped Kodi in anxious embrace, likewise reciprocated. Kodi held him hard. "Say nothing until your mind settles."

Nikal continued to hold Kodi like a lifeline. Slowly, he became aware of the other men looking at him, and Rusty's massive presence. "Curdoz. Shane. What happened to me?"

"The Staff fell against your skin as you were dreaming," said Curdoz.

"The touch of your skin initiated the magical connection," added Shane. "I can't believe we never considered before that that could happen. The dreaming state is such a curious enigma. Conscious yet not. In the deep state of non-dreaming sleep, I don't think it would have triggered the connection."

Curdoz looked all about. He spoke calmly but firmly. "I wish all of you to leave the pavilion except for Shane and Tiliruf. And Kodi of course. I'll come out to retrieve you when we're done here."

"Where's Lumin?" asked Findun.

"Oh, out and about," said Tiliruf. "He'll be back later, eh?"

Findun, Deens, Rusty, Manwul and Hadon left the pavilion.

"Is he going to be all right?" asked Tiliruf.

"He'll be fine," said Shane. "His mind's his own, now."

Nikal and Kodi released themselves from their embrace.

"Praise the Guardian for you, Kodi! You've been my saving grace ever since that damned Prophecy! Lyndz told me you are a great hugger!"

"His humor is returning," said Shane.

"Didn't know he had any, eh?" quipped Tiliruf.

But then a wet tear fell from Nikal's eye. Kodi gripped his hand. "It's all right, Nikal. Take a deep breath. Tell us what happened."

Nikal did so. He wiped away the tear and tethered his emotion, keeping his eyes peeled on Kodi. "They spoke to me. Velus and Strom, both. I could see their bodies and faces. They were so real."

"Knowing what we men know," offered Shane, "let us presume they really are real. Their souls reached out to you through the Staff while you slept. Gosh, Brother Curdoz. I should have foreseen this possibility!"

"More than phantoms, yes," agreed Curdoz. "But it isn't your fault. You know magic, but this is Qeteral magic, and it's different, and there is no way we would have even pondered the possibility before we saw Strom and Velus at the Sanctum the other day. We've only been lucky that never before has the Staff actually been positioned against Nikal or Kodi's bodies while they slept. They've kept it close beside them, but presumably never actually touching them."

"Nope," concurred Kodi. "Don't believe it has. What did they say to you, Nikal?"

Nikal rubbed his face. "It was more emotion than anything. They are trapped and wish...they wish to go on."

"To the Stars," said Shane.

"Yes. And I felt and understood their pain so well. But they also made plain to me that the Staff can do more than what I thought it could."

"You mean it is more powerful."

"Very. And it was almost as though they were begging me to try harder with it, that is should I have a chance to use it again against the enemy. They...they showed me *visions*, Kodi, of what the Staff can do. And...and it's their own powerful anger and aggression in it. Hate and not hate at the same time. Hate for the evil of the enemy and remorse, terrible remorse for...for..."

"Collateral damage." Kodi seemed to know, as it was also on his mind a lot.

"Exactly. The death of innocents in the process. I felt their desperation. Their faces were mad with it. And sad, too."

"I can see it," said Kodi calmly. "I see it, Nikal. Yet, I am not so sure that we should change the way we wield it in battle. Targeted and careful."

"That is wise," agreed Curdoz.

"I do not wish to deny the sadness of their souls, but I have a hypothesis," said Shane. "I strongly suspect that though they may indeed grasp a little of the time that has transpired since they released their souls into the Staff centuries ago, that nevertheless, in a way, their 'awareness' of anything at all is inert when a War Wizard is not holding and concentrating thought on the Staff."

"You mean you believe the Staff only has active 'life' when Nikal or Kodi touches the Staff?" asked Tiliruf.

"Almost exactly what I am trying to convey, a'Terianh. You have more awareness than you might think on these matters. At all other times they, Strom and Velus, for all practical purposes, sleep."

"Yet sleep is not a lack of all consciousness. You just said so yourself," suggested Tiliruf. "Sleep is not always peaceful, eh? Perhaps they, too, dream. Just like you said that Kodi and the Matriarch met each other in Kodi's Vision. They were both dreaming at the same time. Maybe that's what happened here. And Hurlin and the brothers could sense the life in the Staff when Nikal allowed them to hold it when we first met. And that wasn't when either Nikal or Kodi were touching it."

Shane and Curdoz both raised eyebrows.

"I...I think I must modify my hypothesis," said Shane. "You do have a scientific logic about you, a'Terianh."

Nikal spoke. "I believe Tiliruf is right. Based on what I felt, to say the least, Velus and Strom are...discontent. Unhappy. Their desire to exit Dumhoni forever is strong. They may not be suffering at all times, yet even so, as their consciousness comes together in their dreaming, and at the times we wield the Staff, they become aware of the centuries. It has been too long for them."

"Say nothing to the Qeteral princes of this, any of you. Or to the Matriarch," said Kodi firmly.

"Absolutely not," agreed Curdoz. "The struggles and pains of the Staff are yours and only yours to bear, and us whom you choose to share your struggles. Nikal, allow the pain of what you witnessed to wash over you. Meical does not wish you to suffer for the choices He made, I know that. He knows suffering is required, but He doesn't like it. And everything about the Eagle Staff is of His purview. He is not absent from the souls of Strom and Velus. He is present with them, too."

"He is with them, too," Kodi confirmed. "They are as much brothers to Him as we are."

Gwyn received them in her private study. Hurlin stood by. The Matriarch greeted Kodi warmly and touched her youngest son's face with affection. "What did you wish to see us about, Kodi? You said you have a request. Name it."

Kodi nodded his head with respect. "Yes, Madam. It is more appropriate that Lumin himself express it first."

She turned to look at her son. "What is it, dear one?"

Lumin breathed deeply. With great control in a manly voice, he spoke. "Mother, I wish to go on the mission with Kodi to rescue our brothers and sisters in the south."

Hurlin erupted. "Absolutely NOT!"

"Hear us out, Hurlin," said Kodi firmly.

"This is outrageous! I see it was a mistake to allow him to spend such close time with you *Humans!"* He spat.

"Control yourself, my son," said the Matriarch. "It was my decision to allow him that freedom, of course. Do not question my judgment."

"Listen to yourself, Mother! And see! He is being corrupted by Human...by this, by this *War Wizard* and his compatriots. I trusted Nikal! I cannot believe he approves of such a plan! To take my brother, a mere boy..."

"I am not a boy!" said Lumin strongly.

Hurlin ignored him, "...a mere boy on this dangerous quest! A princeling of our kingdom, my brother, your son!"

Kodi, unfazed, replied. "Nikal does not know of this yet. Lay it all on me if you wish, but this is your brother's wish for himself. I did not suggest it. He expressed this to me shortly after the council. I have had to think on it a good deal, but have concluded Lumin, though young, is not without wisdom and bravery."

"Go on," said Gwyn.

"Mother!" exclaimed Hurlin. "Don't let him convince you...!"

"Silence!" she replied with anger in her eyes. "You will say nothing until they have stated this case!"

Hurlin, incensed, turned away angrily, and muttered under his breath.

"State your case," said the Matriarch. It was plain she was not happy.

"Lumin wishes to learn of the world outside. It is his strong desire. Let us not question the Human nature within him."

"I do not question it."

Kodi nodded. Hurlin muttered again. It was all Hurlin could do to retain his silence.

Kodi continued. "And it draws him to the adventure and the bold elements in a Human man's nature. I believe his presence as a royal prince, the son of the Matriarch, among the lost Qeteral, could be of tremendous help in establishing trust. Imagine how frightened they will be when we ask them to give up all and board our ships on a dangerous voyage of return. No one, of course, can deny the dangers of this venture. Yes, it is of great risk, but consider the workings of Myghal. For *He* believes this rescue can be accomplished."

Gwyn turned around and looked briefly out a window and then turned back to look at Lumin. She raised an eyebrow, an indication it was his turn to explain himself.

"Mother, it is not my wish to create such a dilemma for you and the family. But I want so much to see other lands..."

"Those are the most dangerous of all Human lands, my son. They are absolutely not the places you would learn best of Human cultures. They are not taking you to safe places of culture and learning, such as Tirilorin or Nant. Fighting could be involved if forces of the enemy come to know of this. You have not trained in defensive practices as have your brothers. You are an artist."

"He is a superior archer, Madam. The best of any man I know, er, besides myself," said Kodi, winking at Lumin. "He's as strong as any of us, faster than all of us, and can hold his own."

She looked at each of them in turn. She looked briefly at the sulking Hurlin beyond and back. "I cannot pretend I did not wish for Lumin to make strong friendships with you and yours. In fact, I wished for it very much. His Human side is stronger perhaps than that of his Qeteral nature—I know my son and see deep into his heart, so much like his father. He is different than his brothers. I know this. They are strong Qeteral princes; Lumin is more a young Human man. Healer Solone thinks so."

"Healer Shane also thinks so, Madam."

"Powerful mind that one. Bold. Strong Healer with strong magic. Father has spoken to me of his keen wisdom. You have not spoken of this to Nikal, you say? What about Shane?"

"He knows," Kodi hesitated, but then went on. "He expresses also the dangers of this journey but does not deny the Human factors of the need for Lumin to grow into his own."

"And of the Divine's thoughts? You know, Kodi, what He is thinking on this matter."

"He has not contradicted my thinking, Madam. He is aware."

After a pause, she then requested Hurlin to speak. Though with a powerful eye and eyebrow she indicated he had better be controlled.

"I do not, Mother, believe Lumin to be as Human as you say."

"You just don't *want* him to be Human," said Kodi.

"Nor did Grandfather discover his face among those on the ships in the Sage's and the Matrimonial's Visions. It is a critical point, Mother."

She raised her eyebrow and looked at Kodi.

"Admittedly, Madam, it seems Myghal did not, at the time of our Visions, anticipate Lumin's presence on the voyage."

"You then," she stated, "believe things have changed with your coming here."

"Lumin himself is the one who has changed and grown into his Human, manly side. In the Human world he is a man by eight years. Eight years, Madam. And the Divine does not push back, yes."

"But you won't directly ask Myghal?"

"I hesitate, yes. For as I have said before in council I am not meant to know of His hopes and expectations for others. Except more keenly in Nikal's case, for Myghal expects me to speak for Him there. There is also the element of Choice, which the Divine favors. And in Lumin's case I particularly believe that these choices are his to make. Er, with your permission, of course. I believe it should be based on Lumin's choices and his own faith in the Guardian and in himself."

"As War Wizard you could order me to let him go, for I think you understand that we are required to submit."

"It...I...I admit I have considered using my authority but pray it won't be necessary. Please, Madam, let this be your family's choice."

She considered for a moment. "Lumin, retrieve your grandfather."

Lumin nodded and left the room.

When he was out of the room, Gwyn looked harshly at Hurlin. "Why do you speak with such disdain for the Humans? Have you learned so little from me of good manners? Do you not have reverence for the memory of your father and his father? You, too, are part Human, Hurlin. These are your own brethren. Kodi is no enemy."

"Not an enemy, no. But I don't want to be their brother! Aggressive, warmongering fools! Allowing the empire to collapse! Tiliruf is a shadow! And shallow! No hope there! Most of the world's ills derive from Human faults. Don't deny it, Kodi! And here you go trying to steal my actual brother away! You charm, don't you? Carefully chosen words. Practiced facial expressions, charms and flirtations...scheming!"

Kodi's usual hint of smile turned to a strongly sour expression. "I am not the fool here. And I have been as honest with you as I know how. You choose not to know us, Hurlin. You choose not to see our good nature, which is no different than that of Qeteral. I revere you, and whether you will it or not, I claim you as a brother in the spirit of the Divine. The Qeteral world will be subject someday to you. I'm not unaware. I, with all my heart, wish for you to know me. I charge you to reach out to the Guardian and strengthen your faith. He knows your heart. He knows the pains, the sadness endured by your male forebears in the making of the Staff, and you and Olin feeling it so deeply. Seeing Velus and Strom—they even look like you and Olin, don't they?—sleep endlessly on stone slabs in a hothouse, denied long lives of love and cheer with wives and family and friends, and a great and beautiful kingdom meant for them to rule, all in order to save us Humans from the mistakes we have admittedly made. Though there were stronger powers in those days, Siriné corrupting the hearts of our Ralsheen ancestors. So, I cannot understand you pinning all blame on Humans. And dark magic has returned, though never really absent, for Siriné lives and has transferred magic to the khans. A terrible evil. We need you. I need you, for the greater magic is largely in the realm of your people, and without you and yours we cannot fight against them. But it is as much to save your world as mine. That is something you yourself need not deny.

"And since you choose to single out Tiliruf especially, let me tell you something. Tiliruf is no shadow. He is a great man. As a powerful warrior he has already demonstrated it. He destroyed the Alkhaness' giant bodyguard, he and Rainwing. Controls his stallion like you can birds and two-handed like Terianh himself. He's the greatest swordsman in the world. You would have marveled if you saw him at South Fort. Shane says his Terianh blood is perhaps as pure as any of the greatest emperors. Tiliruf resists such a claim to greatness, for he is on a spiritual journey, and his faith in himself has been slow to develop. You only see his Human joking which you cannot appreciate and bits of casual flippancy. Yet even the cynicism demonstrates a kind of awareness. He's not an iota more cynical than you are, Hurlin! And what else? A cheeky Human grin as he attempts to engage you? You don't like that either, do you? Human fun and humor seem stupid to you. And so, you turn up a proud nose and say he's *shallow*. But his scholarly knowledge is almost unbeatable, excellent in languages and history, art, botany. A scientific mind, too. Logical. He forgets nothing that he reads. He has been skeptical of Myghalian Mysticism, the work of the Divine as He moves us in this world, but he is learning, and his limited faith is stronger than yours. I think you have none at all."

"I...I believe in the Guardian," Hurlin said defensively.

"I know you believe in Him. He also knows you believe in Him, and He follows your mind whether or not you know it, and He wouldn't if He did not also value you, your inner goodness, and the love you have for your people. Give Him credit for His workings. If you think I play with people to get what I want, I am sorry. Understand that I try to do my best, and it is all for Him."

Gwyn added. "Kodi's faith is strong, Hurlin. Someday you will see that if you don't now. Learn to have faith in those presented to you by the Guardian's Will. Through Visions and Prophecies, dangers and sacrifices, Myghal brought them here. Brought Kodi here. Brought Tiliruf here. So we could know them and develop trust in them. And they in us. I expected you, a king in the making, to establish strong rapport with them, and you didn't. At least Lumin and Olin have done good duty by them, and Ryn has done likewise with the women and Rainwing."

Hurlin retained a most unhappy expression, but he had lost the capacity for words just then. He stared fixedly at Kodi.

The door opened.

Gwyn proceeded to elaborate the situation to her father. "...and so Kodi requests rightly that this be the family's decision."

Hakonn hesitated, looking at the other men. As usual, he did not display emotion. "And what does my daughter the Matriarch think at this stage?"

"I am inclined."

"And Prince Hurlin?"

"I am strongly disinclined."

Hakonn looked at Lumin.

"I strongly wish to go, Grandfather. It's important to me. I am immeasurably grateful to you and Hurlin and Olin for everything you have ever taught me. But I want to grow in other ways."

Lastly, Hakonn looked at Kodi for a long while, though he did not request him to speak. Instead, it appeared that, staring into Kodi's eyes, he was delving into his mind.

Retaining eye contact, Hakonn nodded at Kodi and spoke aloud. "He is the Brother of Myghal, Matriarch. If we cannot trust the Brother of Myghal, then whom do we trust? Not denying Prince Nikal's equivalent status, it is nevertheless Lord Kodi here who is closest to the Divine and hears most clearly His Voice. In a way, Nikal is the war leader and the great Polemarchian strategist as the Etoppsi label him, but Kodi is the spiritual leader and the one given the quest by the Divine as confirmed in your Vision. I have begun to see why the Divine chose two War Wizards this time, as they complement each other with different talents and strengthen each other in great friendship. Kodi's request should perhaps be looked upon as coming from the spiritual plane from where he gains his wisdom—that place where Myghal dwells. Let us presume also that Kodi sees Lumin through a light, through the light of Humans, which the rest of us only nominally touch upon. Lumin is more Human than not. Not so different at all from Mabelin when he and you Bonded. You and I have noted this in many conversations. Let us allow Lumin to continue to explore that side of his nature. There is great danger, but also great reward forthcoming."

Hurlin looked down. He had lost.

Gwyn looked at Lumin. "Then it is decided. I do not wish you to go, and you must understand the fears we all have for the danger. But I will not deny that you can make that choice, son. As Kodi has rightly said, this is a matter of your own faith in the Guardian and in yourself. I think you perceive a mystical Calling here. That is what your grandfather is saying, and as I too know a little of Myghal's mind I see that Calling, and perhaps Kodi only confirms my own thinking. I offer all blessings to you. Tomorrow, I wish you to spend the day with me. I will clear my schedule. I have much to say to you before you go. Perhaps I can explain to you how you should present yourself to the lost ones. They will know little of the common Anterianhi tongue if any, having continued to use Ulaki. Let us brush up on the language. You have some magic in you, as do some of the others, I think, to transfer some of the new language into their minds. Great assurances you can offer, a prince sent to rescue his people. For you are Human but also *are* a prince of the Qeteral, and it was right of Hurlin to remind us. This is serious business, the most serious business that has ever come before the Qeteral in five-hundred years, and you mustn't forget that."

Lumin nodded deeply. "Thank you so very much, Mother."

"Kodi, I wish for you to extend an invitation to dinner with me tonight: you, Nikal, Shane, Tiliruf, and Lord Curdoz. I have so delightfully gotten to know the Human ladies and Rainwing but fear I have not done so with you men. Father and Hurlin, remain in the room, please. Kodi, Lumin, you may go."

Shane listened to Kodi's story in private. "So, it was not as fun as you imagined."

"I would have preferred a straight-on boxing match with Hurlin. That would have been fun. It was awful."

"Hurlin is learning more about you, and I think that is important. You stated your case firmly, under the Guardian's instincts with which He gave you, and under Curdoz' teachings, too. No doubt you have grown. Acknowledge your deep wisdom. I doubt Hurlin will ever forget anything you said to him."

"Am I really so wise, Shane? Hurlin thinks I am a manipulator. A schemer."

Shane nodded. "If we're honest with ourselves, everyone is a manipulator at times, and that doesn't apply only to Humans. Hurlin sees you as a manipulator because he himself often acts as one. The key, then, is in the underlying cause. You persuade. You charm. These are not evil things when it is not entirely about yourself. You value the other person, Kodi. You're not trying to be deceitful or mean. You are, as you told Hurlin, doing the best you know how in order to bring about the Guardian's wishes. If anyone is the manipulator, it is He, Meical the Guardian."

"Yeah, and that's why Tiliruf resists getting close to Him."

"And so also Hurlin. Tiliruf and Hurlin struggle to see beyond the maneuvering. Yet Tiliruf is coming around as he begins to see the great good the Guardian is trying to bring about. The idea, really, of manipulation, is in whether it leads to that which is good for all involved and thus in our attitude about it. You've never before considered Meical to be a manipulator because the word typically implies something unkind and selfish. I think...I think perhaps it is in the perception of being used or being misused. No one wants to be misused, and you were convinced from the beginning you were not being misused. But Meical does use you and the rest of us to try to achieve His will. We are all He has here on Dumhoni. We are His friends. His brethren. He deserves loyalty, and we act with obedience to His overarching wisdom, whether or not we are privy to all the knowledge He holds. The women too, as you have pointed out, are acting on His authority. His sisters. They won't tell us of their Visions, but we cannot deny they are up to something they too are Called to. Kodi, you are trying to make the world safe again from the khans and slavery. Lyndz likewise, as you have admitted she must be a counter of sorts to the Alkhaness, which we cannot foresee. A return to the Ralsheen Dark Times would be a horrible tragedy. Hurlin is a good man. He will come around. It's not going to be easy. He is jealous, and what he is seeing right now is that, from his point of view, you are taking his baby brother away and subjecting him to terrible danger."

"Er...and I'm not so sure he doesn't know a little bit about Ryn and me."

"Really? Well. Again, Hurlin needs to grow. You are essentially forcing him to do so before he's ready. I encourage you to let the scene this morning leave you. Treat Hurlin as warmly as you can. Don't bring up today's arguments unless He himself forces it. I wonder if he will be at this dinner tonight we're invited to."

"You and Nikal can sit by him, ha! I am really surprised Hakonn came around so quickly. I was afraid it wouldn't go well when the Matriarch sent for him. I figured he would take Hurlin's part."

"He's a reader of minds, Kodi. Which is what *gods* do, you hear me? I think I would be terrified for Hakonn to place his hands on my head if he were not so supremely self-disciplined. I'm not even sure he needs to touch a person to do it. He sees much that others don't. And wise, very wise. I begin now to see why he didn't want to be king when he surely could have been. With mind powers like his he really would have been the ultimate manipulator, but he knew better than to allow himself such control. Therefore he stepped aside and instead promoted his daughter. He became then a teacher and advisor. He may not have liked Humans very much before. Hurlin learned prejudice from him. But then...we came. He has learned a thing or two. For which you deserve much credit."

Kodi reached over and pinched Shane's shoulder.

"And so do you. I appreciate your insight, Shane, and your advice is always what I need."

"Thank you. It has always been my purview to observe, analyze, and summarize."

"I think you read minds as well as Hakonn. Certainly for any Human you do. You really seem to understand what drives others. And you care. You deeply care."

"You're too kind..."

"No, Shane. No doubt every Healer has a caring disposition. But you're not only a Healer of the body; you're a Healer of the troubled spirit. I know it, and so do the rest of us. That, and every other excellent thing about a man is wrapped up neatly in you."

Shane nodded his gratitude. "And every man appreciates being affirmed so by those he admires and respects. Thank you again. So, you said all that you did about Tiliruf?"

"I'm afraid it kind of fired me what Hurlin said. *Shallow...*"

"Well, it was important, too, if you ask me. Tiliruf is far from shallow. I would have said to him exactly what you did."

Yet if anything, Hurlin became more aloof than ever. And he was not at the dinner that evening. He went about his business of informing those Qeteral who were to go on the voyage and preparing them all with defensive tactics. He would on occasion send for Nikal to come to him to consult about the quest, but the other Humans almost never saw him now. He spoke little even to Lumin. It did trouble Lumin a little. Yet Olin made effort to take up the slack and spent much time in personal training with his younger brother. In his wish to spend as much time as he could with Lumin, he started spending even more time with the Humans. Though he was not a conversationalist, he engaged in swims and some play, and certainly they welcomed his company at the pavilion. He even spent a couple nights with them staying up late in conversation, and on those nights Lumin would not disappear and would sleep next to his brother rather than Kodi, and they would whisper long into the wee hours. Olin made strong effort to demonstrate pride and faith in Lumin and offer reassuring statements. Those two grew closer as the time came nearer for their separation.

"You don't think you should tell Olin, at least, about Fal?" asked Shane once.

"No," Lumin said flatly.

"I won't press it, of course."

"We wear these on the hunt, you see. Qeteral boys and men," said Lumin.

"You made these for us?" asked Manwul.

"I did!"

Lumin had, unusually, spent a night at the palace, and when he returned the next morning before breakfast, he presented to Nikal, Kodi, Tiliruf, Manwul, Hadon, and Shane necklaces made of irregular wooden beads strung on leather. The beads were of different colors, made from different kinds of wood, all polished to a high gloss.

"They're wonderful," said Hadon with wide eyes.

"A princely gift. Thank you," said Shane, who proceeded to bow. They all did likewise, each understanding with Shane's words that a prince had given them gifts, and they were to be treasured as such.

"Don't mix them up," said Lumin with a smile. "I considered each of you as I made each one, you see. For example, I used some of the biggest beads for Manwul's. I've been crafting those beads for months now. I didn't know you were coming, but it was fun. I knew I'd give them away eventually, and I honor you as my closest friends."

"I'm never taking it off," said Kodi who was the first to put it around his neck. The rest followed his example. Hadon now wore two necklaces, as he of course always donned Sturla's gift of the gold link chain.

"Well, the leather will wear out," said Lumin, "and you will have to restring them eventually. The use of leather rather than string is a connection to the animal world, you see. Make sure you keep the beads in the same arrangement. It's important!"

"You bet," said Tiliruf. "I'll pretend they're like the antler collars that Rusty and the Stags wear!"

"Certainly a strong symbolism of your brotherhood," admitted Rusty as he watched them put them on.

"Yes," said Nikal. "What excellent symbolism."

"You all are much too good looking like that," said Curdoz. The chunky beaded necklaces on their bared torsos only added to their overall handsomeness. The Sage was reminded of Modela saying how the men appeared as Modelo's first sons. She was speaking of Kodi and Nikal at the time, but to Curdoz all those present fit the sublime description. *Gods,* he thought. He added, "I envy your youth. I was never like you. Was never so confident in my appearance and have always been reserved. You are all beautiful and full of youth and vigor. I always wanted that for myself, you see. It isn't only that, but also the self-confidence and willingness to face...to face whatever comes. I wish...I wish I were...as you."

The men looked at him and smiled. They all looked to Curdoz as a father, and he was giving them the supreme compliment that all sons wished from their own fathers, but which some of them never had received. What young man doesn't wish to be handsome and strong and confident in demeanor, and for that to be acknowledged by those they respect? They nodded thanks, but no words were necessary. Kodi wrapped him from behind in a big neck hug, and Curdoz' eyes grew watery.

Lumin had his large drawing pad, too. "And I've got something for you as well, Curdoz and Deens and Findun and Rusty! And as soon as Stormgale returns I'm going to draw one of him, too. But I feel I need to see him again to get it right."

And then he proceeded to present three portraits. One contained Deens and Findun together as they sat at the little table at the council meeting writing down notes on parchment, their beards trailing. "You'll have to trade it off with each other like Manwul and Hadon!"

The one of Curdoz showed him stately in the Human clothing he wore, along with his Sage stole the women had knitted, on the night of the reception. The one of Rusty was exquisite, his great fierce head and face, his antler collar, and behind were feathered wings that disappeared off the parchment. Though the first two drawings were in gray pencil, the one of the Etoppsi utilized colored pencil and showed his stunning red fur and brilliant shimmer on his black feathers.

"I'll bring you all cylinders to keep them in!" said Lumin happily. He was like a boy again. "I'll show you how to roll them up properly between other sheets, and that will preserve them until you get home!"

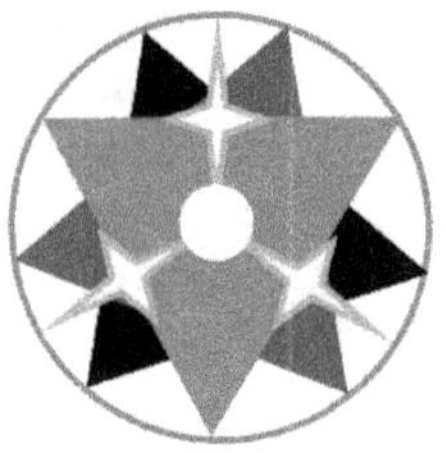

Chapter 23—Nightingale and Lily

The other men had been asleep for a while. Yet slumber eluded Kodi tonight, rare for him. He was wide awake when Lumin slipped out yet again, earlier than usual, to make secret love to Fal in the night. Likely his friend intended extra time and repetition of pleasures over the long hours. There were only ten days and nights remaining to their stay. Kodi smiled as Lumin walked out but retained his silence. He himself was thinking of Ryn. Surely Lumin's exit from the pavilion encouraged these thoughts to deepen. He lay quietly, hands behind his head. As there was bright moonlight coming through the open window flap, he gazed at the scene of the hunt painted by Qeteral artists above him on the canvas.

In truth, Ryn dominated his thoughts in the day and his dreams in the night, she, a vision of exotic loveliness and a presence of joyful companionship. All the moments they shared together now replayed in his mind. After a time, and quite naturally, he began to focus his inner eye on her face and body. Her vivid blue eyes in contrast to her brown skin were mesmerizing, along with the luster of her ebony hair, her shapeliness set off by the drape of the linen she wore, and her scent, like that of the crushed leaves of wild ginger, permeated the space around her. He could smell it even now.

Thinking like this set his soul afire. He wished he could capture Solvermoon or a handful of distant stars, and from their radiance craft a silver wreath by his own hands and place it on her head to demonstrate his love for her. He could hardly bear the thought of leaving the land of Ulakel without expressing himself. Somehow. He had allowed her to take the lead in the relationship, but was it appropriate now to speak his love more plainly? Would she wait for him? He could go happily into the South of the World and with the Eagle Staff conquer the enemy realms, if only he could come back here and find her again.

As his mind wandered into these heroic scenes, the adrenaline flowed, and he quickly realized the hopelessness of falling asleep. He got out of his comfortable bedding and put on his Qeteral pant and Qeteral sandals. Perhaps solitude was what he wanted. He stepped out of the pavilion. His eyes were immediately drawn upwards. Solvermoon and Orohmoon, both near to the full, fired the night, and a myriad of stars glittered, countless diamonds. He paused, had a thought, then went back to retrieve a blanket. Perhaps he would try sleeping under the stars in the meadow. He knew where the copse was where Lumin would escort Fal from her farmhouse, as Lumin had told him, but he would steer away. He draped the blanket over his shoulders, then climbed out of the hollow.

Though the night birds, owls and nightjars, could be heard, nothing moved in the moonlight. He found himself heading in the direction of the moons; both were in the western sky together and were quite close to one another. Was tonight supposed to be a two-moon eclipse? These occurred with some reasonable frequency, usually twice, sometimes three times in a Dumhoni year, but they were always interesting to watch. He found what he believed to be a perfect spot in the field in which to lay his blanket, when out of the night he perceived the piercing sound of the oft-heard nightingale. It was coming from his left, not from the copse where Lumin surely was by now with Fal, but rather in the direction of the greater forest that edged the Plateau. Drawn to its music, he draped the blanket over his shoulders again and followed.

Soon as if by accident, his feet came upon a path of white stone through the field. Looking the other way, it appeared to come from the end of the village where the palace lay. He then turned in the direction of the woods and followed it. Upon finally reaching the forest, the stones continued in unique pattern through a glade of tall hemlocks and pines, translucent now in the dappled moonlight. Kodi felt compelled to continue as it wandered its way toward a bubbling brook at the bottom of a gentle slope. The trees grew closer together, yet there was still good light. The nightingale continued to sing, almost as if it were leading him. Perhaps the brook led to a little river with a pool to swim, and he could watch the moons and sleep on its banks. The hum of field crickets and the calls of other birds faded behind, and the only other sound now, besides the nightingale, was that of the water at his feet.

After a little, he found that the track crossed the brook on a footbridge of one massive stone, and here the water began to cut its way through the Plateau's surface in a sharp gulley. This soon opened out into a little canyon with walls of shiny black rock. It was as if one of the World Gods gouged it with a fingernail, and as he followed the path down, the water rushed forward in miniature waterfalls every few yards in a tune as delightedly soulful as that of the nightingale. It was an enchanting place of laurels and other leafy green flora that shone in the night. At the base of each fall, water sprayed outward in magical bright droplets of emerald and beryl, and other greens that Kodi did not even know existed. In many ways it reminded him of places near to the Wolf River in far off Felto, favorite haunts. Yet here in this miniature canyon every surface of every leaf and stone was misted, creating a sparkle in the double moonlight like nothing he had ever experienced.

The nightingale flew close, the first time he had ever actually seen it. It then landed on the bough of a tall azalea and began such a tune that Kodi paused to stare and listen. Before long, however, the bird flew off again, and Kodi continued to follow the stone path as it stepped ever downward. Soon, he saw that the canyon closed in before him. The tall walls of stone came within a few feet of one another, here creating a lovely archway, and the little stream plunged noisily over a precipice. The white stones of the path became a series of steep stairs leading from this doorway down to a sparkling pool twenty feet below. The light from the moons shone brilliantly into this hollow, revealing a sight the memory of which forever after smote him with deepest longing.

Upon a flat rock in the middle of the silver pool sat the form of the Princess of the Qeteral. Her skin glistened copper in the light of the two moons and the stars. Kodi's breath caught, for he had never before known a face as beautiful as Ryn's when he met her on their first evening in Ulakel. Now before him in the twofold moonlight was not just a face, but a vision of feminine perfection. He was reminded of the sensuous marble statue in the fountain in the palace garden in Tirilorin. Desire and longing such that he had only ever imagined in the fantasies of his dreams stirred his core.

He stood entranced near the head of the waterfall looking down, well-hidden by the archway. Ryn's jet hair hung long and wet, forward across her breasts, and the spray from the waterfall misted her body, the graceful, feminine curves of which moved his body to respond. Despite the noise of the water, he could hear the beating of his own heart.

Yearning spread through Kodi's whole being as he watched the Princess. Then suddenly she stood and her whole glorious form was revealed to him. She was the most perfect of all the Children of the Mold that had ever been made, and his heart was awakened in a way he had not known could ever be. He had no thoughts whatsoever of ole Jonell, none. Rather, he was reminded of the Vision, when he had plunged into the Lake in the middle of the Valley and felt the Power of the Guardian surge through the Voice into his body. If possible, he now felt even more alive and vibrant, and manlier too, for there was a key difference. Like Curdoz had said, that element of the Vision, though powerful, was metaphor.

This was real.

She dove suddenly into the deep pool, an action that promptly took Kodi's breath away. He continued to watch as she surfaced and swam towards the base of the waterfall almost immediately below him but at an angle at which he could not see without stepping out and risking exposure. Yet, drawn by the fire in his chest he did so anyway, moving out to the point where the stairs began, right to the lip of the fall. She was swimming in and out of its curtain, the force of the water not so strong as to cause any harm, falling rather in a playful shower of sparkling gems. He continued to watch as she dallied, her hair flowing behind, and after a time, she swam back to the rock in the center of the pool. Stepping out, she sat again in the warm night air, facing the western moons.

She began to sing.

It was a song that etched itself upon Kodi's heart, and he remembered and hummed it to himself forever after on his travels. Was she singing in Ulaki? For a moment he was convinced she was. And yet it seemed to translate magically into his mind in his own tongue. In common Anterianhi he heard it:

I listen in the water for the song of the Star.
I long for the music from the heavens afar.
Sing to my heart of the first love on the Night.
When He came to Her in the double moonlight.
His smile to Her was as the sun in the day.
A lily He bore in His hand of clay.
In a pool of diamonds They swam together.
The Star sang a song of love forever.

Her voice was more melodious than even the nightingale, and when she stopped, Kodi was surprised to find himself still standing on the top step by the head of the fall. He swallowed hard. If she but turned she would discover him. Was she in fact calling in the song—for him?

His longing intensified if that were possible, and yet it was one of the rare times in his life he was torn. Whereas he was one who believed that well-meaning action was a risk always worth more than the safety of hesitant uncertainty, he felt a wrong choice here would be uncorrectable. Was it too soon? Having allowed her to lead the last two weeks, would it be presumptuous to approach her alone in her nudity? '*When you most need Me, call for Me.*' And though it was not a moment of danger or gravity, it was nevertheless a decision so ominous he chose to rely on the Guardian's promise to him and closed his eyes. Reaching inward with his mind he pleaded his case. "Brother. Meical. Brother, what do I do? I love her. I love her so much."

His beating heart stilled. The sound of the waterfall was lost.

And in that silence, he heard the always-promised Voice. It was youthful and jovial, as a fun big brother revealing his latest trick to his favorite little brother. *Ha! Open your eyes and turn around.*

He opened them. Sounds returned and the princess sat unmoving, looking still in the direction of the double moons which were now close to touching. The anticipated eclipse was near. He then turned, and his breath caught for perhaps the tenth time in as many minutes. Before him, growing out of the edge of the rock wall, was a beautiful white flower.

A lily.

Can you guess now, Kodi?

Kodi reached out his hand and the lily fell loosely in it. Despite all the gardens he and his twin sister had visited in all the lands they had traveled, before him was the most perfect flower Kodi had ever seen, and every pearlescent petal, every leaf, and even the strong root attached to it were full of vigor and life.

"You hoped for this! You wanted this!"

The strong confidence that usually defined Kodi now fully restored, he grinned—a bit rakishly perhaps. He winked knowingly at his invisible Brother, turned, and descended.

At the bottom, next to the moonlit pool, and hidden by the sound of the waterfall, he removed his sandals and pant and entered soundlessly into the water. It was warmer than he expected, about as perfect as the Lake water in the Valley he remembered from his Vision long ago. But instead of absorbing the mountain sunshine, here the starlight and moonlight of a late summer night mingled in the water, sending silver rays to and fro. When he dipped his head under, he could hear the muffled sound of that light and the waterfall as they penetrated the surface of the water.

...the song of the Star...music from the heavens afar.

When he surfaced, the piercing blue eyes of Ryn, Princess of the Land of Ulakel, were on him.

"Kodi!"

With a free hand holding aloft the white lily, he made his way to the rock. At its base he held the blossom up to her, and as she took it, her hand touched his. She returned his smile, and the Qeteral Princess and the Human Man from the north stared longingly into each other's eyes.

"Wait!" she said finally. She took the lily and set it lovingly upon the rock, its root dangling in the water, and to Kodi's enormous satisfaction, her beautiful brown body slipped into the water and came to him.

Together they swam naked in the pool, under the two moons and the stars. Though they represented two different races of the Mold, their joy in the presence of one another was as the first Male and the first Female Humans in the Valley from the Song that the Matrimonials sing at the Bonding Ceremony.

The summer air spoke in warm whispers across their bodies as they lay in the moon shadow of tall pines upon a bed of soft needles and fern, upon which Kodi had spread the blanket he had brought. Their passion was like that of the two moons now glimpsed through the boughs, Solvermoon brushing Orohmoon, they embraced and paused. But the eyes of the lovers were only for one another. An incomparable quarter hour of rapturous naked physicality paired with emotional euphoria was followed by exquisite long moments as a thousand stars burst like arrows through their conjoint bodies. In their perfect timing they called out in mutual joy. Then the two wrapped themselves together in blissful sleep.

They were awakened when the nightingale returned and made its presence known. It sang from a bough just above them. The nearby waterfall, having composed its eternal melody long ago, went about performing as if it had never before been heard. The moons seemed not to have moved. The Princess looked at their light and smiled.

Kodi asked her, "Is it...do you understand what the nightingale is saying?" He drew the Qeteral Princess tightly into the crook of his body and cupped her breasts. He knew no treasure in the world was equal to the body he held now so firmly.

She grinned. "It's Tanter."

"Tanter?" Yet his moment of confusion was gone. He leaned up and looked in her face. "She led me to you! Ryn! She's your own bird! You have sent her every night to sing to me!"

"He. Only the males sing so." The princess laughed, then sang softly until the bird flew off again. Kodi thought Ryn's voice the most beautiful he had ever heard, even among the other Qeteral, who all spoke and sang so divinely.

"Thank you for loving me, Princess."

"And you me, my Human princeling."

"Ah, I am not a prince, you know."

"Neither was my grandfather. Yet your high nobility is established through your Calling by Myghal. Not that its lack would have stopped me. For I knew I was in love with you, Kodi, when I saw you at the reception. But it was important that we grew to know one another."

"Yes. Even tonight when I saw you, though I longed to come down to you, I feared overstepping. I did not wish—the Human phrase would be, *to press my luck*. It just seemed too good to be true. Meical then spoke to me."

She turned around completely to face him as they lay on their sides on the blanket. She held his warm hands to her breasts. "What did He say?"

Kodi repeated the short conversation.

"You heard my song? In your own language? And the Divine prepared the lily?"

"He did."

She beamed. "Kodi, I need to tell you something. This place, this pool and garden carry great magic. I've always wished to experience it. All the tales agree that when lovers come here, time is altered. Vanaratu himself created this garden ages ago for a Qeteral princess and put great charms on it."

His eyes went wide. "This is the Diamond Pool! From that storybook in the pavilion! I, uh, haven't read it yet."

She laughed. "Grandfather had me choose the books to send for the men's entertainment. And as much as I might have hoped, I was not expecting this night, but it was nevertheless a wonderful story I hoped you all would appreciate. It is a true story, Kodi. Beautiful, though Vanaratu's love for her was unrequited. And it is like a window to the Cosmos. Myghal may have sent that flower, for lilies surely do not bloom this late in the summer. But it was an added blessing that may only have occurred within this place."

She is right, Kodi. I am glad to have had this chance to touch you both so closely. I can see everything clearly in Vanaratu's wonderful garden. That is, when two lovers meet here, and you are not the first. Many of Ryn's forebears have come here, among a few others.

Kodi shared Meical's words. Happiness showed in her blue eyes. She drew even closer to him. "You have wonderful hands, Kodi. Large. Warm. You heal me with your touch."

He couldn't stop his grin. Were his hands really as magical as all that? He remembered his sister saying something of the same sort long ago, as he held her hand at a time she was grieving leaving home. He reached up and placed his right hand on Ryn's face and stroked her cool damp hair, running it between his fingers. After a time, he then moved it to play a tune on a nipple. She let out a sigh as her body reacted happily to his touches. He then engaged her other nipple with his tongue.

He then looked up into her happy face and chuckled. His own body was fully renewed. "Well, you know," he said with a wink. "I can do even better than that!"

She laughed too as he reached behind her and drew her atop him. As he leaned upward and kissed her with an unbridled fierceness, their bodies connected once more in the cosmic romp.

"This night is long, my love," she said, as they again lay together after a revitalizing swim in the pool. "It is a great gift. For you and me to be here."

She was referencing Solvermoon and Orohmoon, for they still were connected, having moved only a little. Vanaratu's long ago magic was giving them the happiest night of their lives. As they watched, Solvermoon shone its shiniest silver, Orohmoon a burnished gold. They appeared enlarged in their embrace, and even the colors of stars demonstrated themselves, reds and blues among whites. As a ship on the sea, the garden floated above the world. Beyond its airs the light of the universe shone unfiltered and crisp, sparkling and alive. Kodi would have to tell Lumin. He wanted Lumin to have such a long night with Fal, just like himself with Ryn, whereby they could rest and bathe and even sleep together without concern for the passing hours and make all the love they wished. The slowness of time reminded him a bit of when Theneri took him into the Mode in order to experience Moment-mastering.

But Ryn was no mere portrait of a moment. She was all the moment and more. She was the future. "Ryn, what will you do when I am gone? I will miss you and long for you, but please stay here where it's safe and not try to follow after and find me. The dangers we are heading for, you know."

She looked at him with a bit of a knowing smile.

"What?" he asked. "Why are you looking at me like that? You won't follow me, will you?" He was suddenly concerned that she was indeed plotting such a course.

"No, no, my love! No. I will stay here. Though I am not so sure that any land is safe. The time may come for me to defend my people if the enemy should come this way. The Barrier is powerful and defeated Siriné long ago. But even so, we do worry that the khans are crafty. There are dangers for us as well. And so, you are not the only one who may find them. Myghal has set you on a quest to seek them, but I will not. You misunderstand. I only smiled because of your loving wish to protect me. Instead, focus your protection on my dear Lumin when he goes with you."

"That I will do."

Kodi relaxed now, his momentary concern already forgotten on this otherwise perfect night. He then lay back and folded his hands behind his head.

She sat up and gazed lovingly at Kodi's body, and using her own soft but strong hands, she began to caress it tenderly and with her warm lips to kiss it affectionately. His skin was only a little lighter in shade than her own. She was drawn to its texture, soft in places and rough in others. Even the tufts and lines of dark hair on his body, exotic to Qeteral eyes, seemed deliberately set in place to delineate his musculature and male features. Lumin's necklace, the only thing he now wore, added to this quality. Too, a musky aroma arose from Kodi's warm Human body, which she found intoxicating.

And his face! As his dark eyes watched her, she could not help but to think that before her lay the incarnation of one of the World Gods from the deeps of time, those of course that Myghal Favored. And of course, Kodi was Favored. The most highly Favored of all men.

"I carry your seed, Kodi Fothemry."

He grinned hugely. He, and Ryn too, understood the magic of the water restored them completely each time they swam or drank from it. Each connection, then, held fresh intensity. Which, in Kodi's case, he swore was ever more incredible as the night went on. It built on his pride in the erotic function of his body. He felt a kind of spiritual connection to his perfect animal maleness, though this was not at all dependent on the magic. He'd always had strong body self-love, but it had now achieved an ideal in its union with the female (universes different than his romp with Jonell as a boy, the memory of whose face and form had almost entirely exited his subconscious). These feelings were a key part of the man's perspective behind the Qeteral phrase, which he spoke now through that grin. "Ryn of Ulakel *carries my seed*. And I have never been so happy."

"And through my inner magic will retain its vitality, Kodi, Mated One, whom I love beyond the stars. At the time we choose it, I will conceive and bear your children. Our children."

For Kodi these truths were both terrifying and wonderful. But the wonderful was so wonderful he sat up straight. He touched her face and then lowered her gently on the blanket. Returning her favors, he caressed her lovingly and grazed her curves with his tongue, tasting the wild ginger. In yet a new state of eagerness, he again coupled his body to hers. He remained for a while unmoving, savoring the incredible connective oneness of their bodies and their claim on each other.

Gazing into her eyes he said, "Ryn, my Mated One, I want you to choose it now. I don't want to wait—not for the quest to your kin in the south to be accomplished, not for the war to be over. I am ready. I am ready to be a father. The father of your children. Our children." He leaned down and kissed her compellingly.

"Why are you so sure, Kodi?" she asked with a smile when he ended this particular kiss.

"I knew what I was doing. What we are doing now." His moved his pelvis up and down and put on that euphoric look. "Ahh, yeah, this."

She chuckled. "Mmmm, yes. I'm listening."

"Well, a Human woman wouldn't have that choice you have. I'm Human, you see. And I know what this means."

"This?" She winked and teased as she moved her fingers sensually over his back.

"This." He licked a hardened nipple causing her to groan and then kissed her once more. He slowed his movements again, relishing the steady level of intensity in his groin enhanced by her sensitive touches. "And so, my willingness to become a father was made when I took the lily from the rock and brought it to you. Let's not wait."

Ryn realized indeed that a simple rearrangement of the facts made their lovemaking different for him. Delaying birth was not how Kodi's mind worked. There was the Human woman's cycle which offered a measure of control, but Kodi had no concerns for timing she realized. In Qeteral society it was typical, at least for the commoner couple, to spend perhaps years creating a home filled with all the trappings of household living and plant gardens—for the man to become expert at trapping and hunting or a trade, and for the woman to become adept at gardening and weaving and cooking or in her own art. For the two to come together at the potter's wheel and design from colored clays the wares for the table. Only when all was as it should be would the woman then choose to bear their first child.

Humans were apparently less particular about these things. Their lives were shorter. The bonded couple might control a pregnancy with care, but it wasn't always a consideration when love and passion ruled. For Kodi, plainly, love and passion ruled. There was something primordial here in the Human male mating experience that needed additional expression. Nor was it absent in that of the Qeteral man: a need for his seed to achieve its intended purpose. Kodi was openly expressing something of an inner longing.

Kodi was Chosen by Myghal Himself not only to attempt to bring back the trapped southern Qeteral, but also to fight the evils in the South, and it seemed odd to Ryn to conceive his child while he was gone. Her initial thoughts had been to wait till a safe time in the future, possibly even after the war. If she did as he asked, they would be obliged to tell all now and request her mother's blessing and the ceremony before Kodi left Ulakel. And of course, that didn't give them but ten more days. All these thoughts went through her mind in mere moments as Kodi awaited her response. And in the meantime, she too was basking in the joy of the physical connection between them, his weight carefully pressed against her, his hugeness filling the needfulness in her groin, and also of a deep, female spirituality (little different than what he was also experiencing in that sublime body unity).

And that spiritual quality allowed her to hear the Voice herself this time, though no words were spoken. Instead, she was granted a viewing in her mind of the night behind them. She saw again Kodi's grin as he swam to her sitting on the rock. She recalled the song she sang of her own deep longing—for him of course—and the magic flower he then brought to her. The power of the night and how her body responded to his with an intensity beyond what she'd ever imagined. A night that was even now not yet over, of sanctioned ecstasy, of a love that was encouraged, consecrated even, by Myghal Himself, He who knew the Mind of the One. It was not to be denied by any power in the universe.

A night when the two moons, Solvermoon and Orohmoon, male and female, came together...and paused. So much symbolism. So much realism. As they made perfect love in a garden crafted by a god.

Oh! We have made a vase! She said this silently to herself. And then she realized she could make a home with that one vase. She would plant that lily—that sacred lily—in her garden. Their garden. Her grandmother would let them take possession of her cottage. And then like a Vision—perhaps it was a Vision—she saw a baby, pretty and perfect.

This was a moment as symbolic as it got. As real as it got.

"The Human warrior departs with the joy of knowing, and of the hope of what he returns to," she said, reaching up to touch his face.

Kodi grinned again. "To give him strength and courage in the fight. I realize now this is what Myghal wanted for me. But He wants it for you, too, Ryn. Will you do it for me? For your Kodi? For us?"

His grin was infectious. "Yes, Kodi. I will bear our child now! You must come to Mother tomorrow and do your part, and we will Bond before you go. You are right, my love. I'm sorry I hesitated. In my heart perhaps I too did not wish to wait! For I am part Human, too, you know!"

"Please, love, my Mated One. My precious Ryn! Don't ever be sorry!"

As their minds merged in the mutual consciousness of shared yearnings and hopes, their vibrant young bodies moved rhythmically within that gravitational pull of male and female. Tanter the nightingale returned to watch and to trill a new melody. When they again together came to that rapturous moment of physical bliss, the joy of Kodi and Ryn burst the confines of the Dumhoni sphere. It reached out to a point in the furthest heavens, and there, a billion years of distance, a galaxy of stars ignited, blazing anew in celestial celebration.

It was still dark when Kodi at last returned to the pavilion where the other men were sound asleep, Lumin too, a dreamy smile on his face that surely mimicked Kodi's own.

How 'bout it, Lumin buddy! We're really going to be brothers, you and me! The two determined rascals in the family!

As Kodi lay upon his bed, the muscles throughout his body finally wound down. Yet his skin felt as though it were moving, as if it were a live thing that in and of itself missed its long connection with the body of the Qeteral Princess. Kodi allowed his thoughts to stray—upon all the waters he had ever swum in, across mountains he had flown over in his Visions, into the night sky and to the stars that encircled the heavens. There they skipped from star to star. But finally, they returned to the rocky hollow with its Diamond Pool and its tall pines and the presence of the face and form of the princess. He was grateful for the gift of the long night and the warm breeze, and of the stars and moons, and the little stream and the white stone path, of the pine trees and the ferns. Of the nightingale and the lily.

He was mated—bonded—to the one true love of his life. And he was going to be a father.

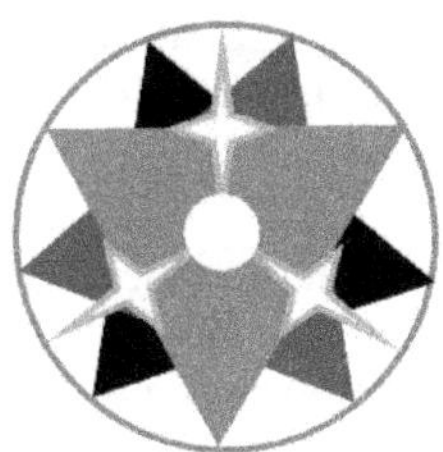

Chapter 24—Caramel Cake

Pr..pr..preeettiest lovemaking you ever did show me on that thing. But wh..what else would I expect from ole Kodi."

"It was wonderful. Meical so hoped for this, and when He told me I knew what He had in mind. More Human blood in the Qeteral. And only the best blood would do."

Two thousand miles away on a tropical island, two individuals, naked and beautiful in bed, having finished up only minutes before their thousandth round of their own unbridled passion, were watching relaxed through a sort of window contrived of the woman's powerful magic. The strong scent of Hralindi Oil infused the air. It was dark outside. A Common Grayhawk sat on an open windowsill, watching silently, occasionally pruning a wing feather.

"It's time, now, Vaaa...nayema, my love. Follow Mmm...Meical's bidding."

She nodded and the magic window evaporated. "The Gifts, yes. But only one at a time, my dear Aron."

"I rr..reckon I trust you."

"It is wise that you do, my dear. Though I may want your advice on one or two." She winked and without another moment's hesitation, her voluptuous form flung itself over and straddled his muscular frame. She placed her hands straight on his chest and used her special magic to return him to his fully restored, buck-ready mode.

"I'm the most blessed man in the uuu..niverse to have you, Vaaa...nayema! Ah...always thought I'd be stuck with some little damsel I'd have to be eeextra careful with. Considerin', ya know..."

"A thousand and one, my love." She winked again.

"Yep. Bedposts all scarred up with mm..my artistic notches. Well, er, Lumin's the artist with those drawings. That boy knows egg...exactly what life's about. Anyways, Tiliruf would be j..jealous."

"You like that don't you?"

She enveloped him and watched that happiness grow on his face. After that exquisite moment, she raised herself up and down.

"I c...c...can't...I c...c...can't get enough of this," he said. The first half minute always made him feel like the whole world belonged to him. Leaving his left hand behind his head, he reached up with his right to play a tune on her breast.

"Ahhhh. Mmmm." She sighed gratefully. "Love makes my world go around! And I'm no damsel."

"On ah..nother rr..related note, I can't believe what you said earlier y..you kept Tiliruf's seed from working in all those w...women."

"A few times I did. He's only half fool. And Kodi too with ripe Jonell, both at Meical's bidding."

"Rah..rrreally?"

"Really. But I was beginning to lose patience with Tiliruf. Meical and I fussed about it, because I thought the boy should start dealing with the consequences. Meical never flat out orders me; He's always polite, so I usually do what He says, of course. He said, 'Consider Róssela's hopes for him.' And for her, He knew I'd do anything. I believed she was the most beautiful Human woman ever until Lyndz grew up. Charming and gracious. Not that I'm oblivious either to the poor girls of North Bend; they suffer enough. But it's not a problem I'm meant to fix with a wave of my hand. But I could have fixed it so he'd have to acknowledge a misbegotten child and maybe start behaving himself, and he'd be obliged to provide a good life for the child and whatever poor girl was involved. He does have a decent sense of duty, even though he surely wouldn't Bond her. Anyway, Meical said that wasn't what He wanted for Tiliruf. He wishes to renew that bloodline not weaken it. Of course, He knows I want the same for Tiliruf, but that boy has a lot of growing to do and key choices to make. Now, Kodi was easy, an otherwise good boy *feeling his oats* as you Human men say. I always understood that notion and can't say it was a flaw in my design for Humans. Meical was a heavy part of that design, too, of course, at the Great Molding. Look how much Kodi learned from it and the self-discipline he then developed. He was better prepared when Meical Called him. And Jonell didn't need that. Sweet girl with a sweet heart, just a little too immature at the time. She only thought she knew what she wanted. *I* knew what she wanted. Esseth was perfect for her. I attended their Bonding Ceremony as an old, gray-haired lady. I'd decided they were special to me."

"I'm glad you d..don't have to do that extra ww..work for us, my love. I like what each thump means." He thrust deep. "Gyah!"

"I am the Mother of all."

"And being Dad gets me all egg..excited and hot, knowing I'm doin' that to y..you. Whah..what's this one's name?"

She again moved up and down and squeezed her inner muscles like an Easterner. He liked that. "I imagined you would name him, dear. He's special."

"Oh! He's male this time? Been a ff..few since the last. I already ll..love him, too. Name this one Aronson. No, put the ah..accent in the middle. Arónson, gives it a bit o' flair, and I w..want him to be their first king. You said I could pick him or her. But the ff..first should be a *king* on Meical's world, in His honor. I ww..want to honor Him in that way. And let the buck have black cur...c..c..currrly hair, wet and beeedrazzled when he comes out of the water, and a wild roguish grin."

"You seem to want that on all the males." She chortled. "Going to be hard for the other races to tell them apart."

"That's your prah..prroooblem, not mine. You always fix their looks different in subtle ways. But they miii...might as well all be as good-lookin' as what you're a'lookin' at just now. Whyyy would ya start 'em out the first set all ugly? And anyways I know which is which. Err...puh...put a silver streak in his hair if you like, and mm...make him bigger than the others. If you know what I mean." He reached up now and gripped both her breasts, his thumbs twirling around and over her rigid nipples.

She moaned happily and then chuckled. "They're a huge race anyway, considering. Meical wanted them so. He had several good reasons, and I agreed."

Her next movements on him were sheer delight.

"D...d...daaaAAAaannng! That's so gooood, my anti-damsel. Www..would you make me c..caramel cake for breakfast? Ole Grrr..randma's was real good but ain't as real good as what yours is. And me mum always scorched hers. T..terrrrrible cook."

"That's a most interesting story about my caramel cake I never told you." She then looked at him most seductively and applied some different moves.

"Aayayayaaaaaahh! Ya got me goin' and an untold t..t..taaale besides!"

She sat up with a wink and returned to a slow pelvic rhythm. "Oh, yes. Caramel cake. Actually, your grandmother got her recipe from *her* grandmother, and *I'm* the one who first gave it to *her*. About a hundred years ago."

"No!"

"Yes! Of course, I used to just make it special for the goats before you came along when they'd get a sweet tooth and bleat at my door. But you see, I liked her and went to her Bonding Ceremony guised as one of her girlfriends who couldn't be there. I love Essemarian Bondings. They know how to dance. Westerners don't have rhythm, don't even know what it is!"

"I got rhythm. Dancin' unnnder the stars with you!"

She winked. "Because you've got strong Eastern blood. Stronger than your Nantian, really."

"Ya know, I always th..thought so. It shows in me curly hair!"

"They were writing recipes in a book for her at the reception, and I put mine in it for caramel cake! And so, you see, she used to make it, your grandmother liked it just like you do and copied it for herself and used to make it for you. But it was always *my* recipe."

Aron looked at her with googly eyes. "Thaaa....thaaat's somethin' else! Yur...yurr sex tales get me ah..ah..alll happy!"

"That wasn't a sex tale, silly boy."

"It's a tale yurrr tellin' me while we're goin' at it, so it's a sex tale."

She leaned up a little, and he started humping more rapidly up into her.

"Ohh, oh, oh, sweet Aron!" She let him go at it for a minute until he slowed down. Their mouths met in a tonguey wet kiss. "Mmm. I suppose I will allow him to be first king. Yes, Meical says He's much honored by your designation for Arónson, but that when he chooses finally a consort, she will reign in full measure with him. Females are to have more of their due in the future, and the eldest will inherit the rule, male or female, but the royal house will be forever in your name."

"Ha!" And with that happy affirmation, one last thrust was all it took. Grasping her body tightly to his, he yelled loudly past her ear as his groin burst in a series of throbbing explosions.

She kissed him again and leaned up. "That was quick for you, my dear."

"C..caramel cake did it for me." He sank into the pillow with an ecstatic smile and put his hands behind his head. "Th..thumping Th..thumper makes a Th..thousand and one. Arónson, have my blessings and make it all good. Damn glad I don't have to be sss..subtle with you, V."

"Subtle was never your great quality." She winked.

"Nope. But I w..w..waited years for this. And subtle ain't you either when it comes to this." He then flipped her wildly over and went to her groin with heavy tongue.

"Ahhh...my own Aron. That's always so grand!"

In mere moments she buckled. She erupted in a wild, definitely-not-damsel scream, beating the sheets with her forearms.

He let her settle for a few moments. Though her beautiful full breasts still heaved, and she was still a bit twitchy. He suckily removed his tongue from her caramel spot, got up close to her face and looked down.

"The One knew what the One was doin' when the One made you, woman o' mine. I love you so, Vanayema of the Mold and Mother of my children," the man said without a stammer. Dark eyes glittered on his smiling, brown face.

She reached up and touched his cheek.

"Likewise you, man of mine, sweet Aron!" replied the magic woman, her own eyes full of love.

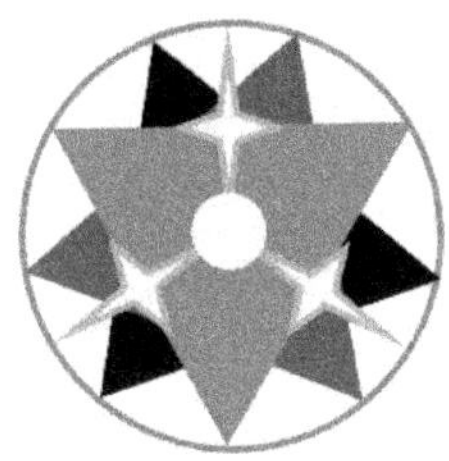

Chapter 25—Morning of Surprises

"Boy, is Kodi ever sleeping late this morning, eh?" Tiliruf's face puckered. "I know the older blokes like to sleep late. And Nikal loves to sleep late when things are peaceful. But that's not like Kodi. He's usually the first one up. Old farm boy instincts. Crack o' dawn."

Only Shane and Lumin heard this.

Lumin whispered. "He wasn't here when I came back."

Shane appeared to be ignoring them. Then his eyes went wide. He had a hard time whispering just then despite the other sleepers. "What did you say? He wasn't here? Oh, my!"

"What's the matter, Shane? I guess he's just tuckered if he went for a long walk in the night, like Lumin said. It's curious, but it's not like he's broken a damned Discipline or something. The stars are incredible here."

Shane glared at him. "Lumin didn't say that. He didn't know where he was."

"You do, eh? Tell us, mate."

Shane said nothing. He got up and paced like Curdoz sometimes did.

Manwul and Hadon walked in with towels around their waists. They'd just taken their morning bathe in the pool.

"What's the matter with Shane?" asked Manwul. They stood there watching him pace.

Tiliruf shrugged.

Hadon and Manwul looked at each other and also shrugged. Everyone thought the world of Shane, but he did have a few indecipherable eccentricities that didn't seem to require too much questioning. They went into their partitioned space to put on clothes and comb out their wet hair.

Shane looked at them and seemed annoyed with himself. "I'm going to swim. Let me be alone in the water for a little before you come out."

"Sure, mate. Whatever you want. I can wait." He then whispered so Manwul and Hadon wouldn't hear. "Lumin took his little bath last night, or rather early this morn...as usual."

Lumin grinned.

"You know I'm surprised you don't need more sleep. Considering all," Tiliruf added.

"Like Kodi might say, I'm always good to go. I love early mornings."

"I thought you like the nights."

"I like them even more, eh?" Lumin whispered back and winked. "And the moons eclipsed last night!"

"Ah, those old romantic notions. Male Solvermoon and female Orohmoon making love."

"It was perfect," said Lumin.

"Only you would know."

Shane paused again as he heard this. Then he walked out.

It wasn't long before Nikal was next to rouse himself. He saw Kodi still snoozing and raised an eyebrow. He walked out into the living area of the pavilion. Lumin, Manwul, and Hadon had left to retrieve hot breakfast foods from the palace. "Kodi sleeps late this morning."

"You noticed, eh?" said Tiliruf, smoking his pipe and still keeping his voice low as the older three gents were still asleep. "Maybe we should wake him up. Lumin said...oh, never mind."

Nikal didn't notice the almost slip-up that might have exposed Lumin's own absence in the night. "No, let him sleep. Maybe he took a hike in the night to look at the stars."

"Actually, that's what I said, too. Shane's all up in *oh's* and *my's* over it. He thinks it's a great sin."

"He doesn't think anything of the sort, Tiliruf. Is he out at the water pool?"

"He wanted some alone time. But he said I could come out after some time had passed, and I'd say it's been a good twenty minutes."

Nikal looked at Tiliruf curiously. He looked back towards the curtain behind which Kodi still slept and raised an eyebrow again. A little higher this time. "I'll go. You stay here."

Tiliruf put on a befuzzled look. He drew several puffs on his pipe.

Nikal stopped first at the privy, then walked to the pool and plunged into the water. He then sat by Shane on the great rock. "You suspect something odd about Kodi sleeping late."

Shane was gazing into the distance. He was not unsmiling. "Rather."

"Well," Nikal said. "I've decided you're the great secret keeper in this bunch. I've got one to share with you."

Shane turned to him. His eyes came into focus. "Certainly, Nikal."

"I believe our Kodi is in love with Princess Ryn. I saw how he looked at her at the reception. And she him. Slipping off every other day or more. Not really telling us where he's going. He always returns with a dreamy sort of boyish grin on his face." He paused and gazed long at Shane who was trying hard to keep a straight face. "And then, as I have noticed, he seeks you out in secret chatter. Do I approach the mark? He was gone most of the night, wasn't he?"

After a long moment, Shane looked away and grinned. "And the moons eclipsed last night. Do you know what they often symbolize in poetry? Think long before you answer."

"I need no time. Kodi and I have spoken of the moons together and explored their meaning because of Solvermoon carved on the Staff. It was after the Installation, and we grew especially close that night. I'm right, am I not? You are giving me my answer. Solvermoon is male and Orohmoon is female, and when they eclipse it symbolizes lovemaking. Yet also, as from the Ancient Book, the stars are for the Etoppsi as they are highest in the sky. The Sky Kings. Solvermoon is for Humans and is closer to Dumhoni and so waxes and wanes in a month, symbolizing our shorter lives. Orohmoon with its long slow orbit is for the long-lived Qeteral."

"You have answered your own questions, my friend. I have said nothing."

Nikal smiled happily. "Kodi sleeps late."

"Kodi sleeps late after a two-moon eclipse. It's cosmic, Nikal! The Guardian's hands are all over this. It's like how you all described that Aron and his Modela..."

Nikal interrupted, "Say instead, that Modela and her Aron."

Shane laughed. "You said there was a great meteor shower at their Bonding Ceremony, as though thousands of bright stars were shooting across the night sky, the most fantastical any of you had ever witnessed or even imagined."

The two men looked at each other with great grins.

"Perhaps a great story is forthcoming, you say. Our Kodi will awaken."

"Our Kodi will awaken, yet remember. I did not say any such thing."

"You are the secret keeper. Kodi's always honest with us anyway. The most honest man alive. He just controls his timing."

"Yes, exactly. Which is why I'm not especially concerned about this little conversation."

The older gents awakened and prepared for the day. Rusty had gone for his morning fly. Kodi still slept. Tiliruf grew more suspicious, though his thoughts didn't remotely approach what Nikal and Shane suspected. They all ate an enormous breakfast with added warm sausages to supplement the bread, nuts, and fruits that the servants always kept resupplied on a sideboard in the pavilion. So far, there were no special plans that day for any of them, though Nikal decided now to see what Olin had been teaching Lumin with a long knife. Having witnessed his shooting, he knew Lumin would be perfectly steady as a bowman. Nikal's military instincts told him the young man was ever as supernatural with that talent as Kodi but wanted to see if he understood defense in a hand-to-hand situation. Those two went outside on the lawn. They practiced for some time. Nikal was pleased. Lumin handled himself with strength, stamina, and some cunning moves.

"Will you work with me with a sword? I really want to handle one!"

"It certainly takes some skill. Maybe when we get back to the ships, I'll have Tiliruf work with you. He's been an excellent teacher for Kodi. Though it is not desired for you to fight at all except as an archer, I think. You will stick close to Kodi or me at all times. You will sleep in the ship's cabin with us. I promised Hurlin the best protection possible. If danger presents itself and we're not present, draw close to Rusty or Stormgale. They will be under orders to fly you away from danger if there is need. And finally, if not them then Tiliruf and the Swordmasters will defend you, along with Nantian knights and some of your own Qeteral defenders. You are much too valuable for us to leave you to your own devices. I know you have a strong and fast body, Lumin, but I don't want you pretending you have your brothers' years of solid training."

"I understand, sir. I am sorry for the added burden."

Nikal smiled. "I'm not. I think it's good you're going. Kodi knows what he's doing. And we will work on your training. Now. Is there other magic you have as a Qeteral that perhaps we haven't witnessed?"

"I can control whole flocks of birds. Most Qeteral can only sing to one creature at a time."

Nikal couldn't really envision where such a Gift could be helpful in Lumin's self-defense, but he nodded and winked. "Splendid. I've not heard you sing magically before, only in normal tongue when you try to pick up on Manwul's soldier tunes at our campfire."

Lumin then produced the most beautiful tone Nikal had ever heard come from a male Qeteral. As he listened to the magical song, his soul was moved. And then two, ten, thirty birds of all kinds and colors, were drawn from all around the trees surrounding the hollow and began flying around the two of them in a tight circle like a whirlwind. And upon a new note off Lumin's tongue they all landed at his feet. He stopped his music, and then each and every bird began to trill and chatter in its own unique call, performing an avian symphony to the one who called them.

Nikal smiled hugely as he witnessed this most incredible sight. It was like something out of a children's storybook. Then Lumin raised his hands, and they all flew away back to the trees. Nikal had a sudden, interesting thought. Would Lumin be amenable? It had nothing to do with children's stories.

"I know it is most unusual, but could you call birds to attack in your defense should the need arise? Even as distraction it could prove useful."

Lumin's face turned to a puzzle, but then he raised his eyebrow. "I think that I could. But...but I don't think it is something I could practice in advance of such a need, sir."

"I understand you would care for the welfare of the creatures, as that is second nature to your kind, but Myghal wishes for your safety above theirs. Remember, He is the Taxiarch. He leads in a Cosmic War against the evils of the universe, as the One has designated. You are of the Divine Mold, descended from the First Pair, Modelo and Modela, and shaped by the Mind of the One and of Myghal. The birds were made by the World Gods to enhance the beauty of Dumhoni. Given life, yes, by the One, they are nevertheless lesser creatures than yourself. And so, you must use them to fight for you if necessary. Just as the Matriarch your mother knew many ravens would die on the dangerous journeys to your kin in the South to send messages, she nevertheless called them to her greater needs."

Lumin considered these words and then nodded. "I can do it, sir."

Nikal was pleased. He then considered Lumin's perfect, half-clothed manly form.

"When we get to the ships, I'm giving you Human man's clothes. They will better protect that pretty skin of yours. Yours is not a body on which anyone would like to see scars."

"Eh? Can I keep them afterwards?" Lumin was thrilled. "To go with my boots, you know! I want a long-sleeved linen shirt, white, with the funny *round* buttons, and a leather vest with pockets, and thick-woven trousers! And a belt with a big silver buckle!"

Nikal laughed hugely. "I'll make it happen, my young friend. You're slightly larger than Kodi, and I think you'd fit best in some of my own. And a silver buckle with an engraved Nantian seagull from me to you. But often on the ships the sailors are half-bared still if the sea spray isn't too cold. You're nearly impervious to temperature extremes anyway, so while we sail on peaceful days you can keep showing off that excellent physique."

Kodi awakened. He sat up. He put on a big grin. Then he noticed Tiliruf staring at him as he sat on Nikal's bed.

"'Bout time, eh?"

"What time is it?"

"Four hours past dawn. Why the big smile? Good dreams?"

"You could say that. I'm starving."

Ignoring Tiliruf, he walked out to the sideboard and gorged himself on cold sausages and bread. Everyone else was gone by now, off on his own venture. He didn't speak to Tiliruf, who sat in a chair. When he was finished eating, he finally said, "Takin' a bath. Let me be alone for a bit."

"Seems to be the order of the day. I took mine already anyways, when Shane and Nikal finally let me."

Kodi wasn't paying attention. He cast off his night pant in the living area and marched out.

Eh! Must have been a damned good dream.

"Where's Shane?" Kodi asked when he returned.

"Probably visiting Healer Solone."

Kodi retreated behind the curtain. He made up a paste with salt and soda and brushed his teeth. He rinsed with strong mint water. He found a dressier, heavy-woven linen Qeteral pant, worn for more refined occasions. He put on a Qeteral open-fronted vest, also meant of course for dinners or meetings at the palace. It was cream, embroidered with green and gold threads. He put on the sandals. He then peered in a tall looking-glass and grinned at the reflection. He shook out his head, ran fingers through his hair that he'd mostly dried with towels and made his natural dark waves re-form properly around his face. He had freshly shaved at the pool. She liked his Human scruff, but today he needed to appear as much Qeteral as he could. And scruff had to start somewhere. He wore Lumin's necklace. It seemed to crown his appearance: like a Prince of Ulakel.

When he came out again from behind his curtained partition, Tiliruf puckered at his vest. "Lookin' right smart. Something special going on at the palace?"

"Will be shortly." Kodi winked at him and started to exit the pavilion.

"Would you want me to come along?"

"Not yet." He then paused and turned to Tiliruf and looked him in the face. "Listen, buddy. I'll be back as soon as I can, and I'll tell you. I promise. But some other people have the right to know first. I need to find Idamé. Don't think I mean anything by it. You're my bud, and you're gonna know real soon."

He grinned and winked again and raced out of the pavilion.

Tiliruf came to the tent flap and watched in stunned curiosity as his friend ran out of the hollow.

Idamé? Whatever the heck for?

Just before the running Kodi got to the edge of the village, to his surprise there before him walking briskly his way was none other than the first object of his day's quest. He yelled in delighted greeting.

As they stood facing each other, her eyes wide and the most unusual look on her face, Idamé spoke. "Kodi! I slept very late you see, but I must tell you something! I came right away. It's much too important to put off! I had a dream last night; I must tell you of it!"

"You mean a Vision, don't you! Meical gave you a Vision!"

She looked all around making sure no one was near to overhear.

"Yes, Kodi!" she said almost breathlessly. "And I don't know why I didn't see it before!"

Kodi grinned hugely. "I know just what you dreamed, dear lady!"

"It's true?" She stared with both eyebrows up. "Oh, Kodi! You're in love with her! With the Princess Ryn! But Kodi I want to let you know, my Vision made it plain that she is very much in love with you, too!"

Kodi laughed loudly. He looked at her goodly face and laughed again. "You're behind the times, Mother Idamé, by a good spell. Your Vision wasn't of a *future* moment."

"What? But Kodi, you must take these things slowly! She's a princess! She's a Qeteral! Royals are the worst! I thought I should warn you, and I want to help you with this if I can."

Kodi laughed and laughed. And laughed. And though Idamé couldn't understand what he was being so silly about, his laugh was so infectious, she herself began to chuckle. "Kodi. You need to be more serious about this. Now, really. I've thought of a plan. Together, you and I will go speak with the Matriarch. You must first get her permission to court the lady Ryn..."

Kodi's heehaw interrupted her discourse. Finally, "Oh, Mother Idamé! I love you so! But like I said, you're behind the times. We're waaay past the courting phase, you see! Way, way past."

He winked at her with a big, expressive double wink and created a Manwulish rogue grin. "Way past."

Her eyes turned into saucers and her eyebrows went to her hairline. "KODI!" She turned beet red, and her jaw dropped to complete her utterly over-stunned look.

"Er..as of last night." He double-winked again. "But I ain't giving you the details. A mother never needs to hear about such things."

He could hardly control his laughter. Finally, he grabbed her up in an enormous bear hug. As he held her, though her eyebrows stayed way high, she smiled. And then she too began to laugh. She pushed him back and held his shoulders, and then she drew him back to hug him again. "Oh, Kodi! My dear sweet one, like a son to me! You've found her! The love of your life!"

Her chubby body shook, and she began to cry enormous tears. And then Kodi, overcome by her joy for him, found that tears were also falling from his eyes. They hugged ever so tightly as he spoke in her ear. "But you *are* going to help. I was coming to find you first! Yes, the first part of your plan is right. We're going to the Matriarch, you and I, together. Right now. Right now!"

"Yes," she stood back and smiled. "Oh! But what if she's not alone in her study?"

"I don't care who's there! Come on!"

He grabbed her hand and together they walked and talked their way to the palace.

"... and if I have any say in the matter, you're going to be the one to Bond us."

"Oh, Kodi! I so want to!" She beamed. "But without my old Gift, I don't know if I really have the right credentials! I know I promised I'd do Hadon's for him, but I've often wondered if I really could, you see!"

"Credentials! Mother. The Guardian gave you a Vision, didn't He? And I want you to sing the Song! I want it bad, and I bet they don't even know it here, because it was meant for Humans, and I'm Human, and Ryn's part so, and she'll love it."

She started with the happy tears again, though she didn't lose control. "I will sing the Song for you, dear. Of course, I will."

They arrived at the doors. When Kodi asked to see the Matriarch, the servant said, "She has gathered a few of the ladies for an impromptu brunch, Lord Kodi. On the verandah by the back garden. Mother Idamé, we tried to find you, as you were invited, but we could not discover where you went to."

"Excellent," said Kodi. "Take us there, please."

"It was meant only for the ladies," said the servant. Yet she quickly reconsidered. "Of course, Lord Kodi. She would never deny your request. I'm sure they will all be delighted to have you join them."

When they arrived at the rear patio, they discovered not just a few, but quite a number of ladies, and Rainwing, too. Long tables were set in the form of a square, a near square, as one of the lengths was shorter than the rest, and so there was an open space by which the servants could enter the little area and serve. Those present included Lady Mishoo, Halta, Frith, Ulna, Maru, Rainwing as stated on a larger stool to accommodate her size, though her legs were definitely full under the table, the elderly former Matriarch, and the High Princess Linea, and 'Grandma' Manoo, along with a few others Kodi did not know.

Idamé whispered. "They are Matrimonials and scholars I met recently. Oh, my!"

There was Lyndz who beamed at him when she saw him. She sat beside the Matriarch on one side.

And the Princess Ryn, who sat beside the queen on the other.

He gazed into Ryn's face from the distance, and she gazed back and smiled a lovely smile. She nodded almost imperceptibly. And was that a wink?

"Kodi!" spoke the Matriarch who stood. They all stood. "How lovely to see you! Mother Idamé, there is a chair for you, dear. The servants shall make a space for you too, Kodi. Give them but a moment."

"I don't need a chair, Madam. Thank you ever so kindly. I intend only to stay for a little. May Idamé and I come into the square as to address you?"

The Matriarch tilted her head a little at the oddity, but nevertheless she replied. "Certainly, Brother of Myghal. We are ever happy to receive words from you. Sit, everyone."

Kodi held still to Idamé's hand. It trembled, yet he squeezed it with his big brown sturdy one and brought her into the middle of the square where together they faced the queen. The servants retreated out of the inner square and to the rear.

The Matriarch then lifted her punch glass and drank. The rest did likewise. She then nodded to Kodi.

Nor did he lose a beat. Ryn had said to him the night before, *Be bold, my dear. With my mother that is always best.*

He bowed first to Ryn, which caused Gwyn to raise a slight eyebrow. And then he bowed deeply and handsomely to her.

"Matriarch of Ulakel, Gwyn of the Qeteral, Myghal's Blessings ever be upon you."

She nodded. "Thank you, Brother of Myghal."

"Idamé stands with me as like a parent, like a mother to offer blessing to me in my own mother's absence." He looked warmly then into Idamé's face and lifted her hand to his lips to kiss it. He then indicated for her to stand slightly away, and he stood center stage.

Lyndz' eyes became saucers. *OH...MY...STARS!* She kept her silent scream to herself. She turned her eyes ever so slightly as to see the princess on the other side of the queen, and found she bore the beamiest smile she'd ever seen on the young lady, her eyes fixed upon her twin brother. *OH, MY STARS! KODI FOTHEMRY! OH, MY STARS!* She looked at Kodi. Was that the quickest side eye in her own direction and the most imperceptible wink?

"I have come to ask your gracious permission to Bond your daughter, the Princess Ryn. As soon as may be before I leave on the quest. Ryn and I, by Myghal's great blessing, have been brought together and hold the deepest love and affection for one another."

He then went to one knee, folded an arm before himself like a knight to his king, and lowered his head.

There could be heard the intake of female breath around the entire square. In the subsequent silence, only the many birds of the garden could be heard.

The Matriarch slowly stood, though no one else dared move. She stared wide-eyed at the bowed Kodi for a long moment. She turned to her daughter, who then stood and faced her mother. She, too, bowed.

"It is as he said, Mother." Ryn bowed again.

After another long moment, the Matriarch spoke. "I take it then you have been spending some time these last two weeks with Kodi?"

"Yes, Mother. We have spent many long hours together. Always at my personal invitation."

Gwyn nodded. "I do not know of a certainty that this is wisdom, daughter. Are you so sure this is the right step to be taken at this anxious moment of our country's need?"

"The moment is notably an anxious one, Mother, yet it is not without hope. Myghal Himself has, in symbol, come into our midst in the form of Kodi of Solanto, His own Voice, His own Claimed Brother whom He has blessed and on whom He has bestowed all talent and courage...and joy. Joy which you have seen in Kodi's good face. Which I have seen. Which I cherish and always will. Take heart, then, Mother, that the Will of the Divine is at work. His own Brother kneels before you. Yet...it would be most disrespectful not to make plain the whole matter. I..."

"Ryn carries my seed, Madam," Kodi announced clearly and with very Qeteral-like manly claim.

Though he kept his head bowed, Lyndz noticed he wore a caddish half-smile.

There was uttermost astonishment displayed by many exclamations around the tables. The servants were in a chatter.

Gwyn's eyes went wide, and she took in a deep breath. She looked from Kodi to her daughter, "Do you say so, Ryn!"

"Yes, Mother. Let all here be witness to the truth. I do. And it makes me so happy. Will you please share in our joy, Mother? And at his sweet, love-filled, and bold request, I have chosen to conceive. At the proper time, a grandchild will be born to you. Let that knowledge be the strong symbol for you of the hope that it is."

All this time, Lyndz' jaw was dropped, her eyes wide, looking first to Kodi, then to Ryn, back to Kodi, then to the Matriarch, then to Mother Idamé (who was dabbing tears), to Rainwing who was looking just as astonished as she, back to Ryn, back to Kodi, back to the Matriarch...

...whose reply was generally anticipated now by all present, as there were no words left to be spoken by anyone else.

Finally, Gwyn turned to Kodi, still kneeling, his head still bowed in respect.

"Stand, Lord Kodi."

Kodi stood tall and looked straight at the Matriarch, his cocky half-smile gone, his face now displaying the most handsome sternness Lyndz had ever beheld on him. Royal as a prince, king even, wisdom of a sage, confident, and father to be. And Lyndz knew, that he knew, there was only one conceivable reply that could come forth from the tongue of the stately queen before him.

"Come," said Gwyn.

Kodi stepped to the table before her.

"Ryn, give me your hand," she said.

Ryn came close and put her hand into her mother's.

"Kodi, give me your hand."

Reaching partway across the table, Kodi put his own into the queen's other hand.

"I hereby grant consent for my daughter, the High Princess Ryn, to Bond his Lordship, Kodi of Solanto, Brother of Myghal. May the Divine shower His great blessings upon their union."

She then placed Ryn's hand into that of Kodi's.

"Step back, Matriarch," said Kodi with a hint of smile. "If you will, please, Madam."

Gwyn put on an unusual pucker, but she granted Kodi's request and stepped back.

Without letting go of Ryn's hand, Kodi leaped over the table, over the dishes, over the glasses, with perfect muscular grace and instantly drew Ryn to his body in powerful embrace and kissed her on the lips with the most passionate kiss.

"Oh, Kodi!" Lyndz exclaimed loudly and stood, no longer able to contain her emotion.

With that, there was the sound of many voices, the scrape of chairs on the stone of the patio, and then somebody clapped, and then somebody else clapped, and suddenly all stood and were applauding.

Nearly all, for there were two women who could only dab at great tears, Idamé and Grandma Manoo.

Then, suddenly, there was a change in the sunlight. The applause stopped. The lovers paused in their kiss. All eyes were drawn to the sky.

Like a window of a different shade of blue, surrounded by rays of light and white cloud, from it descended an enormous, winged creature, a scarlet bird with fancy crest and a long, flowing-feathered double tail. In its large beak it carried a draping thing, a shawl of many colors. They all stood in astonishment as it swept the airs around the luncheon setting. It then fluttered with its great wings above none other than Mother Idamé. The shawl dropped lightly around her shoulders. Then the bird produced a powerful trill, flew high and disappeared into the other-blue window. The normal light of the sun returned, and all stared at the stunned Matrimonial.

"It's the one my grandmother made!" She whooped. All tears gone, she looked around at the crowd staring at her...

...and she saw it. There, above Kodi with his arms still around Ryn, it shone bright.

"It's there! It's there! Oh, my! Oh, Kodi! Oh Ryn! It's there, it's there!"

And that was not all.

"Look at it!" said one of several Qeteral Bondswomen who were present. She was pointing.

"She's right!" said one of the others.

"The brightest I've ever seen!" said a third.

"Myghal on High," said Bondswoman Vitalle. "An Aura! The high favor of Myghal is upon their union! Let there be no doubt, Madam Matriarch! He has favored them in holy union!"

Nor was there ever any doubt who saw it first.

"Oh, Mother!" yelled Lyndz. "It's back! It's back! Your Gift is back!"

She raced around the tables, Maru and Ulna, too. They ran through the little separation between the tables and overcame her with hugs and kisses.

All the other men had returned to the pavilion by now. Though Lumin wasn't among them, as a servant had come to fetch him about a half-hour ago. He was wanted at the palace. The rest now intended to eat a lunch and then go to the village swimming place.

"Kodi went to the palace, did he?" asked Shane of Tiliruf.

"I keep telling you he ran there, eh? Ran!"

"I imagine he was in a hurry," said Nikal with a smile on his face.

Tiliruf couldn't contain himself anymore. "WHAT DO YOU BLOKES KNOW THAT I DON'T!"

"Calm your mind, Tiliruf. We actually *know* nothing. Though we have a suspicion or two. You said he promised to come back and tell you as soon as may be, so let the truth come about on his own good timing, shall we?"

"This is making me crazy."

They heard voices. A cacophony of female voices. Descending the path into the hollow were the Human women, Rainwing, Kodi and...

"The princess, eh?" The three men stared. "Spikeshafts and blazes! Kodi's holding her hand!"

He looked at Nikal and Shane who were grinning from ear to ear. Manwul, Hadon, Curdoz, Deens, Findun, and Rusty all came out of the pavilion at the sound of the female voices. They found themselves almost forming a line as the group approached, Kodi leading, with Ryn's hand in his.

Tiliruf's jaw, his eyes, his eyebrows were all mimicking those of Idamé and then Lyndz only an hour before.

Kodi's grin was magnificent. Ryn's smile was extraordinary. At that moment there was not a more handsome couple standing side-by-side and hand-in-hand in all Dumhoni, possibly in all its history.

Kodi spoke. "My friends, my great friends, I wish to introduce you to my newly betrothed life-mate."

There was a long pause. Tiliruf continued to gape.

"This is most excellent news, my brother!" proclaimed Nikal. "I was beginning to guess. Congratulations, Princess Ryn. What great joy you bring to Kodi and by extension to us all."

"Congratulations," said Manwul and Hadon together.

"Most excellent news, son," said Curdoz. "I must admit as did Nikal that I was beginning to suspect something on the order."

More congratulations were offered by Rusty, Deens, Findun and Shane.

Shane, smiling, added, "I admit I knew a little more."

Kodi reached out and put his hand on Shane's shoulder. He used a quiet and personal voice. "Only thirteen, fourteen days? But it was my happiest journey. And you were my confidante, Shane. You steadied me and gave me courage along the way. You and Nikal will stand with me."

Shane nodded. Replying with words was unnecessary, but he was very moved.

Kodi then turned to Tiliruf with a great grin. This was met with a most weird rascally smile on his friend's freckled face. "Will you stand with Nikal and Shane at my side, great buddy? Ryn's brothers will be standing with her. The Bonding Ceremony is in three days. Idamé's doing it."

"Eh? Blazes, Kodi! I hardly know what to say!"

"That's rare."

"Shut up, Hadon. Kodi, mate, I have never been so surprised about a surprise in all my whole life! It's the greatest honor ever to stand with you! It always has been and will be in three days."

"There's something else you all need to know," said Lyndz, beaming.

It was as though none of the men had yet noticed that someone was being hidden behind the massive Rainwing.

The female Etoppsis, a great smile on her furred face, something they almost never saw, then stepped aside, revealing Mother Idamé.

Not all the men there understood the significance of what they were seeing just then, but some—those who had traveled to Modela's Island—knew.

Curdoz exclaimed and walked over to her. He looked with shock into her face. He then lifted the end of the shawl. "It's the one your grandmother made for you! Ida!"

"She sent it back to me, Curdoz! Modela! She sent it back!"

"And her Gift, Curdoz," said Lyndz softly who walked up and put her hand on Curdoz' arm. "She proclaimed the Aura over Kodi and Ryn. But an hour ago."

Curdoz looked around at the women and all their smiling faces. Then he looked back at Idamé, shock still on his face. "Describe it, dear Ida! Tell us all!"

There was much coming and going in the early afternoon. Kodi and Ryn went on a walk together in the fields and returned to the pavilion after about two hours, at which point she returned to the palace. The Matriarch wished to have private conversation with her daughter, and then all the females were going to celebrate with her into the night in the palace garden. Kodi would remain one more night with the men, and they celebrated, too. Much mead was consumed and most got quite tipsy, the first time they'd allowed themselves such freedom, but no Qeteral aside from Lumin interrupted their fun. They swam, played games, and sang around a campfire. Kodi told them tidbits about his days with Ryn and even a little about the magic of the Diamond Pool that previous night. He described the setting and somewhat of the magic, but for now his emotions held close to a vision of Ryn in his mind, and he was not going to elaborate. At a later point Kodi did share with Shane a little regarding the evolution of his thinking since he was a boy. It seemed important to him to share it, and the Healer would write this in his journal:

...and this mindset was not unique, for there are many I know like him. Early days of boyhood bawdy talks around campfires and male minds often focused on sexual fantasy, experience with a willing girl or two, but a growing respect for women leading the young man out of earlier self-centered desire.

Kodi was that way. Like others of his young Felto friends he did indulge himself. Once. He hesitates to use the word considering how willingly he gave in to her, but I would call it 'seduction' on her part, and her intent was obviously entrapment. It scared him when he realized this, broke it off, and his thinking shifted. What helped in Kodi's case was a father whose devotion to his mother served as an example, and he realized he wanted that more than he wanted to play around. Even so, though he was then determined to be, in his words, 'a monogamous good boy' and harness himself until he committed to a life-mate, he admitted he still had privileged thinking and partly objectified this imaginary life-mate: she would satisfy his desires, dote on him, and raise a family to him. He would remain the center around which all revolved. This is common, as I have described elsewhere, of male mentality in the Western kingdoms. He told me he knew early on this was not right thinking, that it reflected the chauvinism shared among some of his Felto friends. He fought it, and yet it still colored the image he had of what it meant to have a wife. But his experiences on the journey grew him, and when he met Ryn, he came into full maturity. Falling in love is often the catalyst that redefines a man.

Their courtship was short, though concentrated in many hours together. It was plain Ryn knew what she wanted. She initiated and directed the courtship. And to him she was much too wonderful to objectify. She would not be a mere 'consort.' She would be his equal. It makes sense to me that a life-mate for Kodi would turn out to be the highest royal princess in all Dumhoni. And their bonding, of course, was of an Aura and was precisely what the Guardian wanted—for both of them. He didn't do it just for His favored brother Kodi. He did it for Ryn, too.

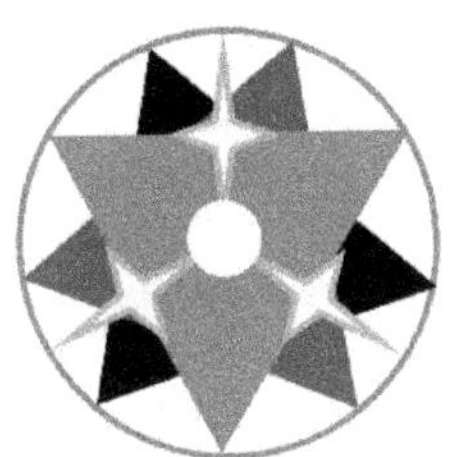

Chapter 26—The Hunt

"You're actually going, Curdoz?" asked Tiliruf. "It doesn't seem your cup of tea, eh?"

"It isn't, but I'm going as Shane's companion. I will not be hunting, as I told him. He says I can be his assistant. He and I have some things to discuss as we walk to the fields and await the deer to come out for their evening grazing. Considering your own history, I wouldn't say deer hunting is your cup of tea, either, city boy son of Genehbro."

"I will, though. And since you bring up my House, my forebears used to hunt game in the reserves of western Lorinth and in the forests of Lintiri, and so why shouldn't I give it a try? I'm excellent with a bow."

"You are not excellent with a bow," said Kodi with a laugh. "You are mediocre with a bow. There isn't a boy over thirteen in Felto who couldn't beat you in a tournament."

Tiliruf put on an annoyed expression. "What's the purpose of this 'tradition,' anyways?"

Manwul answered. "Male members of the betrothed's families, or of their close friends, are meant to bond in companionship as a symbol of the new connection."

Tiliruf looked aghast. "You mean Hurlin's going?"

"I am his companion," said Nikal, putting on his boots. "Hakonn and his father the old Patriarch are going. I wish you to pair up with Olin."

"Why not Lumin?"

"Kodi and Lumin chose each other."

"Sure did," said Kodi, unconcerned. He was examining his bow and quiver of arrows that Nikal had given him. "He's my own little brother now. Er...even if he is older by five years...and a size bigger. Anyway, we're stickin' close."

"It isn't fair."

"Kodi gets first choice," said Hadon. "And you can't have Manwul, so don't even think about it."

"And you can't have Hadon," added Manwul. Manwul reached behind his buddy and wrapped his arm around his neck. "So don't even think about it."

"You and Shane and I are Kodi's chosen witnesses at the Bonding," added Nikal, explaining further his reasoning, "Shane and Curdoz have things they want to talk about. So I see it as our duty to pair up with the brothers. You can have Hurlin, then. I'll trade."

Tiliruf's eyes went wide. "Er...Olin's fine by me. Perfectly fine. He just hardly ever says anything."

"And sometimes you talk too readily, so it's an excellent match."

"There is more to the competition, actually," said Shane, interrupting a round of laughter. "The man who downs the largest buck is to craft a song and sing it at the Bonding Ceremony in the couple's honor."

"Oh, that's excellent!" said Hadon. "I'm great at verse."

"Comic verse," said Manwul with a chuckle. "*Ole rooster looked around the pen and peckered the lazy, fattest hen. The chicken sat and spread her legs and laid about a dozen eggs*. Shall I go on?"

They all heehawed.

"I promise," said Hadon, also laughing, "I promise I can do much better! Certainly so for Kodi and Ryn."

Flamefur, Deens, and Findun would not be participating. Rusty was off delivering supplies to the ships. The Scribes were spending the afternoon writing in the palace library. They had no interest and zero skill for hunting.

It wasn't long before the Qeteral men arrived, along with a coterie of male servants bearing food provisions and hunting gear for all. Kodi was the only one of the Human men who typically carried a bow, the one given him by Nikal, though some had such gear back on the ships. The Humans genuflected to the former Patriarch. He bore a smile, and aside from the servants he was the only one besides Curdoz who donned a shirt. He would not have a great many more years before he danced the stars, but even into their last decade of life Qeteral still had energy, including those like himself who had grown heavy.

Hakonn's face bore its typical dispassionate expression, though he was engaging during the greetings.

Hurlin's expression was stony. He was there only because of the tradition of the Bonding Hunt and for his sister's sake. Nevertheless, he returned a jovial greeting from Kodi with a decently respectful nod, nodded also to Curdoz, but then he positioned himself within Nikal's space and spoke almost solely to him the rest of the day, aside from his Qeteral family and the servants.

Olin was reasonably cheerful. Tiliruf would come to appreciate him more than he expected.

Lumin, of course, displayed enthusiasm, and he and Kodi kept calling each other 'brother.' It was as if those two were the ones being Bonded, and their handgrips and shoulder bumps were ever more commonplace, truly as if they had grown up in the same household.

They were also the best bowmen.

They marched in the pairs appointed, and there was much conversation. There was some mixing but mostly when the old Patriarch wished it. He engaged in polite tit-for-tat with each of the Humans. He especially wished to speak with Curdoz and...Tiliruf.

"I never met your great-grandfather, Zarelio. Though I sent him one or two letters bearing formalities."

"I've seen them, sir," said Tiliruf as they walked. To him the Patriarch spoke, well, patriarchal. Tiliruf was uncomfortable but tried his best to bear himself as nobly as he could. "They are preserved in the palace records of Zarelio's reign."

"You are a scholar of imperial history Curdoz tells me."

"Most of my studies focused on the history of Tirilorin and the emperors. That is true. I also studied the Ralsheen language, and the evolution of the Anterianhi tongue. I also quite like botany."

The Patriarch continued to engage him for a quarter hour. But his final words were well beyond Tiliruf's expectations, and he wasn't sure how to take them.

"Greatness still lies in the House of Terianh, I see. And it is plain your family is still revered in Tirilorin as it is here."

Tiliruf blinked, but shoved emotion away. "You are gracious. My father uses his position and wealth always to the benefit of the city and the people. He is certainly well-respected."

"Yes. But it is of you that I am speaking, Lord Tiliruf. The blood is there. It is through you that greatness will return to your House. I will have you foremost in my thoughts when you all leave here."

Again, Tiliruf blinked. He forced a gracious smile. "Then let us hope your faith in me is well-founded, m'lord."

He was exponentially relieved when Olin returned to walk at his side.

The group paused halfway to their destination and rested by a stream. The servants introduced the food provisions, and they all ate in little groups. The conversation was merry and relaxed. Nikal and Kodi sat shoulder to shoulder under the bole of a large tree, Lumin and Tiliruf in front of them, and Tiliruf was able to set aside his ruminations of his conversation with the Patriarch. Nikal threw off his boots and socks to cool his toes and drank from a water bottle. Tiliruf did likewise. There was much laughter as they ate and talked.

Tiliruf lit his pipe after lunch.

"You haven't smoked, Kodi, since we came to Ulakel. Relax and share mine, eh?"

"Nah. I might when we get back to the ship though. I don't want to smell of it for Ryn's sake. She says I smell clovey and likes it."

"Clovey? She hasn't got a good whiff of you all sweaty, has she?"

Lumin chuckled.

"It's probably just the soaps they give us here." Kodi winked.

"I'm beginning to understand your recent pattern of constant bathing here," said Nikal.

Kodi winked again. "Yeah. But she don't care if I'm sweaty, either. Lucky for me."

"I'll try it, Tiliruf," said Lumin.

"No," said Nikal with a firm eyebrow when Tiliruf started to hand the pipe over to him. "It isn't Qeteral, and you know it. Don't overdo your newfound sense of Human independence while your brothers and grandfather are so near. And I don't want to be on the receiving end of another diatribe from your eldest brother."

"Yes, sir." Lumin nodded respectfully. He had in a way, just like all the rest of them, submitted to Nikal's overarching authority when he determined to go with them on the voyage, and that relationship had already begun. "I'm intrigued, though."

"It's relaxing," admitted Tiliruf. "You get a kind of calming in your head."

"Who else does it besides Curdoz?"

"Nikal and I both," said Kodi. "But not really so often as they. Curdoz is one of the few Order Members you'd ever see smoking. It's really against their Disciplines to smoke, but Curdoz bucks it, 'cause he started it up when he was a farm boy and can't give it up even if he tried. He can get away with it since he's a Sage, although Healer Labert's another. You haven't met him yet. It's kind of addicting. Shane, Manwul, and Hadon don't care for it. Shane's really quite opposed to it, but he doesn't stop any of us. He thinks it's bad to breathe smoke down your lungs and says it's not natural. And it does make you smell bad to the ladies. Smells better than the ship, though, I can tell you that. Nikal runs a clean ship, but it's not the most pleasant place to live. Honestly glad Rusty and Stormy smell so good to kind of cover up the worst. Even if it does make you feel a little horsey as you relax into their scent in the evening. Won't be long before they go rutty again, and it's even stronger. And then it gives you bucky dreams, but I'm not complaining."

Even Nikal laughed.

"Lumin, eh? Do Qeteral get bucky dreams?"

"Well...this one does."

There were more chuckles.

As evening approached, the group arrived at a great grassy land, mostly open, though there were small copses scattered everywhere. It went on for miles, and the low profile of the distant mountains could be seen. Summer wildflowers, mostly goldenrods and purple asters, created a tranquil scene. They broke into their pairs and headed for hiding places to await the approach of the promised herds.

As Tiliruf and Olin marched towards their chosen copse, Tiliruf had a sudden awful thought.

"Olin! Do we have to carry our catch home on our shoulders?" He couldn't bear the thought.

"No, Tiliruf." Olin actually laughed. "There are others who will be driving pony carts this way tonight. They will haul it all back to the palace for the cooks to prepare for the Bonding feast. It is all well organized, I assure you. Be at ease. But, if like me, you do not have the remotest desire to prepare and sing a song..."

Tiliruf laughed. He was glad Olin felt the same way he did. "Don't aim for the biggest buck I sight."

"And we help each other, you see. It sometimes takes more than one arrow to kill it, unless your shot is especially lucky, and we must follow it until the beast drops from blood loss and weakness in order not to lose track of it."

"I see."

"It is often perceived as a courtesy to allow the bridegroom and his chosen companion to be the ones to find the largest buck. But don't underestimate Great-Grandfather. He has always been competitive in the hunts."

"Your great-grandfather..." Tiliruf began but then went silent.

Olin raised an eyebrow. "Pray tell, Tiliruf. I am your friend."

Tiliruf raised his own eyebrow and nodded. "Thank you, Olin! I admit to being a little troubled, eh? It just appears to me that he, and your mother, too, envision a particular future around me. It makes me uncomfortable."

Olin nodded. "Tiliruf, many Qeteral wish for a renewed imperium. Great-Grandfather has many regrets having not stood strong with Zarelio. But he nor Mother can foresee the future any more than anyone else. I apologize for the discomfort they may cause you. Tiliruf, only Myghal can possibly see so far, and maybe not even He. I think I adhere to Curdoz' interpretations rather than the conservative Qeteral viewpoint. I would urge you not to dwell on others' thoughts on this matter. You must focus on the present. The war must be won. It is the only matter any of us should be considering these days. Do your part as friend to the others and continue your efforts as a great Swordmaster."

"Thank you. I feel as though they believe the only way in which Qeteral and Humans will return to a friendly and open engagement with one another is if an emperor sits on the throne in Tirilorin."

"It is a belief some have. It is based, as you may know, on the Guardian having created the imperium and having the Qeteral ally with its emperors. The relationship, then, was with the emperors. And so, admittedly, it is likely the easiest way forward from a political standpoint, particularly for our noble families, many of which are very conservative, to agree to a renewal in the relationship. But if you Human visitors have taught me anything, it is that it does not have to be the only way forward. Your father will not bond again—Nikal made mention Genehbro's union with your mother was an Aura Bond, of which I am not surprised—and so you are the last of the House of Terianh. Your father can have no more children. I now see that it indeed is a great burden for you. I truly wish I could remove the burden. You struggle with it more than I understood before. And coming here, Tiliruf, I realize has added to your burden. As a descendant of Velus, I do understand the burdens of a royal house, that's for certain."

"Yes, you do. I am grateful for your words and understanding."

"I would say one thing to you, however. Being a son of Terianh does have great meaning. You should not discard the pride in it."

"Terianh certainly has great meaning for me. I do, in my way, try to honor his history. I am probably not so good at it, but I do revere him."

"I believe you. Just your willingness to come to Ulakel is proof of it. The nobles who have entertained you at their estates have said good things to my mother. Admittedly those few are of more progressive views, but they have influence with the rest. And we, too, are honored you came."

"Your elder brother isn't."

Olin breathed deeply before replying. "Your Human honesty is striking. I am not bothered by it. Tiliruf, our father's untimely death affected Hurlin more than you realize. But my brother is a good man and can be gracious and kingly. And he has more Human in him, well, I do too, than you might think. We are flawed. I do not mean it that Humans are flawed, but rather that we do not always make effort to discover what being of Human blood means for us. The balance, that is."

"I say you try harder to balance than he does."

"I am not going to say that is wrong. But, look at the way he honors Nikal."

"Oh, so you believe he is learning—about himself—by way of Nikal."

"I believed it would happen. Yes. So, I think there is hope there. Hope that Hurlin will someday find the balance I speak about. It only saddens me that Nikal must leave us so soon."

Tiliruf nodded. "And for yourself?"

"It has meant a great deal to me that you all have come. More than I anticipated. You quickly dispelled any wariness I had. I am sorry he..."

"Don't apologize for Hurlin. I realize I don't need it. Your words have caused me to see much more."

"Oh, but for his slight of you at our first meeting is what I meant. It was his failure, and he used you, Tiliruf, as his excuse to create an almost immediate distance to you Humans. He expressed some shame to me for it afterwards. But I knew you were honoring us by wearing your eagle symbols."

"My father counselled it. But I lost the Eagle Sword to gain the Staff, or I would have had that, too." Tiliruf said this with sadness.

Olin paused, then said, "We are grateful for all the sacrifices made in order for the Staff to be returned, yet we sympathize for the loss."

"So, you talk to Hurlin about some of these things?"

"There is nothing we don't talk about. Though have no fears I will relay your thoughts regarding him. I keep a few secrets. But we share a set of rooms. We haven't parted since I was born less than two years after he was. Lumin has his own rooms. He much prefers having his own space and is several years behind us anyway. Hurlin and I are close."

"Does he ever laugh?"

Olin laughed. "Certainly, he laughs! And we have a coterie of friends with whom we get together quite often and enjoy mead and hunt together. You seem to presume him always...gloomy? You are not giving him due credit, Tiliruf, for ordinary pleasures. He is well-liked by many."

"I should apologize, then. I just am sorry he can't be friendlier with us."

"It probably would be asking too much at this stage. Nikal will have to suffice."

"True. I suppose we must be grateful for that, eh?"

Olin chuckled, and the conversation shifted. "Do you know your *eh's* are quite familiar to my ear and bring back memories of my father?"

"Ha! And Lumin uses it! Olin, it comes from Eleni, eh? Elenites use it all the time! My Elenite ancestry is strong, not just to Terianh, but the emperors often Bonded Elenite princesses. And even since then...er, though not princesses. But my mother was Elenite. My grandmother was Elenite. Father uses it. I took it on when I was a kid, and of course Elenite officials and tradesmen come to Tirilorin all the time. But that's why you don't hear any of the other blokes using it, 'cause they're not Elenite. So, your father used it, and your grandfather used it. I knew where it came from when I first heard it off Lumin's tongue!"

Olin smiled. The two were developing a stronger rapport. "Yes, Lumin does have early memories of Father and his speech."

The two continued to engage in friendly manner. At the edge of a copse they sat and awaited the approaching sunset.

The sun was sinking. The herds entered the field for evening grazing.

"They don't congregate in such large groups in Tulesk," whispered Kodi to Lumin. They were probably a quarter mile away from any of the others. "Just in small families. They're a different kind. Ours are a little bigger, I think. That's amazing! Of course, you eat a lot of venison here. Now I know why."

"Venison is almost required at a Bonding." Lumin spoke even more quietly. "It's the tradition."

They waited no more than five minutes when an enormous shadow emerged from the forest border.

"Blazes, oh!" Kodi pointed. "That one's mine. I spotted it!"

"You didn't. I saw him the moment he came out!" He fisted Kodi's shoulder and grinned huge. And then, to Kodi's shock, Lumin vanished.

"That isn't fair!"

"All's fair, Brother," said an enthusiastic voice. "And I've already got a new song churning in my head!"

Kodi detected an invisible body next to him get up and step out of the copse.

"Dammit, you thumping little...!" whispered Kodi, but he bore a great smile. *Well, heck! But, Little Brother, if it has to be someone else but me...anyways, I got better songs to sing to her. Body songs, ha!*

And there was little Kodi could do about it. The monster buck was still too far away. Lumin had the immense Qeteral advantage of being an invisible sneak.

Kodi could see the huge rack. Still fuzzed as expected for late summer. Sixteen, maybe eighteen points. And it was significantly larger than the others nearby, nearly as big as any he remembered from the north. Maybe his perceptions about the general size of the different kinds were inaccurate.

There was another, and he sighted it. It wasn't as big as the one Lumin was heading for, but it was a presentable catch. More quickly than expected it approached in Kodi's direction.

Come closer, buddy buck!

It did. Very close. Kodi stood silently and took aim.

Probably detecting movement anyway, the beast looked up in Kodi's direction.

Twang.

It didn't stand a chance. It was a bullseye between the eyes. It took two steps and fell.

Yes!

And off to his left he heard a great thump.

Lumin's darkened figure could now be seen in the twilight. The rest of the herd fled back to the forest.

Kodi ran out to him.

"Wow, Lumin! Nobody else will possibly beat you tonight!"

They approached the huge animal. Lumin was ecstatic. But they would have to hide for another half hour to allow the others in copses further away to get in their shots. They couldn't risk showing themselves and disturbing the other herds.

"There's risk to yourselves, though," whispered Kodi.

"No, no, no. Don't forget, Qeteral can still see each other."

"Oh, that's right! Shane will remember. And Manwul and Hadon will, too."

And they did. All was well. In another hour, the attending servants, who had remained separated from the hunters, came out from hiding and worked to carry all the downed prey to one spot. Everyone was in a giddy state of sorts. Even Tiliruf shot one, though Olin had to help him down it with another arrow. Lumin's buck was clearly the largest, and even Hurlin was congratulatory. The competitive old Patriarch seemed a bit disappointed, but he congratulated Lumin as well. As it grew dark, they marched in their pairs back to the village.

It would be another two hours, just before midnight, when they returned. Kodi and Ryn had a 'plan,' and he took leave of his friends as they approached the village. The queen's blessing of their union the day before was all he needed, and he didn't care what Hurlin or anyone else might have thought. The pavilion would no longer be Kodi's home. With his hunting gear strapped to his back, he climbed the trellis to Ryn's rooms and discovered a beautiful princess with a tantalizing smile awaiting him at the balcony door. Tanter had already warned her of his approach.

"The bath is ready for us, my dear."

When the rest returned to the pavilion, the men agreed that baths could wait till morning; they collapsed into their cots and fell instantly asleep. Then, when all was quiet, an elated young Qeteral man slipped out of the pavilion. He too had a plan, having been directly encouraged by Kodi. Exactly as Kodi with Ryn two nights before, when Lumin looked over the waterfall of the Diamond Pool and saw Fal's form in the moonlight, the emotion he experienced just then would return—whenever he was forced to be apart from her—in joyful smile and yearning memory.

Two young men would therefore experience another exquisite night of favored delights. Lumin's would be magically longer. He returned to the pavilion while it was still dark, and unlike Kodi, he did not need to sleep late. None questioned him, therefore. But he had a self-satisfied grin on his face all day long, and with a hint or two, an astute Shane quickly figured it out.

And when late in the morning with sun pouring in the windows and the birds singing, Kodi awakened in a beautifully carven bed in superior comfort, his lover nestled in the crook of his body, he'd never experienced such supreme contentment in all his life.

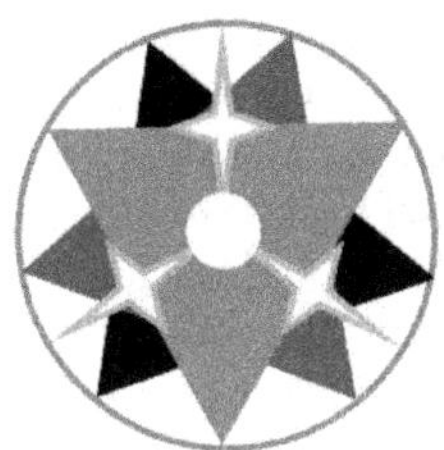

Chapter 27—Royal Surprise

"This is so much fun!" Lyndz said. "Arranging flowers for Kodi's Bonding feast!"

"What's so fun about it?" asked an annoyed Rainwing. She bore in her arms quantities of flowers cut from the palace garden that Lyndz asked her to carry. She was patiently—or perhaps not—following Lyndz and Idamé about. "I feel like an idiot."

"Do you not like flowers?" asked Idamé.

"Yes, I like them, so why do you cut them and not leave them alone to be beautiful in your gardens or to bloom in pleasure in the fields? It seems sacrilege. They do not wish to be picked." She looked at the flowers she bore with pity.

"Oh, yes they do," said Idamé. Among the asters, brown-eyed daisies, sedums, coneflowers, goldenrods, and phlox, she was choosing a combination for the next vase. "Their status rises from common to nobility, because they will grace the tables and bring pleasure to those sitting at them. Flowers are a part of every Bonding Ceremony, Rainwing. Unless it is winter, and decorations of evergreens and winter berries must suffice."

"Why is it sacrilege, Rainwing?" asked Lyndz.

"You end their lives too quickly. I do not like it."

"Oh, I see. But their stems go in water, you see, and can last a long time. Do you not decorate at your Bonding ceremonies?"

"With fruits, yes, in lovely bowls given beforehand as gifts, and then we eat the fruits at the feast."

"Well, that does sound like a nice tradition. I like that. But we put the foods all on one large banquet table. Though here there will be several banqueting tables. I imagine one will be just for fruits!"

Idamé added, "And I think it is remarkable that the Qeteral bring food dishes to share. With Humans, if they are well-to-do, the family provides all the food for the guests. It appears here the family provides traditional venison dishes, the mead, and some special desserts, but the guests bring the rest."

"The whole village is invited, and many nobles from all about. It is an excellent tradition, and it involves everyone in the celebration. It would have been difficult, even for the palace kitchens, to serve so many with such short notice. It will be the biggest Bonding Ceremony I've ever attended. They're expecting over seven hundred! Are you nervous, Mother?"

"I've participated as a Sister in large Bondings, not as a Mother. I've had the Qeteral Bondswomen review my format, and they say it is much as their own and all the elements will be easily understood. They are also perfectly fine with Ulna and Maru doing the dance as I sing the Bonding song. This is a longer format than what was done at your grandfather and Ansy's, and even Aron and Modela's, as the bride and groom are each marched in with presenters. I feel in stride now that I have Grandmother's shawl back. Now, dear. You and Curdoz will walk the central pathway with Kodi. Hakonn and the queen will walk up with the princess. You and Curdoz must make the formal presentation for Kodi. They will do so for Ryn. The four presenters will then greet one another with kisses symbolizing the connection of the families. And then you will sit in the front-row chairs."

"And what of the men?"

"Nikal and Tiliruf will already be standing with me on one side, and Ryn's brothers on the other. The other Matrimonials will be gathered behind us. Bondswoman Vitalle will also offer a Qeteral Blessing, as the queen requested."

"But you are center stage! It is such an honor, Mother. You will be the first Human Matrimonial to ever preside at a Qeteral Bonding!"

"I would have protested to the Matriarch," put in Rainwing, "if they didn't allow Idamé to do it. Considering the Dream she had from the Guardian the other night and her Gift returned in order to see the Aura first! And Ryn is also part Human. It makes all sense. And you being the first Human Matrimonial will add to the memory of it for the Qeteral."

"Vitalle herself promoted my role to the Queen," said Idamé. "She was gracious, particularly as Ryn wanted Kodi to have everything he wanted for the ceremony, since otherwise Ryn is having it here at her home with all her own people present among other Qeteral traditions. I told Kodi to wear his best Human clothing as he did the evening of the reception, but he was insistent he would dress as Qeteral. Who am I to argue anymore when Kodi wants something? He says he is part of them now. He is embracing their people as his own and this land as home. Hakonn is providing him with proper finery."

"He looks excellent in Qeteral attire," said Rainwing, oddly. "It seems a much more natural style for your bodies than Human wear. It does not cover up so much the perfection of your physical form."

Lyndz smiled. "It is wonderful you see us that way, Rainwing. Surely my weeks here have caused me to have a new perspective."

"It works on the young, of course," said Idamé. "The young and beautiful. But Curdoz, Deens, Findun and I will wear Human clothing."

"That several of you are doing so adds the Human element," said Lyndz. "It is good, I think. But you have changed, Mother. Not long ago you would have insisted I too dress more modestly. And Ulna and Maru."

"Well, here you are a goddess among the rest and stand with them. You are as lovely as Ryn, my dear. Everyone says so, and they are right. And there is a healthy, natural look to Ulna and Maru in Qeteral clothing, and so how can I possibly judge such negatively anymore? The culture and expectations are simply different here, and so I made myself observe from the Qeteral perspective. I actually think you helped me, Rainwing, to be less rigid on the matter of clothing."

They looked up as a male servant approached them. "The Matriarch requests your presence in the great hall, ladies."

Rainwing rolled her eyes.

"Mistress Rainwing?"

She puffed up and glared. "*Mistress!* Spikeshafts and blazes!"

"He's only being polite as is his duty, Rainwing. But just call her *Ambassador*, kind sir. That will do."

The servant swallowed and nodded. "Do you mind pointing out to me the ladies Ulna and Maru?"

Lyndz pointed at the Healer Sisters who were in another part of the garden area, also filling the table vases with flowers. The servant nodded his thanks, looked askance at Rainwing, and headed in their direction.

The three gave their flowers to a set of nearby servants and marched towards the rear entrance of the palace. Maru and Ulna met them there.

"You can be too tense with the men, Rainwing! Stop trying to find fault. You don't act that way to the female servants."

"Sorry, it's just..."

"Yes, we know."

"What?" asked Maru.

"Oh, the servant referenced her as a *lady* just now, along with Mother and me, of course, but then he addressed her as *Mistress*. She got her shackles up."

"I see." Maru chuckled.

"Don't lecture me. I said sorry, didn't I?"

"Not to him, you didn't."

"All right. I'll do so," she replied huffily. She looked back at the servant man, who was clearly keeping his distance. She yelled out, "Sorry!"

The man's eyes got wide.

"I guess that will have to do," Mother Idamé whispered.

They went inside.

"I wonder what this is all about?" asked Ulna.

When they arrived, they discovered the Human men and Flamefur, and all the greater royal family. Ryn too was present with Kodi at her side.

All men were wearing the open-fronted vest, always an immediate giveaway that a gathering involved a certain formality. Lyndz walked up and stood with Nikal. "Do you know what this is about, Nikal?"

"I think I might, because I mark certain elements of which I am familiar. I think Curdoz knows, and he had us all wear our Order Medallions. As you see, Kodi wears his, too. But let us watch, my friend, and see if I am right."

On the dais stood the royal family. The women wore circlets of flowers on their heads. The princes wore circlets of silver on theirs.

The Matriarch wore an elaborate golden tiara. The former Matriarch and Patriarch were also wearing gold on their heads. Something of great importance was taking place, for Lyndz had never seen royal circlets on their heads before, only flower wreaths sometimes on the women. A few noblemen and noblewomen were present, some she remembered from the reception, those known to live closest to the capital village. They stood behind the royal family, adding to the formality.

"All are present, Matriarch," said Hakonn. "We can proceed."

Queen Gwyn nodded. A servant then stepped up to the dais carrying a velvet pillow atop which lay a silver circlet. It was precisely of the same simple style as those born by Ryn's brothers and Hakonn.

The queen spoke.

"Lord Kodi, will you please step forward."

Kodi, who had been standing on the dais holding hands with Ryn, his eyes a little wide, looked at the Matriarch with amazement. Lyndz realized he was repressing a sense of shock. She wanted to say something to Nikal, but silence reigned. However, she saw Nikal was nodding knowingly. Then, she too seemed to understand. *Oh, my! Is that what is happening?*

Hakonn spoke quietly and motioned. "Lord Kodi, the Matriarch honors you. You may kneel before her now."

Kodi looked at him. He truly was not anticipating this. "Yes, m'lord."

Kodi then moved out into the center and turned towards the Matriarch. He knelt before her as he had done when requesting Ryn's hand. "Madam Matriarch. I am your servant."

"You serve the Divine Myghal, Lord Kodi, and we know your first allegiance will always be to Him. But this honor we grant you before you take my daughter's hand tomorrow evening. In royal council we have determined you are to be made a High Prince of the Realm. It is the highest honor we can bestow upon you in recognition of my daughter's great love for you and of your love for my daughter. You have made your intent known that, should peace come again, you wish to return and dwell here among us and raise your children and make this always your home. And I, Matriarch of Ulakel, Gwyn, daughter of Hakonn and Linea, love you as a son. When I first experienced your presence in my Vision, I knew your sincere heart and felt the depth of your spirit. A spirit of joy follows you, and you have brought joy and hope to me and mine. I proclaim now that this is your home, Ulakel, Garden of the Gods, which we so cherish. And here you will live as a High Prince of the Realm with your wife my daughter. Your children likewise will be Princes and Princesses of the Realm."

From Kodi's eyes a few tears fell. He still did his best to keep his voice firm.

"My love for you and this place is so very great. It is the greatest honor I could ever receive. These have been most happy days. Madam Matriarch, I find myself overwhelmed with feeling. But thank you."

Lyndz shed a tear and Nikal held her hand. In fact, there were a great many Human tears all around, even from the men, and a few Qeteral, too.

Hakonn took the silver circlet from the pillow the servant held and handed it to the Matriarch. She stepped forward and placed it with both hands on Kodi's head.

She spoke tenderly in recognition of Kodi's depth of feeling.

"Arise my son, honored Brother of Myghal, Kodi of Ulakel, High Prince of the Realm."

He rose. She then kissed him on the forehead. She then indicated for Ryn to come forward. She did so and, taking his hands, they kissed each other lightly on the lips and leaned their foreheads together in tenderness. He smiled and seemed to relax in her love. She led him to stand with her just a little away, for it appeared the Matriarch was not quite finished.

Hakonn spoke again.

"Lady Lyndz of Solanto, would you please step up to the dais?"

Lyndz gasped and froze. Yet Nikal kindly encouraged her and led her forward by the hand. Hakonn stepped forward and helped her onto the dais.

The Matriarch smiled kindly, attempting to put Lyndz at ease. She came and kissed Lyndz on the forehead. Lyndz then curtsied. "Madam?"

"Ah, dear lady, but don't you see? As Kodi's closest kin his sister we designate you a High Lady of the Kingdom, on the order of my mother-in-law Manoo, and our cousin, Mishoo! You are to have all the rights and privileges of your position whenever you come here and will be forever welcome."

Lyndz didn't shed anymore tears. Her smile beamed forth like the sunshine.

"Oh, Madam! It is with all gladness I receive the honor!"

"And so, you are a part of my family, my dear! Though it becomes official at the Bonding tomorrow when our families join in ceremony."

"Yes, Madam. I am much moved by your graciousness."

She curtsied again.

Hakonn, with rare smile, announced loudly. "Let all rejoice!"

There was great applause.

"It is typical in Human kingdoms, as well," said Nikal later in the day to some of the men. He was referencing the tradition to ennoble the male consort of a royal princess prior to Bonding. "To be raised up a duke if he is not so already. Or to be made a prince if his betrothed is a queen or expected to inherit the throne. It is similar here, although they do not call their highest noblemen 'dukes.' They chose 'prince' for Kodi."

"His status already was high enough," said Shane, "as War Wizard. He is the Brother of Meical. With you, Nikal, Kodi stands at the side of the Guardian."

"And so the Matriarch believed so, too," said Curdoz. "But there were political considerations due to his Bonding Ryn, and she told me she wished to honor him anyway, as the Orders have done and as the Etoppsi did by proclaiming him Polemarch. Hakonn and his father the old Patriarch also thought it was important. I was in on the discussion with the family. They wished to understand from me Kodi's current position in Solanto and Nant and within the Orders. It was decided that designating him High Prince of the Realm was the worthiest honor that could be given, and that it was within the Matriarch's prerogative. It was what was done for Linea when she Bonded Hakonn, although unlike Kodi, Linea herself was of royal descent. The other princes, however, are also known as High Princes of the *Qeteral*, which here means being born to the monarch. But in a way, Gwyn was claiming Kodi as her own royal son, almost like an adoption. It was an expression of love for him. There are many subtleties and differences among all the kingdoms in how they go about establishing titles. They are different here, too. In any event, he is raised to the same rank within the kingdom as Ryn. And nobody anywhere misunderstands 'prince.'"

"You can't give him enough honors, eh?" added Tiliruf. "He deserves every one he gets. If anyone has royal blood, it's Kodi."

"I agree with you, Tiliruf," said Nikal. "I have never thought of him as less than my equal in any regard. If anything, I compare myself to him. I have learned in my years that true nobility is of the heart. A generous spirit. We, all of us, believe him Favored. Rank, whether he had it or not, hasn't stopped Kodi from being and doing what he sets his mind to."

"Certainly, since we left Solanto that is true," agreed Curdoz. "He has become one of the great men of history. Yet plainly today's honor had tremendous meaning for him, connecting him to Ryn's people and this land. He was deeply affected."

"What was Hurlin's thinking, Curdoz?"

"There were six in the meeting besides myself: the old Matriarch and Patriarch, Gwyn, Hakonn, Hurlin, and Olin. Hurlin was not in agreement with their thinking, but he did not force the issue. But he felt designation of High Noble, rather like Manoo as the queen's mother-in-law was sufficient. And Mishoo, who is closely related to Linea, and also descended from royalty. That was definitely discussed. He agreed his sister's consort should have higher noble status than that of a Human count's son, but probably more as a means to camouflage Kodi being a Human and make him seem more palatable to some of the more conservative noble families in Ulakel. But I am just guessing that based on his earlier behavior."

"Almost assuredly a part of his thinking," agreed Nikal. "But I actually think Hurlin has come to believe Kodi really does hear the Voice of Myghal. That he stands in a place of Favor. Hakonn has convinced him of it. But I don't know that he will ever feel especially close to Kodi."

"At some point, what Hurlin will see," offered Shane, "is that no matter how disagreeable he might sometimes act towards Kodi, Kodi's going to love him as a brother anyway. Bonding Ryn will make him Hurlin's brother by the common rules of family, and, like he's already displayed with Lumin, Kodi will take the connection to heart."

"Yes," agreed Nikal. "I think Hurlin might also take the connection seriously. Might. I'm sure he never wanted his sister to fall in love with Kodi. But he did not interfere."

"True," added Shane. "Kodi thinks Hurlin knew of their attraction for each other from the beginning. Hurlin did not interfere, and he could have. He could have discouraged Ryn. He could have gone to Hakonn or his Mother and essentially 'warned' them, and his Mother might well have intervened and insisted on a longer, slower courtship. None of that happened, as we know."

"I wonder if Olin might have stopped him from doing something like that, eh? He says there is almost nothing they two don't share."

"Possibly, Tiliruf," said Nikal. "Olin certainly tries to soften his severity. Neither brother would have wished to prevent their sister from any happiness. She was of an age to make her own choices, and Qeteral men as you've noticed do not dominate women as is more typical in the Human West. Hurlin might not like Kodi, but I think even he sees Kodi's innate nobility whether or not he openly acknowledges it. What he cannot dismiss is his mother's Vision in which Kodi appeared to her. Obviously, he doesn't like much of any of us except possibly me. I really cannot understand why he keeps a distance from Kodi who attempts to express warmth, except it's almost as if he fears something about Kodi. Not his character, or at least not anymore, but perhaps something else."

"You've pinpointed what I've seen, too," agreed Shane. "He has come to acknowledge Kodi's good character, but still fears or is anxious about something regarding Kodi."

"Well, it's beyond me, eh?"

"True, Tiliruf. These are surely unnecessary musings. Only time will tell whether Hurlin will warm to Kodi. No doubt the two have different personalities. Kodi basks in the joy of blessings and sees blessings everywhere all the time. It isn't that he doesn't have concern for the future, but Kodi understands fully the value of the present moment. It is hard for most men to dismiss the weight of the future, and Hurlin struggles to do so. And so, his soul is more troubled. And trust me, I am convinced Hurlin's responsibilities, and the constant and powerful use of his magic, do weigh on him."

"Precisely, Shane," agreed Nikal. "Like me fighting battles, he too is fighting. The Barrier magic might come naturally to him, but it is surely burdensome in addition to his other responsibilities."

"As for Lyndz," Curdoz said, "know this. The queen was determined to honor her, too. That she said, 'on the order of Manoo and Mishoo' meant of the highest order of nobility, as they do have some distinctions within their noble classes."

"You mean as a duchess, or a Cee Amirah in the East," said Shane. "How excellent!"

"Yes, and *in her own right*, rather than by way of Bonding a duke and assuming his title. Gwyn said, 'Lyndz may prove the greatest woman of our time.'"

"I'm going to tease her and call her 'Duchess' from now on, eh?"

Nikal chuckled. "Don't do that, Tiliruf."

"Or she'll start calling you, The A'Terianh, like others do," Shane winked.

"Er, no, I guess I don't quite deserve that from her."

"You deserve it. But it's good you put her on a pedestal."

"For sure, I do. Who wouldn't, eh?"

"She is certainly a queen among queens. I've told her so myself," added Nikal. "But tease Kodi with 'Your Highness' and 'Lord Prince,' by all means! That will get his goat!"

They all laughed.

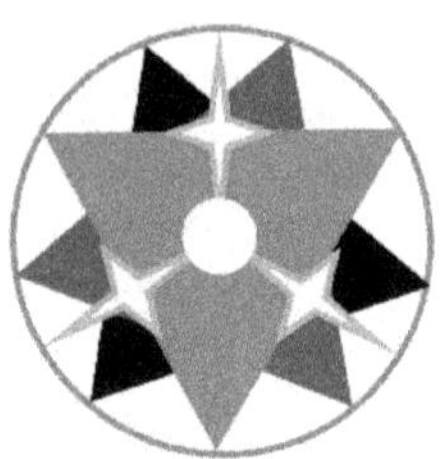

Chapter 28—Royal Bonding

"The weather is always perfect here," offered Ulna in a soft voice.

"It truly is," agreed Maru, also keeping her voice low.

The two were lovely in Qeteral finery standing together a little behind Mother Idamé. They liked Qeteral clothing very much, less for its revealing nature and more for its cool simplicity. But they had nice figures for their age, now toned even more from all their secretive training, and even the normally sun-careful Maru had developed a tan over the last two weeks. Tiliruf noticed all this, and as the group had started gathering a little while ago, he eyed them unabashedly and told them they looked 'damned healthy.' They grinned at the compliment, and certainly tonight, being barefooted and with daisies gracing their hair, they appeared youthful.

Behind them stood a stately line of some six Qeteral Bondswomen dressed a little more formally, as they wore their sandals, and their breasts were fully covered with the loops all buttoned on their shirts. They ranged markedly in age from young to quite old. Such a number was only because this was a royal affair, adding to its overall grandness.

Idamé was forward and center. She was wearing a Human dress and more importantly her grandmother's multi-colored shawl. Under favorable circumstances she would rarely part with this anymore. In future she might come to additionally treasure the one knitted special for her by the Healer Sisters and Lyndz on the Modela voyage, but for now the one returned by Modela's tropical bird on that most splendid morning a few days before would hold paramount symbolism. Certainly today it would. The object had itself become part of a grand romance.

On her left stood Prince Nikal, Shane, and Tiliruf. They wore this evening their Human best. Nikal wore his gold Order Medallion as War Wizard, and Shane his silver one as Healer in the Orders. They both looked regal, Shane no less so than the prince. Tiliruf wore his eagle embroiders and looked for all the world an imperial prince, though his loose blond curls and a one-sided smile perpetually lent him that touch of rascality. On the front row in chairs before them the other Human men—Manwul, Hadon, Deens, and Findun—also wore Human clothing. It was understood that Kodi would be dressed as a Qeteral, and so the men agreed that for the Bonding Ceremony he should stand apart as a Prince of Ulakel, that which he was now proclaimed to be. The Scribes looked perfectly well, just as they had at the reception over two weeks previously, but Manwul and Hadon looked particularly rich with their bleach-white linen shirts overtopped with the fancy red damasked vests. The necklaces from Lumin were visible, too, and Hadon's gold chain from Sturla. He would finger it throughout the evening, for the grand event would cause him to think often of her.

He whispered to Manwul. "First chance we get I'm Bonding Sturla. I miss her something fierce."

"Aye, friend. And I miss Steffy. Would they were here to see this!"

At the end of this row sat Rainwing with Flamefur, slightly apart on a large bench where their massive frames would block as few spectators as possible. Rusty wore his Stag collar and looked irrefutably the *Sky King,* an address used often by the Qeteral since he came. (In healthy pride he loved this, and when the children used it, he would sometimes explode in booming laughter, causing them to laugh despite what might otherwise be his intimidating immensity and a certain fierceness in his large, sculpted face. Rather, they liked getting close to him, feel his red fur and even smell his interesting musk. However, they would hastily scatter when he spread wide his wings in order to launch himself into that sky he ruled.) He and Rainwing stood guard over the Staff of Terianh as it lay at their feet, and Musca himself sat there on the ground, in and out of a doggy snooze. He'd been given a bath and a brush by the breeder, and his silver fur glimmered much like Rainwing's.

The Etoppsi were pleased to observe the present event. It was possibly the only Bonding of any sort since prehistoric times in which all Three Races of the Mold were present together to witness. Rainwing did her best to whisper into Rusty's ear. "I am beginning to worry for Stormgale. He should be here with us to see this."

Rusty nodded his agreement.

The picturesque palace garden glowed golden and green in the half light of a late-summer sunset. All-men flute players, perhaps fifteen altogether, barefoot, shirtless, and bearing wild crowns of goldenrod in their dark hair, mimicked mythical fauns as they leaned back against the nearest garden trees. They were the first Qeteral musicians the visitors had actually seen. Their muscularity and relaxed poses as they held their reed flutes added an unusual artistic and sensual quality, very Qeteral indeed. In silhouette with the trunks of the trees they were like living sculptures in the background of a theatrical set. The music they played was as a flock of melodious birds in magical symphony. All the Qeteral and some astute Humans like Shane or Lyndz understood that by being all men they symbolized the fact that it was male birds of most species (like Tanter the Nightingale) who tended to sing the more beautiful songs, and their music was intended to represent the call of the bridegroom for his bride. Yet it was not only musically stylized bird calls, for it was of complex composition and contained other sounds recalling forests and waters. Their harmonies mingled, and it often seemed as though they were passing the music among one another, as some would trail off and others with different tune would come into greater emphasis. And indeed, birds all around the shrubberies and trees, along with the breezes, added their own nature songs to that of the players.

It was an enormous semicircle containing row upon row of chairs, where some seven hundred sat, including virtually every villager and some noble families who lived in the vicinity. There was only limited whispering as all were enjoying the enchanting music of the flutists.

On Idamé's right stood Ryn's brothers, their princely silver circlets on their heads. Lumin's superiorly handsome, dual-race face demonstrated just now his Human grin. To the Humans it seemed always to give him a hint of mischievousness and a sort of perpetual joy. Olin and Hurlin were not grinning, but Hurlin, interestingly, was not frowning. It may have been that the union about to take place was not to his liking. Yet his gentlemanly instincts told him that this moment, to honor his sister, he should not express even a morsel of resentment. Maybe Olin had lectured him beforehand. And like Olin, he stood tall like a young king with serene expression. Earlier he had escorted Lady Mishoo to sit on the front row, notably very handsome together as they walked, and Olin and Lumin had escorted their grandmothers Manoo and Linea to sit with her.

The flute tune changed subtly, and yet it was clear the moment had changed with the change in the music. Everyone stood as the aging former Matriarch and Patriarch walked down the central aisle. They wore gold on their heads. All turned towards them and bowed as they passed. The two smiled and nodded at the crowd as they went by every row, and eventually they made their way to their chairs in front.

The crowd remained standing as Kodi now made his way. He wore Qeteral linen of a rich blue, heavily embroidered, blue being his favorite color to wear at fancy occasions and of which he requested from Hakonn who cheerfully provided. On his superior bared torso with its open-fronted vest were Lumin's gift of the wooden beads. He did not wear the Order medallion tonight. It was excellent symbolism on Nikal and Shane as witnesses, but its imagery on Kodi as bridegroom wasn't quite right. In fact, it was Tiliruf who puckered with distaste when Kodi was about to put it on. "Don't wear it, Kodi. You're the perfect stud without that fancy gold thing covering half that pretty chest. She ain't Bonding you 'cause you're a War Wizard, eh? She's Bonding you 'cause you're *you,* charmer boy." Curdoz and Shane agreed he was right. For this event Kodi was to be a Prince of Ulakel, nothing more and nothing less. His face was shaven perfectly smooth, then, and the silver circlet he received the day before crowned his dark, wavy hair. The people on the rows' edges nodded as he passed them, some softly addressing him, "Brother of Myghal," though, rather than title, tonight it held tones of affection. The villagers had come to love him as he had them. Some of the little children, whom he had blessed or played with at the swimming hole, aimed big smiles at him. He winked back.

He was flanked just behind by Curdoz and Lyndz. Curdoz wore his Human best and the stole knitted for him by the women on the Modela voyage. Lyndz, as a new noblewoman of Ulakel, wore Qeteral clothing. Pink linen draped over her breasts, loops buttoned for formality, and in her black hair was a lovely ring of yellow and white daisies. Like her twin she too looked exactly like a Qeteral, and the Qeteral saw in her both youthful beauty and regal splendor. The three made their way and stood in front and slightly to one side.

And then she came.

Ryn, too, wore blue, paler in shade than on Kodi, also embroidered, and trimmed in white silk ribbon. The loops on her shirt were held by carved and painted buttons resembling songbirds. Her ebony hair was crowned by an arrangement of flowers interwoven in a silver tiara and cascading down her tresses to her waist.

She was escorted by her mother, Matriarch Gywn, and her grandfather Hakonn. Hakonn wore his princely silver circlet, and the queen wore a more elaborate golden one. She looked quite young herself, and it was mostly her eyes which demonstrated additional maturity. Had there been Human strangers present they otherwise might have believed her to be of the same generation as her princess daughter, an older sister maybe, serene, beautiful, and regal as any moon or star. As when the former Matriarch and Patriarch processed, all bowed as these three passed.

Kodi, his eyes only on Ryn now, was enamored as always by her mesmerizing blue eyes, exquisite face, and that supreme figure, decorated now in traditional royal Qeteral female perfection. The world's most gorgeous woman, and as far as he was concerned extraordinary in every other way in addition to her beauty, was about to become his legal Bondmate, this to be proclaimed to all the world and written down in its histories. *She carries my seed,* he said to himself in that fullest sense of Qeteral manly pride, not with any false sense of male dominion over women, typical of many Human men, but rather of the superior, almost indescribable emotion of being the healthy, virile, male-half creator of ongoing life through and with her. The relationship was all gift, mutual gift, claimed in most-valued monogamy, but not in the sense that either owned or possessed the other. (Shane could have exposited on a dynamic here of animal and spiritual values.) And she was allowing a life to gestate inside of her even now, that which they had created together in the sublime magnetic union of fun-filled body bliss. Masculine joy shone in his face: youthful excitement and a confident roguish sexiness, these moderated by respect for the moment and an overarching awe for the approaching princess.

Ryn saw the sparkle in his brown eyes. She beamed in recognition of the look he bore her, experiencing as she was equivalent emotions of the Qeteral feminine: *I carry his seed.* In the woman the balance of the spiritual and the animal is subtly different—more spiritual on her part, and nurturing, whereas the animal more so colors his perspective. Having grown up around a lot of boys and men she could appreciate the subtleties and believed them to be good. It made life more interesting and enjoyable that men and women were not the same. The point was that she knew she had chosen the best man in all Dumhoni, Qeteral or Human, to be her husband and the father of her children.

Now gathered before Idamé, the escorts used formal words to introduce the pair and then proceeded to kiss one another on both their cheeks. This was a Qeteral tradition to symbolize the union of families. Curdoz may not have been a relative, of course. Yet as the Sage, he was the allegory of fatherhood, and to Kodi much more than that—a spiritual father, yes, but one who favored Kodi with a true father's pride-filled love.

As they kissed, Hakonn whispered in his ear the most unique of Qeteral jokes, and certainly the only joke ever uttered by him of which any Human knew. "Most interesting it is to kiss an old man with a scruffy beard!"

"I ran out of time to shave this morn!" Curdoz chuckled at this humor (and also at the Qeteral vanity, as Hakonn was over twice his age and knew it) and patted Hakonn on the shoulder. The four then took seats on the front rows, Curdoz and Lyndz by the Humans, and the Matriarch and elder prince with their family.

It was not something that took place at Qeteral Bondings. Yet the Human symbolism was important to Idamé (and to Kodi), and she had beforehand requested them from the Bondswomen, and they had agreed to make it happen. Two of the Bondswomen—Vitalle and another—reached back to a white bench and from it lifted medium-length capes of beautifully woven linen. One was blue, the other white. They and a third Bondswoman then stepped around the Bonding party, down a level from the specially built dais. The third Bondswoman helped to carefully lift away Ryn's hair while Vitalle and the other placed these 'mantles' upon the couple, tying them in the front, the blue one of course on Kodi and the white one on the princess. Ryn's hair, with its interwoven flowers, was then allowed to fall behind. The Bondswomen returned to their positions, and the betrothed couple then proceeded to face Idamé and hold hands.

One by one, the flute players ended their song until only one was left. For two more minutes this one continued the music in captivating solo, and then the six Bondswomen lifted high their arms. The final flutist ended his tune, the last tranquil notes recalling something of a loon on the water. Then Idamé too lifted high her arms and spread her hands.

It was then that something extraordinary happened.

Something magical.

As Idamé lifted her arms above Ryn and Kodi, before her shone a bright green light. And yet not only could she and the Bondswomen see it, so could everyone present! For a moment Idamé could not understand the whispering clamor from the crowd and pointing fingers, until Ulna stepped up and spoke into her ear, trying her best to cover her own sense of shock.

"We can all see it, Mother Idamé! All of us! We can all see the Aura! And it was as though it came forth from your hands!"

Maru with gumption turned around and spoke hurriedly to the Bondswomen. Obviously, they and Idamé, since they always saw Auras, did not understand at first. Yet too, Kodi and Ryn, even as they continued to hold hands, looked above them with astonishment at what looked like flickering bright green flames. Kodi smiled enormously. Quickly, Bondswoman Vitalle stepped up to Idamé, and they spoke to one another in whispers.

"I suspect, Mother Idamé, Vanayema has herself done this! I believe she may have added something to the Divine's own magic allowing you to reveal it to everyone! It apparently occurred just as you lifted your arms and opened your hands!"

"I can't believe it!"

"Believe it, Idamé! Believe it! I'm telling you your magic has been changed! Think of it as a good thing and a blessing of uttermost magnificence! Consider this extraordinary union about to take place between our two peoples! Now take charge, my dear! This is yours!"

Vitalle stepped back.

Idamé's eyes were wide, and her eyebrows were at her hairline. But all in a moment she did consider the amazing events of these last days and the significance of the couple before her. She put on her happiest smile and exclaimed in a great voice.

"The Blessing of the Aura is shown to all! Understand ye witnesses! Question not what you see before us, that which the Bondswomen and I can always see when man and woman are Blessed by Meical Himself, Myghal the Divine!"

She then nodded to Ulna and Maru, and those two stepped forward and began a dance.

They were as lovely to behold as any trained Matrimonial Sisters, and as Lyndz later suggested, they in a powerful way provided a feminine balance in their art to that of the male flute players. In bare feet and with fluid waving involving their arms and torsos, as woodland nymphs they made themselves round and round Kodi and Ryn, as those two held hands and beamed at each other with superior faces.

And while they danced, Idamé sang...The Song:

In rapturous morning, under golden sun,
The One stood in a Valley of Gold.
There was joy in the heart of the One,
And from that joy sprang the Mold.

With clay at hand, the Mold was imbued
With the shape of two, yet the essence of One.
Female and Male mirrored the Mood,
She was called Daughter and He was named Son.

Daughter was draped in garments of white.
A mantle of blue was born by the Son.
Together they stood in the morning light.
One had made two. The two now became one.

Side by side they wander the Earth.
The Son is the hunter and fights the foe.
Daughter is gatherer and to their children give birth.
Together they love. Together they grow.

Created for Human Bondings and translated from ancient times, there were smiles and nods of approval among this Qeteral crowd, too, and Idamé had a lovely singing voice. Maru and Ulna ended the dance and went back to their places behind her. The Matrimonial then spoke her beautiful words. Kodi would remember them.

"What joy! What joy! Let it be known to all that in a Vision in my sleep given to me by the Divine but a few nights ago, Myghal made known to me His own joy that these two before me had pledged their hearts each to the other. High Princess Ryn of the Qeteral and Kodi, Brother of Myghal. Kodi, as a dear son to me, that morning confirmed for me his great love for our beautiful Ryn, and in the presence of the Matriarch they displayed openly their affection and commitment. A great miracle then occurred. My Gift was returned, that which had been taken from me, and the Aura was seen first by me and then by my Bondswomen Sisters, even as Kodi and Ryn displayed their love to all present. The Divine has shown His favor. Indeed...indeed you now see it for yourselves.

"As you all now know, a task, the greatest of tasks is at hand, as our Human, Qeteral, and Etoppsi world faces a threat, the gravest threat we have known in many centuries. Yet this union tonight is a sign, a sign of the presence and favor of the Guardian. He is with us tonight, this especial moment, as we see His Aura above the betrothed. He reaches out to us in this oldest symbol of love and union. It is love that drives the Divine, and it is love He wishes us always to know and to have in our forethoughts during these tasks ahead. It is not only the love which we witness before us between Ryn and Kodi, but a love that surrounds and connects us all here together in a valued unity of friendship. Etoppsi, the First Peoples, Qeteral, the Second, and Humans, the Third, we of the Divine Mold have come together in union too this night!

"And let me now speak to these two before us. Ryn and Kodi, do you yourselves see the symbolism of what your union demonstrates to us?"

"We do."

"I charge everyone present to stand now and witness!" When all stood, she continued. "Kodi, do you then take Ryn forever after to be your cherished Bondmate?"

"With all my heart and body and soul."

"Ryn, do you then take Kodi forever after to be your cherished Bondmate?"

"With all my heart and body and soul."

"Please turn around now and face these witnesses present."

Switching the hands they held, the two, Kodi and Ryn, then turned and faced the great crowd.

"As Mother Matrimonial of the Orders of the Guardian on High I now proclaim to you the Bonded Union of Princess Ryn and Prince Kodi. In witness then let all proclaim aloud their joy!"

And every last individual present proclaimed some words or yells of joy, and the applause was thunderous.

Bondswoman Vitalle then came forward as planned to offer a Qeteral blessing. The two turned to face her, and she placed her hands on their heads. The crowd grew quiet.

"May the Garden of the Gods enrich your lives always. May your home be filled with all happiness. May your children bask in sunshine and sing in the rain. And may the Affirmation of Myghal the Divine give you joy throughout all the days of your life together."

She stepped back, and Kodi and Ryn held each other and kissed most superbly.

As a preplanned surprise on his own volition, Lumin at that moment sang very quietly, but magically. Abruptly, from all directions of the garden, songbirds of many kinds came and flew in great circles above the couple. Responding to his will, through the green light of the Aura they passed, and like a column they rose high then flew away back to the trees.

The happy couple kissed again, and the applause reignited.

The feast began. Tables had been spread wide over the gardens, and the larger crowd slowly gathered their foods at the great banqueting tables and dispersed to these. Whereas on the stone verandah facing out to the garden were set close tables in a semicircle meant for the Bonding party, families, and friends. And here, servants did the work, bringing food, fruit punches, and mead.

"The words were good, Idamé," said Curdoz. "You referenced some Meicalian Mysticism which I thought quite appropriate for this."

"Thank you, dear. And yet I admit I wished in my heart to do differently. I wished to be much more personal for dear Kodi. But I didn't feel it would work right."

"I understand. You had to consider the Qeteral audience and the meaning behind our coming here. Besides, there were many Human elements which Kodi will not forget. And even a personal touch or two. Now tell me of the Aura magic!"

"It overwhelmed me nearly!" She then went on to describe the experience and what she and the Bondswomen now believed. Finally, she added,

"And as you can see it only demonstrates itself to others when I wish for it to. You don't see it now. I think it would be a bit distracting, don't you think?"

"I called him *My Own Brother Hurlin* when he gripped my hand after." Kodi spoke over Tiliruf's shoulder as the latter sat at the table.

"You didn't!"

"I did! He didn't return the favor quite, but at least he spoke nice words. *I know you bring joy to my sister, Kodi. May the Guardian favor you both.* He smiled decently, then turned away."

"Well, that's something, then, eh?"

"I think so."

There was a reception line of sorts, though a bit more informal. It wasn't really a line. As Kodi and Ryn stood and greeted the verandah crowd they came up in ones and twos and threes. Some nobles also came forward whom Ryn knew and Kodi had met. One couple greeted them quite affectionately. They were the epitome of Qeteral good looks, he with smooth muscular build and she shapely with lovely brown skin and gorgeous face. The woman kissed Ryn on both cheeks and spoke as though they'd known each other years. The man gripped Kodi's arm in Human soldier manner, a natural movement like they were good friends meeting again after a long absence. The couple then went off to the banqueting tables on the lawn.

"Who were they again?" asked Kodi. "Their voices were familiar. Were they at the reception two weeks ago?"

But Ryn didn't seem to know, and memory of the strange but handsome couple faded quickly as they continued to greet others.

"Y...you took my sss...stammer away wh...when I spoke to him. Wh...why won't you take it ah...away alllltogether?"

"And just why would I do that, love? You're much too precious for me to change you, other than disguise, of course. Your voice is sexy and warm. To me you're perfect, and though you look quite nice like that, I'm putting you back to your Human form the instant we get back. I miss the beard."

"Ah, V, I love you so! Th...this has been fun, though. Hardly www...wait to g...get you home! Rrrrromp by the stream tonight, ah...under the stars."

"I was thinking something of the same sort, dear! But the food here's free in the sense I won't have to cook tonight, you see, and I might learn a new recipe! Let me know if one of these casseroles is exceptional. Try this one with the tomatoes and late summer squash. Looks promising. And I want to hear Lumin's song in person. We'll stand by that tree just there by the verandah when the time comes."

"Oh, yes. Lumin's song. Www...wouldn't want to miss that."

The greetings were pleasant, but finally all had taken seats. Kodi and Ryn were centered together at the top of the half circle where all could easily see them. Nikal sat at Kodi's other side, then Tiliruf and Lyndz, followed by Shane, Idamé and Curdoz. By Ryn was Lumin, followed by Olin, then Hurlin, and then Lady Mishoo. The rest of the royal family were at the next table over on that side, and beyond Curdoz at the next table were the other Human men and the Berugians. The Eagle Staff lay on their table like a centerpiece. At another table were the Healer Sisters and the six Bondswomen with their husbands. There were certain others in the verandah crowd, specially invited guests, and Healer Solone with his wife were two of these, and also Halta and Frith. There was much conversation, light-hearted and happy. Even Hurlin, with Olin on one side and Mishoo on the other, demonstrated an actual chuckle from time to time. In fact, he and Olin engaged continually with Mishoo, a favored cousin. Any of the Humans who looked in their direction were amazed to see Hurlin so engaged with another and without the straight face or the frown which they had grown used to.

Servants served, and all ate and drank, but toasting possibly with mead cups was apparently not a Qeteral tradition, and so there really were no speeches offered. It suited Kodi. One never knew if Tiliruf might get it in his head, say, if he drank a bit more mead than he should, to offer up something too Humanly silly. Kodi really needn't have worried. Tiliruf had never the remotest intention of embarrassing his best friend on this most glorious of nights.

The flute players returned and sat before them all and played. As it grew dark—though lanterns were everywhere lit and hanging from the tree limbs—Tanter the nightingale came and perched for a few minutes on Ryn's shoulders. He sang a lovely song to which they all found themselves mesmerized. The bird then flew off.

Finally, the Matriarch stood.

"It is my understanding the Bonding Hunt was won by our dear Lumin!" She looked at her youngest son with affection. "And so, he now wishes to present the gift of original song to Ryn and Kodi."

She sat, and Lumin proceeded to leave his chair and come around to the middle, whereupon he looked at the newly Bonded couple and began.

None of the Humans there had ever in their lives heard a male voice as melodious and stirring, and none present would ever forget it.

A ship upon the churning blue,
High rode the sun, not knowing me.
Whether an east wind or a west I heeded not,
For white sails carried a troubled heart.
The tossing waves reflected my thoughts;
My loneliness was heard in the cry of the gulls.

Upon a green land I disembarked.
Paths I wandered, meandering and lost.
Searching, I knew not what I sought.
A kind little bird kept me company.

Then, at my feet, arose the lily!
Its brighter green captured my eye.
My soul was captured by its perfect flower.
You were there! Let it not be a dream!
Yet, beholding the flower, I struggled with doubts.
Assure me, I pray. Do I seek too high?

A sailor I was. I believed me a knight.
To greatness I aspired. I am but a babe.
Dare I reach for you?
A star in the firmament?

A song I hear. Is that your voice?
Are you aware of the fire you kindle?
I will take this lily, this magical flower
And race upon the path appointed.
I am a man, now, and you draw me to you.
I grow. I see. I draw you to me.

Thoughts break into hearts! No dream is this!
As the cosmos shifts its moons and stars,
Our bodies travel newfound paths
Of warmth, of joy, of glorious flesh.

You, my love, are more than a blossom.
Blossom and stem, root of life.
And so, rooted in you I see all.
This path and green land, and the ocean wave.
The sun was smiling all along.
So, too, the moons in lusty embrace.

Now, the blue of the sea and the cloudless sky,
and the land of green with its golden sun.
Then, diamond waters and the light of night.
And in that light, we love.

As Lumin sang he lifted his arms in poetic performance and turned this way and that so as to include the whole of his audience. There was also a sizeable number of listeners just off the verandah. Upon completing his song, and while facing Kodi and Ryn again, his arms dropped, and his eyes closed. After several seconds he opened them again.

There was silence all around, and many mouths were agape in uttermost astonishment.

Hadon whispered to Manwul. "It was art! I never knew a song could be sung without any rhyme. Yet rhyme would have distracted from it, I think."

Deens spoke to Shane. "I've never heard a more extraordinary love song in all the days of my life."

Shane only nodded and did not reply. He understood more from the words in the song than Deens ever would.

"That was stunning," whispered Lyndz to Curdoz.

"Absolutely incredible."

"Damn!" Tiliruf found himself deeply moved, but no other words would come to him. Like Shane, he knew more of what underlay that song than virtually everyone else.

Universal amazement except for one. Hurlin whispered to Olin. "It's well beyond him. A boy singing of love as if he were a bonded man. And too Human. Ships and sailing. I should be ashamed."

Olin turned to his brother and gave him a sharp look. "No. It isn't. And you are a great fool to think as you do. It is you of whom I am ashamed. I will never be ashamed of Lumin."

None but the intended audience of these various whisperers heard any of it. And though no one knew it, when the two elder brothers would finally retire to their shared rooms that night, Olin, perhaps for the first time, displayed open anger with Hurlin and had many more words to add regarding Hurlin's recent behavior towards Lumin.

Finally, Kodi reached for Ryn's hand and stood, and she with him. He nodded deeply and said, "Thank you, my Brother, Lumin. With all my heart I thank you."

Ryn added, "It was the most extraordinary gift, Lumin. Kodi and I will cherish it forever."

Then Olin immediately stood, then Lyndz, then the Matriarch, and when she stood, all the rest then stood.

"It was marvelous, my son. The words of your song are to be added to the annals of this day. Though there will never be a one, Qeteral or Human, who will ever sing it as superbly as you. Yet from you, my son, both Qeteral *and* Human, I am not surprised. Your father the king, who blessed you last and not least before he left on his final journey, would be most pleased."

She then began the applause, which grew swiftly to include everyone there.

Lumin looked straight at Kodi and grinned.

Kodi nodded and winked.

The handsome couple listening with others just off the verandah then walked behind the trunk of a large tree. In its dark shadow they began kissing each other with uncontrolled fierceness and vanished from the scene. They left nothing behind, but with them they took full bellies, more than one new recipe, a decanter of Qeteral mead the man had snatched from a table, and an ever-increasing fondness for all those who were present at the royal Bonding.

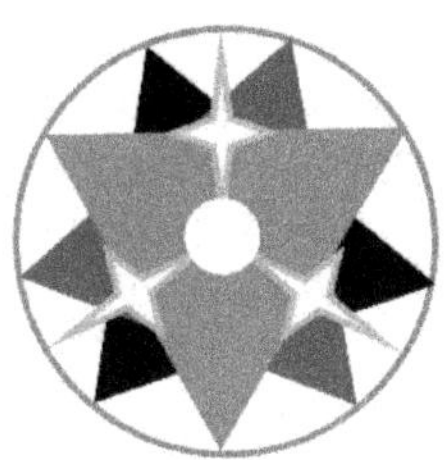

Chapter 29—Stormgale Returns

Two days later when he had the chance to do so, Kodi said to Lumin in private, "You're exceptional in all the arts, Lumin. I envy your talents. I could never draw like you, and certainly can't sing like you. That was amazing, that was. You personalized it with the lily, I know, for Ryn and me, but you were singing to Fal. Am I right? I'm sorry she wasn't there to hear you."

"Ah, but she did hear me."

"She did? How so?"

"She was standing close, just off the verandah, as I had asked her to. And when all had settled late that night, I met her again at the Diamond Pool. Our new favorite place. And I sang it to her again."

Kodi, filled to the brim with all the joys of the last many days, discovered a tear had overflowed and fallen from his face. He reached forward and the two embraced. "That's so happy, Little Brother!"

"You know me," Lumin said with a telling wink, "I made sure it was the best happy all night, eh?"

Kodi chuckled. "Yeah. Trust me, Little Brother. My happy late that night well compared to your happy."

Lumin got a sudden mischievous twinkle in his eye. "Ah, Kodi. Just like the other arts you're but a novice compared to me."

Kodi guffawed. "Oh? The multitalented magic man here putting me in my place, ha!"

"You begin to comprehend me now, eh? See you later, *Little Brother*." Lumin grinned, and proving he had become expert at Human humor, he reached out, placed a willful double slap on Kodi's cheek, and vanished from his sight.

Kodi's heehaw just then would have split ears. He raced off to inform Tiliruf of the superior joke. Tiliruf was gleeful at the retelling.

With Hakonn's permission that same morning Rainwing ordered Flamefur to fly northwest across Ulakel in search of Stormgale. "Go all the way to the Corellyan if you have to. Fly as high as you dare in order to try to sight him." And low and behold, that evening the two returned together. All were relieved and greeted Stormgale warmly.

He carried a packet for Curdoz. But it was soon apparent that his news from Solanto was distressing, to say the least.

The Escarantines were shocked at the appearance of an Etoppsis when he first landed at Mannago's palace. Mannago was absent. His wife, Merelda, was intelligent and discerning. Though she too was shocked, she reassured everyone, knowing quite well he had to be a messenger of the gravest importance. She welcomed and fed him and directed him on to her husband who was with the king in Ferostro. In Ferostro he engaged in many a conversation with those two and Father Marco, expounding upon every morsel of news from the south and receiving all the news from Solanto. He would in time explain further the high and gracious manner in which he was welcomed, the feasting, and the pilgrimage of curious Humans who came far to see their first Etoppsis. But for now he cut that piece of it short in order to tell Curdoz and all the rest what he had learned.

Curdoz was beside himself with fury, and some grieved, particularly Lyndz, when it was understood Princess Isatura had been abducted and was being held by Filiddor as a means to give him leverage over Carlomen. The Ramp was closed, and little word had been heard from Mannago's ring of spies he had sent there months before. However, Filiddor was allowing Order Members on pilgrimage to leave the principality permanently. Father Marco had ordered an end to new pilgrimages there anyway, although for now he had not ordered a complete withdrawal of the Orders from Hesk. That would have been an extreme measure until it was perceived Filiddor was acting with hostility to the Orders. So far, all indications were their work there was continuing. There were messengers between Aster and Ferostro, usually knights in the service of Filiddor or the barons. They were assured safe passage, and negotiations—of a sort—were ongoing.

But without Isatura, Carlomen was in great grief and could make few decisions. Mannago had been doing his best to gain time and not allow the king to give in to any of Filiddor's demands. It was plain to him that Isatura was, for now, completely safe, even if she was a prisoner. The situation would have to be dire indeed before Filiddor would actually threaten her person, for without her he had nothing else whatsoever to negotiate with.

In secret, Mannago told Stormgale that his own sons, Matteo and Olaron, were involved in an attempt to enter Hesk by the secret way behind Felto and try to recover the princess. The king was completely unaware of this, and Mannago believed it best not to tell the old man for now. He told Stormgale when, in the need to gain more time, should Carlomen get too desperate, he might then tell him this in order to give him some additional hope. But for now, the secret of the rescue attempt must be kept. None knew of it aside from Captain Santher in Thorune (promoted now to General), and it was from him that Mannago had received the secret information from Matteo.

Kodi was glad he had told Olaron about the trail behind Felto, and Curdoz was also glad they had given that information too to Danly and Xeno. It represented a means for potentially rescuing the princess, and also possibly to get troops or at least other spies into Filiddor's territory. Though news had been sent back and forth too between the neighboring kingdoms of Eleni and Solanto, the passes from the former into Hesk would be just as impassable as the Ramp. But the king in Eleni was also attempting to coordinate a plan. He had allied fully with King Carlomen, was infuriated with Prince Filiddor, and had now sworn him as his enemy. Isatura was his cousin through close royal ties. He would at the least be working to gain information on Ice Tribe movements and had ceased all trade with the principality. He also pledged troops and was sending these to the passes in order to press Filiddor too from the east and make it plain to the prince that Solanto would not be alone against him.

All understood, even Carlomen now, that Filiddor had treasonously sided with the old enemy, and that the Ice Tribes were offering the prince their support. What little news they did have from Aster was that Tribal troops were on the move in Hesk. The Hescian commoners and army, though they may not have liked Tribesmen, were too much yoked to Filiddor and his barons to even feign resistance to his will.

Unclear still, was Duke Snoffit of Ascanti. He had been summoned forthwith to Carlomen following the battle at the Ramp whereby they had tried to rescue the princess, but though he pledged public support for the king, he was for now refusing to believe war was required, and was urging the king, even openly now, to turn the Tolosian Peninsula over to the prince and end the need for further conflict. In addition, he refused to agree with the belief Count Ostin was in league, saying it was total conjecture. Yet he could not deny that Counts Mere and Nees had sided with Filiddor. He said he had summoned them upon hearing the news of the battle at the Ramp but believed they had taken their household of knights and disappeared behind its gates. Trying to deflect blame, he attempted to pin the dissension of these barons on the king and his unwillingness to do right by Filiddor. Mannago would not have it, however, and reminded him that Mere had killed old Count Ilmore, in fact calling it outright murder, and that Mere had openly assisted in the abduction of Isatura. Nees had allowed them to cross his lands and had issued no warnings when he could have. It was high treason. The king made it official that Mere and Nees were under sanction, used royal law to remove their titles, ranks and privileges, and took possession of their estates. Their castles were now occupied by Solantine captains with Kingsmen guards, all now under General Santher's authority, and these were patrolling the lands in the vicinity of the Ramp.

Siding with Duke Amerro of Tulesk, when the king wished also to summon him to court, Mannago put his foot down and convinced the king that Amerro had every right to remain in Tulesk in order to monitor Ice Tribe movement in the mountains and protect his own from Filiddor. Until Carlomen was actually willing to take the Peninsula away from Amerro, for now Amerro was the king's man and must protect them and the status quo. And of course, Mannago wasn't letting Carlomen get close to that decision.

It was tricky, for Mannago knew in his own heart that Amerro would go to war, even against the king's express wishes. King's man, yes, but only until his own sense of honor had to be upheld. Amerro believed, and technically he was right, that he had never done anything wrong. Tolos was legally a part of his duchy. All blame lay with Filiddor. And if the king gave in to Filiddor's demands for Tolos, Tulesk would surely be next on the prince's agenda. Tulesk, old Ice Tribal Stavenland, was just as much a part of the supposed old Terianh document Filiddor had brought to the King's Council all those weeks ago.

Now, on that, when Mannago and Carlomen understood through Stormgale that the document Filiddor had brought to the earlier council meeting was fake, it opened their eyes further to Filiddor's treachery. And even as Stormgale was himself in Ferostro, messengers sent by Enric and Genehbro in Tirilorin came to Carlomen with proof documents and histories confirming that Terianh had never given those lands to Filiddor's ancestor T'vani.

King Carlomen was infuriated, for all along he had allowed himself to believe the Filiddor document carried ancient weight and should be considered. It seemed genuine, and Carlomen had wondered if he should abide by it.

Filiddor's expressed will that he only wanted Tolos and not Tulesk had seemed to him at the time to have the quality of a grand and noble gesture. Carlomen thought he was being wise and fair regarding Filiddor's desires, in light of the document, allowing for the three-month time frame in which to issue a decision. And now he knew all along he had been completely duped despite the warnings given by Curdoz before he left, and the council of Mannago, Marco, and of his daughter. His desire for peace had overruled his wisdom.

And in a way, as Mannago told Stormgale secretly, it made Mannago's position even better with the king, because for now, the king was so angry he vowed never to allow Filiddor a square inch of Tolos. Mannago believed fully now that the king would almost certainly adhere to Mannago's advice on all matters, though of course that depended still on the situation with Isatura, and the king could always change his mind. Mannago's fear, which he hardly dared speak aloud, was not that Filiddor would threaten Isatura's life but that he would force her into Bonding him and by it make a claim on the throne of Solanto. He also let Stormgale in on another secret of which the king was unaware and was not common knowledge: the princess's servants who had returned from the escort told him that Isatura and Matteo had pledged troth to one another the actual day on which she was later abducted.

"If they have pledged troth," Idamé said, "for royalty it is as binding as the Bonding itself."

"Except that Filiddor has Isatura captive, and has the advantage," said Nikal bluntly. This possibility carried strong emotion for him as much as it did for those who essentially knew Isatura, and Idamé reluctantly admitted he was right. There were legal methods involving the Mother Superior that would allow for royal trothplight to be made null, and even annulments following Bonding, even though these were exceedingly rare.

"Why won't Mannago tell the king of this?" asked Kodi.

"It is plain," said Curdoz, "that Mannago is being careful regarding the facts he is allowing Carlomen to have in order to keep him from making rash choices in his communication with Filiddor's messengers. I can see he has explained some of this in the missive he sent me in Stormgale's packet. In part it is to ensure it all remains secret from Filiddor as well. Mannago has ordered all the princess's servants and Kingsmen in the know to keep the betrothal secret for her safety, as the information might also cause Filiddor to react rashly if he were to learn of it. The more secrets Mannago is able to keep and dole out slowly allows him to gain more time for his sons to attempt the rescue."

In the meantime, the Kingsmen army was mobilizing. Even Snoffit in Ascanti was at least verbally gathering his own men together, and Mannago had agents there who had informed him he was. And all the dukes and barons in the rest of the kingdom were sending troops to Ferostro should it indeed come to full-on war with Filiddor.

But the primary news that Stormgale had brought to Ferostro was a shock beyond anything they could have conceived. The information about a magical Doorway that could open into Tolos allowing the faraway khans to possibly send an army through it and to potentially ravage the northlands was beyond the pale. Carlomen could hardly bear this news, and even Mannago could not find words to address it at first. Finally, he did say that Snoffit's geographical position in Ascanti made it critical they gain his unwavering support. To date, he had been giving Snoffit some benefit of the doubt on the Hescian situation and some leeway to prove support for Solanto without accusing him of possibly being in league with Filiddor, as the evidence on that had definite limitations. But now the matter had come to a head, they would be required to press Snoffit to subdue his pride and comply fully with the wishes of the king. But they certainly didn't (nor did Curdoz suspect they could) offer any inspiration on whether the khans were in communication with the Ice Tribal alliance with Filiddor. It seemed doubtful, and yet admitted, with the realization the khans were the children of the last Ralsheen emperor, and so of the same blood as the Tribal Chieftains, that the possibility of such long-distance communication was surely there. Father Marco also, based on Stormgale's information, suggested that dark magic was involved in making the fake Terianh document appear so authentic, and so dark magic could be involved too in communications between the khans and the Ice Tribes and Filiddor.

But the news also made Mannago realize something else he had heretofore been reluctant to consider, and that was the idea they would be required not only to mobilize the trained Kingsmen and knights of the realm, but they would also have to reach out to the populace and recruit more armies. It would take planning and time. He would be sure also to send the information on to the king of Eleni. Poor old Carlomen seemed altogether to be in a state of unbelief at the full drama of the situation. He kept stating how only a few months before the northlands were in a near full state of peace, and now they were facing the potential for a northern conflagration.

Based on Curdoz' wishes, they allowed Stormgale to fly to Duke Amerro in Cumpero in Tulesk, another lengthy flight, and the Etoppsis had further news from that sector. Amerro was massing rapidly for a war he was almost determined to fight. And he didn't trust Duke Snoffit in the end, believing him in cahoots with Filiddor. He was also sending troops by ship around the Tolosian Peninsula to reinforce those he had stationed at the fort and port village he had earlier established at the mouth of the Tolos River. He had, on his own volition, begun capturing Ice Tribe fishermen that could at times be found in far northern waters in summer. He already had some eighty prisoners and was trying to get information out of them regarding their Chieftains' plans. There were passes over the Northern Mountains. These were being reinforced against an incursion which he fully believed was coming. Stormgale, with Mannago's prior permission, then told Amerro of the secret path behind Felto of which Amerro had heretofore been ignorant. He had been on his way to Felto to meet with Princess Isatura when he received word of her abduction and returned to Cumpero without seeing Lady Elisa and her father whereby he might have learned of it. He was beyond grateful for this superior piece of intelligence. He would send troops to Felto immediately and take control of that trail.

But on the whereabouts of the twins' father, Hess, Amerro admitted to no information. Nothing had been heard, and yet it wasn't expected that any news was to come for a while longer. The plan of course had been for Hess to explore deep into the interior of Tolos, attempt to discover treasure and the ancient city of the Ralsheen and to return in the fall. Hess was not expected, really, for at least another full month if not longer.

Amerro was astounded by all the news Stormgale then gave him from the south. He had heard about Curdoz having come for Hess's twins and departing the country with them, but he knew nothing otherwise. He then spoke of 'Bagarro's own mighty blood' and was awestruck and complimentary in particular of Kodi's great heroism. And then like Carlomen and Mannago, when Stormgale then expounded upon the khans, the Doorway, and all the potential horror of that situation, Amerro paced the floor for minutes on end. He would certainly send more troops to Tolos, and now he realized that even he, despite his current feelings for the wishy-washy Snoffit, would be forced into diplomacy with his southern brother duke and try to make amends and ensure a stronger alliance. Of course, that is what Stormgale told him Mannago wished for him to do. He wasn't happy about that but acquiesced to the need.

When Curdoz heard this, he was immensely pleased that Amerro realized the need to be less hot-headed in his decision-making. His obsession with the potential for riches from Tolos would have to be set aside for now. Amerro then promised Stormgale he would send scouts to Tolos and do his best to retrieve Hess as soon as possible and ensure his safety. He even admitted to Stormgale he was now beginning to feel regret over the level at which he had pressed his cousin Hess into continually doing his bidding. Yes, he believed Hess was the best for the job, but knew in his heart Hess wanted only to reside in peace with his family and administer his county and the ambernut trade. He also realized, considering all the news regarding the man's twin children from the south, Hess's heart would in future be burdened by these ramifications. "Hess should have been at home. He should have been at home with his wife and the twins. I took that away from him. I am regretful of this. Stormgale, you have overcome me with all this news. You must tell them when you see them, the Lord Kodi and the Lady Lyndz, of my remorse. Their father should have gone with them."

"No, he shouldn't have," said Kodi with vehemence, as Stormgale concluded.

"No," agreed Lyndz. "The last thing I'd have wanted would have been for Father to leave Mother and come with us. But yes, Father should have been home with us these years, he should be with Mother now, and Amerro really is responsible. Guardian's Teeth, Stormgale! All your news is an eye-opener for sure. I so wish Father had returned home by now, but I am truly heartbroken for Isatura."

For his bravery, determination, and for the critical nature of Stormgale's journey, Nikal gave him the honors of the Kingdom of Nant, and Matriarch Gwyn did likewise for the Kingdom of Ulakel. Stormgale was not typically of a boastful nature. He didn't have the sort of brilliant charisma of Flamefur or Windsdown that made those two especially popular back home in Berug. But now his sense of accomplishment showed with proud countenance on his severe but handsome furred face.

"They did the same for me in Solanto. They treated me with great reverence everywhere I went."

"They'd better have," said Kodi.

And it was not the only honor he received. Flamefur reminded Kodi and Nikal of the roles they held officially in Berug, and as such they had authority to do something which Flamefur now recommended, and which they fully agreed to. Stormgale was an Eyefeather spy in the Berugian Sky Front with a mission leader specialty rank essentially at the level of a Wing-Sergeant. He had been commended several times already for spy work over West Khestadon.

"It is most fitting we advance your rank to that of Rainstorm-Major. You have leadership capabilities and experience beyond most of your cohorts. It seems you also engaged in some skillful diplomacy."

Skipping past the Cloud-Captain level, Stormgale was now equal in rank to Flamefur. It well fit the value he, like all Feathers, placed on the Taxiarchan Disciplines of the Berugian Sky Front that he looked on this as a great honor. Especially so as it was bestowed upon him by Staff-wielding Polemarchi under the direct authority of the Taxiarch. It was a first for any Etoppsis, at least since the ancient days of Berug the Magnificent. Nikal would have Deens interview Stormgale at length in order to create a full-written account of his journey and deeds, a copy eventually to be delivered to King Eagleron.

All the visitors to Ulakel, male and female, along with Ryn, Lumin, and Olin, together had a late supper by firelight at the pavilion, sitting about on the ground or in chairs brought out from inside. The talk consisted of ruminations over Stormgale's news from Solanto, but also of the happy events in Ulakel over the last several days. Stormgale of course expressed his surprise and hearty congratulations to the newly Bonded couple. He was now asked to describe the journey itself. Beforehand they had been focused on his news, but now they wanted him to reflect instead on the adventure to and from. Much of his description focused on his flight over the Corellyan Mountains. Ryn stated that though Qeteral had many stories regarding them, no Qeteral had set off to explore them in over three-hundred years. There were Ulaki villages in some of the near foothills, and places that afforded incredible vistas, but even those who lived so near were unwilling to venture higher and further in.

It became immediately clear that Stormgale himself had discovered in them a land of magnificence and wonder that reached deeply into his soul and set it afire like no place had ever done before. "Those mountains. You may say they are haunted, but I am here to tell you they contain the most striking landscapes I have ever seen. Four times I landed in order to rest and drink, twice going and twice coming, in high valleys serene and stunning. Waterfalls of unimaginable height and glacial lakes of intense blue. I could not stay, of course, to explore, and yet that is precisely what I wanted to do. And if ever in future I have a chance to return with some friends to see again those places I will consider my life charmed. Or perhaps better my Bondmate Yellowtips. High summer meadows filled with flowers of every color of the rainbow, herds of deer by the hundreds and birds countless and colorful. There were eagles there of great size. They were curious of me and flew with me many miles like an escort. I was moved with emotion and felt like a World God flying the skies in the primordial days before the coming of the Children of the Mold. If the tales are true that it was the home of the World Gods in prehistoric days, then I understand why. The canyonlands of Berug are beautiful to be sure, and I miss them, but I will return to the Corellyan Mountains someday if I am lucky enough to live into a future world of peace. Yellowtips and I would spend a whole summer in one of those green and flower-filled valleys and plunge into those cold lakes and get fat on venison!"

"Your adventures would gain you a place in the Soaring Stags," Rusty said, from his perspective a great compliment. "I will promote your membership upon our return to Berug."

"Thank you, but no. Maybe I envied the Stags when I was a topling, but no more. Again, thank you. I am glad to see you again, Flamefur. And Noble Rainwing."

"And I you," said Flamefur.

"You were greatly missed," added Rainwing.

It may have been before that Flamefur and Stormgale were not close friends. Certainly, they were not. Rather, the relationship contained some aloofness due to strong personality differences. But Stormgale's journey and mission, added to by the affirmation provided by his promotion in rank, had created in him strong self-confidence and even a flame in his soul that manifested in greater willingness to engage Rusty. Likewise, his absence had had an unexpected impact on Rusty. Rusty, with his gregarious nature and big ego, wasn't used to being without a close male companion in order to bounce that ego. It had always been Windy before, or others of the Stags who shared strong alpha-male instincts and machismo-type humor. But he found he had missed Stormgale mightily, even worried for him as though he were family. So as the days went by, it became plain that the two male Etoppsi did indeed become close. They were unique to the present situation, and a brotherhood bond developed to a point the one would not part from the other for long during their tasks, quickly seeking the other out after a separation and engaging in more robust conversation than they had ever done before. That new flame in his soul allowed Stormgale to see Flamefur's animal-driven passions through different eyes, and Rusty began to appreciate Stormy's penchant for philosophical and aesthetic observation, and each began to take on some of these values from the other. Kodi was glad, and maybe he had anticipated some of this. Actually, Nikal accused him of it.

"You wanted them to draw together, didn't you?"

"I did. I knew they were opposites in a lot of ways, but look at it this way. Tiliruf and I are opposites in some ways, too, but he and you are my best buddies. Manwul and Hadon are different, too. Manwul's rough and tumble, and Hadon likes art, music, has an aesthetic eye, and likes comfort and elegance. And Lyndz and Rainwing had nothing whatsoever in common when those two met."

"At the core you and I are much the same."

"We had different experiences, but I think that's true. You and I are a lot alike. So are Rusty and Windy. But I think a man needs 'opposite' friends in order to grow into a bigger man. So why not Rusty and Stormy? But yeah, maybe I did plan it that way on a purpose for those two. I thought each could learn more around the other, but I think Rusty needed to be away from Windy for it to happen. And I didn't get it wrong."

"That is the high mark of leadership. It is kingly and Sage-like to be as you are. You have become a superior judge of men's characters. And not just Human men, but apparently Qeteral men and Etoppsi males, too."

"I've realized, and I think our expert Shane has too, that blokes of all three races are much the same. He's been writing those journals on 'masculinity' like the world's going come to an end if he don't get it all down fast enough. And I guess, logically, that means the 'females' of all three races are much the same too. I'm sure Lyndz would say so. The differences then in what we look like and other tidbits like Qeteral magic and Etoppsi having wings, er, and a few sexual differences, are just artful decoration if you ask me. Remember when Tiliruf said, 'Stoles and shawls, who needs them?' There was wisdom in it, for it's what's under the surface that matters. But we don't deny stoles and shawls are important symbols just like wings are on an Etoppsis and speaking to birds is to Qeteral."

"What do you say they are symbols of?"

"Well, that I learned from Curdoz. The Creation Act by the One Mind. The grand scale of beauty in the world. And it all points to love, if you ask me. That's what we're all put here for, and we're all unique Minds, little Creators, and it's the best thing in the world. We're s'posed to love each other, and that's what I'm trying to do."

"You do a superior job of that, Kodi. And you have taught me more than you can ever know. And though I am sometimes still sad over Dira, a sense of despair has abated. Nor do I deny the friendship of the others, but you are the one who has largely made me a whole man again."

"You're going to make me tear up, buddy."

"And what you have gained here in Ulakel has made you a whole man."

"I feel it. I know it. I also want to see our baby when it comes, and I think it'll add to me even more. But this is part of the thing, Nikal. And that's that we men don't have to be perfect in order to be men. My definition of a man is this: the spirited male with a good will and the creative drive to make a mark and do well by others. Doesn't mean we're perfect, doesn't mean we never make any mistakes, doesn't mean we're always right about everything, doesn't mean we can't ever be boy-like and playful anymore. Sometimes we mess up along the way, but it doesn't take away who we are as men. Sometimes I think we think, at least as boys, and maybe sometimes our fathers tell us this sort of thing, is the 'you'll be a *real* man when...' and then they add in a bunch of conclusions they think are wise. But I don't look at it that way anymore. I was a man before Curdoz came and got me. I was a man before I shot down those Sea Serpents. I was a man before I became a War Wizard. I was a man before I fought the Alkhaness. I was a man before I met Ryn. I'm a man because that's what the Mind made me into, and I've really felt it in my soul since sixteen, I think, maybe earlier than that. Though I think I became a *better* man at each point."

"I like your definition of a 'man.' And what you say is wise. But, too, and I think Shane would agree with me, and that's that you had a Vision from Meical, Kodi. Not all men are so lucky to have that sort of affirmation in their lives, affirmation despite our imperfections. But I do see something here, and this relates to what you said about fathers just now. The pressures of many men keep them from assuming the genuineness of their manhood, keeping them from achieving a sense of purpose and self-fulfillment. And there are those too, who may have all the wisdom like what you have espoused about manhood, know it logically, believe it to be true, and yet still suffer..."

"From lack of affirmation, though."

"Probably so. But not just from others but from within themselves, which is surely just as important if not more so. And so, there are those who suffer from internal melancholy, some worse than others. I do not know, Kodi, that every such man can be fixed, even if he were to experience a Vision. I think I was close to being such a man, but you have been the Vision for me, and for me I think it has worked. But it may not work for everyone. So, you and I really are witnesses of consequence to the workings of the Guardian, and I feel closer to Meical than I did. Men will follow us, and men are inspired by us. And there are other great examples of faith that inspire, and the work of the Orders very much inspires many people. That sense of grand beauty, too, inspires, along with all the creative arts and good works. But then the inspiration leaves some, a black hole widens in their souls, and the melancholy takes hold again. I feel then we are still missing something that truly causes Healing for such people. I don't think it's just choice on their part."

"I believe you. Maybe it isn't just choice. But Nikal, there's still the acts of love, and Meical says, and He's right, that it's actions we take that're more valuable than the outcome. And so, you've suffered. I've suffered a little with Father back home and some guilt over some choices, nothing like what you've gone through, but the point is that we keep on trying. Love and action don't mean we ourselves will always be the ones who benefit, but others will. When necessary, a real man must be able to see the need to sacrifice for the benefit of others. The selfish man is convinced he will be diminished should he sacrifice anything, and he's wrong. I really think that's the way it is. The star points on the Orders symbol, on these medallions of ours, what Curdoz taught us about them, I think are exactly right. We take the steps from one point to the next. Melancholy, yes. It takes hold in everyone, sometimes. But I think it should only lead to despair when we give up trying. I wonder if the melancholy of some comes out of a belief they're completely alone and that no one on Dumhoni can understand the paths they walk."

"And so they isolate themselves."

"Yeah, and it's a mistake. We can't break the melancholy if we remain always alone, even if the loneliness is just inside our heads. We weren't meant to be lonely. The People of the Mold are each of unique value, but that value is only shown in relationship with others. Curdoz taught me that, too. Shane emphasizes it often. It has everything to do with why you and I were Chosen to carry the Eagle Staff. Not every man can do it. We are walking dark paths, Nikal. Very dark, with this Staff. It makes us into mass killers—Velus and Strom, likewise, when you think about it—and killing kills the soul. And so, we have to reach out and love the ones put in our lives and more importantly allow them to love us back and keep us sane and try to close up the dark holes.

"Not every man can keep love in the forefront of his thoughts and actions. Instead, he gets power-hungry and allows pride to take control. He turns himself into a wicked conniver or a spikeshafted bully. Dark paths and dark holes are all he'll ever know. Am I supposed to feel sorry for such a man, Nikal? Like Filiddor? Like your damned peckerjuiced brother? Like the Alkhan? Not sure that I can. About the only thing I feel sorry for in him is that there's no way for him to go back and undo the horror he's made for himself. He's lost. Redemption for the soul is always there Curdoz taught me, and I believe it, but such a man almost never acknowledges it, and in his pride won't acknowledge the need for it. Meical was never going to pick such a man for the Staff. He picked me and He picked you because we know how to love and how to let others love us back. And He picked two of us together, because we know how to love each other, you and I, a deep love that lifts us higher than we each were before we met."

"We need each other; I firmly believe it."

"I'm a better man because of you, Nikal. And about the Staff, I don't think I'd be happy at all if it were my responsibility alone, even with Meical speaking to me. *He knew what He was doing*. If Curdoz has said that once he's said it fifty times."

This was hardly the first deep conversation between these two, nor would it be the last. But it was a demonstration of the growth and wisdom they had gained, particularly in Kodi's case since the time he left home in early spring. His mind had broadened enormously, his experiences had sharpened his wits to the point he was as astute as Lyndz or Shane, and more importantly the wisdom and love of others had played on him and grown him. All the men and the women saw it. He had changed, was more mature and confident, and yet he was just as friendly as he ever was, still playful, still joyful, full of hugs and smiles and handgrips, and now blessings for the children, superior lovemaking with Ryn, dwelling in the moment. Nikal's growth too was marked, Curdoz in particular could tell, as he observed Nikal bask in Kodi's joyful nature and found it seemed also to fit Nikal himself more naturally than the old Nikal who always worried about responsibility and the manner in which people observed him. He had retained an aloofness in part as emotional defense in order to protect himself from others misusing him or misunderstanding him. These pieces were melting away as he found a new self-assuredness. Just as he went most every day to swim and play with the Qeteral children and revel in the cool waters under the late summer sun, Nikal became more and more the openly loving man that was as much a part of his nature as it was Kodi's. He would always maintain a kind of cool reflectiveness and make less use of words than Kodi, but otherwise he'd come to see blessings and joys all around him, in great measure involving him. He too was hugging more, smiling more, handgripping more, laughing more, and also offering blessings to the children as the Brother of Myghal almost as often as Kodi. All those in the fellowship around him had a love for him that wasn't always of the reverential type but rather of the intimate sort, the same sort that was so plainly directed at Kodi. He was finally living the life he wanted to live, surrounded by the best people who were easy to care about and who genuinely cared about him. Dira was absent, of course, and it hurt him deeply, but love all around him had increased rather than diminished since she had been stolen away. He felt it strongly. And he loved others more keenly than ever before.

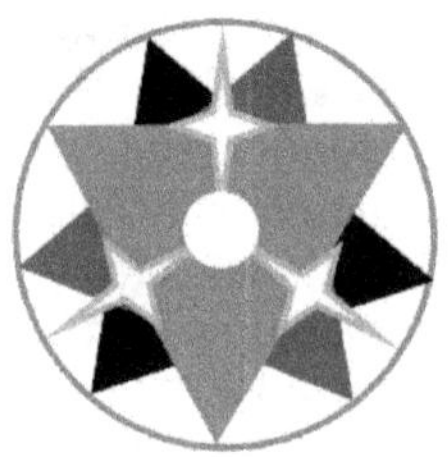

Chapter 30—Azure

As it approached time to leave Ulakel, the Humans and Etoppsi were suppressing sadness and trying not to think of the dangers facing them once they left. They were doing a fair job of it, trying to make every hour count. Nikal would not miss another day at the swimming hole. He'd grown attached to many of the children and become friends with some of their fathers. Short as it was, the magic of the land of Ulakel made it seem much longer, and to him this had become the life he would cherish and for which memories would aid him in the trying days afterwards. He'd been able to discard responsibilities and duty and be the kind and loving man he wished to be—which old Antonin told him long ago he was—and engage in fatherly adoration of the Qeteral children.

The women trained one more day with Mishoo and then used the remaining days to rest and enjoy gatherings. Idamé attended two Qeteral Bonding ceremonies in other nearby villages as Bondswoman Vitalle's guest, and those two had become good friends. Halta came along, as she was Vitalle's granddaughter and wished to spend more time with her before her own departure.

Tiliruf, Manwul, Hadon, along with Lumin, would usually be at the swimming hole in the early afternoon with Nikal, as would Shane and Solone.

Shane and Solone's friendship had grown deep. They hardly hid any secret thoughts. Solone took the deceased Eliander's place as Shane's confidant. Shane was a deeply emotional person on top of his intellectualism, but aside from genuine feelings of fondness and friendship, he rarely displayed intense emotion with the Human warrior set. He felt his strength of mind and will and overarching professionalism was something that increased their own sense of duty and inner strength and that it was a part of his Calling as a disciplined Healer. But with Solone he had found a soulmate, and Solone's wife and daughter also grew fond of him. Shane could share certain worries and anxieties with Solone of which the Human men knew little.

There was also scientific-medical discovery involved for them, for just as Shane had wished to use his magic to examine the bodies of Lumin and Olin, Solone's wife offered herself as a female specimen, and for Solone's benefit, Manwul, Hadon, and Maru, too, were willing to allow him to probe their bodies with his magic. Maru was able to get in some examinations of her own, as she was nearly as interested as Shane was in learning about Qeteral differences. Though Rainwing did not offer, Flamefur was more than amenable and allowed Solone the opportunity to examine his body with magic, too. Solone's notetaking was as intense as Shane's could be.

Those last few days also saw a quick growth in intensity—the happy sort—in the relationship between Hakonn and Curdoz, as those two spent many extra hours with each other in deep conversation, either in Hakonn's study or on walks in the palace garden.

Tiliruf and Lumin spent many hours together, and Tiliruf was able to achieve a sense of lightheartedness as they romped together through fields and on hikes. Lumin taught Tiliruf the names and habits of many plants not known to him in Tirilorin, increasing his botanical knowledge. Once, Lumin took Tiliruf on a longer trek by a river and climbed to a cliff overhang with a beautiful view.

"This is the place."

Tiliruf grinned but was respectful. "Thank you for sharing with me something of great meaning for you and Fal."

Surely Lumin felt a brotherly affinity with Kodi, but his friendship with Tiliruf was nearly as strong. The thing was, Kodi was not seen very much.

Because for Kodi, these last days were largely filled with privacy with Ryn. They spent all their days and nights together. There was a second night for them at the Diamond Pool when Kodi with fun told Lumin he was to stay away.

There was one day in which they were invited and attended a late afternoon lawn party at Grandma Manoo's cottage. This included the Etoppsi and all the Humans, along with Mishoo, Lumin, and Olin. Queen Gwyn and Princess Linea arrived a little later and stayed for an hour. Manoo's servants provided refreshments and mead, and they all enjoyed games on the grass. Lumin wore his boots that day as his grandmother requested.

Two days prior to their departure, a message came one morning for Nikal at the pavilion. He was summoned by Hakonn. Upon arriving at the palace, he was led to the rear verandah where he found Ryn and Kodi.

Ryn explained. "Grandfather and I wish to present the two of you with something of immense value. It is my Bonding gift for Kodi, and yet you, too, Nikal, are meant to share the gift with him."

At that, Hakonn and two male servants stepped around a corner. Perched on the strong arm of one of the servants was an enormous, regal bird. The raptor sported a bright blue tail.

Kodi's jaw dropped, his eyes grew big, and then—he could not help it—very watery. "Ah! Ah! Oh, Ryn!"

Nikal smiled enormously. "He's stunning. It is a 'he' is it not?"

"It is," said Hakonn with rare pleasure in his voice. "The females are larger and much heavier. You would not wish for a larger bird, I think. These bracers are each for you. Kodi, I realize you do not normally wear a bracer as an archer, but you will find wearing one useful as a perch."

Kodi could not speak. Hakonn strapped silver and leather bracers on the arms of both Nikal and Kodi. The image of a hawk was engraved on the silver. Hakonn continued. "The Blue-tailed Hawk is to become the sign and symbol of your house, Prince Kodi. Princess Ryn had the bird brought here when she discovered that Bluetails have great meaning for you. It is her Bonding gift for you and is to become your familiar. He is a well-trained young male of two years. They are used by some few hunters who live north of here for locating prey. But this one will become much more."

Ryn spoke. "Grandfather is capable of instilling a magical connection between you, the two War Wizards, and the Bluetail. His name is Azure, as I requested one with the bluest tail."

Upon guidance of the knowledgeable servant, a trained birder, the great bird hop-stepped from the man's arm to that of Nikal. They peered at each other with what appeared like reverence. "He has great intelligence, I can tell. I allowed Aron to keep our little Greyhawk Letti on Modela's Island. I have missed that bird. What a wonderful, wonderful gift. Thank you."

Then, inevitably, Kodi's arm was graced by the stunning Bluetail. He found the great bird surprisingly lightweight for its size. The look they bore one another was one of affection. The bird nuzzled Kodi under his chin. Finally, Kodi spoke. "I...I just cannot believe this." He looked at Ryn. "Thank you, Mated One. But I have no like gift for you!"

"Ah, Mated One, it needs no reciprocal gift. Just return when all is done, and when together we hold our child, there can be no greater gift."

Hakonn spoke again. "I will be required to touch each of your heads and the body of the Bluetail and back and forth again in order to instill the magic. Though you are not Qeteral, I know it will not matter. By it you will each be able to communicate messages each to the other by way of Azure, whether it be for battle tactics or in any other potential separation. In addition, you will be able to see all the bird sees within a distance of around six leagues, though he will still be able to relay messages no matter the distance. Qeteral will of course also be able to understand your messages. Azure will be loyal to you and in some measure do your bidding within its talents. You understand and trust me?"

"There is more, which Grandfather hesitates to tell you," said Ryn. "For when he does this it is a sacrifice of those pieces of the magic within him."

"You mean, he will not be able to communicate with birds ever again?" asked Nikal.

"It is, I believe," said Hakonn, "a choice the Divine requires of me. Could another do it instead? Probably. But I have chosen this. I have communed with birds for over a century, and it is a joy. But Kodi, Nikal, we of the royal family wish to show our devotion, and also our love for you, and wish to demonstrate some sacrifice, sacrifice along with you, for these events and the war belong to all three races. The enemy must be defeated. Azure will help you along the way. I prophecy he will be of great help to that goal. So, will the two of you accept our gift?"

Both Nikal and Kodi were overcome by these intimate words, so rare from Hakonn, and such a demonstration of his own strong faith in the Guardian. They nodded.

The task took only a few minutes. Several times Hakonn took his two hands and placed them on the heads and eyelids of the War Wizards and also the high shoulders of Azure the Bluetail Hawk. All this time the hawk sat regally and quietly on Kodi's arm.

"Send him forth, Lord Prince Kodi," said Hakonn.

"Fly, my friend, fly!" commanded Kodi.

With that, Azure let go of his arm, and as he dropped downwards a little, his great wings, surely with a five-foot wingspan, spread forth. And he flew.

"It's easy, Kodi. Nikal," said Ryn. "Just 'imagine' and you will see through his eyes!"

"I can! I can! I can!"

The bird flew high and within moments had disappeared beyond the palace.

"There are Stormgale and Flamefur!" exclaimed Nikal.

"They see him! They see Azure! They are flying together!"

"They are coming!"

And very soon, Azure with a great call, the first they'd heard from him, returned, followed by Stormy and Rusty. Azure landed gracefully on Nikal's arm and called again.

"He is happy," said Ryn, smiling. "He has great love for both of you."

Stormgale and Flamefur landed beyond the verandah and walked over.

"Magnificent creature!" boomed Rusty. "It was as though he called for us to follow and we did!"

"Did you ask Azure to do that?" asked Hakonn.

"I think I did!" exclaimed Kodi.

"I am not surprised that Etoppsi would have an affinity with flying creatures and understand them a little."

But Kodi was absent too many words just then, he was so overwhelmed. It was Nikal who explained to the Etoppsi what had taken place. They were awestruck.

"What an extraordinary gift!" offered Stormgale.

For several hours until lunchtime, they all enjoyed one another's company as Nikal and Kodi 'experimented' several times with launching Azure and issuing commands through their minds and 'seeing' all that the great hawk could see. The Matriarch, Linea, Rainwing, and Lyndz came out to the verandah at one point and added their own exclamations to that of Nikal and Kodi. Finally, Nikal returned to the pavilion carrying Azure, for he would be the one to explain to the Human men about the gift. They were all amazed, and many times Nikal would send Azure to Kodi at the palace. Through Azure's eyes each War Wizard could see the great smiles on the other's face and even relay thoughts.

Later, Gwyn privately approached her father.

"It was a great gift. How are you feeling? Tell me."

"It...is hurtful. There is an emptiness. I walked in the garden with Ryn and Kodi after Nikal left, and though I could hear and see the beautiful songbirds, I could not understand their voices anymore. The garden seemed to have lost a great part of its charm. But I did what was right."

"I honor you."

"Thank you, Daughter."

"The latest on our defense?"

"The Barrier is as strong as it has ever been. Siriné herself could come to the edge of the Plateau, but she would be luckless upon reaching it. She cannot do so anyway, but as you and I have discussed with Hurlin and Olin, the wicked khans have subtleties of which we know not. I am relieved neither Hurlin nor Olin were in the Sage's and Matrimonial's Visions. The Barrier would be of minimal value without those two. Also, Hurlin, Olin, and Mishoo have in the last month reached Hurlin's goal of a trained defensive fighting force of some four thousand. It is doubled what it was a year ago when the eastern war began. After the group leaves, at Nikal's suggestion, Hurlin is considering sending forth some five hundred to monitor the Lintiri shore."

"Inform him I approve of that plan. We will take Nikal's suggestion as an order from a War Wizard. Mishoo will be outstanding as a leader on the forthcoming journey. Lumin is determined also to do his duty."

"He speaks with mature demeanor since you gave him permission to go. Letting him go was your sacrifice for the rescue, just as mine was for giving magic to the War Wizards to use the Bluetail. Let us hope our family sacrifices no more. Should Lumin return, you and I understand he will wish to proclaim his manhood early—earlier even than Mabelin his father."

"If he does so, I say we affirm him without question and rejoice with a family feast just as we did with Olin and Hurlin. I told him he must not go with the others afterwards to the war in the east. He assured me of his obedience. He said to me, *Ulakel is where my heart dwells. If we save our brothers and sisters in the south I will return with them, Mother. I will bring them home. I will not go to the east.*"

Hakonn paused for a moment. He then raised an eyebrow and replied. "Those were the words he used? *Where my heart dwells?* Those are the words of a poet, Madam. Since Ryn's Bonding we now know just what sort of poet he is. I wonder..."

Gwyn looked steadily into her father's face. After a moment, she too raised an eyebrow. "You're beginning to think his song may have meant more than...more than a *future* wish for himself? That it reflects something of the present?"

"He *is* Mabelin's son. Not just the stirring words, but also the exceptional manner in which he sang it. There was a depth of passion. Especially for a Qeteral of his age. But not..."

"But not for a *Human* his age." A regal Qeteral queen demonstrated...a grin. "This is entirely speculation, Father. Question him not. The idea raised by this observation is to remain between you and me. Lumin has always been obedient to us and deserves his privacy."

"I do not recall your mother and I questioning *you* until a long time after the fact. You were ever of an independent streak and secretive in your youth." Gwyn actually chuckled and glanced out the window, as Hakonn continued with a rare broad smile on his face. "Lumin is quite obviously *your* son, too. Certain subtleties. I am unaware of a young woman he may be spending time with, but you pretended Mabelin was but a sort of boy playmate with whom you shared interest in hiking the countryside."

"That I did!" She laughed.

Hakonn went on. "I really should have known better, considering Mabelin's early maturity and adventurous nature. I could have read his thoughts, had I wished it, but of course respected his privacy. And yours. In retrospect he had a compelling youthful charm little different than that of Kodi and could charm feathers off a bird. Like Kodi he even smelled of dirt and grass when he sweated. You liked it, you told me, in your attempt finally to explain to us your love for him. You said he smelled like..."

"Summer wheat and sunshine!"

"Your mother laughed, and you were lucky she liked Mabelin so well! And you had been intimate with him already for four years. Four years! I was most unhappy. But in time, I grew to value my son-in-law as a unique treasure with a giving and noble heart. His eyes shone in love for you like Kodi's do for Ryn. Have I ever learned so much more about Humans lately, how similar Lumin is to them in looks, mannerisms, and speech, and his passionate nature, and the young ones who came to us are certainly jewels; Kodi and Lyndz are most beautiful creatures, and Prince Nikal looks much like a Human king *should* look, even with that beard. I cannot believe I am elaborating on Human sweat...and beards! Those few

Qeteral women who Bonded Human men; they would write it up in their silly love poems, ha! Even Manoo's poems about her bearded 'Feleep Pickerman.'"

"You are making me laugh, Father, talking like this."

"I admit I was fascinated by Feleep's beard, though he was otherwise not my favorite neighbor. I regret that, of course. My attitudes. He was ever polite, of course, reverential to Mother especially, even though he knew Father and I didn't much like him and called him 'the goat-faced Human' behind his back!"

"I remember you using the phrase a time or two."

"Father and I always feel guilty when Manoo comes to court and hear her reminisce at dinner. Thankfully, she and Mother get along well, and Linea is willing to charm her, since I seem incapable of making the effort."

"You could certainly be rude back then in family conversation. Grandfather mellowed and so did you, especially after I Bonded Mabelin. Though Hurlin picked up on your continued prejudices of Humans."

"I regret it."

"I know you do. And so it is your task to undo the damage. Grandfather and Grandmother have certainly acted with perfect congeniality with the Humans, and Grandfather spent time with the Etoppsi. He and Grandmother have offered to travel the country and inform the nobles of all the latest. It may be their last long journey while they are still able, and they will be happily received everywhere. I want you here, of course, but was thinking of asking Mother to go with them to attend to their needs."

"I believe that would be excellent. She would enjoy that. They could also escort Manoo back north. I shall speak of it to your mother."

"By the way, I personally think of those silly love poems as high literature!" Gwyn laughed again. "I think I must now read Manoo's recent poetry book she brought for me! I think her writing is quite good. We're all a big family, my dear, even the Human types. Are you pleased by it, or not?"

"It has become my greatest joy, my dear, as it always has been for you."

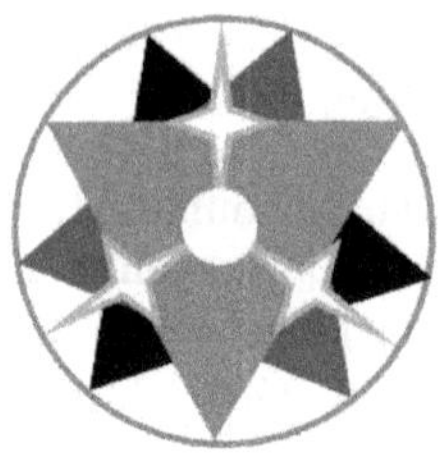

Chapter 31—Return to Sea

The return journey to the ships, even with some thirty well-trained Qeteral defenders, can best be described in one word: subdued. Emotions were mixed. Some of the Qeteral felt anticipation being the first to venture out of Ulakel after so many years of isolation. Mishoo, Halta, and Frith were among these. All thirty did carry with them a sense of duty and understood they were part of a great undertaking, ordained by Myghal. But the Humans and the Etoppsi had few words, except that Nikal, Manwul and Hadon did make some effort in communicating expectations for the ship journey with the Qeteral.

Kodi, dealing with powerful emotions upon leaving Ryn, could not bring himself to engage in effective conversation. He instead focused on Azure the Bluetail, launching him forth and even talking to him as he would sometimes ride on his outstretched arm. Nikal ensured he had all the space and privacy he wished. The exception was at night when the two of them lay their heads together and talked, always with a little distance from the others, though Musca was there, snoozing next to Kodi. Relaxed in the darkness, Kodi shared with Nikal everything that came to his mind. He would speak of his love for Ryn. Nikal was attuned, and though it brought to him strong memories of Dira, it was not painful, but instead made him cherish those memories ever more.

Lumin's emotions were dichotomous. Exactly as Kodi for Ryn, he was anxious at having to leave Fal. On the other hand, this was an adventure he was looking forward to. But he was probably the only one for which 'looking forward' described the emotion. He understood like the rest that dangers lay ahead, but that knowledge could not suppress the sense of adventure. These two emotions really did not mix. Sometimes he was thinking about Fal and, already missing her greatly, his face would turn reflective. At other times he was absorbing every moment of this new world outside Ulakel and smiling a great deal. Yet he did have other thoughts that imposed themselves on each of these ends. They often centered on his brothers. He would think of his sister Ryn and all his other family members, but his relationship with his brothers had largely defined him until the Humans came. He would especially think of their farewells to him.

Hurlin had, at the last, approached Lumin, embraced him, and gave him a blessing along with a newly minted long knife in a sheath. It was meaningful for Lumin, and the long knife became a treasured possession. Olin went out of his way to escort the group for a great part of the first day before returning alone. He descended the Plateau, walking beside Lumin the entire way to the place where before they had camped by the river. Here, he asked Lumin if they could exchange their bead necklaces as a token of affection. Lumin readily did so, and they embraced and said their goodbyes. Neither brother would remove that necklace from his body for the entire time they were separated.

Lyndz was quiet too on the journey to the ships. She felt energetic and strong. Physically she felt like a new woman after training with Mishoo. Every part of her body had become taut with new muscle. She moved with fluidity and never tired. But it was a wrench for her, as it was for all of them, to leave behind serenity. Ulakel was as a utopian paradise where every space was beautiful, the sun was bright, and the few rains, typically at night, never interfered with the memorable days.

A few of the Qeteral did bring along their bird familiars, but only of the kinds specifically trained for working with them, not the common songbird pets like Halta's blackbird. Among them were white ravens and two each of a small hawk variety and falcons, altogether about ten such creatures. Mishoo had a small hawk. They would prove useful in communications. However, on the journey, the Qeteral readily reached out and communicated with the many gulls and waterbirds they encountered.

Nikal wished to have Qeteral on each of the three ships, for he knew they would rely on each other in dealing with the incredible strangeness of a ship journey. They were all in sleeping cabins, but some had to share bunks or sleep in hammocks hung from the walls. There were not so many of them that any were required to sleep below decks in hammocks with the crewmen. Certainly, most of the Qeteral were glad to sleep and talk privately among their own when they could.

The crewmen were overawed at meeting Qeteral for the first time, and the Qeteral dealt with some shock at realizing how physically different all the Human shipmen were from one another. Many were big and burly and had beards, some were lither in frame, some were quite a bit shorter than they expected from their limited experience of the tall friends who had been in the delegation to Ulakel. Many were not good-looking at all by the high Qeteral standard. Some were 'loud,' and all could in less than a day of washing themselves in their bucket baths become rank to the sensitive Qeteral nose. Otherwise, the Qeteral adapted quickly to the constant Human interaction. Maybe a handful of the Qeteral carried hints of Hurlin's distaste for Humans, but mostly the interaction was cordial.

They traveled well. Shane predicted and was correct that seasickness would be entirely absent from them. Their bodies were magically adapted to extremes. Any cuts, scrapes or bruises healed completely within hours, and so rarely did they make use of the Human Healers. They never complained about discomfort.

In general they engaged with the Human crewmen. They all did their best to get along. And inevitably, the Qeteral adapted and learned. Many allowed their innate curiosity to blossom and helped the crewmen as they could, and some became adept at sailing skills.

The crewmen were Nikal's best, with certain gentlemanly instincts. They communicated mostly in calm manner with the Qeteral. They were overawed by their flawless beauty. Though the Qeteral women's shirts typically hung open and loose, revealing much skin and curve, the crewmen forced themselves to get used to this. All knew the seriousness of what was taking place, and rudeness or crude male attitudes towards women were always subject to stern punishment by the ships' captains and officers. Yet certainly the Qeteral were to them a fantastical race, something out of legend that had come to life. There were a few friendships that developed, particularly with some of the crewmen or officers who were of particular intelligence and held within them the sort of graciousness that defined the Human delegation who had traveled to Ulakel. And so those few reached out with strong friendliness towards them, taught them much and learned much from them. On the Qeteral side there were those who were determined to be engaging and obliged the sailors with descriptions and stories of their land.

There were eight Qeteral men on Nikal's ship. He put seven of them into the guest cabin that had, on the Modela Island voyage, been used by the females. But only Lumin among the Qeteral stayed in Nikal's large cabin. He and Kodi intended to keep Lumin close. It was a squeeze, as Manwul, Hadon, Tiliruf and Shane were also with them. Shane was the only Healer who accompanied them for now. Azure, far too big for any cage, was given a large perch near the porthole, and the Etoppsi males slept, 'cuddled,' on the floor, taking up most of that space. Hammocks would not have been a good option to hang here due to the giants' needs to stand up and move around, and so the bunk mattresses were shared by some of the men. At least these mattresses were a little larger than those in other cabins. Lumin would lie beside Kodi while they slept on Aron's old bunk. It was a tight fit, but they were now brothers of the same family. They even 'cuddled,' too. They'd lie there at night, all of them chatting, and Kodi would have his arm wrapped over Lumin, or Lumin with his over Kodi. Tiliruf would tease them, but they didn't care. They valued their new familial relationship and were simply glad to be alive, healthy, and together. The physical closeness represented an unspoken comfort as they dealt with inner emotions that greatly paralleled, reflecting what each left behind in Ulakel. Though not all yet knew this of Lumin.

For that matter, Tiliruf was forced to sleep with Shane. Though they didn't display arm-wrapped affection. Nikal might have been willing to share bunk space with Kodi, but not anyone else. Manwul was too big to share a bunk, and Hadon, though he was of Tiliruf's and Shane's general size, also lucked out with his own. Tiliruf complained that Hadon had a "private" bunk. Nikal gave him the eye.

"But I'm the *A'Terianh,* ha! Hadon's just a little Swordmaster and servant." Tiliruf said, winking at Hadon. Of course, he didn't think of Hadon in any such manner.

"I don't care. Do what your told, or you can sleep in a hammock below deck." Nikal chuckled.

All these quibbles and teases on his part were just Tiliruf's way of creating some lighthearted laughter and interchanges in a less-than-ideal setting.

Once or twice, Shane and Hadon shared and gave Tiliruf a bit more space for a night or two, and Kodi likewise with Nikal for Lumin's benefit. It could definitely be stuffy and uncomfortable, and when necessary, Shane put them all to sleep. He only occasionally allowed late night talks.

The Etoppsi had gone rutty again. Rusty's scent was especially strong. 'Bucky dreams' were universal, even for Lumin. All admitted the dreams were vivid, otherwise giving little detail. However, Shane wrote the experience down in his journals and the effect Etoppsi musk could have. He created a theory that magic was somehow involved in the effects. He felt there was something deeper in the emotions in these dreams than what was typical of youthful teenager sex dreams. Kodi agreed with him and was the only one who gave Shane some limited detail in private. He said his dreams were markedly different from the wildness of the previous time, contained no 'fighting scenes' and were unwaveringly focused now on Ryn. He told Shane what Curdoz had said regarding Nikal's focused dreams on Dira being connected to their Aura. Shane would not press the others to reveal details of their dreams, as he himself had no intention of doing so. And though it was something they would never get a chance to test, he, like Kodi before, speculated in what manner it might affect sleeping women.

At first, some thought they should 'take advantage' of the fun each night and simply enjoy the dreams. But after the second night of the same thing, though they again kidded each other, most were feeling sluggish and knew they weren't getting the restorative deeper sleep they needed. The dreams were all-consuming. One more week of such likely effects while the Etoppsi were at the height of rut would surely make them all quite crabby, and so Shane experimented with additional spells and a stronger 'dose' of his sleep magic. It worked really well for the others; they slept much better. However, a Healer's magic has its limitations in application to the self, and he himself was not as immune.

And so, Tiliruf still had something to laugh about.

He played it up.

"Good dreams?" he joked next morning. "Pretty sure we know who the other blokes dream about. Who's Kalay? You called out in your sleep."

Shane froze. If he had been a white man, his face would have surely shone bright red. "Dammit, Tiliruf, keep quiet. Dammit to blazes!"

As it was, his rare cussing was pure admission.

"You once said nothing ever embarrasses you, mate. Did I misconstrue?" Tiliruf continued to tease, but he had been keeping his voice barely above a whisper. The others were chattering noisily, climbing out the cabin door to head for breakfast below decks. To Shane's relief, they weren't paying attention.

When the cabin door shut, Shane proceeded. "I didn't even...I don't even...I thought I had forgotten her name."

"You remembered her really well last night, I'd say. Was she Eastern or Western? It'd be pretty bad, you know, if you called out, say, *Maru!*"

"Exactly why I'm embarrassed! Rutty blazes, Tiliruf, punch me if you hear me again like that and make me roll over. Promise me!"

"I was expecting to build out the list." Tiliruf then delighted in Shane's responding intake of breath. But when he realized the good Healer was about to explode in more uncharacteristic cussing, he gave in. "Oh, all right, but only if you tell me about Kalay, eh?"

"If you must know, she was Essemarian. Enough?"

"Ummmm. No."

"You thumping pecker!" In spite of his annoyance, Shane was close to a grin. "All right, then. She was superior. We made love at the beach under an ascending full Solvermoon. I really thought I'd forgotten her name; it was a long time ago. But I'll never forget that night."

"I'm sure she won't forget it either, buddy," he winked. "My highest compliment for a *Vow-taker*."

"I certainly hope it is still a happy memory for her. Kalay was the first I made love to after being appointed to Danzilet. She found me at a lonely beach west of the city playing in the waves that evening. She too was wishing to find a private setting to enjoy the water and contemplate the sunset. She liked what she found."

"A likewise *'superior'* black man playing the dolphin. Not particularly common, I'd say, on the waterfronts west of Danzilet. A young bloke from home."

"That's what she found, and yes, we were both amazed by the serendipity of the encounter. I recall her walking out to me in the water as I stared mesmerized. She grew more and more stunning as she approached. It was surreal. She laughed, reached out for my hand, and kissed me on the lips before the first word was ever spoken between us."

"You're joking!" Tiliruf's jaw was dropped.

"You could not have paid me gold to resist. It was incredibly romantic. Undeniably...sexy. We held hands and played together in the waves like children, saying very little as we watched the setting of the sun. Solvermoon came up full as we lay in the sand and talked. The inevitable occurred, and we engaged a great deal in that, until about midnight. We walked back to the city, said our farewells with a grateful last kiss; she was to board ship next day for Essemar, and I never saw her again. Now leave me alone about it and promise me. They're important memories for me, Tiliruf. I often think back on the beauty of my encounters. In these crazy Etoppsi rut dreams I'm living some of them over again. But it's uncouth to give out their names. They weren't prostitutes and they aren't a *list!* They were beautiful, incredible women, and I respect everything about them still. It's true one or two were so long ago and such brief affairs their names left me, but I still think about them and how wonderful they were. Like Kalay. I admit being glad you helped me remember her name. In my journals I give them faux names, so they can never be identified by a future reader, and sometimes the faux names stick in my mind rather than their real names. Now, don't make me regret what I *do* share with you, all right?"

Tiliruf was actually struck by the seriousness of the request. The mention of prostitutes caused his cheeky grin to falter a little. Shane's sexual history (at least since his Calling Vision) was quite different than for the rest of the friends and appeared to affect the Healer in strange but wonderful ways. "No. I never want you to have any regrets, buddy. Not due to me, anyway. Just how hard am I allowed to punch you?"

Shane winked. "I have to admit this was funny, Tiliruf. *'Who's Kalay?'* Considering this *Vow-taker* was the subject, it was classic."

"Your reaction, ha! But Shane. It ain't a classic if it don't get told, eh?"

But Shane shook his head and only grinned.

Tiliruf let it go but wished to ask a question. "Kalay sounds so perfect I'm shocked you forgot *her* name, though. Have you ever regretted not pursuing a relationship with her, or any of the others?"

"It's a fair question. I have." Shane then put his Order medallion around his neck to emphasize his next point. "But for me such feelings come and go, and that I did forget a name or two should indicate to you the *go* is stronger than the *come*. I'm happy with the choices I've made, and I just say those women and I gave each other amazing gifts of understanding, body, and memory. But as I've mentioned before, regarding a future relationship, it is unwise of me or anyone to say 'never,' and so I don't."

The Etoppsi were oblivious to what the men were experiencing. They were the first to depart the cabin in the early mornings in order to fly and monitor the skies, and Nikal told the men it wasn't necessary for them to know their musk caused them to have sex dreams. "They might think it funny, but I think it'd make them self-conscious, too. Kodi and I decided last time not to tell them, although they were near the end of the cycle anyway and it only worked on us a couple of nights. But I say the same goes for now. Keep that particular bit of humor between us men. They can read Shane's book someday if they want. I've come to the conclusion everyone's going to read Shane's book and learn enormously, and everyone's going to read Shane's book and laugh extravagantly. What are you laughing about now, Tiliruf?"

"Nothin'. Just, as you said, keeping the humor between us men, right, Shane?"

Shane might have offered a hint of a wink, but he was much more interested in getting his observations written down about the Etoppsi, sitting as he was at Nikal's desk.

The Healer certainly learned much. He got Rusty's and Stormy's permission to examine them during their rut. He'd already examined each of them back in Ulakel, Rusty several times. He hadn't yet examined Rainwing for contrast, but he knew Ulna had been taking notes on Rainwing ever since their venture to Modela's Island. They'd agreed to share their findings with each other. He was determined to describe—in language probably only other Healers would comprehend—what he could of Etoppsi internal body elements and pheromonal chemicals and especially how the male changed during his monthly cycle. He deduced their musk did have qualities similar to Hralindi Oil with its aphrodisiac qualities, but he wrote, too, of his speculation that a sort of odd magic was involved in how these pheromones worked on the subconscious mind, stimulating the mating impulses.

In addition to the chemical changes inside their bodies he observed several things. They tended to fly more often, as if to deal with pensiveness. They were more talkative, talked even louder and boomier than they normally did, and seemed more attuned, aware, almost jumpy. Yet they were also notably more humorous during rut. He (and Lumin, too) learned what the other men already had learned back in Danzilet about Star Revel and Soaring Stag culture.

They all learned of the intense emotions Stormy carried for his Bondmate, Yellowtips. Normally reserved the rest of the month, during his rut Stormy talked a great deal about Yellowtips and missed her. He missed her company and said that, when together, the two talked to each other almost constantly about every subject under the sun. He also bluntly admitted missing making love to her. He would describe her physical traits and the sexual experiences they shared to a point that would surely embarrass someone like Idamé. And Rusty would talk frankly about Star Revel—sometimes in answer to Tiliruf's blunt questions—creating laughter and reciprocal sharing and joking.

In any event, it was obvious the Etoppsi dealt with a low level of mental and physical angst without the opportunity to mate during rut. They had now experienced two cycles without mating, and it was not easy for them. Shane experimented with each of them with his calming magic, and they appeared to appreciate it and lessened some of their tension.

Lumin truly thrived on this journey. He altogether turned into a curious, adventurous Human man. He adored being on a ship. He wasn't bothered by the smells. He didn't care how dirty he got, or anyone else. He thrilled in the man clothes Nikal gave him. He wore Nikal's trousers and silver belt buckle and often kept the white shirt on his torso, unbuttoned. He loved the way it fluttered in the winds. His dream of sailing had come true.

The crewmen would marvel as they watched him. They marveled at all the Qeteral on board. But it was obvious Lumin had Human blood and had been told some details by Kodi, and in their eyes, just like everyone else's, he stood apart like a primordial god. Like Manwul and Hadon sometimes did, they called him *Torovúr* in honor of the Hunter God, whom all the tales told, and classical art demonstrated, was the most handsome of the male World Gods. He was a friend to Vanayisu Modelo and of Berug the Magnificent during the Great War, had been honored by the Guardian, and was believed to dwell in bliss on the Other Side of the World. Lumin was simply too perfect not to look at as he stood over the rails and looked on the sea. His smile was that of a dreamer. He sang his Qeteral original songs. In contrast to his brown skin and long black locks were his bright blue eyes. He looked on the Lintiri Sea, new for him, like a deeply spiritual man might look with contemplation on the stars at night. He would sing out to the seagulls, and they would come to him. They would sit on the railing, or he would lift one up on his arm and look into its face. It was magical, and the crewmen were mesmerized. At other times he would sit on deck with his drawing pad, recording faces of the others on board, waterbirds or dolphins, and images of sails and ships on the water.

Like Kodi had done long before, he also wanted to learn everything he could about ships and sailing. He worked hard and reveled in all of it. They taught and encouraged. They instinctively loved him and were also determined to be protective without Nikal having to make that clear. They understood he was a young royal prince, the beloved son of a great queen, and a valuable treasure.

Tiliruf worked with Lumin on some sword play, and Nikal continued to help him with long knife moves. His level of concentration was good and he never tired.

One evening, as they lazed about in the cabin after supper, Lumin told the remainder of the men and the Etoppsi the truth. They sat up enraptured.

"You have a lover!" Manwul shouted. Chagrined by his outburst and realizing his word choice was perhaps not best for Qeteral, he lowered his voice. "Be better if I say *life-mate,* friend Lumin. Sorry. More than a lover for you, of course."

"But you're quite young for a Qeteral!" exclaimed Hadon.

Shane spoke before Kodi could. "For a Human man he is mature, Hadon."

"Yes, of course. I'm just shocked by this revelation and that your family doesn't know."

The Etoppsi had a different perspective, and although they had learned of Qeteral traditions, they could not act as shocked at something that seemed so natural.

"I honor your monogamous commitment," said Stormgale. "It sounds wonderful to me. It's plain she brings you happiness from the manner in which you speak of her."

All was quiet for a moment. Most were looking at Nikal.

"I...I...don't know what to say," He did not express it, but the thought went through his mind that he might have refused to allow Lumin to come if he had known. However, he also suspected... "*You* worried I would not let you come if I knew."

Lumin looked down.

Nikal looked at Kodi with 'the eye' and then also at Shane. Both looked slightly guilty. He then looked at Tiliruf. Tiliruf raised an eyebrow like, *Don't think I had anything to do with this!* But he kept his mouth shut.

Finally, Nikal continued. "We don't deny your bond and love, Lumin. Maybe I would have urged you not to come and that you should keep your focus on her at home, being as young as you are and so much emotion involved. But I would have given in ultimately to Kodi's wishes. But I'm not sure how happy I am about this."

"I have wanted to tell you, sir. Perhaps I allowed some concerns to overcome my judgment?"

"Look at it from a Qeteral's perspective, Nikal," said Shane. "But also from that of a Human man's. Have you ever questioned the intimacies of any of your crewmen or denied their services due to being young and bonded? Of course not. Most of the Qeteral who have come with us are Bonded. I am not unaware the delicacy of his station as a royal prince and the relationships we established in Ulakel. But this is who Lumin is. He is as much Human, more Human, than Qeteral, sufficiently mature. He is a man. It would have been an error to deny him his choices. Fal herself was supportive of Lumin's desire to come. Yes, Kodi might have told you anyway, but Lumin made it plain he would eventually tell you once we got away from Ulakel. It was his right to do so from a personal perspective, even if from the diplomatic perspective he might have been more forthcoming. Consider which relationship with Lumin is more important to you, the personal or the diplomatic. You didn't want Kodi to tell you of his love for Ryn one minute before he wanted to do so, *on his own good time,* you said, even though you had suspected for days."

Nikal pondered. He knew Shane was right. This was certainly a piece of Lumin's life for which Lumin should make the rules. Lumin was definitely of greater maturity than sometimes it seemed from his occasional boyish speech and level of curiosity. Lumin lived in a dual world.

He nodded. "I concur. There are not any other great secrets you are keeping from me?"

"Well, it relates," said Kodi, who hadn't said anything until now. "This journey is Lumin's chosen method to return and claim Qeteral manhood, and then Bond Fal in Ceremony, thereby following tradition and honoring his family by doing it this way. Considering Hurlin and others, he wished to take all these steps from the perspective of a twenty-four-year-old Qeteral prince. Otherwise, the nobility, and some of those in his family, might have looked on his claim of manhood and proclamation for Fal, at his age, as out of step with the moral norm. But returning after a journey of exceptional deeds, they would view him differently, and his claims would be accepted."

"I see."

"I find it all strange despite what I have learned," said Flamefur, "that a male coming into his own sense of maturity and finding and bonding himself to a life-mate should ever be questioned by others."

"You see it as I do, Rusty," said Stormgale. "I agree with you."

"Yes," said Kodi, "but he wishes to do this the proper way based on Qeteral tradition, and being of the royal family makes it that much harder to buck it."

"And having Hurlin as a brother, dammit," put in Tiliruf. "Lumin, you and I have talked about this. I know it's important for you to get these steps right of manhood and Bonding. But after all that, I think I've come to know you well. I wish I could go back with you and see the look on his face when you tell him you're going to live your life the way you want to."

"My mother would have stopped me if she had known about Fal," Lumin said. "They all would have stopped me."

"Maybe. Maybe not," said Shane. "I think you only speculate in your mother's case. I'm really not so sure that's true. She had begun to value your Human differences and also to look on Kodi's opinions as ones she could not ultimately go against. And so had Hakonn. But I understand of course why you felt it necessary to keep it secret. There is always more than what is seen on the surface. We need to realize this is also about Fal's reputation, too, and how she will be perceived after the two declare for each other. She, too, is looked upon as a little too young and is not born to a high family."

Nikal spoke again. "Well. I really understand. I am sorry, Lumin, deeply sorry you felt you had to keep the secret of your love for Fal. In fact, if *I* cannot understand that, nobody can. Kodi can tell you my story sometime. How similar your story. Passions in conflict with rules and duty and obligation...not just me, several of us: Kodi, Manwul, Hadon, Stormgale. Yes, we understand it. We've all been there, and some of us are still there, just like you. Like Shane said, on the outside looking in, it's easy to misjudge the issues, the depth of those issues. You have done all you believed was right. We got to know what Hurlin was like. What Hakonn was like. The pressures your mother is under. And you being part Human in a Qeteral world. You lost your father much too soon. He would have understood you. And yet you've done your level best to navigate properly as a Qeteral prince rather than rebel, understanding they all love you and only wish the best for you. It's important to you not to damage those relationships. We understand, and we honor your determination to do what you believe is right. I'm glad you've chosen to come with us on this journey. But quite frankly, I agree with Tiliruf. If you return safely, claim then all that is your right to claim and live your life as freely as you can manage it. I am glad, Lumin, very glad indeed, that Fal carries your seed, and no one, ultimately, will be able to deny the relationship or your love for each other. If all goes well, Lumin, what do you hope for yourself and Fal in the future?"

"A big family, four children, eh! We want to live away from court, maybe in a village near the mountains and start an art school. We talk about that all the time. We want farm animals. And we're going to Eleni someday and see the great apple orchards and try to find my grandfather's people. Grandmother has sometimes said she wishes she could pilgrimage to where he came from, and if she's still able, we'll take her with us."

"Some of those apple orchards have been there since ancient times," offered Tiliruf. "They're famous, eh?"

"Ryn and I will go with you. And return by way of the Valley of the Gifted."

"Yes!"

Nikal was pacified. He would never again question Lumin's choices. It did, however, cause him to think ever more often of Dira, and whenever Lumin spoke of Fal and his dreams of their future, Dira's face would appear in his mind. But if anything, Nikal was encouraging and listened happily as Lumin told them more about Fal.

The two Etoppsi left the cabin for a long evening fly. Rusty was going to retrieve Rainwing and allow her to be aloft and see the stars above and the sea below this one more time while things were still relatively peaceful. It meant much to her to be airborne. The men then sat at Fifty-twos.

They were talkative, and Shane allowed them more freedom that evening with the brandy. Their questions led to Lumin getting quite chatty about Fal. Now he had let the secret out and the others were encouraging and accepting, he was almost determined to 'catch up' with the Human men on their previous discussions. He was honest but poetic. He'd been in relationship with her longer than any of the rest of them had with their respective life-mates. It was funny hearing how he'd deliberately chosen a different palace bedroom remote from his brothers, with a second-floor balcony down which he could easily climb in the dark to rendezvous with Fal. Those two would exchange messages by Fal's little gray owl. Only rarely did he run into a servant but always made up an excuse for why he was out. Twice he ran into Olin who, oblivious, made him go back to bed. But all it really did was delay him about an hour at which point he again climbed down the balcony. And if other night birds he knew, such as Ryn's Tanter, espied him, he would charm them with his mind and voice, and they would not relay any tattletale messages. Only the little owl would know of his approach.

"But that must be powerful magic, really," said Shane with a raised eyebrow.

"Not really. All it is is causing them to focus interest elsewhere. But it's true not everybody can do it."

"Even birds that are at quite a distance?"

"It's true I am very aware of them."

"We all know he has a specialty with birds. Why don't you keep a working bird yourself?" asked Nikal. He looked up at the regal Azure on his perch, who was dozing at the moment.

"I use Fal's sometimes. I say it's hers, but really, we share it. But he's all sleepy in the day, you know."

"I wonder if you've really explored all your magical talent with birds," offered Shane.

Tiliruf felt a qualm in his stomach and secretly praised the stars no night birds had exposed his presence to Lumin and Fal on the night he observed them making love in the copse. He wondered if the little gray owl was even near that night.

"Can I try it now?" asked Lumin a couple card rounds later, when Kodi and Tiliruf lit up their pipes. Nikal decided the moment was as free and relaxed as any, and he too lit up. He was in a light-hearted mood, having just won the last round. By now they'd drunk quite a bit of brandy. Lumin had mead they had brought from Ulakel for the Qeteral. He drank it like water.

"I don't see why not," Nikal said.

"I'm going to probe you, though, while you try it," said Shane. "Tobacco contains chemicals that affect the brain, and we don't know if it might work negatively in a Qeteral."

Tiliruf was gleeful and explained to Lumin about it, little differently than he had done for Kodi back in Tirilorin.

On his first draw, he didn't even cough.

Shane had his hand on Lumin's head; there was a hint of green light. For a time, he said nothing. Lumin drew a few more puffs and grinned.

"Just think, eh?" said Tiliruf. "You're the first Qeteral ever to smoke!"

"Just remember," added Kodi, "Fal won't like to smell it on you. When I live in Ulakel someday, I know I will never smoke. Only when I go visit Tiliruf! For me it's more about the company and the setting anyway."

"It isn't harming him," Shane finally said. He sat back and pulled out a Kings and Castles set in order to challenge Tiliruf. "It seems to be reasonably benign like for the rest of you. It can be addicting, Lumin. Curdoz couldn't give it up if he tried. Perhaps you should confine it to private moments with your Human friends like Kodi suggests. Tiliruf's addicted to it, too."

"Am not!"

"Yeah, you are!" said about four men at once.

Lumin took to it with some relish and Tiliruf promised to get him his own pipe someday. For now, Lumin would share the others'. He seemed to think it one of the most Human of experiences, and he was inclined to try anything Human. The evening altogether was the most enjoyable the men had had since leaving Ulakel.

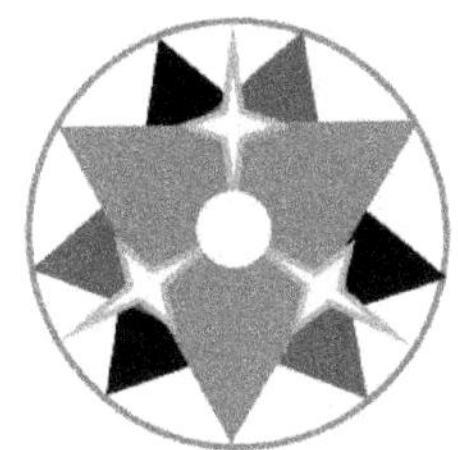

Chapter 32—Expecting and Unexpected

"Nikal sent Flamefur in the night to Danzilet to arrange for the rendezvous."

Lyndz was explaining plans to the other females after she, Mishoo, and Rainwing had returned from a conference on Nikal's ship.

"It grieves me to part with Nikal," offered Idamé. "We must say goodbye."

"I feel the same way," said Rainwing. "We don't know when we'll see him again. Curdoz is sending Healers Gustus and Luwiss with him. That's a good thing. But Nikal is letting Kodi have his ship, and Nikal will board another. Like he's told us before, he's going to personally command the fleet near to the entrance of the Khestadone Sea and await the return of the rescuers, watching for movement by the Alkhaness' navy."

"Yes, and let's remember to be careful about referring to the rescuers as 'them,' as 'we' are expected to be part of it all and return with them all. And be wary how we go about saying our farewells to Nikal, so they don't sound more long-term than everybody else's." Lyndz looked down at Musca dozing beside her. She was troubled. "I don't know yet when we attempt our exit from the group. I expected all along we would stay with the group and be a part of the rescue, but now I am unsure if we ought not to depart on the way there. That is, if a good opportunity presents itself. I am considering Meical's words. What He said about keeping Musca handy after we leave Ulakel was a clue to the timing. I realize that now. He expects Musca to help me with his own magic. I honestly cannot see how we do this secretively. And yet secretively is the only way it's going to happen. I imagine us taking one of the landing boats from our ship, probably at night. But even then, how can we keep Kodi and the rest from knowing about it?"

"I'm not going to say it's impossible," offered Idamé, "because the Guardian Himself wants us to do this. But I'm like you. Kodi and Curdoz, if they know about it, they will try to stop us. They won't be made to see our point of view, unless...unless Meical speaks to Kodi and makes it plain to him. Maybe?"

"Maybe. But we cannot depend on it. And besides, even if we left openly and he agreed to let us go, he would insist on sending male soldiers with us for protection, which would hinder us and go against the Guardian's expectations. No. We just cannot let Kodi know of this. I'm just wondering if, somehow, we could communicate our wishes to Captain Avantrees. From what I can tell, he is a strong believer in the Guardian."

"I really don't think we should even inform him," said Rainwing.

"We can put them to sleep," offered Mishoo.

"Yes!" said Ulna

"That has potential!" agreed Maru. "But Mishoo, are you saying Qeteral have that kind of magic? I thought only Healers and Sages could do that."

"Oh, I can put anyone to sleep," said Feena. She, along with another by the name of Teffi, were the two chosen by Mishoo, who, along with Halta and Frith, completed the set of five Qeteral women Mishoo envisioned for the Guardian's mission to West Khestadon.

The ten females were in Lyndz' cabin conversing under Ulna's privacy spell. The Humans were drinking wine. The Qeteral were enjoying mead. In the earlier conference on Nikal's ship, Rainwing, daring Tiliruf to say anything—he only glared—rummaged in his trunk and had taken two bottles of brandy. She was now consuming one of these.

"Yes," said Mishoo. "Not all Qeteral can do that but many of us can. Halta, Feena, and I can do it. I envisioned us making use of it in Khestadon as a method of keeping from having to kill every individual who spots us. Especially any of the enslaved inhabitants. They are innocents, really. It may be useful against hapless soldiers, too. Another magic I have that was revealed to me in my youth is that I can alter recent memories. It isn't a magic I have practiced, as there are ethical considerations involved, but it is in Qeteral tales, and I know I have it. I think I can cause others to forget we were seen."

"That's even better!" said Lyndz. "We're getting ahead of ourselves on that, of course. We don't know what to expect."

"The sleep magic takes a few seconds of touching," said Maru. "Another couple, really, for them to pass out. Instantly for some. Is that the same for you?"

"About that, yes," said Feena. "It won't stop resistance for those seconds, but then sleep is inevitable."

Lyndz' eyebrow was raised during this. "That could work. At night especially, there are not as many men on deck. I say this is the beginning of a workable plan!"

Upon entering the Central Passage from the quiet Lintiri Sea, it was marked by greater rolling upon the waves. Other ships were sometimes seen, including Nantian warships, and by way of Stormgale, messages were passed. There were those that guarded these waters leading to the Lintiri Sea, but also merchant traffic, mostly from Tirilorin, including supplies of all kinds for the Eastern war.

Led by Flamefur three days later, a fleet of navy ships out of Danzilet met them near to the middle of the Passage. Four ships were to add themselves to the three in order to make up the required seven for the rescue mission, two were heading east with some fresh recruits from Nant and Tirilorin, and finally, Nikal was going to take charge of the remainder, another eight ships. In addition to many already patrolling waters south, he estimated they would create a flotilla of some thirty to watch for the return of the rescuers and be on hand for any challenge or chase by the Alkhaness' navy.

Lyndz, Rainwing, and Idamé watched in the distance as Flamefur flew two men from one of the approaching ships over to Nikal's. He went back and retrieved a third individual. Then, all was quiet for a half hour when they saw Flamefur apparently return the first two to their own ship, and Stormgale came towards the females' ship.

"Nikal needs to see the three of you at once," he said when he landed on deck.

"I should hope so," said Idamé. "We wish to say our goodbyes. But why so urgent?"

"I am not certain, but I think goodbyes are premature. I don't think Nikal intends to depart just yet. Duke Midale from Nant brought messages from King Monticu, and he and another held conference with Kodi, Curdoz, and Nikal in his cabin for some time. The duke and his servant came out eventually, Rusty flew them back to their ship, and Nikal asked Tiliruf to come into the cabin. He told me to fetch you quickly and then he shut the door again."

"I hope there's not some bad news," said Lyndz.

"The duke was exuberant when he greeted Nikal, but when he left, Nikal appeared tense when he came out and hailed me.

Stormgale quickly transferred Rainwing first, then came back and fetched the two women together. Lyndz knocked on the cabin door; Kodi had the three come in and shut the door behind them. Those now present were the seven friends that had returned from Modela's Island.

"Er," began Kodi a bit hesitantly. They looked over and saw Nikal sitting at his desk with his face in his hands, near to the open porthole. "We have some interesting news. The duke had a lot of news, but only one piece of it is, you could say, 'noteworthy.'"

"I know it is certain, but we need additional confirmation, Ida," said Curdoz, "from a Matrimonial. It is, as they say, your specialty."

"Whatever is the matter?" she asked.

"Heh, heh," Tiliruf chuckled under his breath.

"Don't laugh, friend," said Kodi. Though he couldn't stop a subtle smirk on his own face.

"The Princess Dira is expecting," Curdoz plunged on. He watched as the women's eyes grew wide. Lyndz' intake of breath was dramatic. "And based on what is known of it, how far along she is and so forth..."

"But...but! Nikal!" Idamé practically screamed. "It *has* to be...but, how *can* it be?"

"I think we know the *how,* eh?" Tiliruf chuckled again.

Nikal finally took his hands off his face and looked at Kodi. "Don't know what to think. Don't know what to say. What do I do? This is all... This is all...Help me, Kodi."

"Well," Kodi began again. He was not at all unsympathetic, but he had a look that approached Tiliruf's chuckle. "We just kind of needed you to confirm the magic, Mother Idamé. That, because of the Aura you saw, this babe Dira's carrying is surely his and not Lekktor's."

"But how can that be?"

Tiliruf chuckled yet again.

Kodi's smile grew a little bigger. "To ease your mind, I can assure you it wasn't *after* Lekktor Bonded her."

"You mean...?"

"It was before," confirmed Curdoz. "I gather it was less than two weeks before we met Nikal."

"Yes, and before her betrothal to Lekktor was even announced," added Kodi. "Nikal and Dira had been meeting secretly for months whenever he could get back there from the war. They were lovers, Mother. I think that's all you need, ha!"

He winked. Idamé's face was as shocked as ever. Nevertheless, she swallowed and got over it quickly. She walked over to Nikal and took his hands together and held them. She said softly, "You really should have told me this."

"I...I'm sorry, Mother." He then looked at her questioningly.

Lyndz interjected. "How beautiful, Nikal, really. Oh, Mother, surely you realized already the level of their love? Of course he wasn't going to really talk to us women about it. But why else would he have been so brokenhearted if they hadn't been lovers and planned a future together? I can't believe you hadn't figured that out. All the rest of us did."

"Well, I..." She nodded and breathed deeply. She turned back to Nikal. "My dear, the child can only be yours, then. That...that you made love before the Aura was seen by me makes no difference. Before. After. Whether another man was involved. It doesn't matter. It doesn't matter what Lekktor did after they Bonded, even if it was before the Aura. It would not have presented itself if she had conceived another's child. All Matrimonials know this, and the fact has never been in dispute. Never. In fact, that an Aura appears after the woman becomes pregnant is quite typical. This is Meicalian Magic, Nikal. The Aura prevents Dira bearing the child of any other man. Only yours. Only yours, Nikal."

Tiliruf chuckled again. He cupped a hand over his mouth pretending to whisper. "*Thumping Thumpers*...eh?"

Kodi grinned in his direction. He and Tiliruf were just glad Nikal had, since Midale came, been displaying no more than perplexity and wonder. A month or two ago he might have broken down in grief over this news with the presumption the future held no hope of proclaiming and proving his fatherhood and love. Obviously, the situation was far from perfect, but Nikal had cast off the worst of his despair some time ago with Kodi's help. Events had gone against Nikal regarding Dira, but Kodi never once believed it was the end of their story and had worked hard these last months to convince Nikal the same.

And the others felt the same as Kodi.

"You must not think so much on...on what took place after. On Lekktor," added Idamé. She turned to Curdoz. "There has to be a way to fix this. To make it right!"

"Maybe. If enough key persons could be made to believe in the reality of Auras and convinced king and council. Midale was lively with that and other news. Nikal's face went pale when the idiot offered that piece."

"Yeah, and Nikal otherwise hid it until Midale left the cabin. Though I'm not sure we really heard the rest of what he had to say. Midale is not necessarily on Lekktor's side of things, though, from what Nikal has told me about him." added Kodi. "He's just...what Curdoz said. An idiot. Sent by the king to bear messages, and he plans to go east and offer his services in the war. I'll send word and make sure Jaden doesn't give him any sort of high officer position. He can serve as Jaden's messenger to the queen or something. That ought to fit his flamboyant style. Bows and pleasantries." He then walked over to Nikal and gripped his shoulders, even as Idamé was still holding his hands. "Dira loves you, and you love Dira, and she's going to have your baby, Nikal. You keep your focus on that. Listen to Curdoz and Idamé and ignore Lekktor and all that for now. This isn't something we can make right, just now, but Mother Idamé's right. When this is all over, we'll go back to Nant, and we'll work this out. Together. You, me,

Curdoz, and Idamé. We'll make them all see the truth. You need have nothing but hope in this."

"Count me in," said Rainwing.

"I'll go, too, eh?" Tiliruf fingered Aron's blade. "If nothing else works, Lekktor has a date with me. Can I be the one to tell the blokes all this?"

Kodi chuckled. "No. I will. You'll turn it into a joke, which it isn't. Look at the beauty of it, Tiliruf. Their love and a babe they made together. And the hope for Nikal. Get past the *'Thumping Thumpers...'*"

"I'll give the news to Flamefur and Stormgale," said Rainwing, "if you're willing for them to know, Nikal."

"And I'll inform Ulna and Maru," added Lyndz. "The more of your friends who know the truth the better. If something happens to some of us, then there will be others who know."

Nikal nodded. Suddenly, he himself chuckled. He looked up at Tiliruf. "It's what Aron said, too. He gave me that eye and warned me. Right at that very time."

Tiliruf and Kodi both laughed aloud. Tiliruf added, "Call it a prophecy, then, eh?"

Rainwing and Idamé didn't catch it. Lyndz rolled her eyes. Suddenly, her eyes grew wide and she grew animated. "OH MY WORD! The Prophecy! Yes! The *Child!* Remember? That was the hope the Guardian offered at the end, don't you see? *An island kingdom by a child is redeemed; In truth the child was not as she seemed..!* It's..."

Idamé screeched. "It's a girl! The baby will be a girl!"

"And that half of the Prophecy came after...," began Rainwing.

"After the fact, yeah," concluded Kodi, grinning. "The Guardian would have known Dira had just conceived Nikal's babe when He essentially *completed* Deroge's Prophecy and gave it to Rainwing in a Dream! Ha! Brilliant, Lyndz!"

Nikal grinned. It was the prettiest grin on him any of them had ever seen.

Tiliruf had never stopped grinning. "Aron's *Thumping Thumpers* prophecy was funnier, though."

Lyndz rolled her eyes again. "Men can be so silly about that and babies! But it's a joy to see you smile, Nikal. It really is the Guardian's hope that He gave you. I wish we could get word to Dira secretly. It would bring her joy to know. And she would keep it secret and keep the pretense going for now. No doubt she's smart, or Nikal wouldn't have fallen in love with her. She likely knew she was pregnant quite soon and surely wondered if it could possibly be Nikal's. Probably not quite at the time we saw her, and Mother Idamé saw the Aura, but she might have known by the time we came back through Nant from Modela's Island. Of course, she was far away in Hildred by then, and word hadn't come to Sevarr yet."

Curdoz raised an eyebrow. "Ralle. Ralle will realize precisely what we have. Word would have soon come to court from Hildred. Lekktor was proud to announce it as soon as it was determined. Midale said so. Ralle has probably known now for some time. He knew the Prophecy, and he knew of Idamé's Aura. He surely deduced the level of their relationship just as I did. At the time he knew Nikal better than I, and Aron had told him pieces of it. It's true it was our intent at the time to keep the Aura secret from Dira and everyone else, but our thinking was that due to the Aura, she would never have a baby at all. The fact she is expecting will cause Ralle to realize the truth and change our position on the matter. He may have already gotten word to Dira in Hildred."

Nikal looked at Lyndz and smiled. "She might already know!"

He stood up and gave Lyndz a huge happy hug. "If it really is a girl, I'd be so happy if she's only half the amazing woman you are and that Dira is."

"Ah, that's sweet, Nikal! Well, what else *have* we learned?" she asked with a smile as their embrace ended and this part of the conversation appeared at an end. "Anything else unusual?"

"Eh? You hadn't heard? You didn't see her?" exclaimed Tiliruf.

"See whom? We saw Rusty fly over here with another. Who was it?"

"Sturla Keen! Hadon's beside himself!"

"Really!" exclaimed Idamé, throwing her hands in the air with delight.

"Oh, I really, really like her," said Rainwing.

Several of them left Nikal's cabin and went looking for Sturla, Hadon, and the rest. Following sounds of boisterous laughter, they found them below deck eating a meal.

Hadon's plate was still full. He had a grin from ear to ear. He was sitting next to the exotic beauty. The huge pearl necklace he had given her when they pledged their love adorned her dark, sinuous neckline. Through all the chatter going on with Manwul, Shane, Lumin, and some of the others at mess, those two clearly couldn't get enough of each other, their hands, arms...and lips, in constant interaction.

Nevertheless, when they saw Lyndz and the others, they stood, the women embraced, and Rainwing and Sturla bowed to each other regally.

The fleet was to sail due south from this point for the next two nights and the day between before Nikal was prepared to depart. In a way, the news had galvanized him but, as Curdoz had predicted in private conversation with Gustus and Luwiss, Nikal's parting with Kodi would be difficult for him. At least for that one more day they could share in the hope of the news about Dira.

In addition, Nikal was determined to share with all of them in a last celebration.

It was that final evening, the winds had calmed somewhat, and the stars were beginning to appear when Mother Idamé again did her most happy duty by performing the Bonding Ceremony, this time for Hadon and Sturla. The ambassador had brought with her lavish blue and white mantles of the most expensive brocaded satin from the finest tailor in Tirilorin's Central City; it was plain she'd planned to Bond Hadon at the first opportunity. Every lantern on the ship was arranged to add to the starlight. Standing there on the ship's deck the two looked like royals. Manwul stood proudly with his best friend, and Lyndz was given the honor of standing with Sturla. Hadon had begged Idamé to sing the Bonding Song just like she had for Kodi, and Ulna and Maru did their lovely dance. Sturla's coterie of servants who had been brought over to the ship were animated in their sense of fun, and even the Qeteral on board who witnessed the occasion walked up to the couple, bowed, and offered congratulations.

Then, barrels of ale were ordered opened, followed by a magnificent amount of consumption.

"Never seen you so...unreserved, eh!" Tiliruf shouted to Shane over the noise. Shane didn't even look up, but he grinned. The Healer had joined his Essemarian countrymen, Sturla's many servants—all most handsome persons—in great revelry: dancing, of course, and the beating and clanking of Eastern percussions. He was downright tipsy, his shirt was drenched, sweat droplets sparkled like stars on his black brow, and he was drawing almost as much attention to himself as the newly Bonded couple who were currently dancing in the middle. He was all over a set of bongo drums, maintaining a wild but glorious rhythm and moving with energy among the likewise tipsy crowd.

At some point all the 'Western' folks shuffled out of the way. The Easterners now went wild, and all their men, including Shane, were suddenly shirtless and began demonstrating frenzied hip movements. They were moving in a sort of wide dance circle around the couple yelling, "Oom Yah Oom!" The women were swirling up and down about the men, shimmying up against them and shaking their bodies. The drums would pause, the cymbals were exaggerated, then all would go still with a final, "OOOoooOOOoooMMMM, YAH!" the women shouted "LALALALALA!" and then they'd start all over again.

"Spikeshafts and blazes, Manwul! Is that the same Shane we know?"

Tipsy Manwul went philosophical. "Easterners know how to live it up. *Essav Shanna Soor* is his real name, he told us, and that's who we're looking at right now. As disciplined as they come is our Healer Shane, he is. I say his preference is peace and quiet, but he has a hot fire in his soul that bursts out sometimes. Easterners can be elegant and stately, but at other times shock you with a let-loose abandon. Why should Shane be any different? And look. Don't he usually wear his Order medallion for an occasion like this? But instead, he's wearing his Qeteral beads. He's feeling the buck inside him! Like I've said before, he's the most *real* Vow Taker we've ever met."

"And he knows when to set *that* aside, too, eh? Sturla's cooks, maybe? Or Maru again. He could be approaching one of those happy moods that apparently hits him every couple years! Two or three are already giving him the eye!"

"Ha! Female hands feelin' on him while he beats out his rhythms. Eating up the attention, ain't he? Definitely feeling the buck. But pipe down and don't mention Sister Maru. We promised. But I think we're just pretendin', Tiliruf. Shane's never going to do anything he regrets later, no matter how much he's drunk. I don't think any of these are that highly intelligent, artsy female type that appeals to his senses."

"I know you're right. They aren't, and he won't."

All Westerners were applauding and laughing at the revelry, and from the aft deck, the Qeteral observed with a certain apprehension but also much curiosity.

Nikal had already turned the command over to Kodi. It was Kodi, then, who agreed to put the happy couple together on one of the newcomer ships alone in a "tiny" cabin...

...based on *her* insistence. She'd somehow arranged the details already with the captain of that other ship. "Tiny" is how she described it to Kodi. Hadon would shortly discover it was the captain's private cabin! It wasn't tiny at all, with a large bed bolted to the floor, a copper bathtub, and other comforts not typical of most.

Cee Amirah Sturla Keen was a formidable personage. She was used to getting what she wanted, nor was that just because she was rich and carried about quantities of gold and silver like Tiliruf and was willing to parcel it out on occasion. Though that in itself would explain that other captain's willingness to vacate his cabin. Typically graceful and gracious, she could also display a matter-of-fact manner and a certain commanding confidence. Which was why Rainwing liked her so well. Rainwing had seen what she was like back in Tirilorin.

Having docked in Danzilet, Sturla had finagled General Fouch into revealing the whereabouts of Hadon and crew and learned that a dangerous mission was planned in enemy territory. She then tricked Fouch into believing she was only traveling with the new recruits on the ships east—an ambassador returning to her queen in Essemar to give report. He knew she would surely see Hadon briefly and, having a kind-hearted disposition, was not opposed to her getting a chance to see him again. Had he known the full truth, he likely would have forbidden her embarking with this particular convoy.

Brave as Rainwing and with that determined personality, her real plan surfaced almost the moment she arrived on Nikal's ship. She insisted she was going to join them all on the mission. It was questionable, for Hadon had his duty as protector and bodyguard for Tiliruf. Sturla's presence would add a complication. Despite Nikal's happiness for the newly Bonded pair, he expressed this concern to Kodi.

Nevertheless, Kodi had a different leadership style than Nikal. He would accommodate others when he could, and he knew, just as Sturla did, that for three or four more days of travel the danger risk, though heightened, was still limited until they arrived at the strait to the Khestadone Sea. He would allow the pair to remain together for now. He had Rusty fetch her overlarge trunk and take it to their cabin (and when Rusty later informed him it was the captain's cabin, Kodi laughed uproariously). But he made it plain to Sturla she could bring none of her servants, and these would have to return to the eastbound ships. She would have to join with the women and Rainwing before they entered enemy waters, and Hadon would rejoin the men. And he reminded her, bluntly, that Hadon's first duty during dangerous times was to Tiliruf...not her.

She gave him a powerful 'eye' during this speech and looked rather regal. Kodi didn't flinch, and frankly, Sturla was a woman of logic and not unreason. She was also astute as to the political and historical value placed by many, including her queen, on Tiliruf's person as the last A'Terianh. As Hadon honored and loved Tiliruf, she automatically would, too. She had no intention of interfering with Hadon's duty and in fact looked on this and his recent promotion to Swordmaster as the noblest of responsibilities. She'd heard the tale back in Danzilet. That he'd taken a blade and saved Tiliruf's life made Hadon a renowned hero, and in her eyes, sexier than ever. Kodi perceived some of this in her, which is why he was less concerned than Nikal. She nodded with appropriate respect.

In her sensuous voice she replied. "As you wish, Kodi War Wizard. I am a disciplined fighter as required and brought my weaponry for the purposes of being helpful, not a hindrance. I do not need servants, though my cooks could make the offerings of your mess more palatable, ha!"

She then offered Kodi to serve Lyndz and provide her extra protection. This was remarkable, for Sturla was a very important person in the circles she walked, one of the richest noblewomen of Essemar. Kodi had not necessarily intended to assign her any specific duty. Clearly, she saw Lyndz as a key figure in all that was happening, and Sturla was making it plain she was a capable warrior and knew what she was doing. He remembered her archery skills the day of the Grand Dance and that she kept her head shaved reflecting her warrior role. The offer was much more than polite gesture.

Something told him this too was a part of her plan all along—to get herself close to Lyndz—and he raised his eyebrow. Though he was a War Wizard in command now of a dangerous mission, he could see Lyndz beyond, dancing with Lumin's determined Human side to a slower rhythm of Shane's drumbeats and imagined her annoyance should he 'assign' anyone to her without her permission. "By all means, make your offer to my sister, and thank you, Ambassador."

"And thank *you*, Your Highness." She displayed a most charming smile and a little nod.

Kodi rolled his eyes and laughed. "Oh, please, no. Tiliruf keeps teasing me with that."

"But you're a royal prince now, they say, hmm?" She was openly playing with him and swished her head a little. She could definitely apply flirtatious mannerisms. "*Highness,* no? And I wish not to be called *Ambassador* anymore, do I? I stepped away from that role when I boarded your ship. Her Majesty in Essemar will be displeased when she finds out, at least until my barrel of citrus candies arrives from Danzilet. She has a very sweet tooth. I am *Sturla,* Kodi War Wizard, to you and your friends. *Cee Amirah* will suffice for the shipmen. I've already made that plain to the captain."

Hadon was standing beside her during this interchange, looking in her face with half drunk, starry eyes. That he was about to have some alone time with his new wife for a few nights and days was all he could think about. Through the background revelry, Tiliruf and Manwul were teasing him outrageously, walking back and forth behind him and muttering innuendo in his ears: *"Hralindi Oil massages, yah!" "He'll be a 'Keen' observer tonight!" "Star-Revel Sturla!"* And finally, *"The ole' Eastern Squeeze, eh?"*

All the friends gathered together that next afternoon and bid Nikal their farewells. Leaving with him were six of his knights along with Healers Gustus and Luwiss, whom Curdoz had ordered to stay at Nikal's side, do everything Shane used to do for him, and sleep in his cabin. Idamé could not help but shed many tears. But hers were not the only ones. Among them, Tiliruf notably struggled when last they gripped arms and Nikal drew him into an embrace.

"You are the A'Terianh. Never forget that. You are a knight and the greatest of Swordmasters!"

Tiliruf could not speak.

The seven ships left the convoy and headed south. Nikal's fleet would follow along with the two eastbound ships for the day before they too were to make their way southwards. Yet for that day, Kodi and Nikal sent Azure back and forth between them three times with additional messages as a sort of test of the great hawk's skills. Though the two fleets were growing more distant, Azure was swift of wing.

The messages themselves were not so important. Rather, it was just so, through Azure's eyes, each could see the face of the other, his greatest friend and truest brother.

On the third night following Nikal's departure, the captain sent for Kodi. The men had been asleep some three hours.

"What is it, eh?"

"Not sure, Tiliruf."

Tiliruf was too sleepy to move quickly, but Shane and Lumin followed Kodi out of the cabin and climbed to the foredeck to find the captain, several of the sailors, and two or three of the Qeteral. They were all looking southwards. Overhead the stars shone in their multitudes, but far ahead of them was a great gray darkness slowly swallowing the night.

Stormgale and Flamefur landed before them.

"What did you discover, Storm Majors?"

"It is a great fog bank, Polemarch," offered Flamefur. "Very dense. We flew into it a short way but could see almost nothing, though outside of it here, as you can see, the night is bright. Oddly, the winds are strong inside of it, though quite cool. And these waters are quite warm, which might explain it. Yet it is very strange."

"It isn't right for the time of year this far south," added the captain. "And strong winds inside it, you say? Yes, very strange."

"I sense something," said Shane suddenly. "I've never felt such a thing before!"

"I feel it, too," said Lumin. His eyes were wide. Some of the Qeteral were nodding at him.

Kodi looked back and forth between them.

"Lumin, retrieve Azure for me. I want to get an overview with my own eyes, er, or rather his eyes. Stormy, and you Qeteral with your working birds, get word to the other ships to draw into a tight formation. Rusty, go to Curdoz' ship. I expect you'll find him awake now. Have him gather the Scribes and all their belongings and move over here. I think too I must make some other rearrangements."

"Such as?" asked Shane.

Lumin went to retrieve the Bluetail, and Kodi took Shane aside and spoke quietly in his ear. "You are to stay on my ship, Shane, and get Brother Labert over here with us, but I want warriors with the women. Tiliruf, Manwul and Hadon are to share a cabin on the women's ship. Whenever possible, I'll send you over to check on Tiliruf, but you might speak to Ulna of him, understand?"

"I do, sir. I am glad *you* understand."

Kodi nodded. "Have no hesitancies in explaining to her what you know of Tiliruf. The times are now of a critical nature. I know she's not as inciteful or powerful as you..."

"She has great talent, sir, and we've already had a conversation or two about him. She is quite aware. Not everything I know, but I assure you she is not stupid about Tiliruf."

"Excellent. Sturla must move over there now, too, but she cannot sleep with Hadon. She must sleep in the women's cabin. She knows this already. She is wily, but she understands duty."

"All Eastern warriors do, sir. The Alkhan is trying to take away our home and our freedom, and they—we—are trying to stop him. Sturla will be professional, whether Hadon is close by or not."

Kodi nodded. "Nor will Hadon let her one up him! And I say, Shane, you are a Healer, but you are a warrior, too. Now, go and carry out these orders for me. Use the Etoppsi after they get back. Go now and awaken Tiliruf and Manwul and explain." He then walked back to the captain. "Sail on."

Lumin appeared with Azure, and Kodi immediately launched him forth.

“We will be approaching the strait, soon, sir,” replied the captain with no little trepidation. “I expected to sight it by morning. If we can’t see, we can’t navigate it safely.”

“Keep the fleet in tight formation, yet safely apart. Sail on, Captain. Let the winds take us where they may.”

All the ‘rearrangements’ between the several ships were made quickly with the help of the Etoppsi. Tiliruf only grumbled because he was sleepy, but otherwise no one complained and followed the new orders. Curdoz, Shane, and Lumin at last stood at Kodi’s side again on the foredeck.

“He’s here,” said Kodi.

“Yes,” replied Curdoz.

“Vanaratu!” exclaimed Shane, though in a quiet voice. “I cannot believe it! World God of Mountain and Sea! And I *feel* him.”

“Because you are Gifted,” said Curdoz. “I’m sure all the Qeteral sense him, too. And though his mind and thoughts, and of course his power, are beyond ours, Brother Shane, have no fear of him. For he is a god who knows something of what love is. He knows more about the Peoples of the Mold than any other. And, though on a time long ago he disobeyed, he now follows the orders of his Master, Meical.”

“What is he saying to you, Curdoz?” asked Kodi.

“He greeted me earlier but said no more, and though I sense his many emotions, one stands out.”

“What is it?” asked Lumin.

“Determination.”

As Azure returned a quarter hour later to Kodi’s arm, the seven ships were swallowed by a great gray mist.

THIS ENDS BOOK THREE

Continue with

Daughters of Vanayema

Book Four of

Heirs to the Taxiarch

Enjoy a preview chapter of
Book 4

Daughters of Vanayema

Daughters of Vanayema

Chapter 1—Elisa's Resolve

"This is where he lived," whispered the peasant woman to her older companion. "With his mother, Kalemna Deroge. The village of Dunstun."

"Your grandmother, dear."

"Yes," she acknowledged a little reluctantly. "My grandmother. Say nothing of it to our friends. It bears on nothing regarding the task ahead. But I wanted you to know where Pap lived before he made his way to Tulesk. He told me the name of the place, but of course I've never been here myself. It's surely larger than it was then. In those days it was tiny and even more remote. From what little Pap has said about her, I think she was wishing to be far away from Aster and less bothered by folks begging for predictions of their future. It looks like it has become an important lumbering town."

The women's dresses showed torn places and were a little dirty. Kerchiefs covered their heads. But if anyone were to examine them a little more closely and peer into their faces, they might have wondered.

For peasant women, the younger of the two would surely have been labeled beautiful, very. And the older woman smiled a good deal and hummed to herself. Such a cheery disposition was out of character for a poor woman in Hesk.

They were walking with three men in the garb of Brothers in the Monastic Orders, and two burros who bore all their goods. Two of the men were of darker complexion. That wasn't so unusual for Monastics in Hesk, though they did occasionally garner second looks. One of the two was quite young, tall and lean. The third man was of large muscular build, definitely atypical of Monastics.

Their robes covered much of this detail, and they kept their hoods up much of the time.

It wasn't out of the ordinary for Monastics to travel out this way, and the road was busy enough. But they had their alibi and had already used it once.

Hescian soldiers on horseback had halted them on their march on the road and informed them all Monastics were to return to Aster and the Monastery at once or to leave the principality. They feigned surprise but of course promised to do as the soldiers commanded them. They stated they were escorting a peasant woman who believed she had had a Calling Vision to become a Matrimonial, along with her mother, for examination by Father Jarom at the monastery. The soldiers, busy with more important orders—conscripting young men for the army—were not especially interested enough to question them. They nodded and rode on past.

Of course, the young woman was not really of the teen years in which a Calling Vision was likely to appear. Nor were the men "returning" to Aster. Not one of them had ever been to Aster before. But it was certainly their destination.

Rather, Matteo and Olaron, along with Captain Cludder, had come by way of the secret path behind the town of Felto. They then traveled through the woods until they found the eastward trek.

It was their initial intention to come alone as three clandestine men on the most secret of missions, yet it didn't turn out quite that way. For when they arrived in Felto and came to the Fothemry home with the news of Princess Isatura's abduction and for further advice from Yugan on finding the hidden trailhead into the Escarpment, something triggered inside the usually serene Elisa.

Something about the travails of Isatura along with the desperation and yet strong determination in Matteo—her husband's cousin—moved the countess.

But there was more that moved them all. Knowing the Fothemrys were implicitly trustworthy, Matteo had informed them of the betrothal. This created strong feelings for all of them, particularly for Ansy. Also, Olaron reminded them keenly of the absent Kodi. In many ways, Olaron was a four-years-younger version of his "Cousin Ko," not only in personality but also in looks. Elisa would look on Olaron and be reminded of her brave son. It was surely the memory of her absent children, the sacrifices they and others were making in the world, that stirred her into a decision.

And in her keen mind, she foresaw something:

"Matteo, presuming Isatura is being held there, you will not access Filiddor's palace as an obviously southern man. And Filiddor or other lords would recognize you. If this Valgene sees you, he will kill you. A Monastic's disguise is excellent for getting into the city, but you will be handicapped once there. It will be easier for a woman of fair skin..."

When Ansy realized what her stepdaughter was proposing, without even garnering Yugan's agreement, she insisted she would come along:

"And you cannot travel the roads as you are without another. You are still young and beautiful, dear. Even with Monastic Brothers it would look strange and draw eyes, at least among those who care about such things. And those are the ones we should worry about the most..."

Yugan was not happy about the prospect, but what he did know was this: If anyone could gain access to an imprisoned Isatura, his daughter was the one to accomplish it.

Onri, who had come months ago with his letter from Kodi, had been accepted without question into the Fothemry home. They were as much moved by his life story as Kodi had been. Yugan happily took him as an apprentice and quickly found a market for his work. Now that Onri had access to high quality lumber, even ambernut, he was gaining a reputation. More importantly, he was surrounded by a new family.

He was extremely helpful. Woodworking was not his only talent. Having been an innkeeper, he could do many tasks. In large measure, he was capable of doing everything Kodi used to do at home, with the addition of cooking. He liked being in the kitchen and was a great help to Ansy. In addition, living with people who actually showed him support, he was gaining confidence in himself and was less socially withdrawn. He now had a few genuine friends in Felto.

Without Onri, it would have proven nearly impossible for Elisa and Ansy to leave Yugan. But Onri was willing to keep the home going, cook, and help Yugan while they were away.

The element of danger was strong. Lives were at stake. Matteo was opposed when Elisa offered. But his adamancy waned over the hours. The three men remained the night in Yugan's home, and as certain elements of logic and his needfulness weighed in on him, by morning he had agreed. Elisa and Ansy began preparing themselves for the journey. In order to minimize questions, they left Felto in the night so that none would see they had not taken the road, but rather the trail to the Wolf River. Villagers had heard of the abduction of the princess and the talk of war. They would presume Elisa had left town out of need to confer with other high folk and represent her absent husband. Yugan and Onri encouraged this speculation, but in general, the people of Felto were inclined not to question too much into the business of their neighbors.

After topping the Escarpment, they struggled through the forest for two days. They eventually discovered the eastward trek, just as Yugan had said they would. They kept it in sight far to their left and passed several lonely hovels and a few of the tiniest hamlets. They relied on provisions they had brought. Finally, Matteo and Elisa agreed the road had now gained sufficient traffic and that their own little group would not seem out of place or create wonder among the people who lived in these distant reaches of the forest. They would stick to their alibi, and the "Brothers" could now use coins to pay for additional provisions as they traveled along.

Elisa had been a high lady for years, now. But she had resisted having regular servants, awaiting a grander change in lifestyle after the upcoming move into the new manor. Also, as a child in the years before Yugan had built wealth from his woodwork, and from living on a farm with Hess before he was ennobled, she was familiar with a rougher sort of life. Ansy, too, knew how to do without. The two could play the peasant role well. Taking on the guise of Matrimonial Sisters would have required them to be more personable and engaging with others. It would have been a more challenging part to play. As poor women without any social standing, they could move without drawing attention to themselves.

Of dark complexion, acting as Monastics was really the only disguise the two brothers from Escarant could pull off in the Principality of Hesk. There simply were no other darker-skinned men here aside from Order Members. Healers would have drawn even more attention to themselves than the women as Matrimonials. As Monastic robes could hide Cludder's large, muscular build, it was the best disguise for him as well.

Robes could also hide the long knives they bore, and the drapes on the burros hid other gear.

Bringing young Olaron was not Matteo's initial wish. But he really had no choice in the matter. Olaron had proven himself not just capable, but a young man of resourcefulness, determination, and intelligence. He'd also proven himself in battle. Matteo had grudgingly concluded Olaron would be of great help, and of great comfort.

"Father told me...warned me...it might turn out to be my place, depending on the circumstances."

"Your place to do what?" asked Olaron with curiosity and a chuckle.

"To offer you the familial blessing, which I now do. You're a man, Olaron. You're sixteen in two months in any regard. In Father's name I give you your freedom. Whatever you want or need from Father or me, you just ask for it. And you understand, if I Bond Isatura, Father's title and inheritance will devolve to you when she becomes queen. That is now my great wish for you, for that will mean my wish for myself will have also come true."

"Unless I find my own queen, someday, ha! You never know!" He winked, but then he put on a straight face. "Thank you, Brother. It means a lot. Maybe even more than if it came from Father."

"Queens find you, by the way. Not the other way around."

"You flirted with Isatura for ages!"

Matteo chuckled. "Just remember what I told you, and don't ever underestimate any woman. Let her do the 'finding,' and you'll be better off. But certainly, make your presence known so she notices, ha! In a good way. Not as an ass. I've known some of those. And you need to learn to dance well."

"I dance well already. Mother has been much too insistent about it. But I'm not for romance, yet, but I'm going to help you with yours."

As for Cludder, memories of the hijacking of the princess's procession haunted him. Matteo continually reminded him he did the right thing. He was badly outnumbered, and engagement at that time would have resulted in the unneedful death of many soldiers and innocent servants. His choices saved lives. Even so, Cludder was inflamed with hatred for Valgene, Isatura's abductor, and was out for revenge. Determined that these emotions would not interfere with their plans, it nevertheless inspired him to beat Valgene and Prince Filiddor at this game. If Valgene could steal the princess, Cludder would steal her back.

Altogether it had been eight days since they left Felto when they finally approached the canyon of the North River and descended slowly to the great bridge there. As they descended, they took in stunning views. Upstream, the convergence of the two main forks of the river was plain, and looking up, one could see the palaces and towers of Aster. Beyond the city, also on the edge of the canyon above the southerly fork, was the Aster Monastery.

"What a lovely place," offered Ansy.

"A shame it's ruled by rabble," said Cludder.

"Maybe there will be a change in its rule if we get Isatura out and war comes," Matteo whispered. "Now, let us begin using our aliases, and remember, we're making our way through the city to the monastery. Once there, we will reconsider our disguises. Jarom is trusty, and he will provide us rooms and cover for us, but that is all we need expect from him. It is the old librarian, Theneri, whom I'm hoping to meet as soon as ever we can. As I've told you, he is an informant for Lord Curdoz and Father Marco. It is he we can rely on for the mission. He will know if Isatura is being held in the palace, as we suspect, and how to get you inside. This will take us many days of reconnaissance and careful planning. We may be here weeks before we can make our move. Theneri can advise us further. And according to the information my father gave me at the time of the Council of the Kingdom, Curdoz had sent two Healers to work for Theneri. One is a very large man, Brother Xeno, and his companion is short and stout, Brother Danly. But it is supposed they are posing as Monastics, not as Healers. Danly is supposed to be apprenticing to Theneri in order to take his place eventually as head of the library. I'm not really sure what Xeno's part is. We'll find out soon if all goes well. But those are the four persons we can trust—Jarom, Theneri, Danly, Xeno—until we get a chance to speak to Theneri at length and learn more. Father has sent a few spies here, probably as Monastics or common soldiers. But I doubt I will recognize any of them."

There were Hescian soldiers at the bridge. It was crowded here. Other roads converged before this bridge, the only crossing for many miles. No one took any particular notice of the travelers. After crossing the rushing river, they ascended the ravine. The ravine road was well-built, and the ascent was not difficult, allowing for horses, oxen, and wain traffic. The forested region of Hesk from which they had come was a principal source of lumber for the principality. Several wains bore this commodity. Finally, they topped the other side of the plateau and merged with the main Northern Road, coming from the direction of the Great Ramp.

And this was their first sight of them.

"Tribesman warriors!" exclaimed Elisa in a whisper to Matteo. "Out in the open, too!"

He nodded.

Pale white skin denoted two officers from the Chieftain class. They each wore a broad hat of stiffened felt which Elisa remembered her father telling her was to protect their sensitive eyes and also their faces from being burnt in the sun. Those with him were not as white of skin, and in other garb they might have passed for the typical Northern ethnicity. Yet they too were wearing the broad hats, and even though it was warm, they all wore a drape of fur over their shoulders. The officers wore one of white seal, whereas the others' drapes were brown. They carried steel-bladed poleaxes and spoke to each other in their own language. A Hescian captain was talking to the white-skinned man as they marched along the road. All travelers gave them wide birth, many looking at them askance.

Matteo glanced at Olaron to make sure he was not displaying open shock on his face. The younger man looked at his brother, but he kept his eyes and face calm under his hood. Cludder, too. But this was open proof of what was suspected by Matteo's father and others in the Solantine leadership. Though Matteo had not heard spy reports before he began his mission, he suspected word had now reached his father and the king: the Ice Tribes had allied with Prince Filiddor and were swelling his army.

They arrived at the city gates. Just as Kodi and Curdoz were required to do months before, the five travelers had to give some account of themselves and have their names placed in ledgers. It was much busier today, and there were several lines. They chose the shortest, but it was quick and efficient, and they only had to wait in line five minutes.

"Names," said a bored Hescian soldier sitting at a table with a large ledger. He was yawning.

"Olman Harfield," said Cludder.

"Olman Harfield," repeated the soldier, writing it down. "Monastic. Where from?"

"The Monastery. Since spring."

"I mean originally."

"Duranti."

"Next."

"Leef Trant," offered Olaron.

"Fisher Upton," said Matteo.

"You two from Escarant?"

"Donesk."

The man wrote it down. "Those women with you?"

"Potential novitiate in the Matrimonials and her mother," offered Cludder. "Hellin and Magna Farner. They approached us while over in Dunstan and asked us to escort them to the Monastery."

"And two donkeys. Got it. Curfew applies to Order Members, now. Inside closed doors an hour after sunset. Now, move along. Next? Wait a minute, you!"

"What is it, sir?" asked Cludder.

"Hellin Farner. Young lady, come closer and let me tell you something."

Elisa did her best to squelch her sudden fear. She bent over the table to hear.

He spoke quietly. "These days, the safest place for *you,* pretty, is behind the walls at the Monastery. Don't get yourself caught alone and cornered by any of that pale-faced rabble, you hear? City ain't as safe as before. They don't follow the common laws. Heard some bad stories. And more of 'em are on the way, from what we hear. Don't think your ma at your side is any protection, either. Keep an Order Brother handy if you must come into the city. The rabble seems skittish of them if nobody else. Superstitious, see. Now, all of you move along."

Which they did with great relief.

"That was kind of him, really," Ansy offered, as they made their way down the crowded main street.

"Yes, but I nearly jumped out of my skin when he called me back," Elisa replied.

Matteo had more to add. "There was a lot of information in that. Consider his attitude towards the Tribesmen. If he thought his viewpoint was singular he wouldn't have said anything. Many of the ordinary Hescian soldiers must feel the same way he does and are openly griping to each other about them. And Tribesmen avoiding those who show belief in the Guardian. Most obvious in Brothers wearing robes." He then indicated a change in plan. "I will take Leef with me, and we will go to the library now and find Theneri. Olman, take charge of the burros and stick close to the ladies. Mingle in the crowd in the great square around the fountain. Think you can look intimidating enough, Olman?"

Cludder chuckled, "I'll offer a Guardian's Blessing if a Tribesman approaches. That ought to scare him off, ha!"

Matteo winked. "Do it in Old Anterianhi! Make 'em run away! I'll send Leef out to retrieve you all if Theneri says it is safe to do so."

"Whom did you say?"

Old Theneri appeared in a state of shock. He had immediately invited the two 'Brothers' into his private study and left Brother Danly at the main desk. He had known the instant he set eyes on them they weren't who they pretended to be. They explained who they were and their mission...

...and who they had brought with them.

"You'll remember Kodi, who came to you with Lord Curdoz. His mother, Elisa, the Countess Fothemry," repeated Matteo. "Is there something the matter, Brother Theneri?"

The giant Xeno then stood and put a hand on Theneri's shoulder. Theneri looked up at him.

Xeno nodded and spoke in his rotund but quiet voice. "I would look upon this as a gift, Master. A second opportunity presents itself. Cast aside fear, Master, and hide not."

Theneri turned back to Matteo, who was understandably looking at him oddly. "Is...is the lady's father, the one called Yugan Lunder... He is still alive?"

The question was puzzling, but he answered. "Certainly. He walks with difficulty but is otherwise in good health. It is his wife—second wife—who has come as escort to the lady. Ansy is her true name."

Theneri swallowed hard and turned again to peer into Xeno's big, but good face. The big man nodded again.

Matteo and Olaron were both in wonder at the old man's reaction and the strange words from Xeno. Just as Matteo was about to speak again, Theneri turned back to him.

"Olaron, go and fetch them immediately. 'Peasants' are not allowed by the laws here and so cannot enter the front doors. Mark the path to the rear behind the hedge that lines the main walkway, just behind a stone seat. There is a high stone wall with a gate that surrounds my little garden. There is a small rear door into my apartments. I will meet you there."

Olaron left and Xeno proceeded to pour wine for Matteo and for Theneri.

Matteo offered his thanks and took a swallow.

Theneri proceeded to drink half his goblet. He looked out the window for a moment, looked back at Matteo, then downed the remainder of the goblet. "Lord Matteo. We will give you all the aid we can. We've had contact already with some of your father's people, and you are not the only false Monastics walking the streets of Aster. But your presence comes with a surprise. When the ladies arrive, I must speak with them alone." And almost to himself he added quietly, "But...by the Guardian, it must be done. Even though I myself may be undone by it."

Matteo looked at the hulking Xeno hoping to find answers there.

"Fear not, Lord Matteo. He is perfectly well," said the big man.

It was difficult to say which of the two women looked more stunned. Theneri's gray-bearded face was contorted in anticipation. However, he maintained a certain firmness and did not shed tears, despite many emotions attempting to consume him.

Finally, Elisa responded, almost in a whisper. "She told you nothing? You never knew?"

"As I said, we broke the relationship, and I left for the Valley. Nor in all the times afterwards when she came to Aster did she ever mention the existence of a child to me."

"But, why?" asked a confused Ansy. "Why would she not tell you?"

Neither woman had any reason to be skeptical of Theneri's story. It was so incredibly out of the ordinary. These were not facts easily made up. In addition, both women could see Yugan in Theneri's face, better than Kodi did. The shade of blue in his old eyes, the profile of his cheek and nose. Then there was a quality in his voice and the way he shook his hands back and forth when emphasizing a phrase and the manner in which he twiddled his fingers when deciding upon the next thing to say. They knew in twenty years, if he lived so long, Yugan would be exactly as the man in front of them.

Before Theneri attempted to answer Ansy's question, Elisa did. "To protect someone. To protect you. Even to protect Pap. She knew you were spying on the princes for the Sages. She considered your position too valuable. You are a Moment Master, you say? And you say she knew that about you?"

"Yes. I've had these months since young Kodi left to consider all this, and that is precisely the same conclusion I have made. She likely believed entanglement in family would require my removal from my work here. She foresaw certain events as the Guardian gave her to see. She...she sacrificed much, and it pains me."

He could no longer sit. He stood and paced his little bedroom where he had invited the women for the private talk. It wasn't anxiety so much as a wonder on his part what next steps were to be taken. His world was changed, now he had revealed the truth.

But it wasn't the only thing that had changed in the world. Now, there were greater dangers with the conflict between Hesk and Solanto, along with Ice Tribe warriors roaming the streets.

And he was old.

"You must come with us," said Elisa, suddenly.

Theneri stopped short in his pacing and looked at her.

She made it plainer. "Escape Aster with us and Isatura. When we leave here, you must come with us. You must come with me to Tulesk and see...and see your son."

"Yes," added Ansy. "While you still have health and can manage the journey. You would bring him such joy. He never knew you. He wanted to know you. He wonders all the time about you, though he presumed you died ages ago. His mother would never reveal who you were, as you realize. Listen to...your granddaughter and come with us."

It was a long minute in which Theneri stared at Elisa. Finally, he reached and touched her chin. Elisa then took hold of his hand and nodded.

Still holding onto Elisa's hand, he turned to Ansy.

"I expected to die in this great place. All my life's work is here. Yet here, possibly in the last decade of my life I discover I have...," Theneri paused and breathed. "I have a...a son. A son of my own blood. A granddaughter and great-grandchildren. A daughter-in-law."

"You'll have love," said Elisa. She smiled warmly and squeezed his hand. "If you indeed believe this to be the last decade of your life, then...you need to be with...your family. You have overwhelmed Ansy and me with this revelation, and it is difficult to take it all in. Let me tell you something, Theneri. My heart is big enough for the family I know and for the family I didn't know I had. Perhaps you and Kalemna, all those years ago, engaged in an act of passion for which you may have thought afterwards was an error in judgment. And yet, think on it. Think on it, Theneri—Grandfather. Pap wouldn't be here. I wouldn't be here. Lyndz and Kodi would not be here to fulfill the wishes of the Guardian. And so, that act of passion was one that changed the world. We all know the twins have been Called to a great task. We cannot deny it, as much as I, when Lord Curdoz came, wanted to deny it. My world changed. But my heart did not get smaller because of it. It seems to have grown almost to the point of bursting. I miss my children dreadfully, and yet in their absence, and as my husband is still away, I could not be still any longer. And so, I am here. It seems I am meant to be here. To find you at the very least, even though rescuing Isatura was my intent. It still is my intent, of course. I am asking you to come, Theneri. Help us find a way to rescue Isatura and then escape with all of us out of Hesk by the secret way."

After a long moment, a huge grin crafted itself upon the old man's face, reminding Elisa less of Yugan than it did...

...of Kodi.

Works by Terry Lee Martin

Fiction:

HEIRS TO THE TAXIARCH

Book 1: *Seeds of the Guardian* (2021 Silver Goblet Press)
Book 2: *Companions in Prophecy* (2021 Silver Goblet Press)
Book 3: *Brothers of Myghal* (2025 Silver Goblet Press)
Book 4: *Daughters of Vanayema* (Forthcoming)
Book 5: *Champions of Dumhoni* (Forthcoming)

Non-fiction:

Love's Young Dream: The Letters of Dr. Edward Noel Franklin to Miss Nannie Hillman—1871 (2018 Silver Goblet Press)

Journal Articles:

"Newly Identified Images Add to the Story of the Franklin & Armfield Slave-Trading Firm," *The Alexandria Chronicle*, Spring 2025. (Alexandria Historical Society, Alexandria, Virginia)
https://sites.google.com/view/alexandria-historical-society/publications/alexandria-chronicle

About the author:

Terry Lee Martin is an alumnus of the University of Tennessee at Martin, with majors in psychology and history. A historian and former teacher, he lives in Tennessee with his wife, Laura. His first book, the non-fiction work, *"Love's Young Dream," The Letters of Dr. Edward Noel Franklin to Miss Nannie Hillman—1871*, explores two prominent Middle Tennessee families of the antebellum and postbellum South. The book received positive reviews from professors and historians. Martin has presented his research at various historical societies. Martin's venture into fiction began with his fantasy world-building in the early 2000s, coming to fruition in his *Heirs to the Taxiarch* book series. The first volume, *Seeds of the Guardian*, was published in 2021 by Silver Goblet Press. Contact Martin at the following email address: **tmartin@silvergobletpress.com**

Visit the *Silver Goblet Press* website to find Martin's blog, along with details and updates on his publications: *www.silvergobletpress.com*

www.ingramcontent.com/pod-product-compliance
Lightning Source LLC
Chambersburg PA
CBHW070542310726
48982CB00010B/1439/J